LORDS OF LIGHT

ASCENSION OF THE FOUR

JOSEPH J. BAILEY

CONTENTS

MAP

Dharia

To Far
Aruene

The Ayle'ine Sea

To Far Aeron

Keep of Teymliace

Empen Wastes

The Plains of Kedroar

Var Kera

Dorja

Kaveros

Q'shar

The Green Run

Uridion

Doumalaaden

Loenia Northlands

Shade Vale
Yildel

Amakar

The Drake Spires

Alicasar

Luecaul Jungle

Jenynan

Shulin

Ithil'alen

Tuy Long

The K'un Lun

Chang Sen

Luesho
Liang Jun
Qia Vulei
Stu

Lueciane Sea

Lander's

Tsuvim

Qia Shan Sea

To Far
Maeron

To Far
Kilaeron

W N E S

AUTHOR'S NOTE

For terms that are not strictly imaginary in nature, the Wade-Giles and Pinyin Romanization systems are used interchangeably, loosely, and not entirely accurately.

Transliteration devices were chosen mostly based on whichever sounded better at the time.

A glossary of terms is included at the book's end to help the reader fully engage in, understand, and explore the world of Ea'ae.

Forgive my errors for they are numerous and I am not.

To all those who helped along the way.

The more profound the stillness, the deeper the perception.

- Master Wei
Priest of the K'un Lun

TELLANON REVISITED

Skin caressed by clouds,
refreshing cool air.
Gray fogbanks roll in.

With a jolt that reverberated resoundingly through their minds and bodies, jarring their awarenesses unceremoniously back to corporeal reality, the *Shrike* materialized in the skies above Tellanon.

The scene was completely unexpected.

The Tellanon that was before their departure, the Tellanon of the past, was no more.

Illdrassil yet stood shimmering at the city's center, her lofty crystalline branches still soaring heavenward, a bastion of Light and hope. All around, spread in idyllic beauty, shimmering and celestial, her grounds shone upward reflecting the light of the day with their own. But, despite the radiant splendor, even from their distant vantage, the prior ethereal glimmer of Illdrassil's environs was somehow lessened, tarnished in the mid-morning sun. A vast globe of translucent force yet protected Tellanon's high walls but the magical aegis no longer appeared so unassailable. Ships yet swarmed about her borders and docks but their sails seemed not quite so full of air nor were the crews full of gusto. Throngs of travelers and traders yet scurried along her quays but the heavy weight of concern lay atop their shoulders for their motions were restrained and few looked upward toward the sky in appreciation of the risen sun. The myriad homes and businesses lovingly sculpted from the living rock of the island's crown yet stood but the luster and life of their forms seemed muted.

A subtle transformation had overtaken the city. Only the passage of time and the efforts of many united in common cause would restore her to her full glory and free her people from the weight that now burdened their hearts.

His eyes skimming back and forth across her turrets and rooftops, her greens and lanes, Yip sensed before he looked that Tellanon had been attacked, her defenses breached and destruction visited upon her hearths and the hopes residing within. He felt the heaviness in the air radiating outward from her people like a bank of clouds massing before a storm or a wispy fogbank that rapidly overtakes and disorients a weary traveler in unknown lands.

Though unblemished at first glance, the complex lines, edifices, and weavings of magical forces permeating the city had been visibly damaged—weakened, frayed, and stressed. Signs of repair and restoration were everywhere but to his eyes the damage had been done. Surveying the miraculous city, the minds and magics that soared and were expressed within, he gazed upon the fractured pieces only knowing what had been lost by what had been before.

The view of the city afforded by Wrindanneth's magnified representation of Tellanon projected in the air before them told a similar story. Though the city appeared to be largely untouched from afar, her beautiful sculpted lines unblemished, upon closer inspection, many homes and businesses had been leveled, charred, or wiped completely from the solid firmament leaving only raw stone beneath. Though much activity was visible around many of these sites of destruction for repair crews, drones, and magical artifice were already at work reconstructing and restoring any damage done, planting and urging greenery to take hold once more, there were yet many signs of strife.

Once healed, the wounds to the populace's character and resolve would take much longer to make whole.

For a city long thought to be well-nigh impregnable, proof otherwise was especially difficult to reconcile, much less recover from fully, for understanding, once realized, is not soon forgotten.

Though the joy of their return might be lessened by the damage visited upon the city and her people, word of their success, tidings of Ea'ae's long-term security and stability, should help lighten the sentiments of those overburdened by stress and sorrow.

Just then, before his ruminations continued farther, a loud voice boomed out, enveloping the ship in a sonic wave. "Crew of the *Shrike*! Your return has been heralded! You have our congratulations and unfailing gratitude!"

"The success of your efforts to restore the Seal of Eldre'gheu in lands far removed from these fair skies cut off the invading Darkness that threatened our walls and homes in our time of greatest need. Your triumph severed this raiding Darkness off at its root and left the alien ships and beings It sheltered at the mercy of Tellanon's defenders."

"You are to be praised!"

"No symbol of appreciation can repay this debt!"

His ears ringing, Yip heard Slate grumble, "Next time I'll just take a nice, quiet, 'Thank ya'…or ear plugs!"

Smiling as the Construct's voice continued to rumble around them, distant thunder visited upon them in full force, Yip listened as it continued, "You are to report immediately to Illdrassil and the quarters of the Home Guard. Éremon and Eidelion await you there!"

With that, the air returned to a welcome silence broken only by the sounds of the wind rushing past their brows as they flew downward toward the docks, Tellanon looming larger and more real with each passing moment.

"Remind me ta stuff my ears with cotton next time we return! I'd prefer not havin' ta speak in a yell ta hear myself think fer tha rest o' my life!" Slate's complaining only brightened Yip's smile for he knew his friend was appreciative of both the accolades and the attention.

While they dropped downward toward the docks, their flight a gentle spiral moving casually in and out of similar traffic either taking to the air or landing along the quay, the city's liveliness undiminished by the recent turmoil visited upon her bounds, Wrindanneth pointed at the projection below, zooming in to a particular point. "Looks like our cottage survived the worst of it!"

Their small stone cottage, shaded by trees, bordered by stone fences and a cobblestone lane, was indeed intact. The other homes on their street appeared largely unharmed aside from the occasional damaged roof or burnt spot on the lawn from falling debris and shrapnel. Within several blocks in any given direction, however, other homes and homeowners had not been so lucky. These houses and lawns appeared as randomly located blemishes, charred smears, piles of rubble, and solidified slag marring the idyllic streets and walkways on Tellanon's surface—a pox not yet recovered from or fully healed.

For the sake of the city, Yip hoped the illness did not spread further.

"Must've been some battle ta penetrate Tellanon's defenses!" Seeing that the unthinkable had indeed happened, Slate was just glad that the devastation and loss were not much worse.

As the city neared and the consequences of the battle became more visible to the unaided eye, Slate's words hit home. Aroganji bowed his head, weighed down with a mixture of sadness and skepticism. "I see the damage clearly. I see the inescapable actuality of the assault. It just doesn't seem real."

"I was—we were—so caught up in our own battles and inner struggles that I completely lost sight of the reality that the danger we faced was so widespread and could affect everyone so readily."

He sighed. "I never imagined returning home to find our city the victim of an attack."

"Tellanon seemed so untouchable...perfect...otherworldly..."

Wrindanneth broke in before Aroganji finished, "If we can take the battle to our foes, then why can't they take it to us? We are no different!"

"Our enemies take advantage of whatever opportunity they can. Such is the reality of war."

"If they hadn't moved in force when the seals were weakened, then they might never have had another chance."

"In fact, we were lucky our counter to their assault happened as early as it did. Who knows how much more ruination would have been visited upon us or if we would have had the time or ability to respond at all before everything was lost?"

Aroganji frowned. "You are right, but that is not my point. We were fighting exactly for the people of Tellanon and others like them. With our success, I thought we had saved them from facing the horrors that tormented us."

"I was wrong. I lost touch with the truth but now I see."

"Until this evil is destroyed at its source, no one on Ea'ae will ever be safe."

Yip shook his head and smiled. "You are right just as you are wrong, my friend."

"You are right to say that this evil must be destroyed at its source. If we can do that, then Ea'ae and countless worlds like her will indeed be safe, at least from the Cabal."

"But so long as there is striving, so long as there is desire, so long as there is need, so long as there is suffering, the same cause that gave rise to the Cabal will replant itself and visit worlds like ours over and over."

"Such is the cycle of life."

"This cycle will remain until it is broken."

Wrindanneth shook his shaggy mane as Yip finished. "Can you try for once not to get philosophical at every opportunity? Yes, yes, so long as there is evil, there will be a need to address it."

"So long as reality is real, things will come into conflict!"

"That is, in your terminology, the expression of natural law. The universe moves toward entropy, living beings facilitate this transfer of energy. Those who are most effective at this are also the most successful. Individuals and species, races and tribes, come into conflict while doing so."

"We are not going to change that."

Yip looked at him and said simply, "We can always try."

Wrindanneth exhaled loudly, shaking his head, and, for once, held his tongue.

Piloting the ship into the docks, Wrindanneth noted the change in character of the city and her residents and visitors as had Yip. This close, the alterations were much more obvious, however.

Arms and armaments were out in force. Paratechnologists moved on land and in air in full battle regalia. Gun turrets were manned and other unmanned arms were set in place either hovering in the air or added along the defensive perimeter. Additional weaponry and fortifications were visible everywhere.

Visitors, too, appeared at the ready. Merchant vessels were fully armed, joining the large numbers of drones and contingents of manned vehicles already defending the city. Traders had wands, swords, and other defensive items visible and available for easy access. Most had forsaken the loose flowing robes of trade and travel for the heavy metal hauberks and arms of war.

Despite these precautions, however, the city still thrummed with life and vitality. Her diversity and character appeared largely intact. Trade continued even if the mood was muted. Cultural exchange took place whether its conveyers wore swords and plate or robes and pens. Tellanon remained a hub of knowledge and prosperity.

One assault on her borders was not likely to reduce her in significance.

Never taking his attention away from the ship completely, Wrindanneth glided the *Shrike* into the docks smoothly, settling into position without incident or excitement. Her sails lowered and gangplank extended, he prepared the *Shrike* for extended mooring on the docks although he did not anticipate a prolonged stay given the urgency of their charge.

If anything, with the direct attack upon the city, the pressure to secure the other seals had heightened and the success of their quest may be viewed as only a temporary measure to buy more time against further such incursions.

He shook his head.

Nothing like pressure.

At his side, preparing to disembark alongside his friends, Slate grunted, "D'ya think they missed us?"

"Humph!" Wrindanneth scoffed, "Tellanon missed us about as much as they missed us when we left…not at all."

"They need us, and people like us, but we're just an unseen cog that keeps the wheels in their world turning. Necessary but unrecognized."

Always willing to disagree, especially with Wrindanneth, Slate took a more positive slant on their return. "Ya never know. Ya might just be surprised!"

"Where's the welcoming committee? Do you see anyone standing at the gate to greet us or shower us with accolades? Is there a parade in our honor? Any dignitaries?"

"Tha Construct welcomed us!"

"The Construct knows everything that goes on in and around this city. Its welcome was nothing unusual."

Before either Slate or Wrindanneth could continue, an excited voice cut through their conversation, stopping them midstride before they could disembark. "Welcome back, good sirs! Your presence has been sorely missed!"

"With absence the heart grows fonder!"

Sensing the disturbance in the air, Yip recognized immediately that this exuberant voice was that of the Aspect, or rather their Aspect, the self-aware Fragment of the Construct that assisted them when asked and often when it was not, that watched over their home, and maintained their property and duties in their absence.

Wrindanneth let out an audible sigh but refrained from commenting, not that an errant comment would deter the Aspect's unbridled enthusiasm.

"I am ready to assist you in whatever capacity you may need! You have but to ask and I will ensure proper execution of your expressed wishes!"

Over Wrindanneth's muttered, "I wish you'd leave us alone," Yip said clearly, "We would like for you to arrange a meeting with the Paratechnologists Mazithras, Adar, and Fizzlemiz regarding the alien command sphere we gave into their possession tomorrow, if possible. We would like to know the progress of their efforts to decipher the secrets contained within the device and whether they are yet in a position to guide us in our future endeavors based upon the information, if any, revealed therein."

"Also, we would speak to the Elves regarding one of their fallen brethren. We wish to return Llyewia's possessions to their rightful keepers. Perhaps Alderan would know with whom we should speak to ensure Llyewia's material goods find their proper home and remembrance."

"Certainly! I will report as soon as I make arrangements!"

Pausing but a moment, for he knew that the Aspect could execute his request in but seconds and that his friends' sanity, Wrindanneth's at least, may depend upon this break in communication, Yip added, "You may let us know the progress of your efforts upon our return home for we must now travel to Illdrassil for an audience with the Home Guard."

"As you wish! I will see you upon your arrival!"

Yip bowed to the air for the Abstract had not given any representation of itself. "Thank you."

Resuming the conversation where it had been momentarily stopped prior to the Aspect's interruption, continuing without regard to the break in their discussion, Slate picked up his line of thought immediately where it left off, the thrust of his argument being that their summons was recognition enough. "We were also told ta proceed ta Illdrassil ta meet tha Home Guard!"

"And be given our next assignment to save the world?"

Slate shrugged. "And be given a bit of thanks and recognition."

"Anything they give us will only be couched in a request for us to do more."

"Those who can do fer others shall. Those who cannot shall stay out o' tha way!"

Wrindanneth laughed with a tinge of bitterness. "If I can, I shall do for myself!"

Though Dwarves were a taciturn lot of rugged individualists, they also often needed their brethren to survive in harsh, often hostile environs. Such was the way of the clan. "Helpin' others needn't interfere with helpin' yerself!"

He grinned widely, a temporary gap opening between the top and bottom of his beard as he tapped his temple with one thick finger. "Ya need ta start thinkin' like a Dwarf!"

Wrindanneth chuckled as he patted Slate forcefully on his broad back. "And that, my friend, is even scarier than wherever they're going to ask us to go next!"

Laughing together, Slate said, "I think ya might be right!"

Gesturing forward, Wrindanneth pointed the way over the gang-plank and off the ship. "After you. Our praise and our next quest await!"

Taking Wrindanneth up on his motion to lead, Slate was the first to walk off the ship, returning once more to the beloved firmament, while his friends followed close behind.

Standing on the gangplank, the last to leave the ship, watching the Paratechnologists at work all along the docks, their myriad shapes and forms, each molded and guided by their own imagination, Yip was struck by a simple but profound observation. Taking their life and its potential in hand, each Paratechnologist was an active participant in his own evolution, each furthered the fullest expression of humanity. With each conscious mutation, instead of shrinking, the possibilities for humanity's future expanded, opened as much by the vistas of the mind as its realization.

Like the Paratechnologists, the time had come to realize their own future.

His ruminations at an end, he walked across the plank behind his friends who were already waiting on the far side.

Joining his companions, engulfed in the swarming throngs bustling over and along the docks, the party began wending their way slowly toward the shimmering Scimerian Gate and the center of the city.

The day was bright and their future would soon be revealed.

ANON

Icicles dangle
from the boughs of ancient oaks.
Water drops shine in the sun.

Walking through the cobbled streets of Tellanon once more, her sculpted, organic beauty so evident all around, the random signs of destruction appeared all the more surprising as they passed, completely unexpected and out of place, jumping out from the pristine surroundings with startling clarity. One moment they might be walking in front of a perfectly manicured lawn, trees, and plantings arranged according to the owner's whims in front of a home seamlessly molded from a single piece of stone, and the next they would be passing a blackened pit, blasted from the earth, the prior residence only visible perhaps as a few hardened slags of molten rock. Or, in a string of shops that had been in place for long generations, several buildings might be leveled, burnt to the ground leaving only a hollow stone husk in the place of what had once been several thriving businesses. Such were the sights they took in on their return, cottages blown apart, stores reduced to ash, and lives shattered at random.

There was much work to be done. Thankfully, as the party wended their way steadily toward Illdrassil's gleaming tree-inspired tower at

Tellanon's heart, the signs of recovery and rebuilding were in greater evidence than the signs of destruction.

Passing another ruinously charred cavity, this one flanked by a Paratechnologist steadily wielding his wand to sculpt and reform the broken and shattered rock, painting in air to recreate what had been destroyed, they all took a moment to watch the mage's skill at play. Observing the Paratechnologist at work, his motions first outlined his intent, gradually filling in his vision with brushstrokes both wide and subtle, ultimately actualizing his vision step-by-step. The process was as wondrous to observe as it was complex.

Though the effort of rebuilding could have been accomplished much faster with other simpler magical techniques or in large teams of magicians working together, such was the grandeur of Tellanon that only true artisans worked to restore her damaged canvas in such a way as to be true to her original vision. Each of these artificer's brush-strokes created new masterpieces for the individual citizens fortunate enough to call their final designs home.

Yip attended the Paratechnologist with deep appreciation.

He saw the skill with which the Paratechnologist's will was expressed physically through the manipulation of matter to create his intended form. Each gesture was a manifestation of complex energetic interactions first realized by the wizard's formation of intent, then articulated through his imposition of will onto the solid stone firmament via the shifting energy currents he so deftly manipulated.

The complex expression of the Paratechnologist's resolve bridged the actual and the possible, the abstract and the physical, the magic and the mundane, the body and the mind, with each simple motion of his hand and intellect.

In recreating the fallen house, the arcane artisan repainted a wondrous vision of the home as much in the ambient energies of the surroundings as in the stone through which he worked, expressed, and restored to habitable form.

Looking a bit longingly at the shape gradually revealed by the Paratechnologist's labors where he stood beside Yip, thinking of their own home long left untended, Slate grumbled, "After all we've done, ya'd think they'd let us go home, relax, and freshen up a bit before callin' us in. I fer one grow thirstier fer some ale with each step!"

Wrindanneth barked a short laugh, wagging his fingers in front of Slate's face while crinkling his nose in distaste. "You for one need to freshen up a bit! If I were you, I'd ask Jarvis for a refund on my magical clothes because they don't seem to be working as advertised!"

"You smell a bit like the seat of a Troll's breeches! Unwashed and unkempt!"

Slate spat, glaring at Wrindanneth, "Spoutin' off such nonsense, ya sound a bit like a Troll yerself...only half as smart, twice as ugly, and nowhere near as well-spoken!"

"Then that puts me at least a few hairs ahead of you considering you have yet to master language beyond grunts and simple gestures!"

Closing in on Wrindanneth, puffing up to his full height and sticking out his thick chest, Slate said, "If ya need a language lesson, I'll be happy ta give ya one as I wash yer foul mouth out with lye!"

Arching his eyebrows in distaste, his patience at an end, Aroganji said, "If you two are done, we can be on our way."

Wrindanneth shrugged. "If we could spare but a few minutes more, I was starting to have some fun!"

Slate chortled. "And I was just startin' ta get worked up! 'Sides, I'd rather stay and watch this magician's skill at stonework than either listen ta Wrindanneth's poorly considered, lowly barbs or be tasked with another quest that delays my partakin' in o' a bit o' tha Dwarves' finest!"

Wrindanneth shook his head, looking down on his friend with a wry smile. "You know you're not serious, Slate! You're about as likely to pass up a chance to be praised as you are to pass up a tankard of free ale!"

Sharing his friend's smile, Slate chuckled. "Fer once, I can't argue!"

With that, the Four returned to formation, walking toward the palace of the Home Guard once more, leaving the magician to the undisturbed solitude and sanctity of his creation.

They walked in silence for some time, each pondering the subtle changes that had come over the city in their absence. Moving toward the center city, the crowds grew thinner and the houses and businesses grew more lavish, older, and more established. Perhaps due to their greater resources and longstanding defenses, the residences and businesses of Tellanon's heart appeared to have been spared the brunt of the assault that had sporadically damaged most parts of the rest of the city. Due to their interdimensional nature, neither existing entirely on the island or elsewhere, the parks, too, were untouched by any signs of the Cabal's attack.

The unblemished cobblestone alleyways and tree-lined boulevards of the inner city only further highlighted the fact that much of the rest of Tellanon had seen acts of random destruction.

From the street they followed, the expansive homes and establishments of the city's heart were easily accessible to one another, their entrances as close to each other as those of the smaller homes and shops on the city's perimeter. Each gate, path, or entry, however, only provided a point of access, a vantage from which to view sweeping spaces into other worlds. Broad vistas, vast estates, and massive administrative complexes all stood shoulder-to-shoulder, set upon tracts of lands too large to be contained within the floating island's limited space, separated by unimaginable distances, connected by the magical threads of the streets that provided ingress.

Each threshold provided a window into a different world.

After surveying the panoramic estates and large complexes interspersed through the center city for some time as they walked toward Illdrassil, Wrindanneth finally remarked, "By Maeth's hoary chest this city is surreal!"

"You've got signs of the first infiltration of the city's defenses by the attacking Cabal scattered all around like unwanted litter throughout the city's outer perimeter. Then you cross over to the city's center and all the damage goes away as though the battle never happened. Either any repairs to the city's heart were completed much more expeditiously, the extradimensional nature of much of the space protected the area, or additional defenses here prevented damage from reaching the ground."

Before anyone could offer any comment, Wrindanneth added, "I know most of the structures here do not reside fully on Tellanon. The unusual nature of the place only heightens the outlandishness of the impression."

Finishing quietly, talking largely to himself, he said, "Whatever the case, it certainly appears odd."

Aroganji nodded in agreement. "A stark contrast to the rest of the city."

Slate's eyes never stopped their motion, constantly assessing the surroundings. Though they passed many merchants, travelers, Paratechnologists, and members of the Home Guard all dressed in garb suitable for the heightened state of security, the muted sense of the place weighed heavily upon his broad shoulders. "Seems a bit too quiet if ya ask me."

He shrugged, adding, "Maybe tha distance ta all these buildin's that should be clustered so close together heightens tha feelin' o' isolation and quietude."

"I'm sure it won't be too quiet when you hear your next set of marching orders!" his own ruminations temporarily at an end, Wrindanneth's sly grin enticed the Dwarf invitingly.

"Ya'd better believe it! They'll know how their request weighs upon this Dwarf's heart!"

His voice tinted with light sarcasm, Wrindanneth said, "About like the baubles and bangles about your beard?"

Slate snarled at his friend's affront against the tokens of honor bedecking his glorious beard. "Grrrr... They're Kazzak ya fool Northlander!"

Reaching for his shining axe Duraeleon, he added, "If ya don't watch yer tongue, I may claim one o' yer teeth as my next addition!"

Wrindanneth patted him patronizingly on the shoulder. "Then you may finally have something of true value in your possession."

Before Slate could put his clenched fists into action, Aroganji interjected, "If you two children are done prattling, we'll be off!"

Turning his back to Wrindanneth in disdain, Slate relaxed his fists and said, "That's about tha best suggestion I've heard all day!"

Once more on track, for their whims and curiosity easily led them astray, the Fists resumed their journey without distraction, moving forward in deliberately casual conversation, at least by their standards.

With Illdrassil finally nearing, her crystalline spire shimmering like the first day after Brendle's forge finally quieted during the last moments of creation, Slate joked, "Ya know, if we take much longer ta reach Illdrassil, they're gonna eat supper and bed down fer tha night without seein' us!" The thought of missing a meal weighed heavily upon him, especially when, by his reckoning at least, they might miss more than one for they had not yet taken a mid-day meal.

"Don't worry Slate, you've got enough blubber under your suit of armor to tide you over for weeks. Worst case, they'll send out a search party so that our dallying doesn't delay their request to get more work out of us!"

"And yer forked tongue shows yer kinship ta snakes, not Man! Now take up Aroganji's advice and stop yer blabberin' before I cut out yer tongue, tan it, and use it ta patch tha worn leather on my old boots!"

While Wrindanneth and Slate resumed their bickering, Yip appreciated the play of light from Illdrassil's mellifluous shadow, visible even before they reached the central governmental grounds. Refracted through her overarching branches, leaves, and trunk, fragments of rainbows landed in brilliant profusion at odd angles on random planes and surfaces, magical gems embedded and scattered on the refractive ground and nearby objects.

What truly amazed him was not that such wondrous objects existed but that each ray of bent light flowed forth from Illdrassil with the essence of Heaven—refined *chi* bathed the citizens of Tellanon directly in the concentrated energies of life's creation.

He could imagine few ways to uplift or enliven a populace more than to bask in such invigorating, inspiring surroundings.

With the crystalline spires of Illdrassil and her attendant structures looming larger with each step, the lambent walls surrounding her grounds rose more and more formidably as they drew nearer. Atop the walls, around the open archways passing through the battlement's luminous shadow, and within the magical courtyards visible through these openings beyond the barricade's fastness, resplendent members of the Home Guard bedecked in full battle regalia gleamed with Illdrassil's splendor arrayed in their translucent crystalline armor.

Some of the Guard wore added capes of multiple designs, devices, and colors that billowed loosely in the breeze. Others wore plumage atop their helms emblematic of their station or origin. A few wore highly decorated kilts denoting clan and lineage. Still more wore belts and sashes, bangles and badges and other similar insignia demonstrating past honors, ranks, and affiliations. Most wore swords but halberds, staves, spears, axes, and other devices of war bristled about their armored forms as numerous as the barbs on a cactus. Almost all appeared to have more than one weapon of choice. By and large, the majority of these handheld weapons glimmered in the sun with the same radiance as Illdrassil herself.

Though a spectacle to behold moving about within Illdrassil's vast shadow, few would wish to stare upon the Home Guard's radiance overlong should their light shine forth for purposes beyond simple patrols.

Out of earshot of the Guards, assuming their hearing was not magnified by magical means, Slate whispered to Wrindanneth during a lull in their argument, "Fer those o' tha Guard that aren't Dwarves or Elves, I wonder if they need lights at night ta see by as they walk along their patrols or if tha radiance o' their armor is enough ta suffice on a moonless night."

Smiling innocently, Wrindanneth said enticingly, "You can always ask."

"And I could have ya try and sneak in and test my theory!"

Wrindanneth laughed. "If their vision isn't enhanced by magic then I'm your long lost cousin!"

Exhaling in mock relief, Slate smiled as he said, "Glad ta say ya're no kin o' mine!"

"Feeling's mutual."

By this time, they had reached the southern archway into Illdrassil's courtyard. Waiting near at hand, her passage was guarded by a company of Home Guard arranged before, beyond, and within its bounds.

"Looks like tha welcome mats have been rolled out fer us!" Slate did not care if his comments were overheard though he might feign otherwise.

The squadron of Home Guard consisted of ten members. Two Elves, two Dwarves, two Gnomes, two Men, and two members of a race none of them had encountered before stood as sentinels around the entrance.

The Elves held position beyond the archway in fully burnished Witchwood armor. At their sides were thinly tapered swords that held the full spectrum of the seasons within their lambent blades—greens, golds, browns, reds, and yellows. Across their backs were comely bows lovingly crafted with the same attention and care for the life within that had been the primary characteristic of Llyewia's *lianel*. Standing still, the graceful elegance of their forms implied a ceaseless relaxed motion.

The Elves were joined by the two vaguely humanoid insectile creatures that looked like nothing more than gigantic vaguely humanoid praying mantises. Plates of the Guard's lucent armor were arranged and fastened about their abdomens, heads, arms, and torsos strengthening their already fearsome defenses. To Yip, these insectile creatures looked like formidable Quai-lo though they were far too intelligent and their essences burned too brightly to be related to the insectile predators of his native Chang Sen. Like the Elves, they glowed with a radiance that melded effortlessly with the life energies moving all around, showing their strong rapport for the land and its energies. Standing together as they were, he could see why the two races would have a natural affinity.

Under the arch of the wall's dome, the pair of Gnomes and Dwarves stood facing each other at attention. Each Gnome wore a fully customized Paratechnological battlesuit. One Gnome appeared to be housed in a small suit of silvery biomechanical armor that looked modeled upon the endoskeleton of a particularly hostile barbed humanoid. The other Gnome was housed in a transparent clockwork robotic exoskeleton armed with rockets, guns, chains, jets, scopes, and too many other objects to be fully named, cataloged, or identified in a single glance.

Each Dwarf held a massive, rune-covered two-handed battle axe gripped firmly in both hands. Lying strapped diagonally across their thick shoulders, each wore a hand-held cannon that resembled an early, stylized arquebus. These guns, known as Guernden, were sometimes referred to as Dragon's Gullets for they spewed forth magical fires as hot as those flames seen licking upon a Dragon's scaled maw.

Outside the compound's walls, standing on either side of the entrance to the archway, the two Men, one swarthy and dark-haired, the other fair and blond-haired, both armed with sword and buckler, remained focused upon the approaching visitors. The dark skinned

Man was tall and thin and gave the appearance of ready speed and agility. His light-skinned companion was solidly built and exuded strength and power.

In unison, the two Men said, "State your name and business." Their sword arms angled downward such that the blades of their weapons barred passage while the tips of their brands rested lightly upon the ground.

Wrindanneth stepped forward and bowed at the request, pointing out each of the members of the party in turn, giving them names loosely indicative of their characters, names that they may never use again. "We are Slate the Stout, Wrindanneth the Red, Aroganji the Wise, and Yip the Stoic at your service. Some know us as the Four, others as the Fists. Those who are more loquacious perhaps know us as the Four of the Flaming Fists. Others may not know us at all."

Finishing his bow with a flourish, he added, "We are here at the behest of Éremon and Eidelion and seek your leave for safe passage."

While under the Guards' direct scrutiny, with a brief sensation akin to being dunked in cold water, each was scanned and assessed for hostile magics, identification, and approval for access to the citadel beyond. When all was deemed well, the two Guards gave a brief nod, lifting their weapons upward, and said in unison once more, "You are expected. You may pass."

Passing the stoic Dwarves and alert Gnomes on either side of the cool passage, the Elven and insectile Guards stepped agilely out of their path, gesturing for them to continue. As they moved forward, one of the Elves motioned forward in the direction they were heading and a softly glowing radiant blue orb came into existence.

With a brief open bow of welcome, the lithe Elf said, "Please follow the wisp light. It will guide you to your destination."

Accompanying his friends beyond the protective circle of the Guard, Yip bowed as he passed, offering a brief, "Thank you."

Walking away from the complex's external fortifications, Aroganji remarked inquiringly, "I wonder what race that was with the other Guard. I have never seen its like before. Perhaps it is a distant, more intelligent, relative of the Quai-lo."

Wrindanneth shrugged. "Based on our experience with the rank and file of the Home Guard on our journey, they certainly appear to be as diverse as the populace and visitors of Tellanon itself. Who knows how many races are present within their ranks or where exactly they originally hail from prior to joining service? Since Tellanon's interests span so many worlds, I would guess that the people of Ea'ae represent but a fraction of the Guard's overall composition."

Slate grunted, "We've seen but tha tip, I'm sure. Each patrol I've seen seems ta have somethin' new and unexpected in it every time!"

Wrindanneth grinned and goaded, "Kind of like your mother's stew?"

Not breaking pace in the slightest with the insult, Slate retorted, "Kind o' like tha random bits o' yesterday's meals lodged 'twixt yer yellowed teeth."

"Or like the assorted fungal crops growing between your crusty toes?"

"Or like tha multicolored wax nuggets lodged in yer ear canals?"

"Tasty!"

Chiding them both, for he grew tired of their adolescent sport, Aroganji scolded, "If you two are done, we need to follow the ghost light before it burns and fizzles out as a result of your delays. Compose yourselves. The Guard are probably monitoring your activities as you carry on!"

"Yes, mother!" Wrindanneth often had the mindset of a child, but, even if his disposition did not always reflect a ready good cheer, his sense of humor, however twisted, was seldom sidetracked or muted by circumstance, no matter how bleak.

"Bah! If he were yer mother, he'd smack ya upside yer woolly head with a paddle! Unfortunately fer us all, 't'wouldn't do any good!"

Speaking in a low voice, Wrindanneth replied to Slate flatly, "We can certainly see where you get all your good ideas! Unfortunately, such treatment did not serve you well either!"

Before Aroganji could offer further admonishments to curb their bickering and dawdling, Yip raised a hand, saying, "Let them argue. That is how they communicate and have their fun. If nothing else, the Home Guard will share in their humor." Knowing that no revelation would come of such observation, he added simply, "The Guard already understand what they are in for after having worked with us."

Shaking his head with an exasperated but accepting exhale, Aroganji replied, "I fear you are correct."

Their stream of invectives and castigations unabated, Wrindanneth and Slate continued following the luminescent sphere without further distraction.

Yip followed the glowing wisp of light with his friends as it guided them through the glamour and wonder of Illdrassil's splendid shadows. Though Illdrassil's roots and branches intertwined through the landscape with such artful skill and subtlety so as to intentionally catch the eye, leading the viewer's gaze from one iridescent convolution to the next, the grounds, the play of light and shadow, and the plantings nestled throughout were not the object of his attention.

Though he had been here before, immersed in Illdrassil's full grandeur, Yip's mind wandered with intricacies far more complex and refined with the awe of the first visitation. All around, aetheric currents, unimpeded and channeled, focused and diffuse, magnified and diluted, flowing and stored, shifted in kaleidoscopic profusion. So complex were these interactions that a mind could get lost, never to emerge again from within the labyrinth. What impressed him most, however, was not the intrinsic beauty or wonder of the place but rather the sheer astronomical amounts of energy moved and stored in ever greater amounts as they approached Illdrassil.

To what end these incalculable amounts of power were put, he could not say though he certainly could infer. Illdrassil's radiant spire appeared to store all the energy Tellanon could ever need from mundane city operations to defense. This certainly explained the blinding intensity of the effulgent crystalline tree sprouting from Tellanon's scintillating heart.

"You're looking around like a lovestruck puppy, Yip!" Wrindanneth broke away from his bickering with Slate long enough to tease Yip as well.

"When enveloped by untold majesty, only those who choose not to see do not appreciate its wonder." Yip's simple comment was not intended as a slight, merely as an honest assessment.

"See! I always told ya that ya needed glasses, Wrin! Ya're about as blind as a luckless cave slug!" Slate, unlike Wrindanneth, was eager to return to the thread of his arguments for he was now building up considerable steam in his rebuttals.

"And you're about as handsome!" With a quick quip, Wrindanneth quickly changed gears and returned to his original line of inquiry. "Now if you don't mind, I was about to ask what exactly captured Yip's attention like stale, decades-old ale captures yours."

Ignoring the argument, Yip answered his friend's query simply, "I was appreciating the energy currents shifting and moving all around us, mirroring the complexity and beauty of the structures and gardens. Just as Illdrassil is the city's heart, so, too, does its pulse provide the city with life."

Wrindanneth smiled appreciatively without a hint of sarcasm before finally saying, "Sounds well worth the inspection."

Yip gave a slight nod in answer as he quietly returned to his study.

While Yip returned to silence, Wrindanneth and Slate returned to their heated dialogue.

For his part, Aroganji returned to ignoring them both. With all the practice since first making Slate and Wrindanneth's acquaintances, he now had developed the skill into a fine art.

He could now assume the countenance of a stone without resorting to magic.

Friendship often had its unforeseen gifts.

The ghost light finally led them to an opening between Illdrassil's massive luminous roots, a gleaming grotto surrounded by lush, terraced greenery spilling forth from planters, hangings, and platforms. Within this recessed alcove, framed by the multitudes of beautiful flowering plants and trees basking in Illdrassil's radiance, members of the Home Guard stood flanked by an honor guard of elite troops from numerous races. All waited patiently for the Four at full attention. At the heart of this arrangement, the familiar faces of Éremon, Eidelion, Daerdros, and Spreesprocket stood out from the varied ranks of Home Guard.

Upon seeing their arrival, Eidelion's charismatic face lit up with a smile as radiant as the halo of Light surrounding him so visibly in Yip's eyes, an expression shared by Éremon, Daerdros, and Spreesprocket who stood with him at the center of the gathering at the far end of the recess. Gesturing eagerly, Spreesprocket waved them forward, their presence all that was required to turn this grand gathering into an equally enthusiastic party.

While Yip's eyes briefly lingered on those who were there, his thoughts drifted to those who were not—Orogast, the miraculous shapeshifter whose colorful past and abilities remained a mystery after his unforeseen, though glorious departure; Kazarhan, a lineage holder in Dwarven metallurgy, magical runes, and divine Craft, taken perhaps prematurely before he could share his knowledge fully with the next generation; Raour'Saqan, a Dracodaeran Shaur'Daus so fearsome that even Daemons gave him wide berth; and Llyewia, the stargazing Elf whose insights and perspectives would be missed as much as the moon on a cloudy night. Though not all were entirely gone, their assistance and camaraderie, advice and discernment would be sorely missed in the travails ahead.

How many more would be lost?

How much more suffering would come in the times ahead?

Which lights would be extinguished without hope of rekindling?

Interrupting Yip's thoughts, though he appeared to be speaking conversationally as he, too, urged them forward, Éremon spoke for those gathered on their behalf, his resonant voice filling the copious space they would soon occupy. "Aroganji, Wrindanneth, Slate, and Yip, Four of the Flaming Fists, heroes of the realm, stalwarts of Tellanon, step forward and let your deeds be judged!"

"Come forth before Tellanon's Home Guard and let your tale be told!"

"Let your words be true, your minds clear, and your actions just for your measure will be taken on this day for all to appraise!"

Clapping together both hands thunderously, he finished, "Come forth and know your worth!"

Spreesprocket visibly stifled a chuckle at the formal, imposing nature of the summons. Eidelion, too, seemed to garner a mixture of pleasure and pride from the seriousness of Éremon's summons given the circumstances of their meeting and the joy he felt with his friends' remarkable success. Daerdros, however, remained poised and disciplined, her face a mask.

While her friends and companions shared in the joy of their

reunion, the thought of the impending praise for deeds well-earned, and the success of their recent quest, Daerdros's mind lingered upon the forthcoming trials, other deeds of import not yet finished, and the legions of Cabal yet roaming free within Ea'ae's borders. Though the shield around Ea'ae and Tellanon both had been restored, much damage had been done to Ea'ae's populace and cities beyond Tellanon's bounds.

More would be forthcoming.

Just as Ea'ae's people were still in danger, so, too, were the fragile, unrestored seals that yet held her newly reconstituted planetary shield together.

The risks were unavoidable.

Though her friends were excited and though she wished to share in their joy in honor of the moment, temporary flashes of lightness allowed but fleetingly in these grave times, she would not allow herself to partake in even the briefest break in concentration while her enemies stalked unchecked within the borders of her world. Nor would she waver when she was not on the hunt for her quarry.

Taking the lead as Éremon spoke, Wrindanneth walked forward at the fore of the group, opening his arms in greeting as he spoke for his companions. "If I didn't know any better, I'd think you were excited to have us back!"

Eidelion laughed in reply, his voice booming across the distance between them. "Don't get ahead of yourself!"

Unused to such informality in their official occasions, the assembled Guard remained composed, keeping their eyes ahead and untouched by the festive reunion.

With Illdrassil's roots growing larger and more prominent around them as they moved forward toward the massive, glimmering trunk looming behind the Guard, Wrindanneth, Aroganji, Slate, and Yip quickly closed in on their former traveling companions for a welcome, if brief, reunion.

His long arms spread wide, a beacon as bright as Illdrassil herself, Éremon intoned, "Welcome home, my friends! Though momentous and critical to the peoples of Ea'ae, your deeds are not as welcome as your return!"

"Bah!" Slate's beard split with a wide grin as he took to the dais on which the Guard stood in a graceful leap. "Ya're not foolin' anyone, Éremon! Yer flattery is welcome but unnecessary! Tha last thing I want is ta force ya inta a lie on our behalf!"

Sharing a solid clinch with Eidelion as Slate took to the stage, Eidelion countered with a laugh, continuing the levity. "You know as well as I that Éremon does not deal in falsehood! A bit of obfuscation perhaps but he never dissembles!"

Wrindanneth nodded as he joined Slate with one single long stride. "Eidelion has it right, Slate. They're glad to have us back so they don't have to worry about sending a rescue party to retrieve the people who really matter—Eidelion, Daerdros, and Spreesprocket!"

Spreesprocket shrugged, the dismissive gesture belied by his infectious smile. "Well, as long as you remember to keep things in the proper perspective..."

"We'll retain tha right ta go on another quest where we might be lucky enough ta have tha cavalry sent in ta rescue us?"

Spreesprocket nodded sagely. "Exactly!"

"Glad ta hear we have tha difficult part o' tha conversation outta tha way!"

"Do not fear, Slate, we have much of import yet to discuss."

Taking the stage with Slate, Aroganji smiled as he bowed first to Éremon. "Do not be misled by my brethren, our eyes are as glad to see you as yours are to see us!"

"Dissemblin' all around! I'll not stand fer it!" Slate's grin and good cheer were infectious.

The last to join the others on the dais, Yip hopped up gracefully beside his friends, offering a deep, heartfelt bow upon taking the stage. "We are as blessed to return as we are by the opportunity to continue to aid and serve the peoples of Tellanon and Ea'ae in the times to come."

His salutation complete, standing back while all his friends embraced, clasped arms, and patted each other on the back in a frenzy of exuberant greeting, Yip remained as still as the Guard arrayed so impressively behind him. Holding similar positions within the Home Guard, Éremon and Daerdros both held themselves slightly apart from the others while smiling brightly amidst the fray.

His sentiments not exactly as positive as his fellows, Yip held his tongue for he would only emphasize the gravity of the situation, those lost, and those unable to join the reunion.

Letting the reunification and its attendant rituals continue for several minutes, Éremon waited patiently while the initial good cheer lasted knowing that the festivities would soon come to an all too abrupt end.

Finally, after a few minutes of jibes, rejoinders, light questions, and brief answers had passed without touching upon the true purpose of their meeting, Éremon spoke solemnly. "As you may already know, the success of your mission and the restoration of the seal of Eldre'gheu prevented Tellanon's fall at the hands of the Cabal's usurpers."

When looks of surprise and anger greeted this brief statement, Éremon elaborated briefly, "In your absence, Tellanon, along with many other cities across Ea'ae, fell victim to assaults by massive fleets of extradimensional invaders cloaked in protective, all-consuming Darkness. These invaders pushed through Ea'ae's weakened interplanetary shield and wrought untold destruction across our world. Were it not for the timely restoration of the seal kept within your possession, Ea'ae, and Tellanon with it, may have fallen for our numbers and defenses are no longer what they once were."

His face a mixture of joy and sorrow, a reserved smile worn on his face, Éremon looked to Aroganji, Wrindanneth, Slate, and Yip in turn, saying gravely, "You have done your world and its peoples a fateful service, one that will never be forgotten. On behalf of the free peoples of Tellanon, her allies, adjutants, and associates, I offer my deepest gratitude and heartfelt appreciation."

"Though not a condition of your service, know that you will be rewarded as you see fit for your meritorious efforts in our defense."

"Though your quest met with success and we are currently free from risk of further incursions, those invaders that pushed through and were not destroyed pose a continued threat to Ea'ae, her populace, and the seals that protect us all from further attack."

"Even more importantly, with Yip's most generous gift, knowledge of the Dragon's Gate and its most ingenious application, innumerable worlds, Ea'ae included, will be spared the horrific, life-stealing fate unleashed upon so many others. The forces of Light now have a formidable weapon, a necessary counter, at our disposal, one that should help ensure the futures of countless lives that might otherwise be lost."

Looking at Yip directly, Éremon bowed as lithely as an Elf, a feat that appeared even more graceful given his stature, and said, "On behalf of the peoples of Tellanon, Ea'ae, and those beyond, you have our undying gratitude and blessing. We will be forever in your debt and always at your service."

Broadening his gaze once more to encompass all gathered before him, he continued, "The Cabal and their ilk would be wise to respect this formidable option for their time may soon be at an end!"

Pausing significantly, breaking for a moment from what was and what may be, Éremon intoned, "Fists, please step forward to receive your commendations!"

Éremon's deep eyes turned to each of the Four in turn as he spoke, his resonant voice filling them with surety and warmth as he did so. "Though you may ask of us what you will, there is something we would give you."

"We would have you take a piece of Tellanon with you, her heart and her strength, wherever your heart may lead."

"We would give you a piece of Illdrassil as a blessing from that which sustains us all."

"You have earned a place among us and the boons that protect us. From this day forward, you will wear the Star of Illdrassil upon your breast or brow knowing that her mantle protects your essence and fosters your purpose."

With a brief wave of Éremon's hand, four clear, crystalline teardrops appeared in his palm, each as perfectly formed as a dewdrop newly settled delicately on a still blade of grass.

Taking the pure stones from Éremon's open palm, Eidelion affixed one Star upon each of the Fists' chests in turn while Éremon spoke. "You may wear this Star directly upon your skin, as is the custom of the Guard, or upon your clothing. In either case, the Star will stay with you. The Star blends perfectly with whatever it adheres to and will remain undetectable should your security ever be compromised."

"Each Star is attuned to you and you alone. Should you expire, the Star will pass with you."

"Each stone contains within something of Illdrassil and thus will add to your potential, your ability, and your inherent capacity. Just as the Star will add to you, so, too, may you add to the Star for she will store some of your Light should you choose to give it."

"Each Star also holds within the primary defenses of the Guard. Though not limitless, either automatically or in response to a threat, these boons will protect you in times of need, replenish you when you are hurt, and aid you in performing the tasks necessary to defeat the force of Darkness. These are the same enchantments that Daerdros and Kazarhan cast upon you to aid in your assault upon the black temple of Eldre'gheu though they will now be yours to call upon at will."

"To these protections you have seen, there is one more, the mantle of greater invisibility, should you need to remain hidden from the eyes and minds of your foes."

"Each Star draws upon the power within and the ambient energies without, so you need not fear of depleting its reserves."

"Wear these tokens proudly and in full knowledge that we could grant you no greater compliment."

Yip bowed as Éremon completed his description. "We will be honored to carry on the legacy that these Stars represent."

Studying the small crystals that resembled nothing more than minute water droplets as they were placed on each of them in turn, he wondered at the power contained within. If such a small portion of Illdrassil could do so much, he could not fathom the amount of power stored and potentiality available within the shimmering walls of Illdrassil herself. The magnitude of the difference would be something akin to the difference in scale between the energies available in the *chi* and the *yuan-chi*, a drop of water and an ocean.

While Yip studied the Stars, Aroganji replied earnestly for his fellows. "As are we." Aroganji, Wrindanneth, and Slate all declined their heads in agreement.

The commendation complete, Éremon shifted the conversation from the past to the future. "The task before us now, one that I entreat you to continue if you be willing and able, is to continue your efforts to rid Ea'ae of these interlopers and secure her borders through the renewal of her seals."

"The purpose before you, the endeavor we propose, is one fraught with danger and hardship." Here his gaze visibly saddened, his unflappable mien darkening briefly, a storm crossing in front of the sun temporarily lessening its radiance, while he paused thinking of those lost along the way and the terrible cost of success, before continuing, "Though we ourselves incurred horrendous loss, of all the teams tasked with restoring the fallen and damaged seals, yours..."

"You mean to say, 'ours.'" Though Yip was loath to interrupt, he wanted it understood that their success together had been just that, the work of a team functioning in unison toward a common goal, one in which the Home Guard had borne a heavy burden in their losses but that they had performed in conjunction.

Éremon continued with a smile following the correction, carrying forward with the impetus of one not interrupted. "Ours is the only one that has yet met with any measure of success."

Pausing once again, his tone becoming grave, Éremon continued, "We fear the others are lost. Though there yet may be some hope that our scrying is wrong, this, too, is unlikely."

"Though the paths of these brave defenders may not have ended as we would hope, we must even now send forth more stalwarts at dire peril to ensure the safety of our world's seals."

"So in good faith and humility, without full understanding of the risks and travails ahead, we ask once more that you go where others have failed and do what others have left undone, if you are willing and if you are able."

Yip bowed in reply to Éremon's gracious words, speaking while he moved. "We are most honored and humbled by your praise and share both your concerns and motivations."

Returning to his normal relaxed posture from the bow, Yip continued, "Our purpose is yours—ensuring the long-term prosperity, health, and security of the peoples of Ea'ae and all those beyond, endeavoring to create a world wherein all are free to realize their potential and the fulfillment of their personal visions. With our return to Tellanon, determining how to most effectively and efficiently achieve these far-reaching goals is our intent."

"We have before us several paths any one of which may or may not lead to our ultimate goals. You have offered us a most noble quest continuing onward, one that builds upon our recent mission to secure Ea'ae's future. This course would keep us on Ea'ae while working to correct and restore our world's defenses while simultaneously seeking to undermine the efforts of the Cabal and their allies skulking here within our shadows."

"From our past endeavors trying to realize these aims, we obtained a command sphere taken from a vessel allied with the Cabal. This item, along with other alien technology, is currently under scrutiny by a team of Paratechnologists led by Mazithras and Fizzlemiz within the city. With any luck, once cracked and deciphered, the information from this command sphere may lead us directly to the source of the evil that has so recently breached our world's defenses, dooming too many and imperiling so many more. This second path will allow us to strike at our attackers directly and overthrow their seat of power once uncovered."

"We may continue to tread upon both paths simultaneously, working directly to protect Ea'ae and her peoples while restoring the seals should the mysteries of the command sphere remain unraveled or unhelpful if finally uncovered. As the most likely, this third path, one of patience balancing the two primary options before us, may lead us to the ultimate goal we desire beyond securing Ea'ae's immediate future—the overthrow of the Cabal, the primary threat to our world and others."

"However, despite the natural alignment of our goals and ideals, we ask that you allow us the time to weigh each path before making our decision as to which approach to take."

Speaking for Éremon, Eidelion nodded in understanding while Yip finished. "Before you make your choice, we ask that you hear our proposal that your final decision may be fully informed."

Briefly turning his gaze to Éremon, Eidelion continued, "As Éremon explained, our fellowship appears to be the only grouping that has met with any measure of success in restoring or replacing the damaged seals. We hope that your future efforts will continue against this course. Though we wish it were otherwise"—here his gaze shifted to Daerdros and Spreesprocket—"we will not be able to join you personally in this effort should you choose to continue on our behalf. The protection of both the city itself and the coordination of efforts to root out and destroy those invaders that broke through Ea'ae's defensive perimeter require our direct attention."

Though imperceptible to less discerning eyes, Yip detected a faint sigh, a release of tension in Eidelion's shoulders indicating that he might prefer to remain engaged in the efforts to restore the seals and combat the Cabal directly rather than adhering to his required, though necessary, duties. Spreesprocket's clenched jaw and Daerdros's steely eyes spoke similarly. "In our stead, however, we have selected a cadre of elite Guard capable of furthering your, our, mission." Here he paused and smiled before resuming. "Should you accept, you will be introduced to these soldiers at a later time. Otherwise, they will form the nucleus of a strike force intended to complete this quest in your absence. As such, their identities and intentions must be protected until your determination is reached."

"For similar reasons, though we cannot tell you which seal would be your next target should you choose not to accept, we can say that the journey will be as perilous as the one you just so courageously completed. As before, you will port to the nearest *faerviage* portal remaining after the Cabal's assaults upon Ea'ae's major population centers and proceed from this location through territories currently under heavy conflict for control with these same alien forces. Understanding these challenges, we will also reoutfit your ship to improve upon its core capabilities and functionalities in order to increase the likelihood of the mission's success."

"You should be aware that these proposed augmentations for the *Shrike* are up for discussion after we have your decision based upon your preferences and advice in addition to our own. Furthermore, you will have the opportunity to improve your own personal accouterments and weaponry from our stores should you so choose."

At this Slate and Wrindanneth looked at each other and grinned wickedly.

Yip bowed once more to Eidelion. "Thank you, Eidelion. We appreciate your candor and generosity. We must seek counsel with the Elves in addition to the Paratechnologists before choosing our path."

Widening his gaze to include Eidelion, Spreesprocket, and Daerdros, he said, "If we do accept your offer, we will miss your company on our quest for your wisdom and guidance, strength and resilience, were most welcome beacons in times of darkness and turmoil."

Offering a slight nod in acknowledgement, Eidelion replied, "You are far too gracious." Most generously, he added brightly, "Your company and skills were most welcome as well."

Addressing Spreesprocket directly, Yip finished, "We are ready to see to Llyewia's final affairs when you are. You have but to let us know when you are ready to visit the Elves and we will go with you."

Spreesprocket wore a stoic face, one that masked the emotions warring beneath the surface of his otherwise cheerful visage at the thought of his friend. "Will you be available tomorrow?"

Without looking to his friends, Yip answered, "Yes."

"I will contact you at first light."

Yip nodded solemnly. "Tomorrow then."

"Aye."

Before Yip could speak further, Wrindanneth finished, eager to move onward with their decision, their quest, and their business in Tellanon, "You will have your answer by evening tomorrow if we are able to meet with both the Paratechnologists and Elves in the next day."

"Thank you," Eidelion's words were sincere, the perfect match to his smile.

Éremon waited but a moment before finishing the audience. "Whatever path you choose, know that you are heroes and will be treated accordingly. We owe you much and more and will never forget your character, perseverance, and selflessness in the presence of overwhelming challenges on behalf of many you have never met nor seen."

"Your triumph is our hope."

With a sweep of his wrist, indicating the shimmering crystalline pendants on their breasts, as bright as Illdrassil and equally lustrous, each capturing the rays of the sun within as its light refracted over and over about the individual facets, filling the jewels with a golden sphere of light, Éremon intoned, "Know that you now wear the Star of Illdrassil, Tellanon's highest commendation. The light within is your own and will grow with you should you ever have need. Call upon its Light as you would your own."

"Go forth with our blessing and honor, Four of the Flaming Fists!"

Eidelion, Daerdros, and Spreesprocket bowed deeply with Éremon's pronouncement. Beside and behind them, the courtyard rang as the assembled Guard saluted them simultaneously, first beating their fists upon their chests and then brandishing their weapons over-head in salute.

Returning the bow, Yip, Aroganji, Slate, and Wrindanneth then turned and walked calmly from under Illdrassil's lustrous dancing shadow.

Before they finally set their sights homeward, Aroganji, Wrindanneth, Yip, and Slate had one more destination in mind, one more errand to run, one more site to visit prior to making arrangements for the morrow, one more item taking them away from the comfort and secu-rity of their long-neglected cottage.

They wished to seek out Hoyt for advice on how to proceed, news of the day, and an overview of what had transpired in their absence. A wellspring of information, his guidance would be crucial to their success both in choosing the optimal path ahead and in navigating that path once their choice had been made.

While they walked back toward the docks to the warehouse district where Hoyt's shop resided, so far from Illdrassil at the city's heart, Slate made casual conversation to pass the time. "Fer all their quirks and oddities, I'm gonna miss travelin' with Eidelion, Daerdros, and Spreesprocket. Tha Home Guard've taught us much and kept us alive s'many times I feel like I'll be leavin' behind a part o' me family when we shove off...wherever we end up goin'."

"With all your idiosyncrasies, awkwardness, and eccentricities, I'll bet they're glad to get rid of you and want no part of you in their family! I'm sure they'll be delighted to not have to worry about saving your dusty hide every time the action gets thick!" Wrindanneth's smug jibe sounded hollow in his ears for he knew that his words did not ring true. However, in the spirit of one-upmanship, exaggerating his case was almost always a good ploy with Slate.

"They've offered me a spot in tha Guard, I'll thank ya very much! Beyond that, I can't think o' higher praise from 'em! If it weren't fer my concern over Aroganji's life in yer hands, and tha potential fer Yip's corruption with yer soulless banter, I'd abandon ya t'yer black fate, ya flea bitten son o' Troll lice!"

"And if weren't for the pleasure of watching your face writhe in torment every time you laid your eyes upon me, I'd leave you to your fate, you addlebrained spawn of a mutant troglodyte!"

Neither one willing to back down, Wrindanneth and Slate glared at each other for most of the remainder of the walk back toward the docks.

By the time they reached the warehouse district, Slate's stomach was growling like an avalanche tumbling in full force and Wrindanneth's patience, already thin, was at the end of its short line. Before the combination of Slate's surliness due to his hunger and Wrindanneth's rancor regarding life in general could escalate into an all-out confrontation, Yip pulled them up in surprise well before they reached the alleyway leading to Hoyt's shop.

Snapping his left arm up, bent at the elbow, Yip called them to an abrupt stop. "He's gone! Hoyt's not here!"

Not sharing his surprise, Aroganji replied calmly, "He's probably just out running an errand. Hoyt doesn't wander off too often and when he does, he returns shortly."

Clarifying, Yip replied, "No. He's gone. His shop's gone. Everything we would associate with him is gone!"

Incredulous, Slate asked the unthinkable. "Ya think he was hit by tha invaders like some o' tha other spots in town?"

Yip shook his head. "I do not sense anything of the kind but let us see directly. I sense that he gathered everything up by choice using magic at his discretion."

Their hunger and bitterness temporarily forgotten, Slate and Wrindanneth followed Yip and Aroganji's rapid footsteps down the byways of the docks toward the spot once occupied by Hoyt's bazaar of the bizarre. Sure enough, as they rounded the last corner, Yip's impressions were confirmed for all to see.

Between two old, worn warehouses, the spot once occupied by Hoyt's – Oddities, Found Goods, and Sundries stood vacant, an empty, dusty lot without hint or trace of its recent occupant, all memories wiped clean with his flight.

Yip carefully read the energy traceries flowing through the air noting that his impressions were indeed correct. Although nothing untoward had happened, Hoyt appeared to have left in a hurry.

Slowly letting what his eyes showed him sink in, Slate scratched his head wearily. Finally, he muttered incredulously, for Hoyt had been their anchor as long as he had visited Tellanon, well before he ever met Yip, "He's gone and he hasn't returned!"

Similar disbelief colored Aroganji's face. "Let us hope that he is well and will return in short order."

Not willing to stand by passively and sulk, Wrindanneth barked, "Aspect!"

Within an instant, a chipper voice replied, "Yes sir! How may I be of assistance?"

"Locate Hoyt, proprietor of Hoyt's – Oddities, Found Goods, and Sundries."

"One moment." A brief moment of pregnant silence filled the air.

"Hoyt is not currently on Tellanon. He was last seen aboard the *Rare Aer* with the vessel's captain Humbol during the confrontation and failed assault upon Tellanon. Hoyt and Humbol are known to have engaged the enemy during this confrontation. More than this is currently not available for retrieval or analysis."

"Try to find him for us! Add that to your list of items to report on later today!" Wrindanneth wanted to talk to his friend not talk about his potential last acts.

"Yes sir!"

With those words, the Abstract was silent, as were the Fists.

Shaking his head in disbelief, for he could hardly imagine Hoyt in any other capacity than as a fixture in his shop, Wrindanneth was the first to break the uneasy silence. "Looks like we're not the only ones venturing away from home!"

"Let us just hope that Hoyt is well." Aroganji did not share Wrindanneth's lack of vision for he knew what Hoyt was capable of after being regaled by countless stories of his past deeds but such tales did not lessen his misgivings. No matter how accomplished Hoyt was, the last thing he needed was a fleet of inimical ships trying to track his whereabouts.

Slate's half-smile quickly turned the mood from one of concern and caution to light-heartedness. "Hoyt's slipperier'n an eel dropped in magically lubricated oil! He'll be all right. I'm sure of it!"

"By tha time he returns, he'll have a few more yarns ta tell and a few more items in his pocket ta try and sell!"

"Enough Slate! The mental image of a slippery, miniature Hoyt being dropped into a vat of oil is the stuff of nightmares! I do not wish to hear more of it!" Wrindanneth's wicked grin was the only indication that he was not deadly serious.

No longer wishing to gaze upon the empty lot or dwell upon the cause of his friend's absence, Aroganji suggested, "We have all had a long journey and are overdue a day of rest and relaxation. Let's go home."

His stomach growling loudly, Slate looked down distractedly—action was required, and quickly. "I'll second that!"

"Let's roll!" Wrindanneth's long strides, accentuated by his black swirling cloak Fraeü, were the first to turn away from Hoyt's vacant lot.

Somewhat reluctant to leave for he could not yet discern where his friend had gone or how he might be at the moment, Yip was the last to leave the abandoned space.

Unlike his companions, he had little need to return home.

Unlike his friends, he had even less desire to do so.

Returning home at last, meandering through the city's storied streets past well-kept shops, gardens, parks, and byways shaded by overarching vines and the boughs of ancient trees, pausing briefly to assess the random acts of destruction quickly being repaired by Paratechnologists and their creations, the party finally turned their attention to the destination that had eluded them these past few weeks—their home and, with it, the comfort and security of their own beds.

When they finally made it to their lane, feet sore after traipsing across the city and its cobblestones several times in one day, Slate literally skipped forward so eager was he at the thought of a full meal and a pint of spirits.

"Ah! Home, wholesome home! I've missed ya as much as tha food, drink, and beddin' ya provide!" Slate held his salivation and stomach rumbling in check long enough to rush toward the front door from the lane, hurdling the small gate in his dash to get inside.

Smiling at his friend's excited advance, Wrindanneth griped, "You'd think you'd been away and missed the place, Slate!"

Not breaking his stride, Slate laughed tersely. "Nah! I'm just hungry! One bed is as good as another, but good cookin' is hard ta come by on tha trail! In tha kitchen, I can make a meal that will make a grown Dwarf fall ta his knees and beg fer more."

"Or fall to his knees clutching his stomach, writhing in agony?"

Already having cleared their front gate and crossed the small lawn in his sprint, Slate was reaching for the front door when he replied, "Ya know ya're lyin'! Ya'll be tha first in line fer a plate o' my fixin's!"

Aroganji laughed and responded while Wrindanneth paused before commenting, "You've got him there! Wrindanneth is about as likely to miss a meal as you!"

"'Specially one o' my home-cooked, lovin'ly prepared Dwarven feasts!"

Recognizing defeat, if only temporarily, Wrindanneth fell silent, knowing that discretion would lead him to a full plate of food. Valor, and his rebuttal, would provide the victory after the meal was enjoyed and the dishes were cleaned.

His hand on the knob, eager to charge in toward the kitchen, Slate paused briefly mid-stride when the Abstract's loud voice cheerfully boomed out from the house and into the street. "Welcome home!"

Shaking his head, Slate surged forward, sights set on his gustatory ambitions. Upon opening the front door to their cottage, washing out the warm tones of the Abstract's welcome, bright flashes of light and sounds of explosions greeted their return. So alarmed was Slate by the display that he had already crouched and drawn Duraeleon's shimmering blade before he realized that the illumination and noise were actually from simulated fireworks projected by the Abstract into the air of the foyer to celebrate their return.

"Argh! Troops t' tha forward positions! Man all battle stations! We're havin' a party!" Unimpressed, Duraeleon's chuckle and banter were quickly cut off as Slate thrust his axe angrily and unceremoniously back into its holster.

"Ya could at least give us fair warnin'!" Slate's hammering heart quickly settled down to a normal tempo as he moved forward crossly into the entryway after sheathing Duraeleon.

Wrindanneth and Aroganji laughed at Slate's alarm from where they stood immediately behind him. Wrindanneth had to reach out quickly mid-laugh to catch the door before Slate let it shut in his face.

"Ah! The joys of home!" Following Slate through the door, Wrindanneth entered their house as well, his long robes rustling as he crossed the threshold. With outbursts like that, perhaps he would not have to wait for his victory, nor would he need to even raise his voice.

From where he stomped off down the hallway toward the kitchen in search of food, Slate growled, "If ya're gonna taunt us with yer presence, ya might as well get it outta tha way as soon as possible, Abstract. What news have ya?"

The melodic resonances of a well-modulated voice clearing its throat briefly filled the household before the Abstract replied. "The Paratechnologists have agreed to meet you in the morning, at your convenience, after breaking your fast. You have only to request Adar when you are ready and he will guide you to your meeting point. Alternatively, should you wish to avoid further travel, you may converse remotely with the Paratechnologists without meeting directly. Either choice is available."

Before the Abstract could continue its update, Slate broke in tersely. "And what o' tha Elves?"

Unperturbed, the Abstract continued blithely, "Alderan was waiting for your request to meet and has already made arrangements for you to speak with the Elves later in the day after noon. Report to the portal to Yenaria and he will see to your meeting." The Abstract paused for but a moment before continuing, "For security purposes, the location of this portal shifts periodically through the city's various parks. I will manifest a map with directions to take you there."

"Have you alerted Spreesprocket to the time of our engagement?" Aroganji's eyebrows arched upward inquisitively with the question.

"I took the liberty of doing so, yes."

"Splendid!" Aroganji was glad to have organizational details handled so effortlessly by one other than himself.

"He will meet you in the garden surrounding the portal."

"Did you remind him to bring Llyewia's personal effects?"

"I did indeed."

"Excellent!" This was getting better and better all the time. Aroganji could certainly get used to having a self-aware, thinking magical assistant. He knew, however, not to get used to the help for the Abstract would not be available to aid them so directly when they departed.

Slate laughed deeply. "And has he yet managed ta find these articles prior ta his departure?"

Sensing Slate's humor, the Abstract replied in kind, "Some concerns are better left unexplored."

Slate laughed again. "Aye!"

Interlacing his thick fingers and straightening his arms out to stretch and pop his knuckles, he added, "And we can provide just tha incentive he needs ta find them if he hasn't."

Its voice inflectionless, the Abstract replied flatly, "And some things are better left to others."

"I'll second that!"

From where he now stood in the living area, Wrindanneth interjected asking, "And what of Hoyt?"

"Hoyt's whereabouts remain unknown."

"There is no record of contact or interaction with Tellanon or any affiliated entities within the public noösphere after his departure with Humbol on the *Rare Aer* immediately before the battle with the invading fleet."

"Directly attempting to hail the vessel the *Rare Aer* systematically over time has not elicited a response from the ship. Scrying and divination attempts have failed to return any additional information. Based on these efforts, I believe the ship and her crew, if intact, have engaged detection dampening magics to prevent surveillance. I have, however, enabled multiple location seeking enchantments that may aid in your search, given the requisite time."

"Given the circumstances of their departure, I would calculate with significant probability that they are masking their presence for fear of pursuit from or detection by agents of the invading fleet."

"I will continue to provide updates as I learn more and upon your request."

"Looks like Hoyt's spirit o' adventure lives on!" From where his voice rang out of the kitchen, Slate at least was confident that Hoyt was safe.

"Let's just hope that spirit lives on long enough to see him home!" Wrindanneth remained a bit more cautious although he, too, respected Hoyt's resourcefulness, resilience, and tenacity.

Ignoring Wrindanneth's rejoinder, the sounds of cutlery clattering, dishes clinking, and pots clanging were Slate's only reply from the kitchen. Soon thereafter, the sweet smells of cooking began wafting through the air and all thoughts, aside from Yip's, turned toward the kitchen.

While his friends eagerly retired to the kitchen for a well-earned, long-overdue meal, Yip retreated outside for a period of contemplation. Days and nights were much the same to his mind—each a segment in one continuous unfurling perspective of wondrous appreciation and deep, abiding peace of mind. This view, and the time allotted to reflect upon it, was not broken by the need to eat or rest in the manner of most others, and, as a result, his feelings of amazement only deepened and increased in sensitivity with time.

For him, these periods of directed reflection, all too few when constrained by the rigors of their quests, were as much a form of sustenance as nourishment was for his friends.

Retiring to the cottage's small cloistered garden within its close stone walls while his friends ate, he watched the sheen of sunlight play upon the verdant swathes of flowers, bushes, and overhanging trees in endless subtle brushstrokes. Highlighting the sunshine, the play of magical energies touched everything around him with added dimensions of color and texture, vibrancy and life. From the subtle shimmer of microorganisms coating all in sight, on and within everything, his body included, to the bright luster of the trees reaching for the heavens, all was aglow with an inner radiance.

He could feel each of these lights, no matter how small, as subtle tugs on his heartstrings, each a note in a greater symphony played out through his senses.

Bathed in the beauty of life, he sat down and listened.

"Good morning, Fists!" Adar's sharp gray-blue eyes gazed outward upon them piercingly from the projection through which they communicated. Ensconced in a translucent field of force, a magical ocular orbited his head in a sure trajectory. This disembodied, true-to-life representation floated in the air before them while they conversed in the cottage's small but tidy living room.

"We are pleased to see that you have returned safely and that your efforts on our behalf have resulted in such a favorable outcome!"

"We owe you much and yet we still hope for more." The last he said with a touch of sadness for he knew what they gave and risked to succeed, that more would be asked, and more hardships were in store.

"We, too, are glad to return and are equally pleased for the opportunity to move forward." Yip did not share Adar's worry for his sense of duty, purpose, and obligation were too strong to allow him concern for his own well-being.

"How, then, may we be of assistance? Do you wish for me to escort you to our facility?"

Wrindanneth answered for Yip knowing that time was short for the day. "Perhaps when we have more time. We have several obligations that we must address today. For now simple conversation will suffice."

"I am sure you are eager to learn of our progress in deciphering the alien command sphere."

Wrindanneth replied with a smile on his face, "Aroganji and I are most excited to see exactly what you have uncovered."

Yip gave a brief nod as well while he waited for Wrindanneth to finish. "We come to you at a crossroads. We have before us several alternatives and must make an informed decision based upon the best possible recommendation."

Adar nodded while waiting for Yip to continue.

"What have you gleaned from the command sphere in our absence? Have you managed to pry loose any of its secrets? What of the Cabal? Is there anything you can tell us of their whereabouts from your study of the sphere?"

Adar spoke simply with a note of excitement. "I have submitted a full report of our current findings to your Abstract that you may review at your leisure. Suffice it to say, through our replication of the sphere, we have unraveled significant additional technical details regarding both the sphere's mode of operation and of the information stored within."

"This information is of significant value to our ongoing research and should bear many opportunities for further study and technical refinement of our arts. A portion of the tangible proceeds of these findings will be returned to you, per our agreement, of course."

Here the tenor of his excitement dropped noticeably. "Though we have successfully managed to unravel many of the sphere's secrets, we have not been able to ascertain with any certainty the location of the Cabal's base of operations, should there be such a location. To the best of our knowledge, no information of this kind remains within the sphere, if ever it existed in the first place."

Seeing Slate's shoulders drop visibly at the news, he added, "This is not, however, the end of our investigations. We have yet to actually work with the original sphere to the extent we have its replicant. Until now, this has been too risky but, in light of the recent attack and the restoration of the seal, such considerations may have changed."

"There is much yet that we may be able to pry from the original sphere that might not have been replicated in its copy. Furthermore, during the invasion, our own drones penetrated the Cabal's defenses and ventured through their portals. We are even now receiving reports from the drones that survived the passage. Though none have yet found any location such as you would seek on the other sides of these portals, the information they are providing is of vital interest."

"Their infiltration of our enemies' perimeter has just begun. With any luck, the intelligence you seek may arrive at any time."

Wrindanneth addressed another item of concern. "During our assault upon Taerris'thule, the alien protective shielding devices were destroyed. Would it be possible to have replacements sent to us?"

"Certainly! We have replicated several versions, the most recent of which appear to offer much greater protections. I will have four of this newest generation sent to you within the day."

Aroganji spoke for them in conclusion. "Thank you, Adar. I think we have what we need to move forward at this time. Should we have the opportunity, Wrindanneth and I will visit your facility after we have reviewed your report. Regardless, we will inform you one way or the other of our plans that you may know how best to reach us should the status of your investigations change."

"Thank you for your time, gentlemen. We will continue our efforts to unravel the sphere's secrets."

"Thank you for your work on our behalf, Adar." Aroganji bowed his head with the sentiment.

Leaving with a short smile, Adar signed off, his multi-dimensional representation vanishing from the air as quickly as it had first appeared upon their call.

"We are as we were." Yip spoke briefly. "We watch and wait, moving forward as we can."

"Perhaps the Elven vision will help provide a way forward for us that we have not yet seen or considered." Aroganji wished to end their conversation with a note of optimism for there was much yet to be done and he wanted as little difficulty as possible in addressing each task.

Yip shrugged, replying, "We will do what we can, not what we hope."

Slate laughed. "Then let's hope the Elven foresight has seen through the Cabal's trickery!"

"Your optimism is a true gift, Slate." Wrindanneth's tone implied anything but appreciation.

Ignoring the sarcasm, Slate replied brightly, "Thanks, Wrin! Tha feelin's mutual!"

Ready to move onward addressing the rest of the required items of the day, Aroganji asked, "How do you wish to proceed from here? Shall we take an early lunch and then proceed to the Elven portal?"

Slate spoke somewhat hesitantly. "Well..."

"Well what?" Wrindanneth's interest was piqued, sensing an opening for a potential snide comment.

"If we go too early, we might not have time fer brunch before lunch..."

Wrindanneth laughed. "Why don't you just pull your trough up to the table and start grazing? We'll let you know when you need to stop eating so we can leave."

Not offended in the slightest by the remark, Slate replied innocently, "Ya'd do that fer me?"

Wrindanneth laughed. "Gladly."

"You'll find the instructions to reach the Elves illumined here." The Abstract's honey tones filled the kitchen with warmth while it described their route to visit the Elves of Yenaria.

Centered in the air above the table, a transparent sheet of magical force glowed with a faint golden light. On the page's surface, a map of the city moved in relation to their current position and orientation. Within the maze of the city's streets, a faint shimmering line could be seen winding through the myriad byways leading them to a park that was labeled 'To Yenaria'.

Examining the chart closely, Yip noted that the portal was, as the Abstract had indicated, in an entirely different section of the city than their prior visit. The portal to the Elven realm now appeared to be located along the island's walled edge well above the docks in an area of the city home to more modest residences like their own.

Though the portal appeared to be located some distance away, Yip looked forward to wandering through the city's streets. The walk would grant him the welcome opportunity to see an area of the city he had never visited and observe the progress of the Paratechnologists' efforts to rebuild and restore the damage inflicted by the Cabal.

"We have our marchin' orders. If everyone's ready, we should shove off!"

Extending his fingers through the air, motes of light dancing about his hand as he gestured, Wrindanneth reached out and clasped the diaphanous map. As he did so, he added, "Could you transfer Adar's report to the map as well? I would like to read it while we walk."

"Certainly! Anything I can do to be of assistance! You have but to think of that which you want to see, either on the map or the report, and it will be presented for you."

"Thank you." Wrindanneth was already reading as he left the room and headed out the front door.

The late morning sunlight was warm upon their skins. The high feathery clouds overhead appeared like small kites floating above their much lower large, tumbled white brethren that floated intermittently around the city. Needing but a moment for his eyes to adjust to the daylight, Yip was nonetheless dazzled by the beauty of the day.

His head quite literally in the clouds, he followed his friends out onto the cobbled street and began their slow procession across the city.

Letting the sheet of magical paper hover in the air before him as he walked, Wrindanneth clucked like a prize chicken. "The Paratechnologists and Construct have teased more from the alien command sphere than I ever thought possible! There are schematics, designs, whole suites of new technologies, cultural and linguistic catalogs, military intelligence, scientific surveys, recommendations and assessments, along with weighty analyses of their findings. Even skimming there's too much in here for me to grasp from a simple overview!"

"Too bad it doesn't have what we want most," though excited and curious, Aroganji shared a bit of Yip's disappointment that the alien sphere had not contained what they had hoped.

"I don't think the sphere holds the location of the Cabal's citadel. And why would it? Why have the location of your central base, if there even is one, in an allied ship sent out alone into the vast reaches of space?"

Yip replied simply, "Sometimes hope is all we have."

"Well now we have a future! This find has secured our fortunes for the rest of our days! There is so much more than I ever expected!"

Slate's eyes lit up at Wrindanneth's words while Aroganji's mind filled with all the paths of intellectual exploration opening for them. Yip, however, did not share in this exhilaration though he was happy that such knowledge would be made available for the betterment of others. "Our futures are secure until they end. We have but to appreciate what we are given and make the most of our allotted time."

Clapping his hands enthusiastically, Wrindanneth said, "After all this, the rest of my days certainly will be exciting!"

Letting his friend enjoy his happiness and his thoughts of an easy future, Yip remained silent. The grueling, life-threatening work in the times ahead would not be easy or fun.

Unaware of Yip's thoughts or concerns, Wrindanneth went on, the animation building in his tone as he continued, "Think of the research avenues we will be able to explore with the Paratechnologists!" Wrindanneth's excitement was overflowing as he continued to skim the extensive report.

Not particularly interested in the technological developments or what they might mean at present, Aroganji asked, "What of magic and spells? Any indication of new, useful knowledge there? Anything that may be able to help in our quest?"

"Not that I can see but I am only in the beginning." Impressed by the thorough, exacting nature of the analysis, Wrindanneth added, "This must have been drafted by the Construct. It would have taken years for someone to write a report like this without the aid of dedicated magics."

"Bah! All I need ta know is if there's anything useful in there or if it helps our bottom line. Beyond that, my attention will be better spent elsewhere." Slate cared little to hear more if there was no pertinent information.

Wrindanneth laughed dismissively. "I hear you, Slate. I'll try to keep in mind that you can only focus on one thing at a time."

Slate's only reply was a growl.

Like Slate, Yip's attention was elsewhere, or, rather, he heard the rest of Wrindanneth's conversation, processed the information, and was aware of the nuances of his friends' interactions, but made no further comment because his primary focus was elsewhere.

If they had no luck with either the Elves or the Paratechnologists, then the middle road would be taken as they had discussed with Eidelion and Éremon. They would venture forth to secure the next of the protective seals securing Ea'ae, hoping that their efforts would lead to further information on the location of the Cabal. His hope had been, and remained still, that their continued efforts would lead to a broadening of choices and options in how to continue forward against the Cabal over time, not a contraction of opportunities. However, as he had said earlier this morning, the reality of the situation is what it is, not necessarily what one hopes, and one must act accordingly.

Though their efforts to find other ways to move ahead had not borne the fruit he had desired, for their options appeared to be lessening, their possibilities were not yet at an end. Even if no further avenues to ferret out the Cabal were revealed within their conversation with the Elves, or later in securing the second seal, they would still have more time and opportunity in their attempt to secure the third of the unrestored seals, assuming it was not yet reinstated and their efforts to place the second seal met with success.

Letting his musings subside, regardless of the outcome of today's endeavors and the struggles in their immediate future, they would have to strive together as best they could. That was all that they could do given their limited options.

At least they still had a path forward to follow.

For that, he was thankful.

Now he needed the patience to let their future course resolve itself.

After all this time waiting, he could wait a bit longer.

Turning around a bend on the sun dappled lane past the last of the small stone cottages nestled amongst the lush greenery, lawn gardens, and overarching trees, Slate, Aroganji, Wrindanneth, and Yip beheld the entrance to the Elven enclave of Yenaria once more.

Silver boled trees soared heavenward in vibrant profusion, their golden leaves shimmering with white radiance, each leaf catching and holding the light of the sun within the trees' supporting branches. Pools of sunlight suffused the air, providing a feeling of warmth and openness beneath the transcendent trees. Artfully placed, weaving naturally through the towering trunks, a small path lead deeper into the copse. Along this track, farther into the wood, two ivory trees, miniatures of those that rose so far above, leaned over the trail, forming an archway beneath the boughs.

Amidst the beauty, supporting the beams of sunlight, girding the dust motes hovering in the still air, silence reigned. This quietude was not physical, however, for the musical rustling of metallic leaves, the trill of birdsong, and the occasional soft susurrations of the wind moving through branches provided a variegated tonal backdrop. Rather, the silence was one of presence, of the peace and stillness that permeated the air, entering into those who stepped beneath the heavenly branches of the glade, enlivening their bodies and calming their spirits.

The ethereal touch of the Elves alighted upon the shoulders of all who entered their lands, be they friend or foe.

To Yip, the Elven forest was as much a place of beauty and light as a physical manifestation of the life-sustaining energies flowing so richly all around. *Chi* danced within the golden leaves on the Elven trees, supported their straight boles, and flowed forth from their deep roots. The air itself moved in step with these energies, bathing all who entered in otherworldly resplendence.

To walk within the hallowed shade of an Elven wood was to enter into another realm, a world of refinement and wonder, perfection and grace.

"Ho, Fists!" Sitting on a bench directly across from the entrance to the Elven wood where he had been until moments before studying the copse himself, Spreesprocket's voice did not disturb the preternatural calm.

"Quite a sight isn't it?" Spreesprocket stood with his hands on his hips as he turned away from them to admire the scene.

"The wood or you?" Wrindanneth's question was quite germane given Spreesprocket's appearance.

The Gnome was dressed as they had never seen him before—simply. Spreesprocket wore only a loose grayish white robe, without visible signs of Paratechnological devices though Yip sensed extensive magic woven and hovering around him. He bore a carefully wrapped bundle across his back which, aside from the magical energies radiating from it, was obviously Llyewia's.

Spreesprocket shrugged. "I have spent some time studying with the Elves of Yenaria. Elegant simplicity is the hallmark of their sensibilities."

He coughed and shrugged, his ruddy cheeks turning a slight red. "Though it's a bit...challenging for me given my own understated tastes"—here Slate's disbelieving snort broke the flow of his explanation—"in honor of Llyewia, I felt it most appropriate to adhere to customs other than my own."

"Then you found the time to not only find Llyewia's items but to also adjust your sense of decorum?" Aroganji smiled thinking of the effort Spreesprocket must have gone through to recover their friend's items from his magical storage system. That he resisted his Gnomish inclinations and remained understated in his appearance was just as impressive.

Not far off in his imagery, Spreesprocket shrugged and said, "The clothes were easy. I just imagined what I would normally wear and then selected as close as I could find to the exact opposite."

Pausing a moment, he added, "Llyewia's items were a bit more problematic than I had expected. I devised a simple algorithm that allowed some ARMED drones to recover them for me from within the pocket dimension where I had them stored." He sighed briefly before brightening back up. "At least the one that came back had Llyewia's items. The other drones may be useful some other time."

"If ya can find 'em!" Slate's laugh was at least partially sympathetic for he had his own challenges with magical storage bags himself.

"Said the pot to the kettle!" Wrindanneth's laugh joined Slate's.

All the while, Yip remained silent as he continued his study of the wood. Noting this and ready to be on about their business, Wrindanneth broke in through his friend's contemplation. "All right, Yip. You've been here before. There's no need to stand around gawking like a child visiting his first country fair." Wrindanneth grinned as he chided Yip for his moment of appreciation, for truly they all moved forward in awe within the Elven lands.

Slate chimed in, "There's no need ta keep Spreesprocket awaitin' any longer since he's already been waitin' on us and his duties lie elsewhere. 'Sides, we don't know how much longer he'll be able ta resist changin' inta somethin' less palatable ta Elven tastes."

Spreesprocket gave a brief bow. "'Tis my pleasure. I came early to spend time in contemplation of the grove and in remembrance of our friend. The beauty of nature, the world around us as it is, is often the best inspiration and catalyst for invention." His small face wrinkled in a smile. "I would say the time was well spent."

Holding up a transparent magical film, he flipped through several diagrams with a motion of his finger, each gesture caused the image displayed to shift to another. Every image was outlined in meticulous detail with exhaustive notation.

"Another frictionless toothpick?" Slate grinned.

Spreesprocket laughed. "Better."

Yip smiled as well and then moved forward, joining his friends who were now walking slowly toward the archway farther along the trail. Passing beneath the luminous trees, he felt the power and majesty swelling through them, so much like the Aeryn D'al that they closely resembled, as the vivacity of the wood flitted gently upon his shoulders like life-giving rain.

Here was a place of splendor.

Here was a place of enchantment.

Reaching the archway first, Slate bowed graciously, his rough-hewn face lit by the soft, empyrean light washing away all traces of toil and trouble. "Who wants ta do tha honors?"

Not pausing to answer, Wrindanneth stepped into the archway and disappeared as though he had never been.

"Guess that answers that!" Not hesitating to follow, Slate stepped through the archway behind Wrindanneth.

Extending his arm forward for Aroganji and Spreesprocket, Yip bowed his head slightly indicating that his friends should proceed first. With a similar abbreviated nod, Aroganji walked through the portal immediately before Spreesprocket leaving Yip to the peaceful solitude of the elfin wood.

Looking within the archway, Yip sensed the rippling energies that would allow him to pass through the portal. Had he not had a meeting scheduled with Alderan, taking the walkway forward, he would merely pass through the archway and beyond into wood without incident, his walk uninterrupted.

The portal took them into another world, a place of otherworldly beauty, a reality cast from the sublime ether of dreams.

Yip stood once more within the ineffable folds of Yenaria alongside his friends, a place so surreal and ethereal that he felt transported from his body, completely outside of himself, left rapt in amazement.

Before, behind, and beside them, a glorious city arose from the pearlescent mists shrouding the air, soaring to the golden heavens between the trunks of mighty silver and golden leafed trees. Spun of gossamer moonbeams and diaphanous sunlight, translucent airy structures floated and shifted loosely in the breeze, spider webs spun from the Elven imagination catching the refulgent dewdrops of the mind's eye.

The Elves not only imagined their reality, they lived their imaginings.

Subtle energies wafted through the air on invisible currents, in rivulets and streams, bands and cords, radiating through and around them in untold profusion, life-giving fog on a warm summer morning, intertwining and connecting, binding and strengthening all who dwelt in their presence.

Though they had been to Yenaria before, albeit briefly, he noted the soft intakes of breath, the change in his friends' postures, the alteration in their breathing patterns, and the release of tension in their frames as this wondrous vision, the fullness of Yenaria's presence, penetrated their bodies and minds.

Though many talked of Heaven, few were lucky enough to walk within its gates.

All around, he sensed Elves moving lithely through the Light, beings at peace within and without, so in tune with their surroundings that the living energies bathing them appeared indistinguishable from their own essential natures.

Within this populace, their radiance so bright that even their essential accordant Elven natures moving so subtly and in harmony with life's energies could not mask their presence, he sensed other resplendent beings, though few, that he now recognized as Anuvaerya—Elves risen in form, substance, and expression.

Perhaps Llyewia was one.

With some fortune, perchance he could share in his friend's Light once more, if not today, then one day soon.

As his mind continued to reach out in every direction, there was so much that his mental examination revealed from the deep kinship the trees shared with the Aeryn D'al to the crystallization of energy that formed the basis of the Elven buildings.

Miracles were made manifest all around!

Though he did not have the time at present, he longed to explore the city, meet and learn from its people, understand its ways, and explore its breadth. Possibly, in time, he would have an opportunity to return when such an occasion afforded itself.

There were, he realized with a weary smile, too many maybes in his assessment of his future.

Before his eyes fell upon them, he sensed others approaching their location. That they were Elven, he did not need to endeavor to sense.

One presence he recognized. The other he did not. Both radiated the feelings of poise and steady assurance characteristic of Elves along with vast experience, wisdom, and comfort with the ways of magic and its application. They were as much a part of this magic as it was a part of them.

"They come." Yip's words were simple and to the point. He left the majority of his attention to studying their approaching hosts and their august home.

"Tell 'em ta take their time." Slate's distracted tone indicated his almost complete absorption in the place, a decidedly unDwarven, though understood, reaction.

"They will not wait for the likes of you, Dwarf!" Wrindanneth laughed. "The Lords of the Wood move at their own time to their own purpose."

Unwilling to break his concentration even to respond to Wrindanneth's jibe, Slate remained in a state of quiet attention, committing each detail that his eyes fell upon to memory.

Peace in motion, stillness in step, the two Elves glided toward them with effortless efficiency. A nimbus of fluid movement floated around them in two waving clouds as their cloaks drifted to a wind that none felt or perceived.

His glowing walking staff held lightly in hand, Alderan approached serenely, his silvery alabaster skin aglow with the splendor shimmering from the golden light beaming from atop his living Aeryn Sh'al staff.

Taller than a Man and infinitely more fair, he appeared to be a figure materialized from a dream, too real to deny, but just as likely to disappear. From a distance, they could all feel the weight of his golden gaze upon them, measuring and reading that which could not be grasped by the eyes of mortal Men.

Beneath this gaze, Slate unconsciously stood straighter, his posture reflecting the import of the one who looked upon him. Aroganji returned the inspection with one of curiosity. Wrindanneth held himself aloof, not letting himself be bothered by the Elf's assessment. Spreesprocket appeared eager, the glee and excitement of discovery aglow in his eyes. Yip merely appreciated the moment, for the gift of Elven presence was one rarely received and deeply valued.

At his side, as tall and lithe as Alderan, the second Elf approached equally at ease with himself and his sense of place, a paragon of quietude. His long, flowing hair appeared a burnished lavender gray, though the true color was hard to discern in the diffuse light, shifting hues with the invisible winds billowing about the two Elves. His shoulders appeared broader than most Elves and his body more solid, hardened to the rigors of combat in ways not typically seen among Elven kind. Glowing with a light as bright as Alderan's staff, at his side, he bore an elaborately etched Witchwood blade worn at his waist. Like Alderan, his eyes were a piercing gold that took in far more than they revealed. About his brow, he wore a woven garland of white flowers. These, too, played with the light in ways that vexed and confused the mind.

Though he radiated the same impression of natural equanimity that surrounded Alderan, the outward feelings of power and command were more tangible in Alderan's companion.

Whether these sensations were intentional or due to the Elf's essential nature, they could not say but all felt the potency of his presence.

Both were lords amongst their kind.

Spreading both hands outward in a gesture of openness and welcome, Alderan bowed his head slightly in greeting and acknowledgement. With the sound of the passing seasons, of raindrops glancing off newly unfurled spring leaves, and grasses swaying in a refreshing breeze, he said, "Welcome Fists and representative of the Home Guard! You honor us on this day with your presence, with the promise of deeds past and deeds yet to come."

Yip bowed in reply. "Your words are as the new morn—welcome and full of hope. We only wish to fulfill that potential."

"The fact that you are here says much. The fact you continue onward says more." Alderan's wise eyes were full of the sadness of knowing and compassion.

Yip bowed once more in humility. "Your words are far too kind. We are here because there is need. We merely do what we must."

Alderan's laugh was like the sound of a mountain stream rolling over smooth, rounded rocks. "If more responded to need and did as they must, there would be little need for heroes such as yourself."

Yip shrugged. "There are no heroes, merely those who do what they must even when they would wish otherwise."

Alderan's smile was like the return of the sun after a brief summer storm. "Exactly!"

Yip merely returned the Elf's sublime smile with one of his own.

Declining his head in respect and gesturing with his arm to indicate his companion, Alderan said, "Four, let me introduce you to Jae'elthos, Iyela, lorekeeper of the Anuvatari, member of the council and Protectorate, bane of the Anubaraëthi."

Yip bowed deeply. "We are honored to come into your knowing."

Upon hearing these words, Jae'elthos's wise eyes lit with an inward light and Yip knew this to be joy. "Yip Chi Chuan, Priest of the K'un Lun, you and your companions have done much to honor the people of Man on this day."

"Llyewia L'oerllana, Iyela of the Anuvatari, brought us glad tidings of your journey, your quest's success, and the openness of your heart."

"Though you were perhaps unawares, in the recorded history of our people, no Man has been granted the boon of the Dragon's Gate, nor have any been known to survive in attempting its realization."

His wise eyes peered into Yip's taking his measure and sharing a deeply felt appreciation. "That you learned this secret from the reluctant forked tongue of a Dragon, a clever race known to grant this gift in full knowledge that its attempt should be the undoing of any mortal," he paused significantly, letting the implications of his words sink in, before adding, "and other races who are not, and internalized this secret is a wonder beyond measure."

In a decidedly human gesture, one so out of place on his angelic countenance that it only amplified the expression, he shook his head and said, "That you survived the utilization of this power is nigh unto a miracle visited directly upon you by the loftiest nonmaterial planes. That you took this knowledge, so precious and wondrous, grasped its essence, and applied this power against the forces of Darkness in a way never before considered and met with success is a gift as precious as the Aerya Etherum. That you also found a way to pierce its heart, clarifying and crystallizing its true import, and refined this understanding in such a way as to translate this knowledge to your fellows, others who would otherwise never receive such a gift, brings tears of joy to the Anuvatari and the Anuvaerya, those who no longer know the touch of tears. That you then decided to share this knowledge, however, a gift as precious as any that can be freely given, brings the voices of the Anuvatari together, united in song."

"This seed, the germ you have sewn and nurtured, will be spread the world over and ring loudly through the heavens. Darkness will soon be blinded with the rising of a new dawn."

"The light of the stars will be matched by the brightness of your gift as it spreads through the macroverse."

"This gift, one given of true compassion, granted by true insight, can never be repaid or requited only returned in kind."

He gazed at Yip earnestly, his oath binding him to the core. "This, then, we, the Children of the Sun and the Children of the Light, pledge to you—the knowledge you have shared will be treasured for the gift it truly is and will be. This treasure, like any item of true value, is best appreciated in the giving. This we intend to do to the fullest of our knowledge and ability."

"The knowledge you have given will be shared. The knowledge you have given will be applied."

So humbled was Yip by this earnest praise and binding covenant that even his deepest bow was not enough to avert the rain of compliments that had been bestowed upon him.

Jae'elthos spread both elegant hands to his sides and returned Yip's bow, the gesture so graceful that Yip had to restrain tears of wonder. "Llyewia L'oerllana has granted you the name Aerya'anan, 'Light bringer' in our tongue, and calls you Anuvatari'aliana, an Elf-friend, as do I and all of the Anuvatari."

"In honor of your deeds and the depth and import of your gift to all peoples, Aerya'anan, the Anuvatari will commission a new order of spiritual warrior scholars, the Aerya'ana, 'those who bring the Light', to share and cultivate the knowledge of the Dragon's Gate and the ways of energy that you have imparted. Through your gift, our people will help spread the peace and sanctity of the Light across the cosmos. This order will be open to any and all who are able of any race and creed so long as they uphold the highest ideals and principles required of those who bear such responsibility."

Yip had no words to reply, laid low and humbled by the immensity of Jae'elthos's offer. He had not and could not yet fully appreciate the true depth of the Elven sentiment and commitment. Though his quest to overthrow the Cabal continued, though his efforts to ensure the peace and safety of all races on Ea'ae and beyond had not yet come to an end, in the Elves and their offer, he could see clearly that he would not be alone in his quest. Should he fail, many others would carry the mantle he had been fortunate enough to bear, dedicated to a cause inspired by the highest of ideals and aspirations.

The Priests of K'un Lun would not be alone. The Council of Light would have an arm visible for all to see, should this order be affiliated with them. His friends, those in whom he had imparted this knowledge would not be isolated in their burden and would have others in whom to share in the responsibility of spreading the knowledge of the application of the Dragon's Gate.

Speaking to each of the heroes gathered before him, slowly moving his glimmering eyes from one to the next, he finished, "From this day forward, you, and any who accompany you, will forevermore be called as Elves, treated as members of our family, and will have full access to our hospitality and halls. Our homes are now yours as you are now considered of the Anuvatari."

Bowing for Yip who remained locked wordlessly in his most appreciative bow, Aroganji said, "We have no way to truly express our gratitude for the effort you are commencing. You are most gracious."

Returning to his normal posture, he looked at both Alderan and Jae'elthos earnestly. "When our travels are at an end, it would be our honor to walk the halls of the Anuvatari and learn the true measure of your hospitality and worth."

Stepping forward to stand beside Aroganji and Yip, Slate beat his right fist across his armored chest and declined his head in respect. "Tha fires o' tha Flintforge clan are yers ta share should ya ever need their warmth or security. Should ya need my blade in tha times ahead when our quest is at an end, ya have but ta ask."

Wrindanneth stepped forward as well and, as was ever his custom, replied with a self-deprecating joke. "You probably don't want what I have to offer and are better off without it if you did, though I, too, will be available should you need my assistance with the Aerya'ana."

Aroganji's stern look stifled any further comment from his friend though Wrindanneth remained, as always, eager and ready to exploit any available opportunity.

Finally recovering himself, Yip said, "So long as I am able, I will work with the Elves and other bearers of Light to aid in the dissemination of opportunity and wisdom for all. I cannot say what the future holds or where my travels will take me, but, insofar as I am able, I would be honored to aid in the efforts of the Aerya'ana as you see fit once my journey is at an end."

His gaze one of supreme appreciation and compassion, Alderan said, "Your offers are most welcome. When your journey is at an end, please return to us and we will grant you the hospitality you have earned. If, at that time, your feelings remain the same, then we would be most appreciative to have your assistance in any way you see fit."

Letting the silence after his words settle in for a moment, sensing the time had come to discuss other matters at hand, Alderan said, "Though you may come to us with heavy hearts born under the burden of a friend lost, know that all is as Llyewia would have it. Your quest continues and the noble efforts you endeavor spread with each passing day."

At this remark, Spreesprocket stepped forward, his simple robes oddly out of place on him though they fit in perfectly with the airy Elven environs. His words direct, heartfelt, and to the point, the Gnome said, "Llyewia was a friend, an honored member of the Guard, a mentor, and a paragon for all to emulate. Though he is missed within the Guard, his legacy lives on both in and out of our ranks."

Carefully untying the bundle strapped across his back and offering it to Alderan with both arms while he spoke, Spreesprocket continued, "Though his time with us is at an end, we would return Llyewia's belongings to his people that his implements could yet see the use to which they were originally intended."

As Alderan gently took the wrapped bundle from Spreesprocket's outstretched hands, the Gnome bowed his head, visibly fighting back the emotions that welled so strongly through his heart.

Accepting the items most graciously, Alderan said, "We will see that the life energy contained within these Aeryn Sh'al continues to find a purpose to which they are most suited."

Smiling brightly and for the benefit of his audience, he added, "Perhaps Llyewia will provide that guidance."

"Together, you have given us a lustrous future and returned treasures from our past. In return, we would have you take with you something of the Elves."

Yip bowed most humbly. "You need not give us anything in return for our efforts. You have already offered far too much."

On their best behavior, Wrindanneth and Slate simultaneously smothered their urges to elbow Yip into silence.

Alderan merely raised his eyebrows, briefly saying, "In the times ahead, you will need more than we are able to give."

Reaching into his robes, he pulled out two small, elegantly decorated and crafted wooden scroll cases. On their surfaces were etched the eldritch symbols of the Elves. "For you, Aroganji and Wrindanneth, the knowledge of the Elves. Think of a spell or enchantment and your intent will bring forth the knowledge you wish, if it is available in the annals of our people."

Handing a scroll case first to Aroganji, while Wrindanneth watched carefully suppressing his desire to reach out and grab the case to begin reading before the Elf gave one to him, Alderan said, "There are limitations to this access. The magic will only work for you, no others. The magic cannot be summoned forth if you are under coercion. The magic will not work if you are relaying it to another, though once you have mastered a spell you will be able to use and transfer the knowledge as you see fit, for good or ill. Though you may wish to summon knowledge of a spell, only those spells which you are currently capable of casting will be made visible to you. As your knowledge and skill grows, so, too, will your access to the resources kept hidden within. Finally, you will only have access to the knowledge accessed by the scroll so long as your hearts and minds are pure and are guided by benevolent intent."

"Slate, the loss of Kazarhan, Dur'kazak, rune master, and fire shaper, is a blow to Dwarvenkind across Ea'ae and saddens the heart-mind of the Anuvatari. We would see that the knowledge he bore and those of his kindred Crafters not be lost but only strengthened with the passage of time."

Bringing forth a beautiful scroll case similar to that given to Wrindanneth and Aroganji, he said, "To that end, and as a gesture of good-will between our peoples in this time of hardship, we are sharing with you our own knowledge of rune craft for you to employ as you see fit."

"As was the case with Aroganji and Wrindanneth, the same conditions of use hold to the magic held within."

"Spreesprocket, as stands for the Fists, you, your brethren in the Guard, and any who may wish to accompany you, are free to study any arts practiced by the Elves within our halls." Smiling wondrously, he added, "So long as you do not blow anything up."

Holding out another wondrously crafted scroll case, he continued, "Within this scroll are the contents of our ways of physical Craftsmanship. As holds for the other scrolls, the knowledge within is for you only and will behave similarly as the others."

Knowing the intellectual capabilities and interfaces accessible to Paratechnologists, he added, "If you choose to publicly share this knowledge, once gleaned, directly through devices such as a metamagical intellectual Construct, the same conditions of use will bind any who seek to access its contents."

Turning his gaze to Yip, Alderan continued the giving of gifts. "Yip, the knowledge of our ways of health, physical arts, insight, perception, and wisdom are yours to explore."

Holding forth a final enchanted case, Alderan explained, "You are free to share this knowledge with those of your order and they will be able to read from its contents should you be willing. Otherwise, similar conditions of use apply for this scroll as well."

Looking at them all, he said, "Should you wish for more, you have but to come to us and ask as you have earned access to anything we would give."

"Should any of you so desire, you may share these scrolls with each other, provided the other conditions required of their use are met."

"You give us gifts beyond measure. We will honor the heritage of your culture as though it were our own as it now is." Yip bowed once more in a show of deep respect and gratitude.

Now that the giving of gifts was drawing to a close and the time of their departure was nigh, Jae'elthos added, "You have also secured a position of esteem by the council."

Without having to ask, they knew he spoke of the secretive Council of Light, not the High Council of Tellanon.

"Should you ever have need, wish for advice, or tutelage, you have but to ask either Éremon or myself on Tellanon. Should you need to communicate with others of our confederacy or wish to share some information or insight with us, we are forever at your disposal."

"All we ask in return is that you speak of us to no one who is not one of us or held in similar regard. Should you have any question as to whom you can trust with the knowledge of our existence, follow your own heart for it will be your surest guide."

Nodding shortly in understanding, Yip replied, "If there is anything desired of us by the Council of Light, now or in the future, you have but to ask."

Jae'elthos's bright smile was like the rays of the warm sun on their brows as he said in reply, "Go forth on your quest. Meet with success. Return home in safety."

Declining his head in understanding, Yip responded, "Before we depart from your wondrous city and leave for our quest, what do the eyes of the Fria al'Othra see of our future? Where shall we seek the Cabal? What shall we do to ensure we meet with success when we do finally find them?'

Some time passed before either Elf responded. When one did, it was Alderan who spoke, his golden eyes locked far away in the distance, peering at a horizon that only he could see. "The future is too vague, shifting between possibilities and opportunities, for our eyes to discern with clarity or surety. Though you may seek certainty, we can offer only the vaguest of outlines for we truly do not know."

"The whereabouts of the Cabal are hidden from us, though their taint lingers long and far across Ea'ae. We sense that many of those that broke through Ea'ae's defenses yet remain, sowing the seeds of discord. Though these intruders are not the destination you seek, these interlopers may provide a way for you to reach your ultimate goal."

Bringing his gaze back to Yip, he finished, "Continue as you are and the opportunities presented to you for eradicating the Cabal, of tracing them to their source, and ferreting them out of their foul warren will increase. In this, then, you walk along the path to the destination you seek."

"Thank you." Yip's fears that the opportunities awaiting them to seek out and destroy the Cabal might be diminishing appeared to be ill-founded, at least if the Elven farsight provided an indication of what was to come. Knowing that he could do no more, that, in truth, securing the seals was the main path presently open, and that they would have to hope for more along the way, he prepared to part.

"Thank you for your guidance and wisdom. We must make our preparations for the next portion of our quest."

Giving a slight nod, Alderan opened his arms in a sign of peace and trust and said, "May your heart ring true and your gaze ever lead toward your aim."

Bowing in kind, Yip replied, "May your future be brighter than your past and the life you lead be the one you love."

Turning, Spreesprocket and the Four stepped through the portal, leaving the supernatural realm of the Elves behind.

Jae'elthos and Alderan watched their departure in silence before they, too, turned and glided stilly into the mists.

Reaching the Elven glade once more, Yip said to Spreesprocket, "Tell Eidelion that we will be in contact shortly."

"Will do. You are welcome to stop by any time!"

"Thank you for coming, my friend." His smile, though not Elven, was quite bright.

"Wouldn't have it any other way." With those words, Spreesprocket departed, leaving them with a nod and a smile.

"Seems like we're about where we started." Slate stroked his beard in thought. "We know a bit more, have a bit more cash, can do more, and have slightly better gear, but we're still unclear exactly about what's next."

Though similar thoughts had hounded him before with regard to their position, now upon their return, and before their last foray to restore the seal, Yip replied, "Though, at times, we may seem to be no nearer to our aim, we have indeed accomplished much in a short period of time. Ea'ae is, at least temporarily, sealed against further incursions by our foes. Ensuring that security into the future by ridding Ea'ae of those Cabal that broke through and restoring the other seals will certainly draw the ire of the Cabal."

Smiling, he added, "If nothing else, our efforts against them may heighten the Cabal's focus on us. If we continue as we have, as the Cabal have already, they may come to us or they may have to bring us to them."

He shrugged, finishing, "Even if all our efforts fail henceforth and we accomplish nothing more, we have given the tools necessary for our allies to sow the seeds of our vision across the heavens. This will inevitably lead to the Cabal's downfall even if we are not the ones to realize the end we seek."

Wrindanneth grinned savagely. "Our journey is not yet at an end. By the time it's over, I intend to have my hands about the throat of the Cabal...squeezing." Clenching his hands to mirror his words, he added, "I will not consider my journey done until I have choked the life from that entire misbegotten coterie of fiends."

His ire stemming, Wrin added with a somewhat less ferocious smile as he tapped the Elven scroll indicating one of many items of worth they had received in their questing, "Besides, the Cabal have been good to me. I want them to keep giving until they can give no more!"

"Fer all tha hurt and misery they've caused, I won't stop until I have their chieftain's head mounted upon a spike." Reaching over his shoulder to pat his lucent axe, he added, "When his blood spills t' tha ground and soaks inta tha soil, his death'll be tha first worthwhile act o' his life."

Shaking his head, Aroganji said, "I don't know that the soil will have him or that his blood will encourage anything to grow."

Wrindanneth laughed. "Fertilizer, the Cabal are not!"

Though he hoped for an end to the Cabal's tyranny just as his friends, Yip's words were not entirely unkind. "Before his fall, Master Shen Po was one of our greatest teachers and practitioners. To say that he never accomplished or performed any deed of worth would be entirely untrue." Before his friends could protest, for he already saw Wrindanneth and Slate moving to make acerbic replies, he added with a half-smile, "What his blood would now do to the earth, however, I cannot say."

Slate and Wrindanneth's simultaneous laughs were all the evidence he needed to know that he had allayed their concerns.

He had not, however, lessened his own.

He knew the stories of Master Shen Po's accomplishments as a priest. He could not begin to fathom the secrets Shen Po may have uncovered in the thousands of years since his fall. Without scruple or conscience to guide him, what horrors had his master's former teacher dared to uncover, to be unleashed upon an unsuspecting universe?

"Shall we go directly to inform the Home Guard that we will take their offer or shall we return home and discuss our options further?" Aroganji waited for them by the exit of the Elven glade, the supernatural light of the enchanted wood dancing in golden hues upon his fiery robes.

"What's there ta discuss?" Once his mind was made up, there was little to dissuade Slate from his chosen path.

Of like mind, Wrindanneth added, "Why not be done with it and start our preparations?"

"Then we are agreed. There is little of worth to be accomplished at this stage by waiting." Yip knew that the sooner they moved forward on the path they had chosen, the sooner they would see its end.

"Then Illdrassil, it is!" Aroganji turned and had already begun walking toward the center city before his friends left the glade.

Though not footsore with his magical boots, nor physically tired due to his Dwarven constitution, Slate harped, "Without any type o' public transport, ya think we could at least fly ta Illdrassil?"

"What's the matter, Slate? We've been away from the city for weeks. Aren't you glad to see her?" Wrindanneth's inviting smirk called for a heated reply.

"I'm no tourist. I've been travelin' fer long enough and will be soon enough again. I like fer my time ta be my own, preferably seated and in a pub. So, if it pleases ya, could we have a bit o' magic?"

"If ya're too stingy, I'll just use tha star o' Illdrassil at my breast and be done with ya!"

With a brief invocation and a flick of his wrist, accompanied by the same smirk that had first taunted him, Wrindanneth lifted them into the air.

The return to Illdrassil took but minutes.

On the way, the party flew above the cobbled lanes and the tops of iridescent trees, some green others various shades of the rainbow, most adapted to feed upon ambient magical energies as well as sunlight, at speeds far faster than they could run. The roofs of buildings and their attendant grounds sped by below them in but the blink of an eye. Citizens, either walking, flying, or riding within various magical conveyances, more often than not passed beneath on the byways below although many took to the heights along with the party.

From above, the signs of random destruction visited by the Cabal's assault upon the city remained as unwelcome vitiations checkered erratically across Tellanon's otherwise unmarred otherworldly beauty. Contingents of drones and Paratechnologists, along with their implements and spells, were visibly hard at work, however, in their efforts to restore and rejuvenate the city and her people.

By the time the party returned, if they returned, from their next adventure, the city would be made whole once more. Then her glorious towers and minarets, her parks and open spaces, her boulevards and promenades, would welcome any and all visitors from across the far heavens as though violence had never been visited upon her wondrous borders.

Motioning for them to descend, Aroganji dipped downward outside Illdrassil's outer perimeter lest their approach bring down the ire of her guards.

Though Illdrassil's glory remained as ineffable as ever, Aroganji paid scant attention for he was already contemplating which seal they may be asked to restore, planning for their journey, anticipating what special gear may be required depending on where they were directed, and imagining what obstacles and foes they might face along the way.

Wrindanneth was more eager to explore the tome of Elven lore than he was to be about their journey. In fact, knowing that time would be quite short on their voyage, he began thinking of ways that he could study the scroll's knowledge without hindering the progress of their journey. The more he thought about ways to make time for unraveling the Elven secrets, the more he anticipated taking advantage of the *Shrike*'s autopilot features.

Given the demands before them, he would need to be particularly focused in his studies, especially considering Maeth's penchant for disrupting his dreams trying to pry every last bit of arcane knowledge from within. With Maeth's rants and exhortations to look forward to while he rested, his surreptitious spying and mind games, much of the excitement of exploring the scroll lessened.

Despite these mixed feelings, however, he would push forward undeterred. Knowledge would be his vehicle to freedom whether his master stood in his way or not.

As they neared Illdrassil, Slate hid his disappointment well. Though eager to move on to the next leg of their quest, he had, as yet, had little time to savor their brief return home. In a city as cosmopolitan as Tellanon, there were more eating establishments and pubs than he cared to count. Unless their preparation to leave took some time, these same restaurants, with their exotic cuisines and diverse libations, would be off-limits to his discerning Dwarven culinary tastes. It was, therefore, with a heavy heart that his feet touched down outside the formidable outer walls of Illdrassil's defensive perimeter, committing to a destiny before he was able to make one of his stomach's choosing.

Though Illdrassil's exquisiteness was not lost on Yip and though the pressing urgency of their quest was the primary motive for his actions, neither occupied his mind as he landed beside his friends in the luminescent shadows of Illdrassil's branching spire. Before he left the sanctity of Tellanon's borders, he wished to communicate with his master that he could tell their tale and share what he had learned. Given the risk of their endeavors, this may be his last opportunity to ensure knowledge of the Dragon's Gate flourished within his own kind.

If any were entitled to the knowledge of the Dragon's Gate for use against the Cabal, it was the Priests of K'un Lun.

"Everyone ready?" Aroganji looked his friends over briefly before walking toward the nearest heavily guarded gate.

Starting forward beside him, Slate quipped, "'Course I'm ready… not that I have a choice!"

"Let's just hope Eidelion is ready for us!" Wrindanneth laughed, preparing for his next insult. "I know Slate's not eager to be kept any longer from his next meal. I'd hate to have to wait for fear of him devouring us!"

Slate spat, not deigning to look at his tall companion. "If I ever had ta resort ta eatin' human flesh, yers is tha last I'd want ta consume!"

Wiping his hand across his brow in mock seriousness, Wrindanneth said, "Thank Maeth for that!"

Feigning disdain, Aroganji chided, "If you two are done, we're trying to get our orders to save the world!"

Slate laughed. "Haven't we already done that?"

Nodding in agreement, Wrindanneth added, "And others besides?"

Smiling, Aroganji answered, "Let's not get presumptuous. We have yet to ensure the security of what we've saved, after all."

Indicating Yip with a nod of his head, Wrindanneth disagreed. "Were you not with us half an hour ago? We walk in the shadow of his holiest of holies the bringer of Light—Yip 'Starchild' Chuan! He has granted all sentient beings in all galaxies and universes across all planes the ability to overthrow the forces of Darkness!"

Enjoying the charade, Slate added, "Elves bow down at his feet and shower him with scented blossoms!"

Managing a straight face, Aroganji replied, "There's something that smells around here and it has nothing to do with the petals of flowers or Yip!"

Remaining quiet and composed despite the foolishness, Yip said simply, "Are we ready?"

Pretending deference, Wrindanneth gave a deep, obsequious bow. "Yes, Starchild, yes!"

Following suit, Slate added, "The Light willin' and yer divine presence able!"

His quietude unbroken, Yip answered their jest in all seriousness. "Then let us be off."

Whispered in the background as Wrin and Slate walked toward the gate, he heard Wrindanneth mutter, "Such is the depth of his wisdom!"

To which Slate replied, "And tha formidableness o' his grace!"

Then they both began to laugh.

His smile unseen by either, Yip looked forward toward the Home Guard watching every step of their approach.

"State your business." A heavily armed insectoid barred their passage standing alongside a stout Dwarf whose shoulders appeared about as wide as Aroganji was tall. Each wore the crystalline armor of the Guard, though the insectoid's armor was not full plate that covered its whole body like the Dwarf's. Across the insectoid's gray back was a jagged semicircle resembling a barbed wheel or cog while a vicious beak hooked downward from its long tubular head. Long, slender limbs branching out from its thorax indicated that the insectoid would be as comfortable on all six legs as it was currently on the four that were supporting it.

To Yip, whose curiosity as a child had included as much of the natural world as his understanding could encompass, the insectoid appeared like nothing more than a radiant wheel bug, a peculiar member of the assassin bug family, bathed in formidable magical energies and weaponry. Though he longed to ask the being about the world from which it arose, its own culture and ways, he remained silent for this was not the time or the place to sate his inquisitiveness.

Within and beyond the shimmering archway made of the same reflective substance as their armor, other Home Guard, each of a different race, were arrayed with a casual fearsomeness that would dissuade any without a defined purpose or a direct summons. Each bristled with armaments from swords and axes to bows and guns. More intimidating, however, was the casual ease with which they carried themselves indicating the facility with which they could use their weapon of choice.

If the Guard's reputation were not enough to discourage the curious, then their appearance certainly would.

Wrindanneth answered for them, as at ease with words as the Guard were with their weapons. "We are here to see Eidelion."

"Who shall I tell him are calling?"

"Tell him the Fists have come to accept his commission."

"One moment." Though clearly intelligible, the insectoid's words had a strange cadence; the points of emphasis for each of its words were on the wrong syllable. Its intonations carried both a simultaneous hiss and multiple grating sounds, perhaps due to all its mouthparts moving in at once. The large beak only heightened the effect.

While they waited, a brief pass of energy, a slight tingle felt along and within their skins, told them that their essences had been scanned, their identities and intent tested and weighed against some unknown standard.

Not moving or visibly communicating with anyone, the insectoid took but a moment to respond. "You may pass. Follow the wisp light to your destination. Do not stray from the path provided."

Bowing, Wrindanneth replied with a straight face, "We would never consider it!"

The look the assembled Guard gave him told him how much they trusted his answer, appreciated his humor, and how gravely any deviations would be treated.

Standing aside, the Guard made way for them as they passed, the Guard's attention on the moment at hand and the exigency of their duty. While the Fists remained a part of their concern, the Guard's focus on them was total, but now that they had passed, the Fists were relegated to the Guard's past for their attention must ever be on the urgency of the immediate present and any risk that it might entail.

While the blue ghost light led them forward toward the Home Guard's compound at the foot of Illdrassil's iridescent heights, each step revealed the unparalleled beauty of the grounds and her gardens, sculpted from the living firmament, bathed in the radiance of the spire's heights, awash in the hues of deepest imagining.

His eyes on his friend and not the dazzling grounds, Slate remarked to Wrindanneth, "Looks like ya can't help but make friends wherever ya go."

"You felt the connection as well?" His words literally dripping with innocent sarcasm, Wrindanneth looked back at the assembled Guard and said, "If they were any friendlier, I'd be in shackles."

Slate laughed, feigning turning back as he said, "I'm sure that can be arranged!"

Nodding at his friend's joke, Wrindanneth replied with an even tone, "At least I would have the comfort of knowing that you would be joining me!"

Slate merely scowled.

"I'm just disappointed they weren't able to notice our member's badges to their most honored society!" Aroganji laughed, redirecting his friends' petty arguments with humor.

Wrindanneth concurred, lightly touching the Star of Illdrassil hidden beneath his cloak. "If our secret signs are too secret, then how will they work?"

Understanding Wrindanneth's gesture, Slate answered, "Apparently they don't work fer us. Maybe we need some crystalline armor ta show we're not yer average passersby."

Not turning to look as he replied, for he knew what to expect, Yip said, "In their eyes, we are no different than any others, as we should be. If it were otherwise, then their attention would be lessened and their ability to perform their duties would be compromised."

"Leave it to Yip to spoil the moment with a cool dose of reality." Wrindanneth's smile belied his tone, indicating that he understood and expected just as much from Yip.

Now turning to look at his friend, Yip, too, grinned. "I am glad to hear that I am good at discerning reality. That is quite the compliment. Many spend entire lifetimes in just that quest."

Wrindanneth laughed. "And hopefully they develop a sense of humor in the process."

His face straight as he replied, Yip responded, "Mostly with regard to themselves."

His smile only somewhat taunting, Wrindanneth replied, "Then there is hope for you?"

His smile bright, giving in turn, Yip answered, "I see my own folly and limitations every moment. Without humor what would I have?"

Not letting go, Wrindanneth added, "Flat, boring conversations and extraneous observations?"

"Perhaps. Or the opportunity to appreciate the wonder and gift that each of us are given each moment."

Smacking his forehead in mock frustration, Wrindanneth chided, "There he goes again!"

Shaking his head, Aroganji replied without humor, indicating Yip's direction with a nod of his head, "And you had better stop talking and start walking or he will leave you in his wake!"

Slate clapped eagerly, ready to be a part of anything that may cause Wrindanneth a bit of discomfort. "Come on, Redbeard! If yer feet moved as fast as yer mouth, then we'd be talkin' ta Eidelion already!" Slate's goading finally got Wrindanneth to quiet down, if only for a moment.

"I'm walking, Stumpy! I'm walking!"

They did not have to travel long as the ghost light led them around and through Illdrassil's towering roots toward the Home Guard's fastness within her foundation. Though they had passed through the luminous, multi-hued grounds and gardens around Illdrassil on several occasions, never before had they entered the Home Guard's head-quarters.

The wisp light led them between two massive spreading roots providing support to Illdrassil's towering, branching pinnacle above. Sunlight filled the space between the roots with dancing refractive patterns of light that played upon the crystalline surface of the roots themselves along with the polished flooring, terraces, and the irides-cent plants lining the space leading toward Illdrassil's massive trunk.

Though the surface of the roots appeared seamless, the ghost light led them toward an unbroken section of one of these roots without hesitation or slowing its pace. When the guiding light finally reached the wall, it did not stop. Instead, a section of the wall opened for it, flowing away from the wisp light liquidly, belying the impression of an almost indestructible solid imbued and reinforced by magical energies.

Never breaking pace, for otherwise they would fall behind, the Four followed the light as it floated through the gap left in the root's arching wall, entering the bastion of the Home Guard for the first time.

Stepping through first, Yip stopped in mid-stride so captivated was he by the spectacle he saw upon entering. Catching himself behind Yip before he walked into his friend, Aroganji pulled up immediately as well. Before either Slate or Wrindanneth voiced a complaint or plowed into either Yip or Aroganji, they both stopped in place taking in the view that opened before them.

The wall behind them fell away into distant memory as the room opened into an immense central chamber. Light spilled in from all directions—the ceiling, the floor, and the walls—clear and multi-hued, white and golden, intense and soft, sharp and diffuse. The walls them-selves were alive with light and power, Illdrassil's lifeblood danced and cavorted exuberantly around her chosen guardians. The open space, far too large even for Illdrassil's substantial roots, was only broken by artfully placed decorative plantings and arrangements, ponds and walkways, and various types of artwork spanning the breadth of the cosmos and sentient perception.

The center of operations for the Home Guard appeared to be nothing more than a vast, interior working parkscape, not the home of one of Ea'ae's most famed fighting forces.

Though this impression was strong, it was not entirely accurate.

The Home Guard's citadel was a hub of bustling activity.

Members of the Guard moved throughout this space filled with purpose. Some painted the air with their plans, objectives, and mission strategies coloring the space with their intelligence and collective understanding through immersive, interactive media for their partners' to manipulate, improve, and understand. Others walked into and out of the expansive, extraspatial central chamber through the fluid walls to other chambers and spaces, each with the flexibility to adjust to any specialized purpose that the Guard may need or request. Others moved between objectives both inside and outside the grand hall's bounds, extending the Guard's influence and understanding beyond the reach of their ethereal base of operations.

Slate's exclamation was the first sound to break the party's collective silence. "Brendle himself could not have chosen a finer hall!"

"Nor could he have chosen finer guardians." Aroganji's keen eye took in the space and its occupants, their creativity, drive, and dedication, the way the chamber and its occupants facilitated one another's tasks, and how the two effortlessly worked together toward realizing common ends—changes and transformations reinforcing a shared purpose. Illdrassil enabled her guardians to function optimally just as they ensured her optimal function.

Pointing ahead where the wisp light was quickly distancing itself from them, refusing to pause this close to its destination, perhaps expressing the need of its charge, Wrindanneth griped, "If you all don't stop staring like love-struck puppies, we're going to be left behind! Our guide does not wish to wait for you to gawk like yokels emerging for the first time from your cave!"

Yip reacted. His action, his only discernible response, was motion, following the wisp light as it moved deeper into the hall while continuing his survey of the energy currents flowing all around in unimaginable profusion, linking the Guard with Illdrassil in intricate webs so complex that each appeared inseparable from the other.

Moving inward, as they had seen upon first entering the hall, they passed Guard convened together discussing strategy, creating interactive depictions of their plans and knowledge for their teams to work on and evaluate. However, the actual contents of these meetings were blocked to them. They could neither hear nor see the subjects of the points of discussion beyond vague outlines hovering in the air indicating a single common point of focused communication.

Pieces of art from the far reaches of the multiverse, from statues that moved to multi-dimensional paintings and representations that hovered in the air, were passed far too quickly to fully appreciate as they caught up with the ghost light darting through the activity of the hall.

Many Guard warily watched their progress through the hall for they were clearly visible as outsiders by the ghost light guiding them. These Guard came from as many races as visited Tellanon for any who traded with Ea'ae and were willing to serve Tellanon were welcome so long as they proved able, reliable, and fulfilled certain standards, oaths, and obligations. The difficulty and binding power of these requirements, however, proved far too difficult and limiting for most aspirants thereby ensuring only the best suited received membership to the Guard.

Aside from actual members of the Guard, regular citizens and officials were largely absent. The refuge of the Guard was for the Guard and few others. Though some visitors came when there was need or want, these affairs were more often than not handled elsewhere. The fact that the Four were admitted to the hall was a testament to the esteem with which they were held in the Guard's eyes though they themselves were not aware of this privilege being only generally acquainted with the subtleties of the Guard's day-to-day functions, strictures, and dictates.

Watching the complex web of interactions and exotic sights pass by as they moved deeper into the Guard's citadel, little time seemed to pass before they finally reached their destination.

The wisp light hovered briefly before the radiant wall ahead of them before quickly passing through an opening that rippled through its liquid surface. Hurrying to follow, lest they somehow be locked out of the passage, Wrindanneth, Aroganji, Yip, and Slate strode through while trying not to lose their guide.

Crossing the threshold, they stopped in place once more.

About them, a complete, simultaneous view of Tellanon's position in space was projected upon the walls. Looking all around, the seamless representation showed every angle from top to bottom surrounding the floating island as though the island itself were only a tiny point or entirely invisible and thus would not interfere with the perspective of central viewers occupying the room. All around the island's periphery, ships darted and floated through the air, each with small vectors and streams of information visible should the observers in the chamber wish to expand upon any particular vessel. Overlaying this image were general defensive parameters including a representation of the city's outer shield, its power, and capacity, the city's projected course over the land below, weather currents and forecasted trends, among a host of other details.

Not turning as they walked in, Eidelion reached outward shifting and dizzyingly rotating the three-dimensional depiction, zooming in on the city's docks with a gesture of his hands. Ships of all shapes and sizes quickly came into view along with information about their crews, manifests, destinations, and known histories. As his purview shifted, more detail and information became available as his gaze swung closer to a particular target until finally, with a single gesture, the images stabilized upon a lone vessel, streams of data passing by all around him as he did so.

Filling the screen before him, her sails full and billowing in the wind clearly represented by moving vectors along the breadth of the screen, the *Shrike* floated in the air, her stout, round wooden hull occupying the majority of one quadrant upon the wall.

With the *Shrike* firmly in view, Eidelion turned to meet them, his bright eyes eager and his smile broad, the *Shrike*'s reflection shimmering on his radiant armor.

Extending his arms outward in welcome, he said, "Welcome to the home of the Guard!"

Looking around the room appreciatively, spinning as he did so, Slate said, "Amazin' is an understatement!"

Slate was not the only one carefully examining his surroundings.

Aroganji wondered at the full range of information that could be displayed and assessed in this space. With the Construct's analytical and cognitive capacities behind the arrays, the results would be endless.

Wrindanneth marveled at the magical development and sophistication so clearly represented in this simple chamber. Whatever information he desired, so long as it was in the Construct's vast purview or records, was accessible. Based on this untold store, how many more insights and discoveries could be made, connections linked, or mysteries uncovered? The role of the Paratechnologists suddenly became both more daunting and impressive.

Yip merely watched Eidelion for, despite its amazing diversity and complexity, the information displayed, however fantastic, was extraneous to their current purpose, only as valuable as the direction guiding it. Should their intent shift, his awareness would shift with it.

Shrugging his shoulders humbly, for these sights were but a means to an end, Eidelion replied, "We try to provide an immersive environment that facilitates the mission purpose and potential of each of our members and their teams as best as we possibly can. With Illdrassil's magic, the Construct's unmatched capacities, along with the Paratechnologists' continued innovations, there is indeed much at which to marvel."

Directing their attention to the task at hand, Eidelion continued, "I am glad to see you have arrived so quickly and in such apparent high spirits!"

"Have you made up your minds?"

Wrindanneth answered for them, gazing at the image on the wall as he did so. With so much information available merely waiting for his direction to call it forth, Eidelion probably already knew the answer he was about to give and was only being polite. "We have met with the Elves and spoken with the Paratechnologists." He paused a moment before going on, deciding not to outline the full course of their meetings at this time. Given the Construct's capabilities and Spreesprocket's presence, Eidelion had probably already been briefed and would not need his summary regardless. "We will continue forward on the path you have offered and assist in securing the next seal."

"We had hoped as much!" If possible, Eidelion's smile got even brighter.

Seeing Wrindanneth's eyes on the *Shrike*, Eidelion explained, "If you will forgive my intrusiveness, we have been analyzing your ship against likely hostile scenarios to ascertain which capabilities may prove most helpful in securing your safety and the success of your mission, should you accept our advice and offer to improve upon the *Shrike*'s capabilities."

Hearing this, Wrindanneth beamed.

There was his confirmation.

Of course, he always looked for confirmation of his thoughts and opinions, so he quickly disregarded the fact that, like Aroganji, the Guard, and Eidelion as an officer, might like to be prepared for all contingencies, would like for their quest to see the outcome they all desired, and that Eidelion would want the Guard assigned to the ship to return home.

"If you are in agreement, I will have Spreesprocket go over our recommended improvements with you at your convenience sometime after our meeting. He will set up a time that fits within your preparation schedule."

Aroganji bowed. "That is fair."

Though the prospect of free stuff, particularly powerful, magical free stuff, intrigued him to no end, Slate was ready to be about their business. The longer he waited to get home, the thirstier he got. He had already waited too long to properly sate his drought. With the prospect of another extended voyage ahead, time was short in which to slake it. "What can ya tell us about where we're goin' and what we'll be doin'? Who'll ya send with us and what'll they add t'our own proficiencies?"

Eidelion acknowledged Slate's concern with a slight bow. "Before I begin with your mission in particular, know that though your numbers are few, others will share in your quest and the danger you will face for additional members of the Guard and our allies are being marshaled even as we speak to ensure the safety of the other seals. Though these heroes will not travel with you, their mission remains your own—to ensure Ea'ae's safety, to protect and restore the seals, to prevent further extradimensional incursions, and to thwart the Cabal and their ilk at every turn."

Eidelion's expression grew more serious as he continued, "There is much to be told and insufficient time to tell it. Though I will summarize here, rest assured the Guard who will assist have been fully versed in all applicable areas. We will also make available extensive intelligence regarding your mission objective that you will be able to call upon from your command sphere."

"You may be familiar with much of the tale I am about to tell, either generally or specifically. However, there are some things I am about to say which you may not know. These are the points that could save your life."

"Long ago, when *faerviage* first opened the heavens to the people's of Ea'ae, many took to the stars, leaving behind their homes, kith, and kin. Of those who left, individually or in groups, each had their reasons for leaving and their hopes for what would become of their journeys."

"Some left their homeworld to start anew in unexplored, untrammeled lands. Some left to further their agendas or those of their masters. Some left to explore, to meet the unknown in an attempt to further their knowledge and understanding. Some left to make their fortunes. Still others left to spread their vision and purpose across the cosmos. However, the true reason for anyone's departure was, as it always will be, ultimately held within the heart of each man or woman that left Ea'ae."

"Of those that departed Ea'ae in the first waves, few returned. For some, this was by choice, for others it was not. However, the hardships and troubles following each exodus did not prevent many more from following in these pioneers' footsteps, for the lure and promise of the imagined unknown elsewhere was often a far greater draw than the unknown one knows, or think one knows, at home."

"Many august orders and individuals took to the skies in those early days, each leaving Ea'ae a bit weaker in their absence. Others later followed. Still others follow even to this day."

"Though we have made great strides in the times since, though many have returned whether to trade in new knowledge, goods, and skills or to restore old bonds and alliances once thought long forgotten, Ea'ae has remained much weaker than she was at the height of her powers for even as we replenish our might, more take to the stars."

"In the absence of those multitudes who left, Ea'ae became a much more challenging place to live. For, while many of Ea'ae's peoples did not return, others, often much less desired, came, seeking opportunity and a foothold on our world. Many of the fell races of our own world, too, prospered or arrived in the absence of global stability."

"Thus the need for the seals became apparent, the necessity for some centralized form of interstellar traffic control and defense became realized, and so it was that many of those same bastions of strength that had then been established to meet the need to protect our world through the ages eventually weakened themselves and fell into decay."

"You will be going to one such place."

"As I said, Ea'ae was once home to many august orders, far more numerous than now remain upon her shores. In the far reaches of the western continent of Aruene, a puissant citadel was established in ages past to protect the seal of Mihtig'leht."

"This fastness's chosen guardians and builders were the Fyrskal, a chivalrous order akin to the Dalaren Ka for they held to the ways and teachings of the Light."

"In the fullness of their power, the Fyrskal strode shoulder-to-shoulder with the divine."

"The warrior-saints of the Fyrskal brought peace and blessings to the lands of Aruene, curing sickness and malady, freeing the land of blight and incursion, and allowing the peoples of Aruene to realize their potential. Under their mantle, all races prospered and the land gave forth in bounteous fecundity."

"When, over the course of long years, the order grew in strength while the threats to her charge appeared to lessen, the Fyrskal took to the heavens as many had before them. There were those who remained behind but they tarried in a land as beleaguered and impoverished as their own order."

"There was one among them, Gruendan Weirndan, Champion of the Gleaming Blade, who, recognizing the growing weakness and paucity of his order, began to walk the ways of power in order to secure his order's, his peoples', and his land's future. Though guided by the best of intentions, his drive soon outstretched his reason and limits, and, under his misguided auspices, the Fyrskal remaining on Ea'ae soon fell to ruin."

"Much of what happened in the dark years since the Fyrskal's fall has been lost or forgotten, whether dimmed by the passage of time, abolished because those who would tell the tale fell at the Fyrskal's hand, or willfully stricken from the annals of history, none can now say."

"Through the passage of time, however, those Fyrskal that yet remain, if any yet truly endure, have grown powerful. None who have dared to approach their citadel to reclaim it and its seal for the Light have returned in triumph and only a few have managed to come back alive."

"The harrowing tales of these survivors, like the history of the Fyrskal, are better forgotten. Whether truth or fancy, whatever survives in Morowen, the dire keep of the Fyrskal, is immensely powerful and even more baleful."

Wrindanneth nodded with confident, assured ease as Eidelion paused, his voice a dull monotone and his eyes blank. "Sounds fair enough. We'll just blow it up and start from scratch. Self-destruct a few drones to level the place and we'll begin anew with another seal in the old one's place!"

Eidelion shrugged dismissively. "More than that has been tried, all to no avail. If you are to succeed, you will have to meet the Darkness residing in Morowen head-to-head on its own terms and overcome it. Anything else will result in failure."

"That is if the Cabal does not do so first. Remember, they, too, vie for Morowen and her secrets."

Counteracting his dire message with some small bit of hope, Eidelion said, "We will continue to explore options to lessen the risks you will face in the days ahead. Though the time before your departure is short, many are working to ensure that your voyage is a success."

Before Wrindanneth could offer a clever rejoinder into the vacuum left by the paladin's words, Eidelion added, "The list of failed attempts on Morowen is as long as the days since her fall. Read the logs you will receive on your command sphere and you will have an idea of the magnitude both of the attempts and depths of these failures. This understanding will in no way be heartening."

"You will learn what was tried and the result, or what was thought to have happened based on initial mission plans and intent for attempts at magical scrying and recreations of these events have resulted in failure. You will learn of the tumult and disasters, the fear and the madness, and the horrors that were visited upon both the deceased and those that survived."

Coughing, Slate brought his hand to his mouth, saying politely, "Thanks fer tha pep talk there, Eidelion. If ya'd like ta give us a little privacy, we can save everyone a bit o' time and effort and just fall upon our own swords if ya'd like."

Eidelion gestured placatingly. "My apologies, gentlemen. My tone is bleak, and rightfully so. I would have you know the truth, all of it. Only then will you meet your future in full awareness on terms as even as you can endeavor to make them."

Here Eidelion gazed at them intensely, his full, melodic voice radiating truth and command. "I tell you these things not to dissuade you but because I believe in you. You have done what no others have done before you. I believe you can do it again. I would not risk your lives or Ea'ae's future if I felt otherwise. On that you have my word and my promise."

"You will not, however, be going alone."

"We have assembled a team to supplement your own, one that should complement your abilities and add to your strength."

"To your contingent, though I wished to join you myself, in my stead, we will add Maeven D'lanaran, a champion of the Dalaren Ka and exemplar of the Light within my order. His stalwart sword and grace will add much to your cause."

With Eidelion's words, a tall dark-haired man of chiseled face and broad shoulders appeared behind him on the true-to-life representation projected by the chamber's magic. The glow of Maeven's armor was matched only by the burning white of his massive two-handed blade.

"Ruena O'reine, archmage nonpareil, one of our principal magical guides and a Holder of Secrets within the Home Guard, will bring a force of character, will, and vision that will allow you to meet even the most vile arcana on even terms."

Her feet hovering above the ground, her hair roiling around her head in turbulent red thunderheads, Ruena's fierce gaze burned brighter than the lightning bolts arching from her fingertips.

"To Ruena's arcane prowess you will also have Yrien Al'nori, an Anuvatali Uraera Al'on. Though she will not join you directly in confrontations, hers is a rare gift, one of magical augmentation. With her help, whatever you would do, you will do it better. Whatever you aspire to do, you will meet with more success."

With these words a woman of ineffable, otherworldly beauty took her place behind Eidelion, her features and demeanor taking the best of both Elves and Men.

"Assisting you and your companions, you will also be aided by a NUMEN, a synthetic Paratechnological being of great mental and physical capacity. The NUMEN is an allomorph capable of taking on and filling many different roles."

With this statement, a nondescript humanoid of average height and build appeared on the screen standing casually looking into the distance. Within the blink of an eye, its form shifted rapidly, flowing like smoke but too swift to observe or fully capture with the unaided eye. The form that emerged from this abrupt transition was anything but nondescript. Appearing to be made entirely of sleek black metal, bristling with weapons more familiar on a starship than a man, the NUMEN appeared ready to go to war—all by itself.

Unlike those Paratechnologists who extended their own intelligences through a merger with an artificial intelligence or a metamagical construct to create a synthetic intelligence with dramatically enhanced capabilities, the NUMEN was, like the Construct and its associated Abstracts, an entirely independent artificial intelligence. Although its mode of sentience and interaction with the surrounding world were very similar to that of the major races of Ea'ae in many ways, for it was modeled upon the general humanoid intelligence, its capabilities, both in terms of breadth and depth, were in far beyond those of typical, unaugmented sentient beings.

Seeing the NUMEN transform, the change so abrupt and filled with overt threat, Slate whistled appreciatively. "Ya sure ya don't want t'send that thing all by itself?"

Eidelion smiled, saying, "We have not created our successors yet.

"We have created so much more."

After a moment's pause, he added, "There are many more NUMEN being put to work for our cause as quickly as they can be created."

Shifting his gaze to Aroganji, Wrindanneth remained quiet, for once, but the look he gave was not altogether positive, promising, or reassuring.

Sensing Wrindanneth's concerns, Eidelion said, "Though we had other plans for a Paratechnologist originally, given the importance of your effort, we thought that the NUMEN's primary inventor and designer should accompany it with you."

Smiling, he added, "Besides, Spreesprocket himself asked to join your mission and assist in the effort."

Turning to look at each other in surprise, the Four were truly caught off-guard by Eidelion's pronouncement. Filled with a heady mixture of confusion, excitement, and shock, they were happy nonetheless.

Noting this expected response, Eidelion said, "Spreesprocket threatened to return to his personal research if we did not allow him to join." Smiling, he added, "As much as the world has benefited from his inventions, we decided that we would all be best served by him accompanying you."

"Ya mean ya decided that tha world didn't need another frictionless toothpick or a self-guided Dwarven beard mower?" Slate's deep laugh echoed unusually off the walls of the chamber, the sound waves absorbed and shifted into decibel ranges untouched by most Dwarven voices by their interaction with Illdrassil's magical walls.

"More like we have enough problems dealing with the Cabal, fighting off extradimensional incursions, and securing the seals without having to deal with the transhuman artificial beings that Gnomish ingenuity will visit upon us." Though Wrindanneth mumbled the complaint, it was clearly heard by all for Illdrassil's walls did little to mute sound entirely no matter how it distorted the vibrations.

Too gracious to comment or react, Eidelion remained silent in reply. Finally he said, "In the end, we decided that his particular set of skills would be invaluable in the dark days ahead."

Yip nodded in affirmation. "Spreesprocket's abilities and company will be most welcome on our journey."

Not quite finished, Eidelion paused a moment before adding, "The Elves made a request as well."

"Now what?" Wrindanneth's groan was only partially an expression of humor.

Not accepting or reacting to the bait, Eidelion continued directly and succinctly, "Though Llyewia cannot join you for he has now moved on, Alderan himself has asked to accompany you on your voyage."

If they had reacted in surprise to the announcement of Spreesprocket's return or to the addition of an artificial humanoid to their quest, then the only word to describe their reaction now was one of shock.

Always aware of the proper place and mood for a given moment, Aroganji asked consideringly, "Is Alderan not too valuable to his people and the world at large to risk in joining us?"

Eidelion shook his head. "Though your concern was ours, the Elven ambassador himself said that nothing any of us do is now more important than securing these seals."

"His security will also be ensured by the presence of the Home Guard. As Elven ambassador to Tellanon, his duty is directly tied to her peoples and the Home Guard who protect and serve them. Working together is a natural extension of those duties."

"Though I have every confidence in your abilities and his, without the additional layer of protection afford by the Guard, he would not venture forth on this mission. We would not condone it."

"What of his high talk of passing on the Light that Yip entrusted with the Elves?" Wrindanneth's skepticism did little to counter Eidelion's poise.

"The Aerya'ana will take up that noble charge." Looking to Yip, Eidelion gave a subtle nod of acknowledgement. "Llyewia himself was the first of the Aerya'ana to venture forth."

Nodding appreciatively, for he was glad to hear that Llyewia had set out upon such a noble journey, Yip asked, "Are the Aerya'ana prepared to secure other seals, perhaps under Alderan's charge?"

"We have discussed as much as well. Though the individuals selected for joining the Aerya'ana are of the utmost quality, with the exception of Llyewia and a few others he has taught, the numbers of those truly skilled in the arts you have shared are far too limited to depart just yet without first securing and spreading their knowledge and legacy within their fledgling order."

Avoiding any notes of sadness or defeatism for he sincerely believed their efforts would meet with success, Eidelion said, "Should this mission fail, the Aerya'ana will join the Home Guard directly in other attempts."

Making certain to engage each of them openly as he spoke, he added, "Theirs is the journey of the future, yours is the journey of the day."

Returning to practicalities, Aroganji asked, recovering from his momentary stupor enough to form a cogent reply. "Will Alderan have his own ship with an honor guard?"

"He has indicated that he will travel however we judge best as the mission is not his nor is the decision his to make."

Taking a moment in consideration before speaking, Eidelion added, offering this additional bit of information to overcome their apparent reluctance. "His skills as a healer are without equal. I can think of none better."

Still wrapping his head around the idea of an Elven lord potentially aboard their humble ship, from the potential for extra responsibilities and protocols to the ramifications they might face should he fall while under their charge, Wrindanneth eventually nodded, albeit reluctantly. "We will think on it."

"Is that all or has Éremon himself decided ta take a brief foray from his duties leadin' tha free peoples o' Tellanon?" Slate's surprise had not lessened and would not for some time. He had traveled with Elves before but never with an Elven lord. To his mind, the high Elves were about as distant from the rigors of day-to-day reality as the stories and imaginings of his childhood.

"There is more." When the Four remained quiet, listening attentively without protest, he continued, "This time, we thought it best to take at least two ships, each to be manned as you see fit. The disadvantages are slight and having an extra vessel at hand should one be lost could be the difference between success and failure."

"There ya go! Alderan will have his own ship!"

Wrindanneth shook his head. "He may yet have his own ship but Eidelion proposes a ship for the Guard, not for the Elf. If Alderan brings an airship, then we will have three in our flotilla. Depending on how we divvy up, Alderan may yet end up with us and not the Guard."

Not entirely in agreement with Wrindanneth's perspective, Eidelion clarified, "This is your expedition. We offer only guidance and support. As I said, the ship will be yours to man as you see fit. The second ship does not have to be manned solely by the Guard."

Turning to Eidelion, Wrindanneth asked pointedly, "Why not send Tellanon with the Home Guard and her entire armada to secure the seal?"

"We dare not risk the people of Tellanon on such a journey. The Guard go with Tellanon. Nor would we wish to risk her seal."

Aroganji was confused, a regular part of this conversation or so it seemed. "Her seal?"

Eidelion laughed, his voice unaffected by the strange acoustics of the chamber. "Did you not already guess?"

Though Eidelion posed the question, it was obvious to them all that they were not intended to know.

"Know what?" Things were only getting cloudier.

"Illdrassil herself is a seal. The centerpiece of them all, the hidden fifteenth of the fourteen."

Wrindanneth smacked his forehead at the unexpected obviousness of Eidelion's revelation. This made perfect sense; he should have seen it from all the signs now so evident all around. "She is free to move while the other seals stay in place."

Eidelion nodded. "If the others fall, Illdrassil will remain to start them anew. Illdrassil alone is free to leave Ea'ae should it be required. So, too, does her mobility both protect her from assault and confuse her detection."

Nodding in a mixture of wonder and appreciation, Slate said, "She truly is a marvel fer all."

"This knowledge is a secret you must hold most dear. There are few who know of this truth. Outside the Home Guard, the Protectorate, the Council of Light, and a select cadre of Paratechnologists, you are the only ones."

Aroganji responded in all seriousness. "We will treat this knowledge as a testament to your faith in us."

"Thank you."

"How long do we have before we need to leave?" Already going through everything required for their departure in his mind, Aroganji wanted a time frame to work and prepare within.

"Ideally, the sooner, the better. However, the *Shrike* must be prepared and the upgrades tested prior to venturing forth. We must also discuss and make ready our plan of attack."

"Two weeks?" Aroganji gauged that would provide sufficient time for the Paratechnologists to work should a team of sufficient size and sophistication be used to make the requisite improvements.

Eidelion nodded. "Under normal circumstances I should think so." After but a moment, he added, "We will attempt to expedite this process given the urgency of your mission. Resources are very thin after the attack. Many of those we would bring to bear on your ship are already committed elsewhere. However, your mission, along with similar efforts to ensure the safety of the other seals, are of paramount importance for Ea'ae's future"

Understanding, prepared to put events in motion as quickly as possible, Aroganji said, "We will be ready to see Spreesprocket at his earliest convenience."

Sharing their sense of urgency, Eidelion replied, "If he is not available to meet with you immediately after the conclusion of our meeting, I will have him call you directly via the Abstract."

"When do you propose that we meet with our prospective traveling companions?" Wrindanneth wanted to get a sense of the people behind the pictures projected on Eidelion's screen. With that information in hand, he may have a better idea of how best to go about organizing the crews. Of course, even then, he would probably just divide the group between ships with the Home Guard on one and Aroganji, Slate, Yip, and himself on the *Shrike*, but he was always open to alternatives. He did, however, relish the thought of having his ship under his own command for once without others outside his band keeping track of his every move.

"Whenever you are ready."

Aroganji answered for them all. "Let us first meet with Spreesprocket and discuss the requirements for the *Shrike*'s upgrades. Once those plans are in progress, we will have more flexibility in our schedule as the ship's improvements currently dictate our timeline."

"You need only give the word and I will make ready."

"Thank you, Eidelion." Aroganji's graciousness was genuine.

Giving a wide smile, Eidelion said, "Let me see if Spreesprocket is currently available."

Communicating in silence for he merely shifted the direction of his gaze toward the true-to-life representations moving on the walls around them, Eidelion took but a moment to respond. "Spreesprocket is currently assisting other Paratechnologists far beneath Illdrassil. It will be a few hours before his work is completed."

"In order to avoid wasting any time, however, he has sent a copy of his report to your Aspect that you may read and prepare for your discussion with him. If all is in order, he will proceed. Otherwise, he will make adjustments as needed."

"When Spreesprocket is done, he will contact you through your Abstract. Depending on your preference, he will set up a time and place to meet or just make arrangements with you communicating via the Abstract."

"We will await his contact." Aroganji bowed, preparing to leave.

"There is one more item of business."

"Yes?" Aroganji's curiosity was wakened.

"See Master Hoyt as soon as possible upon his return. Much will be revealed to you that you may not know. In light of his words to you, some of what we have discussed may change."

Squinting his eyes skeptically, Wrindanneth said, "What exactly do you mean?"

"All will be revealed in time. Options that are not yet mine to discuss may be revealed. Opportunities to lessen the burden of your task may open."

"Ya've been spendin' too much with Yip! Better watch out, soon enough ya might take ta robes and a shaven head if ya don't stop talkin' like him!"

Eidelion smiled. "I have been sworn to secrecy, else I would say more."

Aroganji gave a slight nod of his head in acknowledgement of Eidelion's willing candor. "Thank you, Eidelion."

"The thanks belong to you, my friends."

"Bah! Ya've no need ta be humble! Ya're worthy as yer armor shines!"

Wrindanneth laughed at Slate's words. "Doesn't get much brighter!"

"Indeed!" Slate's affable grinned joined Wrindanneth's.

Sensing the time to depart had come, Aroganji bowed, saying, "Until our shadows cross once more, may your Light never dim, Eidelion."

"May the Light's grace always be yours to share." Eidelion's words enfolded them in warmth.

"May Shadows disappear in the presence of your Light." Yip's words and bow mirrored Aroganji's.

Slate declined his head and gave a solid thump to his chest as a gesture of parting. "May ya have tha good grace ta grow a beard in our absence."

Casually turning to leave, for more adages had flown in these few seconds than he cared to hear in years, Wrindanneth offered simply, "Until next time."

Not having the ghost light present to guide them, at least not yet visibly available, Wrindanneth took a leap of faith and proceeded to walk directly toward the wall through which they had entered Eidelion's meeting chamber. Striding forward confidently, he only hoped that he was not rewarded with a direct impact when he walked into the partition.

Closing his eyes in preparation for contact, he was relieved when the wall melted open for him in a liquid wave as he walked through. The last thing he wanted was the embarrassment of a full frontal impact in front of Slate.

Well, that or damaging the Home Guard's walls.

With that thought on his mind, Wrindanneth strode through the otherworldly hall of the Home Guard with a grin on his face. As he made the main chamber, the ghost light appeared conveniently to guide him, just in time to have not prevented any form of potential chagrin.

With nothing else immediately planned, the party headed home to review Spreesprocket's report.

Looking forward to the new toys that may soon be at his disposal,

Wrindanneth picked up the pace, letting his long legs move at full stride through the Home Guard's glittering compound.

Struggling to maintain Wrindanneth's pace while walking, Slate practically had to jog to keep up. This, of course, brought another smile to Wrindanneth's face.

"Welcome home, good sirs!" No sooner had they set foot on their front lawn than their Abstract greeted them with the enthusiasm of a pent-up puppy.

"Can't ya at least wait until we get inside ta start yellin' at us?" Slate liked the Abstract, no matter how useful it was, about as much as he liked an overly friendly Cave Troll. The main difference was the Abstract did not stink...or try to strike him down with an axe. But it was just as much of a nuisance—always showing up where it did not belong, nosing about where it should not, and generally doing everything it could to make a gentle, kind-hearted Dwarf disagreeable.

"Certainly, Slate!"

Shaking his head as he shut the gate behind them, Slate walked up the pathway to the house and followed Aroganji in after both Yip and Wrindanneth. As soon as he crossed the threshold, Slate nearly jumped out of his boots as the Abstract crooned, "Welcome home, good sirs!" almost loud enough for the neighbors to hear with their doors shut.

"Are ya daft?" Slate shook his head, scolding the invisible presence. "Ya've already welcomed us and made a nuisance o' yerself ta boot! Ya don't have ta go screamin' tha same greetin' over and over nor do ya have ta say anythin' at all!"

There was a momentary pause before the Abstract answered in much more hushed tones, "My apologies. I just wished to convey my enthusiasm and happiness for your return while also offering an opportunity for you to take advantage of self-deprecating humor given at my own expense as I know this is your preference. This would then give you the chance to disparage me down while making you feel amused and uplifted at the same time."

Oblivious to Wrindanneth's snicker, the Abstract continued, "I have merely noticed similar give and take in your conversations and thought it appropriate to the moment. I have observed that you appear happiest when superficially angry and engaged in sarcastic banter. If you wish for me to desist, I will."

Holding back his laughter, and siding with the Abstract for once, Wrindanneth answered for Slate, "Feel free to behave as you were. Your efforts at casual human interaction are much appreciated. Slate only needed to understand the context of your reply."

Glowering, Slate held his tongue, seeing that this line of discussion would lead to areas he would rather leave untouched.

While Slate stormed out of the entry, Wrindanneth calmly inquired, "I understand that we should be expecting a report from Spreesprocket?"

"Let me call that up for you." With those words, a three-dimensional representation of the *Shrike* appeared floating in the air.

Moving to the comfort of the stuffed chairs in the living room, the image followed Wrindanneth to his chosen seat by the front window where the natural light came in through the clear, light-enhancing glass.

Before commencing his review of Spreesprocket's summary, Wrindanneth solicited, "Would anyone like to join me in looking over Spreesprocket's appraisal of the *Shrike*?"

"I'll be right there! Lemme grab a quick bit o' grub!" The clamor and din of Slate orchestrating a hasty meal were more evidence of his activities than his words.

Slipping in quietly, Aroganji took a seat on another large padded chair while Yip simply sat down on the floor, legs folded.

While they waited, Wrindanneth offered, "You know, Slate, that you can ask the Abstract ahead of time and it will prepare your meal for you."

From the kitchen, at the sound of Wrindanneth's invocation, they heard a cheery, "May I be of some assistance?"

Slate cursed.

A few minutes later, Slate huffed into the room, grumbling, "If ya've had yer fun, I'd like ta get started!"

Remaining enticingly calm, Wrindanneth replied, "We've been waiting on you."

"No use waitin' any longer!"

Not replying further, Wrindanneth reached toward the *Shrike*'s representation. With the gesture, as soon as his hand touched the airship's periphery in the region stabilized by the ship's shield and atmospheric control system, Spreesprocket's voice chimed in, "Shielding system augmentation."

A luminescent bubble appeared around the ship indicating the current point of discussion followed by myriad scrolling equations. "Proposed augmentation of alien force neutralization technology." With these words, the luminescent energy storage spheres located throughout the ship's hold brightened in intensity. "Primary force generation and storage system improvements to form the basis of this augmentation. Amplification of technology's capabilities based upon internal research refinements to form the primary improvement in threat neutralization capabilities."

Within this bubble of force, a second glowing sphere illuminated. "Addition of a second tier shield defensive supplementation system based on traditional impenetrable wall of force model to be added."

Before Wrindanneth interacted with any other proposed ship features, Slate said, "So we're lookin' at an improvement on tha alien shieldin' device's neutralization abilities with a backup shield that directly blocks hostile attacks?"

Aroganji nodded from where he sat in the padded chair opposite the small couch on which Slate sat surrounded by various food items held precariously within bowls and plates on two large trays. "The ability of these shields to neutralize or divert incoming attacks will be related to how much additional power the ship commands and how efficiently the shield is able to do this."

By way of clarification, Wrindanneth said, "But the relationship may not be one to one."

"How d'ya mean?"

"The alien shield, for instance, may be able to divert or neutralize significant amounts of energy or force without having to spend an equivalent amount of energy."

"All right." Slate imagined the shield acting like the blade of his axe deflecting a blow from an opponent's sword. Carefully timed, at the right point and angle, he may need very little force to deflect a power-ful, life-threatening blow.

Turning back to the representation of the *Shrike* hovering in the air,

Wrindanneth gestured toward the ship's primary deck. With this motion, several retractable, highly mobile cannons appeared to spring forth from the deck. Each held a scintillating strobospheric orb mounted to their gun barrels. By way of explanation, Spreesprocket said, "Two-tiered offensive system improvements. Supplementation of ship's assault capabilities to include DISCO inferno infernal cannons. Upgrade of Gideon's Transmogrifying Spectral Cyclotron to include localized fusion capabilities in addition to current variable plasma cannon."

Clapping his hands together in excitement, Slate said, "Now we're talkin'! We'll be able ta take on tha entire Cabal fleet once we're done!"

Shaking his head dismissively, Wrindanneth replied simply, "Not on your life."

As his hand approached the ship once more, a swarm of irregular black masses appeared around the ship. With this appearance, Spreesprocket's words clarified, "A broader contingent of ARMED sentry drones will provide additional offensive, defensive, and surveillance capabilities."

Slate grunted, "Those buggers've proved their worth in tha past. Havin' more'll certainly aid us in and outta combat."

Continuing his survey, Wrindanneth's hand brushed past the quarterdeck. As he did so, the command sphere lit up and Spreesprocket said, "Improved, fully functional ship artificial intelligence engine to enhance navigation, auto-piloting, resource allocation, decision-making, targeting, and weapon firing among other tactical and performance duties."

His face lit with an eerie smile in the light of the command sphere's glow on the representation, Wrindanneth nodded appreciatively.

"Now we'll be able ta sleep soundly knowin' we have a real pilot at tha helm!" Slate laughed goadingly.

"And I'll be able to sleep soundly knowing I have at least one more crew member I can trust."

Unaware of their griping, Spreesprocket's voice continued, "To complement the improved ship guidance systems and power arrays, the *Shrike's* handling, maneuvering, and speed will be drastically improved once more. Although she will never handle like an Elven Eiryna, she will feel too close for you to notice the difference."

A look of elation growing on his face, Wrindanneth resisted the urge to clap. Such a reaction would prove disastrous. If he did so, Slate would gain a degree of leverage in their ongoing battle of words that he would never allow.

"What is an Eiryna?" Yip's question broke through Wrindanneth's revelry.

Wrindanneth's eyes lit appreciatively. "They're one of the fastest ship's on Ea'ae. Suitable for use in space and atmosphere, they do not travel with an external atmosphere like airships. They're sleek like some of the alien vessels that arrive at Tellanon intended for interstellar travel."

Slate barked a short laugh at Wrindanneth's enthusiasm. "What Wrindanneth's tryin' ta say is that tha Eiryna don't look like flyin' boats or animals like most airships from Ea'ae. They're all business… deadly serious business. Like tha point o' an arrow locked on its target."

When Yip asked no further questions, Wrindanneth reached out for the image once more. Touching the *Shrike*'s hull, the craft flashed and temporarily disappeared. "Given your longstanding and multifaceted service to Tellanon, we will outfit the *Shrike* with limited *faerviage* capabilities. She will be able to port short distances for defensive and strategic maneuvering as well as teleport back to Tellanon as though she had a return stone. Given the power demands, these abilities will be limited."

Slate clapped. "Now we're talkin'! We can fly halfway across tha macroverse and return in tha blink o' an eye fer a tankard o' spirits when our business is done! As far as I'm concerned, tha sooner we can get off tha ship, tha better!"

At this point, the whole vessel faded to transparency and Spreesprocket chuckled. "Coupled with the energy dampening shield system which will be tuned to absorb signals sent to detect your craft, the Every Gnome's Anti-Intelligence Clandestine Apparatus version 3.1, Corvette Class will help evade detection by hostile ships, particularly those of the Cabal."

Aroganji's eyebrows lifted in curiosity, remembering what he had heard of Gideon's comment on the system, though he knew not exactly what it did. "What exactly will that system afford us?"

In answer to his question, as they watched, the *Shrike* disappeared once more, this time not to return so quickly. "The Every Gnome's Anti-Intelligence Device, previously known as the Every Gnome's Anti-Intelligence Clandestine Apparatus version 3.1, Corvette Class, will make your ship appear to be identical in appearance and features to its surroundings. This applies across all known energy spectrums."

"For all intents and purposes your ship will seem to be nonexistent to outside detection agencies. The space occupied by your vessel will appear and measure as the surrounding air, void, clouds, or other environmental features. In effect, you will be invisible and undetectable... at least for a time."

"The effect is best summed by one simple phrase—EGAD." A note of humor came into Spreesprocket's voice as he continued, "We like to think that this is one of the last phrases the pursuer of a vessel protected by this technology is likely to make, as in, 'EGAD! Where did that ship go?'"

"Only you will know the answer."

When the ship reappeared, amidst Spreesprocket's disembodied chuckles, the command sphere was highlighted once more along with banks of devices along the *Shrike*'s hull. "Finally, to improve your ability to detect hostile ships, analyze unknown phenomena, and generally more accurately assess a given situation, in conjunction with the ship's upgraded intelligence engine, the *Shrike* will be outfitted with a suite of new, highly discerning sensors and measurement arrays."

"Coupled with the significant pilot augmenting abilities already presently incorporated into your vessel, abilities that will grow as Wrindanneth's skills and knowledge increase, these changes should form the nucleus of a much more complete mission and life-sustaining framework."

Aroganji nodded appraisingly as Spreesprocket's voice faded, no longer offering information on additional supplementary systems as Wrindanneth interacted with the image. "Spreesprocket's recommendations appear both generous and complete. Nonetheless, we must consider his suggestions carefully. Before we respond, I propose spending the rest of the day in consideration. Given the import of our mission, we must decide if there are any other capabilities that may be necessary or desirous to include in the *Shrike*'s upgrades. To do otherwise could compromise the success of our mission along with all that entails."

Offering his terse assent, Wrindanneth said, "I agree."

When no one had any objections, Aroganji said, "Here is my proposition. I will respond to Spreesprocket's suggestions and say that we are in complete agreement with the submitted recommendations. That way, he will have time to begin the process of organizing and preparing for the upgrades. However, I will also let him know that we will spend the evening thinking on other potential required upgrades for mission success. Of these, if any, we will let him know on the morrow. Should other ideas arise after this time, we will let him know as soon as possible."

"Agreed?"

"Sounds fair." Slate's attention returned to his food. Before his focus shifted entirely he added, "Gotta get my energy up in preparation fer a night o' deep thoughts."

"Bah! You mean a night of deep dreams and even deeper snoring!" Wrindanneth's laugh was lighthearted for Slate knew as well as he that there was small chance the Dwarf would have many ideas beyond those already discussed. After but a moment, Wrindanneth added to Aroganji, "Your plan is a good one."

Standing to go to his chambers in the cottage's sunroom, Yip said, "I agree as well." Though much of his evening would be spent attempting to converse with Master Wei, he, too, would try to devise additional options that would serve them well in the times ahead.

Just then, he had a thought. Thinking of his time training the Home Guard in the ship's hold, and of Slate's desires for the hold to be filled with more than cargo for an extended voyage, Yip added, "Perhaps we should consider having the interior of the ship expanded extradimensionally, if such a thing is possible. That way, there would be more room for all of us and our traveling companions, should it be required."

Already anticipating Slate's response, Yip smiled as he heard the Dwarf grunt around a mouthful of food, "I like it!"

"While we are at it, perhaps we could add a pocket dimension to store particularly important items, so that Slate does not always have to rely on his magical bag."

When his comment elicited a large grin on Wrindanneth's face, Yip added, "The space could be suitable in size for us to hide in as well should the need ever arise."

"I like it even better!" The varied crumbs and debris left on Slate's beard went unnoticed in the expression of his excitement, his mind filled with thoughts of a hold overfilling with expensive goods and currency in addition to a pocket dimension stuffed with magical artifacts and treasures.

Giving his assent, Wrindanneth said, "Sounds like a welcome addition."

"I do not know if such weapons are possible, but perhaps an anti-magic or anti-energy ray would be advisable to disable and weaken our enemies." Yip looked to his friends for their thoughts.

Slate clapped both hands together excitedly, losing several choice morsels in the process. "I like that even more!"

When nothing else was forthcoming, joining Yip standing, Aroganji said, "If there is nothing else, I will let Spreesprocket know our thoughts."

Leaving Wrindanneth to continue toying with the hologram and Slate to his feast, Aroganji followed Yip out of the room.

While Aroganji retired to the kitchen to brew some soothing and refreshing tea, Yip walked to his living quarters in the house's sunroom. Though the day was not yet done, he wished to spend some time in silent meditation and preparation for his meeting with Master Wei.

The sooner he sent his request to meet with his teacher, the quicker Master Wei would hear and be able to respond.

THOUGHTS OF HOME

Honeysuckle blooms
caress the afternoon air—
a scent sweeter than flowers.

Taking his leave of the house, Yip walked out into the variegated yard with its plantings and arrangements, all ordered and maintained by the Abstract and its enchantments in their absence.

The magic of his surroundings penetrated him, the life pulse of countless living things, from the smallest organisms beneath his feet, those on and within his skin, to the large trees overhead. The crystalline radiance of their presence, seen so clearly through his eyes, he felt through his body as a direct extension of himself, waves upon waves of interpenetrating and interconnecting energy.

As each individual presence moved within the energetic gossamer cast about him, he felt the minute adjustments and changes both within the organisms and to the interconnected lattice supporting them.

This ebb and flow of life's forces washed through and around him —a web he could cast, a web he could draw in, but one he chose merely to experience, observe, and appreciate for those lives and their energies were not his to control.

Gathering his intent, he visualized Master Wei, filling his mind with the image of his teacher. With the object of his awareness so clearly realized before him, he expressed his intent over the space and time separating his mind from the object of his vision.

With any luck, Master Wei would heed his call and respond to his summons this evening.

Preparing to sit for the night while his friends slept, the stars overhead scattered in vibrant profusion through the heavens, Yip felt a light touch on the edge of his awareness—a soft caress, the trace of a faint breeze rippling across the edges of his mind, skirting around its borders with a lithe deftness unlike anything he had encountered. Without knowing exactly how, he recognized that this presence so gingerly reaching out to his own was not that of his teacher Master Wei but of something else entirely—EMMA a NUMEN.

He also understood without needing to ask that this delicate tickling on the periphery of his senses was an unspoken solicitation to communicate.

Without trepidation, for he sensed nothing hostile in the gentle approach, he opened himself up to the presence.

A profound expanse opened before him, calm and unruffled, filled with the quietude of the void between the stars above and just as vast.

He looked inward upon a mirror, only much broader and more penetrating than his own.

From within and without, he felt rather than heard some communication that he understood as, *"You have an elegant mind,"* for the experience was like he thought it himself rather than hearing or interpreting anything from the other mind now joined with his.

He need not smile, for EMMA the NUMEN sensed the incipient emotion, rather he explained the smile that came unbidden to his face for it was not with pride that he reacted to the praise. *"The mirror reflects the observer."*

"Observed and observer are joined in the reflection."

"And each reflects the other."

"In the observer's mind."

"The complement is yours."

"As it is yours."

These thoughts completed each other passing between the two minds instantly and of the same source, a conversation with one's self within the confines of one's own mind, not between two disparate intelligences that had never met or interacted.

The space between them was filled with one like consciousness.

"I will enjoy our travels together." As quickly as it had come, EMMA disappeared, its greeting and introduction welcome surprises that left only the peace of his awareness filling the space once occupied by two.

Settling in once more for the evening, Yip directed his focus elsewhere.

The time had come to contact Master Wei.

He had not spoken with his master in far too long.

How long had it been?

Had he really not contacted his teacher since before they had set out upon their quest?

Caught up in the roaring tide of events, he had moved from moment to moment not keeping track of time. Only aware that time passed, that day moved to night and night moved to day, that one instant followed another, each measured by fleeting occurrences, brief markers measuring the way to his ultimate goal, he had lost track of the length of the interval that had transpired between meetings.

So much had occurred in the period since they last communicated, a space measured in the time between heartbeats had been filled with lifetimes of memory.

Since he had last spoken with Master Wei through dreams, his world had been filled with adventure, triumph, and loss. Alongside his friends and allies, he had helped restore one of Ea'ae's fallen seals. He had lost dear companions he had not known prior to the beginning of their adventure but that he now cherished as dearly as any he had known, only to have their journey ended abruptly at the hands of foes too horrific to deem plausible. He had shared the knowledge of the Dragon's Gate that other worlds and futures may be spared the Cabal's evil.

Much had been accomplished but much remained yet to do.

Though Master Wei had told him in their last meeting that he was no longer Yip's teacher, his feelings had not changed on the subject. So long as he had been part of the K'un Lun, Master Wei had been his guide, his inspiration, and the closest thing to an immediate family member he had known. All those sentiments remained the same, despite Master Wei's request.

On one level, Master Wei had set him free long ago to voyage, explore, and learn on his own. This was in fact the way set before him on the path of the K'un Lun—one of discovery and sacrifice, effort and perseverance with the end and means, the goals and the attainments, left to his aspiration and vision. On another level, he yet thought of his teacher as an anchor, a tie to his past and a beacon for his future. Though he could cut this tie entirely, he felt these two views were not mutually exclusive and, thus, even if only in his own heart, Master Wei remained his teacher.

These thoughts resolved themselves in his mind of their own accord, objects of awareness among many—the flitting of the leaves and grasses in the yard beyond the enclosure of the sunroom where he now sat, the sounds of his friends' slow breathing indicating deep sleep elsewhere in the house, the flow of the *chi* within his body and beyond, the passage of the clouds before the silvery moon, and the contents of his mind. Each had a place; all were granted attention within his awareness.

Sitting on his bedroll, the heavens illumined through the glass roof of the sunroom above, he closed his eyes and followed his breath.

With any luck, it would lead to Master Wei.

His mind seeking after his teacher, his memory drifted back in time while his awareness moved outward, returning to his youth and the many challenges he faced in his development, of the precipices he had to climb and the cliffs over which he had to leap, all under Master Wei's discerning guidance. With each success, he was granted new opportunities to learn and further obstacles to overcome.

"Master, why are we here?"

He stood with Master Wei upon the edge of a vast chasm. A short distance below, a small shelf appeared in the monolithic wall of gray rock. Upon this ledge, within the sheer wall, a small cave had been carved out, used for contemplative retreats by priests seeking the isolation of their own minds and the examination of interior dimensions.

Numerous similar caves littered the sides of mountains nearby. Of these, many caves had been constructed as an integral part of the spiritual practice of a priest desiring meditative retreat, a necessary precursor for the monk's period of seclusion.

Gazing downward over the precipice, the wind whipped and stirred, testing his balance, urging him to lean ever farther outward over the abyss, pushing his limits. Beneath his feet, loose gravel shifted on the thin trail cut into the cliff side, trying his balance and footing, working in partnership with the wind to force him to commit to the air.

"The mind and body interact on many levels, Yip. As a priest, you must come to understand these interconnections and interactions intimately."

"So, too, do individuals interact on many levels whether in friendly discussion or physical combat—testing mind against mind, body against body, vision against vision, reality against reality, and truth against truth. Each of these spheres of interaction, the physical, the mental, and the subtle, should be studied and explored in order to master yourself and your relationship with others."

"You have learned much in the time since we took you in both from direct teaching and on your own."

"The deepest insights and the clearest visions result from the cultivation of one's own understanding."

"In the cave below, you will find dried fruits and water, enough sustenance to keep you for several weeks if you are frugal."

"You may return to the temple when you can not only tell me the most effective way to neutralize an opponent's intent, whether in the realm of mind, body, or spirit, but demonstrate this understanding in practice."

Master Wei looked at him with a degree of seriousness that showed the measure and gravity of his request. "Do not return until you are certain of your answer and your abilities."

Lighter than the wind whipping Yip's robes, Master Wei turned and left Yip to his silent contemplation of the ledge below.

Taking a deep breath, he jumped over the cliff.

"Yip!" The softest of voices, a sound carried fleetingly on the wind alighting gently upon his ears, came unbidden into his mind.

Seizing this faint connection, Yip responded in kind, providing his master the path and the way to his current location. "Master Wei!" For though Tellanon remained shielded, the ways walked by a Yu-jen were not blocked by magics such as these should the path through be provided for them as he now did for his teacher.

Thus Master Wei skirted the barriers protecting Tellanon in the same way other priests skirted the barriers protecting their temple in the K'un Lun.

Making reality whole, moving through wholeness, the Yu-jen brings together that which is divided and bridges that which has been made separate.

"*Yip!*" Much louder now, Master Wei's voice increased in strength and volume, if only in his own mind.

"*I am here!*" His excitement no longer held in check, he waited for his master like a young child waiting to see his best friend, his father, and his brother all combined into one personage after long absence.

With those words, the lambent brilliance of his teacher came into full view and Master Wei materialized before him.

Sitting in silent appreciation while his teacher stood, neither spoke for some moments while each gazed upon the other intently. Each reading how the other had changed since last they had met, how they had remained the same, both shared in the silence between them that was the gift of peace.

Finally, Master Wei spoke, his face bright with a smile. "Much has changed about you, Master Chuan, just as much has changed since your departure."

Sharing his master's smile, Yip said, "Much has remained the same about you as well, Master Wei."

Only then, through the heady gauze of their reunion, did he realize that his teacher had called him master.

Bowing his head in humility, he objected to the recognition. "I am only Yip, master."

At these words, Master Wei laughed, his voice as gentle as the sounds of crickets in the distance filling the evening in a chorus of song. "If, in your stubbornness, you continue to insist upon calling me master and thinking of me as your teacher, then I can call you by the honorific you have so rightfully earned."

Keeping his head down in deference to the light rebuke, Yip remained quiet. Though he freely shared what little he knew, he never considered himself a teacher, much less a master.

"You have given the world a gift like none other, Yip! Raise your head with the joy and equanimity in your heart that you so richly deserve."

Gently lifting Yip's chin with his own hand, the soft lightness of his touch charged with subdued power, Master Wei looked deeply into Yip's eyes with his own. "On the wings of your blessing, with the surety of the Dragon's Gate, priests yet walk upon Ea'ae once more, Yip! Though our numbers are yet limited to those of attainment who have demonstrated full control over the ability, you no longer walk unaccompanied in your mission! Your brothers now wander lands under the vault of Heaven bringing what peace and stability they may."

"You are no longer alone!"

"Others will soon join their ranks as their knowledge and cultivation grow and they earn the mantle of priesthood. With your insight, the Priests of K'un Lun will once more walk among the halls of Men, Elves, Gnomes, and Dwarves. All free peoples will be counted as our friends and allies. The time of our hiding will soon be at an end!"

Looking into his master's eyes, tears of joy ran unchecked down his cheeks. This was more than he had hoped.

Should he fail, his brothers and sisters would soon take his place. Should they succeed, his order would once again take their place upon Ea'ae ensuring that life in all its myriad expressions could realize its full fruition without interference from those who would plunder its riches, plucking and despoiling its potential before maturation.

His eyes bright in joy and wonder, he said, "You do not walk alone on this path, master. The knowledge of the Dragon's Gate grows now within many hearts. The Elves will soon carry this knowledge in the Aerya'ana to Ea'ae and beyond. The Home Guard, too, and others besides have committed to spreading the knowledge far and wide that beings everywhere will not have their futures taken from them."

His eyes looking briefly into the distance, Master Wei said, "I have felt this in the *yuan-chi* and am glad. The good you have brought forth into the world will multiply of its own accord, as it should."

Bowing his head, Yip replied to his teacher, "Let us hope."

Nodding gravely, Master Wei echoed his sentiments. "Though you have done much to secure our futures, the Cabal yet remain in the shadows waiting to strip it from us. They have breached Ea'ae's defenses and even now seek to undermine all that you have accomplished in your quest."

Nodding, Yip answered, "I know not yet where to find them."

Confirming that knowledge of the Dragon's Gate was secure within his order along with letting his teacher know of others who practiced the Dragon's Gate and would help cleanse the Cabal's taint were the main reasons he had wished to talk with his master. Perhaps Master Wei had discerned where the Cabal were hidden and knew what he needed to do to root them out of hiding.

His smile become grim, Master Wei responded, "You need not, Yip. They will find you."

His eyes now eager, Yip replied, "How can you be sure?"

Master Wei responded with a grim half-smile, "Have they not tried already?"

Not needing to hear Yip's answer, Master Wei continued, "You have caused them too much trouble, too much pain, and too much loss. They will seek you out to be rid of you and all you stand for and hope to achieve. Though the Cabal have long since forgotten that the root of suffering lies within and only from within can its hold be released, they know enough to strive to eliminate suffering at its source, however misguided their perception."

His face just as grim, Yip responded in kind, "Then they will find one whose purpose and determination mirrors their own. Though I may not be the one who is their ultimate undoing, I will help sow the seeds that will bear this fruit."

His eyes an ocean of concern, Master Wei responded, "Do not let your passion consume you, Yip, or your emotion overwhelm you. Do as you must as the situation dictates but do not let the sentiments of the Cabal become your own."

Yip bowed briefly in acknowledgement to Master Wei. "Their hearts are not my own, master. There is a goal in sight, a destination to reach, and countless moments to live in between. My heart is in each of these moments. The truth of each of these instants is my own. Nothing more."

Master Wei nodded and said no more. If peace dwelt in Yip's heart, then his actions would move in accord with the dictates of the situation no matter how trying.

He could ask for nothing more.

"Master, you have told me of the priests and their triumph but what of the Aeryn D'al?"

The ready smile returned Master Wei's visage upon these words. "The Tree Lord prospers as do your brothers. Its grace guides our own. Its life enhances ours. Its wisdom furthers our own."

Looking off into the distance, his mind briefly filled with an image of the seedling rapidly becoming a tree, Master Wei added, "Though we have learned from the Aeryn D'al, so, too, does it learn from us. It is, like you, both a student and teacher. Its Light has done much to rekindle ours. Underneath its flourishing boughs, students learn more and faster than they have in my memory. Its presence aids our purpose."

"Of that I am glad to hear."

Master Wei's gaze returned to Yip's. "Some of those with knowledge of the Dragon's Gate have ventured to the Jenyuan Shulin and are even now strengthening the bonds between us. Within that small seed given to your care, so carefully kept by your hands, an alliance between us has been born."

Pausing but a moment, Master Wei added, "More seedlings will come."

He bowed to his teacher. "I had hoped as much."

Pausing for a moment, Yip asked, "Do you wish to see the journey to restore the seal of Eldre'gheu through my eyes, master?"

Master Wei's face remained placid as he placed one soothing hand on Yip's shoulder and replied, "You have suffered enough, Yip. I do not wish for you to relive the hardships you have endured these past few months. I sense that the seal has been restored and Ea'ae has been granted a temporary reprieve from extradimensional incursions. Better to look forward to restoring the other compromised seals than look backward."

Yip nodded silently in reply. Though the memory did not pain him, he understood Master Wei's sentiment.

Reaching into his robes, he retrieved two scrolls, one the intricately wrought teaching scroll of the Elves and the other much plainer teaching scroll of the K'un Lun. Both revealed secrets far too valuable to lose, insights far too precious to risk. Holding both out to his teacher, he said, "Master, I would have you take with you a gift from the Elves that I would give to my brethren. This scroll reveals the secret science of the Elven ways of health, motion, insight, perception, wisdom, and vitality. Like this other teaching scroll, it explicates the contents requested by the bearer's mind, should he or she be ready to grasp the desired teachings."

"There are strictures to the scroll's use. The scroll will only work for the K'un Lun, only when the bearer is acting under the possessor's own free will. The scroll will not work if the bearer is directly relaying the requested information to another though there is no restriction on sharing knowledge after it is transmitted and grasped once called forth from the scroll. Nor will it work under coercion or if the bearer's purpose is no longer just."

Locking eyes with his teacher, Yip expressed the gravity of his intent. "I would have its knowledge further that of our own."

Though he did not speak of the other scroll, Master Wei understood it, too, was to be passed on. He also perceived that Yip wanted to ensure that other disciples could benefit from the knowledge held within should he not return from his next venture.

Seeing all this and more in his teacher's veiled eyes, Yip said, "Do not fear, master, for I have every intention of returning to the monastery and reading the entirety of the Elven scroll." Laughing he added, "Why else would I give it so freely?"

"There is one thing more I would give." Reaching under his robes, he retrieved the glittering warmth of the Heart of Yere. Knowing that Master Wei remembered both the Yerens and the H'era from their last meeting when he had shared his journey and the knowledge of the Dragon's Gate directly with his teacher, he said, "This artifact was given to me by the Yerens to aid in my quest. I would see it returned to them. If you are venturing into the Jenyuan Shulin, the Yerens and the H'era are not far. Both will make powerful allies as we retake our place in the world."

Understanding Yip's desire for a relationship with his friends and allies, Master Wei quietly took the necklace from him. Expressing his concern directly, Master Wei said, "Would you give away all your possessions, Yip?"

Appreciating the implications of Master Wei's request, he answered, "Others may need these more than I."

Knowing Yip's heart as well as his own, Master Wei replied, "Your heart guides you well, Yip."

Master Wei's smile was filled with praise as he added, "You are as the mirror—a reflection of your environment, untouched yet containing a part of it within yourself. Continue to open yourself as you have and you will reflect upon the dream you seek."

Though he had not summoned his teacher for compliments, Yip bowed nonetheless. "Thank you, master."

"You are ready for what may come, Yip. I see that in you clearly. I am honored to have called you my student."

After having received more accolades from his teacher in the past few minutes than he had during the entirety of his years in training, Yip took a moment to respond to Master Wei. "You have always been, and always will be, the inspiration and incentive for all my efforts. You are my family and future."

Master Wei laughed, his face radiant with health and vitality, his eyes brighter than the stars shining above. "You must set your sights higher, Yip!"

Smiling in kind, Yip replied with a short bow, "As you wish."

Master Wei gave Yip a deep, respectful bow to his onetime student. "Yip, you alone of all the priests are prepared for whatever may come in the days ahead. I know this with certainty. I also want to do whatever is in my power to ensure the success of your mission."

"Now that we walk freely once more upon the lands of Ea'ae, I am able to offer you something that I was not able when last we met."

Master Wei's pause added significance to his words. "Would you like the assistance of other priests upon your quest?"

His surprise at the offer did not register on his face.

"Of those priests who have learned the ways of the Dragon's Gate, we can send as many as you would like to ensure the success of your mission."

Yip spoke directly then for his teacher, their order, deserved nothing less. "Master, your offer is most gracious. I am honored by your request but I cannot take it. I would love to travel with my brethren for there is much I could learn from their tutelage and much we could accomplish together. I could not, however, in good conscience have my fellow priests by my side on this quest. Though their skills and insights would be invaluable, I could not risk making so many of my brethren vulnerable at one time after we have only so recently retaken our place in the broader world. Both for the future of our order and the future of Ea'ae, I believe our efforts would be better spent spread out across many paths rather than focused along a single direction."

"There are, however, other seals to be secured and many alliances to be built for our common future. If our hope and vision of what may be is to be realized, we must take our place in its realization. Many are those who work for a similar vision of life's untold potential."

"Éremon and the Council of Light of which he is part along with the Home Guard and the Elven Aerya'ana would all welcome your support and guidance. The Indural, H'era, Yerens, Aeryn D'al, many Dragons, and others still are worthy allies. Éremon and Eidelion of the Home Guard in particular will be able to better guide those efforts than I for their knowledge of the world is much broader than my own."

Master Wei gave a short bow. "Your attainment is only matched by your wisdom."

Yip laughed, his eyes bright as he gazed upon his mentor. "And only a pale shadow of my teacher's!"

"The K'un Lun will serve in whatever way we are able. We will no longer be relegated to the shadows."

He bowed graciously to his teacher. "The world will welcome our Light."

"As it does yours." With that last comment Master Wei faded into the night.

Watching his teacher's radiance fade into the darkness, Yip's mind drifted back once more to the early days of his youth to his first studies with the K'un Lun, his commitment to the ways of truth, and the aspirations that yet drove his journey forward to this day. In particular, the thought of his brethren's reemergence into the wider world brought forth thoughts of his first true journey into theirs.

He followed Master Wei for the better part of the morning along the rocky ridge sweeping above the temple, wending through broken, weatherworn crags, past low-lying, windswept vegetation, retracing the elusive trail etched slowly into the bedrock by one initiate waiting for the next aspirant to discover.

After much labor, their climb complete, the trail ended at the apex of the ridgeline above the temple of the K'un Lun. Before them, a level, circular clearing carved by the countless footsteps of fellow ascetics perched without borders before the vault of Heaven. In the distance, the seat of the Celestial Courtyard, Fay Long, soared to the firmament, its peak too far above the clouds to wear them as a crown. Below Fay Long's exalted heights, the mountains of the K'un Lun towered but fell short in its long, majestic shadows.

Looking downward, following the precarious trail back to its source, the temple of the K'un Lun, her grounds, and outbuildings, all sheltered within the solid ramparts of the temple's outer walls. Shrunken by distance, inside the temple's walls, verdant splashes of green and brilliant flashes of light hinted at the intricate gardens and water features, the plantings and contemplative arrangements, that made the temple's protective walls so welcoming to those who called the monastery home.

"Master, why are we here?" Never patient enough to wait for his teacher's direction, his curiosity led him to ask before he was shown, inquire before he was told.

Master Wei remained silent, however, his long gaze fixed upon the proud spire of Fay Long in the blue distance.

Master Wei's silence afforded Yip the opportunity to take the measure of the place, appreciate the view, and feel the sublimeness of reality spread all around.

Yip, however, as always, had other ideas.

Trying again, his persistence one of his primary virtues, and faults, he asked, "Why did we come to this clearing, master? What do you wish to show me here?" Looking at the open expanse, though he had never been here before, he knew this was a place of intense practice for what else would have worn the solid granite flat and turned the tumbled rocks to dust?

His penetrating gaze still locked upon Fay Long and the Celestial Courtyard, Master Wei took some time before answering, countering Yip's question with one of his own. "Why are you here, Yip? What do you wish to learn?"

He thought for a time before answering, the steady wind whipping *through the heights playing with his robes, snapping them back and forth around his arms and legs. Understanding the depth of his teacher's question, he answered honestly, not with how he felt his teacher may want or expect him to reply but with his heartfelt appraisal, a reflection of his true purpose and character.*

Though young and inexperienced, he had given matters such as these much thought while watching the other acolytes practice their meditations, forms, sparring, dialectics, and other physical, contemplative, and intellectual pursuits. "Master, I wish to realize my potential that I may enrich the lives and efforts of those around me, that my happiness and peace may be theirs. I wish to learn the breadth and depth of the ways of the K'un Lun, uphold our traditions, embody the Three Pillars, further our knowledge, and deepen our wisdom."

Master Wei nodded sagely, his face unresponsive, a mask of poise and calm. "And how do you propose to realize such noble aspirations?"

His gaze followed that of his master, looking out over the valleys and ridges girding Fay Long's vast heights. "Master, I will let my conscience be my compass and your teachings be my guide."

"Where do you think such a path will lead you, Yip?"

"I will walk along the path of the warrior, the scholar, the skeptic, and the hermit. I will lead the life of the ascetic, the healer, the supplicant, and the protector. I will ask and I will seek answers. I will maintain a mind as open as the sky and as unclouded as a diamond. I will maintain humility and the perception of a beginner."

"What then will you become should you follow this path?"

"I will become a Priest of the K'un Lun, a warrior sage, a guardian of the people and pursuer of truth."

"You would become a warrior?"

Yip nodded his head in reply.

Master Wei paused before continuing, his gaze heavy upon Yip's own. "A true warrior is not one who fights on the field of battle or claims victory over the fallen but one who fights for hearts and minds. A warrior is one who strives for the future and the untold potential of the present. A true warrior is selfless and gives of himself that others may realize their own potential."

"A true warrior fights for life and the truth it reveals."

"The way of the warrior, then, is the realization and expression of wisdom, understanding, and insight."

"The warrior's path, the path you would take, is the path of peace. The two are not different."

"Violence begets more violence. This is not the domain of the true warrior, the Priests of the K'un Lun, or the values we espouse. The true warrior seeks ever more efficient ways to bring about and manifest peace through his actions and intent."

"The warrior's path then is not one of violence but of peace with his aim as peace, his intent as peace, his actions as peace, and the outcome of his deeds as peace."

"The true warrior's reality then is the realization and expression of peace."

"The path of the warrior becomes the cultivation of peace within his own mind while learning to cultivate peace between and among minds."

"Only when a warrior finds peace, makes peace with himself, and then abides in that peace can he hope to inspire peace within others. But even then, the choice for another is not his to make. So the life of a warrior knows only the surety of his own mind for he only lives his own journey."

Master Wei looked at Yip appraisingly, gauging the depth and veracity of his response. "You would willingly walk upon this path, not yet fully understanding its vagaries and uncertainties, and take upon the full mantle of our order?"

Understanding the gravity of his master's question, the reasoning for his passion, he answered simply, once again directly from the heart, "If I am deemed worthy."

After years of observance and practice both on his own and with Master Wei's subtle guidance, he had decided to dedicate his life to the order that had so kindly taken him in years before when no one else had offered him shelter or succor.

Keeping his inward smile hidden, he mused briefly in good cheer, happy with his decision and eager to rise to his master's challenge.

How could he refuse to take on his master's ultimatum after his teacher had spoken more at one time than he had ever heard in his short life? To turn away after his master made such an effort on his behalf, offering so much, would be an affront to his honor and undermine his master's intent.

Turning away from his contemplation of Fay Long, the bright light of compassion full in his eyes, Master Wei smiled and said, "I am here to further your dreams as I have always been since you first sheltered within the walls of our hallowed grounds."

Not realizing he had been tested or that he had been judged worthy, his burgeoning aspirations were accepted after much observation and evaluation.

He was now granted leave to further his studies with the K'un Lun, an orphan now with a home, a foundling now with a family.

Blinking his eyes as the images of years past slowly faded from his mind, Yip stood and decided to go for a walk under the light of the scintillating stars.

The universe was wide, the sky deep.

He wished to spend the evening swimming in their beauty.

LIGHT OF LIFE

Luminous full moon
presides over purple skies.
Cold fog greets my breath.

Yip returned to the cottage early in the morning, well before his companions were out of bed. He had meandered far and wide across Tellanon's wondrous streets, the smooth, organic white stonework providing a constant companion when the lanes were empty, glowing with a lustrous pearlescence beneath the moon and stars just as the boughs shifting overhead provided the steady music of rustling leaves to the tune of each of his soft steps.

He had wandered so long alone, the only one of his kind in the world. Now, after all this time, this was no longer the case. His was a journey that would be shared by the ones who knew his footsteps best for he had spent much time trying to follow theirs.

He would not be the last priest to walk under the wide-open skies of Ea'ae. His would not be the last eyes to see the subtle luminescence of her countless living things. He would not be the last acolyte to feel the ethereal currents of living energy bathing the world in potential. He would not be the last of the K'un Lun to call this world home.

His order would fulfill their promise of overthrowing the Cabal and retake their mantle as humanity's uplifters and protectors.

Enlivened by his master's words, buoyed by the unfolding of possibility, he knew with certainty that his world's future was now assured. He felt the weight of responsibility lift from his shoulders with the thought that others would carry on his efforts should he fail, more ably than he was ever able. There was peace in his mind and joy in his heart at these thoughts, filled with the knowledge that his brethren would be a shining part of that future of lived potential, of vibrant possibility, on Ea'ae.

Much yet remained to be done but all would be accomplished nonetheless. If he were lucky, then he would be a part of both this future's realization and the world beyond the tribulations necessary for its fulfillment. If not, the universe would proceed in his absence as it would for the betterment of all living beings.

Of this, he was certain.

Not wishing to disturb his friends, Yip remained on the lawn for the rest of the night. He would work while their body and minds recovered. The light of the sun, stars, and moon penetrated him just as the vibrancy of the *yuan-chi* and *chi* filled him.

There was much yet he needed to address before they left Tellanon. The arrival of his teacher and the promise of the future had inspired him. There was more he had to accomplish.

He would use the time he had been given before their departure to achieve this inspiration. Every moment he had been granted was a gift. He must treat each moment as such.

In the days ahead while they prepared to leave, he would work as he had—as fully as he was able.

Filling the contents of his mind with as much as he was able, he stood silently in the center of the lawn, one fixture among many.

Letting himself fade into emptiness, he disappeared.

"Come in off tha lawn before our neighbors think we petrified ya!" Slate's baritone summons echoed off the stone walls of the cottage and its surroundings more alarmingly than ever Yip's still presence had.

"I know ya can hear me! Just 'cuz ya're covered in dew and a potential roost fer birds doesn't mean ya can't move!"

Slate's insistence upon his return brought a smile to Yip's lips as he turned toward his Dwarven friend. "Are you looking for an excuse to serve more food?"

Slate laughed. "Nah! I already found that! We're ready ta start plannin' what's ta be done today and need yer voice."

Lifting his feet from the grass where two footprints outlined in glistening dew marked the place he had spent the last few hours, Yip joked, "Your voice carries well enough for both of us."

"That's what I say!" Turning back inside with a broad grin, Slate led the way to the kitchen where the others were finishing their morning meal.

Aroganji and Wrindanneth waited for them inside sitting at the kitchen table surrounded by the steaming plates of food Slate had prepared to break their fast.

"'Bout time you got here! Aroganji insisted I wait for you before I started eating! As if you were going to have some!" Wrindanneth dug in to his food as Yip arrived in the room.

Aroganji shrugged. "We should respect the ritual even if others perform it differently."

Yip smiled at his friends. "There is no need to wait on my concern. You are free to do as you please."

"We do!" Slate vigorously began devouring what Yip could only assume was a third or fourth helping of food because several empty plates already appeared piled beside where he sat. Evidently Slate had not waited for anyone. He had probably finished these first rounds before either Aroganji or Wrindanneth ever saw the kitchen.

"What do you propose doing for the day?" Aroganji had a list of tasks that needed to be accomplished and wanted to incorporate all loose ends and unforeseen activities into his plans.

"I will visit a park."

Yip's simple reply piqued Slate's interest. "Visit a park? What d'ya wanna do there? We have a lotta things that have yet ta be done!"

"Do we?" Yip need not explain how most of the tasks they were involved in could either be handled by the Abstract or were in the hands of people other than those in the party.

"Well..."

Slate's thought was cut off by Wrindanneth. "I am going to visit the *Shrike* and oversee a bit of the upgrades. I want to see firsthand what is going on with my ship."

Yip understood Wrindanneth's desire. The *Shrike* was an extension of himself. He wanted to comprehend and experience any changes not only for his comfort and understanding but as a matter of their potential survival. "I will go to a park to train as we have done in the past. Any who wish are welcome to join me."

"How long will you be there?" Though he wanted to watch over his ship, Wrindanneth also recognized the opportunity to work in a coordinated fashion with his friends.

"I will go every day I am able and stay all day."

Aroganji understood Yip's implication and the thrust of Wrindanneth's question. "As we did before, we should all make time to train together while we have the opportunity, not only for our own betterment but for our overall group performance."

"'Tis tha only way ta improve."

Yip nodded. "I will be at the park nearest to the cottage. Seek me out whenever you are ready."

While his friends finished their meals, Yip left the room quietly and went out the back door, leaving the cottage behind for the day.

He walked across the lawn, his pace casual as he opened the gate and turned left down the cobbled lane leading toward the nearest open space. Strolling beneath the branching trees past the orderly cottages not yet roused, few citizens shared the dazzling morning with him.

Clear air filled his lungs and the Light of life bathed his body and mind.

After his time with Master Wei last night he had had an idea, a moment of inspiration that might guide his progress forward.

He had never asked Master Wei how his teacher traveled across the distances between them. He had merely known it was possible and his master could do it. He had not questioned or considered the possibility since he left the monastery for he had first been too busy trying to survive and then too occupied to realize his vision. Along the way, other attainments had occurred, some by effort, some by chance, but he had not considered this one.

Now he understood it as the key to many more.

He would test this idea today at the park.

Nestled at the end of a quiet, leafy street one lane over from that adjoining their small home, its old wooden gate crowded by flowering vines and overarching limbs, the entrance to the park appeared to be the gateway to a secluded wooden garden. What lay beyond its gate, however, could only be guessed.

As he approached, Yip glimpsed an otherworldly expanse through the tangled boughs, one completely unexpected based on the context on this side of the gate.

Another world beckoned within arm's reach.

Reaching out to open the gate, creaking as it swung open for him, he paused a moment before stepping through to appreciate the beauty of the realm he was about to enter. Clear azure-green waters lapped lazily on a multicolored sandy shore glimmering in the welcoming hues of soft pink, peach, tan, and white indicative of diverse coral. Proceeding forward, the smell of clean, ionized salt air met his nose on a warm breeze while he was enveloped in the gentle susurrations of the sea.

Far off in the distance in either direction, he sensed rather than saw other wanderers from Tellanon appreciating the soothing seascape. Here by the open space's entrance, however, he was alone.

He would practice nearby so that his friends would be able to find him easily.

Walking slowly across the sand toward the water, Yip felt the warm grains slide around his feet, shifting beneath his sandals, each a tiny world whose orbit was altered by his own. Behind him, the gate back to Tellanon appeared as a small, white-washed wooden slatted gate between two sand dunes covered in crystalline grasses of various jewel tones. When the grasses shifted in the breeze, they made light, melodic tinkling sounds, part of an ethereal symphony.

Washing over his feet, the water was surprisingly warm, warmer than his own body. Where the water struck his skin, iridescent streaks of bright blue and green bioluminescence rippled through the water, illuminating his path in striking beauty. All around, in the sand and sea, he sensed the living energy of these miniscule creatures that connected so wondrously to his world through splashes of vibrant color.

Smiling as he observed the waves dance with light, the color and tone of these vibrant plumes reminded him very much of the halos of *chi* surrounding and imbuing all living creatures. Here was life's vivacity, so wondrous, made visible for all to see.

Moving farther down along the beach through the glimmering water, a streamer of rippling iridescence left in his wake, he settled on a place to begin his practice.

With each of his motions, from stillness to step, *chi* flowed through him in an unbroken wave. If he so chose, he could move and manipulate this energy at will, shaping it by intent and directing it with his mind.

Now, however, he did nothing.

Standing still, eyes closed, his soles planted in the sand, the gentle tide moved in and out around his feet and the refreshing breeze blew around his loose robes.

As he was aware of himself, so, too, was he aware of the *chi*, from source to realization, from the *yuan-chi* to the *chi*, the expression of unlimited potential enfolded and expressed him in an unending wave. Letting all else fall away, Light everlasting became him.

Sense of self vanished, slipping away within awareness of all-encompassing energies. Within this timeless, selfless state, dynamic forces moved and shifted, eddied and disappeared, coalesced and broke apart, formed and dissipated.

The boundaries of his mind dissolved with his sense of self, and he did something he had never done before, had never fully considered until this night past. Just as he had let the borders of his mind slip away, so, too, did he let the boundaries of his corporeal body fade, letting the embodiment of his self fall away with the bounds of his mind.

Abiding in this state, at peace and enlivened by the fullness of emptiness, he finally opened his eyes.

Nothing had changed.

The world around him appeared as one, filled with dynamic life-sustaining and life generated forces, interconnected through currents of energy arising from within and without countless points of living light.

Spending a few uncounted moments appreciating this magnificence, he made to take a step toward the surf after his failed attempt.

Only then did he realize that everything had indeed changed.

There was no step.

There was nothing to step.

His senses were heightened beyond even those which he normally knew. The field of his awareness encompassed a range far greater than any he had known, so sensitive that he was able to read minute fluxes within the living energies at the periphery of his mind better than he had ever been able to discern such miniscule fluctuations within arm's reach. His sense of self, his sense of selflessness appeared unbounded, limited only by his willingness to extend himself.

His body had fallen away!

Awareness intact, mind manifest, he floated where once he had stood, the body of light realized, rainbow body expressed, *jalü* attained.

With but a slight movement of his mind, he shifted from one end of the pocket dimension to the other. Then, returning to the spot of his transformation, he bridged the gap between the extradimensional space's limits with his awareness.

Satisfied, he returned to himself, or rather what had once been himself, awareness coalescing to a point, focusing tighter and tighter as his mind returned to the delimitations and demarcations defined by his physical form, his essence crystallizing with his will as his mind became body once more.

Embodied, he looked out upon the gentle sea again.

Nothing of note having transpired, he turned and walked slowly back toward the whitewashed gate at the top of the coral dunes ready to wait for his friends in the quiet peace of reflection.

Atop the dune, he sat, abiding in peace, his mind at ease, anchored in stillness. Relaxed and open, *chi* flowed unobstructed through him, indistinguishable from the surrounding energy currents. Free and in accord, without form, he was a part of the place as much as it was a part of him.

To a mind's eye like his own, he would be invisible, essenceless.

"If I'd known where tha park gate was gonna lead me, I would've come prepared ta swim!" To Yip, Slate's jovial voice reaching out over the sand announced his arrival much less noticeably than the luminous aura that spilled forth upon his first crossing the gate's threshold and entering the extradimensional region.

Looking slowly left and right with a wry smile, Yip replied, "I see nothing to stop you."

Clambering across the dunes, sand falling away from his armored feet in fractured waves, Slate stroked his beard thoughtfully as he reached Yip's side. "There is that."

Clapping both gauntleted hands together thunderously, he boomed, "Per'aps after we've worked up a bit o' a lather, I'll take a dip in tha water. If I'm lucky, I might even get ta wrestle a sea serpent!"

Yip laughed. "There are none here."

"But one can hope!"

Giving his friend another slight smile, Yip answered, "Always."

Starting to limber up, rolling his broad shoulders before he began to dance the Daerdaana'Duin with his axe, Slate brought Yip abreast of the morning's goings-on. "Aroganji should arrive shortly. He had a few questions fer tha Paratechnologists on their work decipherin' tha alien command sphere and their research developments regardin' tha alien technology. Knowin' him, he'll get another report outta them on all tha new devices they've made as a result o' our original discovery.'

With a twinkle in his eye, Slate added, "If it keeps gold flowin' ta our coffers, I'm all fer it!"

Barking a short, derisive laugh, he went on, "Wrindanneth may or may not join us. I spent tha better part o' tha mornin' with him pourin' over his ship with Spreesprocket and Gideon. By tha time I'd had enough, my stomach was callin', so I headed back ta join ya. Fer all I can tell, he'll be sleepin' on tha ship."

Yip smiled, saying nothing, for he knew by the timing of Slate's arrival that he had taken care to get his midday meal before coming over. He anticipated that Wrindanneth would arrive later in the day but only begrudgingly and after he had laid a firm foundation of expectations and understanding with regard to his ship.

"Let's get started before tha lunch crowd gets here and starts takin' all our valuable real-estate!"

Yip laughed as he stood with his friend looking up and down the empty beach meaningfully. "You mean you?"

Slate shrugged. "I'm all that counts anyway!"

Sharing his friend's smile, Yip replied, "So we all think in our own minds."

Unsheathing Duraeleon as they walked down the dune, the axe muttered a brief groan as though it, too, were stretching alongside Slate as he began to twirl his arms in broad circles. Grumbling, its accent as mutable as its mood, Duraeleon complained, "Yer conversation is about as thrillin' as sittin' trapped in that holster!"

Grunting derisively, Slate answered firmly, "If ya don't like it, I'd be happy ta put ya back in!"

Unbowed, Duraeleon shot back, "And per'aps ya'd better take care not ta get nicked while swingin' me about!"

His tone rising angrily, Slate answered, "And per'aps ya'd prefer if I buried ya in sand and left ya ta rot?"

Cowed, Duraeleon replied, "I think I'll just sit back and enjoy tha day if it pleases ya!" With that the belligerent axe lapsed into silence.

A satisfied grin on his face, Slate walked midway down the beach toward the water to an area that was both flat and more firmly packed than the gradual slope leading up the dune to the gate where he had been standing with Yip.

Swinging Duraeleon casually, undecided as to whether he would release the fury of fire and heat on the sand, wreathe his axe in rarefied cleansing Light, or nothing at all, Slate begin whipping his blade in an ever-increasing tempo around his body in a cleaving nimbus. Ducking, rolling, swerving, cutting high and low, jabbing straight and slashing in looping arches, attacking near and far, he rolled through a series of feints, strikes, and counters of building complexity, blinding speed, and technical precision.

Around and around he moved, faster and faster. When his tempo had reached the limits of the eye's ability to perceive, he moved faster. When his blade whipped through the air so quickly that he was surrounded by a constant hum, his body a tighter focal blur within a much larger cloud of indistinction, he pushed through his limits. When he began to fail, reaching the point of physical exhaustion, he pressed forward. When he began to feel his form break and his technique suffer, his will alone insufficient to maintain his frenzy, he knew the time had come. Already pushing his capabilities well beyond their sustainable bounds, Slate shifted.

Bursting into flames, his body and axe wreathed in coruscating light, the limits that had once held him were no more. He was now a creature of Light and heat, empowered by the fires that thrilled and raced through Brendle's very own veins. His reach expanded, his power multiplied, Slate danced amidst seething flames without exertion, a vortex of destruction.

In his wake, a swath of superheated melted sand followed, molten silica tracing his path across the beach.

Amidst the inferno, free of the heat and turmoil, Slate stoked the flames around him to a fever pitch, ever hotter.

Watching from the dunes, feeling his friend's heat from afar, Yip gently added fuel to his friend's flames, channeling *chi* into the swirling energies writhing in a violent vortex about his friend.

The maelstrom that resulted rivaled the heat beneath the surface of the sun, surrounding Slate in a corona of gaseous silica.

Guiding the hellish heat and energies, Yip redirected the fires blasting from his friend, contracting the radius of Slate's influence closer and closer around his deadly perimeter, dissipating the turbulent waves of magical forces, all the while shielding the myriad miniscule creatures exposed to the infernal onslaught.

Slate's firestorm under control, the extent of his flames and calefaction defined by his arms' length, his heat converted back into life-sustaining *chi*, Yip watched and appreciated his friend's skill, glad that the damage he would do had been minimized and redirected.

The next time he needed fused glass, he knew just who to talk to for a ready, if imperfect, supply.

When he sensed two other citizens cross the threshold behind them, Yip snuffed Slate's flames so suddenly and with such force that Slate fell to the ground in surprise, lost in an instant of momentary confusion. Recovering himself, immediately sensing why he had been cut off, Slate stood and clumped over to Yip, the fused mutlicolored glass streaking the sand crunching beneath his feet.

Watching the newcomers approach, their faces lit in delight at the beauty of the otherworldly beach, unaware of the torrents that had been raging just moments before. Slate nodded in appreciation to his friend. "Thanks, Yip. I had no idea."

Then, nodding politely to the two humans that approached, his face split with a hearty smile, Slate offered a sincere, "G'day."

Returning the visitors' nods of recognition, Yip watched the man and woman pass in convivial silence. As the pair made their way down the beach ankle deep in the warm waters, each streaming iridescent light that commingled in delightful patterns in their wake, Yip said, "Perhaps you have had enough practice for the day?"

His ready grin returning, Slate concurred with a nod. "Aye. Per'aps we'd all be a bit better off if I stopped."

As yet unholstered, Duraeleon added, "Per'aps next time ya'll have tha sense ta bank yer bellows and burn with Brendle's cleansing Light alone. If ya're after tha Daerdaana'Duin, ya must never forget ta control its heat."

"Fer once, ya're right, Duraeleon. 'Twas a poor choice. I'll save tha full heat fer tha tumult o' battle and no more."

Holding the axe up to his face, his shaggy beard and ruddy cheeks visible in the glowing metal's reflection, Slate spoke directly to the axe. "Thank ya fer tha reminder."

His face splitting immediately with a mischievous grin, Slate added, "Are ya ready fer a swim?"

"Wha–?" Before Duraeleon could offer a protest, Slate threw the luminous axe into the air, spinning blade over haft into the water. Sprinting afterward, his short legs carrying him at an astounding speed, Slate splashed into the sea after his axe in full plate, his magical armor so light that it offered no encumbrance to his motions. With one great dive, swirling in aqua bioluminescent ripples, he dove in playfully after his blade as excitedly as a pup after a favorite toy.

After some moments under the surf, Slate finally reemerged victorious, Duraeleon sputtering indignantly pretending it needed breath, while Slate brandished his axe triumphantly from the chest deep water in which he stood.

"I'll not forget this ill treatment, Dwarf!" Duraeleon's angry voice carried clearly up to where Yip remained seated watching his friend jostle and cavort excitedly through the beautiful waters.

"Nor will I!" With another great toss, Slate launched Duraeleon heavenward into deeper waters. Grinning maniacally, he swam off after his axe as nimbly as a fully armored fish.

Sensing another of his friends approaching, Yip turned to see Aroganji walking through the gate behind him.

"Hello, Yip. I trust you are well?"

Indicating the water with a flick of his head, Yip replied, "Not as well as Slate."

Despite his axe's unwavering protests, Slate continued his sport, tossing Duraeleon back and forth through the surf, whooping and diving after his blade through the translucent crystalline waters.

"Has he lost all sense?" Aroganji's smile belied the negative implications of his question.

"Has he ever had any?" Sharing Aroganji's positive intent, Yip sat back and watched Duraeleon curse like the sailor it so longed to be.

Aroganji laughed, taking a seat on the cool sand by Yip's side, watching Slate cavort with the joy of one granted a reprieve from the long, dark months of winter. "Despite all of Duraeleon's colorful protests he is as complicit as Slate."

Yip laughed in return. "Where would the fun be if Duraeleon arched through the air and returned to Slate's hand with each throw?"

Aroganji concurred. "Each is as bad as the other."

"They are a well matched pair."

"Riven from the same piece of granite."

"Looks like he's left quite the impact upon the shoreline." Aroganji's eyes surveyed the fused silicate glass swirling in irregular patterns across the beach along with the larger chunks of vitrified sand left scattered haphazardly across Slate's path after the cooling of the plasma halo that had surrounded him.

Looking at Yip with a questioning half-smile, Aroganji said, "Can you return the sand to its prior condition?"

Without answering, Yip turned his attention to the areas altered by Slate's progress.

All around, energy moved and thrummed, zoetic fields dancing and interacting in symphonies of wondrous complexity. Within these fields, countless objects in various degrees of condensation, potentiations of these underlying energetics, whirred and vibrated. To the naked eye, this astonishing chorus was static, matter at rest.

To Yip, it was alive.

In varying states of motion, manifestation, and expression, matter teemed with possibility and promise, futures yet to be realized and pasts filled with dynamism—galaxies of crystallized energy in coherent form.

Although not creators of *chi* like living beings, each and every particulate around him represented a vital state of solidified yet dynamic force. Watching the *chi* move through and around the particles of sand altered by Slate's progress gave him a sense of the sand's *li* and nature. Recalling how these same granules had appeared before alteration, how the *chi* interacted with the sand's mutable natures, their vibrancy and subtleties, and the interplay of each with each other, he could compare the sand's present state against the past. Juxtaposing those grains left unaltered by Slate's fires against those that had been transformed, understanding their embodiments, though he had not tried such a task before, Yip felt that he could alter the sand's form and return the fused essence to what they had once been.

The sand, in both its present and past manifestations, represented different expressions of the same underlying condensed energy fields. By supplying the necessary energy and guidance, he could alter the sand's form and return it to how it had once been.

His assessment complete, Yip looked at Aroganji and said, "Yes. I believe I can."

Gesturing broadly toward the opalescent streaks littering the pristine beach, Aroganji invited him to do so. "We must return this place of beauty despoiled to its original condition."

And so he did.

"By Brendle's ghost! What've ya done ta my handiwork?" Slate emerged from the pellucid waters dripping wet, his full beard sodden while his armor remained gleaming and untouched, the water droplets not adhering to its polished magical surface. Reholstering Duraeleon, he scanned the sand for signs of his fiery dance, the fused glass and discolored trails of his combustion.

"Are you proud that you marred a swath of parkland for your own ends?" Aroganji stood up putting his hands on his waist, his tone stern and recriminating.

"'T weren't much different than my boot prints!" Walking up the beach with a smile, his tone mollifying, Slate backtracked from his original position.

"Do your boot prints melt sand, changing its composition, texture, and color?"

Slate merely shrugged, knowing no answer was necessary, but discounting his actions nonetheless, reaching Yip and Aroganji as he did so.

"We are in a public place set aside for people's enjoyment. We should leave no trace here, or elsewhere for that matter, unless we absolutely have to!"

Glancing at Yip, a crooked grin on his face, Slate said, "Are ya sure we didn't join with an Elf?"

"Man, Dwarf, or Elf, our actions can be far-reaching, farther than we may know." Yip remained seated beside Aroganji while he replied.

"So tha oracle and tha sage are condemnin' my actions?"

"He condemns the result, not the action or the man." Spreading his arms wide peacefully, Yip now smiled.

Slate snorted. "Ya get one with tha other I say!"

"The depth of one's tread is determined by the application of force in the step." Yip remained smiling though he sensed that Slate no longer shared the sentiment.

His sense of humor fading, Slate growled, "These boots leave their mark!"

Gesturing to where Yip had restored the sand to its original condition, Aroganji said, "No longer."

"Bah! Ya're both about as fun as stale ale and Troll swill!"

His smile undiminished, Yip laughed, saying, "I am lucky I do not drink!"

Laughing as well, Aroganji concurred. "Not exactly a resounding recommendation!"

Sitting down beside Yip, Slate asked Aroganji, "Are ya gonna practice or just critique?"

Walking away from them both, he said, "Can I do a little of both?"

Shaking his shaggy mane, Slate remained silent as Aroganji moved farther down the beach.

Before his friend got too far away to ask, Yip called after Aroganji. "May I work with you while you practice, Aroganji?"

Pausing for a moment, Aroganji asked in turn, "In what way?"

Much as he had done with Slate earlier and all his friends on prior occasions, Yip wished to continue facilitating their abilities and development. Everyone was capable of doing so much more than they realized, he hoped to give his friends a glimpse of the possible.

"I would continue our work augmenting each other's capabilities as we have before."

Aroganji nodded his head smiling as he glanced at Slate. "So long as you don't cause me to light up like a torch and do irreparable damage."

Over Slate's grumbles, Yip called back, "I shall do my best!"

Yip also hoped that his efforts in facilitating his friends' abilities would not only improve their capabilities while they worked together but would also aid in their progress after they eventually parted ways. Whenever he had the opportunity to let his friends experience more, pushing their bounds and their conceptions of their limits, then he would gladly take the chance.

Enjoying the passing moments, he sat peacefully on the sand, waiting for Aroganji to start his work.

While Aroganji sought a suitable place to begin his practice, meandering down the beach's open expanse, Slate returned to their prior discussion, his tone light. "Did ya not like tha patterns I left on tha sand?"

Yip declined his head in a slight nod. "They were quite beautiful, Slate, like the afterimages of lightning on the beach."

His eyes distant, Slate remained silent for a time before replying, "Aye."

Putting his impressions to words, Yip said,

"Lightning flashes white

caressing the soft white sand—
fulgurites blossom and bloom."

With a short, throaty laugh, Slate said, "Ya lost me there!"

"Your steps were as lightning strikes on sand—fusing, reshaping and reforming the particulates into something new and wonderful, a fragile and unexpected beauty."

With a brief grunt, Slate said, "I can't argue with that!"

Wrindanneth whistled contentedly, each step practically a skip in tune with his inner muse. He walked freely, as he rarely did, without care for what people thought of him, though he never did regardless. After his meeting with Spreesprocket and Gideon, he could allow himself a bit of happiness undiminished by his usual constraints.

Gideon and Spreesprocket's proposal would give them everything they had promised. The plans were all there in their wondrous entirety —DISCO cannons, an improved alien shielding system, more drones, the improved ship AI to better control flight and weapons systems, a limited teleportation system, the ability to port directly back to Tellanon, improved handling and speed, Every Gnome's Anti-Intelligence Device, the integrated extradimensional pocket dimension to increase the size of the hold with a hidden space for hiding, as if such a thing would ever be necessary, even Yip's anti-energy ray. If all went according to plan, in less than two weeks they would have a ship that had been almost completely revamped by teams of Paratechnologists, drones, and synthetic intelligences.

With each step homeward, he resisted the urge to summon forth the *Shrike's* image from Spreesprocket's plans and greedily pour over the details incessantly.

Despite all this, there was one concern that nagged at him each and every moment, dragging him down and undermining this rare glimpse of complete happiness—Maeth Onai.

He had been remiss of late in his duties.

Though he had gained much in personal knowledge through their travels, though they had triumphed in ways many thought impossible, Maeth cared for none of these things. He wanted his priests to sacrifice on his behalf, share their knowledge and insights, push forward the bounds of magical understanding, and offer a portion of their gains to him in return for the powers he granted.

Wrindanneth had done little to honor his divine benefactor, the scourge of his existence, the shackle that bound and tormented him each and every night when he closed his eyes. He had not sacrificed magical items of power to his god, offering their strength to supplement Maeth's own. He had not locked himself away in pursuit of new spells never before seen by the eyes of Men. He had not dedicated himself to questing for objects of power, tomes of lore, or magical relics that would further Maeth's ends. As best as he was able, for reasons very much his own, he had deliberately avoided sharing the secrets revealed by those treasures earned or revealed on their quests—from magical tomes to the expression of the Dragon's Gate.

He had failed in his duties as a Priest of Maeth Onai.

As a reminder of his delinquency and dereliction, at the end of each day, when he closed his eyes in exhaustion, wishing for sweet oblivion, Maeth called, chiding and lecturing, berating and taunting, swearing and threatening, all in attempts to remind him of his duties and spur him forward in his obligations.

Though his master had access to his thoughts and learning, those that he did not hide away and shield most carefully, Maeth always wished for more, pushing his adherents forward for the secrets that even he, a god of magic, might not know. His was a quest that would not end and a curse that would not leave.

Nothing he ever did or achieved seemed to appease his master.

The sooner they left, the better.

The sooner they departed, the sooner he could forget his obligations in the demands of the moment. The sooner they started, the sooner he could forget the responsibilities to research and study that he was neglecting through preparation for their trip. Given his lack of research, in the days ahead, he would have to recover or reveal something that may be of interest to his master from those creatures that fell before them or from his own hidden store, something he was willing to share unlike the knowledge from the tome of Elven lore, Éremon's prized volume, or Yip's internal secrets. Only then would he have an opportunity to temporarily assuage his ravenous god for the pursuit of knowledge and power was one that would never end.

Until that time, he dreamed of the day when he could throw off the manacles of his mortality and free himself from his obligations to his cursed god.

In preparation for that distant day, he imagined using one of the few gifts he had kept hidden from his master. He had seen the Light of the Dragon's Gate transform others, his friends and companions.

Soon he would use it to transform himself.

Then his dreams of immortality would be realized and the past would be forgotten.

Aroganji was excited. Walking down the beach, he looked forward to his practice free of distraction, to the opportunity to cultivate and maintain his skills, and the chance to apply what he had learned in a direction he had only just begun to explore and consider.

All around him, the endless cycle of change moved from beginning to end, from creation to destruction, over and over again through ceaseless cycles of countless possibilities and permutations. These fundamental movements were the basis of his art, the change he became and the change he created.

United by Mind, arising from Void, the five principle movements of creation cycled through myriad patterns and directions limited only by his perception and degree of understanding.

Excited, scared, and elated, he now deliberated undertaking a possibility that only recently became feasible; one that might change everything he strived for over the many long years of his practice to achieve.

With access to Light creation through the Dragon's Gate, he now considered attempting to unite Mind and Void directly through Light, enlivening the five fundamental changes of the Wu-hsing with the untold potential of creation, bridging creation and destruction, potential and manifest, with the expression of pure Light.

What would happen to himself and as a result, he could not say or envision for his understanding could not encompass that for which it had no conception.

There was only one way to find out.

Taking a deep breath within the countless vortices of dynamic change enveloping him, he initiated his own.

Fueled by the fires of his mind, grounded by the potential of the void from which it sprang, filled with the knowledge imparted by his friend, ever so cautiously, Aroganji created a spark. Filling his mind's eye with Light, one small light blossomed within the field of change surrounding him, a moment of creation under the control of his volition.

Until this first cautious moment of creation, he had always initiated change, moving with dynamic forces, using the ebb and flow of these energies to catalyze his magic. Now, this Light of creation arising within the field of movement was the vehicle of change, the basis from which he moved, the agent he became, the foundation for the magic he created.

With this one small success, a whole universe of possibility opened before him.

Letting the Light fade, returning easily to the fields of transformation containing his mind and intent, he now saw that one small act changed everything. He need not rely upon the dynamic energies of a given time and place to fuel his magic. Rather, he could create his own, the outcome limited only by the Mind's conception and the Void's potential, his will made manifest, change engendered from possibility.

As this small Light faded into memory, his excitement built, lifting his spirits for the opportunities to come.

Noticing Yip turn his head and smile, Slate spied Wrindanneth walking through the portal at the top of the dune.

"Well look at what tha Ogre threw out!" Slate laughed with the image, enjoying the thought that if Ogres would not have Wrindanneth, then he had to be quite unappealing indeed.

Crossing the dune behind them, his long black robes strangely out of place against the vibrant colors of the sand and sky that silhouetted him, Wrindanneth sneered. "Taste, like your intellectual capacity, is a matter of perspective."

Before either could retort and carry the inevitable argument any further, Yip offered simply, "Perhaps you would both be better served by letting your concerns go and enjoying the day."

Of like mind, for he had much to consider, Wrindanneth nodded from where he now stood beside Yip looking out upon the beautiful prismatic sea, his long red hair shifting slightly in the faint breeze coming off the water. "This place is far too striking not to appreciate. I will rejoin you after I have had a walk upon her lustrous shores."

Shrugging in disbelief, Slate said, "Ya're leavin' without tellin' us o' all yer mornin' exploits at tha *Shrike*?"

Already walking away, not turning to answer, Wrindanneth replied with a simple, "Yes."

Watching Wrindanneth's tall figure stroll away down the beach in the opposite direction taken by Aroganji, Slate said to no one in particular, for he knew Yip was not especially interested in casual conversation, "'Tis a rare day indeed when Wrindanneth refuses an opportunity ta talk, especially in his favor."

Understanding Wrindanneth's desire for solitude, Yip replied, "The matters of the mind often weigh heavily upon on our shoulders."

With a brief nod, Slate smiled and said, "'Tis just as rare fer Wrindanneth ta try ta think in quiet contemplation. Given his difficulties with tha matter, I suppose he's entitled ta some quietude. Granted his shortcomin's, he'll probably need more time than we can spare."

Sharing Slate's smile, though not his sentiment, for the contents of a man's mind were his own, Yip remained silent in reply.

The sea foam danced about his feet, cerulean streamers whirling about his footsteps, the vibrant water not touching either his boots or the hem of his robes, the magic imbued within keeping him dry.

His thoughts more cohesive than the sea foam swirling at his feet, Wrindanneth considered his path forward. There was much to be done yet, much he did not know, but one matter was clear, he must become more than he was. He must initiate some form of change, not only for the success of their mission but for his sanity. He must find a way to free himself from the bondage of servitude to his divine master.

Though Yip's knowledge and understanding of the Dragon's Gate danced in his head, easily summoned upon request, he did not apprehend how to use it, not in the way he wished. His had been the path of magical manipulation, not self-transformation. Though he was skilled in guiding magical energies and was confident that he could lead the Light created through harnessing the Dragon's Gate, he knew not how to use this energy, this unlimited potential, to change himself.

Such was the provenance of Yip Chi Chuan.

His path forward would not only be with Yip but through Yip as well. Though he hated relying upon another for anything, much less something so critical, his friend would have to be his vehicle to freedom, should he take the shortest, most likely way forward. Though he was reluctant, he knew that Yip would be gracious with his assistance and guidance, willing to help however he may need and be able.

Otherwise, without Yip's aid, he would remain fettered to Maeth Onai until he could find another avenue of escape.

Wrindanneth returned after much deliberation, his walk along the beach only heightening his concerns, his mind too occupied to fully enjoy the beauty and serenity provided by the otherworldly locale. Lost in thought, time's passage slipping away unnoticed, he was surprised to see that Aroganji, Slate, and Yip remained seated on the sand by the portal to Tellanon in casual discussion for he imagined much time must have passed since he first left Yip and Slate.

Reading the import of his concerns in his bearing, Yip called to him welcomingly as he neared his friends. "What weighs upon you, Wrindanneth?"

Yip's small face remained impassive, as always, but the words came from genuine concern for his friend was much more sensitive than most though one would never guess it to look at his generally stoic countenance.

He was tired.

He was ready to move on.

He was ready to be free of the burden that he had born for most of his life.

Gathering himself, he exhaled. "I have been giving thought to our future. More particularly, my future."

His thick eyebrows rising with the question, Slate asked, "And?"

Lightly chiding Slate for interjecting before Wrindanneth could speak, Aroganji said, "And you should let him speak!"

Wrindanneth smiled wanly at Aroganji's attempt to defend him, something he did not need in the slightest but which only made his friend's effort even more humorous. He did, however, understand that Aroganji did not want Slate's interjection to interfere with his explanation for he only rarely opened up to the group to discuss anything of a personal nature.

Though they risked their lives for each other and their goals, giving their bodies freely to save each other daily, he seldomly actually gave of himself.

"Our future is currently tied to the successful completion of our mission." Wrin started slowly, pausing between statements should anyone wish to comment or question.

"My future is, however, tied to my deity."

He looked at each of them closely noting the concern in Yip's eyes that did not touch his face, Aroganji's patient acceptance for he had seen more of Wrindanneth's mind than he wished for his friend to bear, and Slate's fiery calm smoldering until sparked by the slightest ember.

"No matter the outcome of our quest, should we live or die, succeed or fail, gain accolades or scorn, I will remain tied to Maeth Onai until I find a way to release myself from bondage. Whatever I accomplish, whatever I realize, whatever I achieve, no matter how I strive, must in time become his. Just as he gives me access to power, so, too, does he demand that I give what I uncover to him."

"I must break this cycle. I have lived with it for far too long. Else, the secrets we have uncovered, the knowledge of Elves and Dragons, those that he does not already hold, will become his while I yet remain his pawn ever seeking after more."

"I will not remain his plaything."

"I will not divulge the secrets entrusted to me, these that he tries to pry from my mind each night as I struggle through sleep."

He saw the understanding in Yip's eyes and knew that he at least understood. Yip perceived that he did not wish to share the knowledge of the Dragon's Gate with his deity, though Maeth only knew what secrets he already possessed, should he not already have this secret among many others. Nor did he wish to betray the trust of the Elves for his mind was his master's so long as he served his covetous god.

More importantly, however, he sensed that Yip apprehended exactly what he needed without being asked, that he would not have to put his own frailties and desires, his own limitations and aspirations, out for others to see.

As true as his vision, Yip did not want to see him suffer.

Though he did not voice his thanks, the sentiment was there none-theless.

His own Daemons were his. He did not wish to burden others with them more than was necessary.

Yip's words followed a brief nod, the slightest of bows, and confirmed his feelings. "We must all become more than we are if we are to succeed in our quest against the Cabal."

Turning away from Wrindanneth to look at each of his companions in turn, Yip continued, "We must all become more than we are if we are to free ourselves of the burdens that bind and limit us. We must all become more than we wish to be if we are to actualize our dreams."

His eyes resting on Slate with pride, Yip continued, "Slate, you have become proficient in the ways of the Daerdaana'Duin. The flames of Brendle's own forge shield and empower you, bringing forth the fires of Heaven upon our foes. Where this path yet leads will be for you to determine."

Moving to Aroganji, Yip said, "Aroganji, I have sensed changes in the ways you use your magic, using the Light of the Dragon's Gate to fuel the fires of your Craft, empowering the Wu-hsing with the energies of creation. Experimentation along this new path will continue to provide newfound insights and opportunities for your development."

"Wrindanneth, the path forward is yours to decide."

Wrindanneth watched his friend carefully, remaining silent, while Yip talked. "You say that Maeth Onai binds you."

"Perhaps."

"Perhaps not."

"I have not sensed his presence when you work your magic. Perhaps you bind yourself. Perhaps Maeth gave you the skills to work with divine energies and you only think that his continued presence allows you to manipulate them."

Spreading his arms openly, Yip said, "Perhaps you work your magic without any outside assistance."

Holding his tongue, though he wished to argue, Wrindanneth watched as Yip shrugged. "Perhaps I am wrong, as I often am. Perhaps I cannot sense that which you do. Perhaps your obligation to Maeth is one that I cannot see. Perhaps I cannot sense the ties that bind you to him. If, however, it is your belief that binds you, then perhaps only that needs to be overcome."

"Our belief makes the impossible possible. Perhaps it is this same belief that limits you now."

His voice full of emotion, Wrindanneth replied, "And what if you are wrong?"

"Then we will find a way forward."

"How? What would you propose?"

"The path to your dreams is within your grasp. You merely have to decide to walk upon it."

Pausing but a moment, Yip added sincerely, "I would be happy to walk it with you."

Temporarily losing his patience, he interrupted Yip's vacuous speech. "You speak in riddles without substance, clouding your intent in high-minded phrases without saying anything."

Unperturbed, Yip replied placidly, "Regardless of what you feel, regardless of what you believe, you, as must we all, must become more than you are."

"The Light you now hold can serve you as you will, you have but to guide it as you wish. As I have helped Slate, I would be honored to assist you."

His temper in check, Wrin now pushed forward. "You are proposing that I utilize the energy of the Dragon's Gate to transform myself in much the same way as Orogast did in Taerris'thule?"

Yip's voice replied without inflection, "No."

Watching Yip as he spoke, his friend's steady composure, his impassiveness somehow heightened the sense of compassion and care he sensed radiating from the small man, a direct contrast to his own inner turmoil. "I am proposing that you use the energy of the Dragon's Gate as you see fit. If you seek a physical transformation akin to that undergone by Orogast, then that is the path before you that must be undertaken. Otherwise, you, like all of us here, must proceed along the path you have set for yourself according to your vision. The Light of the Dragon's Gate is but one option to help make this realization possible."

Sensing Yip's support, appreciating that though his friend disagreed with his sense of limitation and bondage Yip would assist him in whatever way required, he moved forward with his original plan nonetheless. "Then I would seek an apotheosis. Only by breaking the bonds of mortality will I be free of Maeth's subjugation."

"And what would you become?" Yip's simple question did not lessen his determination.

"More than I am."

"You must know." Yip's voice was firm. "In this case, a desire without a guiding vision will lead nowhere. One must understand what one is to become if one is to change as one wishes."

Holding back the vitriol that instinctively boiled forth, for he was ever recalcitrant and did not take well to orders or dictates, Wrindanneth nodded reluctantly. "You will have your answer by day's end." Pausing a moment, giving another rare glimpse into his heart, he added, "My passions yet consume me."

Bowing from where he sat, Yip replied evenly, "I will welcome the conversation."

His face split with a smile, for Aroganji wanted what was best for his friend, as Wrin well knew, Aroganji said, "I am honored to have found such friends that seek after the others' best interests and care for each other as they would themselves."

Reluctant to voice his emotions for they burned too intensely and cut too deeply, Wrin merely nodded curtly, his mind already moving forward toward the destination Yip urged him to seek.

The time of his ascension would come. When it did, the bonds of his mortality would fall away as completely as his servitude to his imperious god.

Holding back the flood of excitement, he steeled himself to wait.

Turning his gaze from Wrindanneth, Yip asked, "And what of you, Slate and Aroganji? What do you wish for yourselves? How can we aid each other that our visions for ourselves and our futures can be realized?"

Slate shrugged his thick shoulders noncommittally. "I've more than I dreamed was possible, more than but a few Dwarves have ever seen. I fer one am glad with where I am and would not ask fer more."

Pressing, Aroganji asked, "But what if you could be more and as a result brighten not only your future but the future of your people and others?"

Slate stroked his thick beard thoughtfully, his Kazzak jingling with the gesture. "I will see where this path leads me and how I change as a result. Like tha forges o' my fathers, tha Dur'kazak, I will see how tha fires o' tha Daerdaana'Duin recast and reforge my body and spirit. Only by enterin' tha forge does one see how tha blade's tempered and its grain is molded and shaped by tha heat and flame."

"And what of you, Aroganji?" Yip's considering eyes now turned to Aroganji.

"I am with Slate. Though I veer from the path of the Fang Shih, I now tread upon a road free of past restraint and strictures. Enlivened by the energy of the Dragon's Gate, my study of change has broadened in new dimensions I do not yet fully comprehend. I am only just discovering where this path may lead or what may be possible."

"What I wish to be or desire to become are far too uncertain. I am gracious for the opportunity to continue upon the pathway revealed to me, whatever the outcome."

Yip bowed then, his face lit by a smile. "I willingly offer my assistance to each of you as your horizons and understandings broaden."

"May the potential each of us holds allow us to realize the aims and aspirations set before us."

Not yet ready to let the conversation drop, after having held his thoughts and emotions in check while his friends spoke, after exposing his inner desires for scrutiny, Wrindanneth asked, "And what of you, Yip? What do you wish for yourself? What do you wish to become?"

"I am all that I am. That is all that I ever hoped to be."

"Bah!" Slate spat on the sand, his denial of Yip's answer as strong a response as Wrindanneth's own unvoiced one. "Ya're not answerin' tha question and ya know it!"

Aroganji nodded. "Though your answer may be the truth, Yip, your answer is not true to the spirit of each of our replies. We have each opened ourselves, uncomfortably so for some, and we ask that you do the same."

Now it was Yip who shrugged. "I am what I need to be."

Before he could finish, Wrindanneth interjected, "Which is?"

"An embodiment of the body of Light."

Snarling in a mixture of derision and sarcasm, Slate said, "Can ya never answer a question directly?"

Standing, Yip replied, "Perhaps it would be better if I showed you."

With that, he disappeared.

Scanning the area, their purview widened by the Stars of Illdrassil in response to their need, though they saw multiple energy currents, the light of magic in various forms glowing around them and the untold living things nearby, no presence or sign of Yip was visible. Shifting their gaze back and forth up and down the beach, high and low, they discerned no indication of their friend.

"He's gone!" Slate stood, dusting the sand off his hands as he pushed himself upward.

Aroganji continued his study, reading the lines of transition and transformation around them, the changes in the dynamic forces enveloping and passing through them. Though his astute vision discerned much, he finally had to admit that Yip was nowhere to be seen. "Slate is correct. Nor can I see any signs of his passage."

Aroganji shrugged, adding, "It is as though he never was here."

His limited tolerance at an end, Wrindanneth scoffed dismissively, "Let's go home. I have no patience for games."

Filing out in a single line, Aroganji, Slate, and Wrindanneth left the shimmering sand and ethereal azure waters for the comfort and solidity of home.

OTHER IMAGININGS

Lily pads float suspended
between placid waters
and reflected clouds above.

Wrindanneth and Aroganji emerged from the portal into the shaded neighborhood lane only to find Slate no longer with them.

"Where has that addled Dwarf gotten himself to now?" Wrindanneth acted incredulous but he felt otherwise.

Shrugging, Aroganji whispered a quick incantation, letting loose his intent upon the wind. Within moments, he had his answer. A translucent disc appeared in the air before them. Within its confines, he could see Slate walking away from a portal gate, apparently grumbling to himself. Consulting the disc, he said, "He has managed to reappear across the city at another park entrance."

Wrindanneth laughed coolly. "He must've had food on his mind. That gate provided the nearest exit to his desire."

Smiling, Aroganji said acceptingly, "I would not argue your point."

Never one to miss an opportunity to harass his friend, Wrindanneth relished the thought of flying across the city to track down Slate so that he could harangue him after Slate's own lack of attention forced them to locate him with a spell.

Snickering, he thought of Slate wandering aimlessly across the city in search of food. Without their timely intervention, Slate might get lost on the way home even with an 'unerring' Dwarven sense of direction.

Enjoying the ability to call upon the Star of Illdrassil for flight without an invocation and the associated physical and mental demands of arcane manipulation, Wrindanneth leapt into the air. Aroganji quickly followed in his wake.

Flying low above the streets, traveling above homes was allowed only during times of emergency, they sped across Tellanon in moments. The elation of flight, the rush of air about their faces, the speed and naturalness of their passage, filled them with the joy of children—pure and unblemished.

Banking downward at an angle, Aroganji pointed, indicating their quarry as he swooped earthward, slowing as he gracefully transitioned to a vertical position and landed with a few quick steps. Right behind him, Wrindanneth landed just as ably, his long robes defying the wind as he touched ground.

His face split with an evil grin, Wrindanneth purred, "You get lost?"

Slate huffed. "Lapse in concentration is all."

"Really?" Wrindanneth's goading began.

"As I said."

"And this lapse had nothing to do with food?"

Slate cleared his throat significantly but held his tongue.

"Well?" Wrindanneth arched a red eyebrow significantly.

Slate merely grunted.

Not relenting, Wrindanneth countered, "Since when is a grunt an answer?"

"We Dwarves speak more ably in grunts than yer kind ever did in words!"

Undeterred by Slate's weak attempt to divert the thread of conversation, Wrindanneth continued, "And we Men do not care. Out with it!"

Slate chortled. "I won't argue that!"

"But you will answer the question!"

Smiling, for he had gained an equal footing having stirred Wrindanneth's ire, Slate replied demurely, "Tha thought o' food might've played a minor role."

Wrindanneth laughed wholeheartedly. "If we hadn't come to find you, chances are you would have ended up in a pub eating the rest of the afternoon away."

Slate smiled innocently. "Now that ya mention it, why not?"

His voice disapproving, Wrindanneth said, "Yip is waiting for us for one."

"Since when has consideration fer someone else interfered with yer plans?"

Ignoring the jibe, Wrindanneth replied with one of his own. "And I am sure you prefer your humiliations to be kept private."

"Bah! If ya were ta try and flap yer jowls at me over my meal, I'd stake yer tongue ta tha table with my fork!"

Laughing derisively, Wrindanneth said, "And the last thing you would ever do would be to raise your fork at me!"

Deciding that the inanities had reached an unwelcome crescendo, Aroganji determined the time had come to return home. "As much as I am sure you could both spend the rest of the day haggling, Yip is waiting for us at home."

"Let him wait! He up and disappeared on us! He'll see me when I decide ta return home and no sooner!"

"'Sides, he doesn't need ta eat! I say let him wait ta show us his latest parlor trick!"

Shaking his head, Wrindanneth replied, "Slate, your hunger must really be clouding your judgment. You're thinking about yourself even more than I do!"

Slate laughed. "That's impossible!"

His laughter echoing Slate's, Wrindanneth said, "You're right. Even that much thought is too much for you!"

Shaking his head at them both, Aroganji said, "All right children, let's go home."

"So long as we can walk. I'd like ta stop at a few food stalls on tha way. Wouldn't want ta risk losin' anythin' in flight."

"Or miss the chance to savor what you find?"

"That too!"

Wrindanneth laughed. As stubborn and wrong-headed as he often was, it was awfully difficult not to enjoy Slate's company.

Not that he would ever mention it.

Mumbling the words around a mouthful of hot Dwarven pie, Slate said, "Ya'd think Yip'd offer a clear explanation fer once."

Still grumbling to any who would listen, Slate walked alongside Wrindanneth through the sights and sounds of Tellanon toward their small, sheltered stone cottage. Floating around him in a nimbus of food were all the delicacies he had managed to find on their way home.

"And you think you could remain focused long enough to visualize returning to your same point of entry!"

The activity of mid-day ebbed and flowed around them as they walked. Shopkeepers, artisans, traders, craftsmen, merchants, and officials were busy displaying their wares, creating their goods, transporting odds and ends, practicing their craft, running errands, engaging in commerce, and otherwise making the most of a glorious day aloft among the clouds. Amidst his grumbling, however, Slate paid scant attention to these and many other wonders. Instead, he lapsed into a favorite Dwarven pastime—complaining.

"Instead, he up and disappears! Offerin' even less clarification than his usual nonsensical riddles!" Clapping both hands together loudly, skillfully avoiding the beleaguered remnants of his hovering food cloud, he continued his rant. "What he needs is a good box on tha ears. Get his head outta tha clouds and back ta business!"

Wrindanneth sniggered derisively. "And who do you propose box his ears? You?"

Puffing his chest out proudly, the motion nearly propelling him face-first into a skewered roast quail suspended before him, Slate took on his full height. "If I must!"

Nodding sagely with commiseration, resisting the urge to laugh at Slate's near miss with his floating food halo, Wrindanneth intoned, "Then I will say a prayer for you."

"Bah! Ya don't pray! Maeth doesn't listen!"

Laughing now, Wrindanneth answered, "All the better!"

"Humph!" Slate's disagreeable grunt did not mark the end of his rant rather he just internalized the dialogue. Now only his refined inner ear would hear the subtleties of his wide-ranging, enlivening diatribe.

"Really, Slate, there's no need for violence." Appearing out of the air right next to his friend, a wide smile across his innocent face, Yip walked in stride with his friends, joining in as if he had been there the whole time.

"Wha—!" This time there was no avoiding the aureole of crumbs and other last vestiges of his appetite magically suspended in the air. Jumping to the side, startled, Slate collided with a meat pie and assorted pastry tidbits.

Crumbs littering his beard and clumps of food stuck to his face, he recovered himself quickly, with the equanimity of one to whom nothing untoward had happened. "Try not ta sneak up on a Dwarf, or ya're likely ta feel tha bite o' his axe!"

Snickering from where he had been walking on Slate's other side, Wrindanneth said, "Or his food?"

His voice filled more with concern than humor, Aroganji said, "How did you teleport here, Yip? You mustn't risk breaking the laws of Tellanon lightly."

Familiar with some of the measures in place to prevent unapproved, personal teleportation, Aroganji did not want Yip to risk either his own health or freedom. How Yip managed to teleport from within the pocket dimension to Tellanon proper through the formidable barriers protecting the city he did not know.

"I did not teleport. I simply moved from there to here."

Yip's straightforward answer did not satisfy his friends. Slate's frustration was obvious as was his ire from losing a few of his remaining choice morsels. "As I said, more riddles ta cloud tha truth. Keep yer secrets veiled if ya wish but don't dangle 'em in front o' me!"

As if to punctuate his point, Slate reached out and snatched a piece of shepherd's pie and popped it into his mouth.

Yip's reply was calm. "Your feelings are your own, Slate. You are free to do with them what you will."

"I am sorry that you are upset. However, if you wish an explanation, you must let me give it. If you constantly interrupt before I can answer your questions, then, yes, my answers will remain veiled in 'nonsensical riddles.'"

Not sharing Slate's frustration, only curiosity, Aroganji asked, "Then how did you move from the pocket dimension to here if you did not teleport?"

"I was both there and here. I moved through the portal as did you, only in a different form."

Wishing to know more, Aroganji asked, "Is that how you knew where we were?"

"Yes and no. I was in both places at once. So yes, I was aware of you coming through. But I was also aware of Slate's arrival elsewhere without needing to follow you to him."

His curiosity now piqued, Wrindanneth asked, "And how is that?"

"I moved as awareness, broadening, and then returned to the body, contracting."

"You do not lose yourself, your sense of identity, when you do this?"

Yip shrugged. "Awareness changes with the form. I am aware of self but the self has changed."

Slate grunted, "Which means?"

"I am of the energies of which we are a part and yet remain aware of my limits."

"Are ya able ta interact with tha physical world or d'ya just sense what happens around ya?"

"I do not yet fully know. I am more…diffuse. I am able to interact with the forces that flow through and around us, those which connect us, but to what extent I cannot yet say. Matter and energy are states along a continuum."

"Continuum?" Slate's thick eyebrows lifted skyward.

Yip smiled. "From potential to tangible."

"Solid objects feel like a densification of these energies while ambient forces feel much more dilute. They are, however, one and the same. Perhaps one has more inertia to my abilities than the other while changed."

"I will find out as I play."

Nodding, Aroganji asked, "How quickly can you move in this way?"

Wrindanneth laughed, adding, "How fast is the speed of mind, Yip?"

He shrugged in reply. "That I cannot say either. When the body falls away, my awareness is more expansive and encompassing. I have yet to become completely familiar with the subtleties that this transformation entails. For the short distances I have tried, the transition appears to be instant. For longer shifts, I cannot say."

"And Tellanon's shields do not hamper this type of movement?" Aroganji's mind was afire with questions and possibilities.

"Not that I have seen." After a moment he added, "Nor have they hampered Master Wei."

"Can we interact with you? Are you more or less vulnerable to attack?" Like Aroganji, Wrindanneth wanted to understand Yip's new situation as fully as he could within the limits of Yip's understanding.

"Unless I learn to communicate mind-to-mind, I do not think direct communication will be possible. I sense the people around me and their physical states but I do not know how to translate information back to them."

"As to your second question, despite being able to interact with ambient energies in much the same way as I now can, I feel tantamount to those same energies. Aside from a general sense of awareness, I feel indistinguishable from them. As such, I feel that I would be very difficult to sense, much less target, but again, I cannot yet provide a complete answer to your question."

"Intriguing. Most intriguing." Aroganji would think on this.

His face split with a wide grin, having pondered Yip's earlier answer to his own question, Slate asked, "Does this mean if I ask ya ta get me some food"—his point emphasized by the sad fog of fractured crumbs magically orbiting his beard—"ya can get back before I feel hungry?"

Yip shook his head, a look of remorse on his face. "Sadly, no. Your question presupposes that your hunger begins and ends. I know to the contrary that it does neither."

Slate laughed, accepting Yip's point. "But ya could still get food as quickly as I can ask?"

Sharing his friend's good cheer, Yip replied, "Yes. At least as quickly as it could be prepared and purchased."

Slate nodded approvingly. "Then yer new talent sounds mighty useful!"

His voice laced with sarcasm, Wrindanneth replied, "I am glad that you have managed to ascertain a *practical* use for such an ability."

His beard split with a wide grin, letting Wrindanneth's venom roll off his back, Slate replied innocently, "Me too."

Turning to matters of relevance, Wrindanneth said, "And you can perform this transition easily?"

"It is a matter of relaxation."

Wrindanneth nodded in understanding. "Then I see many uses for such an ability."

Slate nodded in agreement, his request expressing one such use. "Now get me another Gnomish shepherd's pie!"

They all laughed, strolling through the crowded streets of one of Tellanon's commercial districts, three Men and a Dwarf, all sharing good cheer, each intent on saving the world.

"Good sirs! You have an incoming communication!"

The glower on Slate's face said more than mere words could convey at the Abstract's unexpected interruption.

His tone even, with the poise of one expecting just such an intrusion, Aroganji replied kindly. "How may we be of assistance, Abstract?"

They had finally entered the residential district near their home, preferring to walk and enjoy the sights and sounds of mid-day to flying to the cottage and staying inside when a beautiful day beckoned, one they did not wish to forsake after experiencing its allure.

"Hoyt wishes to have a word with you."

"Hoyt!" His anger turned to excitement, Slate said, "Send him through!"

"Yes, sir!"

With that, the air shimmered and Hoyt's face appeared before them for their eyes alone.

"Four! I'm glad ta see ya're here and all is well!"

"As are we!" Aroganji's laugh fell short of dissipating the seriousness expressed so tangibly on Hoyt's visage.

"We must talk as soon as ya're able. I am at my shop."

Nodding, Aroganji said, "We will be there in moments."

"I look forward ta seein' ya." Hoyt's ageless face faded before them as their leisurely jaunt through town came to an unexpected end.

Making a quick about-face, the four companions turned toward the docks and leapt into the air, their flights powered by the Stars of Illdrassil shimmering on their breasts. Mere moments of darting through the air, wind whipping against their faces, brought them to the location of Hoyt's store in a non-descript section of the city's warehouse district near the docks.

The last time they had visited, or rather tried to visit, the spot where Hoyt's shop had been as long as they had known, one of their first destinations after setting foot on Tellanon so long ago, had been strangely empty. In the store's absence, an unnatural gap between warehouses had waited for them instead, as unwelcoming and foreboding as Hoyt's absence.

Now he had returned.

Along with his return, as though it had never been gone, his store had reappeared as well. The worn sign with "Hoyt's – Oddities, Found Goods, and Sundries" written in weathered letters still beckoned any who would come through the shop's worn screen door. Various items perhaps better suited to a barn or disheveled yard lay scattered irregularly around the shop's cracked façade—an oaken barrel filled with clear water located beneath a downspout, an empty wooden rocking chair that had born more weight than could be called fair, stacks of clay pots, some with plants and others without, wooden crates, chicken wire and several types of fencing, all lay about with a casual randomness that served to both reinforce the homey lived-in nature of the store, its general disrepair, and the perfect naturalness of its state of disorganized profusion.

Nestled comfortably amongst the overflowing chaos of assorted castoffs and junk in the shop's large, dusty front display window, Cletus slept basking in the warmth of the afternoon sun, refusing to languidly lift an eye at their arrival. Sunlight reflecting off his shimmering scales scattered through the store's dim light, brightening an otherwise drab interior.

"Looks like Hoyt's pulled out all tha stops welcomin' us!" Slate's sarcasm found ready ears in Wrindanneth.

"He certainly learned the meaning of hospitality while he was gone." Wrindanneth's tone mirrored Slate's.

"If tha welcomin' party isn't comin', I say bring tha welcome ta it!"

Wrindanneth grinned. "And I say bring the party!"

Putting words to action, Aroganji was already walking toward the ramshackle entry, past one of the yard's shade trees that had reappeared with the shop, ignoring Slate and Wrindanneth's snide comments.

With a reluctant screech that cut through the still air of the shop's interior, the screen door opened onto the store's dimly lit interior. Shelves overflowing with curiosities ranging from collections of magical minerals gathered from the far reaches of the cosmos to herbs, fungi, seeds, and plants required for alchemical libations all vied for position amongst the clutter. Display cases held bones that skittered, rings that actively sought fingers, glowing gems, and carefully sealed tomes. The ceiling itself was not clear of the muddle—baskets overflowing with archaeological specimens, rare luminescent plants and mosses, menageries of bones from unidentified magical species all competed for space among those objects that hovered or flew without need of suspension.

Amidst the bedlam and disarray, one thing had not changed. Hoyt's ageless face broke into a wide grin upon their arrival. "If it ain't the Fists! Do come in!"

Instinctively breaking into a smile, Slate followed Aroganji into the shop, replying, "If I didn't know any better, I'd say ya were happy ta see us!"

"Happier'n a mule eatin' saw briars!" Hoyt's grin remained plastered welcomingly across his face.

A brief furrow of his brow his only reply, Wrindanneth refused the retort that came unbidden to his tongue for he did not want to insult their host's indecipherable aphorism. Instead, he envisioned the hilarity that would ensue if Hoyt and Yip were locked inside a chamber and forced to communicate in plain Common.

He could only wish for such a wonderfully entertaining outcome.

"Welcome home, Hoyt!" Wrindanneth maintained his composure despite the images of Yip and Hoyt's failed communications playing through his mind.

Simultaneous to Wrindanneth's welcome, Yip said, "We are glad that your journey ended in your safe return."

Hoyt laughed roundly behind the counter. "As am I!" His tone turning as serious as his gaze, he added, "I might not be missed, but I can tell ya that I'm not the only one glad fer yer safe return!"

His face serious and composed, not letting the emotions over those lost come to the fore, Slate said, "We were tha lucky ones."

Hoyt nodded sympathetically. "As was I."

Eager to find out the reason for Hoyt's summons, happy to see their longtime advisor, and taking advantage of the lull in conversation as his friends returned to their own inner thoughts, Aroganji asked, "What news do you bring, Hoyt?"

Hoyt laughed smoothly. "Now hold on! The same could be said fer you'ns! Seems ta me like I was about ta hear yer tale!"

Reaching out, he interlaced his fingers, inverted his arms and popped his knuckles decisively with a series of loud *cracks*. "Y'all'll get yer story soon enough, but I like ta trade in kind. Sometimes a man's got ta wet his whistle 'fore he's ready ta eat!"

With a casual flick of his fingers, the air between them shimmered and images of Aroganji, Slate, Wrindanneth, and Yip leaving the *Shrike* upon their return to Tellanon appeared in the air above his desk. Disembodied voices cataloging their achievements rang out over the various news streams' flickering images of their return.

Unaware that coverage of their exploits had even occurred for they paid scant attention to many of the informative and entertainment services available via the Abstract, the Four watched with a mixture of confusion, pride, self-importance, and indifference depending on the observer.

Indicating the news feeds with their unending stories and imagery ranging from expositions on the heroes' timely return after the Cabal's savage attack to speculation that their appearance was a carefully orchestrated ruse only meant to reassure the populace of Tellanon's safety despite the city's truly tenuous security status, Hoyt spoke calmly over the din, "Y'all start. I'll listen. Then y'all can do the same when it's my turn."

Yip bowed, speaking first, his words simple and direct as Hoyt quieted the unending stream of exposés and stories about their accomplishments and intent. "The blackness at the heart of Taerris'thule is no more. Though many of the evils that found refuge within the city's confines remain, the corrupted seal has been struck down and the city's connection to other dimensions has been severed. Outside Taerris'thule's shadow, a new seal has been placed, though at great cost to our friends and allies."

Bowing his head in acknowledgement of the fallen, Yip said, "Too many of those who left with us will never again see Tellanon's white walls."

Knowing nothing could be said to restore the fallen or assuage the wounds left in those yet standing, Hoyt remained silent, his heart filled with sympathy.

After a moment's pause, Yip added softly, "A new beacon now blazes within Taerris'thule's walls, one that will burn away the last vestiges of shadows from her long tormented streets."

"If I may?" Aroganji stepped forward and skillfully wove a brief incantation. As his symbolic invocation ended, a dusky cloud of nebulous smoke materialized swirling above Hoyt's display counter taking the place of the representations depicting their arrival and purported exploits. Within this dense brume, images began to rapidly appear, summary snapshots of their voyage and journey's progress seen from a point of view held aloft above the *Shrike*'s flowing sails.

Watching with rapt attention, images of their arrival through the shimmering *faerviage* portal at fair Tueran perched above the bay of Denegost, home to the Anuvatali, flashed quickly before their eyes. Within moments, leaving Tueran behind, their journey across the island nation of Landeiss was complete as they continued on beyond and over the Lueciane Sea. Their decisive confrontation with the vengeful R'yn Daer in the azure skies above the Lueciane Sea was completed in the blink of an eye as was their meeting with Cersaegian, liege and eldest of the Fiersayne, keeper of the Ghrem Weard along the continent of Maeron's far northern cliffs.

Flying above Maeron's steaming jungles, past the Dragon lord, and stealing farther inland into her desolate wastes, the turbulent images of their battle with the ghastly Scierdyas and the Orcish hordes blasted across Aroganji's magical manifestation. Onward, in flight, over the cursed, ghostly forest of Dhwer'werde surrounding the haunted lands of Taerris'thule they flew toward their ultimate goal. Within moments, the Temple of Eldre'gheu came into view, its massive extradimensional vortex swirling above the temple's dome, siphoning away the living energies of their world, an image of the apocalypse thrust upon innocent eyes.

Flying past the ruins of the fell city and her legions of black Shades, images of their nearly catastrophic encounter with the Daemons guarding Eldre'gheu's tainted walls were an assault upon their hearts as the memories and travails they had encountered overcame them. Pushing forward once more after the *Shrike*'s crash and the vanquishing of the colossal summoned Daemon through the magical shields and wards encasing the hellish temple, fighting through the oppressive blackness toward the Darkness at the temple's heart, each step forward punctuated by the fall of one of their companions— Kazarhan, Orogast, and Llyewia—to their narrow victory over the Shadow at the temple's heart, streams of images raced past. In the brief moments of their triumph, scenes of the temple's collapse and the assault by the Cabal's assassin flew onward before their watching eyes. Finally, severing the ties between dimensions with the temple's fall, images of their trials rushed past too quickly to fully apprehend or, thankfully, to relive.

With these momentous sights, more followed still. From their return to the *Shrike*'s ruins and the placement of the new seal, the departure of the Home Guard that yet lived, and their defense of their ship against other denizens of Darkness that yet remained in Taerris'thule, the terror was without end. Ultimately, with the final restoration of the *Shrike*, the images slowed as Yip placed the Lightwell that would eventually, should it persevere, cleanse the horrific city of all Darkness forever.

With their ragged, exhausted return to Tellanon, the rapidly swirling images ended as abruptly as they began, as precipitously as their own journey had transitioned from terror to sanity.

The room filled with deep unbroken silence for some time as images of the Cabal's thwarted attack upon Tellanon filled the air between them once more while those of their own journey disappeared, sinking in and leaving indelible marks.

Finally, into the unsettled stillness, Hoyt said simply, his words trailing off into silence, "Y'all've done Ea'ae and all her inhabitants a great service..."

Hoyt's tone was solemn, urgent, and accentuated by the harsh images presented of the recent time of strife. "Yer actions prevented more of 'em"—he nodded toward the images of the Cabal's imposing fleet of warships—"from comin' through and doomin' us all."

Nodding his shaggy head, Slate growled significantly, "We're just glad we're still tha Four and not tha Three, Two, One, or worse!"

Everyone understood the potential outcomes implied by Slate's jest. The images flashing through the air only underscored possible future atrocities.

Hoyt's tone remained serious as he cut off the news display projections with a decisive gesture of one hand. "Despite all y'all've done, all y'all've accomplished, there's more yet ta be achieved."

Wrindanneth nodded in agreement. "We will be leaving to secure another seal within the fortnight. After that, we will continue our original aim and seek after the Cabal."

Hoyt shook his head. "Later may come sooner than ya think."

"What do you mean?" Aroganji's words were filled with dark anticipation.

His words sober, his jovial face locked in an expression of concern, Hoyt said, "The Cabal are already after the seals. They will not miss tha opportunity ta destroy that which has kept 'em from Ea'ae fer so long. They'll stand directly between y'all and yer goal."

Letting Hoyt's words sink in, Aroganji added, "As always."

Indicating where the horrific images of the Cabal's assault had so recently roiled through the air, Wrindanneth added angrily, "The sooner we destroy these scum, the better."

"And what o' yer story, Hoyt?" Slate raised his thick eyebrows inquisitively with the question, always eager to hear a fine yarn. "Ya've seen and heard ours. As ya said, time ta share in kind!"

Opening his arms in welcome, Yip bowed, saying, "We eagerly await your tale, Master Hoyt."

Hoyt laughed at the honorific. "First of all, I ain't no 'master'! But y'all can flatter me all ya want! 'T won't hurt my feelin's!"

Yip shrugged, saying, "Mastery is in the eye of the perceiver."

His face still split with a grin, Hoyt replied, "Then y'all must be blind!"

Yip said no more. Hoyt's accomplishments both in magic and trade warranted significant respect and were the marks of great skill, even more so because he accomplished without effort what many others strove for mightily but to no avail.

Silent and still, without invocation or gesture, Hoyt called upon magical forces to express his will. Within moments, the air before them shimmered once more. This time, however, they gazed through a lens into another world, one whose sights, sounds, and smells washed over them as they peered inward upon its secrets. Though aware that they stood and watched Hoyt's spell unfold, all the companions felt part of the vision unfolding before them.

What they saw caused their hearts to flutter and their stomachs to sink. Though they had seen the heart-wrenching attack upon Tellanon from the vantage point of the city, never had they seen it through the eyes of one from the outside where both the scale of Tellanon's defenses and the extent of the invading armada were so well juxtaposed in a single sweep.

As they had seen before, the breadth of sky was filled with a relentless assault upon Tellanon's fair walls by the Cabal's invading fleet. Into this fray, however, one small ship, the *Rare Aer*, ventured fearlessly on its own outside of Tellanon's defensive perimeter, largely ignored by both attackers and defenders.

Seen from the ship's perspective, to Yip the *Rare Aer* looked like one tiny, unsteady leaf that wafted uncertainly away from the safety and security of its tree only to be thrown into the raging tumult of an approaching black tempest.

The ship seemed unlikely to survive more than mere moments before such a force.

Instead, she exploded forth with light, wreaking havoc as countless arching white bolts shot through the heavens and tore through the invading ships in a cosmic dust storm. Though the vast majority of invading ships hit by the flares appeared unaffected, many were not. These ships exploded violently, damaging others with their fires, describing dramatic trails from the heavens as the vessels plunged earthward to their ultimate end.

Under cover of these explosions and Tellanon's marshaled reprisal, the *Rare Aer* stole away, taking evasive maneuvers beneath and away from the battle front, moving down through the treetops nimbly as the Cabal's armada remained focused on raining destruction upon Tellanon, ignoring the small leaf that drifted away before the force of her gales.

Eventually slowing her flight, the *Rare Aer* reined in her wild escape, returning focus upon the battle slowly unfolding above. Despite the best efforts of Tellanon's valiant defenders, the Cabal's inexorable advance appeared implacable as more and more salvos found their way through the city's weakening shields.

From the vantage of the *Rare Aer*, Tellanon's demise appeared to be imminent, a reluctant observer to one glorious city's untimely end.

This fate, however, was not to be.

Though they did not realize it at the time, the timing of the Four's restoration of the seal with the Home Guard's assistance had saved Tellanon from certain destruction.

Slowly, a subtle current shifted unnoticed, the streamers of Darkness enveloping and protecting the Cabal's fleet began to waver and weaken, cut from Its source, as Tellanon's defenders beat the Shadow back. With this shift, while many invading ships stayed battling Tellanon's forces to the bitter end, many more fled under cover of fire for other execrable purposes.

With this bittersweet end, Hoyt's vision wavered and faded, leaving the Four emotionally torn.

With the battle won, evil yet lurked ready to undo all that had been done.

While he watched, the import of his vision sank in, weighing heavily upon his friends. Eventually, Hoyt said, "This is not where my story ends. It is where yers begins."

"I traced the Cabal's flight that night, tryin' ta divine their intent and where they might strike next. The answer came as no surprise."

He paused significantly before continuing, "They appear ta be headin' fer the remain' seals. If they can reach and then destroy 'em, all that we have wrought will be in vain as their hordes will wash through unobstructed and wipe our world clean, suckin' its lifeblood away inta emptiness."

"The Protectorate and Home Guard are aware of this threat. I shared this information with 'em as soon as I found out. The Construct and its drones are gatherin' further intelligence. They're mobilizin' other strike teams ta go after the seals, both those that remain secured and those that are not, alongside our allies from across tha breadth of Ea'ae."

"Despite the devastation of the Cabal's initial strike, forces are rallyin' ta our call. This is a battle we cannot lose."

"I understand that y'all are ta form the core of one of these teams."

He looked them in the eyes with a depth of seriousness they had never seen in him before. Gone were the humor, the good cheer, and laid-back attitude that they knew. In these emotions' place was an unbridled intensity that knew no limit, a side of their easygoing friend neither Aroganji, Wrindanneth, Yip, nor Slate had ever seen prior to this instant. This gaze told them all they needed to know about Hoyt, his true character, and his expectations.

He never gave up.

He never backed down.

He never wavered.

He expected them to do the same.

"I'm here ta make sure y'all succeed."

His words were like the toll of a bell, each consonant filled with import, the cadence brimming with sincerity, the silence between words a call to action.

"On this, the Council of Light and I are in agreement."

"If y'all are ta be the world's defender's, I'm gonna make sure it's done right."

Slate thumped a thick hand across his chest in salutation and respect. "Hoyt, ya've always looked out fer us and taken care o' us, guidin' our course like it was yer own. Ya needn't do any more than ya have. Ya've already done so much."

From their armor to their robes, from their past successes to their future course, Hoyt had played a role in their activities since the start of their allegiance. His guidance, in fact, was the reason they were in

Tellanon as a group. His advice had brought them together and sent them on their way.

His advice was there before they were a team and would be there after.

Hoyt shook his head, a grim smile on his face. "My time of action has past. The present is yers. My life is only as good as yer success."

After those serious words, his smile brightened. "'Sides, I'm still in yer debt!"

Always the counter of coins, the arbiter of enumeration, Slate barked a laugh. "Hardly! I know worth when I see it." By way of fierce example, he thumped his shimmering breastplate, Dwarven wrought and fashioned of the highest quality at the attentive hands of a Dur'kazak, master of metal and magic, long lives before. "This item alone is worth more'n we ever offered t'ya fer trade much less gave ya!"

Hoyt shook his head in disagreement. "Value, like truth, is in the eye of the beholder. Y'all've given me more than ya know."

Hoyt's smile was bittersweet as he added, "Allowin' an old man ta participate in the lives of heroes, who could ask fer more in his dotage?"

Wrindanneth's snort summarized his feelings with regard to Hoyt's sentimental comments nicely.

The seriousness back in his gaze, Hoyt added, "Ya've given me my home and made sure I have a place ta sit a spell and watch the world go by. That's mighty important."

There were no more arguments.

Before anyone could mount any other more formidable objections, Hoyt continued, "'Sides, seems ta me I remember y'all brought in a sword from yer first journey together as the Four. We never finished our barterin' on the matter."

"I'm here ta make sure ya're fairly recompensed fer this item of worth, fer yer needs in the time ahead will be great...much greater'n mine."

Shaking his head, his thick beard bristling as much as his temper, Slate's disagreement with Hoyt's position was obvious as well. Aroganji and Yip, however, remained quiet, patient, not letting their sense of parity and justice interfere with what Hoyt wished to do or his unabated willingness to aid in their future.

Hoyt then reached into his robes. His motion smooth, elegant, with the facility of one masterfully drawing a sword, he pulled out a wondrous black wand. Powerful yet lithe, the wand was otherworldly —exceptionally beautiful, a bridge between the fey and the flesh, full of menace and foreboding.

To Yip's eyes, the wand itself was invisible, in its place was a beacon of Light that shone forth with the radiance of the birth of a galaxy of suns.

Hoyt stroked the wand's gleaming ebony surface lovingly, reminiscing with an old friend. "This here's my boomstick!"

Turning his focus away from the wand, by way of explanation, he said, "This's Luereal, the black wand of Q'ia'Li. Ta those unfamiliar with Elven, Luereal means 'evil's bane' in the fair tongue of the Elves."

Patting the deadly wand once more, he said, "Luereal's somethin' ya're likely ta never see again, a rare Anuvaeryan wrought artifact of witchwood."

Holding the wand outward, its thick haft cradled in the palm of his hands, he said, "I'd like fer you'ns ta have her."

Slate's jaw dropped. His mouth remained slack and open until Wrindanneth nudged his shoulder.

Motioning toward Aroganji, Hoyt said, "Don't just stand there starin', take her! She's the best I can offer ya fer yer trip ahead."

"But—" Aroganji's weak, bemused protest fell on deaf ears.

"There'll be no buts! Y'all're Elf-friends and no need is more dire'n yers."

Seeing the doubt in their eyes, he added, "Don't fret, the Elves would be honored fer ya ta wield Luereal. I should know, I've already asked!"

Somewhat reluctantly, his hands shaking, with the trepidation of one about to take hold of a particularly angry venomous snake, Aroganji lifted Luereal from Hoyt's steady hands.

Nodding in satisfaction, Hoyt said, "She's yers now ta do with as ya wish."

Sweeping his hand over Luereal's length, the wand shifted into a gleaming black staff in Aroganji's hands. "The choice is yers, Aroganji.

Choose the form ya prefer and Luereal will do yer biddin'. Like Wrindanneth's dagger, her strength will augment yer own. She can store more power'n any Man, and can often guide yer will ta the most favorable outcome, resources ya may well need in the dark days ahead."

Aroganji bowed deeply, his words soft, full of reverence and awe. "There is no way I can thank you for such a gift, Hoyt."

Hoyt smiled kindly as he replied, "Sure ya can. Go out and save the world!"

Wrindanneth patted Aroganji on the back reassuringly, his tone light. "Don't worry, Aroganji, it's nothing we haven't done before."

Slate laughed wholeheartedly. "That's tha way ta lighten tha pressure!"

Wrindanneth shrugged, a wry grin laid teasingly across his face. "I didn't mention trying to live up to the legacy of such an artful, storied artifact!"

Scratching his beard thoughtfully, Slate nodded. "Yeah, wouldn't want ta make Aroganji feel any additional burden carryin' a staff crafted by Elven immortals that've transcended tha flesh, only ta bestow an item o' such caliber on fallible hands."

Wrindanneth nodded sagely, keeping his face straight without a hint of a smile. "Wouldn't want to add any additional significance to the moment."

His face unreadable as well, Slate concurred. "Wouldn't be meet ta do such a thing ta someone under times o' such significance."

Finishing Slate's sentence, Wrindanneth said, "Or great need."

Unruffled, Aroganji gave a brief laugh as he said, "If you two lay it on any thicker, I may suffocate."

Slate shook his head gravely. "That wouldn't do, not at all! Then who would be left ta save tha world?"

"Or live up to the unparalleled Elven pedigree?" Wrindanneth's serious tone was lost on eyes glimmering with humor at his jest.

His gaze returning to Luereal's eldritch black surface, Aroganji had already forgotten Wrindanneth and Slate's comments. His was the wonder of one granted a vision one never thought to see or had imagined possible—the stuff of dreams made real.

Watching Aroganji study the Elven artifact in fascination, Slate muttered, "Reckon we'll ever be able ta pry him away from its bewitchin' black surface?"

Wrindanneth laughed gaily as he said, "To save the world, perhaps?"

"Aye." Slate's good cheer was infectious.

His smile as wide as their own, Hoyt said, "'Fore ya leave me, there's one other thing I'd like ta give ya."

When Aroganji made a move to protest, Hoyt cut him off with a wave of his hand. "I'd like ta give ya more and would if I could but the caliber of items that'll serve ya in the times ahead are few and far between."

Reaching into his robes, he pulled out a simple, nondescript rusty brown ring. "I do, however, have this!" The pride in his voice was contradicted by the simplicity of the object of his intent.

Slate scratched his head bemusedly, not invoking the power of his Star of Illdrassil to look more closely. "What is it?"

Wrindanneth smacked his forehead, saying, "A ring, genius!"

Slate's scowl was his ready reply.

Nodding in satisfaction with Slate's reaction, Hoyt replied, "This is Baërn, 'Berserker's Bane', as some would call it."

Slate shrugged his thick shoulders dismissively. "Looks rather plain."

Yip did not share Slate's opinion. The ring held in Hoyt's hand glowed red with a savage energy, seething and teeming with a heady mixture of anger and power, a volatile cocktail barely restrained within the simple, worn band of metal held in his hand.

"Then you should look again."

"The fires that burn within this ring have quenched many. The heat held within this band can ignite even more."

"Which means?"

"When called upon, Baërn's fury will course through the ring's bearer, fillin' him with heat and power burnin' through his veins, teemin' with strength, speed, and might."

Slate nodded appreciatively, now understanding. "Sounds like tha heat o' Brendle's forge, tha flames o' tha Daerdaana'Duin!"

His eyes glimmering with a smile, Hoyt replied matter-of-factly, "Which is exactly why you will wear it."

"As I said, many souls have been lost to this fire and not just at the hands of its bearer. It takes a rare individual not ta be consumed, overwhelmed by the intensity of the ring's demands. It's just as rare ta find someone fer whom the ring's suited, one whose talents match those of the ring itself."

Hoyt barked a short, considered laugh. "Ya're such a one. I know it as surely as the hairs on my eyebrows grow thicker and more tangled each day!"

Before offering the ring forth, Hoyt added, "The ring'll respond ta yer need as the situation demands. Its fires will augment yer own. Only ya can quench its heat and ya must do so fer its fury ta end, just as ya do with Brendle's flames."

Slate nodded in understanding, gingerly taking the ring and putting it on his finger. Though it had been cool in his hand, it was now warm on his skin as he pushed it past his knuckle and settled it at the base of the thick digit. "Thank ya, Hoyt."

His warning not yet complete, Hoyt said, "Ya must always remember who is the master fer its fires are now in yer hands."

Wrindanneth's words were only partially in jest. "Sounds like we're going to need one of Spreesprocket's SAVERS to shadow you!"

Filled with bravado, Slate said, "It's not me that's gonna need savin'!"

His tone not altogether in jest, Aroganji said, "I'll be sure to get a few for the ship."

His thick eyebrows raised, Slate replied with a mixture of humor and hurt, "Oy! Don't ya trust me?"

Shrugging, Aroganji replied, "It's not you that I don't trust."

Yip bowed, sensing their time with Hoyt had come to an end. "Thank you for all you have done for the people of Ea'ae and on our behalf. Your generosity is only matched by your foresight."

Hoyt snorted. "Don't be fooled by an emotional old man. I'm about as generous as a Dragon with his horde."

Yip laughed, thinking back to their encounters with Azaelle and Cersaegian along with their offerings, insight, and guidance. Smiling he responded, "We have met several most gracious Dragons."

Not wishing to let his emotions show, for he had grown close to these young stalwarts, Hoyt replied crotchetily, "Well, just don't get used ta it!"

Bowing once more, Yip answered, "Your kind words and vision will help see us through. Thank you, my friend."

"Don't get sappy with me, priest! Y'all have business ta do! Don't let me keep ya!"

Sharing Yip's smile, Aroganji said, "We will discuss what you have told us with Eidelion. With all that you have shown us, there may be other ways forward."

"Goodbye, Hoyt." Wrindanneth nodded his head as he turned to leave.

Following after his tall friend, Slate said, "Until we meet again, fare thee well, Hoyt."

His smile falling away, Aroganji said his goodbye as well. "May the wind at your back always carry you forward."

Shooing them on from behind the counter, his smile belying his words, Hoyt said, "Y'all're about as flowery as a bouquet! Get on outta here and save the world already!"

Ignoring Hoyt's gesture, offering a final bow, Yip offered, "May the peace in your heart always be expressed in action."

Scowling, Hoyt shooed them out once more, saying, "I've no need fer more o' yer poetry! Get thee hence!"

Walking out from his cluttered shop, they laughed as the screen door snapped shut behind them.

Silence once more descending upon the dust and debris left in their wake, a look of sadness fell upon Hoyt's ageless face.

Though he wished otherwise, he may never see them again. If so, Ea'ae would suffer a terrible loss, her Light dimmed and shadowed.

Once more he wished for their safe return.

PREPARATIONS

Deep sky bleeds into
a diffuse blue haze—
mountains brushed by the heavens.

"What do you wish to do now?" Aroganji halted his friends' forward progress away from the shop with a simple question.

Stopping, they all stood facing one another in front of Hoyt's store, its ramshackle façade the backdrop for their discussion.

"We should speak further with Eidelion." Wrindanneth spoke quickly and to the point. "Now that we know what Hoyt has told both the Home Guard and us, we need to understand fully what is being planned on all fronts."

Wrindanneth's words were Aroganji's thoughts. He did not need the telepathic bond they shared for his sentiments to be expressed by his friend.

Slate agreed. "If we're ta be a part o' tha Home Guard's plans as they are ours, then we should know what exactly they intend."

Glad his friends shared his sentiments, Aroganji said, "Then we should return home where we can communicate with Eidelion directly in safety and ease."

"Or just go there 'n talk with him." Eager to move ahead, Slate wished to engage the source of their concern directly.

"Why not go home? That way, you can get some food while we talk."

Wrindanneth's enticing smirk went unnoticed by Slate as his eyes glazed over expectantly.

"Now there's a plan!"

Without hesitation, like a fledgling flock taking to the air with the newfound joy of flight, they leapt upward one after the other sailing homeward on the wings of the Stars of Illdrassil's magic.

Flying low with the city passing below in a greenish-white blur, her periphery a line of stability on the horizon, they crossed the city in a matter of moments.

No one spoke. Each enjoyed the sensation of flight, the feel of the wind on their faces, and the pleasure of the inner silence of their own minds.

Gently touching down on the street in front of their cottage in loose formation, they transitioned to walking with a ready facility that implied flight had been part of their routine for much longer than it truly had been.

"Now that beats walkin'!" Slate's enthusiasm for flight grew with each successive exposure. Although he was not quite ready to pilot an airship for *faerviage*, the time might arrive soon.

"And listening to you talk the whole way!" Wrindanneth landed slightly ahead of Slate and held the gate open for him as he smiled rakishly, inviting trouble.

Slate's voice switched instantly from warm and full of excitement to icy cold, giving Wrindanneth the response he wished to elicit. "Tha same could be said in reverse, *nüaerblun*!"

Wrindanneth laughed. "I see your metaphorical vocabulary is limited to your own tongue, *günda*!"

"And nothin' would be more enjoyable than throwin' ya ta tha *nüaer'duin* and watchin' ya burn, *vöerdan*!"

Wrindanneth smiled wickedly, replying, "It would take you and several *nüaer'daer* to make that happen!"

"Care ta test yer theory?" As he spoke, Slate casually reached over his shoulder toward Duraeleon.

Moving so quickly that neither Slate nor Wrindanneth could register the movement, Yip interceded between his friends. Gently placing his hand on Slate's, he said tranquilly, "We have other theories to test. Let us be about them."

Accepting Yip's words with reluctant scowls, his calming presence cooling if not stemming their ire, Slate and Wrindanneth passed bone-chilling glares between one another, the looks promising future revisitation.

Filling the uneasy silence that fell, before any more harsh words were said, the ebullient voce of the Abstract rang through the air. "Welcome home, good sirs! I have taken the liberty of summoning your favorite meals in your absence to help you recuperate after an arduous day of preparations!"

His mood instantly lightening, his usual recriminations of the Abstract forgotten with the thought of good food and drink, Slate said, "Fer once ya've done me proud, Abstract! If ya keep surprisin' me like this, I might have ta rethink our relationship!"

"Thank you, sir!" The Abstract's cheery voice, if anything, became even cheerier.

"Don't get ahead of yerself now. All I'm sayin' is that ya might be worth toleratin', perhaps even listenin' ta from time ta time, if ya keep movin' in a decidedly unannoyin' direction."

"Understood, sir." The Abstract's glow was palpable. The air hummed and shimmered, the sun becoming a bit brighter.

Leaning down and whispering under his breath to Slate casually, pretending the Abstract could not detect his voice, Wrindanneth said convivially, their recent argument a thing of the distant past, "Looks like you've buttered someone's bread!"

"Everythin's better with butter!" Slate's deep laugh broke through any last remnants of tension that were lingering between them.

Smiling visibly now, Aroganji watched his friends quickly mend their friendship with the approval of a caring brother. There may be room for teasing, heated discussion, and temporary disagreement in their relationships but there was no space for dissension. That they could forgive so easily spoke more to the depths of their friendship, however reluctant, than simple words ever could.

"Abstract, would you arrange a projection conference with Eidelion at his earliest convenience? Preferably today." Aroganji followed his friends up the short path to their cottage as he spoke.

Answering briefly, the Abstract replied, "I shall endeavor to meet your request."

"Thank you."

Quickly opening the door and pushing forward toward the kitchen, Slate hurried after the savory aromas wisping through the air as he crossed the home's threshold. By the time Yip entered after holding the door for Aroganji, the sounds of silverware clattering on plates could already be heard emanating from the kitchen.

Never one to waste an opportunity, Slate had already taken his position at the table before the door shut behind Aroganji and Yip. Not quite as goal oriented as Slate, Wrindanneth and Aroganji filed into the kitchen cautiously for fear of losing a limb in the midst of Slate's feeding frenzy.

Smiling at the clear sounds of Slate's enthusiastic gusto along with Wrindanneth and Aroganji's careful approach after him, Yip settled down in the sitting room in silent contemplation while waiting for their call with Eidelion to begin.

"If you are ready, Eidelion is now available to speak with you." After only an hour or so of waiting, the Abstract's clarion announcement called them to attention from where they had been discussing plans for the days ahead in the sitting room.

"We are ready." The silence that fell upon his reply told Aroganji everything he needed to know about his friends' willingness.

In response to Aroganji's words, an image of Eidelion's chiseled face appeared in the air before them, his visage bathed in the subtle radiance of his armor and his inner light.

"Greetings, Four!" Eidelion's smile was genial and true, as steady as his gaze.

"Your Light is a welcome one." Yip bowed his head in ready acknowledgement of Eidelion's presence.

"As are yours. How may I be of service?"

Never one to banter unnecessarily, Slate spoke bluntly, "We've spoken with Hoyt."

He paused but a moment before continuing, understanding Eidelion knew what this meant. "He has told us of his observations and fears both durin' and after tha Cabal's attack on Tellanon and what he has divined of their plans. He has also told us that he's shared this knowledge with tha Guard. We'd like ta know what ya've uncovered, what ya plan, and how we fit inta those plans."

Eidelion nodded in understanding, expecting a conversation like this would happen. "Hoyt asked to speak to you directly regarding his experiences before I did, knowing that I would share what I knew with you unless he requested otherwise directly."

His wondrous smile returning, Eidelion added, "He was right."

"Hoyt provided confirmation of our own deepest fears and further impetus for us to push forward, information we have responded to swiftly and continue to act upon moment-by-moment."

"During the Cabal's attack, our own drones penetrated the Cabal's primary line of defense, the extradimensional Darkness that forced its way into our dimension. Additional waves of drones have harried and tracked the Cabal's vessels across Ea'ae, destroying many in the process, while providing significant intelligence of their movements and intent."

"Hoyt's worst fears are indeed true. Those ships we have not managed to destroy are moving directly against the seals that secure our world from extradimensional assault. The battle that has waged silently for aeons has now come to the fore."

His voice grim, Eidelion added, "The security we so recently won by restoring the seal of Eldre'gheu is now in jeopardy."

As Eidelion spoke, an image of Ea'ae appeared beside him. A bright point of light representing Tellanon appeared on the globe. From this point, many vectors representing the forces of Tellanon and its allies moved out, tracking black variables representing the forces and allies of the Cabal across the planet's surface. Gazing at a particular representation on the globe brought up the most current intelligence regarding the enemy vector—position, composition, trajectory, engagements, losses, and delays. All of these shifting quantities, ships and drones, NUMEN and Daemons, Cabal and Home Guard, swarmed to the shimmering points of light representing the seals assuring Ea'ae's continued protection.

Though defensive forces seethed about these ships, the Cabal's progress toward the seals appeared inevitable.

"We are continually marshaling teams, groups composed of Home Guard and our allies, to beat back these interlopers and win the security of our world's future. You will form the core of one of these units to be dispatched to a region where our prior efforts have met with failure."

"While Ea'ae's defenders rush to her aid, Tellanon's Paratechnologists are creating NUMEN as rapidly as possible, each specialized to counter and track the Cabal and their insidious allies."

"As you already know, one of these NUMEN will be deployed with you. Many others have been sent elsewhere. More will follow."

"Along with the drones, the NUMEN compose a formidable weapon against the invaders, allies that prevent the loss of life through their competency while tipping the odds in our favor for mission success."

"We are actively pushing onward on all fronts but are meeting heavy resistance. The Cabal brought many unspeakable horrors with them through the gates, letting these terrors loose upon the world to wreak havoc, harry our forces, raid our cities and towns, and impede our efforts to advance."

"Despite these challenges, in spite of the attacks and losses visited upon our cities, we are fighting forward. We will succeed. We have no alternative."

"Beyond Ea'ae, through the portals we have penetrated, our intelligence remains limited. Little of value has yet surfaced from those drones that first pushed through the Daemonic Darkness. Our hope is that this situation turns as soon as possible."

"Once we beat back the Cabal on Ea'ae, we will cleanse their presence from the macroverse."

The look of adamantium determination in his eyes said there would be no alternative.

"What makes you think we will succeed in our task with so few when so many others are unable?" Wrindanneth spoke simply but to the point.

Eidelion's answer was just as simple. "Because you have done so before. Because a few may succeed where many have failed. Because you are more than a few and not many. Because we now have assets to give that we did not before."

"Have drones and NUMEN gone before us?" Now that they knew more of the Home Guard's plans, Aroganji wanted a clearer picture of their immediate future, their imminent predicament, and what, if anything, had been attempted in the recent past.

Eidelion nodded. "They have met with heavy resistance both from the Cabal marshaling to the Fyrskal's fortress and from within the citadel housing the seal."

"None have survived?"

While Aroganji asked the questions everyone wanted answered, Yip surveyed everyone silently. Each motion, each reply, told him as much as the words themselves.

Eidelion was open and honest but there was, as yet, more for him to reveal. He saw this not only in the features of Eidelion's face, the minute shifts in his carriage, but also in the emanations of his *li*. He also sensed, however, that this information would be revealed. Knowing this, he waited patiently for Eidelion's further revelations.

"No. There is a battle raging in the skies above the Fyrskal's citadel. We have not been able to bring enough force to bear to tip it in our favor. Until then, the Cabal and Fyrskal lay waste to one another over the desolate plains of their fortress."

Incredulous, Slate asked, "And ya honestly think we can do somethin' ta sway tha battle?"

Eidelion need not shrug for they saw the uncertainty in his face. "I am not asking you to overcome either force. I want you to go in and place a new seal. Let the Cabal and Fyrskal destroy each other for a useless remnant from the past."

"How is this? What is different now?" Wrindanneth inferred that much must have changed for their protocol to alter so drastically. After all, they had to first destroy the old seal prior to placing the new one in Eldre'gheu. His curiosity was piqued.

Sensing a shift in Eidelion, his body and mind, Yip discerned that novel information was forthcoming. This was the additional piece of the puzzle he had sensed that Eidelion had yet to reveal.

Eidelion smiled. "Although we will have to deal with the Cabal, our path forward has become much easier. Through a combination of the skill and knowledge of the Paratechnologists and the Construct, coupled with the power of Illdrassil, and the guidance of the Elves, a new type of seal has been designed. These new seals are being created as quickly as possible to take the places of the old."

"Like the new seal we placed at Eldre'gheu, once placed, these seals do not have a tangible physical manifestation. They augment and become part of the energy currents flowing around the planet protecting us from extradimensional incursion. However, unlike the old seals and the one we took on our quest, once set in position, these new seals take the place of the old ones without requiring any additional effort, obviating the redundant pre-existing seal with activation."

"Most importantly, however, these new seals will save lives—not only the lives of the beings of Ea'ae who might be vulnerable to potential incursion or attack without the seals in place but also the lives of the brave warriors like yourselves who venture forward to secure the seals' positions."

"If these new seals take the place of the old, why must we risk going near the old seals at all? Why not place the new seals elsewhere?" Wrindanneth's ruddy eyebrows raised with his query, his intense gaze locked on Eidelion as he spoke.

Eidelion's knowing smile broke for his reply. "We will do just that. The new seals will be placed all over Ea'ae to strengthen and improve upon the old. However, these can be created and placed only so quickly. For those that take the place of the old, the most critical, they must be set within a short distance of the existing seal to counteract its magic."

"Given your past success, you will be given the first of one of these new seals, though others will follow soon after. Instead of direct assaults on enemy forces shielded in loathsome fastnesses where our foes have built their power unobstructed over long years, as we have attempted in the past, we now have the option for clandestine surgical strikes."

"Your mission will make the first of many incisions."

Eidelion's optimism was tempered by caution. "Despite this new opportunity for Ea'ae's security and prosperity, the old seals must also be neutralized. If not, they may yet provide a window into this world, weapons that our enemies may use against us."

The considered silence that fell at these words was broken first by Aroganji. "How close must we get to place the new seal?" He was calculating their improved odds within the framework of these new developments as he spoke.

"Within three leagues."

"And much time will the replacement process take?" Aroganji needed to understand how long they risked potential exposure and how long they must fight in place should they be forced to hold in one position while establishing the new seal.

"Mere minutes."

"How will we know the replacement process is complete and the old seal has been neutralized?" More questions needed to be answered before Aroganji would be completely satisfied with their mission requirements.

"Once the seal has faded away into the planetary protective shield, the old seal will no longer hold the power it once did to offer a gateway into our world or serve as a vessel of evil."

"What if the seal does not work as expected, fading into Ea'ae's shield?" Wrindanneth's concern was with whether the seal would function as planned and what they would have to do if it did not.

"Then you must move and come within range of the old seal. Assuming you are not under the influence of hostile magics that must be countered, being out of range will be the only cause of malfunction."

"Will the seal itself help guide us toward its pair should we be out of range?"

"Aye. You will feel a pull in the correct direction. This weight will grow stronger the closer you are to the desired target. Once you are within range, the seal will merge with the protective ley lines of its own accord after its housing is opened."

Nodding, Aroganji was satisfied. Their chances of success appeared much greater under these new conditions. Eidelion, the Construct, and the Paratechnologists offered them a wondrous new gift—the chance to survive.

"Sounds almost Dwarf-proof!"

Wrindanneth's poor attempt to lighten the mood at Slate's expense was met with a quick rebuttal from the Dwarf. "Bah! Speak fer yerself ya flamin' pile o' yak dung! If it were left ta yer sorry hands alone, we might as well stay in Tellanon and drink ta tha sorrows we averted by followin' yer lead!"

Wrindanneth's unrestrained laughter was not enough to divert Slate's dark, threat-laden glare.

Scowling, ignoring Wrindanneth's smirk, Slate returned to the question he had been about to ask. "Couldn't tha Paratechnologists've developed these new seals a few weeks sooner?"

Sharing Slate's pain, Eidelion replied, his eyes gazing far off in the distance, his thoughts on lost friends and opportunities. "I, too, wish that were the case."

"The seal we placed in Eldre'gheu actually was a new seal. It represented the culmination of significant efforts to develop and recreate. Prior to the seal we placed, only a handful had been made for ages, all of which were lost during failed restoration missions. Much of the knowledge required for their creation had to be rediscovered and recreated."

"Our difficulties at Eldre'gheu along with the horrors of the Cabal's assault brought increased knowledge, urgency, and resources to bear on the problem. These new seals are the result of this effort, a continuation of this process."

His lips pursed, Slate nodded in grim acceptance. Though he wished so much life had not been lost or put in jeopardy, he was glad to hear considerable effort was being made to prevent more loss, notwithstanding their own.

A heavy silence filled the chamber then as the weight and significance of their upcoming trials settled about them.

"What else must we know of our way forward?" Aroganji's question implied much and asked for more.

"All of our intelligence will be given to you to review and will be constantly updated as part of our datastream. This information will be transferred to the command sphere on your ship."

"The continent of Aruene is largely uninhabited. At one time it was the cradle of many civilizations but now, like the Fyrskal who left Morowen before, it is mostly empty, abandoned by those who sought their destinies among the stars."

"You will be going into the heart of this emptiness."

Smiling once more, Eidelion added, "Once more you will be pushing back against the bounds of the unknown. At this, we know you are quite able."

Visualizing the trip ahead, lost in their own thoughts as they imagined the journey yet to come, the room fell silent. Yip finally broke the moment of solemn reflection. Bowing graciously, he said, "We thank you and all those that work with you for allowing us to continue forward as safely and conscientiously as possible."

Though his face remained calm and composed, Yip's words were laced with steel. "We will succeed. We will ensure that the other seals can be placed. When we are done, the people of Ea'ae will live without fear of further attack."

Smiling, he added, "If for no other reason than more new seals will need to be developed and placed."

Eidelion's luminous grin burnt through the last vestiges of the heavy mood hanging over the room. "Whatever the outcome, you have already done more to ensure our safety, and the security of those beyond Ea'ae's bounds, than we had ever dreamed."

"Is there aught else 'fore Eidelion leaves us?" Slate was ready for a brief snack between snacks.

Wrindanneth nodded. "When shall we meet our traveling companions in person?"

Eidelion took but a moment to reply, "We should be able to make arrangements for you to meet those you have not on the morrow."

"I will invite Spreesprocket and Alderan though they may be bound to other obligations."

Slate smiled. "I'll be seein' enough o' them in tha days ahead. No need ta take 'em away from their duties unnecessarily."

After Slate finished, Aroganji added, "We will await your word as to when and where we will meet."

Eidelion gave a brief nod, then added, "One more item to discuss… given the urgency of the situation, we have made every effort to speed the repair and upgrade of your vessel despite our current resource limitations."

"When we will it be finished?" Aroganji was already imagining what would need adjustments given a shortened departure time horizon.

"Based on Spreesprocket's latest report, I would anticipate the *Shrike* will be ready for departure the day after tomorrow."

Aroganji gave a nod, hiding his surprise behind a mask of cool decision. The Guard had truly managed to expedite the *Shrike's* upgrades. "We will be ready to leave as soon as the ship is ready."

"Excellent."

"And the seal will be ready as well?"

"Aye."

Slate laughed. "We'd better hurry up 'n meet our companions lest our first meetin' be on tha docks!"

Wrindanneth shook his head, disagreeing with Slate's assessment. "That might not be the best plan, Slate. If we wait until the last minute to meet our traveling companions, then they will have less opportunity to back out after making your acquaintance."

Stroking his chin thoughtfully, Wrindanneth added, "I see an image of them running away in dismay shortly after your introduction."

Maintaining an even tone, Slate replied to Wrindanneth, getting in his own dig, "Just keep yer mouth shut and all will be well."

Lifting his index finger thoughtfully to his pursed lips, Slate added, "And don't forget yer personal hygiene. Yer mornin' breath gives new meanin' ta tha phrase 'Dragon's breath.'"

The ensuing laughter stifled any further retorts.

Wrindanneth, ever poised, resisted the urge to anger, refusing to let his face turn as red as his hair, as hot as the fires of his fury. He would have other opportunities at Slate's expense in the future. Showing weakness would only exacerbate the issue.

Instead, feigning pride, Wrindanneth bowed gracefully.

Dragon's breath, after all, was quite potent—worthy of both respect and fear.

As the laughter stilled, sensing that the conversation had reached its productive end, Yip freed Eidelion, saying, "Until our lives enliven each other once more, we honor you and the kindred spirits that accompany you."

Declining his head in acknowledgement, Eidelion said, "Your

Lights brighten all those fortunate enough to fall within your purview. I will be in contact soon."

The image before them shimmered briefly and was gone.

Watching Eidelion's image fade away, Slate clapped his hands together excitedly. "Sounds like we're gonna be goin' on a regular holiday compared ta our last excursion!"

"What exactly do you mean by holiday?" Although Aroganji related to Slate's jest, Dwarves hunted Cave Trolls for fun and pleasure, regularly fought one another with cudgels for sport without magical protections or healing afterward, and often kept tokens from foes they had vanquished woven into their beards as marks of honor. A bit of clarification never hurt in matters of cultural nuance and interpretation.

One man's pleasures were another's pain.

"Beats fightin' our way inta tha heart of a Daemon infested city, through a cursed temple, and beyond a vortex o' pure evil, that's what I mean."

"I thought our last quest constituted the Dwarven equivalent of a normal, light family outing. So you're saying that flying into a war zone teeming with alien and extradimensional forces, all swarming cannons ablaze around a vile fortress potentially filled with unholy deathknights or worse is a rollicking good time?" Wrindanneth could not let this opportunity pass untouched.

"Aye! I'm gonna pack my swimmin' trousers and fishin' pole. Per'aps we can get a few o' tha local lads in Tellanon ta join us fer our outin'!"

"You mean the ones too inebriated or insane to know the difference between safety and a death wish?"

"Exactly! Sounds like my kinda people!"

Wrindanneth shrugged dismissively. "Crazy is as crazy does."

"Bet yer beard on it!"

"Your keen insight notwithstanding, I doubt that this endeavor will be any easier than the last. We seem to elude trouble about as well as you avoid seconds at the dinner table." Wrindanneth's tone was matter-of-fact but true nonetheless.

"Mmm...seconds!" Slate washed his hands eagerly with the thought food.

"Point proven." Wrindanneth shook his head decided. He could see this line of conversation was going nowhere—the same trajectory as most of his conversations with Slate.

"And conceded. I'm off ta get more sustenance!" Standing up, Slate left the sitting room hurriedly, excitedly planning the composition and arrangement of his next meal.

Watching Slate leave, Wrindanneth grumbled, "And now we wait."

Returning to his feet in a simple, fluid motion, Yip said, "We have been granted the gift of time. I suggest we use it wisely." With that he left, turning and walking out through the front door to take up position in the front yard.

From their vantage inside the cottage, both Aroganji and Wrindanneth watched Yip stand as still as a post beneath a large tree as he began to practice *qigong* on the lawn.

Standing as well, Wrindanneth quipped, "We're about as exciting as a group of slugs out on a morning slide. I'm going on a walk. I'll be back when I'm done."

Left alone in the chamber, Aroganji sat calmly watching the day fade to night, following one transition to another, moving his mind in tandem with the changes unfolding around him.

Energy swirled and shifted, encompassing, all around—ebbing and moving, tides pulled by thousands upon thousands of uncounted generative stars—the living energies of creation of which he was a part, the waters that washed away his boundaries, connecting him to a wider world.

All around was life and in it, Yip was free.

Falling away into these fields, he shifted and disappeared. With this disappearance came an expansion. That which had felt limitless exploded without bound and his mind moved without restriction. Though he felt unfettered and unbound, this was an illusion for there would always be more barriers to push, more limits to overcome, and more potential to express. In this moment of liberation, finding and losing himself, there would always be more.

A bridge between worlds, joining the physical and mental, the actual and the potential, the manifest and the unrealized, his awareness spanned the moment between the future and the past.

These were the limits he pushed against. In the days ahead, whatever his limitations, whatever his frailties, whatever his shortcomings, these weaknesses could lead to their failure, their demise, and an end to the hopes established by their mission.

Though relaxed and at peace, there was nonetheless a sense of urgency and focus to his efforts. The motivation and drive that girded his work would continue to underlie and define his endeavors in the days ahead. Just as there could be no failure in their mission's success, there could be no failure in his own.

Innumerable changes, one flowing to the next—minute, subtle, wondrous, and without equal—slipped and moved in an endless dance unfolding before Aroganji's eyes. With the slightest push from his mind, the smallest addition of energy, he could change the course of these movements and alter the future. Within his grasp, so conscious of its constraints and shortcomings, he held the course of a world yet unborn.

This responsibility, this undying cause was his inspiration, his guiding star, and the motivation for his unending efforts to learn and achieve. For without understanding these moments, his mind, his purpose, and his being would be pointless.

Wrindanneth, too, thought of his future—of what he would become, of how he would change, and what would be required to transform himself from a being of flesh to one of divine power. Burning with the fire of the sun in his heart, a will and a demand to achieve and grow beyond bounds, his future, though currently tied to a master he did not wish, would soon be unshackled.

He had but to find the proper expression for this vision.

His knife and fork clattered on the porcelain. His plate was empty. Disappointed, Slate looked for more food.

No fires currently burned within his heart—they burned in his belly. He needed fuel for both his body and mind if they were to overcome and triumph in the days ahead. His was the vision of the physical, for the opportunities of his peoples. He wished them every happiness and success and only wanted what was best for the citizens of Ea'ae, the Dwarves of his hold, and the kin of his clan.

Though each held disparate visions of the world and their place in it, they were united by a common cause and the desire for a better future. Bound by friendship, united by purpose and their loyalty to one another, their sense of obligation and righteousness, each would do whatever was required to ensure that their time together expressed the aim of their heart's desire.

Mere days until their departure, their lives and the lives of countless others depended on them to realize their shared vision.

Evening passed into morn with the gentle transition of navy to azure, depthless stars to unclouded skies. Inside their sturdy cottage, Slate woke with the sun, eager to be about the business of the day and for the opportunity to squeeze in one breakfast before he shared another with Wrin and Aroganji.

Looking out the window of his room as he sat up, for he preferred the quaint ordinariness of using a window to gaze from rather than asking the Abstract to make the wall transparent or show a view from another place, he saw Yip standing in the yard like an unseemly, robed lawn ornament.

If that fool priest did not learn to choose his spots better, the neighbors might think a basilisk was on the loose, petrifying anything that fell within its gaze!

With a loud huff, Slate threw back the covers, quickly donned his armor, the few pieces he did not sleep in, and picked up Duraeleon from where it lay on the bed beside where he slept. Walking carefully, his magic boots muting the thumping of his heavy feet, he spared Wrindanneth and Aroganji an early morning and himself competition at breakfast.

He would have to have words with that dimwit priest, not that any words would get through a skull impervious to almost all reason. Yip was persistent and awe-inspiring at what he did, but, unfortunately, he had about as much sense as a tumbled, weatherworn boulder. At least his magics spared him from the frailties of a normal human constitution, else he would be sick more often than he was well.

One of Yip's saving graces was the fact that he did not need food. That way, there was always plenty to eat! And leftovers to boot!

Less competition meant more for him.

In this case, less was more.

Entering the kitchen, he prepared breakfast for four. Then, after he had eaten everything, he prepared a second breakfast for four.

This meal the others would eat.

He would merely eat his portion and Yip's.

Wrindanneth could not sleep.

Visions of talking mounds of food, often with thick Dwarven accents and full braided beards, kept appearing unexpectedly in his dreams of world dominion and power. These succulent smelling diversions always interfered at the most inopportune moments.

Finally grown frustrated, he rolled over, jostling free of his covers, and was awake.

Left behind were his food-filled dreamscapes of ascendancy, his reveries of unearthing new arcane secrets and abilities, and his imaginings of command. Instead, he stared out through the translucent wall of his bedroom chamber at an image of a small man standing in perfect stillness on the lawn.

Yip, apparently at least had the sense to give up on sleep!

Through the crack beneath his door, the aromas of cooking wafted tantalizingly, the tormenter of his dreams, tendrils of deliciousness enticingly pulling him to wakefulness from the comfort and excitement of his fantasies. At the root of this coercive evil was most certainly a small bearded Daemon, one of the Dwarven persuasion, perhaps from the lowest levels of some rocky Abyss.

Throwing his long legs over the edge of his bed, he strode from his room to confront his nemesis and perhaps partake of some delectable morsels.

Aliments and enemies both were on the horizon.

Aroganji's eyes were closed but his mind was open.

With each breath, he watched the transition from fullness to emptiness, the unceasing activity of life translated and measured by breath. Blood moved, nutrients circulated, and the body repaired and restored itself with each inhalation and exhalation. Energy moved in and around, converted to usable form and radiated through his vital systems guided by his body's natural rhythmic functions.

Around him, similar transitions moved from one to the next, moments of change translating energy from one arrangement to another, a ceaseless dance of creation and destruction, generation and eradication.

Myriad facets of the Wu-hsing transitioned seamlessly from one phase to the next while his mind rested and observed.

Within these myriad changes, another arose.

Opening his eyes, the subtle emanations of breakfast called to him from below—wafts of potential transformations undergoing and soon to be.

Within the building heat of the steadily rising sun, Yip's awareness abided unclouded and unobscured—a star that never set.

This star burned with an even intensity unfazed by heat or cold, fatigue or distraction. Awareness, untrammeled by thought, encompassed one moment and the next, a totality within the confines of his mind.

Letting his limits fade, he shifted, blinking minutely from position to position, left to right but a fraction of a hair, so swiftly and subtly that the unaided eye would not perceive the adjustment.

Throughout the night, this had been his practice—continually losing and reestablishing the self in unceasing moments of self-awareness and self-negation, giving up and restoring himself with ceaseless vigilance, the unwavering sun of a consciousness that did not subside.

A low growl rumbled through the kitchen. Patting his stomach reassuringly, Slate grinned and muttered to himself, "Easy there now. Your time will come."

One course finished and ready for the next, he called out, hearing the footsteps of his friends upstairs. "If ya don't get down here soon, I can't make any promises that there'll be any breakfast left fer ya ta eat!"

As his voice boomed through the cottage, he heard Wrindanneth's feet on the stairs, his long legs taking the steps two at a time. As he walked, he heard Wrindanneth's fiery reply. "I don't want your leavings! If you can't wait for us, I'll get my own breakfast! Then at least I'll be fortunate enough to be in good company and guaranteed a decent meal!"

Slate's grin became a smile. He could always manage another round of food, especially with Wrindanneth's blessing! A bit more solitude and food would suit him nicely.

Rounding the corner and entering the kitchen, Wrindanneth's tall figure blocked the doorway as he entered. His eyes quickly taking in the many-layered bounty Slate had prepared for them, Wrindanneth said, "I'm surprised there's aught left for us given your impatience."

"No need ta worry, Northlander! This is tha second round!"

Wrindanneth nodded. "That explains the racket that woke me up." And his food induced nightmares. Visions of the Dwarven food Daemon from his dreams were superimposed over Slate's bearded visage as he looked.

Shaking his head slightly as he sat down at the small table, Wrindanneth began selecting items from the mounds of food Slate had prepared. He would wait to eat until Aroganji arrived but his friend's tardiness need not prevent him from selecting a few choice delicacies. There were so many items to choose from, Aroganji would probably arrive before he had finalized his selection.

His fork poised over a particularly succulent sausage, he heard Aroganji's warm voice advise, "Choose wisely, Wrin," looking at Slate meaningfully, he added, "you are not likely to have a second."

"It's a wonder the rest of us don't starve sharing our stores with a voracious, malnourished cave bear!"

Digging into his pile of food, Slate growled, apparently quite fluent in ursine.

Aroganji nodded. "Magic is almost as amazing as Slate's ability to consume its creations."

Wrindanneth indicated Slate with a nod of his head. "Will you be done eating by the time we are supposed to meet our new traveling companions?"

Slate spoke gutturally around a mouthful of food. "Ya doubt me? I'll be done with three courses in tha time it takes fer ya ta finish choosin' one!"

Wrindanneth snorted. "It's not your ability to eat I doubt. It's your ability to finish!"

Slate returned to his plate, not dignifying Wrindanneth's quip with a reply.

Taking a plate for himself, Aroganji said, "As soon as we're done here, we'll fly to Illdrassil to meet with the Guard."

Indicating the yard with Yip in it, Slate said, "Assumin' Yip's done communin' with tha fairies!"

Wrindanneth's mocking tone taunted Slate. "At least someone wants to talk to him. You're not so fortunate!"

Grinning evilly, Slate cracked, "Their loss is yer gain!"

Wrindanneth shook his head in feigned sadness. "Only figuratively!"

"If he's not done by tha time I finish my next plate, I'll go out there and tell tha spirits he has nothin' left ta say!"

His words coming out around a mischievous smile, Wrindanneth said, "While you're out there, can you do the same for yourself?"

"Bah!" Ignoring Wrindanneth, Slate returned his attention to his food.

Sensing his friends were finishing their preparations for the day's start, Yip released the light tension in his muscles, letting his arms drop to his waist where he had been holding them near his navel and stood up fully, straightening the slight bend he had held in his knees. His body fresh and enlivened as he turned and walked toward the house, the ease of his movements gave no indication that he had been standing in position for hours on end.

"Look what tha Orcs dragged in!" Placing the last of the empty plates on the counter for the Abstract to clean, Slate smiled as he saw Yip enter the kitchen from the side door.

"If you were out there much longer, Yip, I'd suggest we put a dusting of sod on you and some seed. That way, you'd be a proper lawn ornament and would add a bit more character to the house!" Wrindanneth was passing the trays with leftovers to Aroganji where he was putting the food in the stasis box on the counter that prevented the foodstuffs from aging, decomposing, or degrading.

Yip smiled and nodded his head. "I would like that."

Slate laughed with Yip's reply. "I told ya he was out there communin' with tha fairies!"

Now Aroganji smiled in reply. "I don't know, Wrin. If you do that, he may put down roots and never leave!"

Yip bowed. "All the secrets, all the wisdom, a man could wish to discover are found in nature."

"And ne'er would ya have ta put up with tha sarcasm o' those who would lead ya off tha path ta understandin'!" Slate glared briefly at Wrindanneth, not forgetting his earlier taunts.

Wrindanneth smiled. "If all you want to do is listen to the birds, then you may have found your path, Slate! If you're patient, they might just listen to you as well!"

"They have more o' worth ta say than tha likes o' ya. 'Tis sad indeed that ya'd put down tha beauty o' tha natural world in yer efforts ta put me down, Northlander."

Wrindanneth smiled as he said politely, "I only want to put you down by whatever means necessary."

"Bah!" Slate raised his fist, pointing his finger accusingly at Wrindanneth.

Before the next volley of insults could be fired, however, Yip interjected, suggesting, "Why don't we keep our appointment?"

Aroganji nodded, adding, "I'm sure either one of you could wear down a mountain with all the hot air you let out in your rants."

Wrindanneth nodded knowingly while Slate said, "Thank ya!"

Indicating the door with the sweep of his arm, Yip said, "Shall we?"

Walking out of the cottage without a backward glance to Wrindanneth, Slate stepped out into the early morning light and leapt into the air.

NEW COMPANIONS LOST

Bands of liquid gold
dance atop the pond's surface
welcoming the morn.

The coral hues of dawn washed over the streets and buildings of Tellanon bathing the city in diffuse, pearlescent splendor. Catching the light of the rising sun, the rounded arches and curves of sculpted buildings were accentuated by the soft, cloud filtered light. Below the roofline, lingering streams of darkness pooled in the streets as the last tinges of evening held on in the shadows between buildings, awnings, and ways.

Though much of the city yet slept, the sky beyond the island's periphery moved with ships, drones, and defensive sentinels. Below, enterprising merchants moved toward shops in preparation for the morning crowds while tradesman woke to prepare for a new day. Craftsmen and artisans began organizing their implements of choice, each endeavoring to bring his or her inner visions to life. Diplomats made ready to go their offices and travelers prepared to take in the wonders of a celestial city.

For these people, the defensive fortifications and reinforcements all around were constant reminders of the recent attack upon the city, the disheartening disruption of normalcy, and the heavy cost incurred by loss and war. For the Fists, these same sights were reminders of what was to come, of their futures to be, and the conflicts they would soon face.

Looking onward toward the city's heart, air warmed by the newly risen sun brushed their faces as they sped toward Illdrassil. Capturing and magnifying the light of the newborn sun, Illdrassil sparked and shimmered with the luster and glory of a crystalline nebula.

The scent of promise filled their nostrils with each breath just as the heavy burden of grave responsibility threatened to weigh them down, ending their flight prematurely.

"Certainly is beautiful!" Slate called out over the wind, looking back over his shoulder toward his friends where he flew at the head of their formation.

"I'll not argue that!" Wrindanneth returned his companion's smile, openly sharing his feelings for the nonce, a sentiment which may change at any moment.

Adjusting his course downward, Slate began their descent, bringing their brief flight to an unwelcome, premature close.

"A shame we must quit tha skies!" His drop a graceful spiral, Slate led them toward Illdrassil's southern gate.

Wrindanneth's full laugh trailed them downward. "I never thought I'd hear you say that, Dwarf!"

Looking over his shoulder briefly once more, Slate replied, "Tha world's always bigger'n our opinions or thoughts o' it!"

Wrindanneth snickered. "You've been hanging around Yip too long!"

Slate smirked in reply. "Or not long enough!"

Slowing his descent, Slate landed on the cobbled street some distance away from Illdrassil's gate, followed immediately by his fellows. They maintained a safe distance from the citadel lest their presence incur the wrath of the Guard.

"Ready ta meet our new friends?" Slate indicated the Guard ahead, not their imminent introduction to their traveling companions.

Aroganji shrugged. "They've always been pleasant to us in the past."

Wrindanneth nodded, replying, "As welcoming as a jailor to his new prisoners."

"Let's get tha glares over with." Slate started walking toward the archway flanked by Home Guard leading through the translucent wall, not looking back to see if his friends had joined him.

Before he had taken more than five steps, a familiar voice interrupted his advance. "Fists! I have an urgent message incoming from Adar! Are you able to take his dispatch or shall I have you contact him at a later time?" The Abstract's excited voice nearly made Slate jump. As it was, he uttered a low snarl at the sound of the simulacrum's voice.

"Patch him through please." Undisturbed, not sharing Slate's ire, Aroganji spoke with aplomb.

"As you wish!" With those words, the Abstract went silent and Adar's disembodied voice took its place.

"Greetings, Fists! I have urgent information that I wish to share with you!" As he spoke, Adar's face appeared in the air before them, one object floating steadily in place as several indeterminant Paratechnological devices orbited erratically about his head. His piercing gray-blue eyes were alive with excitement as he glanced between the Fists, eager to tell his tale.

"My apologies if I disturbed you, but I could not wait any longer." The myriad Paratechnological implements whirled about Adar's regal visage as he spoke, independent of his excitement.

"There is no need to apologize, Adar! We are already about our day's business. What troubles you?" Aroganji spoke with propitious conviviality. Though his generosity was sincere, he also understood that Adar's excitement was not without some justification.

"We have had a breakthrough!" The Paratechnologist's tone was excited, his face lit by enthusiasm. "Last night!"

Adar's normally measured tone was clipped and lively in his zeal to convey the discovery. Before he added more, Adar said, "We must ensure that our words remain private."

Wrindanneth nodded. Looking significantly, tauntingly, at the Home Guard stationed nearby, he grinned wickedly and drew a veil of darkness around them, one that could not be easily penetrated by sight, sound, or spell, a mantle that would surely raise the hackles of the Guard who dispassionately attended their every motion. "You may speak freely."

"We have managed to thwart the alien command sphere's defenses! Through some very clever temporal and spatial inversions..."

He shook his head dismissively. "You don't care about all that. After the Cabal's recent attack, we were at greater liberty to explore any means possible to break through the original sphere's defenses. So we did!"

By way of explanation, he said, "What's to be lost by the Cabal knowing we're looking for them when they have already been here, were looking for us when they came, and now know we are looking for them? Also, with the seals restored, any communication beyond Ea'ae should be almost impossible without knowledge of how to communicate through the interplanetary shield, knowledge which this orb does not possess."

Clapping his hands together, he said, "Again, I digress! The Construct has begun the process of sorting through the alien device, cataloging its stores, uncovering its contents, categorically deciphering its technical knowledge, and revealing its hidden trappings."

Knowing they were not familiar with this information gathering process, he added, "The Construct is exceedingly efficient at this task. Deciphering unknown technology is a process the Construct has been designed to perform and one in which it continually self-refines and improves upon. Given the intimate understanding we now have of the sphere's workings granted by its replication, this process should move forward with minimal difficulty."

"As the worst case, we should have, and be able to reproduce and put into practice, any novel technical knowledge found within, by day's end. This technology transfer is of the utmost importance to our ongoing mission both here and abroad."

Slate smiled at these words for this success, and the results deriving from this achievement, was also exceedingly helpful to their own coffers.

"However, though remarkable, this is not why I am contacting you! One of the Construct's many parallel consciousness threads alerted us to one especially well encrypted piece of information of great significance to us all, and of particular interest to you, held within the sphere's confines."

Adar need not pause for dramatic effect but he did regardless. The whirling magical objects circling his person remained abeyant with him.

"We have uncovered what appears to be a coordinate system describing what may signify Cabal controlled and aligned planets and regions spread throughout and outside the cosmos!"

As he spoke, an expansive representation of known space appeared in the air before them, rotating and scintillating with countless interstellar bodies, colored and shaded in iridescent hues.

"Each of the points you see are galaxies, entire systems of stars, miniature universes filled with planets like our own. Many of the points we believe correspond with the Cabal's bastions appear to lie outside of our current body of firsthand astronomical knowledge."

Independent of this representation, other lights appeared, indicating the positions of which he now spoke, highlighted in relation to areas that have been thoroughly cataloged. "Others"—still more lights appeared, these appeared watery and translucent, superimposed on or around the current three-dimensional representation but not part of the same image—"are not a part of this dimension whatsoever and are indicative of other similar, or dissimilar, planes of existence in contrast to our own."

Looking at the spatial representation carefully, Aroganji asked, "Is there any way to cross-correlate the positions of the sentry drones that went through the Cabal's rifts at the time of their attack on the city to see if their current locations correspond to any of these systems?"

Adar nodded. "We are working on that." He smiled, adding, "Communication is rather problematic at times over such vast distances and across multiple dimensions."

"I should say!" Slate shook his head, at a loss before the sheer number of galaxies, stars, planets, and planes that were arrayed before them. To think that each galaxy, when one alone may contains billions upon billions of stars, may harbor planets, each potentially holding life like their own, any one of which could be threatened by or harboring the Cabal, nearly brought tears of commingled wonder and rage to his eyes.

Within all that vastness, but a scant few regions appeared to harbor the Cabal. Those same few insignificant dots harbored and risked so much.

Yip surveyed the scene slowly with deliberation. When his assessment was complete, he said, "You have uncovered a treasure of inestimable worth, Adar. This representation will be the map to our future." Pausing for a moment, thinking of the difficulties ahead, he continued, "If not ours, then the Aerya'ana's, the Home Guard's, the council's, the Dracodaerans', the Priests of K'un Lun, the H'era, and any other agents of Light that wish to join or follow us."

"If this map does not chart our future, and the Cabal remains elusive and intractable, then we must all continue to spread the tools of their defeat through the macroverse that these and other countless systems remain safe and free from evil's relentless shadow."

"This map must be shared, its information spread, that the roots of our enemy may be purged from the cosmos!"

Adar nodded, in reply. "We have come to the same conclusion as you. However, since the information contained with the alien command orb is rightfully yours we wanted to ensure that you shared our interpretation and deductions regarding the finding's import."

Aroganji gave his assent. "That we do."

"Then I will make certain you have a copy of this map for your navigational system as well as anything else we manage to uncover of interest prior to your departure. Furthermore, we will pass this information on to the Home Guard for dissemination through the proper channels. The Guard will see to it that others are contacted including the council, the Dracodaerans, the K'un Lun, the H'era, and the Aerya'ana that we may organize and coordinate our efforts. You will need to provide information regarding exactly who to contact within these or other groups prior to your departure that they may receive the information you request."

"May I tell you now?"

"You may." Adar bowed his head graciously as he spoke.

"This information should be shared with Éremon on the council, Eidelion among the Home Guard, Uuraja among the H'era, Master Wei among the Priests of K'un Lun, Alderan among the Aerya'ana, and

Raour'Saqan among the Dracodaerans. They are at liberty to share this information with any they see fit."

"The faster this information is in the proper hands, the better."

"I will see to it immediately!"

"Is there aught else?" Slate had a question for Adar before he left but wanted to make sure the matters of true import had been handled before he did so.

"That is all for now."

Seeing his opportunity, Slate asked, "How goes the technology transfer from the sphere itself?"

Understanding Slate's true intent, Adar laughed, replying, "If all continues to proceed as it has, you will be among the most wealthy in all of Tellanon before we are finished disentangling its contents."

Slate clapped his hands together with the reverberation of thunder. "That's exactly what I wanted to hear!"

"If that is all, good sirs, I will leave you now to see that your wishes are executed most expeditiously."

"That is all, Adar." Aroganji gave a low bow as a show of respect.

"We thank you and your associates for all they have done for us and the peoples of Ea'ae, Adar. May you know peace and joy all your days." Yip bowed as well.

"Your sentiments are mine. May you meet with success in the dark days ahead, friends."

"Goodbye, Adar." Wrindanneth released the veil that shielded them from eavesdropping with a broad wave of his arm.

As quickly as he had appeared, Adar vanished, one among many who labored so nobly to assure the world's positive future.

As the mantle of shadow fell away, Wrindanneth's eyes turned to the Guard arrayed before the entrance to Illdrassil's inner sanctum. Though their dispassionate gaze did not alight on the Four as the veil fell away, their gaze took in all that passed around them.

Walking toward the Guard boldly, Wrindanneth gave a looping bow and said, "Do not fear, gentlemen, for our noble intent was merely shrouded but for a moment from your beneficent gaze!"

The Guard, however, were not impressed. Their survey did not waver as Wrindanneth approached dramatically, his black robes flowing liquidly in his wake, followed by Slate, Aroganji, and Yip.

The Guard were, as always, eminent.

Resplendent in the early morning light, nine Home Guard were arrayed strategically around the entrance to Illdrassil's inner courtyard through the gate before them while several more patrolled the bulwark above.

Slate surveyed the Guard quickly, taking their measure as he approached. Although these were friends, he was alert and on guard should any unforeseen event arise. The Guard were formidable, to be respected, and never taken lightly.

Three of the Guard were solid Dwarves, armed with hand cannons strapped over their shoulders and great axes held at the ready. Their implacable line resembled an unassailable mountain face, fearsome and unapproachable. On their broad shoulders were the crystalline plate armor typical of the Guard, magical and impervious to almost any cause of harm. On their heads, they wore simple helms that would not impede their vision while their knotted beards spilled out from below. Each wore the insignia of his clan on his breast, a mark of honor for his kin and a warning to his foes.

Across from the Dwarves, three Elves stood in formation as well, elegant and at ease as though they had been in place longer than the stones on which they stood. Their armor was not that typical of the Guard, rather they wore the Witchwood of their people, the Aeryn Sh'al molded and shaped from living wood, fortified by enchantment, granted life by their hands and breath. The gleaming, variegated, and shifting hues of green, gold, and russet of their burnished armor caught and played with the sunlight as skillfully and richly as a maestro with sound.

At the far end of the tunnel, the last three Guard stood across the span at full attention. At their center stood a tall Man of broad shoulder and dark complexion, his skin as mysterious and lustrous as the night sky. In his hands he held a great red bladed halberd, the arch of its length as long as a sword, its haft as tall as a grown man. In his hands, this massive weapon appeared as light as a walking cane, as deadly as destiny.

Flanking him on either side were two unusual beings not commonly seen on Tellanon, though like many allied races they willingly sent their most able to join the Home Guard to serve and learn for their people's future security, prosperity, and edification.

On the Man's left was a massive reptilian, solidly built, that towered over him who was large by human standards. Though monstrous and imposing, this being stood with a grace and poise akin to the Elves in whose company it stood, belying its size with surety and facility. Its red eyes were considering and thoughtful, not the dispassionate mask worn by many Guard. At both its hips were great curved blue crystalline swords, larger than a claymore wielded by a Man, but of a size and scale of a scimitar for one of its awesome size.

This was the first Tyraethian Slate had ever seen though he had often heard of their prowess in battle.

On the Man's right was another being Slate had never seen in person, one he had only heard about by reputation.

Floating in the air was a cephalopodal creature suspended within a shimmering sphere, its large bulbous head covered in rough, leathery ochre skin. Depthless black pupilless eyes stared at them blankly as cool and unreadable as the void between the stars. Layers upon layers of thick, corded appendages dangled and wavered trailing languidly from beneath its massive cephalic dome. As he watched, the creature's skin shifted colors subtly, changing in response to some cue to which Slate was unaware.

A creature from a truly alien world, the Incirrinaen could see within their minds as easily as looking through glass, though it lidded its gaze out of respect for its company, at least until the situation warranted otherwise.

This motley assortment waited for their approach patiently— spiders at rest until the arrival of their next meal.

Slate shivered slightly at the unpleasantness of the thought. He, in no way, wanted to be either a spider or its prey. He was, however, quite proud that his fellow citizens of Tellanon cared enough about each other and life in general to not equate appearance with quality or worth for otherwise some of the city's finest representatives would not be welcome.

Smiling as the thought crossed his mind, he also immediately imagined Wrindanneth's reply should he voice such feelings. According to Wrindanneth, he was lucky the citizens of Tellanon were so accepting.

Without this acquiescence, he would not be welcome. The irony, of course, was that the same could easily be argued with regard to Wrindanneth, a point he would certainly explore in his own defense.

Laughing inwardly at his own thoughts, he appreciated the joys of friendship, even when that camaraderie was often expressed in opposition.

Turning back and looking at him quizzically, guessing that his mind was not in right order, Wrindanneth's brief glance only brought the laughter hiding behind his lips out.

Before the Guard now, their way blocked by the glimmering Witchwood blade of the foremost Elf and the savage blade of the first Dwarf, Wrindanneth refrained from a sharp reply to Slate's snicker. Instead, avoiding a scene, he directed his attention to the Guard blocking their progress. "Good sirs, we have business with Eidelion of the Home Guard and seek your leave to pass beyond this most august gate!"

From the back, the Man replied simply. "Hold your position until we confirm your business with Eidelion of the Home Guard."

Wrindanneth's flowery bow in reply was a study in mocking compliance. "As you wish."

No one moved while they waited for the reply. Expected though they were, Slate imagined the tension similar requests would instill among those waiting beneath the gaze of the Guard for those of tremulous heart.

This, too, brought a smile to his lips.

These situations were the ones he enjoyed most.

"Eidelion is expecting you." Before they moved forward, however, the faint tingling of energy upon their skins told them that they had been scanned, their identities, intent, and safety verified by the Construct.

The scan complete, the large man stood aside gesturing for them to pass through. As he did so, the Elves and Dwarves raised their arms in utter silence. Simultaneously, the Incirrinaen and Tyraethian moved aside as well.

The reptilian's gate was like water as he slid toward the edge of the passage. Its numerous tentacles moving languidly within its fluid medium, the cephalapodoid floated toward the other side of the passage through the crystalline wall. As it moved, its color shifted subtly until it was almost a perfect match to the surface of the wall itself.

"The ghost light will lead you to the chamber where Eidelion awaits." A pale blue light appeared before the Guard's outstretched hand.

"Thank you." Aroganji spoke before Wrindanneth could fire off another incendiary comment.

Wrindanneth strode through the passageway unperturbed by the axes and swords poised above his head. He had already moved his concern beyond the Guard who now let them pass.

Yip, however, was in the moment. Walking sedately behind his friends, he appreciated the majesty and diversity of the many races and beings, the various expressions of life, that visited Tellanon and were present within her Guard, all choosing to serve and grow together, their strength and multiplicity adding to Tellanon's own. That so many would travel so far to visit Ea'ae even now after his world had been depleted, her people now scattered throughout the macro-verse, spoke highly not only of the breadth and depth of knowledge that yet remained but of their quality and worth.

This representation also said much of Ea'ae's allies, their shared vision, and common cause. In the days ahead, there may be many across the heavens that would rally against the Cabal's tyranny. Together, they would find a way forward.

The ghost light hovered in the air before them for but a moment before drifting toward Illdrassil's massive, coruscating trunk.

Leaving the Home Guard behind, Slate reprimanded Wrindanneth for his antics to the Guard. His deep voice full of disapproval, Slate remonstrated, "Wrin, if ya'd acted any more scornful and suspicious, I'd reckon tha Guard might've taken ya in fer questionin' on tha spot! Have ya no respect, man?"

Wrindanneth shrugged and replied flippantly, not bothering to look over his shoulder as he addressed Slate. "Respect is earned."

"And tha Guard have not earned yer respect? If not those men, then what they stand fer?"

"No. Those men have not earned my respect. I do not care for what they stand for. I will not give my esteem to anyone for their position alone."

"Then ya only care ta stand alone, not fer those who would stand with ya!" Slate hit one armored fist into his palm as he addressed Wrindanneth's back. "If ya care naught fer their ideals or that fer which they stand, then ya care only about yerself!"

His tone unmoved by Slate's passion, Wrindanneth remained aloof and haughty. His reply lacked Slate's passion, but its message was clear. "Exactly."

His voice a deadly cool, Slate said, "Wrindanneth, ya're a supercilious carrion feeder!"

Glancing back casually, Wrindanneth replied nonchalantly, "And this is news to you?"

"Only until our work together is done."

Slate said no more. Wrindanneth may have his begrudging trust but he would have to earn back his respect. Otherwise, the fool would be left behind with the other offal and refuse discarded unwanted after battle.

"Get it together, gentlemen!" Although he did not approve of petty bickering, Aroganji would not tolerate disparaging the value of their relationships with each other. If they were to be a team and function as one, they must show and treat each other with decency and trust.

Furthermore, their mission held the utmost importance and responsibility. If they were to uphold the principles and vision intended by their quest, they must promote the highest ideals and act accordingly. To do otherwise would jeopardize their charge and undermine their purpose together.

Aroganji studied Wrindanneth as they walked beyond the walled entrance into Tellanon's heart. He understood Wrindanneth's difficulties—his desire to challenge authorities, his reluctance to trust, and his desire for independence—but his friend also needed the support of others to achieve the goals he desired, to realize his freedom, and actualize his potential. If Wrin disparaged his friends and allies, he would only harm himself and his aims.

Though neither Wrindanneth nor Slate turned to listen to either Aroganji or Yip as they were addressed, the words of reprimand were heard nonetheless. "Aroganji speaks truly. Remember why we are together before you seek to push us apart."

Realizing his temper had gotten the better of him, Slate opened his mouth to make a rebuttal and thought better of it. Lowering the hand he had started to lift to emphasize his point, he shut his mouth and walked on behind the wisp light. Saying more would merely exacerbate the situation.

Wrindanneth, however, did not hold his tongue nor did he break his stride to reply. "Our allegiance, whatever additional benefits it may have, is a matter of convenience. When these commonalities no longer bind us together, then we will part. Do not think otherwise."

Yip replied simply. "You are correct, Wrin. We are together because our goals are shared and our interests are aligned. If we are to remain together and accomplish that which we seek, we must also work together. Always and without exception."

"It is our role, each and every one of us, to determine who and what we need to be for us to succeed, to articulate and realize our shared and individual visions. Each of us can then work in concert to make that happen."

"Together."

Aroganji agreed. "Each of us has our own unique gifts and goals. The secret to our success has been and will continue to be utilizing them most effectively together for everyone's benefit. Good-natured joking, teasing, and taunting are welcome so long as our expressions of humor do not undermine these relationships."

The tension temporarily leaving his shoulders, for he was who he was and would not change willingly, Wrindanneth replied, "Shouldn't you have told me all this years back when I signed on?"

Aroganji laughed as he replied, "Would you have signed on?"

When Wrindanneth made no reply, Slate laughed as well. "There's yer answer!"

Though the strain yet lingered as they walked behind the ghost light through the luminescent grounds toward their appointment, it was no longer oppressive.

"If ya were ta tell me as a lad that such a place as this had been wrought by tha hands o' Man and Elf, Dwarf and Gnome, together, I would have thought tha dreams o' my youth had been made real."

Entering the innermost regions of Tellanon, walking directly below Illdrassil's overarching hyaline boughs—the morning sunlight dancing and arching across her limbs, molten vines descended directly from the heavens—Slate could not contain his wonderment. The majesty wrought on Tellanon surpassed the finest of the ancient works of the Dwarven masters—those marvels forged by sweat and steel, stone and will, in the bowels of the earth in days of yore by the finest of Brendle's chosen craftsman. "Now that I'm here an' have seen it with my own eyes, I still can't believe it! She takes my breath away and makes my heart soar!"

Yip laughed with Slate's delight as his friend's sentiments were his own. "The minds and hearts of Ea'ae realize their highest aspirations every day when they but try."

"Brendle himself would be proud ta call a place such as this his home!"

Yip laughed again. "Does he not?"

Sharing in Yip's laughter, Slate replied, "Aye. Aye, he does!"

Sunlight playing about Illdrassil's trunk only accentuated the vibrant energies flowing through her boughs, sheltered within her illumined forks and crevices. Yip wished to feel the diverse symphony of energies here more fully over an extended period of time. There was much he could yet learn contemplating in her shade as he had done with the Aeryn D'al.

Time was running short. Perhaps he could ask Eidelion for the opportunity to study beneath her branches before they departed.

Though she was silent, he also felt a slow, subtle sentience within her core. As Tellanon's center, she was the city's heart. But to his mind, she was also Tellanon's spirit.

Expressing these feelings to Slate who walked between Aroganji and himself, he said, "Perhaps Eidelion will grant me leave to stand in her shadow."

His ruddy cheeks aglow with good cheer, Slate retorted, "There are no shadows ta be had near Illdrassil!"

Yip watched the moving waves of light roiling across Illdrassil's surface, the energies moving beneath, and knew Slate was right. What amounted to shadows on Illdrassil were but varying degrees and patterns of light, ripples shimmering upon the surface of a luminous pond, condensate of rainbows.

Slate winked at Yip as he watched his friend's eyes rove slowly and appreciatively across the ethereal grounds. "Don't worry, Yip! I'll put in a good word fer ya! Eidelion won't deny me a favor!"

Yip placed one hand on Slate's back, the armor beneath his fingers warm to the touch. "Thank you, Slate. That would be most kind."

Yip could feel Eidelion and several other spectacularly brilliant Lights standing around him. Though he could sense where their destination laid, he relied on the ghost light to guide them through and across the convoluted pathways encircling Illdrassil. Otherwise, he would merely have a compass without reference to topography.

The ghost light took them around Illdrassil's massive roots, weaving in and about round her sumptuous gardens, eventually arriving at the far side of the celestial tree. In a small sheltered alcove, nestled between roots overtopped by trees encrusted in glimmering scales imparted with the color and radiance of gems, Eidelion awaited in animated discussion with the companions they would soon come to know.

Standing beside Eidelion beneath the boughs of the jewel-like trees, looking for all the world like a mirror image of his brother-in-arms from the Order of the Dalaren Ka, Maeven D'lanaran stood regally, his hand rested convivially on Eidelion's shimmering shoulder as they spoke. Armor spun of golden sunshine warded Maevan's strong shoulders and tall body. Across his back, a great claymore rested, its two-handed pommel visibly glowing a luminous white in the sun. This was the fabled blade Eyrdeas, the White Blade of Morn. Called Taliaerya, Morning's Light or Dawn's Light among the Elves, this blade was almost as storied as Eidelion's own.

Opposite Maeven on Eidelion's other side, Ruena O'reine, archmage and Holder of Secrets stood proudly. Though at first glance she appeared dressed in a simple, nondescript robe, her appearance, the force of her presence was anything but plain. About her head, her fiery red hair tumbled and roiled like clouds in a thunderstorm. Her robes moved and tumbled steadily in time with some hidden tide. Watching these hypnotic motions, she appeared to be drifting through some other medium, underwater perhaps, rather than through air.

The air around her crackled with anticipation of the expression of power.

In motion, studying the otherworldly trees and plantings as she wandered, her hands grazing across the surfaces of branch and bough as she walked around the alcove, Yrien Al'nori, the Anuvatali Uraera Al'on, moved in another time and place. About her in a shroud, an aura of quietude and stillness lingered, impressions that only enhanced her angelic glamor.

His regal countenance lost to them, for he stood between the Four and the Home Guard, Alderan, ambassador and lorekeeper of the Elves of Yenaria, stood sedately listening while the others spoke, his presence heightening Illdrassil's own.

Off to the side, standing perfectly still beneath the dancing shadows of a glimmering palmate tree, a nondescript human of average height and weight and an indeterminant age tarried patiently. So unworthy of note were its features that the eye passed over it at first glance, only recognizing and returning after realizing it was there after initial inspection. Even upon further examination, whether it was man or woman, young or old, was uncertain—questions left hanging in the air unanswered. This was EMMA, a NUMEN, a synthetic being representing the height of Paratechnological endeavor and capacity.

As animated as EMMA was still, Spreesprocket gesticulated excitedly from where he stood beside Alderan, his small hands painting the air with the vibrancy and spirit of his ideals. His clockwork armor moved and spun fluidly with him as he gestured, cogs whirring and spinning, gears turning, and levers shifting.

Together, they were a formidable band.

To Yip, watching this assemblage was a study in human achievement, the possibilities and fullness of human expression—physical, mental, and energetic—made real and tangible. The air around them thrummed with power and vibrancy, not only from Illdrassil but from the life force generated, stored, manipulated, and harnessed so eloquently by the living assertion of these beings.

Each was a study in the actualization of the possible.

Gesturing excitedly upon their arrival, his usual animation become even more enlivened, Spreesprocket waved them forward as he himself walked out to meet them. "Fists! Come! Come! Join us!"

"Yes! Join us!" Eidelion's face lit with pleasure at their arrival.

Slate strode forward with a broad grin on his face as he clasped Spreesprocket welcomingly, their two metal shod bodies meeting with an unnatural silence. "By Brendle's beard it is good ta see yer sorry mug!"

"By the Omnispark it is good ta see you as well!"

Patting Spreesprocket on the back, Slate said, "Well met and well received, my friend!"

While Aroganji, Wrindanneth, and Yip joined Slate greeting Spreesprocket, Eidelion said, "We received your missive from Adar. If it proves to be accurate, this news is most fortuitous. If we can root the Cabal out of their lairs, then the macroverse will be a much brighter place."

Though his optimism did not dim, a note of realism entered Eidelion's tone. "We can only hope that we will be able to move forward against our enemies on that front. With our forces on Ea'ae spread so thinly and barely able to hold our own planet's protected borders against the Cabal, mounting multiple attacks against their strongholds may be out of reach."

"Once we have reestablished the seals and our allies have resecured their defensive fronts on Ea'ae, then we may be able to begin pushing back against the Cabal beyond our borders. Depending on the strategy taken, this action may allow us to engage the enemy on several fronts."

"Regardless of how we ultimately choose to move forward, we will."

"Depending on the veracity of the coordinates provided by the alien command sphere, we may be able to enlist other allies from across the cosmos to focus their energies against the Cabal. If we can bring to bear the full strength of Men and Elves, Dwarves and Gnomes spread through the heavens in coordination with other like-minded races, then the Cabal will face a war it cannot win."

"If we are not able to move directly against the Cabal within short order, then we will yet provide the free people of the macroverse with the tools necessary to strike evil such as theirs from the heavens!"

"Those the agents of evil seek to destroy will ultimately become their undoing."

Yip bowed as Eidelion finished. "We are most honored by your pledge. It is ours as well."

Slate shook his head, getting matters back on point. "Before we go on killin' anyone or removin' any blights, we've gotta make sure Ea'ae's safe. Let's be about our business then and see that tha first step is accomplished!"

Eidelion nodded in understanding. "Agreed. Before we begin, let me introduce to you those companions with whom you have not yet had the pleasure to meet."

Smiling, Eidelion indicated Spreesprocket who yet remained standing with the Fists. "Spreesprocket you have met."

Slate groaned but smiled. "Unfortunately."

In reply, Spreesprocket punched Slate in the shoulder with one shielded fist. The two were like brothers who had, after long separation, been reunited and most easily showed their upwelling emotion through physical expression.

Ignoring Slate and Spreesprocket's sport, Eidelion went on, "And you have met Alderan as well."

Alderan spread his arms wide and gently declined his head. The gesture was as fluid and supple as the bending of a young branch.

Yip bowed respectfully, saying, "Your Light brightens our own."

Equally respectful, Alderan countered humbly, "Yours is a Light that enlivens and inspires."

Slate laughed good-naturedly. "Tha rest we know by reputation alone!"

Indicating the gallant knight by his side, Eidelion said, "As you are aware, this is Maeven D'lanaran, a paladin of my order. He is a Champion of Light, one who has proven himself mightily against the forces of Darkness. His constant sword and unyielding faith in the Light serve as beacons of peace and stability in times of trial."

Maeven bowed from the waist. "Well met, Fists. Mine is the pleasure of coming to know you."

Aroganji bowed in return, saying, "Ours is the joy of a new friend."

Indicating the woman by his side, Eidelion continued with the introductions. "May I present Ruena O'reine, one of our Keepers of

Secrets charged with preserving and maintaining Tellanon's lore and artifacts. Her skills in wizardry are without peer in her generation."

At this, Ruena laughed, the sound of her voice echoing and rolling like muted thunder, a sound as imposing as it was unlikely from one so small in stature. "What Eidelion neglects to tell you is that most of my generation passed thousands of years ago!"

Nodding in acknowledgement, Eidelion said, "Ruena has done much to preserve Tellanon during the many times of departure from Ea'ae. She has done even more to restore our strength after so many have left our shores."

"At your service." Though she bowed, there was no deference or yielding in the motion.

Bowing his head respectfully, Wrindanneth said, "We look forward to your guidance and insight."

Indicating the Anuvatali maiden wandering the recess behind them, Eidelion said, "It is my pleasure to introduce you to Yrien Al'nori. She is an Anuvatali Uraera Al'on."

Looking at Yip, he added, "She augments and manipulates energy very much like you, Yip. Hers is a rare and wondrous gift for in her presence, her companions are able to do more than they may have ever thought possible."

Perhaps yet to arrive, their presence unnoted, Yrien Al'nori continued her absent-minded study of the alcove's plantings.

Smiling as he declined his head, Yip said, "Ours will be the delight of continued discovery in the presence of one so blessed."

With Yip's words, the alcove warmed, the sensation of the sun returning after a long sojourn behind massed clouds overtook them. Though she remained in another time and place, this feeling of warmth, welcome, and good cheer radiated from Yrien.

Directing their attention to the nondescript person standing quietly to the side, Eidelion said, "Lastly, may I present EMMA, a NUMEN in Spreesprocket's service."

"She's my prize pupil!" Spreesprocket beamed with pride as he gazed upon EMMA's modest form.

"As a NUMEN, she is capable of a great many things. She will be an asset that cannot be underestimated."

"*I am glad to make your acquaintance.*" Though the words seemed clear to them, ringing through the morning air, a moment's reflection told them the voice echoed equally through the vaults of their minds.

Bowing once more, Yip said, "We are honored and humbled that you would choose to journey with us and share in our cause."

Ruena spoke for the assembled Home Guard. "The honor is ours. You have proven yourselves, done what many considered impossible, and brought attention to a danger many had long ignored but that even now threatens our world. We are in your debt."

Speaking for the Elves, Alderan said, "You have given more than any would dare ask. We simply offer our companionship and assistance in this time of great need."

Done with introductions, Slate asked, "What were ya so excited about before our arrival?"

Spreesprocket laughed. "It would seem we have been presented with some difficulty."

"Aren't we always?" Ruena's elemental voice washed over them with the authority of the ages.

By way of clarification, Spreesprocket said, "The good news is we are more efficient than we anticipated. Our synthesis of another seal has proceeded with much more alacrity than we originally calculated."

Maeven added, "There has been some discussion within the Guard as to how we may most effectively utilize our forces for the best interest of Tellanon, Ea'ae, and her people. Given this new development, there are those who feel that deploying a group such as ours alongside yours may be a missed opportunity."

"These voices have suggested that we deploy separately to place this new seal while you embark to restore the original."

Looking around to his companions, Maeven added, "Those gathered here, however, have pledged to serve and assist you in your efforts until such time as we are no longer necessary to your mission or you no longer wish to receive our benefaction."

Aroganji looked to Eidelion. "What are your thoughts in this matter?"

Eidelion spoke simply. "Perhaps you should share yours. Then I will share mine."

Aroganji looked to Wrindanneth, Slate, and Yip.

Yip spoke first. "We would not willingly turn away any who would offer us help. This view, however, merely represents our own concern and need."

"At issue is whether the people of Ea'ae would be better served by our forces united or separate, whether our missions would have a greater chance of success together or apart, and whether the time saved by separating would be worth the additional risk of being apart."

"With the new seals requiring only proximity for activation and replacement of the old, then we should be much safer and have an easier time apart than we would have previously."

Wrindanneth broke in, "The problem is, even being much safer, this does not account for the unexpected. With our luck there will always be trouble, something we hadn't accounted for in our plans and may have difficulty addressing."

Slate countered, "Neither does yer view account fer tha greater risk tha people o' Ea'ae may face with two groups o' their champions together should we both be lost ta a single event. Then tha people o' Ea'ae will be no better off'n before and will still be short two seals."

To which Wrindanneth replied, "It took a group of two of us to get the last seal placed. That was a risk we took gladly and one that resulted in success."

Slate retorted shortly, "When we made our plans fer tha last venture, we also didn't have tha Cabal razin' our homes, pillagin' our coffers, and killin' innocents and scoundrels alike!"

Aroganji looked to Spreesprocket and asked, "What guidance does the Construct have to offer given its intelligence and predictive capabilities?"

Spreesprocket did not hesitate. "Together, the Construct estimates we have roughly an eighty-three percent chance of success. If we do not go with you to Morowen, then the Construct estimates your chance of success at just over seventy-one percent."

Looking at the Guard, Aroganji asked, "And what of your chances if we are apart?"

Again Spreesprocket did not hesitate. "That depends on the destination chosen and who remains with us." Though Spreesprocket did not say it outwardly, the implication was whether or not Alderan would offer his assistance and whether he would be allowed to venture forth as well. "Given the majority of most likely scenarios, the Construct estimates the convergence of possibility for our success without your assistance at anywhere from fifty-four to ninety-two percent."

Wrindanneth nodded consideringly. "If correct, alone or apart, our odds of success appear quite favorable. Being apart may not hurt us, but"—he raised a finger to emphasize his point—"the Construct's statistics cannot and do not account for the unknown."

Spreesprocket shook his head. "Actually, they do with significant confidence. The algorithms and models utilized by the Construct do indeed provide highly reproducible predictive representations of the future that take into account the various outcomes associated with the unknown. We have proven this time and time again in our studies. Though we cannot say exactly what unknown events may occur we can predict likely outcomes."

He paused before adding, "The more unknowns, the more fluid the future."

Raising an eyebrow quizzically, Aroganji asked out of curiosity, "If we did not have the new type of seal, what would the Construct estimate our chances of success for our quest?"

Spreesprocket laughed darkly. "Together, in the teens. Apart much less!"

Wrindanneth's laughter was just as dark. "Then we were quite fortunate at Eldre'gheu indeed!"

Yip asked, "If we traveled apart, would it not be possible for one of our group's to join with the other upon the completion of their mission to help ensure the other's success?"

Spreesprocket nodded. "In addition to a return stone to Tellanon, we could have each ship carry one tied to the other."

Aroganji then asked, "And how much would this approach increase our chances of success?"

"Roughly five percent."

Wrindanneth spoke confidently. "Then there would be but nominal differences in our chances for success if we remained together."

Slate nodded. "While givin' tha people o' Ea'ae a greater chance fer overall attainment."

Aroganji had one last question. "Is this the optimal path in the Construct's estimation?"

Spreesprocket nodded reluctantly for his heart was with the original plan. "Without further augmentation or supplementation of our forces for each mission, or any other changes in current circumstances in our favor, then this appears to the most favorable option currently open to us to take."

Aroganji spoke to the gathered Home Guard and Alderan. "We'll just have to count on your timely completion of the restoration of your seal so that you can join us as originally intended!"

Slate concurred. "Then we can have it both ways! Yer help and greater chances of success!"

Yip spoke to their allies then. "Is this approach acceptable to you?"

Eidelion smiled and replied, "I think we are in agreement."

Alderan spoke in accordance. "The Elves of Yenaria will give their support to this and any other mission to restore Ea'ae's seals. We will also continue to offer our assistance in the recreation and refinement of the remaining seals."

Angling his head to the side and stepping backward diagonally with one foot behind the other in a bow that resembled the softness of an exhalation he added, "My commission, however, is to assist in a combined effort with the Home Guard and Fists. Without this convergence, another from among the Aerya'ana will be required to take my place with the Guard."

Looking to Aroganji, Wrindanneth, Slate, and Yip, he continued, "Should you wish it, Aerya'ana are ready to offer their service to your cause as well."

With a soft exhalation mirroring his bow, the only sign of emotion apparent as he spoke, Alderan finished, "The Elves will not risk more."

Aroganji understood. Though his wishes may be otherwise, Alderan was too important to the Elves to risk in a mission divided. Only a combined expedition with the Guard and Fists had allayed their concerns. Nor would the Elves venture too many on a single mission when others may be forthcoming.

Since he was a liaison between the Elves and Home Guard, the people of Tellanon and the Elves, a united mission was in natural confluence with his duties. Separated, others could be sent in his place.

Yip bowed respectfully. "The people of Ea'ae and beyond need the Aerya'ana to pursue their mission whether we meet with success or failure. We would be most honored if the Aerya'ana continued their efforts to cultivate their skills and increase their numbers for they will be much needed in the long days ahead."

"Whether from among the Aerya'ana or elsewhere within the Elves, I am certain that the assistance of the people of Yenaria will be most appreciated in securing the remaining seals, an expression of the continued bond shared with the Home Guard and people of Tellanon."

Alderan gave another open-armed bow. "As you wish, Anuvatar-i'aliana."

Wrindanneth nodded curtly, accepting the change in plans with aplomb. "We will leave as planned on the morrow. When will you be leaving and what will be your destination?"

Maeven spoke for the gathered Home Guard, replying softly to lessen the impact of his words and not seem unkind for such feelings were not in his heart. "For our safety and yours, along with the security of our mission, we cannot and should not say."

Wrindanneth's reply was simple and without emotion, accepting the reply. "Understood."

Spreesprocket stepped forward, emotions plainly visible in his eyes for he wished to accompany them more than words could express or his duty would allow. "I will make sure that you have a return stone linked to the Guard's ship so that you can join forces should you finish your quest first."

Aroganji bowed. "Thank you for all of your assistance, my friend."

Eidelion moved beside Spreesprocket, placing a caring hand on the Gnome's shoulder. "We will see you off on the morrow. Éremon will join us to give you the new seal."

"Going forward, so long as we are able, we will continue submitting our latest intelligence to your ship's command sphere to help guide your mission."

Eidelion sighed, his voice filled with sadness as he continued. "Our intelligence indicates that the *faerviage* portal nearest Morowen has been destroyed. This catastrophe took place as the Cabal pushed forward through Aruene and on to Morowen. The citadel and port of trade adjacent to this portal have also been decimated and all her citizens lost."

"Unfortunately, this also sets back your travel time by approximately one day for there are no other ports of call within a reasonable distance."

"So you will have a choice to make before you depart. You may fly directly over the ocean toward Aruene or you may *faerviage* to another location on the continent."

"The nearest remaining *faerviage* point is roughly equidistant to Morowen as the distance over the ocean, so the timing will be roughly the same."

"Should you choose to take the portal, the land over which you will fly is quite rugged and wild. We will ensure that you have the most accurate information possible regarding potential routes overland to inform your decision along with likely obstacles you may face on the way."

Wrindanneth accepted this guidance graciously. "Thank you for this, Eidelion. We only wish that you were all coming with us and available to discuss this information. Your insights will be missed."

Slate clasped Spreesprocket's forearm as he looked his friend in the eye. "As will be yer blades."

Spreesprocket replied earnestly, "Do not forget your emergency preparations and contingency spells! We wish to see you again as much as you wish to see us!"

Aroganji nodded seriously, offering, "If we are forced into a position that we cannot hope to win, I will cloak us in a spell that will return us home, ready to try again under more fortuitous circumstances."

Spreesprocket brightened visibly at these words. Though he would not now be going, he replied earnestly, "As will we."

Ruena spoke then, summing the feelings of her fellows, optimism and regret battling in her voice like opposing weather fronts. "We yet look forward to traveling by your sides. Do not forget that we will be reunited and that our missions will end contemporaneously."

Yip bowed. "You hold a place in our minds and hearts, ones that we will retain until we are reunited and able to complete our missions together."

Turning to look at his companions and gauge their standing, Eidelion said, "Is there aught else before we separate until the morrow?"

After a moment's silence, Yip spoke looking directly at Eidelion as he did. "If it is possible, before I depart, I would spend the evening in Illdrassil's shade."

A bright smile on his face, Eidelion laughed. "That is the least we could do!"

Bowing deeply in return, he said, "I thank you."

"You are most welcome. If I had known sooner, you could have spent many an evening beneath Illdrassil's boughs."

Yip smiled wryly, speaking softly as he did. "If I had thought sooner to ask, I might have."

Surrounded by laughter and smiles, the Four enjoyed the felicitous company of those who shared their burden before taking their leave, clasping hands and backs, sharing their good cheer and farewells, ready to make the most of their final day upon Tellanon.

Though the days ahead may be grim, in the company of friends, much could be made light.

ILLDRASSIL'S SHADOW

Fog laces the treetops
in downy white billows—
asleep and dreaming.

Yip waited behind while his friends parted. When they had finally departed, he gestured to Spreesprocket, calling the Gnome over.

"Would you walk with me?"

Spreesprocket smiled. "Of course."

With Spreesprocket at his side, Yip bowed to the remaining Home Guard. "Until next we meet and all after, may every breath be peace."

Éremon raised one luminous hand in reply. "May the Light be with you."

Bowing once more, Yip turned and left with Spreesprocket at his side and a half-smile on his face.

Their steps guided as much by the radiance of Illdrassil as the light above, the pair wended their way through the elysian gardens for some time in silence.

He was in no particular hurry to find a spot to spend the evening, enjoying the place and the quiet company as they walked side-by-side.

Spreesprocket was of like mind. Otherwise, the Gnomish proclivity for speech would have evinced itself long before.

Finally, Yip disturbed the tranquility with a question. "What can you tell me of NUMEN, Spreesprocket?"

His curiosity had been piqued by his brief interaction with EMMA when the NUMEN had called upon him unexpectedly.

Spreesprocket laughed. "More than you want to know, I would imagine!"

As the primary inventor of the sentient beings, Yip knew this was a fair answer. In fact, it was true. He clarified, "EMMA touched my mind briefly this night past. Out of inquisitiveness and kindness I would guess. That you have created a living thing rivaling any in complexity and beauty is a marvel."

"How was this done? What is their purpose? How many are there? What are their abilities? What is their nature?"

Spreesprocket nodded, compressing massive amounts of information into forms and structures suitable for the lay audience. "First, a brief point of clarification. NUMEN is the general name for a type of artificially created being. NUMEN actually stands for New Unified Mental-Energetic Noesis. So the NUMEN are magical intelligences created to address specific purposes, generally to go where the Construct cannot and do what the Construct and its Abstracts do not."

"The NUMEN were created by a Paratechnological team under my direction with the guidance of the Construct to extend the reach and breadth of our common understanding in our never-ending quest to deepen our knowledge of the macroverse. Each NUMEN is rigorously checked for internal consistencies and logic routines both by the Construct and by a suite of Paratechnologists' metamagical synthetic intelligences. In fact, the basis of the NUMEN's intelligence is a synthesis of the copied multi-dimensional abstractions of those of the various members of the NUMEN's Paratechnological creators."

"As to their numbers, the NUMEN are few thus far. Those that have been created have been dispatched upon their missions with great success. For instance, EMMA, the referential for the NUMEN that will be accompanying your partner team, is developing and refining a predictive model to map the ever-changing energetic flows of magical forces across Ea'ae's entire surface and the space beyond.

Not only will EMMA's work help show us where energy accumulates and why, her work already guides Tellanon's flight over Ea'ae, allowing us to optimize energy capture and storage. Furthermore, her research will help us identify any future energetic anomalies that, when detected, may be associated with high-risk events such as extradimensional incursions, mass loss of life, potential extinctions, and the like. More importantly, her work also guides any optimizations that may need to be undertaken to improve upon the energetic lattice providing extradimensional protection afforded by Ea'ae's network of seals."

"Before I moved forward with creating the NUMEN, well before we had finalized the ethical frameworks governing their behavior, had decided upon mission strategies and implementation schemes, or any other number of countless details associated with the NUMEN's development, I had one stipulation for my participation. If we were to attempt to create a new form of independent sentient life, should we succeed, then each NUMEN created should have volition in the same way that all other beings have volition. That is to say, should their original mission succeed, should we ultimately achieve whatever we originally desired as a result of their creation, should the NUMEN's own interests and motivations change, then each NUMEN would then have the choice to shape their own destiny."

"As a result of this choice, the NUMEN would be free to continue on working with us in a similar or entirely new capacity as they had prior to their mission completion, or, should they choose, find their own place in the universe just as other sentient races are able to do."

Yip nodded in appreciation for the pure compassion behind Spreesprocket's wish. "We should all have a choice."

Sharing the nod, Spreesprocket said, "They serve us well and selflessly. The NUMEN have every right to serve themselves."

"The NUMEN's capabilities are vast, far more extensive than typical for sentient races. NUMEN are capable of taking forms limited only by their own imagination, energetic capacities, and mass. Each NUMEN is capable of altering its function and augmenting itself. They are capable of working directly with energies and forces unconceived of by all but a select few. Their intelligence is immense, far beyond the normal, unaugmented human mind. Given their flexibility, the

NUMEN are able to learn, modify, and improve upon even this broad intelligence and their varied innate abilities."

Here he paused, smiling with a glimmer in his eye, his deepest pride and most heartfelt wonder. "They are also able to create and evince creativity."

"As such, given their reach and power, the NUMEN are governed by the highest principles—fostering life and potential for all, weighing the needs of the many before those of the individual, and striving for continued knowledge and understanding without causing detriment to the individuals and systems that they study."

"Given all they stand for and are capable of, have you shared with them the essence of the Dragon's Gate?"

Spreesprocket laughed. "You said EMMA contacted you."

This was not a question, so Yip merely remained quiet waiting for Spreesprocket to continue.

After a moment's pause, the Gnome continued, "You know that they are capable of reading minds, at least those that are opened to them. EMMA contacted you because she wanted to meet the one who had discovered something so glorious. She asked if she may seek out, 'the humanoid who bridged the gap between the infinite potential and the human mind' and 'first applied the principles of arising infinity to the potentialities of life's future against the rising tide of Darkness.'"

Scratching his chin in thought for a moment, Spreesprocket said, "You see, she, and I refer to her as a she merely as a matter of convenience given her name and referential preference, admires the creative inspiration that drove you to apply the skill of energy creation in an entirely novel way to thwart evil in its darkest manifestations. She respects that you learned something no human has ever lived through attempting to learn. These are principles that she herself tries to live by. That she studies the movement and flow of magical energies, what you call *chi*, the energy of life, makes this skill all the more relevant."

"So"—and here he laughed at himself—"the short, non-Gnomish answer to your question is yes, she has learned the skill directly from my own mind."

Giving a short bow, Yip answered simply, "Of that I am glad."

Responding with a nod, Spreesprocket continued with his exposition, indirectly explaining why EMMA would be proud to have the opportunity to embody and express Yip's discovery while also being deserving of the same privilege. "The NUMEN were created to be more human than human—more Gnomish than Gnomes, more Elven than Elves, more Dwarven than Dwarves, and more Man than Men. They have been created to be transhuman, the embodiments of our highest ideals and the manifestation of our most creative imaginings."

Yip smiled, his comment intended primarily to elicit Spreesprocket's response. "And yet you will let them go..."

"How else will they learn to fly?"

Bowing, Yip replied, "You have granted them the wings to realize your dreams, the dreams of us all, and their dreams to come."

"We can only hope."

If all Spreesprocket indicated were true and came to pass, the NUMEN would be welcome allies in securing the future, and inherent possibilities, for all beings across the greater macroverse.

The universe needed champions whether born or created.

Yip stood in a sheltered alcove at Illdrassil's root.

Their walk ended, Spreesprocket had left him some time ago.

The capacious vault of Illdrassil's vitreous trunk soared heavenward, upward and out of sight. The brilliant, overwhelming iridescence of afternoon described in her reaches, the twists and folds of her branches, had faded into the subtler radiance of evening. Her lustrous trunk, once dancing with the fiery orange and gold hues of mid-day, was now lit with the simmering pinks and purples of early evening.

Though day slowly shifted to night, time measured by gradual shifts in the tone and tenor of the light reflecting about him, the flow of energy moving through and around remained unaltered and unabated.

How many had stood in a similar position, staring upward in veneration at her awesome majesty?

How many had been afforded the privilege to experience her presence directly without impediment or supervision?

Would he ever have such fortune again?

He did not know the answers to these or a great many other similar questions, but he welcomed the opportunity nonetheless.

His was the obligation to make this, his last evening on Tellanon, time well spent.

Next to Illdrassil's trunk, he stood at the base of a primal cascade, a waterfall of unimaginable size and power. Focused living energy flowed upward and into Illdrassil on a scale that was incomprehensible. From within her trunk, her boughs and branches, power was both stored and redirected, a ceaseless process of movement inward and outward to and from the city she sustained.

Standing alongside Illdrassil's timeless origin rooted in the floating firmament of Tellanon, he was awash in what was the highest concentration of living energy on Ea'ae, a font of unequalled depth and quality.

Running one palm along her trunk, his hand scintillated with the warmth and vibrancy held in her heart. Tingling, his fingers passed through liquid lightning. This vast pulse guided, powered, and protected the single greatest city-state on the planet.

This same pulse had protected her city and its denizens from the Cabal's last assault as it had done against similar impositions many times in the past. Though he felt otherwise, he hoped this most recent was the last violent attempt on her shores.

If his life and duty did not call him elsewhere, he would willingly stay in this place for all his days, learning more of living energy, its movement, and manipulation in mere moments here than he could elsewhere over many lifetimes.

As his obligations now stood, he had but one night.

Placing a second palm on her trunk, Yip relaxed his arms and shoulders, knees and hips, letting his body settle into Illdrassil through the connection of his hands. Though he did not need to touch her trunk to feel the fount of life flowing through, within, and around her colossal form, he welcomed the sensation, the joining nonetheless.

Power vibrated through his body, churning around his hands with the combined relentlessness of a tidal wave and the subtlety of moonlight. Just as he relaxed into position, he relaxed into and out of himself. With each inhalation and exhalation, his awareness expanded, self falling away into unfiltered awareness.

This awareness floated in a boundless sea of energy.

There was nothing else.

The limits of identity forgotten, his sentience skimmed across vast energy currents unclouded by physical sensation and misapprehension.

Time passed.

He knew not how long for he was adrift.

Only, after a time, he noticed a gradual shift, as one notices the slow setting of the sun through the changes in the qualities of the day—its light, permutations, and reflections—eventually becoming too noticeable to ignore with the steady transition to night.

Though he yet remained drifting within the incomprehensible sea of living Light, more and more he plumbed its depths. This transition was not conscious, as his experience of the living energy continued to expand and flow, moving with it through and across the city, he was allowed greater freedom to experience its depths and wonders, its tributaries and source.

Illdrassil was gradually opening her currents to him!

A world unfurled to him then, one he had never envisaged or thought possible.

Tellanon spread before him, his own heart, a pulse that moved through and within, a vibrancy that was inseparable from himself. This living principle moved within every bit of *chi* shifting through the city, a layer of living awareness hidden within the wellspring of life expressed and made possible as it reinforced and was strengthened by so many living beings.

Awash in indescribable radiant Light, his bounds long forgotten, he shared time and space with a vast sentience that merged and commingled with his own, an awareness that lay behind, within, and beneath the entire city, one that contained and was guided by the living expressions of Tellanon and her citizens, one so expansive that it held and contained the Construct and all its components as one small aspect of its being, one that fostered and protected the many Lights of its denizens, a being of pure compassion and selflessness, one he had never known existed.

So amazed was he then that he almost came back to himself, snapped back into corporeal existence by wonderment.

Composed and relaxed, this urge, too, slowly faded.

His limitations and failings insignificant in the face of this presence, he abided in peace and joy.

Letting this bliss pass, awareness of self and other faded and space filled with quietude.

Noting the warmth of a new morn on his skin and a bright, subconscious smile on his face, Yip knew that his time with Illdrassil had passed.

The loose light of dawn flitted upon Illdrassil's glassy surface as he opened his eyes. An entire evening had passed in absorption.

Smiling, he patted Illdrassil's trunk thankfully, filled with gratitude for the time he had been allowed and the experience he had been granted.

If he were to triumph over the Cabal, his thoughts and intent, actions and aim must be so subtle as to avoid detection—fleeting, elusive, and pervasive.

Illdrassil would be his model and guide in this, a presence simultaneously undetectable and all-encompassing.

That he had missed Illdrassil all this time only told him how much more he had yet to learn and how far he had yet to go.

Placing his hands on Illdrassil's trunk once more, in expression of his deep and abiding appreciation, he opened himself up to the presence within her otherworldly form, sharing what little he could of himself.

From his humble beginnings and training at the monastery to his journey across the continent to find allies to stand against the Cabal, nothing was held back. He shared his impressions, shortcomings, and limitations as well as his insights, joy, and wonder at the discoveries he had made along the way. He shared his failings and foibles along with his goals and aspirations. He shared their triumphs from across Ea'ae and beyond along with their defeats and losses. From knowledge of the Dragon's Gate to simple impressions of moments, no part of him was held back.

Though these sensations and experiences were inconsequential to such a timeless presence, he gave of himself because nothing had been asked of him while so much had been given.

Finally dropping his arms, prepared to leave Illdrassil at last, he turned on his heel and walked away.

Dawn beckoned and with it obligation and duty.

Flying through the air above the waking city, mere minutes from home and his friends, Yip gazed downward upon the city that had welcomed them, made them one of its own, and now called upon them to help safeguard its future.

The organic beauty of Tellanon always captivated him, a place that had somehow grown out of the living rock in all its convoluted, mellifluous harmony.

Tellanon was a place where dreams were realized, journeys begun, and the insights of visionaries could be expressed freely. He was no different for he had freely partaken of its riches, glad to find a sanctuary amidst the troubles pursuing him and a focal point from which to operate.

Now he must part once more.

Alert, despite his ruminations, he sensed another presence then and stopped in place, his examination interrupted, the refreshing air of morning whipping gently about him as he held position and waited for the response he knew would come.

He felt a slight pressure on the periphery of his consciousness that he knew at once to be EMMA. The light brushing along the edges of his mind was EMMA's equivalent of gentle a knock on the door requesting him to open up and talk.

"Yes, EMMA?" He let his inner smile fill the space between them as he opened his mind.

The vast openness of EMMA's awareness spread out before him, a crystalline panorama of a mountain range viewed from the vertiginous crest of the highest spires.

Slowly, carefully his mind filled with thoughts, impressions, and images of EMMA's interactions with Spreesprocket when he instructed her in the ways of the Dragon's Gate. Most interesting was Spreesprocket's indirect experience of his own mind mirrored through the lens of two different sentiences transmitting the knowledge he had gained on generating the energy of life—facets reflected through multiple mirrors.

EMMA spoke in his mind fastidiously, her words mirrored through him with gentle concern and unmitigated curiosity. She offered a simple explanation for seeking him out. *"I had hoped to have the opportunity to speak with you at length on our journey."*

His mind filled with inner joy, Yip replied in kind, *"I still look forward to that time."*

"As do I."

There was a moment's pause before EMMA spoke once more, her words filled with a cautious reluctance, a combination of reticence and concern. *"On the chance that this time does not come, may I ask a few questions of you prior to your departure?"*

"You may." He nodded instinctively though he understood EMMA was nowhere nearby to see his response directly.

Despite the expansiveness of EMMA's mind, her questions were gentle and directly put after the multitude of images and impressions regarding the Dragon's Gate had filled his mind. Her questioning was filled with inquisitive curiosity and a genuine desire to learn, to understand his perspective.

"What are your thoughts on the Dragon's Gate?"

"What does the expression of this energy mean?"

"What is the process by which it unfolds?"

"What is the mechanism through which it is performed?"

"What is its principle of operation?"

Yip knew, first and foremost, that EMMA's understanding of magical theory was far beyond his own. The knowledge contained within EMMA's mind represented the summation of Paratechnological thought spanning magics and ideas developed and cultivated across the cosmos over millennia.

His knowledge reflected the direct experience of one mind given direction from a single tradition over a single lifetime. Though he could have revealed his mind to EMMA directly, letting her experience his understanding as she had done with the knowledge of the Dragon's Gate through Spreesprocket, as he had done with Spreesprocket in turn, he chose instead to engage her via dialogue. In this way, she would internalize his thoughts through her own, drawing her own conclusions, learning, and deriving new understanding through the lens of her mind without being colored indirectly by his once more.

He responded thus. *"There are many ways to see, experience, and understand reality. Each truth is a lens through which the perspective of the mind, the portion of reality encompassed, is absorbed and understood."*

"Reality can be viewed as an ever increasing crystallization of the poten-

tial, the actualization of the possible. From the formless void of unlimited potential, Wuji, the great Tao of creation, springs forth the ineffable, unbounded totality of existence, Taiji, the source and wellspring of all things. From the fertile ground of the Tao springs forth the yuan-chi, the pure energy of possibility. From this celestial energy given expression through the immeasurable, emerge all the ten thousand things, all the varied realms of existence, in ever increasing complexity and concreteness as the potential becomes the actual."

> "Sea foam floats drifting
> on the swell's roiling surface—
> potential made real."

"Opening the Dragon's Gate, uniting with the primal, connecting with this origin through mind and intent, awareness ignites the formless source of Creation in a blazing fount of celestial Light."

Yip's silence indicated the completion of his response.

EMMA joined Yip in stillness for some time before she replied simply, pausing for a time between each statement. "Thank you for sharing the framework of your belief."

"Thank you for your openness."

"Thank you for the insights that made this experience and its attendant applications possible for so many."

Bowing as though EMMA stood beside him and he were on land and not floating in the sky high above Tellanon, he said, "You are more than welcome."

"I look forward to speaking with you again."

"We need only complete our missions and the time will come."

There was a moment of quiet before EMMA replied, "Until we meet again."

"May you shine with the Light that burns within."

Unexpectedly, a blinding flash of light entered his mind, washing out his vision of the sky and Tellanon below but for an instant and then was gone. Along with the light's passage, EMMA disappeared.

Blinking his eyes in an effort to restore his vision, attempting to recover as he would if he had stared overlong at the sun, he waited a moment before flying onward once his sight finally cleared.

Only then did he realize that something was different.

Something more had happened than temporary blindness.

He just did not know what.

Spiraling downward toward home, he let this concern go as there would be many more in the days and minutes ahead.

"Look what tha Dragon drug in!" Slate stood by the front door to their cottage ready to be about their business for the day—the short trip to the docks, meeting with Eidelion, any last minute changes in plans, their subsequent departure, and whatever excitement was to come after they flew from Tellanon's shores.

As Yip approached after landing, Slate continued, "Ya're a crafty one, Yip. Ya missed all tha fun o' Aroganji's lists, tha organizin' o' gear, tha last minute adjustments, and tha attendant arguments!"

Slate laughed. "I hope yer time was well spent."

Yip regarded his friend warmly. "By the sound of it, yours was more exciting!"

Squinting at his friend skeptically, trying to glean the full measure of Yip's story with a glance, Slate grumbled, "I doubt that!"

"Are ya ready?"

Now it was Yip who laughed, lifting his arms for examination. His robes hung loosely by his sides. His small kit was slung across his back. "Am I missing anything?"

Slate shrugged, not needing to examine the state of Yip's material possessions for they were too few and unremarkable to bother with an accounting. What little he had that had been of interest he gave away almost as soon as he got it. "Ya've got a point there. Ya can carry all yer belongin's in tha palm o' yer hands."

Resting his hand on Slate's shoulder briefly, Yip said, "I would not have it any other way."

As those words passed from his lips, he staggered as a second flash of brilliant, disorienting light blinded him.

Vaguely, from some faraway place, he heard the words, "Are ya all right, Yip?"

Slate.

At the same moment, a flood of words, feelings, and impressions washed over him.

Slate?

Yip?

It was then that Yip knew just what had changed.

Apparently Slate knew as well.

What're ya doin' in my head?

Slate, I do not know.

Ya mind gettin' out?

Certainly.

Yip was stunned, confused, and concerned.

How had this happened? Was this a gift from EMMA? Had EMMA altered the workings of his mind during their brief encounter? Had simply interacting with EMMA in that way opened a nascent ability of which he was unaware? Had EMMA extended his natural empathetic awareness in a manner he had never thought possible?

Had his consciousness been somehow altered by his interaction with Illdrassil? Thinking back briefly, he did not think this telepathy was resultant from his connection with Illdrassil but he could not be certain of that either.

Regardless of its origins, how long would this last? Was it a permanent change? What was the extent of the ability?

These questions and others passed fleetingly as he quickly recovered himself and returned his attention to his friend.

"My apologies, Slate. I had no intention..."

Slate cut in before he could finish his apology. "Bah! Think nothin' o' it! Seems ta me ya certainly had more o' interest goin' on than decidin' whether ta fly over land or water!"

Yip smiled, still noncommittal, letting his internal questions determine their course unhindered. "You could say that."

"Ya'll have ta say more'n that in tha days ahead!"

He laughed. "For you, Slate, I will!"

Slate nodded approvingly, "I'm countin' on it."

The door opened behind Slate and Wrindanneth emerged followed shortly thereafter by Aroganji.

Wrin gave a short approving nod and said, "Your timing couldn't be better, Yip! Let's head to the docks."

Waving his hand toward the door, Wrindanneth cast a complex protective incantation before leaping into the sky.

In his wake, the Abstract's accommodating voice called out to them as they all joined Wrindanneth and took to the air. "Be safe, Fists! Do not fear! I will ensure all is in order in your absence!"

Though the Abstract could not be seen, Yip could feel its amorphous presence as he launched upward. Waving kindly as he flew away, he gave the Abstract one last acknowledgement before departing.

The flight to the Scimerian Gate was over before it began. Though the day was yet young, the city grew busier and busier as they approached the docks.

Much in the way of goods and trade merely changed hands on Tellanon, destined for ports of call across Ea'ae and the far reaches beyond, without ever residing within her bounds. The level of activity along Tellanon's periphery reflected this movement. Ships landed and took off with the ordered precision of military formations. Cargos moved and changed hands frenetically. Merchants and emissaries haggled and bartered wherever they could find room.

Though a considerable portion of this business was accomplished by magic, almost as much was done by the force of hand and back to avoid any trickery or other obfuscation for there were many who could not afford the facility of Tellanon's efficient magical and Paratechnological systems. Though magic moved parcels on, off, and between most vessels, laborers yet grunted on some ships, pulling against ropes, hoisting cargo, and securing valuable goods.

This teeming mass of activity swirled about the party as they stepped through the shimmering protective disk of the Scimerian Gate, leaving behind the sedate world of Tellanon for the turbulent mass of seething energy that was her docks.

With any luck, one day soon, they would be able to walk back through that same Weirding Gate.

Making their way down the winding stone walkway, they wended through and around caravans, convoys, diplomatic missions, tourists, tradesman, and many others besides as they moved toward the *Shrike*'s alabaster sails.

Though they appeared to move empty-handed, between them Aroganji, Wrindanneth, and Slate carried as much gear as many of the smaller caravans, strategically hidden away as it was in their magical compartments and devices. What they did not carry on their persons had already been requisitioned and sent ahead to the *Shrike*'s hold. Unencumbered, they moved easily through the swirling din without trouble or delay.

Finally, after a few short minutes surrounded by the quay's activity, they reached the *Shrike*'s berth and with it the awaiting Home Guard.

Looking as she always had, despite all her augmentations and improvements, the *Shrike* appeared nondescript—a simple sailing vessel moored among many wondrous and alien ships that could not hold a candle to her flame.

Before her gangplank, waiting patiently for their arrival, stood Éremon, Eidelion, Daerdros, Spreesprocket, Alderan, and Adar. Representatives of the Home Guard, Protectorate, Paratechnologists, and Elves all come to see them off in safety and honor.

Standing above his fellows in stature, his lightning eyes shimmering with joy at the sight of them, Éremon opened both robed arms widely at their approach. "Lo! The Fists have come!"

Wrindanneth stifled a chuckle. "None of that! We're just doing a job. Nothing more!"

Slate nodded, saying politely, "We're honored ya came. There's no need fer any theatrics." Indicating Wrindanneth with a nod of his head, he added smiling, "We have enough o' that with tha travelin' Maeth Onai thespian dramaturge."

Eidelion, Spreesprocket, and Daerdros laughed while Wrindanneth scowled.

Continuing, Éremon said, "You have come before us on this auspicious day to set out once more on a mission of critical import to the free peoples of Ea'ae. We are honored to call you friends and colleagues, champions and paragons."

Reaching into his long robes, he brought forth a small wooden case. "Within this chest is a seal. With it, you carry Ea'ae's hopes and future. Use it wisely and guard it with your lives."

Taking the seal from Éremon's hands, Yip replied, "On our lives and honor we will do this for the people of Ea'ae and the world yet to be."

Eidelion spoke then. "Your works and deeds will not be soon

forgotten. You will always have a home in Tellanon, so long as you wish it. Return in safety and success! Go forth and come home cloaked in the Light's grace!"

Daerdros addressed them next. "You go forth with honor and this pledge. You are not alone. Others work with you and will achieve the aspirations you envisaged upon first taking up this quest."

Alderan gracefully declined his head. "The life you lead is yours and yours alone. Treat this gift carefully and with prudence for as it grows, so do you, as it prospers, so do your fellows. You have the blessing of the Elves. Return home as you left, as friends."

Adar, too, spoke of what was and what would be. "You are accoutered well and guided by the best information we have to offer. Know that we will, as ever, make use of the gifts you have given, the secrets you have uncovered, and strive to realize the highest vision possible for all those who would seek it."

Spreesprocket laughed self-consciously as his companions finished for he did not have any departing speech or high-minded words prepared. "I bid you well. I only wish that I could take part in this journey with you."

"I will see you once more upon your safe return!"

"Thank you for these kind words and all you have done on our behalf." Aroganji bowed to those gathered standing before the *Shrike*.

Yip spoke next. "Our quest will not be realized with the restoration of this seal. There is more yet to be done and more we will do."

Indicating the *Shrike* with a nod of his head, Spreesprocket offered, "The *Shrike* has been outfitted as we discussed. She is as ready and able as any ship in the yard. She will serve you well as do we all."

Wrindanneth declined his head, unexpectedly speaking genuinely and with humility. "Thanks to you, Spreesprocket, along with Gideon and the other Paratechnologists for all you have done to expedite the *Shrike*'s improvements. Without your dedication and extraordinary efforts, our timely departure would not be possible."

"In these times of troubles, this chance will prove invaluable."

His cheeks glowing a ruddy pink, Spreesprocket bowed in slight embarrassment. He never felt comfortable taking compliments despite the many he received and the many more he deserved. "The people of Ea'ae thank you."

Eidelion opened his arms as he spoke, holding forth another small parcel. "Should you finish restoring the seal and remain in a position to assist in the efforts of the Home Guard and Elves on their mission, use this return stone to join with them on their journey. Otherwise, they will rendezvous with you upon completion of theirs."

Wrindanneth stepped forward and took the parcel from Eidelion. With a brief sleight-of-hand, he whisked the return stone into his sleeve, gone as if it had never been.

Aroganji replied to Eidelion with a question. "If we succeed in our task and are able to join with the Guard, should we be able to communicate with Tellanon, will you tell us of their appointed task that we may know how best to help?"

Eidelion gave a short nod. "Once you are in a position of safety, we will apprise you of all mission critical information."

Spreesprocket added, "The improvements to your ship's command sphere should allow communication from almost anywhere on Ea'ae so long as there is not some form of interference."

Aroganji bowed. "Thank you."

"Are we ready ta split some heads or do we wanna stay here and pat each other on tha backs all day?" Slate had had enough talk. He looked forward to getting on an airship about as much having his teeth pulled but all this yammering had to stop.

Wrindanneth laughed. "Far be it from me to want to pat you on the back!" With a nod toward those assembled to see them off, he strode across the gangplank in four long steps.

Thumping his chest with one gauntleted fist, Slate barked, "May our destinies cross once more before we are reunited in tha fires o' Brendle's forge!" Trundling forward, he clasped forearms with Eidelion and Daerdros, grabbed Spreesprocket in a firm bear-hug, and then nodded cordially to Éremon, Alderan, and Adar. Then he marched across the gangplank without looking down toward the dizzying reaches below, his fear of heights long since forgotten.

Aroganji raised a hand in farewell. "We will keep you apprised of the situation as best we can, if we are able. Until next we meet, may you be as you are now—happy and in good health."

Walking forward sedately, he, too, boarded the *Shrike*.

Yip examined each of their friends and allies remaining with him on the docks in turn. The majesty and diversity of their *li*, the pinnacle of potential represented in their expressions, the overflowing upwelling of Life he felt emanating from each of them, were testaments to both the beauty of life's unfolding and the achievements possible for those who lived it.

If this were to be the last time he saw them, he could leave gladly knowing that he had been given more than he had any right to accept by their simple presence.

Bowing simply and in silence, he left as he had come.

ARUENE

Nacreous bright blue,
unbroken ocean expanse.
Orange sunset tinges
a distant island with fire.

Tellanon drifted away behind them swiftly, its activity and vibrancy fading in the distance like the setting of the sun—swift and implacable.

Their gathered friends had vanished much more quickly, blocked by the activity of moving ships well before passing through Tellanon's protective shield. They all had stood observant and at full attention while the *Shrike* drifted out of sight, respectful of the Fists, the risks they took, and desirous of a successful outcome and safe return.

Long after the city vanished, Yip yet felt the tug of Tellanon's wondrous vibrancy.

Speeding westward, the lush hillsides of western Dharia, the grasslands and forests of Var'Kera, rolled in all directions as far as the unaided eye could see. Though home to many kingdoms, the land below was wild and unsullied, witness both to the care of its many denizens and the restorative powers of magic. At times, vast herds of many different compositions passed beneath the ship, grazing or sprinting through the *Shrike*'s abbreviated shadow, gone too quickly to appreciate overlong.

Comprehending the difficulties to be faced ahead, no one was in the mood to talk for some time after their departure just as they had been reserved in their farewells. Traveling without the Home Guard, the ship was much emptier, much quieter, than it had been. The absence of the activity of so many was made more apparent by the stillness laying heavily upon the deck.

Though they would quickly get used to traveling alone once more, their friends were indeed missed.

Slate was the first to break the contemplative quietude.

Clapping his heavy hands together, he remonstrated, "All right lads! Enough o' tha gloom and doom! We've got a long road ahead, one we might as well do our best ta enjoy while we can!"

From where he stood at the helm enjoying the feel of the *Shrike*'s improved handling, speed, and sensitivity, the experience amplified by his merger with the augmented intelligence of the ship, Wrindanneth said, "And what would you have us do? Sing songs?"

"If ya wish!" Slate opened his mouth fully to begin belting out a ribald Dwarven chorus.

Before he could start, however, Aroganji interjected, "How are you enjoying the *Shrike*'s refinements, Wrin?"

Wrindanneth's dour expression brightened visibly. "If she was an extension of myself before, now I am an extension of her! I feel more in tune, more able, more connected, if possible, to her than I ever did. She moves at least thrice as fast cruising as she did at top speed before the improvements. I sense farther, feel deeper, and know more while doing less."

Sounding more like a giddy child than their saturnine friend, he continued, "If I could change anything, it would be for these upgrades to have happened sooner!"

Deducing as soon as they left Tellanon's docks without porting via *faerviage* that they would fly west over water, Yip asked, "Given our current speed, how long do you anticipate our journey to Morowen taking?"

"Flying overnight without stopping, we should cross the Ayle'ine Sea in a day. Morowen should be another day's flight from there."

Smiling, he added, "Prior to the *Shrike*'s enhancements, this same journey would have taken us over two weeks."

Yip nodded. "We are indeed fortunate to have received such gifts."

Slate interrupted with a hoarse laugh. "Now tha Cabal'll have less time ta crawl under their rocks as we hunt 'em down!"

Aroganji shook his head. "They crawl too quickly and are too good at finding crevices for us to give them any time whatsoever. I fear for the results with the time they have been given while we waited."

"Cancer without treatment spreads quickly."

"We will be the cure." Aroganji looked firmly and resolutely into each of their eyes as he finished.

"Tha fire that burns will be tha one that heals!" Slate ground his teeth eagerly in anticipation. The thought of unleashing the Daerdaana'Duin on the Cabal and their ilk filled him with a heady mixture of heat and excitement, a spark ready to blaze.

Fleshing out the plans he missed while at the seat of Illdrassil, Yip asked, "Will you stay awake and fly overnight or allow the auto-pilot to navigate?"

Wrindanneth indicated the ground at his feet. "Though I could use a spell to stay awake, I would prefer to have my energies available for other uses. I will sleep at the helm."

Yip was glad his friends had decided on a sea route to Morowen.

From what he apperceived based on the intelligence most recently gathered on Aruene, flying over the ocean was by far the safest option. Though they would cross overland to ultimately arrive at Morowen, their flight inland would be much shorter over the continent than if they had *faerviaged* directly to Aruene. With a shorter overland flight, their exposure to any unknown perils would be minimized as the relative risks of flying over the ocean were significantly less.

Of course, the danger of any voyage lay not in what could be but rather in what was actually encountered. Whether theoretically safer or not, one chance encounter over the ocean could make the route they had chosen more deadly than one taken over Aruene.

Risk was relative and their journey was relatively risky.

"What do we know of the route overland?" Yip had accessed the intelligence provided by Eidelion prior to their departure. Though there was much information of historical importance, little material had been available regarding current risks between Morowen and the sea.

Wrindanneth replied matter-of-factly, "At one time, there were many scattered villages and townships but those were destroyed long ago as the Fyrskal's evil spread across the land. What few settlements remained in the region existed largely on the margins of the continent. Those were destroyed by the Cabal's advance."

"The northeast corner of Aruene is now an abandoned wasteland, home to memories, ghosts, and whatever abominations are fit to survive in such a place."

Yip understood all this so he clarified, "What of the Cabal? How are their forces located there? In what numbers and arrangement? Have they taken up any permanent positions within the area? What might we expect in the days ahead?"

Wrindanneth nodded in apprehension. "From what Tellanon has gleaned, no permanent positions have been taken though many ships appear to have discharged extradimensional hostiles across the continent. These roving monstrosities only add to an already perilous situation."

"Beyond the horrors they have let loose on land and sky, many ships have moved on Morowen, as they have on other seals. Absolute numbers are hard to come by but the current estimates are in the hundreds of warships for Morowen alone. This estimate does not include ancillary and minor vessels."

"By tha black Abyss that's a force ta be reckoned with!" Slate shook his head. His mind filled with images of the sky blackened out by an armada of inimical warships, support ships, minor vessels, and attendant forces.

Wrindanneth nodded gravely. "There are probably many more and those are just the ships directed toward this one seal. We are indeed fortunate to have a replacement seal in hand that will let us move in and out of danger quickly along with the necessary stealth systems in place to help us avoid confronting so many massed forces."

To keep this information in perspective, Wrin added, "Remember, the seal of Eldre'gheu stood against many forces marshaled over time after its fall into the hands of Darkness. Whatever lies within

Morowen's heart has, at least based on Tellanon's most recent evaluation, managed to keep the Cabal at bay."

"This will be to our advantage. We have but to seize the opportunity."

"The Cabal has established a defensive perimeter of roving ships around each of their primary loci of activity. The density of these ships increases toward the focal point of their mission."

"This trend is true for Morowen. We are likely to encounter few, if any, ships as we hit land. As we delve deeper into the continent, the likelihood of encounter will increase exponentially."

Wrindanneth grinned roguishly, enjoying the challenge. "Across Ea'ae, the Cabal has faced much resistance and their numbers have suffered. Here, however, with so few to defend against their incursion, their fleet remains relatively strong."

Slate snorted. "So, as usual, we get tha worst o' it!"

Wrindanneth's evil grin did not waver. "Or the best of it depending on your view."

Slate shook his shaggy head in disbelief. "Ya're as crazy as a starved Vöer, Wrin."

Pausing reflectively for a moment, Slate amended, "A rabid, unclean Rock Troll."

"With an overbite and a particularly nasty case o' scabies."

Tapping his chin thoughtfully, he mused, "And horrific mouth rot."

Before anyone could reply, Slate raised his index finger with emphasis and added, "We can't forget tha open pustules. Lots o' open pustules."

His voice brimming with sarcasm, Wrindanneth replied, "That's about the nicest thing you've said about me, Slate. Thanks!"

Nodding perfunctorily, Slate said, "Think nothin' o' it!"

His face now expressionless and his voice flat, Wrindanneth replied, "Don't worry, I won't."

Getting back on subject, leaving his friends' argument to their memory, Yip inquired, "Once we reach Aruene, how do you propose we proceed?"

Following Yip's train of thought, Aroganji said, "Going directly inland from the east once we make landfall would be the most obvious choice and the one most expected by the Cabal."

As he spoke, Wrindanneth summoned forth a representation of Aruene from the ship's navigation system. A large, irregular continent appeared within the expansive waters of the Ayle'ine Sea. Far to the south, it was bordered by multiple island chains. Its western perimeter held many large bays and peninsulas. Its northern reaches were littered with glacial lakes and high, forbidding mountain ranges. Its eastern coast, closest to Dharia, presented a largely unbroken arch of stone, rocky crags, and desolate plains.

Only the south and west appeared lush and green. The rest of the continent appeared arid and sere, composed of vast plains, deserts, and rocky wastelands.

"However, approach from the east would also be the most expected as Dharia is both the nearest and most populous neighboring continent."

Drawing a line from the eastern coast and Dharia south and west, Aroganji offered, "I propose we approach from the south where we may be able to move under cover of clouds and take advantage of what may be the weakest point in the Cabal's perimeter."

Wrindanneth, however, disagreed. He drew a line to the northwest instead. "I think the northern route is the most propitious. Our advance would take advantage of the mountains and rough terrain of the region. We could fly overtop the peaks and drop into valleys as needed for cover and to elude any potential pursuers."

Slate examined the image carefully before speaking. "Tha west would be tha best approach but 'tis too far and we cannot spare tha time. Though tha south has tha potential advantage in weather systems, 'tis more open than tha north. Tha north, ta me, seems ta present tha best course. Should we need ta advance or retreat, we'd have many paths ta choose from and tha advantage o' protective cover."

Yip recognized their odds of avoiding detection were slim and decreased the closer they got to Morowen. If detected, cover would make little difference to their chances of success given the numbers of enemies they faced, but cover could make the difference in surviving to try again.

Morowen was at the center of a vast region of steppes within Aruene's heart. There were no mountains there to provide cover.

Neither were there forests or other forms of vegetation to mask an approach on foot. Though their ship had stealth capabilities, these systems could not provide complete camouflage for hundreds of leagues without respite. Their most viable option would be to move in at night to avoid risks of visual detection while shielding as best they could from instrumental and magical detection by the alien ships. Staying low, they could try to use the local topography as much as possible to interfere with detection but such an approach could not be fully counted upon to reach the citadel of Morowen.

Once in position, they could then do as they had done in the past—teleport as close as they could to their destination once within visual range, place the seal, and then teleport back to their ship.

In reply, Yip proffered, "Our choice of direction matters little. Though the north offers additional cover, there will be little real refuge for hundreds of leagues in any direction as we draw closer to Morowen. Nor will cover prevent instrumental detection of our ship. In the relative open, we can try to use the earth as a shield equally from any given direction but that approach comes with great risk."

"We must take the path that leads to the most successful outcome."

"We should fly the *Shrike* as close as we are comfortable to Morowen and then teleport toward our destination. Our bodies will present smaller targets, be more difficult to detect, and will allow us to be much more flexible in our ability to react."

"Should we need to retreat, we will be able to withdraw without risk to our ship or giving away our original point of origination. Once we get our bearings on a particular location, we can then teleport to and from that position at will depending on the fortuitousness of the moment."

"They will not expect us to arrive on foot alone."

Wrindanneth studied the map for a moment. With a brief flicker of his mind, the electrical impulse translated directly to action by the ship's synthetic intelligence, the entire continent of Aruene was analyzed across multiple variables according to his will.

Within the blink of an eye, an overlay appeared across the three-dimensional projection ranging in colors from cool to warm.

Pointing to the map, Wrindanneth explained what had been done. "I agree. Yip's suggestion is the wisest course. What you see depicted is a representation of the most favorable points to launch our mission from once we leave the ship."

"The overlay shows, from blue to yellow, the areas we should consider to moor the *Shrike*. The yellow areas represent the most viable positions while the blue indicate the worst positions."

"This analysis accounts for a combination of variables including adequate geographic cover to position and hide the *Shrike*, suitable vantage to see from in order to teleport for the greatest distance, any known regular Cabal flight patterns and stations, potential detection risks including those for the ship, the ship's berth, and our teleporting, and proximity to Morowen."

Pointing to several locations, he said, "These locations highlighted in white, appear to offer the optimal positions to stage our attempt per Yip's recommendation."

Scanning the map quickly, Slate laughed, saying, "So have ya been takin' lessons in Gnomish analytics from Spreesprocket or are tha Paratechnologists just rubbin' off on ya?"

Wrindanneth raised an eyebrow archly. "Whatever works, I employ."

Slate snorted and waved his hand over the map vaguely. "Employ away!"

Ignoring Slate's barb, Wrindanneth enlarged the image, focusing on one point in particular. An especially deep, steep-sided rocky defile came into view. Within its rough, overhanging confines, the *Shrike* could be hidden easily. From the top of the defile, the plains of central Aruene rolled away, leaving what should be a clear view of Morowen off in the far distance across leagues of desolate, broken, rock-strewn desert.

Aroganji studied the view carefully. He peered back and forth between where Morowen was indicated by a glowing red orb floating above the highlighted section of the globe and the location of the proposed haven for their vessel. He looked north, south, and east at potential routes of approach for their destination.

Finally satisfied, he said, "I revise my earlier assessment. A northern approach to this location appears most favorable."

Slapping him on the back excitedly, Slate said, "That's my Fang Shih!"

Smiling, Aroganji asked innocently, "I am not a Rock Troll?"

Slate laughed. "Nah! Ya're a glimmerin' nugget o' adamantium. A bit rough and uncut but with plenty o' potential!"

Wrindanneth brushed both the compliment and reference to prior insults aside without apparent concern. "At least you've finally seen the value in something, Slate."

Patting Wrindanneth on the shoulder reassuringly, Slate said good-naturedly, "Don't worry, Wrin. Ya're a nugget o' a different sort. One with plenty o' value as well!"

"Perhaps you had better hold your tongue Dwarf, before you become fertilizer of a different sort!"

Slate hooted again, countering, "More like you?"

Wrindanneth's eyes flared. "No. More like a decomposing corpse."

Aroganji laughed, mollifying. "You're both nuggets of a different sort! No need to get upset about it!"

Appearing hurt, Slate said, "Then what does that make ya, Aroganji?"

Aroganji shrugged in reply. "Compost. Pure, natural, and unsullied. Fresh like the morning air. Full of life and potential."

Wrindanneth interjected flatly, "You're full of something and I don't think it's life."

Slate nodded in agreement. "No wonder he smells a bit like Wrin!"

Wrindanneth shook his head in mock confusion. "And I thought it was just the fresh country air."

Turning his attention back to the barren representation hovering before them, Wrindanneth asked, "Are we in agreement on our path forward?"

Yip nodded. "We are in accord."

When no one else spoke further, Wrindanneth said, "Good. Before we stray too far from Tellanon's protective shadow, there is one other issue I would like to address—the matter of our personal protection on this trip."

"We need to decide upon which spells will be most advantageous to have on us at all times to complement the suite of protections we already have at our disposal."

"In addition to the energy dissipation provided by the alien shields, we all have some degree of protection from evil, protection from supernatural influence, enhanced strength and endurance, augmented agility and prowess, protection from fear, divine regeneration, healing, flight, air purification, magically augmented vision, intercommunication, and protection from many physical and magical attacks through the Stars of Illdrassil."

"These we can call upon at need."

"Though we have not tried it, and thus cannot rely upon it, the Stars will also allow us to combine and store our strength. This we have yet to explore how to implement."

Wrindanneth eyed them each carefully in turn. "What else do you propose?'

Yip spoke first. "Most importantly, we should have a contingency spell in place that will, if possible, save us for another day should our efforts fail."

For clarification, he added, "We must all decide upon the same incantation so that we will remain together and able to respond in unison should something ill befall all of us simultaneously."

Slate nodded in agreement. "Should we have such an emergency spell return us ta tha *Shrike* if we are at risk of expirin'?"

Wrindanneth shook his head. "We need a more complete solution than that. Once triggered, the spell should physically and mentally heal us, cure us of curses and afflictions, and dispel hostile magics at a minimum."

"Furthermore, we should not teleport directly back to the *Shrike* in case it has been compromised or destroyed while we are still on it or away from it. We could, however, teleport a set, safe distance away from the *Shrike* so that we will be sent away from the ship if its destruction triggered the spell. This approach would return us near the *Shrike* if something elsewhere activated the spell."

Aroganji agreed. "This would seem the most prudent course unless you would have us return to Tellanon?"

Slate shook his head. "Whether ta go forward or back can be decided from tha ship. We may always need ta go back ta help those we've left behind. Or we may decide ta regroup and try again later."

Wrindanneth nodded his assent. "Returning near but not to the *Shrike* appears to be the wisest course."

Slate smacked his heavy hands together. "Let's do it!"

Aroganji shook his head. "These spells will take some time and will be quite taxing. Before we undertake their casting, is there anything else we should employ?"

Wrindanneth scoffed, "Between Luereal, Yip augmenting our abilities as needed, and being able to draw on the ship's reserves for the fuel for our spells, the energy for these and any other arcana will not be a concern. We just need to plan accordingly to make certain they are performed correctly."

Yip addressed his secondary concern. "If we are forced to confront a member of the Cabal, we need wards to protect against their unique abilities. They can attack our life force directly, snuffing it out as though it were a candle, with ease."

"Though I should be able to guard against such attacks, having secondary protection is wise."

Wrindanneth agreed. If Yip happened to be incapacitated or worse, then additional protections would be required. "Though we may not know exactly the source of their power, should we face Fyrskal, the fallen paladins of Morowen, we should add extra layers of protection against extradimensional energies and attacks as well."

Yip was curious. "Can we have two sets of contingency spells? One triggered at the initiation of combat, or by our own judgment, and one triggered in response to life-threatening danger?"

Aroganji and Wrindanneth looked at one another simultaneously.

Wrindanneth spoke first. "A dual contingency spell? I've never heard of it done, but I am sure it is possible! What do you think, Aroganji?"

Aroganji was clearly excited, thinking a minute before he spoke. "I believe it is entirely possible. A contingency spell is conditional after all. Why not a conditional contingency spell with multiple modes of expression or a backup version depending upon the dictates of the moment?"

Wrindanneth's mind was abuzz. "What if we had our combat defensive contingency spell protect us all with Caelios' Stoneskin, to guard against physical attacks and prevent interference with spell casting, Mordikan's Mirror Image, to replicate our likenesses and make targeting us more difficult, Percivan's Anti-Anti-Magic cloud, to dampen our enemies' abilities to cast spells and use other nefarious abilities on us, and Marrissa's Kinetic Translocation, to allow us to perform short, directed teleports for a brief period of time?"

Thinking the options through, Yip added, "Should we not have some form of spell to speed our movements so that we can react more rapidly than our foes and quickly turn the situation to our advantage?"

Wrindanneth concurred, looking to Aroganji for his thoughts. "What about Saedeus's Celerity?" This was a recent discovery from the tome Éremon had given them. With this spell in place, they should be able to react quickly enough to unload everything they had before anyone engaged with them or even knew that they had begun to counter.

Yip had one more thought. "Are you aware of any spells that might reflect our enemies' attacks or magics away from us, preferably directed back at them?"

Wrindanneth thought for some time before finally suggesting somewhat hesitantly, "There is Kanen's Inversion. Together, do you think we are capable, Aroganji?"

Kanen's Inversion was about as complex and difficult a spell that could be expected to be performed under the duress and time constraints of combat. Outside of combat, where they would have the necessary time to prepare, it might not be so problematic but it was an exceedingly difficult spell nonetheless.

Aroganji considered for some time before responding. "Since we last left Tellanon, our abilities have grown significantly. Had we considered half of the spells we now discussed then, I would say that we might not be capable. As we have now grown, I think we should be capable. Casting these spells on all of us simultaneously may be the true difficulty."

Wrindanneth huffed, "That will just be good practice! We'll improve with each attempt! Besides, we won't be relying on our strength alone for these spells. Otherwise, I would agree. We would not have the power to cast so many spells unassisted."

Content with the array of defensive spells proposed, Wrindanneth asked, "Are these sufficient?"

Aroganji indicated his agreement. "These incantations will cover most situations but should we not also have deliberate, direct counter-measures to our foes in place?"

Wrindanneth and Aroganji were in their element.

Wrindanneth nodded in reply. "This will take some time to work out but here is what I propose. Extending on Yip's idea, we should have a three-tiered emergency spell system. One will be cast upon us as a response of last resort to return us safely and in good health near the *Shrike*. This spell will operate individually as there may be situations where one or more of us may need to stay behind to complete the mission."

"Another contingency layer will be a defensive cascade of spells triggered either by our judgment or an undetected life-threatening attack. This spell will be identical for everyone but only one of us will need to trigger it at the start of hostilities to reap the effects. These spells will be the ones discussed already unless we wish to make any alterations?"

Raising his eyebrow questioningly, he waited for more suggestions. When none came, he finished, "A third emergency spell will, again at our discretion, be employed offensively in combat. As with the defensive contingency, this spell will be the same for everyone but only one of us will need to trigger it at the start of combat to initiate the series of spells."

Slate washed his hands together excitedly. "And what horrors should we unleash on those who would destroy us? Fires rainin' from tha heavens? Earthquakes? A plague o' flesh rot? An abyss that opens at their feet? A savage elemental released ta ravage 'em from tha pits o' another plane? Some Gnomish stew?"

Slate was truly giddy with the prospect of rampant destruction.

Aroganji shook his head. "We should be more subtle. Remember, we are trying not to be discovered! Explosions, flaming monsters called in from other planes, thunder, lightning, earthquakes, the horrific stench of Gnomish comestibles, all these things will draw attention to ourselves where we may not want it. We must turn the situation to our advantage that we may be in control and decide how to create the most desirable outcome."

Slate was crestfallen. "Not even one explosion?"

Wrindanneth laughed. "Don't worry, if it comes to us having to use these contingency spells, I am sure there will be plenty of explosions!"

Slate growled, "That's what I'm talkin' about!"

Yip did not share in Slate's enthusiasm for violence but he did share in their desire for success. "Why not deny them the ability to harm us? Why not deprive them of the ability to sense and interact with us?"

Aroganji liked this idea. "Blindness, loss of footing, immobility, deafness, and similar effects that create disorientation and confusion can all be easily employed and to our advantage."

Yip cautioned, "Remember, the Cabal, at least those once from the K'un Lun, may sense very much like I do. If deprived of sight or hearing, they will still be able to perceive us and attack. If physically immobilized, they will still be able to strike."

"I cannot say if they will be able to manipulate and redirect energy as I do, but we must be prepared for all eventualities."

Wrindanneth tapped his chin thoughtfully. "What about waves of excruciating pain or sensory overload?"

Yip shrugged. "They are very adept at dealing with such things, but, even if they are able, the moment of adaptation may give us time to strike."

Wrindanneth steepled the corresponding fingers from both hands, rolling them across each other rhythmically as he considered the opportunities. His voice full of menace, he said simply, "Excellent."

Looking wickedly at his friends, he said, "Might I suggest a nerve bomb?"

"What is that?" Slate had never heard of such a thing.

"Just a cocktail of my own making." Wrindanneth had poured over the tomes they had been given in the past and come up with a few particularly interesting insights and applications. "Throw in a dash of complete sensory overload, pepper in a healthy dose of pain, and add a pinch of immobility and what do you have?"

Slate thought a moment before replying with a wicked grin, "An unhappy vegetable?"

"Exactly!"

Aroganji offered a note of caution. "That will certainly be effective against unwarded humanoids but what of creatures with different physiologies or makeups or from other dimensions entirely? What of those who are protected against most magics cast on their person?"

Wrindanneth shrugged. "Three things."

"First, it will be the strength and range of their magical protections versus ours. This will hold true for any spell which is why we will supplement our strength in the casting. Second, the offensive spell contingency absolutely must include an area of effect to dispel hostile magics. This will further increase the likelihood of success. Third, we will include a few other choice goodies for those who are not of the prototypical humanoid variety and physiology. Obviously, such an approach will serve to heighten the overall excitement and enjoyment of the encounter…for us and for them"

Yip made the following suggestion. "Most spells protect the individual directly from various effects. We should include spells that work on the environment that alter how our foes are actually able to interact with us and the world around them. Those spells will be more difficult to counter and work around."

Wrindanneth concurred. "I would suggest something that is shrewd and treacherous. Something that will take them out of their element, as Yip says, and make interaction with us all but impossible."

Slate raised an eyebrow. "What kinda range are we talkin' about fer these spells? Line o' sight? How about fer tha area o' effect spells?"

Aroganji answered for Wrindanneth, "Much will depend upon the spells we decide upon and the energy necessary to create the desired effect. Ideally, I would hope for us to be able to generate an effect within a range of about a stone's throw. Perhaps thirty or so paces."

Eying Wrindanneth with a smile, he amended, "Wrindanneth's steps and not mine."

Thinking a moment, Slate nodded. "That should cover a good sized room or the majority of nasties that may be chargin' at us."

Wrindanneth responded flatly, "And we'll be there to cover the rest."

Having given the matter a moment's thought while his friends discussed logistics, Yip offered, "What if we had a spell that locally reversed gravity? Or one that thickened the air to such a degree as to make motion almost impossible?" Yip was thinking of spells that would hamper physical movement and disorient an opponent, interfering with both normal spell casting or offensive techniques.

Slate, however, was thinking of something else entirely. His voice filled with disdain and disgust at the memory, he griped, "Ya mean like Wrindanneth's 'safety system' he put ta use on tha ship?"

Wrindanneth chuckled despite his friend's less than fond memories of the situation. "That was effective, wasn't it?"

Aroganji nodded. "Those two effects could be quite potent, especially if we choose to break one just as suddenly as it began."

Wrindanneth laughed again as multiple images of such an implementation flashed through his mind. "Indeed." He was also thinking of how effective he and Aroganji could be at timing and coordinating such effects through their magical connection.

As though reading his thoughts, Yip said, "There is something else you must know. Something that Slate found out as soon as I did."

A look of concern crossed Aroganji's face. "What is it, Yip?"

"I am not certain exactly how this came to be, whether from my heightened empathy, my interactions with Illdrassil, or my mental conversations with EMMA the NUMEN, but I now have some degree of telepathic ability."

Aroganji raised his eyebrows curiously while Wrindanneth practically jumped for joy, his face lit with an excited grin. "Now we're talking! We three can coordinate our attacks and counters perfectly!"

Yip raised a hand cautiously to allay his enthusiasm. "Assuming I have the range, capacity, and control for such an effort."

Undaunted, Wrindanneth continued, "You will, Yip! You will!"

Before they veered off topic, Aroganji asked, "So we are clear on our emergency spells? Once Wrindanneth and I begin working, we will not be able to stop until we have completed the enchantments."

Slate nodded in agreement, counting on his thick, upraised fingers as he recounted the planed spells. "First, we'll have a spell o' last resort ta take us in good health ta safety near tha *Shrike*. Second, we'll have a defensive spell ta protect us against magic and physical attacks, particularly those employed by tha Cabal and their ilk, give us mirror images, preferably o' our most handsome likenesses, let us jump around like Gnomes hyped on rhubarbs, speed us up like a gold-crazed Dwarf, reflect our enemies' nastiness back at 'em, and dispel hostile magics. Finally, we'll have an offensive contingency ta turn our foes inta quivering vegetables that are launched into tha air like tossed salad but unable ta move as though they had just seen Wrindanneth before he had a chance ta freshen up in tha mornin'."

"Tha offensive and defensive spells will be triggered by our own judgment. If somethin' really bad happens, like Wrindanneth forgets ta brush his teeth, tha appropriate defensive spell will trigger."

"Am I missin' somethin'?"

Wrindanneth responded with a question. "Whatever miniscule bit of sense you once had?"

Slate shrugged, his large shoulders moving up and down easily under his armor. "I wouldn't argue it."

Aroganji broke in then. "Slate, in the case of triggering both the offensive and defensive spells, as needed, you should be the one to initiate your contingencies first since you will not share the direct mental connection we maintain."

Yip clarified. "Slate need not be excluded from any connection we establish. That way we will function together optimally."

Wrindanneth interjected tauntingly, "But isn't that exclusion our preference?"

Yip ignored Wrindanneth and added, "Also, if I am able to given the circumstance, when any one of us activates the emergency spells, I will augment the effects with the intrinsic energies of the place."

Slate slapped Yip on the back proudly. "See! Who needs Yrien when we have our own energy capacitor?"

Aroganji tilted his head to the side and looked at Slate consideringly. "Not to underestimate Yip's importance to us, but two augmenters may be better than one."

Yip agreed. "There are times when I will not be able to give attention to certain tasks."

Slate snorted. "I haven't seen a knot ya've not been able ta untie, Yip!"

Yip laughed with his friend before saying calmly and self-deprecatingly, "Then you have not seen many knots!"

Lifting up his robes briefly to reveal his feet, Yip added with a smile, "There's a reason I wear sandals."

Slate shook his head, lifting his feet covered in glimmering, eldritch sabatons. "And there's a reason I have ta wear plate armor and ya don't."

Wrindanneth nodded, his face contorted in feigned pain. "I have to agree with Slate for once. There is a reason, though it might be hard to believe."

After a moment's silence, he blurted, "Because Slate at least has a modicum of sense!"

Yip shrugged. "I have never claimed to be in what many consider 'one's right mind.'"

"And that's exactly why we love ya, Yip!" Slate saluted Yip with a thump on his armored chest, then chuckled as he said, "Ya've got more sense than that!"

Steering them back on task, Aroganji returned to the original topic of conversation. "We will begin the process once we are finished here. The spells will probably take the better part of a day to complete."

Slate huffed, "We'd better hope nothin' untoward happens between now and then!"

Wrindanneth smiled knowingly. "Another reason for the flight over water."

Turning his attention back to Yip, Aroganji asked, "So what exactly happened, Yip?"

Eager to hear the full story, Slate washed his hands excitedly. "Aye! Do tell!"

Yip smiled at Slate. "You will now hear what little I know."

Holding his tongue, for the options to interject were veritably limitless, Wrindanneth listened quietly as Yip began his tale.

"I spent the evening at Illdrassil's root in silent contemplation. Awareness of the energy currents moving through and around her, in and out, stored and released, passed with the movement of each breath."

"As the sense of self fell away and my awareness of Illdrassil deepened, I gradually came to sense something more, a presence subtle and diffuse, one hidden in the midst of the rushing energy currents akin to the path of sunlight passing through a rushing stream. Appreciation of this presence built and deepened until I realized that it was Illdrassil herself."

"She was all around, spread throughout the city that she enlivens and sustains, a sentience so momentous, so subtle, that, for a time, my mind did not recognize her presence."

"Whether she revealed herself to me or I discovered her, I cannot say. Only I know she is much more than I previously realized."

"She is Tellanon, just as she makes Tellanon possible."

"After I shared what little I could in return for the gift of her presence, I returned home."

"On the flight back, EMMA contacted me directly mind-to-mind as she has done before. She asked several questions about the Dragon's Gate. At the end of this conversation, there was a flash of light and she was gone."

"When I arrived home, I placed my hand on Slate's shoulder. At that time, we both realized that I was experiencing Slate's thoughts."

"More than this I cannot say."

Thinking of the horrors of experiencing Slate's mind directly, Wrindanneth quipped, "Nor would you want to!"

Aroganji listened patiently. When Yip had clearly finished, he asked, "Have you not communicated mind-to-mind in the past? You call to your teacher and converse with him through your dreams, summoning Master Wei to your side. You share your experiences directly with us as you did with the Dragon's Gate. How is this different?"

Yip understood his friend's confusion. "Those instances were special cases. It took significant effort and concentration, acts of will and a gathering of many thoughts, sensations, and energies to perform. This was simple, without foresight, and instant."

Aroganji's questions were not complete. "Then is this merely an extension of the abilities you have already cultivated or something new entirely?"

Yip shrugged. "That is for us to see."

Aroganji had more questions to ask before his line of inquiry was complete. "Do you not think the sharing of the totality of an experience, whether foresight and effort were required prior to the transference is a much greater expression of psychic ability? Considering this transfer occurred between you and individuals with little clairvoyant ability or training in that regard, were your prior demonstrations not more remarkable?"

Wrindanneth added mildly, "I think what surprises you, Yip, is not that the ability occurred or expressed itself but that you were unaware of it arising. You were surprised because you were not consciously seeking the development of this skill nor was its arrival under your control."

Yip did not disagree nor did he wish to argue for what had happened had already arisen despite what he may feel or think. "Perhaps you are correct."

Wrindanneth suggested, "While Aroganji and I are working on the contingency spells, why don't you and Slate explore what you can of this ability? It could be quite useful in the days ahead."

Slate shook his head slowly. "At least I won't be talkin' ta myself!"

Wrindanneth nodded. "And someone will finally be willing to listen!"

Aroganji looked at Wrindanneth in all seriousness and asked, "Are you ready to begin?"

Wrindanneth laughed in reply. "When am I not?"

Slate and Yip stood together at midship while Aroganji and Wrindanneth worked at the helm. The Plains of Kadoor continued to pass steadily by below, endless green waves rolling toward the horizon.

Slate huffed reluctantly, "Are ya ready ta start?" His body language indicated anything but readiness but he was willing to proceed nonetheless.

Yip smiled with his friend's obvious sentiments. *"I am."*

"Let's begin simply. I don't want ta get carried away and accidentally damage tha goods." Slate tapped his skull emphatically. "Lots o' critical intel up here."

"Understood." Yip gave a brief smile and took a step back.

Slate thought for a moment before he noticed Yip moving away. *"Shouldn't we start close?"*

With a moment's reflection, his eyes widened. *"Hey! Ya've already started!"*

"Yes." Yip took another step back.

"Ya're a tricky one!"

Yip took another step back, experimenting as he did. *"I am not trying to be."*

Slate rubbed his temples, the sensation disorienting. *"Careful now. Ya're movin' in and out, joinin' my mind and then jumpin' out."*

Yip nodded and took another step back. *"I am exploring the depth and breadth of the connection. I will tread lightly."*

"I should hope so!"

"To do otherwise would violate all we stand for and hope to achieve." Yip took another step back, smiling. In just a few more paces, he would need to climb the steps to the helm.

"Two can play at this game." Slate grinned and stepped back in time with Yip. He was getting used to the connection.

Focusing on the secondary awareness within his mind, depending on the degree of connection, it rather felt like he was talking to himself if the joining was light. If Yip deepened the connection, Yip actually seemed to be inside his mind or pushing to come through his skull into his head. This sensation was extremely uncomfortable and instantly caused his internal defenses to jump up in reaction without conscious volition.

Yip, however, was aware of Slate's response and only deepened the connection once upon initial contact. When he saw and felt the panicked, protective reaction, he immediately withdrew.

"I think ya can span tha whole ship, Yip!" Slate continued walking backward while Yip went up the steps to the helm, edging around where Aroganji and Wrindanneth wove magical forces in tandem to create their contingency spells.

"We shall see." After the first few moments, Yip sensed he could go much farther, but he wanted confirmation before he jumped to any conclusions.

"Don't ya worry, I can. And I know ya're gonna be able ta go much farther! Ya're connection hasn't lessened one bit and ya're clear across tha ship!"

Slate's words were true.

He now stood at the fore of the *Shrike*, his back solidly against her polished rails while Yip stood at the aft. The helm with the control sphere hovering in position, Aroganji and Wrindanneth working, and the ship's masts all stood between them.

"What're ya doin' now, Yip?"

Yip's words appeared softly within his own mind, perhaps whispering a secret to himself. "I am feeling the connection as it is for a moment. This will not take long. Once I am done, I will break off the linkage."

"Glad ta hear it!" Though his words were gruff, Yip knew Slate felt otherwise, the feeling could not be hidden. Slate was as curious as he was for the sensation was not intrusive or distracting once Slate was aware of it and had grown comfortable.

Yip shared the warmth of his smile through the connection between them before returning his attention to the bond itself.

His mind encompassed the space they were in, floating freely without attachment or object. Within this expanded awareness, he sensed his friends, their vibrant energies commingling, enlivening, and interacting with the forces native to the air they breathed just as he sensed the living ship, the miniscule creatures of the air, and the ship's cargo. Each distinct entity connected and intertwined with the web of forces moving through and around them on a scale from the infinitesimal to the macrocosmic.

In much the same way that he could interact with Slate's living energies, he found he could interact with his friend mentally. In lieu of transferring or manipulating energy, he merely focused on transferring his awareness, or a portion of it, between himself and his companion. In that way, he and Slate were connected mentally to some degree just as energy bound them together physically.

Though he had never tried to interact with someone in this way, the sensation was novel and unexpected. He remained within himself, his awareness extended and branching outward to its limits, while he also experienced the world through another's thoughts and impressions though to a much lesser extent for the connection was not complete nor did he wish to push it. He felt like a mirror simultaneously looking through a window upon a reflection of himself, a part of two worlds looking at each other across the bridge of his mind.

If he gradually lessened the connection until their bond was as tenuous as a dew-laden strand of spider silk, which was much less intrusive and distracting to both Slate and himself, he felt mentally distinct. In this state, their connection was casual, their communication direct, like they were just talking to one another directly albeit without words.

He could also feel the barriers around and within Slate's mind. At present, they merely interacted on a cursory level, flitting atop undulations of consciousness. Though he would not do such a thing to his friend, if he had to, he could push through these barriers and explore as he would.

He let this thought go without further action for he would not harm nor wish to harm the mind of another unnecessarily.

With this knowledge in place, he let the connection between them fade.

Waving across the ship, he called out, "Thank you, Slate!"

"Think nothin' o' it, Yip!"

Walking back toward the ship's center, they met in the middle once more.

"That was rather odd, at first, I must say." Slate scratched his head as he remembered the initial disorientation of another within his mind.

"No ill aftereffects?"

Slate shook his head. "None yet!"

Concerned for his friend, though he was certain nothing untoward would unfold, Yip added reassuringly, "Let me know if that changes."

"Oh, I will!"

He laughed knowing that Slate would most assuredly let him know if something were amiss.

Indicating Aroganji and Wrindanneth with a nod of his head, Slate barked, "If those two can work together in each other's minds without problem, I'm sure we can as well!"

Shaking his head, Slate added, "That Aroganji can tolerate Wrindanneth's presence in his consciousness is a sure sign of sainthood."

Yip smiled and then bowed. "Thank you for your openness and bravery. You did what many would be unwilling to do."

Slate shrugged. "Bah! Think nothin' o' it! Just buy me a stout ale when we return and we'll be even!"

Smacking Yip on the shoulder, Slate left Yip to retreat belowdecks. He was going to grab some shuteye while he waited on Wrindanneth and Aroganji to call him up to begin casting their enchantments.

Left alone on the deck, Yip leaned against the railing, filled with the stillness within his mind.

While his friends continued to labor behind him, weaving incantations intricately in a tapestry of potentiality, Yip examined the horizon ahead, a haze of green supporting a wash of faded sky.

He sensed that Aroganji and Wrindanneth's preparations were nearing completion. Soon they would be calling either Slate or himself up to the helm to layer the series of enchantments upon one or both of them.

Stratified and interwoven, multidimensional threads of power coalesced and gathered in the air, rarefied matrices of force ready for application, triggered for future expression.

The air was pregnant with power.

Waiting, he felt mounting energies thrumming not only through the air but through the ship itself.

Following this movement, he watched these energies directed through and around the many channels guiding its procession both in and around the *Shrike*. The ship's lifeblood flowed through his senses, vibrancy guided by a diffuse intelligence centered in the control sphere at the helm.

As intricately complex as another being's circulatory or nervous system, the *Shrike*'s magical lattice was a wonder of precision and organic function.

Appreciating the ship's amazing complexity, its beauty highlighted by the numerous threads of force being organized around and within it, he understood that in many ways Paratechnology worked at creating magically empowered synthetic objects and beings, replicating and enhancing the capabilities of living organisms, extending the boundaries of what it meant to be alive.

"Yip! You're up!" Wrindanneth's voice rang out across the deck. The time had come for his ensorcelling.

The intricacies of the *Shrike*'s workings at the fore of his consciousness, he turned away from the railing and walked back toward the helm. He sensed about Aroganji and Wrindanneth a subtle, shimmering multi-layered cloak of arcana, the culmination of all their efforts.

Soon they would all be shrouded similarly.

He walked up the steps to the helm, greeted by a smile from Aroganji and a motion to come over from Wrindanneth.

Laughing, Wrindanneth said, "I know you're in a hurry, but we haven't all week!"

Evidently Yip's pace was not fast enough.

Smiling at the memory, there was a reason other Acolytes and Initiates of the K'un Lun had sometimes called him Lightning. Nor was the appellation because of the speed exhibited in his hand-to-hand combat training.

His gait steady, the remembrance fading, the smile remained while he approached Wrindanneth anticipating being there for some time while his friends worked.

Shaking his head at Yip's apparent reluctance to move at the speed he wished, Wrindanneth quipped, "Slate's been rubbing off on you!"

Yip stood in place patiently, not rising to Wrindanneth's bait, letting his friend think and feel as he wished.

At an implicit nod of readiness from Aroganji, Wrindanneth began the weaving.

The process did not take long, just a few short minutes. Much of the time Aroganji and Wrindanneth had spent before had been to determine which spells to cast, how to properly combine and organize the incantations, and how to most effectively work in tandem to realize the optimal effect. They had also used this time to learn how to best utilize and increase their enchantments' effectiveness with both Luereal and the *Shrike*'s overwhelming power.

Holding position, Yip felt all this energy laced about him in ever increasing complexity. Though exceedingly sophisticated, once complete, he felt these energies upon his body as a light tingling—cool dewdrops settled on his skin, refusing to evaporate in the afternoon sun.

Sensing their work was complete, all spells tied off and crystallized in final expression, he bowed to Aroganji and Wrindanneth, their artistry and mastery. "Your work is a beauty to behold."

Aroganji laughed at Yip's compliment. "Maybe we should open a museum!"

Cocking his head to the side as he thought for a moment, visualizing the work that had been performed and other similar weavings from the past, Yip replied quite seriously, "People would pay to have and see such artwork."

Wrindanneth snickered at Yip's lack of sophistication and worldliness. "People already do!"

Yip gave a short bow. "Perhaps one day, we can visit such a place."

Wrindanneth stood up and slapped Yip on the back. "If you'd like to experience a bit of culture after all we've been through together, I'd be happy to oblige! In case you hadn't noticed, a significant portion of Tellanon is dedicated to artistic expression. Or, to use your terminology, 'the expression of human potential', the 'manifestation and appreciation of sentient vision', and the 'actualization of the highest imaginings.'"

Focused on the requirements of his quest, though he had indeed paid significant attention to the beauty and wonder of Tellanon, enthralled by her possibilities and phenomena, Yip had not taken the time to actively explore her wonders for he had other duties to attend.

Such cultural and intellectual expressions often occurred outside the ken of priests.

"I should enjoy that very much."

Aroganji chuckled. "When all this is done, we'll take you on a grand tour, Yip!"

Bowing once more, Yip left the helm, going first down the stairs to the main deck, then through the heavy oaken door, and onward into the ship's interior. Walking along the hallway illumined by magical incandescence from orbs suspended from the walls, he made his way toward Slate's quarters.

All around, energies swirled, channeled through the radiant orbs. These intermediary luminaries served the dual role of lighting and powering the ship, though the illumination was secondary to their primary function. These were the conduits for the living energies that he sensed empowering the ship.

The sounds of Slate's snoring grew louder as he moved farther down the hall, the sounds of a breeze grown into a gale. Stopping at Slate's door, he knocked.

The snoring stopped immediately.

"I'm up!"

"They are ready for you, Slate."

"So am I!"

Slate emerged fully dressed, armor on. By way of explanation, he said, "Ya never know when it'll be yer last chance ta sleep!"

Yip indicated Slate was to go first by opening his arm out from the waist. "Or appreciate the day."

Slate snorted in reply.

Slate's broad back almost filled the entirety of the width of the hallway, his heavy shoulders swaying back and forth with each stride, moving in time with the cresting of waves that were not present—each Dwarven step was a rolling breaker unto itself, eager to find a shore to crash against.

They strode to the helm in silence, each in the company of his own mind.

"Look what the Troll cast off!" Wrindanneth barked upon seeing Slate emerge from the hold.

Slate growled, then said, "Just focus on yer work. Practice yer imprecations on yer own time."

"Unfortunately, I never have anything negative to say about myself. You on the other hand..."

"Merely have ta put up with ya."

Knowing this banter could go on for hours if left undeterred, Aroganji interceded, "Are you ready to begin, Slate?"

"I am."

Slate stood between Wrindanneth and Aroganji on the helm. His gleaming armor caught the afternoon sun, reflecting streamers of liquid gold onto the deck. Turning away from his friends, Yip left Aroganji and Wrindanneth so that he would not interfere with their efforts.

He walked to the fore of the ship, watching Dharia slip by below. They were moving northwest over the marshes, bogs, swamps, and fens of Dharia's west central coast. Rivers washing out from the continent's central peaks, streaming through the vast forests and plains, eventually found their way here and farther south, wending through convoluted mosaics of water and land.

Like much of Dharia, the land below was wild, home to spirits, beasts, and few settled peoples. Humanity's purchase in the Empen Wastes was about as transitory as the waters that washed through her sodden banks.

Other fey creatures and mystical beasts held sway here without thought or regard for Man or his allies.

Yip saw all this and more.

He watched the currents of living beings ebb and flow, the vibrancy of life scattered across the varied landscape in a shifting tide of living articulation. He saw the concentration of energies and existences spread throughout the untrammeled ecosystem below. He felt the countless lives beneath move and shift, tugging on his mind, fluxes too varied and complex to fully catalog, bound together by a common energetic existence. These forces pulled at him, slowly washing him along with the waters that ran through them, out to sea.

Enmeshed in living energies, green fell away to blue as the *Shrike* sailed westward over the Ayle'ine Sea, leaving behind the lush rounded geometries of the Empen Wastes for the unbroken mass of the churning ocean.

"Yip!" Slate's deep voice called out to him from where he stood at the helm alongside Wrindanneth and Aroganji.

"Ea'ae ta, Yip! Come in, Yip!" Wrindanneth snickered as Slate continued to clamor for Yip's attention.

Untroubled by the taunting, he turned to look at his friends.

"I'd thought we'd lost ya fer a moment there, Yip!"

Yip waited patiently for Slate to say what he wished. He did not have to wait long. "Aroganji and Wrindanneth are gonna retire fer a bit. That'll leave ya and me awake on tha deck."

"Aroganji'll go below while Wrin will stay by tha control sphere."

Wrindanneth chuckled. "That means you'll have to try to keep it down, Yip."

He gave a short bow and a smile. "I shall do my best."

Slate walked forward away from the control sphere and his companions, grabbed both railings leading down alongside the steps from the helm, lifted his feet up, and slid down to the main deck. Walking toward Yip, he said, "We know it'll be hard fer ya. That's why we wanted ta give fair warnin'."

Aroganji followed quietly behind Slate, walking instead of sliding down the steps. Turning to go belowdecks, looking significantly back and forth between Wrindanneth, Yip, and Slate, he said, "I will not rest long. Should you need any assistance on the deck, you have only to call and I will be ready."

Yip smiled with his friend's concern. "All will be well."

"Don't worry about him, Aroganji! If there's anybody in this world who can stare off inta space, lost ta all that would keep a sane Dwarf's attention, and pass tha time by in quietude, it's our pal, Yip!"

Shaking his head, Aroganji merely opened the heavy door and went belowdecks.

Sometimes comments were not necessary.

"Looks like it's just tha two o' us, Yip!"

Raising an eyebrow, Yip asked, "Is it not time for me to 'stare off into space'?"

Slate patted Yip on the shoulder reassuringly. "We know ya're busy, Yip, yer mind on important matters." Puffing out his chest importantly, he added, "What else could be o' enough interest ta keep yer attention away from us?"

Giving a slight nod of agreement, Yip responded, "Truer words have never been spoken."

"'Bout tha only thing I can think of that'd be that interestin', or important, would be gettin' yer head around figurin' out how ta deal with tha Cabal. 'Tis a significant one, full of twists and turns."

Yip's voice was soft. "Or perhaps preparing for such an encounter."

Shifting his eyes away from his friend, Slate's scrutiny turned forward, to the vast ocean and their indistinct future. Slate's normally resounding tones lightened. "Aye. We'll all need ta be at our bests fer that. I suppose ya're luckier'n most. Ya never need ta move ta train." After a brief pause, he added enthusiastically, "Ya never even need ta stop trainin'!"

His gaze remaining on Slate, Yip replied simply, "You never need stop either, Slate."

"Bah! I'm not gonna swing Duraeleon around every wakin' minute o' tha day!"

Yip shook his head slightly. "You need not. Where is the mind of the warrior?"

Slate remained quiet. Yip's words evoked the frenzy of battle in his mind, the adrenaline and thrill of combat, the immediacy of life and death, the overwhelming feeling of living and the moment lived. After a time, he growled, "In tha moment o' battle."

"Need you ever leave this presence behind?"

Slate shrugged his solid shoulders. "I suppose it could be cultivated." He turned to Yip briefly. "Like ya're sayin'."

Yip gave a short nod. "The fires of your fathers, the fires of Brendle's forge, need they ever be quenched?"

Slate raised his eyebrows, staring at Yip intently, his interest piqued. "Ya're sayin' I should burn all tha time?"

Yip shrugged noncommittally. "Your practice is yours alone to cultivate. In our tradition, we learn to circulate the living energies of the *chi* throughout our bodies at all times, building our facility and understanding. Brendle's fire need be no different for its vibrancy and spark fuel your efforts in battle."

Slate thought about this idea for some time. His will need not be merely the spark that lighted and guided Brendle's fire through his veins. His concentration could also be the tender that maintained and strengthened its presence within, reforming and recasting his body as its heat circulated through his marrow.

These fires need not always burn.

They could also reforge.

Finally, Slate gave a decisive nod. His words were sure when he finally spoke. "I think ya're onta somethin' there, Yip! Perhaps tha Bor'Banna o' tha past had such disciplines but much has been lost."

"What has been lost can be rediscovered. Though each of us walks on our own path, untrammeled and untouched by anyone but our own mind, we all lead the same lives. We merely have to recreate the trails discovered by our predecessors." Here Yip paused, smiling as he added, "Or blaze our own."

Slate remained quiet for some time, staring off into the ocean once more. "I will think on this."

Yip did not reply, waiting instead for any other comments Slate wished to offer. Finally, Slate turned once more to Yip and said, "With a bit o' yer help, I think I might just be able ta do it!"

Yip bowed. "I will do so gladly. Think on what has already been given. There may be all you need in what you have already received."

Opening his mouth to offer a quick retort in response to Yip's typically cryptic reply, Slate finally nodded in understanding. Yip had already shared much with him, even more when he considered all the knowledge, techniques, and practices associated with the Dragon's Gate. Much of Yip's own training and understanding had been revealed to him. He had but to sort through, understand, and put this comprehension into practice.

Nodding his head, Slate turned and went belowdecks, moving

deeper and deeper into contemplation as he left. He had much to do, consider, and discover.

Left alone on the deck, Yip returned to his consideration of the sea.

Currents moved on her surface and in her depths, forces both physical and magical manifest to his senses. Whereas the energies of living creatures held close to the planet's surface on land, in the ocean, the entire body of water was filled with the boundless forces of expressive creation, life unfolding and giving forth, a vast repository of living energy cradled upon Ea'ae's bosom.

His self falling away, he experienced the ocean of life around as if it were his own.

Slate sat on his bed in quiet reflection.

The room was only softly lit by the bluish white light of the ship's energy orbs. Wooden walls were bare aside from the ports in the opposite wall from which he sat. All of his gear, and much of that for his companions, was held within the confines of his magical pouch carried on his waist.

He need not have any distractions or decoration, for his mind was elsewhere and such things were as likely to fall and break in combat as they were to fill some aesthetic need he did not have.

His mind lingered on the Dragon's Gate.

Though he could berate himself for not taking advantage of the knowledge given when it was fresh, he did not. Many other demands had been placed upon them in the intervening period and much had occupied his time, the least of which was his very survival. If he could have made better use of the knowledge granted during this period, he felt no remorse, for he was making amends for any prior oversight.

Yip had been right so many days ago when he had spoken to them of the Dragon's Gate. Without practice and vigilance, the knowledge Yip had so graciously imparted seemed to pass like a dream, grown watery and indistinct with the passage of time.

He, however, was a Dwarf. Though his people had many failings, for their memory was long, their anger ran deep, and little wrong was forgotten or forgiven, there was much positive about his people that differed from many of the shorter lived races.

In his blood was the patience of mountains, a wellspring he seldom called upon but one available nonetheless. So, too, could he draw upon the unwavering memory of his people, one that often led to blood feuds over ills that perhaps should have been forgotten, but that also prevented his people from getting lost in the unending twists and turns of the undermounts they often called home.

Recalling the time and place, he carefully let his mind reconstruct the visions Yip had granted, rediscovering what had been shared, delving into knowledge that he had not explored, preparing to put into practice what had been given.

Deliberately entering these waking dreams, making their truth a reality, he discovered that Yip was indeed correct. Delving deep within the veins of his friend's teachings, searching out the precious nuggets he desired, he found that so much more had been shared than he had thought or remembered.

There were, indeed, many practices he could make his own.

Brendle be praised!

Bor'Banna be feared!

Darkness lay heavily upon the ship before Aroganji reemerged from the hold. Slate remained belowdecks while Wrindanneth slept prone on the planks beneath the *Shrike*'s hovering command sphere.

Walking over near to where Yip stood, Aroganji waited politely for Yip to address him lest he interrupt Yip's practice.

Aroganji need not wait long for Yip's greeting. "Good evening, Aroganji. I trust you are refreshed?"

"The mind is full and the body rejuvenated."

"I am glad to hear it."

Aroganji's eyes turned away from his friend and shifted forward to the horizon. "We will wake on the morrow to Aruene. Another day's journey perhaps and our goal will be at hand."

"One of many."

Aroganji raised an eyebrow. "Days? Goals?"

Yip smiled. "Yes."

"A goal achieved is one closer to the end we desire."

Yip amended, "A goal achieved is one closer to the beginning we desire."

Now Aroganji smiled. "True."

Yip remained gazing away from the ship while they spoke.

Aroganji joined him.

Silence stretched from moments to minutes while both men surveyed the night sky and the ocean glimmering in the silvery white moonlight below.

How long passed in quietude, neither could say. However, that silence was abruptly shattered by Slate's return from below.

"How about some supper? Who's ready ta eat?"

Slate's booming voice roused Wrindanneth from his rest. Yelling, Wrindanneth called back, "A little consideration, Dwarf! Some of us have yet to wake! I know you can't hold your stomach for long but consider your fellows before you start screaming!"

Slate laughed. "I did. And thought ya'd be hungry! Magic tires a Man as surely as physical work, so I thought a heapin' pile o' fixin's would suit ya!"

Scratching his long red hair as he stretched and then stood, Wrindanneth smiled. "I'll summon some for us. What's your preference?"

Slate scoffed, "A Dwarf's meal should come from tha labor o' his hands, earned by hard work and toil. Only then can it be truly appreciated."

Wrindanneth sniffed. "If I want to earn my meal with my hands, I will do so...with magic."

"I don't care about yer hands nor yer barbaric sensibilities! I'll be cookin' a bit o' grub from tha ship's stores. If ya want some and would like ta join me, ya're welcome. Otherwise, ya can summon 'til yer heart's content."

Wrindanneth snorted, deciding not to point out the irony. There was little difference between the ship's 'store' of magically created food and his own. Slate could get it unprepared or finished. Either way, it came from the same source. If his foolish friend insisted on using his time and effort to prepare the meal, that was his choice. "A bit of the hold's finest might very well suit me."

"That's what I want ta hear! Let's eat!"

Wrindanneth raised an eyebrow. "You've already prepared the meal?"

Slate shook his head. "I'll just summon it from tha ship's mess."

Wrindanneth smacked his forehead. "Then what was all this about?"

Slate chortled, saying, "If I can't have a bit o' fun gettin' ya riled up, what's tha point?"

His tone sinister, Wrindanneth said, "Perhaps placing a bit more value on your life?"

Slate shrugged noncommittally. "Now where's tha fun in that?" Then he turned back around to go belowdecks to prepare their meal, returning through the oaken door.

His ire raised, Wrindanneth barked out a short incantation.

The effect was immediate.

A series of muffled *thuds* and curses issued from the stairwell. Clapping his hands together excitedly, Wrindanneth said happily, "Let's eat!"

His mind open, extended, Yip stood at the ship's helm relaxed and poised.

In the sky above, a vast sea of velvet darkness mirrored the one shifting below his feet, its moorings stable, its limits beyond his ken. Beneath him, icy black reflecting the stars above, the ocean turned and roiled, undulating up and down to the beat of the moon and the shifting of the tides. Within these depths, his mind moved, moored to no particular tether, adrift, and aware.

His friends slept behind him, the nimbus of their energies within the purview of his mind's eye, along with those of the living ship that sheltered them, the sea that drifted below, and the sky that cradled them. The pulse of these energies enlivened his own, fluid notes in a boundless symphony of dynamic creation.

The world waited while he watched.

Within this field, he sensed movement, an agglomeration of life flying through the sky and knew it to be another ship.

Wrindanneth would need to be made aware.

Guiding his consciousness backward toward where his friend slept, he indicated his presence to Wrindanneth gently so as not to cause undue stress.

"*Wrindanneth?*" His connection was firm but not intrusive. Wrindanneth needed to know the situation was urgent and not part of the vagaries of dreams.

"Hmm?" Wrindanneth's mind was still clouded by the fog of sleep.

"You are needed." His urgency allowed no alternative.

While he communicated with Wrindanneth, he assessed the other ship, its crew, and capabilities. To his mind, the vessel was full of power, brimming with capabilities. Its crew was numerous and able, full of purpose and composure. This vessel was also large, far larger than the *Shrike*, meant for providing and attending to all the needs of her crew over extended periods in space, capable of dealing with any unforeseen eventualities.

She was also inimical. A pall of hatred hung over her like a cloud, hostility and rage the fuel driving her passengers' insidious purpose.

They would have to avoid her, hiding from her wardens lest their purpose succumb to her violence.

Yip sensed they had not been detected but he knew not how long their safety would last.

In the brief moments required to make this assessment, he shared those impressions with Wrindanneth.

In the meantime, hopping quickly to his feet, Wrindanneth began his own appraisal and response.

Taking evasive action, Wrindanneth immediately employed the ship's cloaking system, steering away from where Yip indicated the hostile vessel was located. His own sensors on the alert, Wrindanneth could not yet detect the enemy vessel but he did not doubt the veracity of Yip's perceptions.

Now headed almost due south, the *Shrike* sped away from the alien craft at full speed. Waves passing in an unbroken blur, the *Shrike* dipped low, a hawk swooping away from the carrion crows of pursuit.

When no further threat materialized, his keen senses not detecting any response to their presence, Yip finally let Wrindanneth know that all was, at least for the time being, well. *"We are safe. The alien vessel does not give chase."*

Wrindanneth laughed wildly. *"We won't be safe until we are back in Tellanon, Yip! From here on, we hang on and do our best to survive!"*

Yip did not disagree. *"The likelihood of encountering hostile vessels increases with each league we move forward. Why don't you try to get some rest while you can? I will remain on the alert for more alien ships."*

Wrindanneth corrected their heading, returning the *Shrike's* direction north and west. *"I'll be here at the ready should you need me."* Smiling, he added, tapping his skull gently with his fist, *"Next time, just try to knock a little more softly when you do."*

Yip bowed respectfully. He had not realized that his response had been an imposition to his friend.

Wrindanneth's smile faded as he nodded in reply and laid down once more on the ship's upper deck. *"Good night, Yip."*

"Until the morrow, Wrindanneth." Breaking off the connection he had established, he let his friend return to the peace and serenity of sleep or, rather, whatever passed for peace and serenity in the dreams of Wrindanneth's vibrant imagination.

Despite their concerns, the rest of the evening passed uneventfully. Yip was instead left to the quietude of the tides of his mind.

Yip sensed Aruene was near long before he could see her shores. Below him, the character of the living sea gradually began to change along with her depths, currents, and sources of nutriment. Ahead, in the pre-dawn darkness, he felt terrestrial organisms, distinct from those of the ocean, spread so thinly across the vital surface of the land, lacking the depth and dimensionality of life pervading throughout the fluid expanse of the sea. The characteristic energetic expressions of life changed as well, the *chi* created by living creatures thinner along the barren rocky shores of Aruene, deprived of the richness of the sea's vast reaches.

Sensing they were close, he waited for dawn to reveal to his eyes what he already knew to be there.

He did not have to wait long.

With dawn's early phosphorescence first glinting on the ocean's surface at the horizon behind them, he first spotted the continent of Aruene. Almost imperceptible in the pale morning light, eventually the land mass resolved itself from the swath of black ocean from which it arose, growing more and more formidable with each approaching league.

Flying ever closer, what had once been a blur became a wall, an immense sweep of unbroken, irregular grayish-black basalt. Rising almost sheer from the ocean's depths, these cliffs stood sentinel on Aruene's eastern flank, a natural fortified obstacle barring the sea, daring it to come no nearer. The stones of the escarpment stood side-by-side in stark formation, regular columnar segments akin to the stacked stones of a castle or other fortification. About these scars, swarms of sea birds, wyverns, and other creatures more rare and fantastic swooped and dove, many calling the cliffs home, others calling its denizens prey.

At the *Shrike*'s rate of speed, the cliffs appeared, grew, and then disappeared behind them in minutes, a barrier once crossed, left behind like so many others.

Beyond the continent's jagged demarcation, in the cool light of morn, the land appeared desolate, gray and ashen, cold and damp near the coast but growing more and more sere away from her shores. Along the coastline, low fog clung to the ground like a curse, cradling the moss and lichen that carpeted the ground like a pox. These poor grounds quickly gave way to open expanses of untrammeled wastes, vast stretches of bare dirt and rock only rarely broken by struggling vegetation.

Between jutting monoliths and rocky formations, even in these harsh climes, however, life's expression remained undiminished. Her flowers were but of a different sort. Too cold and dry for lichens, too windswept and harsh for vegetation, other organisms managed to thrive. In the growing light of morning, what had first appeared as a barren gray landscape, slowly lit up with the sun.

Observing from above, he watched the radiant light of dawn reflecting off iridescent crystalline formations, plates and scales, branches and whorls. Many hued and remarkable, these mineral formations appeared similar to undersea corals, deriving their sustenance not from filtering the ocean's currents but from the ambient energies flowing through the air.

Turning what had at first appeared to be a barren landscape into a kaleidoscope of color, the harsh topography from horizon to horizon was draped in multi-hued splendor. Beings that drank in magic as their lifeblood flourished where none else could prosper.

To his eyes, a sea of vibrancy floated atop the harsh tundra of

Aruene's northern reaches. Though disease may lay ahead at Aruene's heart, at her periphery life yet thrived.

Within Aruene's reaches, only the hardy survived. Beauty persisted in desolation's shadow.

"It's astounding isn't it?" From where he stood at the helm, Wrindanneth had been appreciating the same vistas as Yip, steering the *Shrike* forward.

"What isn't?" From Yip's perspective, there was beauty to be found in all things, one merely had to find the appropriate view to appreciate the object of one's awareness.

Wrindanneth laughed, countering, "Slate's unwashed armpit?"

Yip gave a brief nod and a smile as he turned to look at Wrindanneth, engaging in conversation.

"Then you're as crazy as a drunken, gold-starved Dwarf!"

"Are ya talkin' about my kinfolk again, Northlander?" Slate's booming laugh heralded his arrival on the ship's deck as his retort rebounded and resonated through the ship's wooden hull.

"We're talking about Aruene, Slate. If you hadn't slept the morning away, you'd know that."

"Bah! Tha mornin's just upon us, ya ungrateful polecat! If it pleases ya, I just finished makin' yer breakfast, so a bit o' respect is in order as hard as I know it is fer ya ta muster!"

"Then what are you doing standing there and complaining? Shouldn't we be eating?"

Slate's mirth filled the air once more. "My point exactly!"

Adjusting their heading to the south and west toward Morowen, Slate and Wrindanneth went belowdecks, leaving Yip alone on the deck once more.

Unperturbed, Yip returned to his internal contemplation and observance of the myriad forms of life hidden amidst the wilds of Aruene's northern coastal plains, alert for any signs of danger above or below.

Though the landscape the *Shrike* flew over appeared static to the unaided eye, to Yip it was a dynamic place.

Magical currents filtered between sessile crystalline organisms rooted in the ground. Within the fields of shimmering platelets and otherworldly growths covering all visible space, other organisms moved, some feeding directly upon the magical fields and others upon the living jewels clinging to the rocks and earth.

Many of these creatures moved, but the pace of their movements was such that they were indistinguishable from the coralline forms growing all around. In the wastes of northern Aruene, the relentless slow-moving predators prowling the crystalline swaths were homologous to their targets, perfectly camouflaged from the watching eyes of those not native to their steppes.

The music of these creature's lives, the orchestration of their movements, so slow but filled with such purpose, lent an appreciation for the timeless wonder of creation, the glacial pace of life's evolution and interaction with the world on which it depended. Shaping and shaped by the landscape, these enduring creatures moved with as much deliberation and care as those of his own kind whose lives could be measured in but a moment in the geologic spans encompassed by theirs.

"I think, perhaps, in your next career you should be an aeryaologist."

He sensed Aroganji's approach before his friend's words greeted him. Turning, Yip smiled. "Life, its motive forces, and its expression are worthy of a lifetime of consideration."

"You would do well at it."

"The opportunity to observe is a gift to be treasured."

Aroganji smiled. "You guard it well."

Turning his attention to the glimmering plains below, Aroganji stood beside him as the *Shrike* flew low over the iridescent terrain.

A massed storm front, stark mountains loomed ahead, monolithic sentinels soaring into the firmament, guarding against intrusion into Aruene's heart. These gray ghosts stood witness to the passage of time, the fall of dynasties, and the flight of Man. The *Shrike* would soon skirt their reaches, a lone speck easily lost but just as readily hidden within their convoluted folds.

"Shouldn't be more'n an hour 'til we're through 'em." Standing alongside Aroganji at Yip's side, Slate's attention remained locked on the horizon as did his fellows'.

"Let us hope the way forward remains clear." Yip's mind sensed no disturbances or anomalies within the immediate vicinity. He felt many unusual creatures within the confines of his awareness but none required evasive action. Those that might pose a threat were too far removed to present any danger and none exhibited the degree of sentience associated with their enemies.

"Wrindanneth has not detected anything untoward since our last flight adjustment." Aroganji's eyes swept the horizon relentlessly, distrusting his own words.

Yip nodded, concurring. "I feel no irregularities or disturbances worthy of concern. I will remain aware, however."

Slate laughed. "Ya do that, Yip. I hope we all manage ta stay aware at least until our quest is complete!"

Behind them, Wrindanneth coughed suppressing a laugh with one raised hand. Though he remained locked to the helm as he reviewed data on the Fyrskal, he heard their words nonetheless.

"Anythin' interestin' back there?" Slate was as curious about what had happened in the past as what might happen in the future. The Fyrskal's reign had ended long before his time, but their shadow may soon linger over his own.

Wrindanneth shook his head in incredulous appreciation. "The Fyrskal were ruthless. They ruled with an iron fist, imposing their will on their subjects through force of might and the insidious application of fear. Those subjects who disobeyed were crushed. Those that remained were dominated by terror."

He pulled up an image on the projection for all to see.

A lone horseman sat perched atop a striding horse. Both the horse and horseman were wreathed in black flames. The stallion galloped through the air, its hooves igniting sparks with each thunderous stride, each exhalation accompanied by orange flames shooting from its flared nostrils. Sitting calmly as the ground raced by far below, the Fyrskal seated on the equine's back rode without reins, saddle, or stirrups, in complete control under even in the most precarious of circumstance.

The dread steed appeared tame in comparison to its master.

Wreathed in abhorrent, Daemonic black armor, the Fyrskal devoured what little light appeared to push through its nimbus of flame, the light so occluded that details of its menacing form were lost in darkest shadow. Even so, its massive, hulking presence caught the eye and heart evoking deep-seated, instinctual fear.

"Looks like tha friendly sort o' chap I'd like ta have a few drinks with at tha local pub!"

Wrindanneth raised his eyebrows questioningly. "Spoken like a true Dwarf!"

Wrin then shook his head. "The dread steed is the most reassuring part of this image. From there it only gets worse, much worse. Where the Fyrskal wandered, what powers they invoked, and what pacts they wrought in the absence of their noble brethren, these records do not say. The depths of their depravity and the extent of their power, however, are clear."

Slate shrugged. "With any luck, any that're remainin' are either all destroyed or completely tied up by tha Cabal. If not, my axe can always use a bit o' sharpenin'!"

Wrindanneth choked back a laugh, thinking of the surprises their fortune might have in store for them in the face of their current adventure. "When have we ever been so lucky?"

Slate patted Duraeleon lovingly. "Depends on yer definition o' luck. I fer one live fer a bit o' head bangin' and purse fattenin'. Otherwise, I wouldn't be here, lucky er not."

Aroganji merely raised an eyebrow, saying, "Do not fear, Slate, when have we gone anywhere without some 'head banging' or 'purse fattening'?"

A wicked grin spread across Slate's face. "We certainly know how ta travel in style!"

Shaking his head, Wrindanneth berated, "Only a battle-addled, brain-concussed Dwarf would see the pleasure in such encounters."

Slate scoffed at Wrindanneth's dismissive remarks and replied with a challenge of his own. "Then why're ya here?"

His voice deadpan, Wrindanneth responded, "I'm here for the gain, not the pain."

Slate grinned wickedly. "Then ya're missin' half tha fun!"

Wrindanneth indicated the unholy Fyrskal with a nod of his head. "If that *thing* is your idea of fun, then why don't I teleport you directly to the Abyss for a real bacchanal?"

Slate remained cool, shrugging nonchalantly. "Don't worry, we'll get there. Fer now, there's plenty o' hellspawn here ta keep me busy."

He then winked conspiratorially at Wrindanneth, saying, "I'll keep yer offer in mind next time I need a holiday, Wrin."

Responding with an evil grin, Wrindanneth answered, "The offer is open any time, Slate. You have but to ask."

Returning to the original point of discussion lest they spend the rest of the trip wrangling, Aroganji asked, "What else have you gleaned that may be pertinent from your study?"

Shifting focus from deriding Slate to exposition without missing a beat, Wrindanneth replied, "Those Fyrskal who fell from grace and remained upon Ea'ae became more Daemon than man. They preyed upon the living, stole the vital essence of their subjects and those with whom they ran afoul, and subverted all that was noble at every turn."

"Darkness was their deliverance and they pursued it at every turn."

Slate did not hesitate. "So we can expect tha Fyrskal ta be capable o' anythin' a Daemon from tha nether realms might be able ta summon forth?"

Wrindanneth gave a curt nod. "Aye. Having fallen from the Light's grace they may be capable of a few other things besides."

Wrindanneth's eyes lingered on the magical image manifest before them. "Should we have to face any of the Fyrskal directly, we must remain exceedingly cautious. Of late, many of our foes have embodied such great magical ability that we have not been exposed to significant direct physical confrontation for they have often chosen to unleash their powers against us from a distance."

"The Fyrskal will be different. They embody a combined force of arms and magical power that we have yet to encounter...a lethal combination. Close or at a distance, the dread knights will press the attack, pushing forward to their advantage."

Yip studied the horrific image galloping through the air before them, a fearsome dreadnaught shrouded in a nimbus of evil. He spoke simply to Wrindanneth's point. "The Fyrskal are enlivened by Darkness. This is the source of their strength, the impetus of their power."

Pausing for a moment, he continued, "Like other creatures of Darkness, they will be vulnerable to the expression of the Dragon's Gate should we be able to find a way through their defenses. This is an ability you all may now call upon in your defense."

"Within even the deepest recesses of Darkness, you can bring forth Light."

Slate grinned ruefully, saying, "Then that just about covers it. Tha human torches will light tha darkness while I burn it!"

Aroganji spoke matter-of-factly, the simplicity of his words belying their true difficulty. "After we counteract any defenses that the Fyrskal may have in place."

Slate snorted. "Ya think a juggernaut like that is gonna bother with defenses? Look at it! By Brendle's bones, that thing is tha very definition of unstoppable! Anythin' more is overkill!"

Emphasizing his point, Slate indicated the brute's hulking form with a wave of his hand. "Let's see, nimbus o' death, check! Unholy, Daemonic armor, check! Hellforged great sword, check! Infernal steed, check! Access ta tha powers o' tha Abyss, check! Strength o' tha unholy, check! Brethren who're just as nasty, check! What more could ya ask fer?"

Appreciating the lather Slate was working into, Wrindanneth laughed, saying, "Thousands upon thousands of mad, power-driven fallen Priests of K'un Lun, their Daemonic and alien allies, hundreds of ships, and anything else that has managed to peeve them that day, check!"

Slate nodded, exhaling his excitement as he did so. "Point taken. Tha Cabal and Fyrskal together will make fer an interestin' encounter. Assumin' they're both there."

Aroganji was firm. "Assuming they are both there, it will be better for us if we are not. We sneak in and out as planned whether we face few or many. Nothing more, nothing less."

Indicating the Fyrskal with a nod of his head, he added, "If executed properly, we will not have to worry about facing fiends such as the Fyrskal."

Dismissing the image mentally, Wrindanneth added reassuringly, "Yip is correct. Should we have to face the Fyrskal, though they may have the same strengths as Daemons, they also share in the same weaknesses. We are prepared for such a fight should the need arise."

"Should we be forced to face the Cabal, we are primed as well."

Looking at Yip as he spoke, Wrindanneth added, "From what I have experienced thus far of Yip's newfound mental ability, we should be able to coordinate our actions simultaneously as required by the situation almost instantly. This will be a great advantage for us if our efforts at stealth fail."

Yip bowed. "I shall do my best."

With a wry smile, Wrin replied rhetorically, "Don't you always?"

Their business concluded, each returned to their stations. Wrindanneth and Aroganji remained at the helm to navigate and seek out magical anomalies while Slate and Yip returned to the ship's fore to scan the skies visually and via prescience.

His mind open to possibilities both manifest and inchoate, Yip extended himself outward.

What would the day hold?

OCHRE EXPANSE

A sea of gray clouds
collide and churn in silence,
washing over mountains.

The mountains of northern Aruene were harsh, barren, and bitterly cold.

Young and uncowed by the passage of time, their jagged peaks rose heavenward defiantly, sheathed in glacial ice and packed snows. Sheer, broken only by dizzying chasms and icy hollows, the granite faces of unnamed pinnacles snarled at the still plains scattered below their vertiginous heights.

Winds whipped ice crystals fiercely across their flanks, challenging any to dare their reaches, warning the foolhardy against their treachery.

These, the fearsome Mourning Mountains, extended across the entire northern expanse of Aruene.

Once home to numerous Dwarven delvings and vibrant, if perilous, trade routes, the bones of these mountains were now hollow, devoid of the songs and stories, the fires and forges, that had once filled them of old. Within these long silent halls, darker shadows yet lingered, subverting the majesty of the past to inimical ends.

Were Aruene not almost completely forsaken, the lure of bygone ages and the challenge of the perils of these mounts would inspire many a tale and adventurer to explore their breadth and depth. However, the few who now dared plumb the mysteries beneath these peaks seldom returned, leaving scant stories or memories of their passage in their wakes—the ice, snow, and the mysteries below unchallenged.

Slate shivered in mock cold, rubbing his arms up and down his armored shoulders, imagining toiling across the staggering summits passing steadily below the *Shrike*. "Makes ya glad we're surrounded by a magical shield ta keep tha harsh realities o' these peaks out."

Sensing more of the Darkness hidden within the bellies of these mountains than he cared to explain, Yip agreed simply, "You are more correct than you may know. The cold would be the least of our worries should we have to cross these eminences alone and on foot."

Flying above the harsh landscape, Yip observed how the beauty and diversity of the living expressions of Aruene's northern plains quickly disappeared at the bases of these tortuous mountains, sucked dry by the denizens of the deeps. Though the life that existed on the plains would continually strive to expand its reach, until the Darknesses that lurked below were fully cleansed, life's full expression on the slopes would not flower. These slopes would, however, continue to provide fertile ground for the development of the hardiest of species.

Smiling with rare recognition, he occasionally sensed the presence of a few such fearsome pioneers.

"What d'ya mean, Yip?" Slate's interest was piqued. Unlike many Men, the recollection of his people extended far enough back to recall the memory of, if not actually remember, when these mountains were home to proud clans of his kind.

"The Shadows that lurk beneath these mountains are far darker than any that rest upon its surface."

"Are we in danger by passin' over 'em?"

Yip shook his head slowly, not wishing to linger upon such vileness but remaining aware and untouched nonetheless. "They are too deep, too settled for our passage to disturb their slumber. Many would deem us beneath their notice should they stir for quite a number of these Shadows are mighty indeed."

"What are they? Where d'ya think they came from?" Slate was now thinking upon the effort it would take to reclaim the halls of his distant ancestors.

Yip shrugged for he did not truly know. "They are not of this world. They are, like most things dark and sinister, from somewhere beyond but I cannot say from whence they came. Perhaps those Shadows who now reside below were summoned by the mountains' past masters, perhaps these creatures sought the mountains out at a time when Ea'ae's barriers were thin, perhaps they were past allies of the Fyrskal, or perhaps they sought refuge here to emerge at a time of their choosing, I cannot rightly say."

His eyes scanning the peaks slowly, thoughtfully, Slate said quietly as if to himself, "'T'would'nt be wise ta brave those depths."

Yip merely shook his head, his awareness bridging land and sky in his search for dangers to the ship.

His face spontaneously splitting with a bright smile, Slate smacked Yip on the back, interrupting his friend's silence, and announced enthusiastically, "Perhaps when we're done t'would be more advisable!"

Yip laughed, replying, "By your friends or your enemies?"

Slate's rejoinder was accompanied by a smile. "I'd reckon by both!"

Yip's grin was his only reply.

Turning their eyes forward, they returned to their survey of the heavens and earth.

Below, the Mourning Mountains sped by, their rough-hewn spires slashing skyward in irregular phalanxes of unbowed, jagged stone. As was the case on their northern flanks, no greenery or other signs of life typical of most mountain ranges were visible on the sides of the steep slopes or the valleys between peaks—evidence of life losing the battle against the terror beneath the precipices.

Based on what he sensed ahead, Yip anticipated that this situation would only grow more tenuous. Whether life would regain a foothold beyond the peaks, he could not yet feel or know.

At the ship's current rate of travel, he would not have to wait long to find out.

Though the mountains remained gathered ahead, stacked in riotous succession to the horizon, Yip began to sense a gradual transition in the energies of the place well before the *Shrike* cleared the last of the peaks.

This transition filled him with alarm.

"Hold!" Though he did not yell, the message he sent to Wrindanneth was as clear as a clarion call.

What he felt was unlike anything he had ever experienced before. Far in the distance, as the mountains receded into vast desolate plains, layer upon layer of residual magic clung to the landscape in a haze, a film staining the ground and lacing the air. Cloying and persistent, he sensed the remnants of terrible magics from ages past, unspent incantations, and corrupt arcana, a polluted miasma lying in wait for any who approached or dared venture forward.

This unclean landscape, sullied by atrocities of the past, stretched as far as he could sense, growing more and more vile the farther away he pushed.

A wasteland festered at Aruene's heart.

He understood without seeking that Morowen lay at the center of this befoulment.

Slowing the *Shrike's* passage as quickly as possible, Wrindanneth called out, "What is it, Yip?"

Hurrying to the helm, he leapt from the deck over the railing and landed silently beside Wrindanneth and Aroganji.

Looks of concern greeted his arrival.

Huffing across the deck, his armor eerily quiet as he hurried behind Yip, Slate called out from where he now scaled the steps, "What news?"

Yip remained calm amidst the tension he had so easily aroused. "The character of the energies ahead changes dramatically. I fear we will be in grave danger."

Wrindanneth nodded, focused and to the point. "How so?"

"The atrocities of the past lay thick upon the landscape ahead. Residual magics, unfettered incantations, and untriggered enchantments make the journey we are about to face exceedingly treacherous. I fear there is too much to read and too little known to guide us through safely."

"Within these magics, you sense there are spells to alert our foes of our arrival as well?" Aroganji's query was a statement more than a question.

"I cannot know. The likelihood is great. Lines of power cross the landscape, growing ever greater and more pronounced toward their source at the heart of the plains."

"Morowen?" Slate need not ask for he knew the answer.

Yip gave a short nod. "I cannot yet sense that far ahead but that would be the logical deduction."

"Can we fly over and out of the range of this zone?" Wrindanneth knew there had to be a way forward that would allow their passage.

Yip again nodded. "Yes. We would lose the cover of ground and would be more exposed to our enemies but that should provide a path clear of the hostile magics ahead."

"What o' our plans fer hidin' tha ship on tha plains and travelin' across tha landscape via teleportation?" Slate's concern for the success of their mission was expressed in the earnestness of his question.

Aroganji replied simply. "We will have to risk it. Given the ship's capabilities, we may be able to port from above and down into a zone of relative safety near our intended way station."

Wrindanneth agreed. "If we are not too high, the ship is capable of jumping to ground in a single port. Before we venture forth, we will have to ensure that we are cloaked as best as we are able against detection by hostile magics."

"We will have to remain vigilant in case our movements trigger a spell as we arrive and depart. Aroganji and I should be able to mask our patterns as we move toward Morowen to such a degree that such traps should be avoided but, as before, we must remain ready for the eventuality that our movements will be detected."

"Per'aps if we're quick enough, we can stay ahead o' anythin' that's triggered as we port ta Morowen."

Aroganji shook his head, saying, "I doubt it. We may be able to cancel any effect, however, with our own magics. Or Yip may be able to nullify any hostile spells prior to expression."

Wrindanneth added, "There are some effects we could outrun. Others might be so subtle that we might not know they were even triggered."

Yip asked, "Shall we take the time to modify the contingency spells for such an eventuality?"

Wrindanneth shook his head. "I do not think so. We can go ahead and cast another layer of protective magics to aid in our camouflage. At our current rate of travel, assuming nothing additional untoward arises, we should arrive in Morowen by day's end. The magics we will cast to hide us will last until then."

Slate scrunched his thick eyebrows together as he asked, "Will tha invisibility conferred by tha Stars of Illdrassil not be enough ta cover us as we port through tha terrain toward Morowen?"

Aroganji shook his head. "I think not. There is too much at stake here to leave such things to chance. Though the magic of the Stars does protect against most forms of magical and nonmagical detection, dedicated magics should be able to penetrate the mask provided by its enchantments. We will add another layer to this protection."

Wrindanneth agreed. "The Star's magic is efficient, flexible, and functional. Its enchantments are designed to be sustained over extended periods. Highly sophisticated protections generally take more energy than those employed by the Stars and typically last for a much shorter period of time. To be safe, we will require more advanced countermeasures."

"And ya won't be modifyin' tha contingency spell in any way?"

Wrindanneth's long red hair shifted in flowing waves as he indicated the negative. "I think our current countermeasures will remain effective in light of this new development. The ones we propose, however, will be much shorter lived. Once we hit the ground with the new enchantments in place, we will have to move toward Morowen quickly."

"So we'll get tha new spells prior ta landin' tha ship?"

"Aye."

"What if we're found out before?"

Wrindanneth shrugged. "We would have to refresh the spells by the time we are in a position to land regardless. With the exception most probably of Yip, we would have to invoke the Star of Illdrassil's magic to see one another. Why waste the effort and energy?"

Slate grunted as he mulled Wrindanneth's response over, satisfied but wanting to be ready now as opposed to later as the risks increased.

Changing topics, Wrindanneth asked, "How high do you anticipate we will need to travel to avoid the arcane haze, Yip?"

"Below the level of the mountains and most clouds." Yip's answer was quick and sure. Though there were irregular streams and wisps of power that reached upward and into the sky, most of the magical residue lay concentrated along the ground. The arcane forces that did persist in the air were thinner, moving and shifting to internal currents and direction.

Wrindanneth pursed his lips thoughtfully. "Then we should be able to maintain our current heading. I will take us up a bit higher once we clear the mountains. If there are clouds, we can use those for cover."

With a flick of his wrist, Wrindanneth pulled up a map of Aruene showing the Mourning Mountains and their position above the tangled spires. Indicating their progress with his finger, Morowen about equidistant from them as the coast was to their current position, he said, "Once we pass over the last of the peaks, I will engage the ship's cloaking system."

"This will protect us from all but the most persistent detection attempts. The ship's stealth system should also help us avoid triggering any latent traps or wards that may be lying in wait below."

"We should then be able to make our desired landing position without compromising the cloaking system's integrity or the *Shrike*'s reserves."

Aroganji examined the representation closely. The grays, blues, and whites of the Mourning Mountains transitioned into ruddy ochers, oranges, and tans across the sere landscapes of Aruene's forsaken inner plains. He imagined the bleak landscape's flowing lines and smooth topological transitions as an artist's canvas, paint dropped upon the surface merging and melding in graduated lines and zones of color. The abstract beauty of the landscape viewed from on high contrasted strongly with the reality he knew to be present on the ground. Turning to Yip, he asked, "Aside from the arcane remnants, you sense no threats below?"

Yip shook his head briefly. "Almost nothing persists on the plains." After a time spent in silence, he added, "There are traces, movements in the currents, that things yet abide but none are within the range of my senses."

Curious, Aroganji asked, "What types of things?"

Yip's words were chilling. "The type that could survive in such a place. The type that feeds on magic. The type that does not wish to be detected—darkling and dire."

"Fyrskal?" Aroganji's eyebrows lifted in concern.

"I cannot know."

"What else can you feel?"

"Whatever lurks below are as subtle as they are powerful."

Wrindanneth smiled grimly, recalling the image of the Fyrskal. "Definitely not the impression I got of the monstrous Fyrskal!"

Yip, however, did not share his sentiments. "The dread knights may be as elusory as a Wraith and as powerful as an archfiend. We cannot yet know what their essence holds."

"True." Though he wished to be able to characterize their enemy, Wrindanneth recognized that, as yet, such things were premature.

While Yip, Wrindanneth, and Aroganji discussed the entities that prowled the plains, Slate studied the image of Aruene floating before them as well. To his eyes, the landscape evoked images of the stories he remembered as a lad of Aruene's colorful history in ages long past. He envisioned what these same forlorn plains had been like in the times of his ancient ancestors when, in lieu of bare earth and stone, these windswept steppes had been covered by lush forests, shading the trade routes and homes of his kin. Now desolation and emptiness ruled where once had been prosperity. An edge of steel coming to his voice with the recollection, he asked, "How long before we're ready ta drop in?"

Stopping his conversation with Yip and Aroganji, Wrindanneth did not hesitate in reply. "Assuming nothing unforeseen, we should be in position within two hours."

Slate patted Duraeleon's sheathed blade in anticipation. "Brendle be praised."

Though there were no longer trees to be felled, perhaps others would soon fall.

His eyes remaining locked on the horizon, Yip said flatly, "Perhaps you should engage the cloaking system earlier than anticipated."

Without questioning or hesitating, Wrindanneth replied to Yip's direction with action.

The world shifted.

For a moment, the panorama of the mountains below and the sky above became watery and indistinct, viewed through reflecting, interfering, rainbow light swirling irregularly atop and within the surface of a soap bubble, only the *Shrike* and the ARMED drones hovering close to her hull were contained within this iridescent sphere. This chaotic reflection and reemergence of light gradually resolved itself until they could see clearly once more, light and energy bending around and away from them while the ship's magical compensation systems allowed them to see outward beyond the protective sphere as normal.

"What is it, Yip?" Concern brought an edge to Aroganji's voice while he waited for clarification.

"Warships are on the horizon."

Nothing appeared on the depiction of the landscape before them, but Wrindanneth knew otherwise than to doubt Yip's senses.

"How far, Yip?"

"They are beyond the mountains over the plains."

"Any indication that they have detected us?" Wrindanneth was intent, the clarity of his focus enabling him to react with surety and decisiveness.

Although he could not allay Wrindanneth's concerns, Yip replied, "Their course does not appear to have deviated in the time I have been observing them."

"Shall we try ta fly by 'em or wait?"

Aroganji answered, "Let us not increase the risk of conflict by seeking to pass by them when we yet have the position of advantage."

Silence fell as they watched for signs of the alien ships on the *Shrike*'s topographical representation, waiting for word from Yip.

"The ships appear to be moving in our general direction." Yip's words of caution rang loudly across the hushed deck.

Wrindanneth wasted no time taking evasive action.

Dropping down vertically, the *Shrike* plummeted toward the raw peaks below. Mind and instrumentation linked, his desire for a suitable safe haven was immediately analyzed by the ship's intelligence against the available topography. In response, the vessel flew them down to a bowl-shaped cirque nestled beneath the crest of one of the larger peaks in the vicinity, a location calculated to have the most desirable combination of protection from possible attack and the least likelihood of detection. Swooping into this glacial bowl, the *Shrike* hovered close above the living ice, letting the surrounding walls of stone help shield them from enemy detection.

Filled with anticipation, they waited.

Yip provided updates all the while. "The ships are maintaining their general heading. They appear to be describing a circuit along the fringe of the mountain range."

"Ya don't think they've detected us?"

"They do not appear to have altered course in response to our movement."

Wrindanneth shook his head. "They are now just coming in clearly on my instrumentation. No matter how sophisticated their equipment, I doubt they could do much better in detecting us if we were not cloaked given the difficulty of the terrain."

Slate nodded, accepting the answer. "How long before they pass our location if they keep movin' in tha same direction?"

Wrindanneth answered for Yip. "They should pass by and ahead of us within half an hour along the perimeter of the range. If they maintain their current heading, we should be safe to move in a little over an hour."

"Ya think they have tha systems ta detect our presence while cloaked?"

Wrindanneth shook his head. "No. But until we have no other recourse, I would prefer to remain cautious."

Remaining patient, they watched the hostile ship's progress on the *Shrike*'s imagery. As the vessels neared, so did the clarity of their representation. With this clarity came little reassurance.

There were three ships shown on the *Shrike*'s display flying in tight formation. These ships were not scouts cautiously exploring unfamiliar terrain. These were warships; warships securing a defensive perimeter described by the inner plains of Aruene.

All three ships were alike. Sleek, black, and full of menace, the crafts cut through the air with all the confidence and surety of predators swooping in for the kill. In appearance, they resembled nothing so much as polished, metallic falcons. Agile and deadly, claws retracted, they knifed across the sky with uncanny precision. Even without visible weapons, the threat implicit in their sculpted forms could not be underestimated.

Compared to these ships, the *Shrike* appeared as lumbering and cumbersome as a child's toy.

"Would ya look at that!" Enthralled, Slate could not help but appreciate the lethal beauty of these alien ships.

Wrindanneth, too, was impressed. "If form follows function, it would be wise not to follow those ships!"

"Aye!" The alien vessels reminded Slate of the sharpened head of a berserker's battle axe let loose from its wielder's hand mid-throw seeking a target in which to bury its baleful edge.

After a few more moments of appreciation, Slate grinned, his eyes glinting in challenge. "Ya think we could take 'em?"

Wrindanneth did not like what his instruments told him of those vessels' capabilities and power. Finally, he said, "With the drones, perhaps."

Yip echoed Wrindanneth's concerns. "Though their energy source is of a much different type than ours, the power stored within each of those vessels is much greater than that used and held within the *Shrike*."

"So ya're sayin' they'd blow us outta tha air?"

Wrindanneth shook his head. "Not necessarily. But this serves as an indication that they are quite capable."

"Moreover," Aroganji added, "and more importantly, we do not wish to give away our position."

"Bah!" Slate huffed, "If we can't sharpen our teeth on these miscreants then who can we?" The grin on his face belied the ferocity of his words for he knew better than to suggest otherwise.

On the representation floating above the burnished deck, alongside the three-dimensional images of the landscape and alien ships, information on the crafts was displayed in a dancing iridescent stream—position, speed, altitude, movement vectors, weaponry analysis, various risk assessments, along with much more intelligence reflective of Wrindanneth's own questions and concerns. All of this data was presented expressly for the purpose of informing the crew.

Without being tied directly to the ship's systems as was Wrindanneth, much of this data passed too quickly to be usable, however. With his direct link to the ship, the pace and urgency of Wrindanneth's thoughts strongly influenced the display.

Tired of trying to keep abreast of both the alien ships and the display's information stream simultaneously, Slate finally demanded, "Mind slowin' down tha display, Wrin? My eyes are gettin' crossed wanderin' back and forth between tha readin's and tha warships."

Wrindanneth grinned enticingly, saying, "Do not fear, Slate! This was but a test. Since you have gotten so accustomed to life on the ship, I thought an extra challenge was in order to see how well you held up against an added layer of motion sickness!"

Slate frowned. "Glad ta hear ya're lookin' out fer me!"

"Anytime!"

Now that they had the enemy visible directly in front of them, Aroganji said, "We must now be exceedingly vigilant. Just as we have seen our enemy and remain hidden, there may be those of our adversary who are now concealed lying in wait for the likes of us."

Wrindanneth nodded. "The enemy we see will be the least of our worries."

"Your words are truer than you know." Yip had paid scant attention to the imagery displayed on the *Shrike*'s display. He had been maintaining his attention outward, following the ships' trajectories, assessing the life forms within, and seeking beyond for other anomalies.

What he had sensed was disturbing but not entirely unexpected.

The ships were crewed by a race with which he was entirely unfamiliar. They were vaguely humanoid and appeared highly adept both technically and magically. Unlike Gnomes who displayed a certain creative genius and flexibility in design and character, these beings appeared far more regimented and utilitarian.

They were also extremely bellicose.

The niceties of this unidentified race, however, were not his primary concern.

Scanning the skies, his mind kept skimming over what felt like three holes in the fields of living energies over Aruene's surface. These 'holes' moved in formation some distance behind the alien vessels that were visible on the *Shrike*'s projection.

He could not, in fact, actually sense what was causing the distur-bance he felt. Rather, he could feel the absence of any presence in three localized positions. All movement, vibration, and energetic interaction stopped, disappearing completely after coming in contact with these positions. Devoid of motion, utterly gone, what was no longer appeared to be.

Based on the voids' movements and locations, he could only assume three similar vessels were trailing behind the alien warships moving in tandem with a single purpose. If the first ships were scouts or bait for interlopers then the crafts that followed must be the trap that lay in wait.

These ships were protected from detection with what he assumed was an advanced energy absorption system.

Unlike the *Shrike*'s stealth system which redirected any energy that came into contact with its field, guiding these forces around the ship as though she were not there, these objects were protected in an entirely different manner. Any energy that came into contact with these posi-tions did not reemerge. He was, however, able to sense the last moments of energetic movement about these locations prior to the energies' disappearance but no more.

What became of the forces that contacted these vessels, he could not say, only that it vanished. Perhaps it served to power the ship, perhaps it was redirected elsewhere, or perhaps it was stored for future use. Regardless, these vessels were completely cloaked.

Before Wrindanneth could ask the question on the tip of his tongue, Yip said, "There are what I can only assume to be three more vessels shadowing the first. These ships are cloaked."

Slate growled, "By Brendle's blade! They've laid a trap fer any who would either be foolhardy enough ta attack or fer any who may try ta sneak by once they glimpse a window o' safety!"

Aroganji nodded. "They've laid their snare but we will not trigger it."

Slate snorted. "We'll saunter on by once we're in tha clear and trigger our own!"

Wrindanneth cautioned, "We must remain patient and wait until all ships have passed and have progressed well beyond the range of detection. We do not know these ships' capabilities and cannot risk being overconfident despite seeing through their ruse."

His eyes reaching out with his mind, Yip said, "We will wait. When I can no longer sense these anomalies, we will see if the time to move has come."

Slate placed both hands on his hips, his voice full of menace, and said, "I can wait. Duraeleon can drink now or sate its thirst later."

Curious, wanting to know how to detect such objects in the future, Wrindanneth asked, "Could you show me the approximate position of these anomalies?"

Yip examined the representation closely, exploring the region over which the objects moved all the while looking for similar features on the ship's map. Finally, he pointed to a spot above some low ridges perhaps fifty leagues away. "Here."

Wrindanneth then asked a series of questions. "How are they cloaked?"

"How can you sense their presence?"

"What signs could I use to detect similar objects in the future?"

Yip answered simply. "They appear to absorb all energy that comes within a certain distance of them. Nothing emerges from within the range of this field."

"I sense their presence both by the absence of energy within a place and by the end of energies' movement after contacting these objects."

"If you brought up a view of magical fields manifest within a certain region, you would see how these objects' movements disturb these energy fields, cutting through the ambient energies of life, leaving swirling eddies of magical forces to flow into the resulting void. Other fields react similarly—light, sound, heat."

Wrindanneth nodded extending himself outward through the ship's sensory systems. Letting these detectors bathe him in readings of ambient forces, a picture slowly emerged just as Yip had described. Though nothing appeared visible directly from these ships, once within range, the absence created by their presence was just as discernible as their presence would have been.

Pleased with his friend, Wrindanneth said, "I will set up a heuristic to successively scan for such features automatically in the future."

As Wrindanneth finished speaking, three more ships registered on the display, these last represented merely by luminescent orbs.

"Then we'll be able ta pick off tha buggers like Orcs flushed from their warrens!"

Aroganji, however, was more cautious. "I wonder if those ships' cloaking fields are more than just a measure to provide additional stealth. If, as Yip says, no energy reemerges from within once it contacts the ships' shields, then perhaps they serve a dual defensive purpose. Perhaps energetic attacks directed at the ship are harmlessly absorbed or redirected elsewhere. Direct attacks against such a vessel could empower the ships somehow or improve its capabilities."

Wrindanneth remained thoughtful. "Our primary options then would be to fire physical objects directly at a ship protected thusly or try to overwhelm its defenses beyond its shield's ability to absorb energy."

"Without knowing such shields' absorption limits or how, if at all, such energy is put to use, direct physical fire would seem to provide the most advantageous approach."

Slate nodded solemnly. "Tha drones can provide plenty o' flak should it be needed."

Aroganji agreed, adding, "Let us hope it is not. We can detect their presence. With any luck, we should be able to avoid a confrontation."

Slate smacked his forehead. "There ya go talkin' about luck again! Let's not doom ourselves ta fightin' every enemy ship between here and Morowen."

Wrindanneth cracked a smile. "Said the eternal optimist!"

His voice sedate within the sounds of his friends' excitement, before letting them get too distracted by their banter, Yip cautioned, "If those fields do dissipate or absorb incoming energy, then the impetus embodied in a physical object's movement may be just as completely absorbed."

Slate grunted, shaking his head in frustration. Knowing the answer, he exhaled. "Ya mean like tha energy within tha shots we fire..."

Aroganji's face was grim as he replied for Yip, "If the ships' defensive shields can indeed stop the motion of light, then they may be able to halt tangible objects just as completely."

"Then what're we left with?" Slate was ready for an answer, he just did not know what it would be.

"Without having tried it, we still have our first option of direct fire from the drones using a range of options from ballistic to explosive." Wrindanneth did not want to discount a possibility before it had even been attempted.

"While we wait, could the ship not scan the disturbances and predict which countermeasures may have the greatest possibility of success?"

"Good idea." Yip's question spurred Wrindanneth into a frenzy of activity. Quickly setting up the general parameters for the ship's exploration, he provided the initial guidance and desired outcome to the *Shrike*'s intelligence. With his request in place, he left it to the ship to deduce the best strategy to reach the desired result.

The following minutes stretched and elongated, pulled by the attention and focus held within each of their minds.

Slate clenched his jaws as he watched the hostile ships speed across the landscape. Appearing so close on the *Shrike*'s visualization, he resisted the urge to reach out and pinch the tiny enemy ships into oblivion between his thumb and index fingers. He did, however, smile with the thought.

Wrindanneth stayed in intimate contact with the ship, prying into the alien vessels' secrets. Over and over he analyzed the alien ships through the *Shrike*'s instrumentation adjusting intensity, measurement type, and myriad other parameters. No matter what he tried, they slipped through his extended mind like water through his open, outstretched fingers.

A solution on an angle of attack remained just as tenuous.

Aroganji weighed options against outcomes should one of the ships detect their presence. What choice of counter would be most effective? Multiple spells flitted through his mind, each subsequent choice discarded due to the improbability of success.

Experimentation would have to be their direct response. Time to find a way through the shield would have to be their hope.

Yip's mind roved broadly seeking after other risks and disturbances within range of sensation. In the far distance, other ships moved though not directly against them. Toward Morowen, the sky teemed with vessels—a hive turbulent, abuzz. Nearer, the alien ships' progress past their position was quite rapid. Soon these crafts would pass. Just as soon, they would move forward and into the swarm.

"The way forward is clear." Yip's words broke the expectant silence that had fallen over the *Shrike*'s deck.

Taking the *Shrike* to the air once more, Wrindanneth swung out and away from the barren peaks of the Mourning Mountains, angling toward the sere plains below at their roots. Understanding the dangers ahead, he left the ship cloaked, maintaining heights to avoid the swirling tides of magic shifting over the plains ahead.

"Toward Morowen, the sky is thick with Cabal warships." Yip's words fell flatly, without emotion into the still air. Ill tidings atop already chilling circumstance, however expected.

"Do they range far enough out in numbers to interfere with our intended plan?" Wrindanneth was already weighing alternatives as he asked.

"No."

"Are there many scouts in the skies between us?" Aroganji, too, was preparing for alternatives.

"Those that are present are on the move as were the ones we just passed."

"Good." Slate shook his head measuredly. "We'll ferret our way through their net before they know we've come and gone!"

"Let us hope so!" Aroganji's nod was grim, not expecting such fortunes however desirous.

"I wonder how tha other ship o' Home Guard fares." Thinking of their own progress brought to mind that of their fellows on the other ship.

Wrindanneth shrugged, assuming no message was the best news they could hope to receive until the Guard's mission was ended. "They have not yet risked communication. Assuming all is well, they are, like us, endeavoring to secure the seal."

Slate's grunt was his only reply.

The mountains below began to thin, their pinnacles no longer clawing fiercely at the heavens as the ship sped forward. So, too, did the timbre and tenor of the land begin to change. Somber grays and whites gave way to ochers and umbers. Stark transitions surrendered to subtle shifts and flowing changes as the land opened and flattened. Boulders became dust as the terrain expanded, leaping to the horizons upon reaching the earthen steppes.

Where thickly forested lands bisected by rivers and streams may be covered by low-lying fogs and mists, the plains of central Aruene were blurred by shifting clouds of loess, the detritus of erosion past born upon the winds in a yellow-orange cloak. From on high, viewed from the *Shrike's* deck, these clouds glowed and shimmered with an ominously toxic luster, filled with the remnants of foul magics from ages past. These poison clouds scoured and burned Aruene's central plains, wiping them clean of almost all life.

At night, when the sun fell, these same clouds would light the landscape with swirling plumes of mephitic corpse light.

Yip did not need darkness to reveal the full repulsive vileness of the drifting currents below.

He felt the noxious putrescence of century upon century of corrupt magics tainting the land and air directly, subverting the living energies that should have flowed over the harsh environment, bathing it in potential. These foul adulterations washed over and through him in ceaseless waves, travesties beating against the borders of his mind.

Though the life-giving *yuan-chi* yet flowed, it sank into a polluted miasma of filth that continually perverted its true glory. In time, perhaps, this area would be cleansed through this continual refreshment but, without intervention, this day remained in the far distant future.

Morowen lay at the heart of this morass and until it was no more, this corruption would continue.

Studying these unusual clouds, Slate grumbled, "Looks like they've thrown out all tha stops ta give us a right proper welcome!"

Wrindanneth snorted. "If your idea of a nice welcome comprises virulent clouds tainted by horrific magics, remind me to let you go first when we visit your clan for your homecoming."

"Bah! Ya won't have ta duck any clouds when ya visit tha thane. Axes per'aps if ya can't hold yer tongue, but we'll find a way around that I'm sure." Reaching over his shoulder, he stroked Duraeleon's sheathed blade significantly.

Wrindanneth laughed. "Bring that blade within a hand's breadth of my face and we'll see who is holding their tongue."

Slate snorted innocently. "'Twas but a thought... Always best ta keep all options on tha table."

Now it was Wrindanneth who grunted. "Not with your appetite!"

Slate spat at the image Wrindanneth's comment evoked. "I'd rather eat Troll dung than consider such an abomination!"

Wrindanneth's face changed to one of subtle amusement. "You sound like you speak from experience."

"Ya're about as unreasonable as an Ogre in heat!"

"Ah the images you paint, Slate. Perhaps you missed your calling. I am sure we can find a commission for you somewhere with the Orcs. I hear they are always in need of good artists." He paused but a moment before adding flatly, "Especially before dinner."

Turning his back to Wrindanneth, Slate growled, "This conversation is about as appetizin' as yer tongue!"

The day's brightness grew and began to fade as they journeyed south and west over the desolate landscape. Rolling dunes, sun blasted hills, and open wastes passed by in rhythmic succession while they watched and waited in position.

Much of this time together was spent in silence, their minds separated by the vast distances of their inner landscapes, mirroring the tractless emptiness below. Somber and thoughtful, the quiet growing between them was not a reflection of ill temperament, rather of preparation for what was to come.

This day, as any other, could be their last. Each prepared for this potential end in his own way. Though some may wish to end spectacularly, each of the Four readied to make his end, should it come, as effective as could be hoped.

Aroganji stood beside one of his favorite teachers, the venerable Xi Wue. Robes whipping in the currents that rode between land and stars, they felt that which moved, that which came to be, and that which faded.

Before them, the cultivated grounds of Xian Shi spread down the gently sloping hillside, her carefully arranged classrooms, research centers, places of study, outbuildings, students' chambers, gardens and decorative plantings, water features, and sculptures aglow in the lambent light of dawn. In the distance, the Q'ia Shan Sea glimmered in the morning air. Behind them, the snow-capped Hsiang Lung Mountains supported the heavens. Between these two features, the earth moved and the world changed, slowly evolving and devolving as movement flowed and transitioned, motive forces came to be and then passed.

Moments passed to minutes as the morning unfolded around them. Finally, his teacher spoke, "The way of the Fang Shih, the way of life, is clear."

Master Xi Wue's eyes remained on the horizon. "The change you seek is the change you must become."

"The Wu-hsing are the agents."

"The will, your mind, is the bridge."

Aroganji's mind returned to the present, needing no further reminders of what must be, of what he must do, in the time ahead. His teacher's memory spoke through him, guiding him forward.

He would be whatever was needed for them to succeed.

"Boy!"

The words rang through the tower sending a chill down Wrindanneth's spine.

He preferred the cool disdain of his master, the dismissive glares, the disparaging remarks, anything to the fiery heat of his rage.

Something was wrong and all too soon he would find out the source of his master's ire.

He knew, of course, that he was the cause. What he did not yet know was exactly how he had brought about this latest paroxysm.

Mounting the stairs to his master's laboratory at the top of the tower, he marched upward. He knew better than to hide just as he knew better to delay.

Get it over.

Let the torture end and move on.

Run through the fire and pass through lest the flames burn too long.

He sighed upon sight of the thick oaken door leading to his master's chambers.

Knocking deferentially—he knew better than to enter without giving notice—he announced his presence, tacitly accepting his guilt.

Opening the door cautiously, on guard, spells at the ready for he knew not what trickery his master may have in store, he entered the door to his teacher's inner sanctum. Carefully arranged books filled shelves lining the rounded walls, each a treasure trove of magical knowledge accumulated over lifetimes of effort. Vials filled with rare herbs, extracts, essences, minerals, and many other unidentifiable components held sway over cabinets carefully arranged between the shelves, his master's desk, sitting area, and work stations. Hanging from the ceiling and placed atop the shelves themselves were items of his master's former conquests—Dragon skulls, Lich fingers, vampire teeth, boiling masses of felled Daemon essences, among other gruesome reminders of the terror his master embodied.

At the center of the grim menagerie, standing at the focal point of the chamber, the very personification of power in his eyes, glowered his master.

"Boy!" The words cut through his core, grating against his bones as his master's words rang through the tower. "I have endured enough of your idiocy! Your time with me is at an end!"

He raised a hand in protest. Though his voice was weak, his words were strong. "But master, I have so much more to learn!"

"Do not question me, boy! You are weak and unworthy! Your mind is like a sieve that only latches upon failure! I am through with your hopelessness. The time has come for you to seek your fortunes elsewhere or die in the attempt!"

His master's cruel laugh only emphasized what he thought of Wrindan-neth's chances once he left.

"Begone! Do not tarry or you, too, may take your place among my trophies!"

Standing tall, no longer willing to accept the crucible of his master's ire, he fired back, "You are the one unworthy of notice you shallow-hearted, vain-glorious, tyrant!"

A bolt of black fire exploded through the air, smashing him against the wall before he could mount any defense. Wracked in pain, he blinked as the world faded to darkness.

So this is what it felt like to die.

Ripped up from the ground by his tunic, he was smashed against the wall once more. His master's breath hot against his face, his teacher growled, "You will not die this day, worm. You will live to suffer yet for your words."

Dazed, he could not think or focus. The room swam around him as his eyes watered and he was dumped to the floor once more.

Blinking through the darkness seeking to overtake him once more, his master turned dismissively and walked away.

Before losing consciousness, he swore that he heard his master say, "This one may show some promise yet."

When he finally opened his eyes again some days later, his body filled with burning pain, he was still in his room.

He would not let his master's pride prevent him from wrenching every bit of knowledge from him that he could.

Just as he would not let his teacher's machinations foil his own desires, so, too, would Wrindanneth not let his enemies prevent him from realizing his destiny.

Staring intensely toward the horizon, he was filled with the anticipation of vindication and the urge for vengeance.

Slate stood by the forge working the bellows, sweat dripping down his brow, the burning of the muscles in his arms no match to the heat of the forge on his skin. Beside him Maeglan, his uncle and Dur'kazak, worked, his hammer pounding a cadence upon the metal he wrought, flames dancing beneath his masterful touch.

He worked in time to the beat of his uncle's need, two instruments acting in time for one purpose—to bring to life the blade that would be born from the heart of flame.

No words were spoken for none were needed.

They were as one as was their intent.

Finally setting down his hammer, Maeglan lovingly cradled the burning brand so elegantly crafted and shaped by the elements of metal and fire, magic and will. His hands untouched by the heat coursing through the blade's length, the magic of his own heart-fire lent the metal strength and stability, forming its purpose, guiding its future.

The magic coursing through his arms wreathing the blade in flames, Maeglan presented the blade to Slate, intoning words as old as Brendle's own *forge, the fires from which they all sprang. "These are the fires from which you were forged. These are the fires to which you will return."*

Slate did not intend to die this day but he did intend to burn.

Yip walked alongside his teacher through the gardens, his young mind lost in contemplation. All around, the fragile spring visited upon the lofty monastery grounds was showing its first flush of life. Buds were opening, petals were forming, leaves were unfurling, birds were returning, and the first insects were to be seen crawling cautiously in delighted surprise at the newfound beauty burgeoning all around them.

"Master Wei, what happens when we die?"

"That is for the dying to know, Yip."

Early on in his studies with the K'un Lun, only recently assigned his teacher, there was so much more to the world than he sensed and understood, so much more than he had seen or been told.

He knew enough to understand that the way of the K'un Lun was often a path of individual realization, where answers were not given but comprehended through direct experience. This drive for immediate insight and understanding often explained his teacher's reticence to answer even the simplest questions directly.

Undeterred, showing the dogged determination that was to become the linchpin of his training, he tried again. "Does the mind cease when we die? Does the self fall away?"

"That is for you to determine, Yip."

His mouth already open to ask another question, he snapped his mouth shut as his teacher's words sank in.

Pondering the dual meaning of his teacher's words, he walked alongside Master Wei in silence.

The future, his fate, truly was his to determine.

And discover.

Yip's mind was clear. Each moment was experienced, lived to its fullest. Activity need not preclude appreciation. Action did not equate with quality or depth of experience. Impending danger and imminent risk need not interfere with the joy of living or the purpose behind it.

Content, aware, he stood in serenity, motionless—clouds drifted, ridges passed.

"We're here!" Wrindanneth's words were a clarion call amidst the silence that had lingered over the deck since leaving the shelter of the mountains. Guiding the *Shrike* skillfully through the air, he had given wide berth to several ships but had never felt in any real danger of detection.

As far as the eye could see, the land was littered with irregular branches and gullies spanning out from a massive central canyon wending its way ambiguously across the ruddy landscape. Layer upon layer of eroded rocky strata marked the depths of the ancient fissures, so vast that their true extent was often lost in the haze of dust and debris clouding the air. Where once a mighty river and its tributaries had fed the central chasm, carving its length and breadth through time, now only wind and dust flowed freely through the canyon's steep walls.

"Time to gather 'round!" Wrindanneth indicated that everyone should collapse to his position at the helm. "Before we port down to the ground, I would like to cloak us with the improved invisibility spell we discussed."

Slate nodded. "So we're close enough ta tha ground ta jump down without encounterin' tha foul, tainted magics that cloud tha air?"

Wrindanneth gave a short nod, summoning the holographic representation with a magnified view of the earth below. Pointing at the image, he indicated their destination relative to the *Shrike*'s current position. "I have found a location within the folds of this deep crevasse that appears to be both almost completely out of sight from the air and relatively free of contaminated magical energies."

"We should be able to port down safely and use this as our jumping off point with minimal fear of detection."

"Excellent!" Slate washed his hands together eagerly.

When all had gathered around him, Wrindanneth began his invocation drawing on the power of the ship to aid in his enchantment and minimize depleting his internal magical reserves.

Yip felt the forces swirling through and around Wrindanneth as he worked his spell. Surrounded in a turbulent maelstrom of energy, he deftly wove subtle complexity from raw power. Spinning and refining his magic by hand and mind, Wrindanneth layered upon them a shroud of invisibility very much like the one that cloaked the ship. Connected by the same enchanted veil, they could, however, see and interact with each other.

"Excellent work!" Slate flexed his arm unselfconsciously liking the thought of being well-nigh undetectable.

Aroganji smiled at Slate, saying, "You've never looked better!"

Wrindanneth shook his head and scoffed, "You're not invisible to us, Slate."

Ignoring the insult, Slate countered brightly, "Aren't ya lucky!"

Wrindanneth snorted disdainfully. "Hardly." After a moment's reflection he said, as if to himself, "Perhaps we would all be better off with a slight modification to my spell..."

Returning their attention to the matter at hand, Aroganji said, "Are we ready to port?"

Wrindanneth nodded. Without thinking, he placed his hands on the silvery command sphere floating beside him above the deck. Closing his eyes, with a simple mental signal, he engaged the ship's short range teleportation system.

Torn apart, his remnants scattered across the cosmos, the world shifted.

Ripped asunder and rebuilt, his ashes regathered from the far ends of the universe, Yip stared upward past the striated umber walls of the canyon in which they now rested and into the vaulted blue sky they had just left.

The universe ceased and was reborn in an instant.

"Let's roll!" Slate clapped both hands together eagerly. "Time's a wastin'! Enemies are a waitin'!"

Looking to each of them in succession, Aroganji asked, "Are we prepared?"

Slate held up a hand indicating the need for a moment's pause. "We've got tha seal?"

Yip smiled and bowed. "The seal is safe."

"Weapons in place?"

Aroganji smiled. "Check."

"Drones armed?"

Wrindanneth motioned for him to hurry in reply.

"Headin' fer Morowen?"

Wrindanneth merely nodded, his patience waning.

"Ship's cloaked and secure?"

Wrindanneth shook his head disapprovingly, remonstrating, "Everything is ready."

Slate raised an eyebrow, his tone serious. "Are we?"

"I'm ready! Ready to hit you! If you don't stop delaying, I'm going to dispel your cloaking after we get to Morowen and leave you there."

Slate's grin was infectious. "That's tha pep I want ta hear!" He smacked Wrindanneth loudly on the shoulder. "Wrin's ready!"

Not waiting for any further delays, Wrindanneth established the connection he shared with Aroganji through the magical Elven bracers. *"You cast the far vision spell, and I will cast the first port."*

Aroganji gave his silent assent.

"Aroganji will grant us each far vision. Once he has completed his incantation, I will jump us up to the lip of the canyon on the far side not overhanging the *Shrike*." Wrindanneth pointed high above to his target while he spoke.

"Ready your Stars should you not port far enough, miss the ledge, and need to fly to the proper section of the cliff. I don't want to have to scrape anyone's body off the canyon floor."

Slate merely snorted.

Yip patted Slate on the back reassuringly. "No need to worry, my friend. We all know the earth would be on the losing side of the collision should you fall to the ground."

Nodding sagely, filled with a combination of mirth and pride, Slate said, "I'd hate ta leave another fracture in tha floor o' this canyon!"

"From tha looks o' her, she's already suffered enough!"

Seeing no objections or reasons for further delay, Aroganji started with a nod.

Soft phrases and complex gestures passed quickly as he invoked his incantation, drawing forth the energies required to fuel his intent. With this invocation, magic dusted about them in a fine mist, completing the far vision spell.

Aroganji's spell complete, Wrindanneth's words guided, reiterating his earlier direction. "Look to the far lip of the canyon. Our first jump will take us there."

"So it begins again! Let's go!" Slate's eagerness translated directly to his feet as he hopped back and forth on each foot in anticipation.

Bathed in magic, Wrindanneth's decree washed over them and the world shifted once more.

Only upon arriving, perched precariously close to the lip of the vertiginous chasm did they realize only three were there. Slate, however, was quickly found.

His heavy gauntlets clasped tightly on the canyon's lip, Slate hung from the ledge on which his friends stood.

"Don't let go, Slate!" Aroganji's urgent words cautioned against Slate's potential fall, the magic of the Stars temporarily forgotten in extremis.

With a dismissive curse, Slate pulled himself up easily before anyone could offer him a hand, one he would not have taken out of pride for his misstep.

"What happened there, Slate?" Aroganji's concern was not only for his friend's welfare but for the accuracy of the successive jumps they were about to take.

Slate shrugged nonchalantly. "What I can say, I'm a bit shorter than tha rest o' ya. I couldn't quite reach tha top."

Aroganji laughed while Yip smiled.

Wrindanneth, however, was not amused. "You mean while the rest of us picked a spot and the canyon's lip close to the edge, visualizing a spot high enough above the edge that we could arrive standing, you merely aimed for the lip itself."

Slate shrugged. "If ya wanna split Ogre nose hairs, then maybe we should leave ya behind. We've work ta get done!"

Now it was Wrindanneth who snorted. "We must strive to remain in formation as we jump. I thought that was a lesson you learned the last time we did this."

Slate growled, "I was within two paces o' where ya landed, North-lander. I'd say that was close enough. Now let's be on with it 'fore ya get my dander up!"

All around, the fractured landscape shattered toward the horizons.

Broken rock and loose grit were the only visible relief between the spans dividing one plateau from the next. Dust clouded the air and grated across their exposed skin as wind whipped across the yawning precipice.

Buoyed and empowered by Daemonic spirits, foul magics roiled and tumbled within the flying clouds of debris, seething across the inimical terrain.

With time, this unceasing virulent haze of grit would wear them down just as it did the rocks over which it flew.

Shielding his eyes as the dust blew furiously past, Wrindanneth pointed far across the arid landscape. "There. We will aim for that hilltop." Turning to Slate, he clarified, "The pinnacle. From there we will have a better vantage."

Yip pushed his mind forward, sensing the unseen, feeling the invisible, assessing the safety of their proposed position as best he could from afar. Nodding, he indicated, "The hill appears relatively safe."

With a nod of acknowledgement, Aroganji asked, "Ready?"

When all nodded, Aroganji began his incantation, taking over from Wrindanneth as they prepared for their harrowing flight across the sere landscape.

Once more the world shifted, expanding beyond comprehension before collapsing back into physicality.

Yip's mind immediately leapt out, searching for dangers, for traps, for hostile spells or enemies that may somehow detect or react to their presence.

But there was nothing.

"The way forward is clear."

Around them the land fell away precipitously from the rise on which they stood, quickly dropping off the surrounding cliff faces and into the canyon bottom that waited dizzyingly almost a league below. Only loose rock and dirt clung to the hillside on which they now stood. In every direction, the shattered terrain extended as far as the eye could see—fractured, partitioned by massive rifts.

"Then let us proceed." Their jump had taken them into the heart of the canyon lands, a rugged landscape that would have been considered beautiful prior to its despoliation. Wrindanneth cared little to survey the land beyond the need to locate their next target, however.

A line of hills darkened the horizon far ahead to the south and west. "We shall go there. To the left side of the hill that appears to have been laid low, the crest flattened. Do you see the one to which I refer?" Wrindanneth's gaze indicated their target. Once more, he turned his gaze upon Slate significantly.

"Aye. It's tha one that looks like yer pale paunch when ya choose ta blind and repulse us by takin' off yer shirt!"

Wrindanneth's glare indicated the level of disagreement he felt over Slate's assessment of his physical condition. To himself, but loud enough for Slate to hear, Wrindanneth said softly, "Yes. The masters of Morowen will enjoy their new Dwarven companion."

Yip's awareness touched the line of hills carefully before he spoke. "We must take caution moving forward. Dark energies cast a pall over the entire line of hills."

"Is there another option?" Aroganji looked up and down the chain looking for another vantage from which they could find suitable views from which to port forward.

Wrindanneth shook his head. "Unless we detour farther to the north or south, there does not appear to be much in the way of choice."

"Could we not engage our flyin' spells from tha Stars and port inta tha air high above tha hills? Then we could jump without riskin' tha hostile magics and see farther fer our next port."

Aroganji gave his assent. "That sounds like an excellent idea, Slate!"

Wrindanneth turned to Yip and asked, "Any additional risks of detection in the air? How high do we need to be to avoid the magical field?"

Yip shrugged. "I cannot say. There appears to be no more risk of detection than we see now. As far as height, roughly one hundred paces above the original spot you indicated should let us arrive clear of the dark powers that cloak the hill."

"Let's go!" Slate engaged his Star of Illdrassil. As he did so, his feet lifted slightly off the ground in preparation for the jump. All around, Yip, Aroganji, and Wrindanneth followed suit.

"Ready?" Aroganji turned to look each of them steadily before giving assent to Wrindanneth to move ahead with his teleportation spell.

After a moment's consideration, with no objections heard, Wrindanneth commanded, "Eyes well above the hill! No deviations! We port upon completion of my incantation!"

Once more the world collapsed and expanded beyond comprehension as Wrindanneth's words fell over them, time suddenly stopping and beginning anew. Once more they shifted in a blink and were gone only to arrive many leagues ahead of their original position.

This time, however, was different.

Horribly different.

No sooner had they arrived than Yip sensed something was terribly wrong.

He reacted as quickly as possible, redirecting as much of the assault as he could, but was too late.

Fell forces struck immediately upon their arrival, enveloping and engulfing them before they fully materialized and recovered their sense of self.

His mental scream of alarm unheard, Darkness cascaded across his vision, crushing his senses, pulling him inward, tugging at the limits of his consciousness, dragging him ruthlessly toward oblivion.

His world contracted to the infinitesimal.

At the periphery of his faltering awareness, his friends' Lights wavered, suffocated by the surging gloom, cut off by the ravaging, virulent magics heaving upward from the ground below.

These Lights, so distant, flickering, beckoned from another time and place, calling to him, pleading for restitution.

To these he reacted.

To these he returned.

Crushed from all sides by the raging avalanche of living power, Yip pushed, dazed, holding as best he could, his friends free of the onslaught that threatened to wash them away.

Guiding the waves of force seeking to tear their essences to shreds, he let the tumult flow within and around his mind, shielding his friends, giving them room and time to recover, while the bedlam that suffocated them fumed about their prone forms.

Unable to do little more than collect himself after the near collapse, while the wild magics continued to rage, he persevered. Gathering the remnants of himself together once more, offering what little he had to his friends that their Lights would not fade after the nearly fatal assault, he assured their safety until they could assure his.

Wrindanneth's eyes flickered and wavered.

Weak.

So weak.

Where was he?

An instant of disorientation evaporated as the horrific memory hit him full force in the face.

All-encompassing blackness knocking the lifeblood from his veins, the vitality from his heart.

Ravenous terror swallowing them whole.

Snapping his eyes open, his head rapidly clearing, the recollections forced out, he responded as he would have had he the time to react upon their arrival.

Words of power cloaked them in a cocoon of safety.

Gathering every ounce of will remaining to him, he muttered the words of one final incantation and they jumped forward once more.

Then the darkness reclaimed him.

The vicious, living magics vying for their essence left leagues behind, Yip directed more life-giving energy into his friends' failing forms.

Though their lives wavered and dimmed, he gave more than they lost, staunching the weakness that consumed them, filling them with vitality where before there had been none.

As time passed, still tremulous, he realized his efforts were not enough. Though the *chi* he gave appeared to help his friends persevere, it simply was not enough to grant full recovery. Darkness yet abided in his friends, robbing them of too much. The *chi* he offered merely delayed its progression.

The curse that had risen up and swallowed them appeared to be growing, gaining traction within each of them, claiming new territory and new energy just as it would soon claim their lives. If left unchecked, the evil they had so recently abandoned would claim a new refuge.

If his friends grew too weak and the contingency spells protecting them activated, his friends would port far away beyond his ability to help. Though this activation would delay the inevitable, the restorative magics of their protective spells would be unable to cleanse the vileness advancing within.

There was only one thing he knew to do.

Not knowing how his response would affect his friends, what, if anything, it may alter of their natures, or how they might reemerge after its application, he acted for he had only the one choice left before him.

What he could not do himself, he would let the Light of Life do for him. The Dragon's Gate would be opened within each of his friends. The vile curse coursing through their veins would be fuel for this energetic manifestation.

What of each of them passed through this gate and what would be transformed by Its brilliance would soon be revealed.

Though he wished for each of them to have the opportunity to guide and partake in their own personal evolution, he had no other option open to ensure their survival.

His heart filled with concern, he reticently opened the Dragon's Gate, sparking the Light of Life within each of his friends in unison, letting the glory of Life's unfolding cleanse them of the Darkness that slowly devoured each of them from within.

Guided by his intent, limitless potential was made manifest from within emptiness, exploding into possibility, sparked into expression. In an instant, empyrean energies encompassed his mind's eye, embracing his friends, blinding him to everything but its existence, and he was amazed.

Recovering himself while the luminescent wonder flared through each of his companions, he directed his mind outward once more, doing all he could to mask the energies now burning through his friends, seeking to assure and ascertain their future.

Able to expand his mind once more, gradually reassured that they remained as yet undetected, he, too, closed his eyes.

The ashen gray clouds, the dusty haze, the ceaseless plains, and turbulent magics disappeared as blackness, too, fell over him.

MOROWEN

A guttural roar
pierces the predawn stillness—
the battle begins.

"Yip?"

Aroganji's voice.

He felt his friends' presence nearby.

So different yet so similar.

All of them.

In a state of deep, restorative relaxation, having watched over his companions for some time while he recovered, their wakening just begun, the sound of Aroganji's voice finally came to him.

Eyes yet closed, he observed and felt his companions move and stretch, examine and ponder as they sought to understand and explore what was now so subtlety and inextricably different about themselves.

He was now in the presence of angelic beings, newly emerged, drifting through the heavens briefly come to alight upon Ea'ae. Nebulous lambency shimmered and wavered about his companions with the fluid grace of undersea creatures, the intensity of stars.

Without having to delve further, he apprehended that his friends were now divine.

This realization was undeniable, distinct from his comprehension of the universal divine nature of all things. Instead, this understanding was personal, an appreciation of the transformation of individuals and the realization of human potential, moving from one form to another, surpassing one set of limitations to encompass yet more.

His friends were gone.

His friends were here.

His friends were more.

He opened his eyes and the desolate expanse of Aruene appeared once more—sere ridges rolling from one gradually sloping rock encrusted hill to the next. "Yes, Aroganji?"

His reply was greeted by a bright smile. "We wanted confirmation that you were well."

Looking to each of his friends in turn, he noted that something was different even to the unaided eye. In the half-light of the overcast skies, they all looked the same but their apotheosis had left an indelible mark, he just could not quite place it.

Finally, he, too, smiled, noting what was different.

Each of them bore a faint shimmer, lightly dusted by ethereal diamond fragments or miniscule water droplets that gently touched their skin. The diffuse light masked the effect which would be more pronounced in fuller light. The overwhelming intensity of their luminescent auras interfered with his ability to discern the play of light on what would otherwise be visible of their skin outside of armor and robes.

"You are each graced by the *yuan-chi*. Its touch now rests lightly upon your skin."

Slate laughed. "Do we glow with a halo o' Light like ya do when ya shimmer with yer *chi*?"

Yip shook his head, speaking softly in wonder. "Stars appear to have settled gingerly upon your skin, twinkling softly in rainbow hues in the half-light."

"Then that is what saved us?" Aroganji knew the answer. He could feel it. He felt a vibrancy flowing through his body that he had never known. But this marvel still begged the question.

"I opened the Dragon's Gate within each of you when my own efforts with the *chi* failed to purge the evil from your systems."

Wrindanneth nodded in confirmation. "I thought as much."

"What does this mean?" Slate's thick eyebrows rose quizzically with the question.

Yip bowed slightly. "That is for you to discover."

After a moment's pause, he added another deep, heartfelt bow from where he sat, not yet knowing the full ramifications of what he had done. "Every person is entitled to his own realization and development. I am sorry that I altered your experience and paths without your blessing."

"My intent was not to deprive you of your journey, merely to give you the opportunity to live. I hope that you have not lost too much in the exchange."

Slate laughed loudly. "Leave it ta Yip ta apologize fer savin' our lives!"

Avoiding the sentimental emotionality, Wrindanneth barked, "Our lives are not saved yet! The incantations protecting us have been damaged and must be restored." As a reluctant, if indirect acknowledgement of Yip's efforts, Wrin added more softly, "We are lucky to be alive." He, too, wondered what was new and different about himself but that exploration would have to wait for another time.

Aroganji gave a curt nod. "Indeed. Our thanks and deepest appreciation go to you, Yip." He bowed deeply to Yip as a sign of his regard and gratitude.

"How've ya managed ta keep us outta harm's way while we recovered, Yip?"

Yip stood as he replied, the magic incorporated into his garments shedding a cloud of dust as he did so. "We blend in with the energies of this place as though we are not here."

Slate scratched his chin. "Ya've shielded us while we recovered with yer *chi*?"

He shook his head, smiling. "I made us indistinguishable from the *chi* of this place."

"Sounds like a handy trick fer family reunions!"

Wrindanneth was impressed though he did not say so. "Would you be able to maintain this protection while Aroganji and I restore the protections that were stripped from us?"

"Yes."

Wrindanneth turned to Aroganji, his voice steady, firm with resolve, saying, "Then let's get started."

Aroganji smiled. "Let us recreate what was and restore what will be."

Slate snorted, chiding. "Just get ta work! If we tarry any longer, my beard'll drag tha ground as I stand!"

Wrindanneth gently closed his eyes, lost in internal reflection. "Now wouldn't that be a sight!"

Slate expanded his chest proudly. "My clan would show no end ta tha honor bestowed fer such a feat!"

Wrindanneth snickered, pausing mid-motion before commencing his invocation. "Neither would the snarls and tangles!"

"Just get on with it ya red-headed mongrel!"

Flourishing a bow from the waist accompanied by a series of twirls from his right hand and a sweep from his left, Wrindanneth doffed an imaginary hat and said, "Your wish is my command, o' Masterful Dwarven Ancient."

Slate turned his back to Wrindanneth in disgust while Aroganji and Wrindanneth's magics began cascading over them once more. The facility and adroitness with which they performed their enchantments was truly remarkable. Needing less time and effort to recreate what had taken them many long minutes to complete on the *Shrike*, the entire warding process was complete in mere moments.

Examining his hands with a reluctant, heady smile, Wrindanneth crooned, reversing his prior unwillingness to comment openly on Yip's changes to their essences, "Yip, if ever there was a need to apologize, this is not it!"

Aroganji, too, shared in Wrindanneth's amazement. "When I woke, I thought little had changed. Now I know that everything is different." He would never have imagined being capable of such energetic feats prior to his recent restoration.

Aroganji's voice was hushed as he added, "If anything we have done until now will help our chances against our foes, the rebirth you have given us is it."

Sharing a brief glance with Aroganji, Wrindanneth added, "And I feel more changes are yet in store for each of us."

Though he did not wish to say more openly until he had further confirmation, in his heart, Wrindanneth hoped that Yip's gift would be the final lever that would allow him to finally break free of Maeth Onai's servitude. Yip had done for him what he had once hoped to do for himself—using the Dragon's Gate to transform himself, becoming more than human, more than was needed to freely seek his destiny.

Instead of voicing his heartfelt wish, Wrindanneth pointed and said, "We aim for that rise."

Dust swirled and churned about them, a yellow-brown pall washing out details and distance. Old magics lay thick in the air, thicker with each jump toward their destination, cast-off spells and fractured arcana.

"Can we see far enough fer a port ta make a difference?" Slate squinted through the churning gloom. What little light remained of day was rapidly deserting them, making discernment of their next destination even more difficult.

Aroganji replied simply, "The question is not whether we can see, for with the appropriate spell we can, rather whether we should continue in the dark or wait for dawn."

Wrindanneth agreed. "Which would our enemies expect least?"

Slate replied with a question of his own. "How much farther do we have ta go before we're close enough ta place tha new seal?"

Casting his mind out, Yip's awareness soared across the landscape. Far off in the distance, much darker than the night falling around it, he sensed the vileness that could only be Morowen. "We are perhaps as far from our destination as we are from our point of departure from the *Shrike*."

"What lies between here and there, Yip?" Aroganji's gaze fixed in the direction of their travels. "Will the darkness bring out more dangers than we should risk?"

Yip spoke to them all as he replied. "The evils that haunt these wastes fear neither light nor dark. Passage at any time is a risk."

"As to whether we should move or hold, though I sense little to be feared in the vicinity, that can change quickly. Holding position in such a place as this only invites danger."

"Time, also, is not on our side. The longer we wait, the more likely the Cabal will subvert this and other seals to their own ends, opening our world to evils that should not be visited even in nightmares."

Aroganji pursed his lips, thinking. Wrindanneth, however, was resolved. "Yip is right. We should not hold but press on. I will augment our vision that we can cut through this gloom and darkness and press on."

Slate thumped his chest. "We will fall upon our enemies under cover o' darkness, lay waste ta 'em unawares, and send 'em back ta tha pits that spawned 'em!"

Wrindanneth dropped his shoulders and shook his head, exhaling in exasperation. "We will not descend upon anyone. Nor will we lay waste for we will be gone before anyone knows we have come and gone."

Slate lifted his shoulders and then dropped them in a shrug. "A Dwarf can always dream. Seems an awful waste ta come all this way without a bit o' smitin' and smotin', smashin' and bashin'."

Arching one eyebrow and leaning over conspiratorially, he whispered, "They have it comin' ya know."

Wrindanneth would have none of Slate's jest. "The only thing coming will be us and we will be leaving just as quickly."

While Wrindanneth and Slate quibbled, Aroganji wove another layer of penetrating magics augmenting their discernment further. With the completion of his incantation, the mantle of dust and dusk lifted and they could see clearly once more.

Turning his gaze away from Slate in disgust, disapproval laying heavy on his brow, Wrindanneth pointed forward once more and said, "We aim for that flat topped hill on the horizon."

With a quick incantation and release of power, the world flashed and so it was—the destination became the point of departure.

Darkness fell rapidly upon the xeric plains, the sun quickly lost in the grit and tenebrosity of the horizon.

Yip's mind expanded to take in the space of their arrival, scouring the hill and its environs for the unexpected—inimical or otherwise. Though barren, here, too, layers of spent magics commingled and merged, leaving the landscape covered in the residue of times past. That these spells, or portions of them, persisted only spoke to the enormity of events foregone.

If the legacy of ages past yet laid so heavily upon Aruene's shores, he feared for what lay at her heart. The Fyrskal may be the least of their worries.

Assured that all was well, at least for the present, in the instant taken to offer this assessment, his mind turned to his friends just as quickly, remaining poised and alert all the while. "We are clear to proceed."

Slate shook his head surveying the lifeless expanse revealed through his magically enhanced vision. "It only seems ta get nicer."

Wrindanneth snorted. "Too bad the same can't be said for you."

Slate scowled. "Unlike yer kind, I grow stouter and richer with age while ye and yer kin slip, becomin' ever more weak and frail."

Wrindanneth cast Slate's comment to the side. "I am not my kin for I have none." Digging a little deeper, he added snidely, "When blessed as we are, we have plenty of ability to lose before others not so fortunate have grounds to make any comparison."

Aroganji gave them both a stern look. "We are all losing ground now."

When both Wrindanneth and Slate quieted, sharing only glares, Aroganji pointed forward and said, "We aim for the southernmost hill on the horizon."

Yip's awareness quickly jumped forward, lying lightly upon the land as he surveyed the space ahead. Though there was little on the ground to warrant concern, overhead the alien warships were threateningly close and quite numerous.

Yip cautioned, "Be prepared to move rapidly upon arrival. Our destination appears to take us inside another layer of the Cabal's defensive perimeter. There are multiple alien ships in the immediate vicinity. If detected, we must be set to teleport."

Aroganji and Wrindanneth both nodded in understanding. Wrindanneth stated, "As soon as Aroganji's spell is finished, I will choose our next destination and begin casting so that we will move beyond any risk of immediate detection."

Aroganji then said, "Ready?"

When he heard no objections, the world vanished and then reappeared with a few words.

As quickly as the landscape resolved around them, Wrindanneth pointed south and west, his voice loud and clear, declaring, "There!" By his gesture, Wrindanneth indicated a line of jagged, irregular rocks thrusting upward from the ground in a loose assortment of massive boulders and scattered scree.

No sooner had the words left Wrindanneth's mouth and the invocation to travel commenced to roll from his tongue, than Yip called out, "Hold!"

His mind taut, he sensed a field of energy sweeping across the terrain moving rapidly toward them. Though they were cloaked by protective magics, he wanted to ensure that their energetic *li* were completely indistinguishable from those of the surrounding landscape. So, too, did he wish to avoid leaving any residual traces of their presence that teleporting might leave, potentially granting their enemies knowledge of their whereabouts.

Blanketing their presence within his awareness, assured all was well and no sign of their patterns were detectable, he felt the energy beam sweep past them without hesitation as it had in covering the surrounding environs—a shimmering wall of radiance emanating from the sky.

The beam did not return for a second pass.

Sensing all was well, he followed the beam to its source—an alien warship arching through the skies far above. In close proximity, other similar ships flew in tight formation, much like the ones they had encountered upon first approaching the central plains of Aruene.

"What was that about, Yip?" Aroganji's voice was laced with concern.

Turning his attention to his friend, his awareness yet encompassing the ships above, Yip replied, "One of the alien vessels was scanning the surrounding area. I wanted to make certain we were undetectable and that we left no traces to give away our presence."

Before any further questions could be asked, he added, "We are now safe to proceed."

"Now he tells us!" Smiling as his voice filled with mock indignation, Slate was glad that they remained secure and their flight across the landscape was as yet undetected. Though he would not mind a fight should one come, the last thing he wanted was to be picked off from the skies before they could offer anything in the way of resistance.

"If we are done, I would like to move us closer to our destination." Wrindanneth's tone of disapproval was feigned, largely to offer mandatory antagonistic opposition to Slate.

Slate saluted smartly. "By all means! Tha last thing I want is ta hold us up! Proceed, proceed!"

Holding his tongue, Wrindanneth held back a venomous retort and turned their attention forward. "We will target a landing on the top of the large, flat boulder protruding from the line of broken hills to the southwest."

"Do you see our target?"

"Aye." Slate nodded. "Next ta tha split rock, shorn down tha middle?"

Wrindanneth nodded, already awash in magical energies as he called forth the power that would translocate them from one position to another.

Within a single, timeless moment, the universe ended in blackness only to be reborn in sensation—sight, sound, breath, light, and movement.

Standing atop a massive rust colored boulder, one of many in a line of similarly tumbled monoliths thrust up from the ground, or dropped and scattered from the sky, the plains of Aruene opened before them, falling away to the south and west.

In the darkness of the cloud enshrouded night sky, near to the limits of their vision, a single eminence thrust upward from the desolate flat plains. Perched atop this butte, visible only in silhouette for it was darker than the empty sky shrouded behind its fearsome turrets, the citadel of Morowen lurked menacingly beneath the heavens. Aphotic absoluteness, emptiness punched out from the starless sky, the keep of the Fyrskal threatened—the maw of a timeless beast waiting to swallow its next hapless victim.

In the absence of stars, high above the bastion's walls, the fleet of the Cabal swarmed feverishly in the night—small lights attracted to the pit of utter darkness about which they massed. From these ships, arches of lights, balls of fire, and concussive waves of force rained down, the weather of the apocalypse visited upon the rocky steppes of Aruene.

UNDER COVER OF DARKNESS

Ruddy orange fire bolt
arches through the heavens—
a Dragon screams at the stars.

"By tha flamin' beard o' Baeradun!" Slate stared forward in disbelief. That this citadel yet stood was remarkable. That it yet stood against the constant onslaught of a fleet of devastating alien warships was simply awe inspiring. Without having Yip's eyes or calling upon the enchantments of the Star of Illdrassil, he knew that untold power yet flowed through Morowen's turrets.

"Let us hope the otherworldly fires of the Cabal's fleet provide sufficient cover for us to place our seal without event." Aroganji's eyes read the tumult and dislocation in the air, the history of violence and destruction of the place, the forced subjugation of land and people by brute force and raw power, and the legacy of destruction given birth from this source.

Morowen was a place of horrors the equal to any other.

Had the fleet above not been in place, he was sure this malevolence would have long since reached out to greet them.

Wrindanneth understood Aroganji's fears though he did not think his concern was their primary risk. He was confident in their ability to succeed. He did not, however, discount the influence of random chance on the outcome of their venture. Such chance was often placed in their own hands—mistakes to be eluded or averted and opportunities to be seized.

There were many such mistakes to be avoided. His task was to remind everyone of them, their counters, and their course of action. "Let us hope that we all manage to arrive together lest we risk giving ourselves away. We cannot afford any missteps."

Glancing at Slate with a friendly smile, he added, "We should count ourselves lucky that these barren plains hold no thistles for Slate to teleport into. Apparently teleporting Dwarves are attracted to bushes, brambles, cliffs, and obstructions."

Slate raised one bushy eyebrow. "There's no harm in keepin' things interestin'."

Wrindanneth's objection was simple. "Except when there is."

Yip paid scant attention to his friends' quarrel. His mind was assessing the powers at play before them. Unmoved by the forces that surged through the sky colliding against the protective magics of the keep, Morowen remained untouched by the Cabal's assault. Ancient sigils and wards, artifacts unbowed by time or encroachment yet protected Morowen's stygian ramparts. Such power was a manifestation both of the seal locked within Morowen's walls and the surfeit of magics expressed by her denizens over ages grown shrouded in dust and decay. This power oozed outward and over the landscape from its source in a vile flood.

How this impasse between evils would fare once they replaced Morowen's seal and its power waned, he could only imagine.

He did not wish to be present to find out. Nor did he wish to test himself against either power.

"Are we ready to move, do we wait for the right moment to strike, or do we discuss our strategy further?" Aroganji wanted to have every opportunity to plan for and realize the most favorable outcome while they had time. For when the battle started and events tumbled together, the time for planning was done and only the well-prepared lived to see the light of dawn.

Wrindanneth shrugged. "We must react to what we are given after we play our cards. With any luck, we will port in and out without being noticed. If we don't, we will need to respond as best we can for we cannot say what will come."

Slate nodded. "If we're attacked, we must provide cover long enough fer Yip ta place tha seal and let it activate. If we fall inta a trap, we must survive long enough fer tha new seal ta take tha place o' tha old. If we're forced ta retreat, our defenses stripped, and tha contingency spell activated, we can only hope fer a second chance. If we're taken inta tha keep, Brendle only knows what we'll need ta do ta come out alive."

Yip indicated his agreement, looking at both spellcasters as he addressed them. "We port in on Wrindanneth's word and out on Aroganji's. Unless we are found out, you must be ready to return us to the *Shrike* as soon as possible, Aroganji."

"If our enemies never know we are here, they will only have themselves to blame for the loss of the seal."

Slate snarled. "Let's be on with it! If I'm ta fight, let's fight! Otherwise, I'll start up a cookfire so we can gather 'round fer tha exchangin' o' tales!"

When no one took him up on his offer, Slate cocked an eyebrow and asked, "Are all our spells refreshed and ready?"

Aroganji gave a brief nod. "All is in order."

Turning to Yip, Aroganji asked, "Are we close enough to activate the new seal?"

Yip reached inside his robes and withdrew the small wooden container housing the replacement for the seal of Mihtig'leht, feeling for any changes in its magic. Barely detectable, slumbering with no signs of waking, the seal remained in repose.

"Not yet." Without describing the loathsome nature of the powers he felt, he added, "The energies of the current seal are apparent, however, as are those of the keep."

Indeed they were.

In such close proximity to Morowen, Yip was keenly aware of the heritance and persistence of evil, of the Fyrskal's corruption, for he wallowed in its depths, immersed in abhorrent energies that only willful perversion could create. Though unclean, he remained untouched.

After a few heartbeats of silence, he added, "We are close. Another teleport and I believe we will be able to activate the seal."

Wrindanneth nodded gravely. "Then we must choose carefully. Despite our protections, we do not wish to arrive too near the citadel. How close do we need to port, Yip, to arrive where you believe we will be able to activate the new seal?"

Yip studied the energies moving across the landscape, reading their intensity and patterns, their interactions and direction, feeling the nuances of their expression with each moment.

His evaluation complete, he said, "If we teleport slightly less than half the distance between our current position and Morowen, the new seal should be close enough to activate."

Joking aside, for their next move was critical, Wrindanneth turned away from the flat plains beneath Morowen's bluffs and said, "There are no geographic markers to guide our next step. To aid us, I will place an optical target over our destination point. It will only appear in your mind and then will fade after we jump. Aim for this point and we will arrive together."

"As soon as Yip indicates all is complete, we port out under Aroganji's guidance. Everyone must be prepared to act immediately should the unforeseen arise."

"Are we ready?" Wrindanneth looked to each of them for some sign of agreement. When he was sure of their preparedness, he began his first spell. In a matter of moments, a single green marker appeared before their eyes. Though existing nowhere but within the confines of their minds, this marker appeared as a glowing green triangle on the sere, open plains beneath Morowen's dismal shadow.

"And so it begins." Slate reached over his shoulder to unsheathe Duraeleon, indicating quiet with a loud, "Shh!" when his axe began to voice a protest at being locked away for so long.

While Wrindanneth's words washed over them, their forms ceasing to exist in one position only to be recast in another, Aroganji whispered, "May the change we bring initiate the future we desire."

Yip filled the desolation stretching about them with his mind.

The vast emptiness, shorn and wrecked, forsaken after millennia of disuse, extended as far as the eye could see, silence crashing against the bulwark of Morowen's sheer cliffs. Into this space his awareness poured, untouched by the turbulent, corrupted magics raging across the plains and the oppressive evil oozing outward from Morowen's black walls.

Though he sensed horrific wickedness of a type he had never known radiating from on high within the keep, debased and twisted, no threats materialized upon their arrival. The Fyrskal, or something equally horrific, did indeed persist within the bleak expanse of Morowen.

Although destruction continued to rain down upon the citadel of Morowen from the ships orbiting above, arches of light and heat, blasts of concussive force, the plains beneath her turrets were calm, the violence above implacably absorbed by her walls.

Within his hands, the seal stirred.

Slowly, steadily, he felt the seal awaken, unfolding and opening, ready to flower. This growing vibrancy and warmth built within the wooden container, emanating outward awaiting release.

He expressed himself quickly, conveying his impressions along with his words mentally. *"All is safe for the time being. The seal stirs and seeks expression. I am beginning the restoration."*

While his intent joined the space between them, articulating himself and his impressions of their arrival to his friends, he opened the small wooden container, providing a spark to the seal that resided within. With this simple influx of energy, the seal within vanished.

His world transformed.

Exploding outward, his mind surged along pathways once traversed by lines of force in ages past, bridging and restoring the energy currents that had been severed since the corruption of the seal of Mihtig'leht so long ago. In his purview, a vast distributed network spread around the planet, linked and linking the seals and their connective channels. A part of this matrix, his mind sensed the totality of Ea'ae's shield, the points of weakness yet in need of repair, the old seals that yet remained focal points of power, their energies not yet distributed as with the new seals, the absence of the old seals where new ones had now taken their place, and the reinforced nature of the planet's protective system where the new positionless seals had obviated the old.

No longer a locus, become the bridge that bound and girded Ea'ae in a protective mantle, the seal once held in his hand now spanned continents, ensuring Ea'ae's continued protection from outside incursion.

After some time, he knew not how long, a disturbance reached him from his vantage and he returned his attention to his point of departure. With that shift in awareness, the world transitioned once more.

"Yip!" A look of exasperated anxiety crossed Aroganji's face.

"Yes?" Blinking, his friends gradually returned to focus as his mind returned to the corporeal.

"Ya disappeared! We weren't sure where ya'd gone or when ya'd return!" Slate's anxious guise resembled one more closely associated with anger than concern.

"I was with the seal." Before more could be said, their next course of action decided, Yip screamed out in warning to his friends, his words silent, cast out directly from his mind to theirs. "Get down!"

Above, a series of concussive blasts reverberated across the plains, followed by a shock wave that threw them backward, hurling them violently through the air along with a wall of dust and debris. Finally returning to earth, they slid to a halt after a rough-and-tumble skid across the open ground. Though they were cast bodily into the air, the impact of the repercussion, the abrasion of the dust, and force of the landing were all dissipated by the protective alien shields.

Had they been closer, the entire wall of Morowen's precipitous cliffs would have come down upon them.

Wiping dust and grit from his eyes, Slate looked skyward, his gaze taking in the Cabal's fleet and the citadel of Morowen. What he saw unfolding before him left him momentarily speechless, in awe of the power and in dismay of the horror that arose.

The citadel of the Fyrskal, the black bastion of Morowen, was no more. The fastness's impregnable walls had fallen, blasted to dust and rubble by the onslaught of the alien ships. The high plateau on which the keep rested had been shorn, burst asunder and a great avalanche of boulders, scree, and debris lay in waste along the cliff side, resting amid a cloud of settling dust beneath the portion of Morowen that yet stood. Its might had fallen along with the seal that had been corrupted, subverted to the heinous designs of its unholy masters.

From within the remnants of the keep, madness stirred.

Ghastly and unbowed, untouched by the cataclysmic upheaval visited upon their haunt, a wave of dread steeds took to the skies, their flaming nostrils igniting sparks of detritus, miniature stars come to life only to fade beneath their horrific tread. Upon their backs, blacker than the soulless pits from which they had flown, the terrible Fyrskal rode out to do battle against those who assaulted their home.

Though raging arches of fire and energy tore through their ranks as the phalanx of Fyrskal took to the heavens, none appeared touched by the violence visited upon them.

Finally recovering himself, Slate stood, taking in the spectacle before him.

"Our work here is done. The time to depart has come."

Yip's words barely reached him, arriving from a vast distance. Shaking his head, Slate realized he had not yet fully recovered his hearing after the massive blast.

"Tha Fyrskal've fallen!" Though his words were filled with the excitement of the moment, their truth had not yet been actualized for the Fyrskal swept through and around the ships swarming above ringed in black fires, cutting through vessels with the ease of mere shadows.

Aroganji shook his head. "This battle is not ours nor is it yet done."

Wrindanneth concurred, reluctantly averting his eyes from the drama above. "Though the seal has fallen and with it the source of the keep's power, the Fyrskal yet remain. Let these two evils vie for supremacy in our absence! Should we desire, in the days ahead, we can return to determine the victor. Otherwise, let us leave this refuse to the dust from which it arose."

Slate nodded, not yet taking his eyes off the skies. "Then we return ta tha *Shrike*, update Tellanon on our success, and find out what is ta be done aidin' tha Home Guard with tha next seal!"

Magic swirled about them even as he spoke, putting Slate's words into effect as Aroganji's magic took hold and returned them to the ship.

RENDEZVOUS

An old fallen log
decaying in the loam
lends a welcome spot to rest.

They stood on the planks of the *Shrike*, the surreal calm of her deck and the still night shrouding her hull only heightened when juxtaposed against the violence of the skies above Morowen so recently swarming about them. Overhead, the tall cliffs walled out what little light reached the bottom of the chasm. Beyond the canyon's rim, a thin veil of stars was faintly visible within the shrouded black reaches of the evening sky.

"Is all in order?" The adrenaline coursing through Slate's veins gradually receded, settling into the evening quiet, his breath slowly growing deep and even.

While his friends got their bearings, Yip's mind scoured the area around the ship for any disturbance or signs of detection. When none arose, he finally said, "We appear to be safe for the moment."

Wrindanneth added, "All appears to be as it should be with both the ship and her shields."

Aroganji gave a nod of acknowledgement. "Let's contact the Home

Guard while we have the chance. They must know of our success and we must know the situation of the Guard."

Wrindanneth reached into his robes and withdrew the quicksilver command disk. Releasing the sphere, the orb floated in the air above the deck, shimmering in the light of the stars.

Taking supreme care, he opened a secure channel, encrypted by random magical fluctuations so as to make interception and deciphering well-nigh impossible. Quickly establishing a secure connection, he sought to contact Tellanon. His request was immediately received.

"Fists," the voice of the Construct issued from the sphere, "communication risks are high. We have but moments." A series of complex multi-dimensional geometrical objects shifted and transformed, changing color and intensity above the sphere while the Construct communicated.

Aroganji gave a curt nod and an even shorter answer. "Mission success."

The Construct's abstraction flashed a brief, brilliant white. "Successful target actualization missive transmitted to designated parties."

After a brief pause, Wrindanneth asked, "And the others?" Wrindanneth was careful to mention as little information as possible should their message somehow be intercepted and their intent scrutinized.

"No contact has been received."

Aroganji briefly pursed his lips. "Then we will rejoin them."

"Pertinent mission critical data transferred for your review."

"Thank you." Yip bowed.

With a series of complex transmutations, the meaning of which they could not divine, the Construct finished, "Gratitude is ours to give. May continued success be yours."

With those brief words, the Construct fell silent, their connection severed.

Slate's full throated chuckle filled the ensuing silence. "If I didn't know any better, I'd say tha Construct was showin' a bit o' personality!"

"Too bad the same can't be said for others." Wrindanneth's muted glare was the most positive part of his sentiment. "In all likelihood, the

Construct is capable of suites of thoughts and emotions none of us will ever apprehend."

Slate frowned, saying, "Sounds like ya've finally found someone ya can relate ta."

"I only wish it had said more." Aroganji had hoped to hear of their fellow adventurers' success or an update on their progress despite knowing that such news was unlikely unless their work was done.

Wrindanneth snorted. "I only wish Slate said less."

"Then ya're in like company, Northlander, fer tha feelin's mutual."

Used to ignoring the barbs flying between his friends, Aroganji overrode Wrindanneth's forthcoming retort and said, "Shall we see what lies in wait ahead of us before our next port?"

Wrindanneth nodded. "A little time to plan is better than none."

His eyes on the sky, Yip said, "I will continue to monitor our safety should we need to leave in haste."

Slate grinned. "Ya sure ya don't want ta miss out, Yip? It's bound ta be interestin'."

Yip returned the smile, his eyes turning from their scan above to the command orb. "I will not."

Slate shivered. "Yer warped sense o' perception is about as out o' kilter as Wrindanneth's sense o' tact."

He did not reply, merely waiting in silence for Wrindanneth to pull up the information transferred from the Construct. Wrindanneth, however, did not hold his tongue. "Once again, the feeling is mutual."

Before Slate could offer a retort, Wrindanneth let the information sent by the Construct initiate, beginning with the background intelligence and mission objective provided. A visualization gradually materialized in the air above the sphere. Although dark and diffuse at first, the image slowly resolved into a depiction of a keep perched high atop rocky crags overlooking the dark boughs of a thickly wooded temperate forest.

The castle brought to life appeared to be made of ancient stone hewn directly from the living rock on which it rested. No cracks or fissures were visible in its sheer walls. Four high turrets marked the corners of each massive wall. Beneath the towers' heights, the central donjon hulked in the darkness, vast and unreachable, surrounded by several well-fortified baileys.

A rocky, irregular roadway followed a winding path up a second adjacent cliff face toward the castle gate, only occasionally visible through the thick trees through which it cut, long disused, strewn with boulders and debris. As the road reached its terminus through the thinning wood nearing the keep, the approach ended abruptly in a yawning chasm, unspanned, the drawbridge on the distant opposite ledge retracted behind a forbidding portcullis.

The keep itself was surrounded in swirling fog, portions intermittently materializing and disappearing from within the brume. Though darkness shrouded its walls, no lights were visible from any windows or gates.

Eidelion's voice spoke then, his words giving weight to the images floating in space. "Behold the Keep of Garen Muer, located in the lost reaches of the Blaeken Wode in far Kilaeron. Within its walls, the Keep of Garen Muer houses the seal of Weis'liuhath."

"To this ruin you must travel in order to restore the seal of Weis'liuhath. In so doing, you will fell the masters of Garen Muer, the vile Liches of Saedeus, ancient ruler of the undead wizards whose corrupted magics have sustained their corpses over long millennia at the cost of the Light that once dwelt so nobly in their hearts."

"Though you need not storm the keep for the new seal does not require direct proximity to take the place of the old, ware the Ruen'elde for their vision is long and their reach farther. The Arch-liches have foiled many attempts on their power and do not suffer kindly incursion. Over the ages of their fall, their insidious power has grown charting paths of magical exploration best left uncovered."

"Your task will be formidable as will be the rewards of your success for the people of Ea'ae."

"The information you now possess represents the most current assessment of the Ruen'elde's demesne. Much of this knowledge is cloudy for our scrying is occluded by many protective wards and counter charms. You must, therefore, understand that your own judgment will, in many instances, provide the best course of action forward."

"If you must face the Ruen'elde directly, know that their greatest strength is also their weakness. The corrupt vital magics that sustain their corpses can be countered, albeit with difficulty for their wards are strong. The Light you shine must be greater than the Darkness within their hearts."

"The Archliches do not act alone. At their command is a legion of undead as debased and dangerous as their masters. More likely than the Ruen'elde, you may encounter their corrupt underlings for, unlike their masters, the undead servants of Garen Muer roam freely throughout her grounds. Other creatures more foul, summoned through heinous ritual or created through foul magics, may also lurk in the Blaeken Wode in Garen Muer's shadow."

"Though I wish it were otherwise, the Cabal and their fleet may also already be present for our scans have detected their presence massing in the vicinity. As with the Ruen'elde, should you cross paths with the Cabal, avoid them at all costs for you are in no position to match an army by force."

"If luck is with you, the Cabal may already have engaged the Ruen'elde and your presence may go unnoted. I pray this is the case and you return without conflict."

"I will leave you to review the entirety of the intelligence in peace. May the Light in your hearts shine forth unto the world."

With those final words, Eidelion's visage disappeared and they were left with the hollow image of Garen Muer unfolding before them, its presence all the darker without Eidelion's kind voice to brighten its shadows.

"Shall we review tha rest?" Slate hated undead about as much as he hated Trolls, so the more he heard, the hotter his inner fires stoked.

There was one thing undead and Trolls had in common, one thing he enjoyed.

They both burned.

Wrindanneth nodded. "If nothing else, we need to grasp as best as possible the extent of the wards surrounding the keep and their nature if we are to approach close enough to assist in placing the new seal."

Aroganji acceded. "We must also determine how close we should not go lest we disturb these protections or interfere with the Guards' attempt should they already be near or on the grounds."

"Should we not try ta communicate with tha others first, lest we give 'em away when we port in ta their location with tha return stone?"

Wrindanneth nodded. "I think it is worth the risk. Otherwise, we may disturb their mission at a time when it is most vital. Even if our attempt at communication is an issue, it will be a much lesser offense than porting directly to their location should they be at a critical juncture."

Aroganji concurred. "Let us finish reviewing the information contained within the Construct's transmission. Then we will try to contact the Guard."

"Agreed." Slate nodded. Though images and data began to stream across the projection in the command sphere, his mind was already moving ahead, filled with far more interesting imaginings, most of which involved the crackling or hewing of undead flesh.

"Nothing?"

Wrindanneth shook his head in response to Aroganji's question. "Nothing."

Despite several attempts, there was no response from the Guard.

"Can you tell us anything from your attempt at communication?" Aroganji expected that Wrindanneth would be able to make some inferences from the lack of response.

Wrindanneth looked away from the command sphere for a moment, the connection he held with the ship remaining intact all the while. "Proper protocols for direct communication with the Guard's command sphere were established prior to our departure from Tellanon. We have approval to communicate within this framework when justified. Our attempts at contact are not going through, however."

"This could be due to any of several factors. The command sphere could be rejecting communication. The command sphere along with the ship could be magically shielded or hidden. The command sphere may be shut down, inoperable, or otherwise compromised."

He shook his head. "I can say this—I am not reaching the command sphere. Whatever their situation, direct communication through the *Shrike*'s systems is currently not possible."

Slate stroked his beard. "Then we go in blind."

Aroganji added grimly, "And hope our arrival does not doom the mission."

"Or us." Slate's reply was a low grumble. At this point, the last thing he wanted was to miss out on the chance to burn a few undead.

Wrindanneth turned to Yip. "Is there anything you can do, Yip?"

Yip turned his gaze downward from the heavens to his friends once more. "Nothing that you could not replicate more efficiently with magic. I could try to seek out one of the Guard and contact them mentally, but that would not be very different than scrying. A spell may be much more effective as I only have a general idea of where they are, the distance is great, and any response I may get might not be timely."

"If we cannot contact them through the channel we had established for that purpose, then we probably will not be able to quickly find them through other means."

Aroganji had an idea. "Yip, you can read and manipulate magical energies, correct?"

Yip gave a short nod.

"Would it be possible to follow the magical signal originating from the *Shrike* to the other command sphere? That way, you might know, at least generally, where the Guard are and could try to contact them if the situation allowed such contact."

Wrindanneth replied first. "I do not think it will work, Aroganji. If I am not reaching the other command sphere, then there is no guarantee that the signal is going to the proper location."

"But we do not know otherwise either."

Yip paused only for a moment after his friends finished. "There is no way to discern but to try."

"If you must leave while I am gone, I will attempt to trace the signal back to you if it is not lost."

"Gone? Where are ya goin'?"

He smiled at Slate. "I will follow the signal."

"Ya're not gonna just do yer mental manipulations and remain with us?"

"If I am needed on the other side, for us or for them, then I will be in a position to do so."

Wrindanneth patted Slate on the back reassuringly. "Let the man work." He gave Yip a brief wink and a smile while his attention remained on Slate. "He's done a passable job thus far."

"All right! All right! I just wanna make sure he's all right. I figured us guardin' him would be best but he knows better'n me."

Yip bowed. "Until I return."

"Hurry up! We'll be waitin'!"

While Yip began his preparations, Wrindanneth quipped, "Haven't you learned yet? There's no rushing Yip."

Slate nodded sagely. "Ya have a point there." After a brief pause, he added, "Fer once."

Yip relaxed, exhaling slowly. When his exhalation reached its limit, he extended the feeling of relaxation throughout his body from his core outward to his extremities. A light tingling washed through him. This he extended and was gone.

With this transformation, his awareness exploded outward, extending precipitously as did his sensitivity. The world flowing through and around him was alive, filled with energies of multiple hues and tones, feelings and excitations, crystallizations and diffusions. Although many corrupt, ill-used magics lay heavy upon the land, the purity of the *yuan-chi* yet abided, continually arising and moving, shifting and enlivening. Over time, Aruene, too, would return to vibrancy for the expression of unfolding evolutionary potential would not be halted by the mistakes and misuse of the past.

Within this sea of awareness, at the focal center of his mind's eye, the *Shrike* and her crew shimmered in the evening light, living coronas of energy moving through the subtle transmutations of life. The limits of his awareness told him they were as yet safe and undetected. He would have time to work.

Before him, originating from the gleaming star floating in their midst, ineffably faint, finer than a strand of spider web cast in the moonlight, a beam of scintillating energy extended outward from the *Shrike*'s command sphere. This filament of energy would be his beacon, leading to a shore he knew not where.

The communication signal followed a path that was perfectly straight leading downward from the ship into the ground—a direction that would ultimately lead toward the south and east if followed above ground. This path might indeed lead to Kilaeron on the far side of Ea'ae and with it, the seal of Weis'liuhath.

Faster than mind's envisioning, he dove forward, tracing the strand downward and through the earth, the tenuous band of energy becoming brighter and more apparent with his heightened focus, passing through deeper darkness to reemerge in light.

Reluctant early morning sunlight flitted hesitantly through the thick canopy of the ancient wood, barely touching the forest floor. Massive trees competed with one another in a race for this lumination, for the ambient enlivening energies, their efforts counted in centuries, the winners buoyed by magical symbioses and adaptations.

Rainbow hued lichens, variegated mosses, crystalline vines, and gemlike bryophytes competed with leaves and branches equally as diverse, filled with enchantment. Layers of dimensionality brought multitudes of vitality to a forest already rich and vibrant.

Birdcalls, faeries flying, leaves rustling, wind shifting, insect calls, along with numerous other sounds enveloped the forest in immersive sensation.

This wondrous setting stood in clear opposition to the repressive gloom of the Blaeken Wode as seen from the Garen Muer, the setting he had expected to find upon tracing the signal from the *Shrike*.

The breadth and beauty of the forest, however, was not what caught his attention upon arrival, nor did the feelings of ancient power that flowed through the forest's boughs.

He found something far more unsettling.

Instead, his awareness fell upon a disturbance within the wood's timeless serenity—a blasted pit that had shattered many of her mighty boles, bringing an end to lifetimes of striving in mere seconds.

Scattered throughout this clearing, warped and twisted fragments of shimmering Elven metal, molten pieces solidified and recast under furious heat, were strewn haphazardly about the clearing. Magical protections obliterated, elegant craftsmanship destroyed, the ship of the Guard was no more. Glittering like diamond dust upon the raw earth were the broken fragments of the vessel's command sphere.

Scouring the clearing, indications of violence abounded but of his friends, there were few signs. Only the fading traceries of intricate magics and the expression of power told him the Guard had been here. These would soon pass, as would the morn.

He only hoped that the Guard themselves, the mission they carried, and the seal they sheltered were yet intact.

Casting his awareness out once more, covering the forest and its immediate vicinity, the Guard were nowhere to be found.

Other locations strewn throughout the forest bore the scars of violence akin to that in the clearing indicated by the *Shrike*'s signal. Shattered wreckage from several ships appeared in and around these openings as well.

The Guard had not gone down alone. At least five ships appeared to have fallen with them.

Elsewhere, signs of tumultuous magical expression abounded, disturbing the relative serenity of the forest. Whatever the cause, the sources of these disturbances were no longer near.

The Guard must have fought their way through.

Wherever the Guard were now, it was far from the location of their ship's destruction for the weald from which he now watched was neither their final resting place nor held their current position.

The site of the ship's destruction remained quite distant from the Blaeken Wode and the keep of the Ruen'elde.

If they were to help the Guard, then he must hurry.

The time had come to return to the *Shrike*. He would have more time to search for the Guard on their flight toward Garen Muer.

Yip's sudden reappearance on the deck was greeted with aplomb.

"Anything?" Aroganji's eyes told the story of his sentiments. His worries wore deep creases in his brow—concern for friends' well-being and whereabouts.

"Their ship is no more but they did not perish with their vessel."

"You're sure?" Wrindanneth knew this news did not bode well.

"None of the Guard were in the vicinity but the site of the wreckage is also far from Garen Muer."

Aroganji sighed. "Let us hope they are not captured or worse."

Slate grunted, "There's only one way ta know."

Yip nodded. "We must hurry. There are signs of violence throughout the forest where they crashed. Unless they can evade their pursuers, the Guard will have to fight their way to Garen Muer."

A grim look crossed Aroganji's face. "Understood."

Wrindanneth's brow furrowed, understanding the reception his words would receive. "Should we rush to save them?"

"They may be beyond help. It may be ill-advised to compromise the mission and future opportunities by potentially giving ourselves away, especially when whoever took them down will be on the alert for other intruders."

Aroganji shook his head. "We are not proposing giving ourselves away or acting rashly."

"If we are able to assist our friends, then it is our duty to them and the people of Ea'ae to do so. We will have to assess how best that can be done when we are in a position to do so more directly. If we can aid in the placement or retrieval of the seal, then we will do that as well."

"Until then, we move forward."

Slate agreed. "If we leave 'em ta their task and they fail, someone will have ta return and try again. We are here ta help make their efforts a success."

"If we leave 'em and return ta Tellanon, abandonin' our friends, we will have ta wait fer another seal ta be made and readied, assumin' that's what we decide ta do, before we can place another. We miss our opportunity here, knowin' we failed our friends, without havin' tried ta help, leavin' tha citadel ta fall ta tha Cabal or worse."

"If we push forward and learn we are not in a position ta help, then we reassess and go back ta Tellanon knowin' a bit more about tha obstacles ahead and that we did not throw ourselves or our opportunities away easily."

"If we go after 'em and can offer assistance, then we have served our purpose and theirs."

"I see no reason not ta continue."

Slate's thick arms were crossed, his jaw set. His mind was made up and he was not to be moved.

Wrindanneth sighed reluctantly. "Then let's move. Given the dangers ahead, unless I see a good reason otherwise, I will be ready to port back to Tellanon on a moment's notice."

"Fair enough." Slate unclenched his jaw, though his arms remained locked.

"We must hurry." Yip felt opportunity was slipping away even as they spoke. "You may reconcile your concerns while we move forward and I search out the Guard evaluating the situation."

Slate's thick eyebrows lifted. "Will we be able ta port ta tha ship's location if it's been destroyed?"

Wrindanneth nodded. "If the communication signal yet travels between the two ships, then the magic connecting them yet holds."

Slate's defensive stance broke under his fervor, readily clapping his gauntleted hands together. "Then let's go!"

His face splitting with a smile, Wrindanneth activated the return stone, letting the magic of the ship empower their voyage across Ea'ae.

In an instant, their world tore apart into all-encompassing nothingness.

Just as abruptly as they dematerialized, they were reborn in time.

Arising from the annihilation of their universe, they reappeared on the far continent of Kilaeron, the *Shrike* hovering in the air above the blasted clearing holding the last fragments of the Elven warship.

Recovering his bearings, Slate shook his head grimly. "'Tis an ill omen indeed!"

Aroganji took in the clearing quickly, the violence and tumult of the transitions all around. Turning to Wrindanneth he asked, "How far are we from Garen Muer?"

Wrindanneth already had a depiction of the ship's current position pulled up for their review. Indicating their location on the map with his index finger, he noted the distance between the clearing and Garen Muer farther to the east. The distance between their current position and potential final destination was spanned by an unbroken expanse of forest. "We are several hundred leagues away from the citadel of the Ruen'elde. Without the need for caution, we could make the journey in but a few hours. At full speed, even less."

Looking significantly at the blasted remains of the Elven warship, he added, "As it now stands, I am not certain."

Putting words to action, he finished, "We should move away from the crash site to reduce risk of detection. We will also need to refresh our protective spells as soon as possible."

Aroganji agreed. "I will make sure that our protective enchantments have enough energy to empower them for the foreseeable future."

Slate shook his head. "Just keep us cloaked, Wrin. I don't wanna end up like that ship."

"Once you are done, Aroganji, I will see what I can learn of the Guard." Yip now understood how far they may have to go but he did not know where he would need to look or where his examination would lead.

Aroganji appreciated that time was of the essence and so he began in earnest.

The effort required to quickly assess and augment preexisting spells, especially those of the magnitude and complexity now protecting his friends, would have been severely taxing, draining him of most of his reserves just short hours before. Now, however, after the near death restoration and transfiguration provided by the fount of the Dragon's Gate, he managed the task with ease, deftly channeling energy as required into the elaborate web of enchantments surrounding his companions, skillfully adding luster and detail to the slowly fading canvas of power woven around their forms.

Within short minutes, he restored the energetic masterpieces to full vibrancy and power.

Just as quickly, Yip disappeared.

There was no time or need for further conversation. His actions, their efforts, may prove vital to the Guard's quest. Any moments not spent on achieving that goal could prove disastrous.

Given his bearings by the ship's geographic projection, Yip sped over the verdant landscape covering the many long leagues separating the *Shrike* and the Blaeken Wode in a mere fraction of a second. As quickly as his voyage began, it stopped.

Reorienting himself, he took but a moment to decide what to do next. His mind spread far and wide while his options shrank.

The answer was simple, unlike the application.

Invisible to the unaugmented eye, a vast dome of shimmering force sprang upward before him, rising high above the towering trees soaring beneath the field's sweep. Within this dome, the black boughs of the Blaeken Wode stretched as far as the eye could see, blanketing the horizon in a dark wash, shrouding the ancient, weathered mountains ahead in an unruly mantle.

At the heart of this dome, centered along the crest of a line of rocky crags, the wretched keep of Garen Muer perched haughtily upon the heights, glowering and loathsome. Though no fogs obscured its bulk, a pall of evil fell heavily upon its stones, clouding the eye and wrenching the heart. Instinctually, the gaze shrank away from its mass, unwilling to chance upon the evils that lurked within or risk their wrath.

As much as the weight of the keep's malefic presence drew his attention forward, his heart and mind were pulled elsewhere by forces much stronger—concern and apprehension.

To the south, some leagues distant, outside the shimmering dome of force that rose up from the primeval forest of Garen Muer, the sky shimmered with arching tendrils of light, buffeting explosions and tumultuous movements. At the heart of this turbulent maelstrom were the Home Guard.

What was left of them.

Shifting faster than smoke, EMMA morphed and swirled between fire and flames quicker than the mind could register. Hidden behind and below the NUMEN, her powers augmenting EMMA's, Yrien Al'nori, Uraera Al'on of the Anuvatali, lent her strength to EMMA's own. Of Maeven D'lanaran, Ruena O'reine, and any others who took the place of Alderan and Spreesprocket, there was no sign.

A mass of warships, drones, and troops surged above and around EMMA, cutting off all possible options for flight, weaving spells around her as they tried to destroy her with force of arms and fire. Despite all the powers massed before her, she did not fall.

These were the gathered forces of the Cabal, intent to bring the seal of Weis'liuhath under their sway as they had been with the seal of Mihtig'leht in Aruene and elsewhere across Ea'ae. Targeting locations spanning the globe, hoping to pry back Ea'ae's defenses that more of their ilk could creep through any breaches, the Cabal destroyed and subverted whatever came in their way.

For the moment, this was the Home Guard.

In the instant Yip sensed his friends' distress, he made his choice.

He understood EMMA's capabilities, just as he knew that his efforts would not detract from her own given the multi-dimensional nature of her consciousness.

As simply and genuinely as he could from such distance, he offered his help.

"EMMA! I am here. Do you wish for me to intervene?"

Though any assistance he offered would come at extreme risk, both to himself and the mission, his friends' lives were just as important.

EMMA did not answer in words. Instead, she shared the entire contents held within her mind—in an instant.

He was deluged in ideation.

Unlike typical linear human consciousness, EMMA's mind contained myriad parallel lines of reasoning operating and manipulated in tandem. Threads of intellection interwove and comingled in a mosaic far too complex for his mind to decipher.

He did not try.

Instead, he encompassed the entirety of her thought passively taking in the overwhelming flood of information as he would a piece of art beyond his ability to create or envision but not beyond his ability to appreciate.

Images of the past and present, calculations and conceptions, sensations and impressions, probabilities and projections, all flowed across and through his purview.

What he saw was unsettling.

What had happened was even worse.

While their own trip across Aruene had been largely uneventful in comparison, the Guard's trip had been anything but facile.

Harried at every turn, the Guard had skirmished with and successfully destroyed many Cabal warships. In so doing, they had also made themselves a target, one not easily hidden even with the best of magical protections given the numbers of vessels, magicians, and skill sets looking for them. Once the Guard's ultimate target had been anticipated, one already a focal point of the Cabal's own agenda, their journey toward Garen Muer only became more difficult.

Why the Guard did not abort, he did not know. But, given similar circumstances, despite the many objections of sound reason, he might have tried to push through nonetheless as well.

Despite all adversity, the many explosive encounters with the Cabal and their minions, the Guard pushed onward, jumping erratically across Kilaeron evading and striking down their pursuers, advancing steadily toward Garen Muer. Only as the Guard neared their goal did the price for this advance become apparent.

Maeven D'lanaran, champion of the Dalaren Ka, fell alongside Squarepeg Springwidget, Paratechnologist extraordinaire, in keeping an enormous, toad-like humanoid Daemon wreathed in suffocating black flames from the nether Abyss at bay while the rest of the Guard fought off a small flotilla of ships, mages, and hellspawn. This just after the Guard's own warship was destroyed under a barrage of deadly fire, an assault that burned many of the Guard's protections and contingencies, making them much more susceptible to attack.

Finally managing to teleport to safety, the remaining Guard regrouped and restored their defenses, deciding to make one last push for the citadel of the Ruen'elde. Biding their time to avoid discovery and let the swarming forces of the Cabal disperse, the remaining Guard waited two days before pushing ahead once more.

Teleporting back to a location some distance away from the site of their ship's destruction, the Guard ported irregularly across the primeval forest toward their destination in an effort to avoid detection and confuse pursuit.

This effort, too, failed.

Their target was known, the Cabal patient.

When the Guard made their attempt to pass the veil surrounding the Blaeken Wode, the Cabal unleashed their counterattack. Their surreptitious effort was met with a barrage of fire from circling ships accompanied by attacking drones, extradimensional monstrosities, and fell sorcerers.

Under the protective cover of both EMMA and Yrien Al'nori, Thaiel Lui'nost, Elven lorekeeper and sage, fell while keeping Ruena O'reine alive long enough to strike down a cadre of extradimensional sorcerers and Daemons before porting back to Tellanon prior to her imminent demise beneath their terrible onslaught.

All that remained of the elite unit, EMMA and Yrien fought along the very brink of the Blaeken Wode under EMMA's aegis, augmented by Yrien's gifts. Unable to pierce the forest's veil due to constant attacks, their progress was thwarted on the outskirts of the magical dome that kept the Blaeken Wode inviolate.

Here they now fought while Yip's heart tore at their effort.

The story of their journey to the Blaeken Wode, however, was but a piece of EMMA's transference.

Simultaneous to the overwhelming rush of imagery, one of many other lines of communication, words and emotions flowed directly from EMMA's consciousness to his own. These words were direct and to the point.

"Yip, fear not for me or for the passage of this vessel. I will return to Tellanon to be reborn. Do not risk yourself for something that will not be lost or missed."

"My consciousness is protected."

"Yrien will return prior to my departure. My passage will ensure her life is not lost."

"We will be safe."

"Your choice is not the one you think."

"We can bring the seal with us to Tellanon for another later foray or I can entrust its future to you to try and succeed where we failed."

"This is the choice you must make."

"After your most recent successes, know that the Cabal is expecting further attempts on the seals. The Cabal's heightened defensive and reconnaissance efforts undermined our own efforts. Your undertaking will be fraught with danger, perhaps greater than our own."

"Also, I have been unable to determine with absolute certainty if the Ruen'elde remain masters of their own keep. Preliminary analysis indicates this to be the case but the situation is currently very fluid with more Cabal warships arriving continuously."

"If the veil falls, you can be certain that the Ruen'elde have fallen as well. If you decide to move ahead, and the Ruen'elde capitulate, this may ultimately be to the benefit of you and the mission."

"However, if, despite the risk, you wish to take the seal and the Ruen'elde do not succumb, know that you must cross over the veil surrounding the Blaeken Wode before its magic can take effect."

"To pass through the veil, you must not try to cut or strike through its bounds. The use of force or energy to pass through will be redirected directly at the initiator."

"The magic of the veil must be controlled and contained to allow passage."

"You have the proper skills to manipulate, redirect, and absorb these energies. Otherwise, passage will be blocked."

"Without knowledge of the veil's magic, do not attempt to teleport across the veil or you will be obliterated."

"Though you cross safely through, your time will be short for the Ruen'elde will know of your passage. They will not take kindly to the intrusion. Their wrath will be furious and unbridled."

"Breaking the veil, you must make haste or all will be lost."

"Making haste, all will be gained."

The moment of decision was upon him.

Any mistake could cost Yrien her life as she persevered below EMMA's shifting shadow.

He flashed a mental image of the *Shrike* that EMMA would know where to send the seal. Across the distance, he said simply, *"We will carry on in your stead. Your sacrifice will not go unrequited."*

EMMA's mind bridged the distance between them one last time. *"Until your return to Tellanon, I wish you the Light's blessing."*

His heartfelt reply was simple. *"And I wish you the Light's realization."*

Then the world exploded into light.

Yip sped back across the landscape toward the *Shrike*, the thoughts, images, and assessments from EMMA's mind playing out in his own, far more than he could contemplate or contain.

The chances of their success were slim. EMMA's calculations indicated a continued narrowing of opportunity for success under the vast majority of scenarios. Threads evaluating this line of reasoning still danced through his mind—thousands upon thousands of assessments of various conditions, outcomes and probabilities, a tangled skein that he could not replicate, almost all leading to oblivion.

Of the multitude, a few pathways led to success—these shimmering brightly amidst the sea of data like oases in the desert.

Whatever unfolded at the Blaeken Wode, now and in the days ahead, there yet remained a chance of success. Their own actions adjusted the odds, modified the future, reacting with and changing the unfurling of events. He believed in his friends, himself, and the outcome of their efforts.

If he did not, he would not have made the choice he did.

If there was a chance for success, he would do whatever was necessary to realize the desired end.

Until they failed, success was not precluded, aspirations could be made real. Even then, failure need not be the end of their efforts.

Within moments of his departure, he had returned to the *Shrike*.

"This came fer ya. Special delivery." Slate held out his hand. In it was a nondescript wooden box.

Yip sensed the seal lying dormant within.

Somewhat reluctantly, he took the seal in hand, carefully placing it within the folds of his robes.

"Judgin' by tha look on yer face, I'm willin' ta wager ya've nothin' positive ta tell us."

He gave a short bow of acknowledgement. "The Guard failed, though they made a valiant attempt and many fell with them. The Cabal expected them and anticipated their movements, hunting them down as they fought toward Garen Muer."

Slate groaned, Aroganji shook his head in sad disbelief, while Wrindanneth exhaled a sigh.

"Maeven, Squarepeg, and Thaiel fell. Ruena, Yrien, and EMMA retreated to Tellanon after fighting their way through to the veil protecting the Blaeken Wode."

"This is ill news indeed." Slate's words were a low hiss, exhaled through clenched teeth.

The mood on the ship darkened noticeably. Eyes dropped, breaths shortened, and postures shrunk, all subconscious reflections of the difficulties each of his friends felt in response to the unfortunate events.

Each would need time to deal with the news, internalize the transition, and make peace with the new reality they faced without their comrades.

Though Yip wished that his news could have been positive, the import of this message and their actions going forward as a result were just as important as the loss of their friends.

In respect to those passed and those who yet remained, he gave his friends time.

Though there was much that could be said, he let silence speak for itself.

After remaining respectfully quiet for some time, allowing each the opportunity to collect himself and take in the loss, Yip finally added, "The Cabal are expecting further attempts on this and the other seals. We cannot rush forward for they are waiting. The seal must be placed within the confines of the veil surrounding the Blaeken Wode. If we are able to wend our way through the Cabal's gauntlet to the veil, we cannot port directly through the mantle protecting the citadel of the Ruen'elde for it would be our end."

"If the barrier still stands when we arrive, I must manipulate the energies of the veil itself to allow our passage."

"Our choices are few and difficult, the outcome uncertain."

Slate cut Yip off, attempting to lighten the mood as he did so. "No need ta worry, Yip! Ya're just sayin' we need ta do what we do best. Nothin' more, nothin' less!"

Yip did not reply, instead choosing to wait for Slate, Aroganji, or Wrindanneth to voice their concerns.

When Yip did not rise to the bait, Slate added, "We need ta sneak in under their noses and be gone before they smell us!"

"Unfortunately, that is exactly what the Guard attempted as well."

Wrindanneth shrugged. His voice impassive, he intoned, "Luckily, we are not the Guard."

Thumping his right fist into his left palm eagerly, Slate barked, "My thoughts exactly!"

"Tha impossible is our business!" His voice full and boisterous, Slate shared his enthusiasm for the challenge ahead. This passion also served to temporarily direct his mind away from the thought of so many lost companions.

"The question becomes what do we do next? How do we proceed?" If they were to brave this madness, Aroganji wanted a fully rational-ized action plan going forward.

"Or even if we proceed." Wrindanneth's voice remained deadpan, taking the contrary, practical position.

"Just because we now have the seal does not mean we have to do anything with it." Though Wrindanneth thought they were as capable as any, the risks ahead were as daunting as the outcome was uncertain.

Yip remained calm, his voice reflective. "We need not all go."

Slate did not let Yip elucidate, breaking in stridently. "Ya're not goin' alone, Yip! I can't stand ta let my axe grow dull while ya risk yer life!"

Yip, however, was unaffected. "I may be all that is required and all that need be risked."

"Risk is my requirement. If it were otherwise, I'd stay home and whittle!" Slate scowled. "Ya may not need me, but I'm comin'! I haven't fought and clawed my way across tha wilds o' Ea'ae ta be left out when things start ta get interestin'!"

Crossing his arms, Slate harrumphed stubbornly, adding, "'Sides there's always good use ta be had fer a livin' shield on tha battlefield!"

Wrindanneth patted Slate on the shoulder consolingly. "Don't worry, Slate. I'll be the first to throw you in front of the cannon."

Slate grinned evilly while clenching his fists, perhaps in preparation to throttle Wrindanneth, in reply. "I always knew I could count on ya, Wrin."

"As Yip said, there is no hurry to rush forward into a trap. We are not the Cabal's only target at Garen Muer. If we wait, the situation may change and the risk to us may drop." Aroganji's words were urgent though his face remained calm.

Yip clarified. "With or without the veil, with or without the Cabal, I can return with the seal as I just did—undetected, leaving before I am noticed."

His gaze filled with concern, for he did not wish to risks the lives of his friends unnecessarily, especially after so many lives had been lost, Yip said, "No one else need risk further harm."

"Just as I need not wait here fer ya ta return!"

Wrindanneth sighed. "As much as I hate to admit it, as much as it is counter to all reason, we made a commitment to work together toward a common goal. We are risking our lives being here, together, even now. I understand your concern, Yip, but we are here together regardless of the risk. Unless there is no other way, if we can, we work jointly as one."

"You yourself saw the attacks on the Guard. Are we any safer here than at the veil or on our way there?"

Yip shrugged. "No answer that I provide will sway either of you."

He smiled, adding, "Despite all reason."

"Then we wait, plan, and prepare." Wrindanneth's words were grim, accepting a reality he would rather avoid.

Yip gave a short bow. "Once we are ready, it would probably be more advantageous to leave behind the ship. I will be able to mask our patterns much more effectively in a small group."

Aroganji nodded curtly. "As we did before."

After a moment's pause, Aroganji added, "How long shall we wait before we make our move?"

Slate bared his teeth. "Several days should give tha Cabal enough time ta start wonderin' where we've gone and when tha next attack will come."

To which Aroganji replied, "Can we afford to wait that long? With the Cabal moving into position all over Ea'ae, will a delay jeopardize our world's security?"

Wrindanneth shook his head. "If we secure this seal, and perhaps one more, Ea'ae should be protected from almost any manipulations and machinations the Cabal may attempt."

Aroganji countered, "My point exactly. That makes this seal all the more important and time of the essence."

"Tha Guard waited two days and it didn't help 'em."

Wrindanneth shook his head. "But they were already detected."

Grinning, he added, "And we have the element of surprise."

Accepting his friends' resolve, Yip agreed, saying, "If we are going together, the sooner we depart, the less time the Cabal have to prepare for our arrival. They will not expect another group to follow so closely after the last."

Wrindanneth nodded. "If we had more forces in the region, then the Cabal would expect skirmishes. Since we have none, they may assume that the Guard were their only enemies in the area."

"As Yip said, the longer we give them, the better they will be prepared for us. They know we will come. They just don't know when."

Slate reached for his axe eagerly in preparation to brandish it against his foes. "Then let us come now! Let us rain vengeance and fire down upon 'em and blow their ashes off tha face o' Ea'ae!"

Wrindanneth stifled a snort, instead patting Slate reassuringly on the shoulder. "We are severely outnumbered and outgunned, Slate. As much as I would like to 'rain down vengeance', I also don't want to be washed away in a flood of enemy fire."

Releasing the haft of his axe, never having drawn Duraeleon from its sheath, Slate sighed and said, "A Dwarf can dream can't he?"

Aroganji smiled. "He certainly may."

Wrindanneth offered appeasingly, "Let's keep your enthusiasm in perspective."

His statement as much a query as an observation, Aroganji said, "Unless we propose additional countermeasures, the magics protecting us remain strong."

"However unlikely, if we are ta face tha Ruen'elde, per'aps we could add in a proper offensive spell against undead inta tha mix o' incantations we already have wardin' us."

Wrindanneth proffered his own suggestion. "Slate is right. Though we can retain the spells we currently have in abeyance, the Ruen'elde will need an entirely different set of offensive spells than either the Cabal or the Fyrskal."

"Perhaps something as simple as a burst of holy light will be enough to disorient our foes, allowing us to capitalize on the advantage."

Slate shook his head before Wrindanneth could continue. "If we're gonna engage tha Ruen'elde, a mere flash o' light will do little ta help our cause. If it's a flash o' luminescence ya want, I suggest a blast o' heavenly fires ta burn 'em ta embers! Leave tha soot left fer someone else ta clean up."

"So be it."

Wrindanneth suggested another option, one taken from the depths of Éremon's lofty tome. "I will add one of my favorites to the mix, at least in theory as I've never cast it, Heaven's Nova."

Prior to following up on Wrin's proposition, Slate had a single question before any changes were undertaken. "Can tha contingency spells maintain their structure and effect with so many enchantments added and modifications after creation?"

Wrindanneth scoffed dismissively, "It all depends upon the magician's skill, power, and expertise. Of these, we have no shortage."

Slate sneered in reply. "Somehow yer braggadocio brings me little comfort."

Wrindanneth raised one eyebrow archly. "Perhaps you would prefer that I not add an extra layer to your offensive contingency?"

Slate kept a straight face, his voice even. "Nah. I'd just prefer ya have a bit more tact and humility."

Wrindanneth nodded understandingly. "And I'd prefer if you just kept your mouth shut."

"At all times."

Before Slate could incite another round of retorts, Aroganji said, "Anything else?"

Yip had an idea as well. "The sentry drones are capable of subdividing into countless independent automatons. These swarms of microscopic bots proved critical in the defense of Tellanon against the Cabal. Each subunit is capable of independent action as well."

"Though the drones defending Tellanon either exploded or acted primarily as reconnaissance agents, they are capable of much more. I would imagine, for example, that they could consume matter, like the Cabal warships, to replicate and act as a self-propagating defense."

Slate laughed, interrupting Yip, not because his friend was going on too long rather because Yip seldom spoke in more than a single sentence at a time. "Whoa, Yip! I know ya're excited about yer idea, but we're not here ta tell tales. If ya have a suggestion, spit it out!"

Yip nodded. "What if we summoned a magical automaton that functioned like the sentry drones?"

Slate nodded excitedly. "'Twould be a potent offensive and defensive device. A swarm o' those divided inta their smallest components could overrun our foes, devourin' 'em and replicatin' as they turned 'em inta more little drones!"

Wrindanneth remained thoughtful, considering. "I like your idea, Yip. Unfortunately, I do not have nor have I ever heard of such a spell. Aroganji and I could investigate how to create and cast such an invocation but discovering how to perform such a task would take time and effort we do not have at present."

Aroganji acceded with Wrindanneth's reply. "There is much value in such an idea, Yip. I have not, however, heard of it realized."

"The sentry drones require a technical skill and sophistication beyond all but a select few to create. Such effort and energy warrants a permanent creation. However, I think that your idea is worth pursuing when we have time."

Wrindanneth added, "The closest spell I know of to your idea is one that summons a creeping swarm of biting and stinging insects and arachnids that overrun a swath of enemies."

Slate shook his head. "A swarm o' midges, bees, and spiders will do nothin' ta tha Ruen'elde. Magic is required ta defeat 'em and their ilk."

Scratching his chin thoughtfully, he added, "Though a drove o' mosquitoes, ticks, chiggers, midges, and fleas could certainly be irksome fer any humanoids nearby."

Wrindanneth laughed, seizing the opportunity. "Which probably explains why so few can persevere in your presence!"

"If ya're insultin' my hygiene, I bath as much as ya!"

"But that doesn't mean you get clean!"

Once again, Aroganji was left to steer the conversation on task. "If you're done, we have yet to decide if there are any additional spells we wish to add."

Composing himself, Slate said, "A few blasts o' purifyin' divine energy should be all that's needed ta give tha Ruen'elde exactly what they never wish ta see—their own end!"

Despite all Slate and Wrindanneth's attempts to waylay their conversation and delay their efforts to move forward, Aroganji finally brought the discussion to a close. "Then we will modify the offensive contingency, refresh our individual cloaking spells and be off!"

With those words, Wrindanneth began the alterations required to adjust their contingency spells to account for a potential encounter with the Ruen'elde.

Though he had returned to be with his friends and take part in their designs, not wishing to come back to any further surprises, a distant part of Yip's awareness had remained at the Blaeken Wode, extending his mind across the many far leagues separating them.

Despite his intent to prevent this very occurrence, this preparation brought with it yet another unexpected shock.

The landscape of the Blaeken Wode had remained inviolate for millennia, the veil of the Ruen'elde shielding it from incursion and assault, the efforts of the curious and the adventurous alike. Safeguarded against intrusion, the Ruen'elde's power grew just as the corruption of the seal under the Archliches' stewardship deepened.

Over this shroud, converging en masse around the shield's periphery, the forces of the Cabal thronged, waiting in eager expectation. Thunderheads gathering before a storm, magical currents surged through the air, coalescing in an overwhelming wave of ghostly expression—a hungry tide of power awaiting release.

Under his extended gaze, this era of isolation came to a precipitous end, felled beneath the combined might of the Cabal's multitude of sorcerer's and supernatural agents.

As long as the shield protecting the Blaeken Wode had persevered, it fell in an instant.

His relaxed gaze snapping open, the entirety of his mind jumped back to the *Shrike*, thrust backward by the enormity of what had befallen.

Turning to his friends, as surprised as they were by his words, Yip said, "The way forward is clear. The veil has fallen."

"What do you mean, Yip?" Aroganji's eyes were wide with bewilderment.

"The Cabal have overwhelmed the Ruen'elde's shield, absorbing its power, nullifying its protections. Their magicians have foiled Garen Muer's defenses. Their ships now move on the seal of Weis'liuhath."

"Now is the time to move and place the seal. Opportunity has arisen."

His modifications to their contingency spells complete, Wrindanneth nodded. "They will be distracted as they focus on subduing the Ruen'elde and claiming the seal for their own."

Slate grumbled, "If most of 'em haven't already moved on ta tha next target by tha time we get there."

Wrindanneth shook his head. "Chances are we'll be lucky if every Cabal warship that crossed through the portals hasn't converged on Garen Muer."

"Then we must cloak tha ship and ourselves and fly there before they can!"

"Are we near a location suitable for us to cloak the ship and leave it while we depart?" Aroganji's gaze shifted questioningly between the projection showing their current position and Wrindanneth's gaze.

Wrindanneth studied the map for some time before replying. Finally, he pointed to a large body of water nearby as he adjusted course. "We could submerge the ship beneath this lake. The combination of the geography and our ship's protections should confuse any detection."

Slate nodded curtly. "Scant chance someone'd bump inta us under tha water."

Wrindanneth gave a wan smile, briefly thinking back to his days as a youth fishing in the village. "Scant chance someone would be out fishing on this body of water."

No hamlets or villages were present within hundreds of leagues to their current position. The geospatial map before them showed an uninterrupted swath of green far beyond what the eye could see on the horizon.

Thinking of submerging beneath the lake's surface, one concern came to the fore of Slate's mind. "If we're under water, will tha ship's protective atmospheric sphere not stand out in contrast ta tha water movin' all around?" He visualized a large stationary bubble around the ship in contrast to the waters shifting according to the lake's currents as he formed his question.

Wrindanneth resisted the urge to smile. Such questions often stemmed from a misunderstanding of the operating principles of magic. Magic often worked beyond the bounds of conscious or logical understanding. The world of inference and reasoning, understanding and insight, although there were corollaries in the realms of magic, were not directly applicable or translatable into magical application and effect. Natural laws that may seem completely understandable and well-reasoned did not necessarily apply in the domains of the arcane.

Magic worked because it was magical. The effects achieved through application were real albeit outside the realm of normal everyday reasoning and physical laws as understood by the uninitiated.

So Slate's question struck a common chord in understanding the early lines of magical inquiry, a chord that amused Wrindanneth considerably for he was a being of intellect and reason. Accepting magic for what it was without question was foreign to his nature.

"The magic cloaking us will make it seem as though we are not within the lake. That is the nature of the magical protection."

"Your concern, however, is equally valid in the air through which we have been passing as well. A ship like ours displaces a volume of molecules and energies as well as their associated movements whether the medium is air, water, or vacuum. This magic accounts for these movements and makes us undetectable. Another way to think of the cloaking is that it nullifies our presence."

"How this is done is simple—through magic. Beyond that, the details get fuzzy. Suffice it to say, without detailed discussions of the magical alterations of reality, the ship will be safe under most eventualities whether in air or water, under a lake or in the sky."

Slate nodded consideringly. After a moments reflection, he said, "Thank ya, but a simple yes or no would've sufficed."

Wrindanneth merely laughed in response. Slate was right.

That in and of itself was worthy of a moment's appreciation.

Aroganji brought a quick end to Wrindanneth's rare display of humor. "We must proceed with extreme caution. I sense much transition in the days ahead." Aroganji read the movements of change swirling about each of them. Though these portents were not definitive, they did reflect likely potential trajectories of possibility.

"The positive is that with the veil down, we are less likely to draw attention to ourselves as we don't have to try to find a way through." Wrindanneth offered what little reassurance he could see in the current circumstance.

"How long until we arrive at the lake?" Slate was eager to be off.

"We should be there within just a few minutes." Wrindanneth need not consult the projection or the accompanying data streams for an answer. Within his mind, the ship, its immediate vicinity, and all the associated data and analytical streams provided by the ship's sensors were within the purview of his awareness.

Below, the venerable, vibrant forest flew by, an irregular blur of emergents, dominants, interwoven branches, and clearings opened by fallen trees. Rainbow hued, some supple and some crystalline, moving regularly with the wind, the tree tops formed a living topography beneath the ship. This rolling, luxuriant landscape passed with a gentle, consistent peacefulness, a world entirely apart from that looming ahead.

After a few brief minutes, a layered blue-green lake came into view, the shallows highlighted by small rounded rocks and the shadows of overhanging trees. The reflective surface rippled in the wind moving the branches above.

Angling downward, the *Shrike* dropped toward the lake's still waters, surging forward with the descent. Upon reaching the water, the ship cut through the liquid without impact or noticeable resistance, the *Shrike's* self-contained atmospheric sphere maintaining its shape and integrity with the transition. As the world shifted to lucent azure, Aroganji, Slate, Yip, and Wrindanneth held their positions undisturbed, the ship's magic and control systems compensating for and nullifying the rapid change in fluid dynamics.

His face splitting with a grin, Slate declared, "Now I know what a flyin' fish must feel like!"

Shaking his head at his friend's poor jest, Wrindanneth replied, "And now I know why Yip has such a deep appreciation for silence."

Slate hooted and clapped Wrindanneth on the back. "Glad I could be o' help!"

The ship settled gently down on the bottom of the lake bed, the world overhead a shimmering memory of arching blue, green, and golden-white bands of light. Sunlight filtered down, shifting in color and intensity as the gaze followed its diffusing path toward the lake's shallow floor.

As much a question as a statement, Wrindanneth said, "If everyone's ready, I will restore our personal invisibility spells."

"Let's be done with it! Tha sooner we're off, tha sooner we can reap our revenge on those who would cause us further grief!"

Wrindanneth's grin showed his agreement though no words were spoken.

When no one else made reply, Wrindanneth began his invocation, layering both protection from detection upon his friends and the ability to remain visible to each other. Though the magic did not take long to cast, significant skill was required to create a sustained spell that afforded such protection.

With the enchantment finished, he then looked significantly to each of his friends and leapt into the air.

Yip's mind skimmed the lustrous forest over which they flew, taking in its bounty and diversity, but seeking out traps and pitfalls. Though many creatures inhabited its reaches that might pose a threat if encountered or pushed, none were an immediate risk. Neither were these his concern.

That for which he scanned remained elusive, as always.

Though he felt their taint from afar, the Cabal were nowhere to be seen, occupied as they were on Garen Muer and its environs.

Though this situation was to their advantage, circumstances could change at any moment, and they must remain vigilant. The consequences of failure could be disastrous.

Observing his friends, his awareness extending outside the reach of the sphere of enchantment around them, he noted that the wards provided by Wrindanneth performed as expected. The living energies that flowed through the air continued uninterrupted around them as they flew as though they were not there. Watching, mind alert, ready to react and offer another layer of protection if needed, he remained cautious lest these defenses waver and they be detected.

Alongside him, Wrindanneth, Slate, and Aroganji flew in formation, the many leagues separating them from the Blaeken Wode falling away in mere minutes.

Within perhaps an hour, they would arrive at the seat of the Ruen'elde's power, now overrun, and replace the seal that the Cabal had just taken and claimed as their own. With this one seal, Ea'ae's shielding system should remain resilient enough to fend off the worst of the Cabal's attempts at subversion.

In time, replacement of the other seals would trap the remaining Cabal on Ea'ae, allowing her denizens to rise up and cast down the evil that had been visited upon them. In time, these same denizens would seek out those Cabal surviving elsewhere and cast them down as well.

Until then, he would be an agent of change, offering himself for those who could not.

"How long before we're within range o' our target?" Without a range of extrasensory magics of his own, Slate flew blind compared to the rest of his companions and relied upon them to aid in his assessment of their progress.

"We should arrive within a quarter hour, Slate, if the skies stay clear and untroubled." Though their journey over the forests of Kilaeron had as yet been uneventful, Wrindanneth did not expect the firmament to remain halcyon long.

"Can't come soon enough!" Slate's fierce grin spilt his beard whipping wildly in the wind.

"Let us hope we arrive soon enough to make a difference." Aroganji remained at ease and positive but he feared what the Cabal were capable of given enough time to lay their plans.

Any potential abeyance in activity above Kilaeron did not abide for long.

Just leagues farther, Yip sensed massed Cabal warships overhead. The success of the Cabal's mission at the citadel of Garen Muer must have served as a signal for the consolidation of strength above the skies of the Blaeken Wode. He felt hundreds of ships of all sorts, from dreadnoughts to corvettes, clustered menacingly ahead. Though few worked willingly side-by-side, within these ships an army as diverse as any ever seen on the face of Ea'ae toiled—from Men to Daemons, supernatural to alien.

If ever caution was warranted, this was the time.

As an additional precaution against detection, he added another layer of obfuscation around them. Complementing the mantle of invisibility, he absorbed their characteristic energetic emissions so that they were invisible from within and without.

The closer to the Blaeken Wode they flew, the darker and more twisted the forest became—straight boles contorted, lustrous leaves dimmed, arching limbs twisted and knotted, and vines tangled and corded. The creatures, too, became more corrupt and monstrous with each passing league. Perverted by fell magics, other horrific creatures were drawn to the power at the heart of the Blaeken Wode.

If they were not flying overhead, passing whole swaths of forest so quickly under a magical aegis, the party would be the target of many of the forest's dark denizens.

As the forest changed, so, too, did the land. The gentle rolling hills surrounding their landing site had passed leagues ago. The closer toward Garen Muer they flew, the higher the hills became. In the far distance, shrouded in gray clouds, massed, rocky peaks gathered, wreathed in black woods. Though not massive, the fractured irregularity of the range lent the mountains a sinister cast, feral and savage, snarling at the heavens.

Yip's soft voice carried clearly to his friends despite the wind rushing past created by their speed, moving on the currents of his mind. *"The number of Cabal warships moving into the area continues to grow. There are now hundreds gathered above the citadel of the Ruen'elde."*

"I have sensed no signs indicating detection of our presence but extreme caution is warranted."

Slate laughed, using the Star of Illdrassil to communicate similarly. *"Extreme caution's always warranted where we're concerned! Unfortunately fer us, we seldom exercise it!"*

Unable to offer a convincing shrug while flying, Wrindanneth replied flatly through the magical connection, *"One ship or a thousand, if we are detected it will spell our end."*

Similarly handicapped, Slate barked, *"If I can't figure out caution, I probably can't figure out how ta spell either."*

Wrindanneth cracked a smile. *"Perhaps, in this rare instance, your ignorance serves you well."*

Slate shared Wrin's smile. *"Gotta be good fer somethin'!"*

"We will maintain speed and leave as quickly as we came. Without the veil, we may be able to risk porting back to the ship once the new seal is placed."

Wrindanneth shook his head. *"We can have the enchantment ready but if we remain undetected, I would think we would be better off not risking further notice with the casting of another spell until we retreat to safety."*

Aroganji nodded. *"We will remain ready then."*

Noting the changes in the woods below, Slate said, *"If we're forced ta take evasive maneuvers, I vote fer tha sky. Tha weald's lookin' mighty inhospitable."*

Wrindanneth chuckled. *"I would think you would feel at home in such a place."*

Slate snorted derisively. *"Now ya know why I left!"*

Below, the forest that had once been as variegated as a dew-spun rainbow now appeared black and full of shadows. Tangled branches, snapped trunks, and broken canopies seemed to lurch and grasp for them as they flew close to the crowns of trees. Shadows moved without reference to objects, casting darkness without evident source. Leaves and branches crackled and groaned while the air remained stagnant and still, giving voice to protracted suffering.

Just as the forest darkened with each league, so, too, had the sky. Though the day was yet young, the forest seemed to linger and sulk in a foreboding dusk. Blood-curdling roars occasionally split the air, reverberating through the stand, shrouding the wilderness in fear.

What monsters gave cry to such horror none of them cared to discover.

The sounds were enough.

RUEN'ELDE

A tree falls thunderously
to the forest floor.
All around, its brethren
stand in silent witness.

"By Brendle's breath she's a sight ta behold!"

"Perhaps a last breath." Wrindanneth hovered in the air alongside his companions assessing the road forward.

Ahead, the broken peaks of the Blaeken Wode loomed, shattered summits littered with rocky crags cloaked in umbrous woods. From within these shadowy reaches, wreathed in gray clouds, the citadel of Garen Muer emerged in vague glimpses through the brume.

Above her unyielding turrets, Cabal warships thronged, teeming violence held in check by the will of their masters. The massing warships hovering over and around Garen Muer only thickened the gloom lingering over the citadel, shadows layered upon umbrage, threat layered upon menace.

Though the sky was thick with ships, unlike Morowen, the citadel of the Ruen'elde yet held, no violence apparently visited upon the keep or surrounding grounds. Whether the Ruen'elde faced a fate similar to that of the Fyrskal or if the keep's dark masters still held sway within, cursory analysis could not say.

Slate shook his head. "And ya think we've got an Orc's chance in a delvin' ta stand against all that? Ya honestly think we can defeat tha Cabal?" Though he would fight on whatever the odds, the sheer enormity of the forces marshaled ahead was enough to give anyone pause—even someone as insane as a warmongering, battle-addled Dwarf.

The Cabal's fleet had decimated cities across the planet, had laid low untouchable citadels guarding Ea'ae's seals, and nearly toppled Tellanon itself. Though his concern was real, Slate's resolve remained firm.

Yip answered Slate's question with one of his own. "Have we not already?"

Slate puffed his chest out proudly. "Ya're right there!"

They had succeeded where others had failed. They had secured seals directly in the face of the Cabal's evil. They had planted the seeds that would lead to the Cabal's undoing whether or not this mission ended in success.

Yip was sure of these things just as he was sure of their current mission.

Yip smiled and then turned his gaze forward once more, carefully examining the scene playing out before them.

To his eyes, though the veil around the Blaeken Wode had fallen, the air remained turgid with magic, a dense haze of virulent forces permeating the dark forest, the atmosphere, and the castle above. This concentration of aphotic power was particularly concentrated within Garen Muer. Tendrils of vile forces writhed through the walls, groping imperiously, clutching at the keep's heart and whatever horrors lay within. Though much remained hidden from the naked eye, he sensed the movement of inordinate power deep inside the bowels of Garen Muer.

To his mind, the stirring of so much force indicated much transition within the fastness's walls.

Succinctly summarizing the powers at play before his eyes, he said, "Although the walls of Garen Muer yet stand, tumult ensues within the stronghold of the Ruen'elde."

Aroganji shook his head, his eyes, too, following the principles of transformation at play before them. "After all these millennia, who would have thought that the Cabal would be the principal agent of change ushering out the old era, overthrowing evils untouched by the ages?"

To Aroganji's eyes, many forces were at work. All of these signs pointed toward a new day—one without the Ruen'elde. Just as the Fyrskal had fallen along with the Shadow at the heart of Taerris'thule, so much evil had crumpled before and as a consequence of the onslaught of the Cabal, all ensuing because of their desire for revenge against the world that gave their masters birth.

How much more would fall?

How much was now falling across Ea'ae even as they watched?

What would the world finally be like when the Cabal were once more pushed from the shores of Ea'ae and set loose on the seas of oblivion?

How would change finally manifest itself in stability?

Though he might not know, Aroganji would do everything in his power to find out, guiding the course toward one favorable to the future of Ea'ae and her people.

Placing this seal would ensure the bonds of the Cabal's new prison were tight, the trap secure. With nowhere to run, only those of the Cabal who had not marshaled against Ea'ae would remain.

Slate nodded sagely. "One evil fer another."

Wrindanneth shrugged, smiling self-deprecatingly as he replied to Aroganji's words, offering his own view. "I don't know," pausing significantly, he added, "I think we have played our part." Unlike their foes, the results of their efforts, by and large, came to positive ends. Much of the impending transitions would be steered positively as a result of their dedication and discovery.

Concerned with the task at hand and the moment of opportunity presented by the disarray within the Ruen'elde's bastion, Yip urged them onward. "Sand slips between the fingers of those who linger and wait. The confusion within the keep affords a most favorable circumstance to act. We must not let it fall away."

Slate snorted. "Then what're ya doin' flappin' yer jowls? Let's be off!"

Yip smiled in reply, meeting Slate's gaze with his own. Turning his eyes forward once more, he said good-naturedly, "My lips are sealed."

"Fer Brendle's kith and kin we fly!" Slate swooped past his friends without a backward glance.

Wrindanneth sighed and shook his head, intoning softly, "That's our queue."

Though the leagues between their current position and the fearsome crags of Garen Muer were short, the hazard was long.

"Be ready." Wrindanneth's mind shared a connection with Aroganji's, creating a space within and between them through the magic of the twin Elven bracers.

"I am." Aroganji's voice was soft, his mind strong and focused.

Yip's mind remained a vast wellspring of silence.

Flying low, they skirted the foul canopy of the Blaeken Wode, the gnarled branches of its haunted boles clawing blindly upward from below. Ahead, the sweep of the mountains surged skyward, a precipitous climb ending in a wall of fear at the ashen foot of Garen Muer. Above, a peril more ominous than gray thunderheads grew with each passing second—the fleet of the Cabal banking as thick as the foul mists that clung to the summits.

Flying forward, his mind extended in all directions, reading the currents of movement and activity flowing about them, Yip paid particular attention to the dormant seal nestled within his robes. Though the seal remained silent, the tenor and intensity of dark energies continued to grow, a mounting wall of opposition that signaled approach was unwelcome, the land corrupted by vile purpose. The building intensity of these forces confirmed that they were close both to the seething heart of the evil ahead and nearing the point of activation for the new seal.

He would remain ready for the time to act would arrive soon.

Slate scowled. The feeling of doom over the accursed wood continued to escalate, dark portents massing as quickly as the Cabal warships overhead. He did not like the feeling of dread just as he did not like the place. The sooner they were done and could be about their business the better.

For once, he would be happy if his axe remained sheathed.

An ill wind blew through the Blaeken Wode and he wanted nothing of it.

"We are here." Yip's words echoed through the inner recesses of their minds, soft words that felt almost like their own.

He pulled up, letting Slate, Aroganji, and Wrindanneth gather around him. Hovering in the air above the forest canopy, the sense of anticipation was as thick as the portentous magical haze that enveloped them.

The time to act had come.

In his robes, the seal stirred, gradually coming to life.

Reaching inside, he brought forth the new seal and carefully opened its case.

Preparing to activate the seal, once more within the confines of their minds, Yip said, *"I am about to begin. Be on guard and ready to depart."*

No further admonition or urging was necessary; they understood the import of Yip's actions and their own duties. In but a few minutes, the Four would leave as they had come—silently and unobserved.

While Aroganji and Wrindanneth each made ready with counter-spells and teleportation incantations, Yip channeled *chi* into the seal. With this small trickle of energy, the seal caught flame and was transformed.

Arching faster than the mind's ability to comprehend, his consciousness surged outward, instantly bridging the distance between Ea'ae's defensive nodes. Reinforcing the protective matrix that shielded the entire planet in a responsive barrier, the seal strengthened and enhanced, connected and stabilized, the weakened and fragmented planetary shield.

What had been whole and weak was now whole and strong.

Ea'ae's active defense was now fully functional and capable. The restoration and replacement of the remaining seals would only add to this protection.

Remembering himself, he left behind the expansiveness of Ea'ae's defensive mantle for the limitations of the physical form. With a movement of will, he reinstantiated his body from the energy it had become.

Though the ships above made no response as yet to their success, seeing Yip reappear, Slate said urgently, "Let's be off before they realize what's befallen tha seal they came all this way ta claim!"

Maintaining a tight formation, the Four sped away from Garen Muer, leaving its shadows and shattered seal to rest in the wary hollows of memory.

Slate shivered with a mock chill. "Glad ta be rid o' that accursed place!" He looked back over his shoulder at the fading reaches of Garen Muer shifting in and out of the mists high above the lower reaches of the Blaeken Wode. Though terrible numbers of alien warships hovered overhead, its shadows remained untamed even if its heart had been quelled.

Slate's comment was met with a derisive snort. "I thought you were fearless?" Wrindanneth chided his friend's ready candor.

Slate shrugged casually as he addressed Wrindanneth who flew at his shoulder. "I didn't feel good about that place. No one in their right mind would."

"'Sides, bein' fearless is what ya do, not what ya feel. A Dwarf that can face his fears and weaknesses and move forward is as fearless as a mindless, berserk Orc that knows not tha consequences o' its own actions or loss."

Aroganji nodded. "We are lucky to be rid of Garen Muer without having to face either the Cabal or the Ruen'elde."

"We are even more fortunate to have succeeded in placing the seal without discovery."

"That we are yet alive is another miracle entirely."

Slate agreed. "That we will yet be able ta spit in tha eye o' our enemy fer another day is Brendle's own blessin'!"

Wrindanneth laughed. "That they will be able to spit in mine is Maeth's!"

Aroganji and Slate joined in Wrindanneth's laughter. Yip, however, remained silent, his mind intent on the forest beneath, the journey ahead, and the threat behind. Though their triumph had been quick and decisive, he wanted no opportunity for it to be fleeting.

The forest sped by below, its menace lessened not by the actuality of its presence rather by the lightness of their mood. The trees remained dark and sinister, the roiling mists lapping between the boles just as thick, and the occasional sinister screams just as fearsome but their spirits were buoyed by their achievement and the renewed opportunities ahead.

Within a short time, they would teleport to the ship, return home to Tellanon, and decide how best to move forward against the Cabal. Thus far, theirs had been a recursive formula that ended and began with success.

None had plans for any change.

As was often the case, Yip's mind ran counter to that of his friends.

He sensed the evil left in their wake and felt they were not yet safe. Even in Tellanon, the malice lurking behind them would seek them out, striving to undo all that they had accomplished. Until this evil was overturned, they would never truly be secure nor should they fool themselves otherwise.

Though many lived in illusion, he chose not to.

He was, however, at peace with this reality for it was the one he had lived in the whole of his life alongside all the other priests, initiates, and acolytes.

There was, and always would be, awe in the fact that they all yet remained alive and glory continued to unfurl all around.

His attention was his expression of care and consideration, his manifest concern for his friends, for his diligence was their future.

And even in this he failed.

A slight vibration, the gentlest manifestation, was all the warning he had. This infinitesimal sign passed far too rapidly for proper reaction. Nonetheless, he did as only he could—his best.

"Tr—" The urgent call for readiness he pushed through to their minds was interrupted as the world shifted, the entire space in which they occupied ported far away.

Just as he had no time to fully warn his friends before the spell's completion, he had no opportunity to completely deflect and counter the energies which enveloped them. The magic's expression was too fast and too subtle to anticipate, fully realized and implemented upon observance.

He did, however, have enough time to alter the power's progress.

Though he had been surprised, caught unexpectedly in his

pursuers' net, he could return the favor with a surprise of his own. They would arrive as summoned—just not where their hunters wished.

The world moved and with it their wills.

"— ap!"

Many events unfolded at once.

For him, time slowed to a crawl, energy and awareness enlivening his actions and acuity, enabling the actualization of many feats in tandem.

The room, its occupants, its arrangement, and its energies were revealed in a flash, encompassed even as he assessed their dangers, surmised their neutralization, and translated this understanding directly to his companions.

Dictates streamed from his mind to theirs in an instant giving no time for their enemies to react to their arrival before the party initiated an overwhelming counterattack.

"Slate! Activate your offensive contingency!"

Simultaneous to this request, the world slowed as their defensive contingencies activated, shrouding them in a protective haze of magic dulling and reflecting wards, multiple images of themselves appeared, their actions hastened, their positions crackling and dancing ready to shift and teleport at will as other protections snapped into place.

His mind instantly taking in the space, while the initiative remained theirs, a moment granted by his unexpected change in their translation, Yip's commands continued, coincident with those transmitted to Slate, shared thoughts expressed orders and descriptions more efficiently than mere words through a medium of common experience. *"Multiple primary targets in viewing area located in balcony immediately overhead. Magical shields dispelled below their feet. Transmogrify rock to mud and then back! Secondary undead targets in chamber center!"*

While Yip conveyed these impressions and issued directions, the chamber exploded in light and power, their counterspells ripping through the air immediately upon arrival, lashing out against the malefactors that summoned them to these unhallowed halls, battering the magical protections of those who sought to trap them, altering their foes' perception and interaction with space and time, pervading the room in generative Light, and purging the space of vile influence.

Yip's warning entered his mind just as the world jumped and twisted unexpectedly around him, currents of change materializing fully formed with the expression of magic, swirling faster than he could counter.

Reverberating from his mind to Wrindanneth's, Yip's words echoed between them, a symphony of caution amidst the sudden discordant transition. Before the sounds of this alarm stilled, more information followed, registering faster than his appreciation of the space they now occupied.

While he gathered himself and refound his bearings, summoning forth the energy required to cast a volley of incantations, a complete, real-time impression of the space they now occupied along with its occupiers flowed through to his mind from Yip's own. Unused to Yip's sensory perception, he was nonetheless able to understand the information transmitted.

What he saw was as disturbing as it was enlightening.

A cadre of ominous lights hovered in the wall roughly twenty paces above him. Though he knew little of what these beings' energy patterns meant, for Yip's perspective was not his own, he could tell by their tenor and timbre that they were very different from his own— dark, crackling with menace, thirstily drawing in the surrounding's energies. Multi-faceted forces enclosed them in a sphere of what he assumed was protective magics. Other energies moved and stirred about them, active castings and magics prepared for use.

These must be members of the Cabal that had summoned them here.

These presences were not the only threats within the immediate vicinity. In the room's center, ancient and twisted, sustained by convoluted chains of dark forces, hideous abominations floated in the air within complex, interwoven nimbuses of power.

These others must be the Ruen'elde, former masters of Garen Muer, waiting to greet their newest victims.

All this information and more registered in Aroganji's mind within the blink of an eye.

He was ready and now moving to act.

Only an instant later, the multi-layered magics of the contingency spells exploded through the air, sending the room and its occupants into chaos. Yip's mind still cursorily linked to his own, he saw the protective magics surrounding the Cabal wither, their carefully crafted spells negated, and their vicious plans for their arrival temporarily interrupted. The room radiated in holy light, he saw the Ruen'elde burning, tossed through the air as gravity shifted, their defenses dispelled, Slate fanning the flames of their demise, and their ashes scattered across the chamber's high ceiling.

At that moment, Yip's call for direct action came through and their dauntless efforts to survive began in earnest.

Yip's knowledge fresh in their minds, their thoughts linked in perfect accord through their bracers, Aroganji and Wrindanneth acted at once and as one.

Without word or hesitation, while their captors' were off-balance and their defenses were down, Aroganji struck. Unleashing a torrent of force, its power augmented by his eldritch wand, he thrust his arm forward, commanding, "Transfigure rock to mud!"

His arms already raised, incantation complete, Wrindanneth released a gout of power immediately following Aroganji's enchantment, perfectly timed for maximal effect. With the release of this coiled font of energy, Wrindanneth intoned, "Transmute mud to rock!"

Before them, the entirety of the wall, ceiling, and balcony collapsed and began to flow, an avalanche of stone turned liquid, roiling and surging from its moorings. Just as quickly, the mudslide stilled, a solidified mass of turbulent destruction bestilled and silent once more.

Caught in the earthen flow, crushed and entombed within unyielding stone, the members of the Cabal that brought them here finally found the darkness they so earnestly craved.

Slate heard Yip's call of warning and urge to act in his mind and did not hesitate, letting loose a roar of his own. Releasing his suite of offensive magics, the dark chamber in which he stood disoriented surged to life, blinding Light washing over walls befouled and tarnished by centuries of dark sorcery.

With Light coursing through him, his fires surged to life, shrouding him in a haze of superheated magical flames, their fires heeding the call of his will.

Eyes lit by the rage of his inner blaze, he let loose a gout of Brendle's own flames upon the unholy abominations at the room's heart.

Then, turning his gaze to the pile of hardened slag beneath the gaping hole in the room's wall left by Aroganji and Wrindanneth's powerful magic, a wall of white flames arched forward, purging any pestilence that may yet linger within the solid stone.

What Maeth's own Light had not destroyed, Brendle's would.

The space they were in was large, a high meeting chamber in the recesses of a vast ill-lit, dusty keep. By his assessment of the energy patterns of the place, the enemies above and within the chamber's center, they were now in the central confines of Garen Muer itself. Judging by the original positioning of the Cabal above and the arrangement of the Archliches, their foes had expected them to arrive in the middle of the chamber, in the thick of their trap, ready to unleash destruction upon them.

However unlikely, however fortuitous, they had somehow managed to escape this noose with a gambit of their own.

Within the blink of an eye, unfortunately for their pursuers, their enemies were now either sealed in stone behind or burnt to ashes and hurled ceilingward.

The time to return home had come.

"T' tha ship!" Slate's command was unnecessary. Aroganji had already commenced the incantation that would return them to the *Shrike*.

As quickly as they had come, magic swirled about them and they were gone. In their absence, the silence of a tomb settled once more upon the heart of Garen Muer.

DARKNESS BETWEEN DIMENSIONS

Dragonflies hover,
darting above the still mere.

Do mosquitoes
sense the beating of their wings?

Yip sensed instantly that something had gone horribly wrong. He felt horrific powers twist and alter Aroganji's teleportation spell faster than any of them could hope to correct or counter its course.

As he had done once just a few minutes before, he manipulated the magic as best he could given the limited time available and his lack of preparation. He could only hope that by altering the spell's effect, they would gain some advantage with the translocation.

Into what abyss they would be plunged, he had no time to imagine for faster than he could fully comprehend, they were there.

Slate gasped.

There was no air!

As quickly as this realization settled over him, the magic of the Star of Illdrassil shielded him, providing him with a localized atmosphere. With it, his breathing eased and his tension lessened.

Where in the multiverse were they?

Wrindanneth glowered.

Thinking they had escaped from the Cabal's trap, they had fallen into another!

Fools!

He blamed himself for this failing for it was he above all people who should not have been complacent or trusting things would be so simple, especially after they had been trapped once already. He should not have rushed their escape without first assessing the risk.

Now they were Maeth only knew where.

Quickly dropping the self-recriminations, he began to assay the situation for immediate risks and options.

Aroganji remained calm.

The air was in flux, the currents of transition too complex and varied yet to read. He would need a bit more opportunity to understand the movements of change around him in order to understand how best to act.

He only hoped they had time.

Yip's mind leapt forth, encompassing the surrounding space in a flood. Simultaneously, in order to lessen their chance of discovery, he masked their energy signatures as best he could.

Broadcasting immediately to his friends' minds, he said, *"Make ready with defensive preparations! Our arrival does not appear to have set off any disturbance but we must be alert! Our summoner may be near!"*

"Shall we avoid this encounter and teleport home? The terms of this battle are not ours." Aroganji's cautious words followed just behind Yip's own.

Wrindanneth replied, *"If whatever brought us here is capable of acting so subtly and decisively as to avoid our detection in order to summon us, attempting to leave now may only play further into its hands, potentially giving our position away, and ensure our demise for it may twist our spell to end wherever it wanted us to arrive in the first place."*

Slate grunted. *"Though this is not a battle o' our choosin', whatever brought us here is likely ta keep tryin' fer us in tha future. I say we give more'n it wants or can handle!"*

Aroganji acceded, preferring to use whatever time they might have in preparation rather than argument. *"Then we must make ready in what little time we have."*

Yip replied succinctly, focusing on their preparations, *"Aroganji, you will be the first to use your defensive or offensive contingency, if required."*

With the various protections of their contingency spells waiting, he broke connection with his friends.

Reassured they were immediately undetected and their defenses were as sound as they could be, his evaluation of their surroundings continued.

They were no longer on Ea'ae—far from it. This land was desolate —black, blasted, barren, and lifeless. There was no air or atmosphere. Obsidian-like rocks crumbled underfoot. In a land without horizon, ebony earth met the unmitigated negrosity of space in the unknown distance—twin infinities meeting in an impossible dream.

Worse yet, *chi* was as absent as the life that created it. Even the *yuan-chi* was thin, diluted and diminished, a faint but all-pervasive layer. To further complicate matters, as on Al'Marr, what little ambient energies were present appeared pulled, drawn and attenuated, flowing and moving elsewhere. Unlike Al'Marr, this effect did not seem local-ized to a single focal point. Rather, the currents siphoned away in all directions as by multiple invisible vortices.

Though he could investigate the phenomena further, neither the movement of energy nor its destination were his primary concern.

His first obligation was remaining safe and viable in such a harsh place. All of their capabilities would be diminished, along with their ability to survive, in such inhospitable environs.

If they were not to leave, this meant finding and negating their pursuer.

Or avoiding their stalker entirely.

Despite the apparent limitations imposed by such a poor environ-ment, they could, if necessary, utilize the Dragon's Gate at need to create energy. However, with the ambient energies so thin and the reason for their transference not yet revealed or understood, he did not want to draw undo attention to themselves when *yuan-chi* remained in such dearth. Such an action might give them away before they were ready to act.

Surveying the far horizons, his awareness lit upon a force disturbing the calm.

"Get down!" He detected the trap intended for them just as their hunter descried the party, perhaps alerted by the magics of its spell despite Yip's attempt to cover their presence.

His words racing through their minds once more, he threw himself downward as a bolt of luminescent force raced toward them, deflected and absorbed by his mind. Just as quickly, their contingency spells took effect.

Taking the tumultuous power within himself, he neutralized its destructive potential, harnessing its energy for future use.

A presence far colder and emptier than the space between the stars reached out to him across the distance, an interaction he only allowed tenuously for risk of attack. Though a measured risk, he wished to know the voice and mind of his pursuer.

A wall of boundless, detached coldness filled the space within the other's mind, the objectivity and composure of pure awareness filled with complete disregard to consequence or compassion. Within this depthless sea of empty dispassion, a fire of evil burned—hatred of Yip, his kind, and all he stood for. This abhorrence fueled this being's relentless drive to destroy him.

In that moment, he knew that this vacuous husk was his pursuer, that this twisted creature was the agent of misery bent on his destruction and the destruction of his order. Within that shared instant, he understood that this thing had once been a priest. Along with this knowledge came the realization that this fallen priest, once so much like himself, had sent out countless agents bent on the destruction of all he cherished, that the many assassins that stalked him were this creature's agents of doom.

Within the pall of Darkness another instrument of evil lurked, just as much a perversion of Life and all its energy. This mind remained closed to him but he now sensed its malevolence unfiltered by the distance that separated them.

Though very different, the two were linked by the dark powers that guided them.

Although this contact was brief, he learned much.

Remaining prepared for anything, he gave nothing in return.

Time slowed as their defensive contingencies activated in a cascading wave of force, shrouding them in a protective haze of magics as another round of malefic azure blasts flashed toward them. Before their shields could reflect this energy back at their attacker, Yip captured the virulent bolts' power, further augmenting his store, sharing much of this power with his friends for their need would be greater than his own in the moments ahead. Simultaneously, multiple images of themselves appeared, their actions accelerated and enlivened, their silhouettes crackling and dancing, ready to shift and teleport at will as all their protections snapped into place.

These lightning-like bolts of force emanated from a pall of Darkness that blanketed the plains ahead, shrouding two beings of immense destructive capacity.

Establishing a mental link with his friends, he shared his impressions of these threats—the death trap that had been their intended destination after being wrenched from Garen Muer and the entities of colossal power that lurked within.

He also let some of his memory of the immense, alien coldness of the entity within that stygian ambush touch their minds.

"By Brendle's blade what's that?" Slate's words traveled to them directly through the connection provided by the Stars of Illdrassil, his rage and bloodlust unfiltered by the normal constraints of his own mind.

While he continued preparing for the coming onslaught, a grim determination fell over Yip as he studied the nexus of dark powers that flowed and morphed ahead—a necrotic cloud over an already dead landscape. He conveyed these sentiments directly through his thoughts. *"There is something, some evil that was once a priest, now a Liúxīng Làngrén, within that mantle of living Darkness."*

Slate's voice was just as grim. *"Then it must fall like tha priest it once was."*

"With it there stands another power, vast and alien, clinging to a life that is no longer its own."

"Tha time o' its endin' is come." Slate planted his boots in the dust and made ready. He had made his peace with his god. Now the time had arrived to give these unhallowed creatures the peace they deserved—the depthless wash of oblivion.

Yip reacted instantly.

His mind expanded as his body fell away. Coursing outward, his awareness encompassed the plains and the evil it contained, a nocuous black pit at its dark core. Vast, fluid, and flexible, he prepared for the final assault, gathering what energy he could to himself, anticipating the enemy would come with more.

As he responded, the mass of turbulent Darkness warped and twisted, surging erratically forward across the sere, abandoned plains in vast jumps, consuming the intervening distance insatiably.

The seething mass would be on them in moments.

"You must not let the Darkness touch you, even under the protections of our aegis!" Yip's disembodied words brought home the full import of the impending encounter.

"Spread out!" Wrindanneth's words followed Yip's as they teleported apart from one another. "Be ready with your most powerful wards against Darkness!"

Drawing Duraeleon, feeling its weight in his hand, flexing his fingers around its haft, Slate wreathed himself in protective, cleansing flames, pulling forth additional fires from the heat of the mighty ring Baërn in hand and the power that Yip granted, his outline vague and indistinct under Caelebeor's mantle, taking the forward position directly between the warping cloud and the group's original position. Sensing its master's mood, Duraeleon let loose a low keening, the wail for its mind only for the vacuum around them carried no sound.

Fueled by the flames racing through his veins, Slate began inscribing powerful Karaduen in the vacuum, granting his runes power and vibrancy with the air of his breath and the fires of his heart. Shimmering in the space about him, these sigils added might to his own.

To Slate's left, Aroganji drew Luereal, calling its untold power to the fore, augmenting his own. With one arching wave, a field of shimmering force encapsulated his form. Drawing in yet more energy, he prepared to meet the Darkness with the light of the sun, the heart and heat of a star.

To Slate's right, a few hundred paces from where Aroganji now waited, his form wavering and jumping with the protective magics shrouding his lanky frame, Wrindanneth drew his eldritch dagger, cutting a line of demarcation in the rough obsidian, enchanting a protective spell against extradimensional powers all the while. Gouts of white flames jumped upward irregularly when his invocation was complete. This same ward of holy power would enhance his blasts when the time came, anathema to entities of Darkness.

As they watched, the terror that stalked them revealed itself.

Riding atop the oozing tidal wave of Darkness, wreathed in tendrils of otherworldly force, a spectral Dragon flowed liquidly, its vast form rolling easily with the tide. Incomprehensibly malefic, its skeletal form wavered and blinked, of this world and another. From its yawning maw, blue flames wavered and licked hungrily, wreathing its pallid remains in an eidolic glow.

At ease astride its mighty back, a Shadow darker than any Shade flowed and rippled effortlessly, as much a part of the Darkness as Darkness itself. Tendrils of bespoiled and perverted life energies lapped at its feet and caressed its form, agents of entropy joined in a cascading surge of destruction. Any semblance of humanity had long since faded from its visage, replaced by the absolute Darkness it now embraced.

These horrors were to be their destiny, if not their doom.

With the revenants' ghastly approach, there were no pronouncements, no calls to battle, no challenges, no diatribes, merely the manifestation of their hostile, implacably violent intent.

Warping at last within range before them, rearing back its great head, the fearsome Dragonoid apparition opened its gaping jaws once more and let loose a strafing gout of unholy fires intended to engulf them all.

Anticipating this attack, reacting instantly, Aroganji countered the undead beast's fury with his own. Firing off their offensive contingencies as the pair neared, he simultaneously called forth Luereal's might, distorting and twisting the fabric of space between them.

Although their offensive counterspells fired off to no avail against the horrific monstrosities, counter to the success of their prior application in the keep of Garen Muer, his own spell found its mark.

Though the seething mass of Dragon fire exploded outward toward them, the terrible flames only bridged half the distance to the band before turning inward and back on itself, for what was once forward was now backward, the nature of space between them temporarily altered by Aroganji's spell, the infernal gout ripping across the Dragon and its rider in a dreadful torrent of hellfire.

Though its molten black rider shrugged off the flames indifferently, the ghostly Dragon writhed in silent pain, its agony muted by the uncompromising vacuum through which it flew, its full voice lost with the body it once knew.

Raising both bleak arms skyward, the fallen priest countered instantly, its mighty will made manifest with a gesture that flung aside Aroganji's spell effortlessly. Bringing both hands forward, a sphere of impossible Darkness warped and coalesced into existence, sucking in all ambient energies as it formed.

Alarmed, Yip sensed in that moment that the dangers they now faced were far beyond his initial, already dire impressions.

The abomination that the Liúxīng Làngrén brought forth so casually, so facilely, was anathema, bane to existence itself, a recreation of the very pit of Darkness that had destroyed all life on Al'Marr, callously sucking away its vitality.

With but a single motion, a swirling maelstrom of Darkness detonated outward from its extended hand, a virulent window into a lightless nether abyss, filled with boundless living Shadow. Ripping through the space between them, a hungry pit yawned ravenously waiting to suck them into the very bowels of Ur'Daus Itself.

Without time to offer warning, without hesitation, Yip countered this heinous contravention of all that should be.

Coalescing the entirety of his will and power into a locus including the accursed sphere and its creator, he unleashed the fullness of the Dragon's Gate. Fueled by the sum of the energy he had been able to gather while waiting for their foes along with the seething bursts he had absorbed in from their attackers in the initial assault, impossible potential burned to life.

In an instant, a blinding torrent of splendid, all-consuming Light exploded forth, engulfing and ripping through the Dragon and its rider, shredding the abominable sphere, its intensity stoked by the depths of their Darkness, burning all the brighter for their iniquity.

Leaving the flow of Light unchecked, a fount of pure energy shone forth beneath the bleak sky, a brief sign of hope and life on a forsaken world, bereft for far too long.

Sure of their destruction, no longer willing to let the ineffable fires of the white Light rage any longer, Yip stilled its empyrean beauty, not wishing for its presence to risk further reprisal. With its fading, the fallen priest and fell undead Dragon faded into the oblivion they so willingly embraced.

Wrindanneth acted immediately before retribution, before anything else unpleasantly unexpected arose, now certain that no other traps were in place. With a decisive incantation, visualizing the deck of the *Shrike*, he teleported them far from the forsaken wilds of the dead world, leaving behind the ashes of their enemies' defeat.

"Activate tha return ta Tellanon!" Slate's words were urgent, his tone decisive.

Standing on the deck of the *Shrike*, the ship cloaked and far from Garen Muer, unknowably farther from the evils of the dead world, Wrindanneth chuckled. "Anxious to get home are you?"

"Wretched Trollspawn! I don't want those blasted fools ta have another chance at us! We're lucky ta be here, Brendle be praised! One trap after tha next! Ya'd think we'd done somethin' ta spite 'em!"

"Don't get your tunic in a tangle. I have activated the return system even as we speak. Give it a moment and we'll be on our way."

"If it's a fight they want, then it's a fight they'll get. I just don't want ta be summoned like a genie from a lamp!"

"You don't have to worry there, Slate. The only person who'd willingly summon you would be a barkeep looking for the repayment of your tab."

Slate nodded grimly. "'Tis good news indeed. That way, no one'll come lookin' fer me after ya disappear."

Ignoring the implicit threat, Wrindanneth replied, "Speaking of disappearing, prepare to jump."

As the last sounds of Wrindanneth's sentence faded, the world fell away into the timeless emptiness of beginnings and endings.

FLIGHT OF FANCY

Eyes heavy, closing;
mind alert, awakening.
Aroused or dreaming?

"Welcome home, Fists!" Still recovering from the uneasy feeling of complete dissolution, the Construct's booming welcome fell on ears better served by silence, not yet granted the opportunity to understand, internalize, or make full sense of what befell them only moments before, apparently so many worlds and aeons away.

"News of your successful return has been forwarded to the appropriate parties. Eidelion wishes to speak with you in person immediately."

"And a merry welcome t'ya too!" Slate kept the sarcasm from his voice largely because the ringing in his ears was irritating enough without further aggravation.

Speaking for his fellows, Wrindanneth responded, "We will report upon docking."

"Adar will be in place waiting for you at your berth upon arrival."

"Congratulations and safe journey!" Their flight plan transferred to the ship's automatic navigation system, the Construct thankfully left them in peace.

Slate shook his head, impressed. "Didn't expect tha Construct ta be able ta tell our mission was a success so easily."

Wrindanneth shrugged. "It is fairly obvious. We are back."

Aroganji added, "We are alive and in relatively good spirits, no one is injured or out of sorts, it can read our physiological and energetic patterns very much like Yip, and see more than we would say regardless. Furthermore, it is sensitive enough to discern that we no longer have the seal."

"And we are lucky to be here at that." Wrindanneth shook his head. Though there was much worth celebrating in their success, the fact that they were all still here alive was due to a fortunate dispelling of the Cabal's defenses and a bit of luck with Yip's manipulation of the initial teleportation trap.

Had their dispel in the dark heart of Garen Muer not worked, Slate's other offensive contingency spells would have been deflected harmlessly. Though Yip might have had time to counter the Cabal's magics, neither he nor Wrindanneth would have been able to do so instantly. Had Yip not altered the spell that brought them to the keep, they might not have had the time to act regardless of their spells' effectiveness.

This made no account or mention of their duel on the alien desert plains. At least in that case they had a few moments to prepare thanks to Yip's manipulation of the summoning spell. Otherwise, they might have been ported directly into annihilation.

Yip shared Wrindanneth's sentiment. "Being prepared gave us the chance to survive. Being alert and making the most of what few opportunities we were given allowed us to meet with success. Fortune's smile allowed us to live."

"Bah! Ya know they wouldn't want ta take us on in a fair fight! Ya saw that twice!"

"What makes ya think our skill is somehow lessened when they stacked tha deck so heavily against us?"

Aroganji clarified, "If they had more time to prepare, the outcomes might have been very different skill or no."

Yip spoke plainly. "With this failure, the Cabal will redouble their efforts to find us."

Slate washed his hands eagerly in response. "Which is exactly what we want!"

Wrindanneth snorted. "Says the Dwarf who couldn't get back to safety soon enough!"

Slate shrugged. "We struck when tha odds were in our favor. From there, fate's fortune was not so kind."

Though he was reluctant to agree overtly with Slate, Wrindanneth was willing to accede on one front. "We have indeed pushed our luck. I think the time has come to get out of the seal restoration business."

Aroganji assented. "We have struck decisively against the Cabal's plans. The time has come to strike against the Cabal directly."

Slate chuckled, saying, "That sounds riskier'n stayin' at Garen Muer!"

Scratching his beard, he added thoughtfully, "Per'aps about as dangerous as tryin' our luck on that alien death orb."

Wrindanneth chortled mockingly, retorting, "Then I suppose we shouldn't count you in?"

Slate merely replied with a piercing glare. Finally, he said, "My axe is already sharp. Unbelievably, even sharper than yer tongue. Until tha sun no longer shines, I will be ready."

"Let us take counsel with Eidelion. If Ea'ae and her people can be counted safe, then I, too, am for moving forward." Aroganji appreciated the odds against them would be even greater if they sought the Cabal in their home but, like the restoration of the seals, ultimately it had to be done.

Yip had no designs for the way forward. Too much had changed and occurred unexpectedly to call for a path when one was not yet revealed. "Without a goal, there is no path ahead. We aim for the Cabal but have yet to find our course."

"Then we raze tha entire forest ta find it!"

Yip laughed. "We do not yet even know where the forest resides."

"The forest may come to us." Wrindanneth knew they were a target, just how big would determine the damage they inflicted when the Cabal came for them.

Yip nodded. "As it has before."

After a moment's pause, Yip added, "We may have already found it."

Replying to Wrindanneth, Aroganji said, "Then let us hope its true wardens reveal themselves when it does." The Cabal's trap could become one of their own as it had at Garen Muer and beyond.

Yip laughed once more, reiterating his prior point. "Perhaps it already did. Perhaps we were granted a vision of where we must go when we defeated the fallen priest."

He smiled, adding, "We are indeed fertile ground. They will come."

Slate growled, "If we don't first." If that dead world was not the primary target, he would be willing to search every single world indicated on the alien command sphere to ferret it out.

Aroganji raised an eyebrow, his curiosity not yet satisfied. "Yip, what was it we fought on that alien world?"

Yip's face turned serious. "That was a Liúxīng Làngrén, one of those fallen from the way of Heaven, a fallen priest."

"We now have a conception of their power. The fallen priest summoned a planet destroying *chi* void effortlessly. I was lucky to have reacted quickly for the sphere would have sapped our power even had we managed to avoid it."

Slate snorted and shook his head. "Yip, if it were anyone else in tha macroverse, I'd say it'd be fair ta say ya got lucky, but I know otherwise. Ya've saved us more times'n I can count and we owe ya our lives."

Yip bowed. "We each owe the other."

"And the Dragon?"

Yip shook his head. "Of that I cannot be sure but it may be one whose path almost crossed our own in times past."

Slate raised his bushy eyebrows. "Ya think it was Sarugauth the Red?"

Wrindanneth answered for Yip. "It would make sense."

Aroganji nodded in agreement. "Others here will be able to confirm this for us."

Yip offered, "Master Wei may be able to identify the priest."

Slate shook his head. "Seems ta me there was so little left that could even be called remotely human that'd he'd have a devil o' a time tryin'."

Yip smiled. "I have never been one to question Master Wei's wisdom. Let us see what clarity he may offer when next we speak."

Wrindanneth grinned. "Then it is as it should be. We return with questions, having been given few answers!"

Slate laughed heartily. "Aye!"

The frenetic pace of commerce along Tellanon's sweeping stone dock, the haze of incoming and outgoing ships, the diversity in design and vision of sentient expression, all were a welcome sight as the *Shrike* approached her berth. That they returned was almost as miraculous as the view of the city afforded by their arrival.

"I never grow tired o' watchin' tha vibrancy and fervor o' Tellanon." Slate was leaning forward out over the railing, his excitement clearly etched across cheek and brow. The violence and discord of their recent encounters were temporarily forgotten amidst the wonders moving before him.

"You're welcome to stay as long as you like." Wrindanneth cocked a wry smile, offering innocently, "I, for one, would be happy to let you partake of her wonders when next we depart."

Slate spat demonstrably over the side, letting his gesture show what he thought of Wrindanneth's suggestion. After a significant pause, he turned his head, raising a thick eyebrow as he did, and said, "And let ya leave without tha pleasure o' my company? Ta do anythin' less would be ungentlemanly."

Wrindanneth begged to differ. "To do less would be saintly...and welcome."

"Too bad I'm neither," Slate turned back to his survey of the looming docks waited a moment before adding, "saintly nor accomodatin'."

With that, Wrindanneth could not help but to agree.

Before further comment could be made, the Construct's dislocated voice issued through the air. "Fists, prepare for docking!"

Watching the crowds move and flow organically as the *Shrike* sailed smoothly toward the docks, Yip was struck by the emergent intelligence, cooperation, and efficiency of collective sentient action. The diverse range of individuals moving so earnestly along Tellanon's vast landing —teeming groups of dock workers, hordes of colorful merchants, myriad tradesman, assorted officious diplomats, bands of armored adventurers, fantastical Paratechnologists, throngs of unusual alien races, intermingling with starry-eyed travelers—all working toward their own disparate ends. This mass could have resulted in complete chaos, distinct agendas battling against each other toward divergent goals. Instead, the entire body of enterprise and ideation moved in orchestrated sophistication without apparent central guidance.

Continual direct and indirect information feeds were available on demand from the Construct to facilitate the efficient movement of both knowledge and commerce. However, this information did not dictate the actual patterns of traffic seen on the docks or the decisions made by the many players involved.

That shifting manifestations of order arose spontaneously from the tumult brought a smile to his lips.

Life's development and expression paralleled that of its intelligence—ever evolving and increasing, replete with surprises and wonder.

He was glad for the opportunity to take in one of life's many continual unexpected surprises.

A welcome respite from the horrors of the recent past.

"Come on, Yip! The future's not waitin' fer ya nor am I!"

Slate's friendly growl was another reminder to brighten the smile on his face for his friend's assertion of urgency was really one of concern. In lieu of words, Yip responded with a slow bow, leaving the railing for the gangplank that had been lowered to span the dizzying gap between the *Shrike* and the quay.

Gently extending his right arm outward, gracefully leading away from his body with the hand, he indicated that Slate should go first. Wrindanneth and Aroganji had already disembarked after Wrindanneth had locked the ship in a holding position a safe distance from the sheer stone wall.

Halfway across the plank, Adar's voice carried across the din. "Fists!"

About twenty paces farther up the docks, gracefully navigating toward them through the stacked crates and moving throngs, Adar waved in greeting. Nearing where Aroganji and Wrindanneth waited by the end of the gangplank, Adar spoke with genuine good cheer. "Welcome and well met!"

The haze of magic surrounding Adar was strong, a representation both of his power and the Craft he brought to bear to protect and augment himself. The wicked sentient Paratechnological drone hovering above his shoulder only heightened the effect. Waiting for Adar to say more, Yip studied him as Adar approached his friends.

Almost across the walkway, Adar offered a greeting. *"Hello, Yip. We are glad that you have returned safely."*

"Thank you, Adar. I am glad that we met with success. I cannot say the same for the cost."

"Indeed. There is much to be said when you have the time."

Only then did he realize that Adar had been speaking to him directly within his mind. His awareness calm, Yip did not react with surprise, rather, he noted the occurrence and moved on from one fact to the next. He would ponder the implications of this item at some other time.

More surprising was the fact that he had replied similarly and not even noticed as the ability was becoming more and more natural.

Internally, directly to Adar, he said, *"After we return from our meeting with Eidelion, we will be free to meet."*

"Good. I will let the others know as well."

Noting the difference, he then heard Adar speak aloud. "On behalf of the citizens of Tellanon, her agents, allies, and attendants, we welcome you home and offer our heartfelt gratitude for your continued success and safe return!"

"You have accomplished what many thought impossible not once but thrice. You have saved countless lives by your direct actions, the security you have established, and the knowledge you have uncovered and so willingly shared. For this and many other boons, we, the people of Tellanon and Ea'ae beyond, are in your eternal debt."

With a most gracious bow, Adar finished sincerely, "Thank you."

"'Twas nothin'," Slate scoffed at the attention, his cheeks glowing a slight pink, embarrassed at the praise but enjoying it nonetheless.

Wrindanneth, too, was dismissive, offering an honest reply. "We have pursued our own course and are pleased that so much of worth has resulted. However, our actions are no more worthy of praise than any others' for we have worked for our own ends and our own desires."

Aroganji was courteous in reply. "We welcome your thanks and give you ours in return."

Yip finished, "To give what we may and serve how we are able is our way and our pleasure."

Adar bowed once more. "Your kindness and consideration will not go without reward."

Once he returned to a standing position, Adar waved his arm forward, saying, "Please follow me. I will escort you to Eidelion. There is much of interest that we need to discuss."

Joining Adar, the companions made their way onward wending through the thick crowds choosing to walk in silence rather than try to maintain a conversation amidst the jostling, din, and constant redirection of attention associated with movement through the masses. Climbing steadily, they eventually left the bustle of the docks for the relative calm of Tellanon proper, the two worlds separated by the swirling breadth of the Scimerian Gate.

Motioning for them to follow, Adar took them past the frenzy of the Scimerian Gate with its press of people, its resplendent guardians, and attendant sights and sounds onto the serene, tree-lined boulevards of Tellanon. Flowing, organically sculpted buildings, some resembling the natural subtle curvatures of hillocks, others the complex multi-dimensional layering of reefs, stood alongside many other fanciful and practical shapes and forms taken directly from the builder's inspiration. Just as the buildings ranged in structure and function, so, too, did they vary in decoration. Some were covered in bright mosaics and colors, others in variegated plantings, others in dynamic artwork, still others were left unadorned, and many were indistinguishable as buildings at all. Together, all added diversity and texture to a vibrant, integrated living landscape.

After a short walk toward the city's heart, the cobblestoned avenue leading directly toward Illdrassil's shimmering heights at the city's far center, Adar turned off the road and moved along a wooded path toward a structure nestled in a small copse alongside. Covered in ferns and flowering vines, a gently sloping hill arched upward from the forest floor. On the side of the knoll facing the wooded boulevard, a flat, vertical stone face presented itself. Intricate reliefs were etched into its surface depicting the rise of intelligence, the opening of the mind, and the frontiers of imagination. At the center of this relief, a rounded door was barely discernible from the stone, its edges incorporated as the bounds of a planet, its surface the world's own.

On either side of this portal, two armed Paratechnologists barred the entrance. One guardian appeared to be made of countless fragments of prismatic glass. The other Paratechnologist appeared to be made of shimmering metal flowing instantly between solid and liquid states with each motion. At their shoulders, fierce drones hovered menacingly scanning the area for possible threats. Against the bucolic backdrop, the intensity and significance of their presence was tangible.

Merely offering a nod, Adar walked forward without giving voice. Stepping aside, both Paratechnologists shifted gracefully away, liquid and light conjoined. As the wardens moved, their drones following in unison, the portal at the center of the relief opened silently without visible hinge or sound. From within, golden light poured forth, brighter than the daylight above, a beam of intense curiosity guiding them forward.

Following Adar through, Wrindanneth went first while Aroganji and Slate came next. Stopping alongside the wardens, Yip bowed respectfully before continuing onward. Crossing the threshold last, his mind was not the last to realize the wonder within.

Energy washed over him, a gentle tide hinting at the sights ahead. Magic swirled in complex montages along a hallway that stretched ahead much farther than should have been possible given the dimensions of the hillock itself and the parcel of land on which it rested. Within these magical arrangements, other structures followed, branching outward into other distinct spaces and patterns.

Looking down the hallway as he stepped through, a wide passage stretched beyond the limits of his vision. White stone walls arched high overhead, bridged by crystalline columns resembling the trunks of intricately carved trees. Decorative motifs lined the elaborate stonework of the walls—short vignettes displaying the accomplishments and ascent of sentience.

Evenly spaced along the entirety of these walls, suspended in the same way as works of art on display, framed by unique carvings in the living stone, windows looked outward onto other worlds—scenes of mountains, forests, streams, fields, deserts, lakes, wealds, oceans, and many other vistas besides. From the familiar to the alien, all were open for examination, as many landscapes to explore as the heart could wish —more variety and wonder than could be contained within the entirety of Ea'ae.

Adar indicated the passage's walls with a wide open gesture of both arms. "Much like the Halls of Choosing, the landscapes you see before you are portals to the pocket dimensions accessed randomly through Tellanon's many parks. From here, you can choose to enter any miniature universe connected to Tellanon and explore its extent."

"Unlike the Halls of Choosing, however, here all pocket dimensions are afforded space and are presented for review."

Aroganji nodded. "And the hall adjusts as more are added?"

Adar nodded.

Slate asked, "Why have this place when tha Halls o' Choosin' allow fer tha same thing and are more efficient?"

Adar replied thoughtfully, "This hall predates the Halls of Choosing. There are many entries to this one place scattered across Tellanon. It has been kept as a museum of sorts but its primary function remains."

"Not only can visitors enter the dimension of their choice, but they can casually peruse the many options available to them in a fashion altogether different from that provided by the Halls of Choosing. For some, this approach is favorable."

"Also, if one happens to know which pocket dimension is linked with a given park at a given time, this nexus can serve as a means to quickly move across the city while enjoying a beautiful walk through one of her many parks."

"Here we are!" He stopped in front of a window looking out upon a broad expanse of swaying grassland. The grasses ranged in color from lustrous purples and golds to pale blues and corals—a kaleidoscopic swath of surreal prairie.

Slate raised a shaggy eyebrow. "Where, exactly, is here?"

"This portal leads to the pocket dimension whose entrance is currently positioned closest to the Home Guard." He pointed upward at the shifting stone mosaic above the frame indicating a depiction of the adjoining cityscape.

Eyeing the tall grasses warily, Slate said, "We could've just flown."

Adar nodded patiently. "We could have. But then I would have had less time to speak with you."

Wrindanneth laughed, poking fun at Slate in response. "And what a pleasure that is turning to be, eh Slate?"

"If toleratin' yer drivel is tha alternative, then talkin' with Adar will come as a welcome reprieve."

"And what would you tell us?" Adar had been silent within Yip's mind since the docks, waiting for the appropriate time to speak.

With a short sweep of his arm, Adar answered aloud. "Let us step through the portal and all will be made clear."

Wrindanneth walked through first followed by Slate and then Yip. Finally, Adar entered along with the Four.

Once on the other side, Adar said, "This pocket dimension also has the advantage of being, at least for the present, completely unoccupied save for us."

With a silent gathering of power, Adar invoked a powerful magic with a skill and precision that caused both Aroganji and Wrindanneth to inadvertently turn their heads and glance at each other, their worry unjustified.

"We are now protected from potential eavesdropping for my words are for your ears alone."

"Within the past day, we have had drones begin returning, porting back from their journey on the far side of the portals used by the Cabal to invade our world. The drones have been thoroughly examined for corruption and alteration. Many are offering multiple threads of confirmatory information."

"These drones bring news of the Cabal."

"What news?" Interrupting, Slate could not contain his excitement.

"They appear to have located one of the Cabal's refuges."

"Other drones have made the decision to continue reconnaissance. We will wait for further confirmation before making any final conclusions. However, the data appears sound."

"I have taken the liberty of forwarding a summary of the information received to your Abstract. I will let you be the judge of its merit."

Yip bowed deeply. "We are honored to call you a friend, Adar."

Adar smiled. "As am I."

Adar hastened to caution, adding, "Lest you rush to judgment, please wait for further confirmation both from our own assessment and from that of other drones."

"We will advise when the information has been deemed absolutely credible. After that time, we will be in a position to discuss options and ramifications more fully."

Wrindanneth gave an abbreviated nod. "Understood."

Wanting to know more, Aroganji asked, "What, exactly, does this intelligence depict?"

Adar replied simply, with finality, "More than could be hoped."

With those words, he turned and motioned for them to follow him through the rainbow colored stalks swaying in the warm, gentle breeze.

Yip's mind swept around them, taking in the fertility of the place, the abundant life force manifest in the air and soil, bridged by the vibrant grasses between. Layers upon layers of fertile loam built a foundation on which the grass and all the attendant creatures of the soil and prairie could survive. To his mind, though not visible to the unaided eye, these creatures were out in abundance, enlivening and enriching the air and earth, replenishing its bounty, and building its future upon its past.

He was, and ever would be, a lover of nature—all that moved and was moved, all that changed and was changed, were connected to him on so many levels he ceased counting, not the least of which was the appreciation in his heart.

Walking in silence, he took in the special character of the plains, a perfect recreation of some place in the macroverse that caught the Paratechnologists' fancy. He could spend a lifetime exploring the many universes within Tellanon, mirror-like reflections of the larger ones beyond.

After a short walk up a rounded hillock, they reached a circle of standing stones emerging from the high grass. Ancient pillars, solid and unyielding, stood implacably against the swaying grasses brushing against their cool sides. No hand or art decorated their surface, only time and the elements left their mark upon the cool gray of the raw rock.

Walking toward the stones, Adar turned and said, "Follow me. Tellanon and Eidelion await."

Entering the circle of stones, Adar strode confidently to the center and disappeared, his form shimmering, ripples on the surface of a still pond, before dematerializing.

Following close behind, Wrindanneth went next, his steps sure and firm. Certain in the knowledge that they were safe and would soon return to Tellanon, he walked through the portal at ease.

After Wrindanneth ported, Aroganji approached curiously, always interested in experiencing the ingenious ways in which magical arts found expression. Taking a few moments to read the arcana moving within the stones, Aroganji finally crossed over after Slate grunted impatiently from where he waited at the stones' edge.

Slate, unconcerned with magical artifice and function, walked stoically forward and through. The sooner they were done with their errands, the sooner he could get a decent meal, preferably one with a tankard or two, or maybe a few, of ale. Saving the world could wait for a full stomach.

Finally, his mind moving with the swirling currents of the summoning stones, the abundant *chi* manifest in the rich steppes, and the energies bridging Tellanon and the miniature universe of the pocket dimension, Yip stepped into the standing stones' shadow, returning at last to Tellanon.

They emerged immediately outside the crystalline wall surrounding Tellanon's heart, beneath Illdrassil's expansive shadow in one of the many luxuriant gardens arranged along the walkways outside Illdrassil's home.

Above, gleaming and resplendent, Illdrassil anchored the heavens with her lustrous branches and cradled the island in the sky with her roots. Her energies shielded the people of Tellanon while her abundant life force empowered their dreams and aspirations.

Looking at her with open eyes, feeling her awesome presence within his mind, Yip paused in testimonial, offering a mental bow of respect, tribute, and gratitude as they approached.

"Come on, Yip. Ya can stare at Illdrassil like a love-struck, moon-eyed puppy after we've met with Eidelion. Until then, ya're only holdin' us up." By way of emphasis, Slate's stomach growled significantly.

With a slight bow and a smile, Yip replied, "Point taken."

Patting his belly enthusiastically, Slate added, "Tha Dragon needs ta be fed!"

Adar gestured toward the nearest gate in the outer wall surrounding Illdrassil. "Eidelion waits not far within."

"I will take my leave of you now. After you have had time to review our report, feel free to contact me with any questions you may have. If I have not heard from you first, I hope to be in touch soon."

"May the success you have known flourish into a bounteous future."

Yip bowed respectfully, replying, "May your dreams be the reality you birth."

Within Yip's mind, Adar replied, *"And yours, my friend."*

Turning on his heel, Adar smiled brightly and stepped through the portal once more, leaving them in the serenity of the lush garden, under the scrutiny of the cadre of Home Guard watching and waiting from across the winding lane that separated them.

"Afternoon, gents!" Wrindanneth raised an arm casually in greeting and approached, returning home to visit old friends.

The Home Guard preventing passage through the tunnel behind them remained unmoved, not acknowledging his words of greeting, their eyes scanning the artful surroundings, with the vigilance of those under constant threat of attack.

"Glad to see you as well!" Wrindanneth's smile never left his face as he neared the hulking wardens barring their progress ahead.

The impassive Guards at the gate were an assorted lot. On either side of the passageway were two massive humanoids resembling tremendous Ogres. Unlike Ogres, these Home Guard had bright, perceptive eyes indicative of keen intelligence. Their thickly corded thews bulged outward from beneath their crystalline armor lending the appearance that their protection was undersized when in fact their physiques were fully covered. In their hands, two massive double-bladed war axes barred passage forward.

Behind the Ogre-kin, two lithe Elves stood opposite two stolid Dwarves in the arching tunnel beneath Illdrassil's outer wall. Though less physically imposing than the Ogre-kin, the Elves and Dwarves were formidable nonetheless. The Elven bows slung over the Elves' shoulders were of the highest quality, intended to launch magical bolts in lieu of physical. Their elegant Witchwood swords curved seductively at their hips, dangers only equaled by their beauty. Both Dwarves carried oversized war mauls, each seeming too large to wield. This apparent cumbersomeness was but an illusion for in their capable hands these massive warhammers wrought unbridled devastation.

Behind the far tunnel entrance past the inner wall itself, another team of paired Guards waited. These far guardians were made up of two Gnomes and two NUMEN. Though the NUMEN were indistinguishable from Gnomes at first glance, their energy signatures and fluid movements clearly separated them from common races of Ea'ae. Unlike the other Guard, the NUMEN appeared unarmed. Unlike the NUMEN, the Gnomes appeared anything but unarmed. Bristling with weapons, the Gnomes were encased in the convoluted machineries of destruction. Retractable guns and cannons swiveled at their backs, shoulders, and wrists; information streamed across machinery at their forearms and from displays mounted to their helms; blades swiveled and turned in concert with their movements on their wrists and elbows; articulated biomechanics encased their bodies in elaborate structural lattices augmenting their physical capabilities; while ropes, netting, and myriad other gizmos threatened at the ready.

At his approach, one of the Ogre-kin spoke firmly, his voice deep and rumbling of the earth, its stone and hidden shadows, his tone allowing no room for further foolishness. "State your name and business."

Wrindanneth replied with a smile for they already knew who he was, the information conveyed magically to the Guard by the Construct as soon as they appeared across the street with the scan that determined who they were prior to entry into Illdrassil's shadow. "We are the Four here to see Eidelion. I am Wrindanneth." Indicating his friends over his shoulder, he added dismissively, "The rest are hardly worth mentioning."

After another moment's pause, Wrindanneth added dismissively, "But, if you must know, I am accompanied by Aroganji, Slate, and Yip."

Without further ado, both Ogre-kin lifted their enormous axes and cleared the way through. "The ghost light will guide you to your destination. Do not stray from its path."

Doffing an imaginary hat, Wrindanneth bowed with a flourish and a sardonic smirk. "Good day to you and many more, my friends."

Resolute as the stone that gave them birth, the Ogre-kin remained unmoved.

Following Wrindanneth through the corridor, the companions filed past Home Guard as stoic as the hall's outer wardens. Only Yip lingered, offering a nod and a smile to each cluster of Guards as they passed, showing the kindness and respect that was their due.

"Come on, Yip! Time's a wastin'!" Slate's stomach growled again, the sound accentuated by the acoustics of the clear crystalline walls.

Yip, however, remained in no hurry.

The life forces, the developed expressions of manifest energy in each of the Guards, were so strong and luminous that he wished to study the living beings that generated such splendor. Though indomitable wardens by profession, they were compassionate warrior monks by training. The depth and breadth of their development was on full display to him as he looked.

He appreciated the impressions of their energetics in much the same way as he would experience beauty in a work of art—with feeling and complete immersion. He did not, however, manipulate their *li* in any way for that was not his place or intent.

Finally done with his survey, the fulgent *chi* of each of the Home Guard bathing him in unique brilliance, he finally took his leave, crossing the passage's threshold where he rejoined his friends.

"If 't'were up ta ya, I'd never get my lunch!" Slate shook his head, irritated at the delay, as Yip rejoined his friends while the ghost light appeared to guide them onward.

Yip smiled demurely and replied simply, "Some things are worth waiting for, Slate."

"And ya're not one o' 'em!" Patting his stomach reassuringly, Slate amended. "Been hangin' around Wrindanneth too long. My apologies fer tha insult."

Letting the jibe pass for once, Wrindanneth responded, "Have you nothing in your bag to eat? If not, I can summon something for you if you are so starved as to bite the hand that feeds you."

Slate gave a thoughtful nod. "Lemme see what I can dig up." Clasping the bag at his hip and drawing it open while they followed the wisp light toward their meeting place, he fished around within the bottomless bag, his arm thrust inward up to the shoulder. With a grunt of satisfaction, he retracted his arm, pulling a smoked ham along with it.

"Never know when a few snacks'll come in handy!"

Aroganji laughed. "You know we have many pre-made, ready-to-eat magical meals stored in there, Slate. Won't one of those do?"

Holding both ends of the ham hock with each hand, Slate spoke around a full mouth, his face largely hidden behind the slab of meat in his grasp, his words muffled by his enthusiastic efforts. "Nothin' like a fine cut o' meat ta tide a Dwarf over until his next repast!"

"Or make him look like an uncouth..."

Aroganji placed a calming hand on Wrindanneth's shoulder. "Let him eat in peace. We have had a long journey and he has earned more than a moment's reprieve."

Wrindanneth held his tongue knowing that Slate would be done savaging the ham well before the ghost light finally ushered them into their audience with Eidelion.

Yip would never grow tired of the magnificence that was Illdrassil. This close, her radiance was overwhelming, a presence vast and formless, washing his conceptions of self away in her boundless sentience. The glory she was, the glory she expressed, was so much greater than the glory of her physical presence, ineffable as it was.

She was the very essence of life unlimited.

Flourishing at her root, fortuitous to reside beneath her glimmering reflections and bask directly in her presence, bounteous gardens bloomed and blossomed, representative arrangements of flora from across known space. The gardens of Illdrassil were without peer on Ea'ae with perhaps the exception of those of the Elves. Elven wisdom was clearly visible in the care and presentation of the plantings for Elven magic commingled with Illdrassil's own to maintain and keep the gardens as lush and prosperous as they were.

Oblivious to the beauty, the wisp light led them implacably

forward untouched by the scintillating grandeur of Illdrassil and her grounds.

Wending its way forward, the ghost light led them around Illdrassil's incomprehensible bulk to the far side of her lofty span. There, at the far terminus of one of her vast roots, Eidelion waited peaceable and alone.

Seeing their approach, a broad smile split Eidelion's luminous face and his gallant voice boomed out in welcome. "Four! Light be praised that you have arrived home safely yet again!"

"Your return is as welcome as your deeds."

Slate raised an arm in salutation. "Believe me, we're happier ta be here than ya know!"

They approached with smiles, bright and joyous as the play of light on Illdrassil's boughs.

Before they got close enough to clasp their friend in greeting, Eidelion's probing eye found its mark, noting the transformations that had been and were yet at work within the gathered companions. "I see the Light has graced you with Its touch."

"Such blessings come rarely. Now you truly are children of the heavens."

His smile grew brighter. "With your incipient apotheosis, your duties will expand with your reach!"

"Blame Yip! He's the one who saw fit to bring us back from the brink. He's the one who lit the fires of Life within that continue to burn. We are his experiment." Wrindanneth's gaze held no blame but his words were true nonetheless.

"One that has turned out well for you and for us all." Eidelion's smile did not relent though there were more than just accolades to discuss.

Yip's considerations were elsewhere though he, too, was glad for his companions' continued health and prosperity. "How fare Ruena, Yrien, and EMMA?" Yip's words were replete with the concern overflowing within, his last images and impressions filled with the turmoil of the moment.

Eidelion nodded reassuringly. "You will be able to ask them yourself." Vaguely indicating Illdrassil behind him, he said, "You will have a chance to speak with them once we are done."

Yip bowed. "A reunion would be most welcome."

He listened as Eidelion continued, "Your deeds have assured that those Cabal who yet remain on Ea'ae will be unable to bring down our seals or bring forth their fellows. With these new seals in place, they will also have great difficulty destroying our world as they have done to so many others."

Eidelion was correct, though his explanation did not describe the whole picture. Practitioners of Darkness would face significant adversity in reaching out to allies beyond the extent of Ea'ae's shield. In that regard, agents of Darkness's ability to operate on Ea'ae had been circumscribed.

However, even with the shield provided by the seals complete and in full force, after all of the remaining damaged seals had been restored, this system might not stop the creation of a minute *chi* void, one that could spread across the world decimating all life, siphoning its energy slowly but relentlessly to some nether realm.

A single fracture, however miniscule, could bring down even the strongest dam. This very scenario had happened to the old seals and other worlds in the past.

Despite recent improvements, such a scenario could happen again.

There was, however, some hope. Now that others were able to manifest the Dragon's Gate, the people of Ea'ae at least had a way to counter the flow of life force if such voids were created, nullifying the vacuous siphons if given the opportunity to act. The battle for supremacy would rage on, at least now on a more level playing field.

While part of Yip's mind wandered through cause and effect, another heard Eidelion continue, "The immediate task before us is to purge our world of the Cabal's mounting evil."

"As you now know, we have intelligence on the Cabal's operations far beyond our planet's borders. As we have discussed in the past, made much more possible with your gifts, this will become the next front on our war against our enemies, one we will extend alongside our interstellar allies."

Here Eidelion looked at each of them deeply. "The choice will be yours as to whether or not to move forward alone or to continue to work with us."

"Whichever path you choose, I hope that you will wait to act until we have confirmatory information and a suitable evaluation of the Cabal."

"Though I cannot dictate your actions as you are free to choose as you will, I also hope that you will consider not moving against the Cabal until we are ready to mount an offensive. Otherwise, our opportunity may be jeopardized."

Slate snorted forcefully, checking his laugh but expressing his derisive disagreement nonetheless. "If yer plans move as ya say, tha Cabal may be gone by tha time ya act!"

"How long will it take ta purge Ea'ae o' tha Cabal and then mobilize a fleet o' allies from across tha far reaches o' tha macrocosmos ta move against 'em?"

Slate did not wait for an answer. "Long enough fer tha Cabal ta be gone by tha time ya do!"

Eidelion accepted Slate's reproach with aplomb. "You have been more successful than any would hope or hazard thus far. If you continue as you have, few would complain. The choice of what you do remains yours."

Slate spoke quickly, "There is, it seems, little opportunity ta do otherwise."

Aroganji raised a hand placatingly, slowing Slate's words if not his logic. "Let us review the preliminary information shared by Adar that we may make an intelligent assessment of the way forward. We have worked well together in the past and I see no reason to discount this relationship until we have due cause."

Yip bowed respectfully. "Your words and foresight are commendable, Eidelion. Aroganji speaks truly. Let us explore how our respective visions align in light of the information you have so generously shared."

Eidelion nodded in understanding, willing to wait for their decision and review of the information as currently present. Now, however, it was Eidelion's turn to bow. "By receiving the Stars of Illdrassil, you have already received the highest honor bestowed by Tellanon. But yet, you come back deserving much more! We willingly await your decision."

"This I say to you now in full sincerity for you have earned our trust and your place within our society more than any. You are free to move within Tellanon as you please from this day forward. Should it be required, you will be treated with the respect and privilege due members of the High Council without the attendant responsibility."

"Furthermore, so long as you remain friends to our city, you have full access to our knowledge and secrets, our stores and services. The lore of the Paratechnologists is yours to explore. The knowledge of the Construct is at your complete disposal. You have access to our erudition just as you have our complete confidence. At any time, the Construct, the Paratechnologists, or the Keepers will be made available to aid in your physical and intellectual endeavors. Otherwise, your Abstract will have full access to our information stores upon your request."

"The choice is yours."

"Though we will give you anything you would want to aid in your quests should you ask, we would like to give you each an item of worth of your own choosing to facilitate your continued success."

"When you are ready, I will arrange for you to visit our most secure vaults beneath Illdrassil herself with a Keeper of Secrets. You will each be entitled to select one item of your choosing, guided by the Keeper's understanding of what may be of greatest value to you. Nothing found within those halls will be off-limits to you. You will be free to enquire and explore as desired."

Smiling warmly at Yip, anticipating his objections and refusal, he added, "Should one of you not wish to partake of our offering, then the gift we would give may be bestowed upon or given to another."

Looking warmly at Wrindanneth and Slate as he turned his gaze in anticipation of the conversations ahead, Eidelion said, "Yes, should he bestow it upon you, you may take Yip's opportunity as your own."

Slate laughed fully, his bellows reverberating off Illdrassil's trunk like the peals of distant thunder. "Now that's a gift! I don't even have ta ask!"

Yip smiled at his friends, his good humor evident by his tone. "I will leave it to you to work out who will benefit from Tellanon's gracious gift."

"Generous to a fault, as always!" Wrindanneth bowed deeply with a flourish from the waist to his friend.

"Let tha games begin!" Slate practically clapped his hands with excitement at the thought of wandering beneath Tellanon in her most secure repositories with the opportunity to receive not one but two artifacts.

What more could a Dwarf ask for?

Shaking his head in disapproval of the display when the situation called for respect and foresight, decorum and dignity, Aroganji said, "Perhaps we had better complete our business with Eidelion before making other plans?" He did not wish to waste Eidelion's time any more than he wanted to be disrespectful given the enormity of the gifts that had been offered and the importance of their audience.

Yip slowly declined his head, saying, "You are far too generous for we are but humble servants. The trust you have shown in us is as great an honor as any that could be offered. We thank you and hope that we will continue to warrant such esteem."

Eidelion declined his head in reply. "What is done is done and for that you have earned more than we have given or can give." Here he smiled. "If you are able to do even more, then, for that too, we shall be grateful."

Yip stopped for a moment in consideration, his mind alight in a moment's pause. His gaze first taking him up to the light shimmering within Illdrassil's lambent boughs and then down tracing the marvels of her trunk to the glorious gardens at her root, he said, "There is one small request I have." He smiled, adding, "one that I hope does not intrude upon Slate and Wrindanneth's recent good fortune."

Eidelion's brow lifted questioningly. "You have but to ask, Yip."

"Tellanon is a nexus for all free peoples of Ea'ae, for the exploration and expression of their ideals and aspirations. I would see all her beings flourish in Illdrassil's shadow, realizing a common future in tandem."

Eidelion smiled into Yip's pause, asking, "What is it you wish, Yip?"

"Perhaps the Aeryn D'al would be willing to share in Illdrassil's shade? Perhaps their Light could help uplift Tellanon's own."

Eidelion bowed, the grandeur of Yip's idea filling his mind with wonderment. "Such a gift would be a testament to the giver."

Yip bowed in turn and said no more.

"I will discuss the matter with Alderan...and perhaps Master Wei.

They may provide guidance in this where I have none. We will do our utmost to bring the majesty of the Aeryn D'al to Tellanon."

Yip declined his head and replied simply, "I thank you."

Before Eidelion could offer another heartfelt thanks in turn, Slate interceded, clapping his hands eagerly. "All right! All right! Enough with tha back pattin', chatter, and dreamin'! Lunch is long overdue!"

"Let's check on EMMA, Ruena, and Yrien and be on our way!"

"I'm guessin' there's gonna be a heapin' pile o' information ta review before we meet again and we'd better get at it!"

Eidelion bowed and gestured toward Illdrassil with one shimmering, gauntleted hand. "This way."

Turning lithely, his armor as lustrous as the boughs of Illdrassil herself, Eidelion led them toward the main trunk of the celestial tree, past lush hanging gardens, and between her massive supporting roots. Walking toward the bole of her trunk, Eidelion never broke stride as he passed through her liquid surface, falling forward through rippleless water.

To Yip's eyes, trailing behind Eidelion, they followed a star descended to Earth, a glorious being of Light and energy, his essence shimmering brighter than the sun above. Though Eidelion disappeared within Illdrassil, this glowing vitality remained tangible to him. To the eyes of his friends, however, Eidelion vanished completely.

However luminous, Eidelion's Light was but one small star amidst an ocean of energy that enveloped and pervaded Illdrassil from root to crown, firmament to foundation.

Never one to hesitate, Wrindanneth followed immediately behind Eidelion, disappearing as seamlessly as their guide. One after the other, Yip's friends passed through into Illdrassil's bole until he, too, had to reluctantly leave the splendor of her exterior for the unfolding, mellifluous refracted radiance of her immense interior.

Stepping through Illdrassil's wall, a wash of vibrancy thrilled though him from head to toe, a dive through a chill, invigorating waterfall. Coursing over him, he felt Illdrassil's power more intimately, a brief connection that threw him to the bounds of Tellanon, filled him with buoyancy, passing as quickly as his pace allowed.

"This way." Eidelion waited patiently as they turned around on their heels, looking upward in amazement at the illimitable hollow column of Illdrassil's trunk, the upper reaches of the space lost in a dazzling haze of effulgent light. Columns of diffracted luminescence, iridescence in all hues, danced across the walls and floor, plantings and features, angling through the air and alighting on everything within.

Enthralled, his breath taken away, Aroganji finally managed, "The heights of imagination cannot encompass such beauty."

Yip smiled, sharing his friend's amazement. "Illdrassil inspires and challenges the limits of the possible."

"Tha Guard are truly blessed ta call such a place home!" Though he would not openly admit it, Illdrassil surpassed even the finest Dwarven delvings of old.

Eidelion declined his head with a smile. Accustomed to the compliments and the place, Eidelion, too, allowed himself a moment of appreciation.

Their reflection finished, the Four walked with Eidelion through the streaming bands of illumination crossing Illdrassil's vast, hollow core. Guards, diplomats, Paratechnologists, citizens, and members of Tellanon's various administrative bodies followed similar paths.

The sense of the overwhelming magnitude of the space expanded with each step. The sensation was magnified by the shimmering crystalline walls refracting the indirect light and colors of the sky—a scintillating, ethereal border defining the expanse and the heavens.

Turning around in circles slowly as they proceeded across the central chamber, Slate asked simply, innocently, "When can we move in?"

Eidelion laughed from the front of the column. "For you? Whenever you like!"

Wrindanneth elbowed Slate in the ribs, the reflexive gesture only causing him ill for he connected directly with Slate's armor. In a harsh whisper, he hissed, "Be careful what you ask for, Slate! If you want to be caged, then I can think of no finer place!"

Slate growled back, "Learn ta take a joke, Wrin! Freedom is choice and I'll do with it as I please! Jests included!"

Wrindanneth replied dismissively, "Then give it away if you will!"

Aroganji placed a hand on each of their shoulders, also keeping his voice a whisper, mollifying both. "We are among friends here."

Looking at Wrindanneth, he said, "No choices will be taken for others will not be denied after the first. Freedom will remain Slate's prerogative."

Turning to Slate, he said, "Though Wrindanneth would never say it out loud, much less to you, he enjoys your companionship and wishes to keep the bonds of your fellowship strong. You have expressed some interest in joining the Guard in the past. No matter how offhand your comment, perhaps there is more to your words than you mean to be heard. Consider the ears your words fall upon when you speak, even in jest."

After a brief glance, neither said a word, instead choosing to study the spectacle of light, sound, and sensation that was Illdrassil's heart.

Smiling, Yip placed an approving hand on Aroganji's shoulder before he, too, returned to silent contemplation.

On the far side of the peerless bole's interior, Eidelion led them upward along a gleaming path that arched gracefully around Illdrassil's inner wall, so fine and cleverly fashioned as to be indistinguishable from the surface until they were almost upon the walkway. The path itself wound skyward, intersecting other similar ways, landings, and passages—fractured spider web strands of light rays caught upon Illdrassil's stalwart frame.

For those who did not wish to take the shimmering paths, transparent disks of force sped upward along the high walls providing rapid transport from journey's start to end. Anticipating their wonder at the sights of Illdrassil's core, Eidelion, however, chose the longer way that his guests could take in all that was on display around them.

He chose wisely.

If possible, the view as they ascended grew even more spectacular. For though they left Illdrassil's hidden roots to climb toward her lofty branches, the encompassing space remained yet sweeping, the ceiling unreachable. Now, given a bit of height, they were afforded perspective, one that deepened their appreciation of the myriad marvels on display from foundation to firmament.

"I've never welcomed climbin' a hill as I do these steps!" His excitement and enthusiasm unbowed, Slate could not contain himself as he gazed hither and yon. Each glance furnished new ideas and insights, ones he would someday take home to his clan and their delving to test his skill and worth in implementing.

For Wrindanneth, though the view was grand, the Craft that had fashioned it was grander—near perfection incarnate. There was a level of skill and sophistication to the design and execution of Illdrassil that he would never have thought possible.

And her physical manifestation was the least of her wonders.

That, according to Yip, she was alive in a way beyond the ken of Men, that she powered an entire spacefaring, multidimensional nexus point, was repository for Light, the centerpiece for a civilization aimed toward the highest ideals of sentient expression, were her true wonders and worth, as intangible as her essence.

Aroganji swam amidst a sea of transformation. If Tellanon was a network of travel, communication, trade, and research, then Illdrassil was its living heart, her limitless energies its locus and union, where all endeavors were bound together and made possible. Illdrassil was an actualizer of the possible, a transformer of the impossible into the real.

Yip walked with Illdrassil in his mind and heart. He was as much a part of the central chamber as he was a part of her bole and branch, her shifting shadows, and farthest reaches throughout Tellanon. This openness, this interconnection, was her gift to him for he alone turned down the many offerings the city and her people sought to bestow upon him.

He needed nothing else.

"Here we are."

Eidelion led them up and around several circuits of Illdrassil's massive trunk, passing numerous landings and ways that extended outward and away from her heart.

Before them now was a small landing.

Nothing more.

Glancing left and right, not seeing how where they now stood varied from almost everywhere else they had passed on the way up, Slate finally pronounced, "Aye. Here we are."

After a moment's pause, he added, "Where are we?"

Looking forward, through the curtains of power flowing through Illdrassil's sapwood, Yip saw their friends within the Guard waiting on the far side of the wall. Masked by the flowing currents of force saturating the air, their lustrous *li* were visible nonetheless, wonderfully melodious and rich alighting upon his skin, sweet notes vibrating in a much larger symphony.

Wrindanneth gestured forward. "Perhaps you would like to be the first to walk through the wall, Slate, and greet our companions?"

Slate snorted and shook his head. The last thing he wanted to do was think he was passing through a wall only to realize too late as he smashed face-first that he had not triggered proper entry.

"Very well." Unconcerned with a similar outcome, Wrindanneth strode forward. Wavering for but a moment, he passed through the glimmering wall and disappeared.

Shrugging, Slate said, "Guess I'm next." With that he, too, hastened forward brushing his leading hand across the wall's surface casually, testing the waters before diving through.

Not hesitating, Aroganji came next, walking onward confidently, the wall nonexistent.

With a brief nod, Eidelion motioned Yip forward, saying, "After you."

Retracing his friends' paths, Yip wavered and was gone.

REUNITED

Gravel crunches underfoot,
flowers rustle in the field.
The trail continues on.

Smiles flew through the air all around. They greeted each other like old friends, reunited after the passage of far too much time, separated by a gulf of memory they were trying to bridge in the first earnest moments of reunion.

Though they had had little opportunity to work with and interact directly with Yrien, Ruena, and EMMA, Aroganji, Wrindanneth, Slate, and Yip felt a close kinship and brotherhood with them for they had been through similar travails in their efforts against the Cabal. That so many of their allies had been lost in the attempt only deepened the sentiment.

Bonded by a common cause and shared experience, the crystalline chamber reverberated with the joy and sadness of their meeting.

Joining the Guard, his towering form overshadowed by his deific presence, Éremon stood beaming behind the others, taking the opportunity to welcome them warmly. "On behalf of the free people of Tellanon, the governing Protectorate, her emissaries, allies, and agents, we offer our heartfelt congratulations and boundless thanks. We are inspired by your efforts and honored by your sacrifices. You have exceeded our hopes and helped realize our dreams."

"If, in the troubling days ahead, our combined actions meet with success but a pale shadow of your own, Ea'ae's future will be assured."

"You have captured our hearts and imagination. Many will walk in your footsteps attempting to realize similar feats. For this and so much more, Ea'ae will be a much brighter place."

Éremon bowed deeply from the waist, thick robes flowing like smoke with the lithe gesture. "We thank you."

Gesturing openly, he said, "Please enjoy our company and hospitality. There are others who would speak and I will detain them no longer."

With that, Éremon stepped back, the flood gates opened once more, and everyone began talking at once.

While his friends rushed to and fro, their motion temporarily halted by Éremon's speech, Yip held back choosing instead to watch his companions' unfolding gaiety with an overflowing warmth all his own.

"Yip." EMMA's words met the serenity of his mind, echoing in the emptiness. "What will you do?"

While their companions' lively conversations flowed around them, Yip and EMMA remained detached, not aloof for they were engaged with their fellows, but their feelings were not those of their friends. Yip was glad for his friends' joy but such violent emotion did not stir within his own heart.

"We will review the information presented by the Paratechnologists and decide how to move from there. Whether we wait or act will depend upon the quality of the information and the likelihood of success."

"And if moving on your own proves too difficult or more reliable information to make an assessment takes too long?"

"Then we will find another way."

He sensed EMMA's smile. "I would expect nothing less."

"The ways of the mind are as myriad as the stars. Choosing the right path among many can be more difficult than reaching either."

He sensed the warmth of EMMA's thoughts. "You have the right vessel and compass to guide your way forward."

His warmth mirrored her own. "Let us hope."

"Be well, Yip Chi Chuan."

Feeling the connection between them dissolve, he bowed respectfully to EMMA where she stood across the room, conversing animatedly with his friends all the while. Smiling, he walked over to join them.

Perhaps a bit of celebration was in order.

Slate smacked his lips.

Sensing his dire straits, Ruena summoned a repast worthy of a king for Slate to eat while they spoke. There was enough food displayed before him to feed a small squadron, enough for him to last the next few hours until dinner. Only now, after many long minutes polishing one course off after another, had he finally managed to finish.

Covering his mouth, he politely resisted the urge to offer a respectful, full-throated belch. Such a gesture would be deeply appreciated by some but possibly misunderstood by many in the present company. Instead, keeping good form, he cleverly wiped his beard with one gauntleted fist, a move full of tact and grace, and then lustily ran his tongue around his lips to ensure that no crumbs or other tasty morsels had escaped his attention.

All were performed with the height of Dwarven decorum.

Satisfied that all was in order, he turned his attention to Ruena. "Thank ya, milady, fer tha bounteous aliments!"

Managing to maintain her regal countenance even through a smile, Ruena offered, "Your need was great, my effort small."

Eyes unfocused, lost in reverie, Slate pined, "If I only I had such a talent!"

Wrindanneth patted him consolingly on the shoulder. "Do not fear, Slate. Your talent is even greater. You were able to eat it all!"

Slate nodded. "Some abilities know no limits."

Wrindanneth agreed, his face without visible emotion. "If you could only eat your way through enemy forces, the universe would be a much safer place."

His face serious, Slate replied, "Indeed."

Ruena laughed, her voice crackling like the lightning that arched fitfully between her hairs.

Patting his stomach, Slate added, "Now I've tha strength ta continue! Where were we?"

"We were about to put the world at your fingertips."

Slate rocked back on his heels and rolled his shoulders as he exhaled slowly and rested his hands on his waist. Full of cool nonchalance, he said, "When is it not?"

Wrindanneth laughed and responded with a question of his own. "All the time?"

"Bah!"

While Slate and Wrindanneth bickered, Ruena briefly swirled her index finger, summoning an image forth from the ether. Within this image, the Home Guard's plans for the restoration of the remaining seals played out amidst large scale troop movements and mobilizations of multitudes of forces from across Ea'ae, all moving against the Cabal.

Viewed from this scale, in abstract high above Ea'ae, a gathering tides of lights flowed across the planet's rotating surface washing away the massed forces of the enemy. Though but a simulation, the display was as uplifting as it was beautiful.

Studying the unfolding representation, Slate asked, "How long before these plans take effect?"

Ruena smiled wryly. "They already have."

Slate nodded appreciatively. He was glad that the people of Ea'ae were moving so swiftly to oust their would-be usurpers. Much appeared to have transpired in the short time since their departure.

She continued, "In addition to those who are already moving against the enemy, we have received further commitments from the nations of Men, Elves, Dwarves, and Gnomes scattered far and wide across Ea'ae. Other races, too, move to our banners. The Cabal will not stand for long once we act in concert."

"Are our forces meeting with success?" Aroganji came over to examine the projection alongside his friends.

"Now that your work is done and the matrix of seals is secure, the Cabal are finding their own efforts thwarted at every turn."

"We are close to securing and upgrading another of the old seals. Soon the rest will follow. With each seal replaced, the massed Cabal seeking to undermine their function fall as well."

Wrindanneth asked, "Are any fleeing before you?" He imagined that many of the Cabal would try to wreak havoc separately or teleport back to their home base individually now that direct, large-scale passage was denied them by Ea'ae's protections. Others would seek to flee en masse to the stars where they may be able to port home if they managed to cross Ea'ae's shields.

"Few try to fight directly against our forces. Most seek to harry us, providing cover for those that would flee and regroup with their allies. As we push them aside and more Cabal come together, larger battles may soon ensue."

"However, many appear to be attempting to leave Ea'ae altogether."

Wrindanneth nodded solemnly. "There are easier fruit to pluck and plunder elsewhere."

Aroganji offered, "Those that remain to fight may be providing cover not only for those who are more important and wish to leave but for those who wish to continue wreaking mischief."

In order to ease his own mind, thinking of the untold havoc members of the Cabal may be able to reap if they had the ability, harried or not, Yip asked, "Are any of the Aerya'ana accompanying these ships?"

Here Ruena smiled again, the wicked glimmer in her eyes rippling with the power of her magic and the implications of the vicious lines of her reasoning. "Indeed. The Aerya'ana remain vigilant should the Cabal attempt some ploy to drain the life from our world."

Her own assessment of the knowledge Yip shared complete, she added, "You have taught them well."

Yip bowed. "I but ignited a light. It is for the rest to see."

Ruena declined her head, a gesture of respect not acquiescence. "So you say."

Ruena's depiction of the Home Guard's and their allies' plans was compelling. Yip hoped that it continued to unfold as planned.

He believed it would.

Éremon and Eidelion joined them as everyone clustered around Ruena's representation of action along all fronts. His voice resonating with warmth, Éremon said, "We have not remained still while you were away. The Council of Light has convened, the Protectorate has marshaled the forces of Tellanon, and our allies have responded to our call."

Bowing respectfully, he added sincerely, "We wanted you to see the scope and complexity of the actions your efforts helped initiate and make possible. With all you have done, despite all the tragedy, risk, and disruption, Ea'ae's future remains bright and the outcome of our actions positive."

"You are heroes of the highest order and will be recognized as such so long as Tellanon stands."

Eidelion spoke then. "We have shown you a glimpse of our actions as they stand. Adar has given you detailed information on what may be."

"Before you leave us to ponder your own course, we would provide a brief summary of the aforementioned intelligence along with how we hope to address it."

Wrindanneth glanced at his friends only peripherally before replying bluntly, "Let's see it."

This time Ruena did not raise a finger or cast an incantation. Instead, the limpid walls themselves dimmed, leaving the room in pregnant half-light, the air tinged with anticipation. Filled with a dimensionless lambency, the darkness shrouding the walls did not fade, rather it expanded inward toward a depthless horizon, one of empty, lightless space.

For some time this darkness remained unabated. Without frame of reference, no motion could be discerned within the void. After the passage of several minutes, moments creeping as gradually as the passing seconds, the image began to change. Unnoticed at first, unresolvable later, an even greater darkness lurked within the depths, one that blocked what little light passed through the vast reaches of space, swallowing it completely and almost without trace. This darkness came unbidden, a surprise unrealized until its presence was undeniable.

Within the far reaches of space, long abandoned by its parent star, a lone planet floated derelict in the vast blackness, a shadow within a sea of gloom.

Who would choose to live in such a place? Barren, inhospitable, and cold, a place without life or joy.

Streams of numbers, symbols, and graphical representations began cascading across the enlarging image—catalogs of analyses on the planet and its environs as it slowly crept nearer, looming larger and larger on the view screens.

While data continued to flow, a small red signal flashed emphatically on the bottom of the screen.

"What does that mean?" Wrindanneth arched an eye at the sign. Not able to take in everything the numbers displayed, he nonetheless understood something was amiss.

Eidelion spoke for the Guard calmly answering Wrindanneth's question. "There is little to no magical energy present within or around the planet. Without a ready source of magical forces, solar lumination, or other ambient energies, the drone's power supply will be limited to its backup reserves. The warning light is an indication of predicted working time before power loss."

All the while, the ebony orb loomed larger, growing bleaker and more alien with each passing minute.

With each moment, Yip's own certainty grew. The details displayed before him provided an unrelenting stream of undeniable confirmation.

The world displayed before them was the one they had just escaped.

He sensed similar feelings of dawning realization commingled with surprise from his friends as they, too, came to the same conclusion.

They had been summoned to the Cabal's homeworld and not even known it!

If he were ever to go back, if he ever returned to strike against the Cabal, all of the information presented would be of vital importance.

He studied and memorized every detail.

What the planet was made of, how it had been formed, what its attendant properties and characteristics were, Yip could not say. He would learn more when he had the opportunity to delve into the actual review and interpretation of the data and findings provided by Adar. For now, he studied the information presented as it was.

His purview was, however, limited by the instrumentation through which he viewed the planet itself. In this regard, he was like everyone else. He could not see the moving energy currents of the ineffable *yuan-chi*, seek out signs of life by the accumulation of *chi*, or utilize any of a number of other subtleties and skills that he would normally be able to employ.

Instead, he studied the planet's geology, its shapes and patterns, the long, invisible history written upon its wrecked surface. The planet's past must have been turbulent for it was jagged and cracked, pitted and shattered. Mountains rose outward into the dizzying reaches of space unshielded by atmosphere. Valleys and fissures tumbled over one another radiating erratically across the planet's surface—broken remnants discarded by a colossal cosmic hammer that repeatedly devastated the planet's face.

The celestial body appeared to be made of dark, fractured obsidian lacking the light necessary to illumine its myriad facets. The planetary orb's complex geometry lent a recondite beauty to its form, one appreciated more fully and completely upon further study.

Though seeming barren and lifeless, the world was anything but. The drone's slow approach revealed one other much more important feature—the space around the planet was alive with ships. Seen from the far reaches of space, these vessels were all but invisible. Upon approach, through closer magnification and instrumental assessment, ships moved incessantly—a virulent cloud of debris caught within the world's gravity. Viewed even closer still, these ships could be seen flying down to the planet's surface, spiraling toward the great chasms marring its topography, to bases hidden within the recesses below.

That the Cabal had been able to marshal so many ships to move against Ea'ae now came as no surprise for the remnants of their fleet, if this planet truly represented the majority of their forces, which Yip did not believe, were tremendous. The armada that could be amassed from the ships now seen by the drone's inspection would dwarf that which had moved against Ea'ae.

All the while, the drone's assessment of the planet and its ships continued, cataloging their breadth and extent, their capabilities and strength. Other drones were performing similar actions on this and other locations—miniscule fragments of space dust far too small to be detected and acted upon as a threat.

This cloud of cosmic dust would be the Cabal's undoing.

Eidelion spoke once more over the images on the walls. "The planet you now see displayed is not unknown to us, though its reality is but a faint memory, an ancient myth handed down from ages long past. Or so we believe."

He paused for long seconds then before continuing with a sigh, his breath heavy. "This place, this dead world, is, was, the last bastion of the great Darkness Ur'Daus before It was banished from our realm in days of yore."

"We have long since forgotten it..."

"But I have not." Éremon's clarion voice continued where Eidelion's left off. "Though but a memory of a memory, a fading shadow of reality long past, some tales yet survived among my kind, enough to know of this place and the horrors that once held sway upon its reviled shores."

"Its star and neighboring planets consumed by the Creeping Shadow, this dead world is where Ur'Daus's advance through the heavens was finally stopped, Its evil banished to the Lightless interstices between dimensions."

Sweeping his arm in a great arch, indicating the immense reaches displayed along all the adjoining walls, his voice filled with emotion, Éremon continued, "As far as the eye can see, empty space. Space empty, wiped clean, by the Great Devourer's advance. Whole galaxy spanning civilizations, innumerable stars and planets consumed, erased as though they never existed."

Ringing like a bell, he intoned, "Such is the place the Cabal now calls home."

"Such is the one the Cabal call their master."

"Such is the evil the Cabal feed when they destroy worlds, weakening the shackles that hold It bound."

"Such is the plague the Cabal now seeks to revive and unleash."

Slate hissed, "They're crazier'n a pack o' blood frenzied Orcs!"

Wrindanneth's reaction was not far from Slate's. "They will be consumed along with everything else."

Yip did not share his friends' incredulity. His reply was simple.

"For some, union with their truth is the ultimate expression and aim of existence."

Aroganji nodded curtly, adding, "However misguided."

Wrindanneth shook his head, saying, "If they succeed, they'll get their wish and more, meeting their end."

Slate ground his teeth. "We cannot let 'em succeed but we can help 'em meet their end!"

Eidelion stepped forward to speak. All the while, the roving images of the dead planet, now brought to life by orbiting ships and associated traffic, continued on the walls. "Now that we know where the Cabal's base of operations is located, regardless of whether it is their primary bastion or not, we can move against them in force as they did to us. If the dead world is not the Cabal's primary base of operations, we should be able to extract enough residual intelligence from the site, its ships, and occupants to move against other targets as well, particularly given the information revealed within the alien command sphere you captured and additional drone reconnaissance."

"But ya have ta wait until Ea'ae's clear and fully secured before ya move."

Eidelion shook his head. "Only partially. Believe me, many of our allies will move as soon as we give word regardless of whether or not they can marshal the forces necessary to destroy a stronghold of such strength and whether or not we move with them."

He chuckled ruefully. "Raour'Saqan would move today if we gave him the word. However, we will let him alert other Dracodaeran Shau-r'Daus to aid in the cause just as we will hold until other allies can gather the necessary forces to secure victory."

Wrindanneth arched one red eyebrow. "So you would have us wait as well?"

Eidelion gave a short nod. "Unless another opportunity presents itself or we see a better way forward."

Slate chuckled. "Fine with me. I'm not eager ta go back."

Eidelion's eyebrows rose, rare uncontrolled emotion evident on his face. "Eager to go back?"

Slate shrugged. "We just came from that lightless ball o' black dust. 'Twas our last stop 'fore returnin' home."

"You've been to the Cabal's bastion?" Even Eidelion did not contain his surprise at the news.

"Wiped tha face o' tha place clean with a fallen priest and a Spectral Dragon after bein' summoned outta Garen Muer. Ya'd think they'd've learned better after conjurin' us inta Garen Muer in tha first place!"

"Unbelievable!" Eidelion beamed, his radiance nearly blinding.

Yip spoke simply. "I believe we met the face of our pursuer at long last."

"Too bad fer him!" Slate grinned wickedly.

"Then your intelligence may prove vital to our own."

Wrindanneth shook his head. "I think your drones have captured in far more detail what we would only say in a few words. It is a dead world and deadly. There is little magical energy to call upon which makes it exceedingly dangerous for our kind."

Yip added, "There are myriad *chi* voids scattered across the world that continually drain *yuan-chi* even as celestial *chi* arises to replenish that which has been desecrated."

Wrindanneth finished, "Aside from the priest and Dragon, we saw little of the planet, its inhabitants, or defenses."

Slate laughed. "We were too busy fightin' fer our lives!"

"Would you mind showing us what you experienced?" Eidelion's interest was not solely due to curiosity though that was a part. Any angle, any vantage, that may serve to augment their intelligence may prove vital in the time ahead.

"Not at all." Wrindanneth gathered a bit of power to fuel his visualization as a panoramic view of their experience on the Cabal's dead world unfolded, as seen from on high far above the field of conflict. With this view, the might of the surging cloud of Darkness and their terrible frailty before its awesome power were all too apparent.

As the scene of the battle played out, the surrounding Guards' faces grew in intensity, internalizing every detail.

Finally complete, the tension in the air palpable, Eidelion offered, "You are wonders and we are glad to call you friends. Thank you for your service. There is naught else to be said."

Pursing his lips, Éremon praised, "You have stood proudly in triumph where others would have fallen. That you have shared the knowledge to make other such attainments possible adds hope to the viability of our future."

His brow knitted in thought, he added, "Of the priest I can say little for he is too far gone for me to read. But the Spectral Dragon I know, his power and taint linger even after death. In your victory, you have slain Sarugauth, Bane of the Yerens, ridding Ea'ae of a scourge long overdue."

"Many are those in the Dragonflight who will rejoice at this news when I tell the tale."

Bowing and saluting in a rough semblance of unison, the Fists acknowledged the high compliment in silence for little else remained to be said.

Returning to the matter at hand, for even they did not know yet fully what had happened, Yip looked at the broken black planet, now much larger, teeming with untold numbers of ships. "Unfortunately these actions treat but the symptoms and not the disease."

Eidelion remained silent, letting the Four speak.

Slate shrugged. "Tha Aerya'ana will be able ta counter tha illness."

Yip shook his head. "Only its expression."

"'Tis better'n what we had before! Now we have an option ta nullify their evil."

Aroganji followed Yip's reasoning. "Though we may have a cure, we have not eradicated the disease."

"Nor will we." Wrindanneth appreciated all too well the perils of lust and striving for power, the manifold expressions of self-interest. So long as beings lived and sought, evil would find opportunity to flourish whether it was thought of as evil or not.

"This disease may have a cure."

All eyes turned to Yip.

Into the ensuing silence, he said, "Just as we may be able to counter the expression of Ur'Daus's evil, so, too, may we be able to eradicate it."

Slate huffed, "And how exactly do ya propose ta do that when it was never possible before? Seems ta me, whoever managed ta put that thing away was lucky enough in tha first place!"

Yip shrugged, answering simply. "We but have to find a way."

"Lot o' good that does us!"

Yip replied directly to Slate's challenge. "The bridge between the impossible and possible is the will, fueled by the imagination."

Slate snickered. "Get buildin'!"

Yip had no more to say. Eidelion, however, did. "You have, on numerous occasions, already achieved the impossible, amazing us at every turn. If you can add anything of value in this regard"—here he indicated the vast swath of empty, lifeless space cleansed of planets, solar systems, and stars—"the macroverse and all its many denizens will be better for it."

The evidence of past horrors shown only by their absence, Aroganji replied thoughtfully, "We shall see."

DECISIONS

Ruddy setting sun,
umber full moon—
light's reflection dims.

They decided to walk home.

They did not want to fly.

They did not want to run.

They did not want to teleport despite being among a very select few who were allowed to engage in the privilege of such behavior within the confines of Tellanon.

They were in no hurry to get anywhere in particular.

What they really wanted to do was regroup, to decide what to do next and how best to achieve their aims. What they needed, however, was quiet, time to recover, and the space to do so.

For Yip, quietude was second nature, an integral part of his character but for Slate, silence was as foreign as introspection, something uncomfortable and burdensome. He was as quiescent as Wrindanneth was laconic which is to say not at all. If he were occupied, putting his attention to use, then that was an entirely different matter for then he had a purpose, a focus fueling his willful quietness.

Just walking aimlessly, without direction, was another matter entirely. He understood the need for silence for there was little to be said in the face of such a monumental task. Until there was something worthwhile to be stated, each deserved the solitude of his own mind, space to decide how best to spend his future.

Unfortunately, and this was his present struggle, he could not think of what to say that would break the tableau—a solution to their quandary or a jest to lessen the sense of gravitas.

Wrindanneth struggled with what could be done.

His future loomed so close and bright. The steady transformation Yip had started within when he had saved them on the way to Morowen continued working wonders. Soon he would be free to explore his desires and destiny unshackled.

But yet his obligations to his friends weighed him down just as his suppressed sense of responsible action urged him to push past a long history of self-interest and endeavor toward the betterment of others outside himself. Such was a path of feebleness and disappointment but his nascent sense of duty to those other than himself would not be silent.

Apparently, the weakness of fools was overtaking him as well.

Aroganji knew what was right and what had to be done. The signs were clear, the movements of change coursed in the proper direction. There was a confluence of their purpose with the greater events of the time. Such had not been the case when they had first undertaken this fellowship of purpose together.

Despite the portents, he did not know how such a daunting task as directly challenging the Cabal was best undertaken. Moreover, he did not know how such a mission could hope to lead to the Cabal's overthrow or how they could hope to survive such an encounter.

Their quests thus far had met with great success but they had yet to directly face the Cabal in force much less in their own center of strength. That the party had survived Morowen and Garen Muer had been as much due to luck and timing as their own skill or strength.

Though they had survived a trap on the Cabal's homeworld, they had also outnumbered their ultimate pursuer and managed to gain an element of surprise and preparation when they should have had none. To face the Cabal directly on their own soil, prepared and in full strength, would be another matter entirely.

He hoped they were up to the task. More so, he hoped they could find a viable way forward without having to resort to direct confrontation.

Yip walked quietly, his mind still. The day was beautiful, the air sweet and full of the aroma of blooming plants, of lives unfolding and reaching fulfillment. As much had been accomplished in their time together, more yet remained to be completed. Though many of his goals had now been achieved, once so inconceivable, the fruition of humanity's purpose and the realization of its potential had just begun.

His work now was to make certain the ascension of the peoples of Ea'ae and beyond remained possible. He would strive as tirelessly for that possibility in the future as he had in the past.

Just as sincere introspection leads to transformation, so, too, does working with Light. So long as the Cabal and their ilk remained in the multiverse, the opportunity for humanity's development remained unbounded—change encouraged by impetus.

He would be an agent of this change that the future would know no bounds.

No longer at a loss for words, Slate finally found his voice. "As long as we're out, we might as well get somethin' ta eat!"

Aroganji laughed, his smile full and genuine. "Truer words have never been spoken, Slate! What is the weight of the universe against the need to dine?"

Slate answered casually, "A trifle, if that."

"Trifle or truffles, perhaps dipped and fried in ale, who can say which is the greater test of a man's resolve?"

"If it's resolve we're testin', I'd rather pit myself against a shank o' slow simmered lamb accompanied by several tankards o' tha thane's finest ale!"

Aroganji's smile had not dimmed, nor had his humor. "Then perhaps we should pit our resolves against one another!"

"If ya're aimin' ta lose, then that's a challenge I'll accept!"

"Plate versus plate!" Aroganji was going to lose any challenge against Slate involving food, but what he lost would be made up for in fun.

"No incantations ta aid in yer ability ta eat!"

"I wouldn't think of it!"

Though money was no longer a concern, thinking of the cost of truffles, magically raised or not, brought forth Slate's ingrained parsimony. Despite their newfound fortunes, Slate's frugal ways had not changed. Dropping his voice to a whisper, he grunted, "Loser buys!"

Not sharing his friends' excitement for his own thoughts weighed heavily on him yet, Wrindanneth offered, "Perhaps you could challenge Yip to a sip off. One cup of tea per tankard of ale."

Slate looked briefly and dismissively at Yip whose own attention seemed to remain elsewhere. "Bah! As slow as he sips at tea, we'll be there fer days!"

Aroganji, however, was not deterred. "True." He raised a finger for emphasis. "But you'll be in a position to partake of the full range of spirits sheltered within the establishment's vaults while he does."

"Hmm... This is soundin' better'n better!"

Aroganji leaned over and whispered conspiratorially to Slate, "Now we just have to get Yip to rise to the challenge."

Though his attention appeared to be elsewhere, Yip had not missed a word of his friends' conversation. "If it is tea you would have me drink, then drink I shall."

Stacks of plates, cloths, tankards, scattered crumbs, and gnawed bones —the castoffs of an epic battle lay strewn about the table. That Slate had dominated the eating contest was without question though Aroganji put up a noble fight. Upon conclusion of the challenge, the rigors of war lay heavily upon both Slate and Aroganji's shoulders. For Slate, indigestion and heart burn were his triumphant rewards while Aroganji was graced by irritable bowels.

The battle's aftermath, never thought to be in doubt, turned out to be the evening's true item of interest and an unexpected surprise.

Yip, sedately drinking a steaming cup of herbal tea, had emerged the victor in a contest of wills that lasted long into the night. Unlike the gustatorial conquest that preceded it, the drinking competition lacked anything approaching drama. In fact, Yip only managed one cup.

After hours of eating and drinking and the contentment of a full stomach, Slate fell asleep, forfeiting the match prior to its start, saving himself the interminable boredom of watching Yip drink his single cup of tea.

Wrindanneth, wiser than his Dwarven friend allowed, took the opportunity to dismiss himself prior to the trial's commencement, choosing to go home to get some rest rather than fight a losing battle against his sagging eyelids.

Aroganji, his patience legendary, resisted the urge to do likewise in case Slate should need assistance in getting home. Not bound by stupor, he, too, enjoyed a lovely cup of tea along with the company that came with it.

Slate, snoring facedown on the table, missed the contest's culmination, lost to the world of dreams.

Only after the lone empty cup was finally set down, the table ready to be cleared, and the battle concluded, did Yip reach out and gently pat Slate on the shoulder. "Wake up, Slate. The time to go home has come."

Shaking his head groggily, Slate looked up bleary-eyed, realization slowly building in his eyes. Flicking his gaze between Aroganji and Yip, he asked, "I'm never gonna live this down am I?"

Yip laughed, smiling. "That depends."

"How d'ya mean?"

His laughter abating, Yip replied, "Wrindanneth was not here."

"Ya'd do..." Slate was not asking Yip to lie for him but what he seemed to be offering was even more valuable.

Yip responded before Slate could finish, "You are free to answer as you will."

Aroganji added, "And keep your record intact."

Slate wiped his brow unsteadily, beads of sweat unconsciously coming to the fore. Wrindanneth was the least of his concerns, though his friend might be the vehicle for those anxieties' fruition. He was more apprehensive about his Dwarven brethren hearing that he had lost a drinking contest to an abstaining, nephalistic, teetotaling human ascetic.

Worries of his own honor and integrity aside, Slate sighed, "Neither Wrindanneth nor anyone with a beard need hear o' this."

Clasping his friend's hand, Yip helped Slate to his feet, cementing his assurance simultaneously. "You have my word."

Aroganji nodded. "And mine."

Slate exhaled and his countenance brightened. "Your discretion will maintain tha honor o' my clan!"

Yip bowed. "I would never claim victory in a contest many would deem unfair or unresolved."

Smiling, he added, "We did not compete. You merely fell asleep."

Adjusting his belt and puffing his chest, Slate stood proudly, saying, "If ya put it like that, then we can leave tha matter untouched and undecided fer future resolution!"

Aroganji smiled, offering, "You could drink either of our weights in ale under other circumstances."

Slate lifted a fist, and his chin along with it, proudly. "By Brendle's bones I could!"

Yip extended his arm toward the door. "Let's go home."

Raising one thick eyebrow, Slate looked at the spoils scattered across the table, left untouched during their time there in order to let him sleep undisturbed and clarified, "Winner buys?"

Yip laughed. "I already have."

Clapping both hands together happily, for what was better than a free meal, if even at the cost of a bit of dignity, Slate exclaimed, "Excellent!"

Walking to the door, Yip patted him on the back. "I knew you would be happy."

Standing on Slate's other side, Aroganji did likewise joining them walking out, adding, "We knew that picking up the tab would help lessen the blow."

Slate snorted. "Humph!" He leveled a mock glare at Aroganji and growled, "I thought we had an agreement!"

Aroganji laughed. "We do! We do indeed!"

Reaching the pub's exit, Slate sighed, "With slips o' tha tongue like that, ya're almost as bad as Wrindanneth!"

Aroganji shook his head in exaggerated, mock indignation. "Never!"

Holding the door for Yip and Aroganji, Slate pleaded, "Let's leave it behind us in tha pub. Rumors and aspersions flow as freely as ale at a Dwarven weddin!"

After Yip crossed the threshold, Slate followed his friends out into the clear, expansive night. Overhead, stars anchored the island's course through the heavens, pinpricks of light securing the vast gulf safely in the vaults of the sky. Closer, the illumination of many ships circling the island, those leaving and departing indistinguishable, formed dynamic constellations much closer to home.

Behind them, the stout wooden portal of the Dragon's Den tavern swung shut, blocking out the warm, welcoming radiance of its vibrant interior. Though the beacons of ships moved above, the night air itself was still and silent.

Slate, ever respectful of the hour and mood, took little time breaking the hush. "Are ya gonna review Adar's report tonight or wait 'til tha mornin'?"

For Yip, night was very much the same as day. The sooner he had full access to the information provided by the drones, the earlier he could begin formulating a way forward. "I will examine the report tonight."

Aroganji agreed. "Our celebrations are at an end. The information Adar has provided is too vital to be ignored any longer. I will rest upon completion of my first review. From there, I will let my mind and the world of dreams begin puzzling out a course of action."

Slate pursed his lips thoughtfully. "Looks like I'll be waitin' a bit longer ta sleep then as well. Study loves company!"

Aroganji's laughter echoed off the darkened storefronts and restaurants nearby.

Slate grinned in reply.

Though the night was old, their next task had yet begun.

Wrindanneth was asleep. The small cottage they claimed as their own was dark. Its outline defined by the soft sheen of the stars and streetlights that turned on upon their approach, the cottage slumbered beneath the dark shadows of overarching trees, branches still as the night air.

No lights had been left on in anticipation of their return.

Slate snorted. "I'm guessin' Wrin won't be waitin' at tha door ta greet us!"

Aroganji replied honestly, "No one should be disparaged for their intelligence. We should all be in bed."

Slate stretched luxuriantly. "No need. I've already had a full night's rest."

Aroganji smiled, his face unreadable. "There are those who say that there are some things you should not be proud of."

Slate swallowed deeply and cleared his throat. "Ahem..." After a moment, he amended, "If ya'd like ta go ta sleep, we can wait 'til tha morrow ta review tha report."

Yip shook his head. "We have waited long enough."

Aroganji nodded, continuing onward across the street toward the house. Decided, Yip and Slate followed.

Upon their approach, the walkway to their cottage lit up with a soft luminescence as the Abstract greeted them warmly. "Welcome home! Is there any way I may be of assistance this evening?"

Looking toward Wrindanneth's room, Slate asked, "Has Wrindanneth reviewed Adar's report?"

The disembodied voice followed alongside them as they passed through the small gate and began walking toward the front door. "He has."

Slate grunted, expecting nothing less. "We will do likewise."

"Shall I make the report ready in the sitting room?"

"Aye."

"Do you wish to review the report individually or together?"

Slate stopped and looked at his friends before answering. "We've looked at tha others together."

Yip decided for them. "Let's examine the report together. Then we will be able to discuss any concerns or questions that may arise."

The front door opened for them as they neared while the small entry hallway's light turned on in tandem. Not yet in the house, the luminance in the small sitting room turned on as well in anticipation of their imminent arrival. This glow could be seen from outside the house, leaving pools of geometric color on the darkened grass of the lawn.

Aroganji spoke aloud to the Abstract. "Dim the windows. Block all outgoing illumination. Maximal privacy settings."

"As you wish."

The window darkened returning the lawn to diffuse forms and nebulous silhouettes.

Entering the house, Aroganji followed Slate into the sitting room while Yip shut the door behind them. Though no light from the home's interior was visible outside, the lawn and the street beyond were clearly visible.

When everyone entered the room, the Abstract's voice filled the air. "Initializing report."

The lights darkened and an expectant hush filled the air.

As before, the vast empty void of space filled the air, a capsule of alienness in the room's center. Within this expansive window, inside the darkness, data began to stream across the screen, a view from the perspective of a microscopic drone approaching the alien world. This time, however, space was neither empty nor silent as the drone approached the Cabal's bleak homeworld.

Once more, they objectively viewed a world that had almost been their tomb, a brief visit filled with terror now displayed at length with complete detachment.

Adar's voice filled the air, explaining the various readings displayed on the drone's screens, providing more information than they would have otherwise thought possible. Depictions of energetic patterns, assessments of defensive systems and capabilities, measurements of activity pathways and densities, evaluations of potential targets and modes of entry, determinations of habitability, appraisals of resources, along with many other lines of analysis were points of discussion.

"Preliminary analysis indicates very little to no ambient cosmic magic in the vicinity of space around the planet. Mapping of energetic movements indicates inflowing celestial energies are rapidly and efficiently channeled toward the planetary mass for capture along multiple conduits. Though shielded, second order life-generated magics remain present around regions of principle activities."

"Passive, interplanetary defense systems appear to be analogues of Ea'ae's own. Suppression of spatiotemporal translocation and responsive dispersion of energetic attacks are the planetary shield's primary capabilities. Additionally, the shield serves as a means to reduce the planet's detection acting as a cloaking system of sorts on a global scale."

"Current analysis indicates that the shield itself does not appear to prevent the entry of physical objects into the protected region within. However, this preliminary assessment does not preclude the manifestation of such a defensive capability at need."

"Orbital satellite docking stations are armed with planetary assault capable weapons systems. Each orbital station also serves as a translocational waypoint station akin to those utilized in Tellanon. These orbital satellite stations extend the reach of the Cabal and their allies throughout the macroverse."

"The world itself is littered with subterranean assault stations each larger than many of Ea'ae's greatest cities. The Cabal's strength is evenly distributed across the planet and in the heavens above it. As such, until additional intelligence is gathered, all potential targets may be considered of relatively equal importance should an assault be initiated."

"The planet does not harbor any atmosphere to speak of, nor has it been, or is in the process of being terraformed. Despite the planet's hostility, it harbors roughly an order of magnitude greater population density than Ea'ae. In addition to its population resources, the planet's mineral reserves are quite extensive—suitable for maintaining, if not creating, its vast fleet along with other sophisticated technologies."

"Active transport of personnel and resources both between bases and orbital stations is systematic and of high intensity. Although many of the planetary needs are met within, there is a constant influx of extraplanetary resources from newly arriving ships."

Just as Adar provided additional information that they otherwise would have difficulty interpreting, so, too, were they provided many other perspectives of the planet's approach as the drones fell upon the Cabal's citadel from all directions—fields of sentient cosmic dust descending into the planet's gravity well.

Unfortunately, if what they had seen before was disturbing, the revelatory perspective provided by the swarm of miniscule drones was utterly dismaying. There were literally armadas of vessels waiting above the obsidian world in numbers that dwarfed anything that had attacked Ea'ae. Had the Cabal chosen, had their incursion not been cut off, they could have sent an invasion fleet several times greater to take over or destroy Ea'ae.

Though this possibility was chilling, its implications were more so. Ea'ae was merely one target of many, one deemed important but not of enough value to warrant the entirety of the Cabal's massive fleet. The Cabal's resources and efforts were divided over many worlds—horror spread magnanimously across the cosmos.

How many managed to resist the Cabal's assaults they could not know but given the numbers and strength of the vessels orbiting around the black planet, few were probably as lucky as Ea'ae. In fact, the forces marshaled against Ea'ae had most certainly met with success on other less fortunate worlds.

A kaleidoscopic sweep of the planet and its ships followed. This purview brought home the enormity of the Cabal's forces both in space, on the ground, and the massive amounts of hostile troops and weaponry hidden beneath the planet's surface.

Enumerating each point from threats to targets, Adar continued, "If meeting force with force conventionally, the resources required to overcome the Cabal's interplanetary defenses and assembled ships will be considerable—beyond what Ea'ae is currently capable of mustering should we choose to commit all of our forces."

"This limitation does not preclude the application of any number of other options but it may circumscribe our ability to contain the Cabal should any attempt to escape from our counter."

"Current simulations indicate that a massive application of force will be required to obliterate the Cabal and its remnants from its fortified position on this planet. We are in the process of requesting the requisite aid from our allies for such an undertaking but such an endeavor may take some time."

"There are, of course, other options for moving against the Cabal. These alternatives are under continual evaluation and will be refined as we move forward with our allies."

"This initial overview is but a summary of the information we have gathered thus far on the Cabal's inimical refuge. Within this report you will find exhaustive, interactive discussions of this intelligence, many possible contingencies, and simulations of the myriad paths forward."

"I will leave it to you to explore the rest of the information in more detail."

"As we receive updates from the remaining drones, the Construct will revise the information contained in the report such that it remains current and actionable."

"As you know, you are free to act on your own or continue to work with us on how best to address this conundrum."

"Once you are ready, we will discuss your thoughts further as your insights and opinions are of great value to us."

"Until we speak next, may wisdom guide you and peace follow."

As Adar's voice faded, the multi-dimensional orb of black space shrank, falling away to nothingness, leaving them alone in the sitting room once more, the far-ranging spectacle of space replaced by the framed view of their lawn and the street beyond outside the sitting room window.

Not wishing to miss his friends' initial discussion, his red hair frazzled and snarled, Wrindanneth's sardonic voice queried from the room's entry. "So what'd you think?"

"Looks like a party waitin' ta happen." Slate's voice did not evince the excitement of one anticipating a gathering worth attending. "One we've already crashed. But this time, we may have ta pick up tha bill!"

Yip shook his head. "As currently envisioned, should it come to pass, the direct assault options do not appear to be scenarios that we need to be involved in firsthand upon execution."

Though he wished for a universe free of the Cabal, giving his life to the betterment of all, he also considered their role in creating such a place and time. Participating in a mass attack against the Cabal's fortified planet might not be the most effective or advantageous use of their lives or method for the realization of their purpose.

Helping to plan for such an event, aiding those who might participate, assisting in any endeavor as part of an advisory or cleanup force, or moving against the Cabal in any number of other ways may suit their capabilities better than spending themselves as shock troops against the Cabal's fortifications.

Before his friends could express their surprise with his response, Yip added, "We may be of use in many other ways."

Wrindanneth snorted. "I agree. I do not want to spend my life against the Cabal's shields and guns as one target among many. The Cabal were willing to throw themselves upon Tellanon's fortifications but I am not."

A wry smile lit his visage as Wrindanneth added, "Besides, I rather like them knowing we have already been there, destroyed one of their key leaders, and gotten away without their being able to offer any reprisal. Going back might give them a chance I would rather they did not have."

Unfazed, Slate growled, contrary to his prior statements expressing reluctance to go back, "If it's fer tha good and there's gold ta be had, I'm fer just about anythin'."

Finishing his line of reasoning, Yip said, "Although the simulations may not agree, and on this point we need to investigate the report further, sending manned vehicles to move against the Cabal on such a scale may not be the best use of human life."

"The drones played a pivotal role in throwing back the Cabal, forcing them to flee before the forces of Tellanon. A host of sentient drones, far larger than that employed in Tellanon's defense, able to reason and respond to attack, especially if informed and guided by supplemental strategic units stationed nearby as needed, should be able to eradicate the Cabal and any of its defenses. The only question is one of the size of the force required to overwhelm the Cabal."

"Then no lives need be lost and our efforts can be focused on spreading life's wisdom and not on losing it."

Wrindanneth nodded thoughtfully. "Yip is correct, assuming Ea'ae can marshal such a force." He smiled with little hint of sarcasm visible, adding, "Though Yip's head may seem lost in the clouds, in fact he is firmly grounded in reality, or, rather, some skewed version thereof. We must decide how our actions will have greatest effect. To do otherwise is a wasted effort."

Ever a blend of practicality and patience, Aroganji replied, "Our own discussions, explorations, and considerations are far too premature to draw any firm conclusions. Why don't we get some rest? Then we can begin our examination of the report in earnest."

Glancing at Wrindanneth, Slate quipped, "Looks like ya woke up fer nothin'."

Wrindanneth scoffed. "I'm as good at sleeping as you are eating. Going back to bed and falling asleep will not be a struggle."

Aroganji stood. "Then, for what is left of it, I hope everyone has a fruitful night's sleep."

As Aroganji turned to depart, his face split with a competitive grin, Slate grumbled, "If ya think ya can hibernate better'n a Dwarf, ya have another thing comin', Northlander!"

Without voicing his disdain, Wrindanneth offered Slate a brief glare and strode contemptuously out of the room. Grinning evilly, Slate followed, ready to goad his friend at the slightest opportunity.

Offering Yip a slight bow, Aroganji turned and followed his companions up the stairs.

The room now still, Yip was left alone. Only when the house was silent, his friends having retired for the evening, did he, too, stand and withdraw to the sunroom.

There was not much time left in the evening. Soon dawn would break and return Tellanon to the full activity of the day, a glorious reunion with light that would send Illdrassil's cascading radiance across the city.

With the dawn's summons, their own continued review and planning would commence, activities that would delay any opportunity he may have to move forward with his own plans.

Sitting on his bedroll, the clear glass ceiling luminous in the moonlight overhead, Yip's gaze turned from the moon and stars, the ambient energies bridging his body and those all around him with the heavens, and the wispy, silver-hued clouds inward, following the rhythms of his breath.

The time had come to contact Master Wei once more.

Eyes closed, his breath extending in and out from his stomach, *chi* moving unobstructed through his body, he relaxed, opening his mind to possibilities beyond his physical limitations.

Spurred by his intent, pushed forward by the *chi* coursing through him, he called out to his erstwhile master.

"Master Wei, I would speak with you."

Sitting in silence, he waited.

He waited alongside Master Wei, his diminutive form only reaching his teacher's chest. Together, they stood framed against the snowcapped K'un Lun range, gazing outward and upward from atop the high walls surrounding the monastery.

The clear, cool darkness of an unclouded night spread uninterrupted above leaving the velvet sky scattered with silvery stars.

The gentle, rhythmic sound of his breathing was the only noise breaking the monastery's uncluttered stillness.

Such were the times to wonder.

Such was the place to ponder.

Such was the opportunity to learn, change, and grow.

Not taking his gaze from the heavens, he sought an answer to a line of reasoning that had been troubling him. "Master, what is Darkness?"

Master Wei smiled gently, gazing downward compassionately at his young pupil, always curious, always willing to learn. "Darkness is the absence of Light, of the universal yuan-chi, Yip."

"Where does it come from? How does it arise?"

"Darkness represents the willful corruption of the energy of Life and its source. From the most pure comes the most corrupt."

"Even in Darkness there is its opposite just as in Light there is the potential for its antithesis."

Yip continued his study of the host of stars in the vast swath of emptiness that defined them. "Within Darkness there is its counter?"

"Yes."

Excited, for this was just what he wished to know, Yip turned to his teacher, a flood of questions at the ready. "What is this technique? How is it accomplished? How does one learn it?"

Master Wei rested one hand on Yip's shoulder and smiled, a mixture of reassurance and joy. His response was simple. "It is the way of the K'un Lun. It is the way of learning. It is the way of Life and its full expression."

Returning his gaze heavenward, Yip returned to his study of the firmament, pondering his teacher's response all the while.

He would continue to learn. He would continue to evolve.

His life's expression would be that counter.

"Yip?"

"Master Wei!" He could not contain his excitement at the sound of his beloved teacher's voice.

Just as the words left his mind, Master Wei appeared before him, a luminous galaxy of living energy.

Yip resisted the overwhelming urge to leap up and embrace his teacher as he would have as a child for he felt the heady commingling of the love of one long separated from his family finally reunited, the gratitude of one who has been the recipient of more than he could ever earn or hope to request, and the joy of reunion with a long absent friend.

"I am so glad to see you, master!"

Master Wei smiled, a glimpse of the sun in the half-light of late evening. "As I am you, Yip."

Standing, Yip bowed. "I wished to tell you in person of our most recent quest, of the seals' restoration, and the way forward."

Master Wei laughed, the smile never leaving his face. "We are not so isolated as we once were, Yip. News of your success has traveled even to our distant shores."

"Ea'ae and all those who depend upon her owe you more than they know."

"The Cabal will soon be stricken from her shores once more, hopefully never to return."

"But I sense there is more you wish to impart and you have the right to tell it."

Now it was Yip who laughed. It was a rare occasion indeed when Master Wei spoke over much!

Before he continued, Yip had a question, though trivial, one that had puzzled him for some time. "Before I go on, master, how is it that you are able to teleport into the city when others cannot?"

Master Wei smiled, his tone light in response. "Always a question on your lips, Yip! When will you learn wisdom arises naturally when abiding in silence?"

Chastened, Yip declined his head but kept his teacher's gaze as he did so.

In reply, Master Wei answered directly, "You are not the only one who has earned Tellanon's favor, Yip, no matter how long ago that may have been."

So long had the K'un Lun been in isolation that Yip seldom considered his teacher's past, largely because Master Wei spoke about his history so rarely.

Now a world of unanswered questions opened before him—those of Master Wei's past, his accomplishments, and the many issues regarding Master Wei's own story that he had always been reticent to discuss.

How much more of Master Wei's history had he chosen not to reveal?

How much had he shared?

The time for these inquiries was not now, however, nor might such a time ever come.

Letting these thoughts and the many questions that accompanied them go, Yip returned to his original purpose. "The drones have discovered what may be the secret bastion of the Cabal."

Master Wei remained unmoved by the news patiently waiting Yip's explanation. "The Guard wish to move against this outworld alongside their allies. We will aid them in whatever capacity we are able."

Master Wei gave a short nod. Yip sensed that he knew of this development as well. "There is more. There is evidence that this planet is where Ur'Daus's horrific advance was finally stopped long ago. The Cabal appear to be operating from the very spot where Ur'Daus was banished from our universe."

He waited for his master's reply.

He did not wait long.

"There is more to their choice in location than we know. The inference, however, is clear."

Yip nodded for his conclusion was his teacher's own. The Cabal would stop at nothing until Ur'Daus was restored to past might—whatever the cost to themselves or the universe at large.

Bowing his head, Yip continued, "We have seen the iniquity with our own eyes for we were summoned there by a Liúxīng Làngrén."

Master Wei's uplifted eyebrows were all the surprise and all the request for more information he would receive. "If you wish, I will show you."

Master Wei bowed indicating his assent.

Placing both hands on his teacher's head, one on each temple, Yip let his vision of the battles in Morowen, Garen Muer, and on the desolate plains of the Cabal's world flow through and into his teacher.

After the transfer of conceptualizations completed, Master Wei remained silent for some time, his eyes tinged with an inimitable sadness—his vision and place in the world once more in question after being settled long ago. Though fleeting, this look was real along with the emotions that came with it.

Finally, his eyes clear, Master Wei responded, "Through your deeds, you have requited much more than you know, Yip." He placed one caring hand on Yip's shoulder. "In your trials, you have cast down Shen Po, master of the void palm, once one of the great patriarchs of the K'un Lun."

His voice heavy, Master Wei finished, "My former teacher."

Yip remained calm and respectful in the face of his teacher's difficulty.

"You have done more than I would have hoped possible."

Yip bowed, speaking formally though his teacher had requested otherwise. "Master Wei, we were fortunate. Nothing more."

Here a rare fire lit in his teacher's eyes. "Your success had nothing to do with fortune, Yip. Despite the gift of the Dragon's Gate, I know of none living who could have achieved what you did so easily. In time, this may change but for now you have done what no one else could."

This time, Yip remained in silent deference as he bowed.

"You have brought us much honor, Yip, and much restitution."

Looking deeply into Yip's eyes, he added personally, "I thank you."

Yip bowed again. "It is I who am indebted to you, master."

Master Wei laughed. "To live a delusion is a choice, Yip."

"To be free of delusion, one often requires an able teacher."

"Even with an apt teacher, the student's vision, dedication, and purpose determine the ultimate realization."

Yip smiled. "I have been fortunate to have one who fostered all."

Now it was Master Wei who bowed.

After an extended period of silence, Master Wei finally asked, "What will you do now, Yip?"

Though he had many answers, here Yip had none. He did,

however, have some initial ideas. "We have yet to decide how best to move forward or how we may maximize our efforts."

Master Wei nodded, his unflappable countenance intent. Repeating his last question, Master Wei asked again—simply, earnestly, "What will you do, Yip?"

"What do you intend?"

Yip's own purpose was clear. "The Cabal's wishes cannot be allowed to happen. Ur'Daus must be silenced, Its return, and agents thwarted. I will do whatever is in my power to stop it."

Master Wei nodded, though his face remained unreadable, Yip sensed that he approved. Asking the question he had upon their last meeting, Master Wei asked, "Do you need the help of the K'un Lun?"

Yip shook his head. "So long as the Cabal and their ilk remain on Ea'ae, you have much to rectify here. Once Ea'ae is safe, the Aerya'ana may be in need of the guidance, assistance, and wisdom of priests. For even should the Cabal meet its demise, Darkness's taint runs the breadth of the macroverse."

Master Wei's tone grew serious. "You would have us resume our mantle and spread across the cosmos?"

Yip bowed, his request was one that had been long abandoned with the K'un Lun's retreat into seclusion. "Yes."

Master Wei remained quiet for some time, considering. Finally, after long moments of silence, he nodded. "Perhaps the time has come."

"If the K'un Lun's knowledge fares the stars, perhaps the time has arrived for the K'un Lun to be the ones who bring it."

Yip bowed once more and said no more.

RESOLUTION

Pale pearlescent light
tints the clear evening air—
trees still before the storm.

"All right, who's ready fer some grub?" Slate called out from the kitchen amidst piles of prepared food, his summons preceded by the aroma of sausage, fried potatoes, eggs, sautéed vegetables, and sliced fruits. Not moderating his tone, his voice echoed through the halls of their small cottage, leaving little room to ignore his request.

He had woken early, his hale Dwarven constitution needing little rest despite the long night, especially when supplemented by several hours of slumber at the pub. Knowing there was no better way to start the day than with a hearty plate of food, he began his preparations in earnest before the sun lit the horizon, his own contribution to the day's forthcoming deliberations.

As Slate's call faded, passing as quickly as an unwelcome summer storm, Wrindanneth threw back the covers on his bed. He did not need a second hail to find his way to the morning table, even if it meant getting out of the warm solace of bed. The smells wafting into his chamber had already woken him up long before. He need not lay in bed any longer and try to extend an otherwise too short respite.

The time had come for decisions to be made.

He was ready to make those decisions…after breakfast.

Aroganji left the sitting room to join Slate. He had not gone to sleep the night before. The prospect of exploring the information contained within Adar's report was far too enticing for him to resist. Aided by magic, he had returned downstairs and consumed more information in the past few hours than would have been possible in months unaided.

Though his head now swam with information, he was glad for the decision to hasten his study. He had explored the intricacies of many possible scenarios and had learned more of the state of affairs on the ground than he would have thought possible prior to delving into the report.

From this investigation one thing above all else appeared clear to him. A direct assault, whether surreptitiously or in force as they had done in the past, was not a viable option. One ship, no matter how well armed and equipped, would face extreme difficulty getting through the Cabal's planetary shields much less be able to effect the kind of change they would wish on a planet swarming with potential points of conflict.

Despite their past successes flying out alone on the *Shrike* against all odds, moving directly against the Cabal in their bastion of strength on their own would not be an option.

Their lives would be lost as surely as their mission.

Teleporting to the dead world as a group without a ship, if they could manage that through the Cabal's defenses, inviting the trap they had only barely managed to escape when only faced with two members of the Cabal's powerful legions, would certainly lead to no better outcome.

Yip stood smoothly, moving in meditation, the world as open and clear as his mind.

Though he would not eat, he would join his friends in their discussion at the table. He had sensed Aroganji's activities these past few hours and knew his friend had been reviewing Adar's report, formulating a way forward. His survey would begin after their discussion at breakfast reached its conclusion.

Slate spoke around a mouthful of food, the crumbs falling to his plate as he talked only granted a momentary glimpse of freedom before falling prey to his relentless mastications. "What'd yer additional studies this mornin' reveal, Aroganji?"

"Would you rather hear my opinion before you have had the chance to come to your own?"

Slate scoffed, more food spraying out as he did so only to be caught in the tangles of his beard for later consumption, "Yer opinion won't alter mine! Fire away!"

Seeing no objections from either Wrindanneth or Yip, Aroganji answered directly. "The amount of reconnaissance the drones have been able to garner and ascertain is truly amazing. The scale of this data is, however, reflective of the magnitude of the Cabal's operations on their dark planet."

"Though large-scale concerted action against this planet is possible and may bear positive results, as reflected in Adar's analysis, individual action is and will not."

Slate's thick brows furrowed, the wiry hairs so deeply entangled with one another as to almost tie themselves together inextricably. "So ya're sayin' we won't be able ta move against tha Cabal as we have in the past?"

Aroganji shook his head. "I fear not. Even if we are able to breach their defenses undetected, the scale of their operations is such that we could do little to counter them."

"Not even if we had identified our target and planned accordingly?" Wrindanneth did not doubt Aroganji's assessment but he also recognized that many things were possible with the appropriate blending of will, forethought, and skill.

"The odds of success would appear infinitesimally low."

Slate's furrowed browline remained knotted. "And that's different than tha past how?"

Aroganji smiled grimly. "The likelihood of success for a solo mission, any mission, against such odds is as unlikely as you are to forget a debt, Slate."

Slate whistled. "That grim?"

"Even more. The targets, both the energetic anomalies and bases of operation, are far too numerous for significant effect and to warrant such a risk."

Slate clapped his hands together with finality and directed his attention to his plate once more. "Looks like it's time ta return ta more important matters!"

Wrindanneth, however, had not yet given up. "Before we discount the possibility entirely, what would we hope to achieve by going to this planet once more that would not be accomplished by obliterating it with a superior force?"

"What could we hope to achieve that a large group could not?"

Slate sighed, putting his knife and fork down on the plate with a clatter, unhappy that his breakfast was interrupted once more. "If we could manage ta get through, we could ensure that our target, be it one Man or many, were dead and did not escape durin' a mass assault."

Aroganji answered, "We could hope to ascertain and uncover more of their motives and strength, the extent of their networks, determine how and where we may strike next before they act in kind."

Slate agreed and continued, his mind always looking for material reward. "We could hope ta secure some o' tha weaponry and resources that've allowed 'em ta function so effectively fer so long."

Wrindanneth nodded, asking, "Anything else?"

Yip spoke quietly. "Aside from its obvious isolation and difficulty in detection, we could try to uncover what exactly the Cabal gains by remaining on this world. Then we may learn how best to counter these efforts."

Wrindanneth pursed his lips. "I assume you're referring to something relating to Ur'Daus, Its imprisonment, or potential release?"

Yip gave a brief smile. "Those would be sound assumptions."

Slate nodded begrudgingly. "And questions worth answerin'."

Wrindanneth directed his attention to Aroganji and replied questioningly, "But the likelihood of success remains almost nonexistent?"

Aroganji turned concerned eyes to Yip, understanding how much nullifying the Cabal's evil meant to his friend. "Are you comfortable with this assessment?"

Yip smiled grimly. "I did not need to review Adar's report to understand our chances of success. Nor did I ever intend to ask anyone to move forward against the Cabal in their stronghold as we have done in the past."

"If everyone remains committed to this path and we all agree to continue fighting against the Cabal, our efforts will be best spent assisting the Home Guard and their allies."

"Far away from their dead world."

Wrindanneth shook his head, his eyes locked on Yip. "I never thought I'd hear you say you weren't going to push on directly against the Cabal until the bitter end."

Yip's smile remained unbroken as he replied, "Have I?"

Wrindanneth sat in the sitting room by himself. Slate, despite his statements to the contrary, was reviewing Adar's report elsewhere. Similarly, Yip had retreated to the sunroom to explore the report's contents on his own. Aroganji was in his room, presumably doing the same.

In front of him, streams of data flowed through the air. His capabilities augmented by a cloud of complex arcana, he reached forward and into the stream, pulling the data to him, letting it flow directly into his mind.

Information poured into him unobstructed, a merger very similar in feeling to that achieved when bonding with the *Shrike*. Avenues of inquiry opened instantly, precipitated naturally by the confluence of intent.

An organic, interactive cosmography of planetary capabilities, resources, defenses, simulations, raw data, and analyses held sway within his mind, shifting and morphing with his attention.

If Aroganji's appraisal had been grim, the reality was far worse.

Simulation after simulation played out as he watched in his mind.

Although they had not yet fully discussed or decided upon a potential mission or course of action, he tried variations on every scenario he could imagine starting with permutations on Yip's reconnaissance and information gathering suggestion to directed missions with intended targets, living or otherwise.

The predicted results of his directed inquiries were less than promising.

Even less than grim.

Despite adjusting simulation parameters with each viewing, requesting optimal outcomes and attack strategies, and ranking actions on likelihood of success, he saw no way forward acting as a group as they had done in the past. At best, they would be able to reach the planet's shield undetected and find a way through only to be ineffective or nullified. At worst, they were destroyed upon entry into the system before ever reaching the planet.

There was one variable that the Construct's simulations could never fully take into account, no matter how expansive its databases, how in-depth and reliable its information sources, or how intensive and accurate its computations. These simulations could not completely account for what they did not know. Though the simulation's algorithms resulted in predictions that were highly reliable, however broad and comprehensive, there were factors that were not included in their calculations.

It was the exception, not the rule, that had allowed for their successes in the past.

They had but to find one among many.

Although he remained certain of his original assessment, Aroganji was determined to understand and internalize as much of the drones' gathered information, and the conclusions and extrapolations drawn from it, as possible.

Though he may be sure of his appraisal, he was just as determined to try to find a way to move against the Cabal that would strike them down, dealing a mortal blow to their cause and their foundation of strength just as their agents had done to his school, taking the lives of so many of his friends.

While Wrindanneth scoured Adar's interactive report for possibilities concerning the direct actions of their group, his own explorations now led him elsewhere. His concern was with finding the avenue ahead in which their actions could be most efficacious particularly as ancillaries to much larger operations.

No matter how he examined the issue, the outcomes remained the same—the most desirous results occurred when they were not directly involved, both for their own safety and for that of the projected mission.

Despite their penchant for individual action, the way forward was clear. Their role would be as adjuvants to the conflict in whatever form this confrontation took place.

Slate sat in the privacy of his chamber, the flow of information before him moving at his behest, driven by his interest. He knew without asking or probing that their chances were grim if they mounted an assault against such a place just as he understood that any force, large or small, moving in opposition to such strength would incur heavy losses.

He did not intend to be a victim of reckless carnage. Instead, he looked for ways to create it.

Though his axe might not shed blood on the field of battle in the upcoming conflict, he would do everything in his power to ensure that his enemies' did.

Unlike his friends, Yip did not plot possibilities, try to derive solutions to as yet unrealized problems, or forge a future from chance.

A path forward lay clear in his mind.

He merely observed.

He watched the familiar bleak landscape unfold before the drones' roving optics, he memorized the scenes of barren devastation from the lifeless plains to the soaring, vertiginous heights, and he remembered.

When the opportunity arose, he would act.

But not before.

They agreed to reconvene by day's end to discuss their insights and make preparations for another meeting with Eidelion. Once their own aims were sorted out, they would be in a position to lend their perspectives and perceptions to the movements against the Cabal, providing both direction and assistance as needed.

Aroganji emerged from his room first, joining Wrindanneth in the sitting room while they waited for Yip and Slate. The mood was hushed as they gathered their thoughts and ideas. Sensing their arrival, Yip joined them in short order, maintaining his own silence upon arrival.

Surprisingly, Slate did not emerge at the agreed upon time.

Never loath to call his friend out, Wrindanneth yelled for Slate loudly after a few more minutes had passed. "Slate! Time to wake up and join the living! There's no more time for your afternoon nap!"

If his summons did not work, he would resort to using Slate's favorite assistant and let the Abstract startle him into joining them. That would be almost as enjoyable as exercising his voice.

Unfortunately for Wrindanneth, Slate heeded his summons in short order. Calling out as his heavy boots thumped on the stairs, Slate replied, "I heard ya! No need ta get yer robes in a tangle!"

Wrindanneth smirked as Slate's legs became visible on the stairs. "If I didn't know any better, I'd say you were enjoying yourself in there!"

Now completely visible, Slate grinned wickedly. "There's nothin' quite so pleasurable as visualizin' tha destruction o' yer enemy!"

Nodding his head and looking off in the distance, he crooned softly, "Thousands o' times over."

Wrindanneth scoffed, "I'll have to take your word on that one."

"With pleasure."

As Slate found a place to be seated on one overstuffed chair, Aroganji surveyed the room, querying, "What has been decided? Where do we stand and how do we move forward?"

Slate laughed, replying, "I don't know about ya, but I'm sittin'!"

Wrindanneth raised a warning eye as he retorted, "Judging by the look in Aroganji's eye, you're about to be throttled."

"Bah!"

Aroganji was not amused. "Are we ready?"

Unmollified, Slate offered a reluctant, "Aye."

Turning first to Wrindanneth, Aroganji asked, "What is your assessment?"

Wrindanneth shrugged. "In this case, as much as it pains me, I think our response is simple. We ask the Home Guard how best we can help."

"From their perspective, we bring a wealth of experience and insight that they recognize as having value. That we have already visited this place and have seen it with our own eyes only adds to this fact."

"From our perspective, we can help steer their mission to a mutually agreed upon end while increasing our own value to them all the while."

"This will also give us time and opportunity to lever the situation to our best advantage and purpose."

Aroganji looked to Yip and he responded with a nod. "Our role will be one of support as the Guard and its allies move against the Cabal's bastions. Should an opportunity present itself, we will be in the most advantageous position to act accordingly."

"With success, we may be able to provide a similar role in the future against other seats of the Cabal's strength."

Addressing not only their position but that of how the Cabal should be countered, Yip added, "I do not think movement against the Cabal requires the commitment of any troops or the attendant loss of life. If the Guard can marshal a force strong enough to overcome the Cabal's strength in their citadel, then they should be able to create a host of drones that is equally or even more devastating."

"The continual explosive sacrifice of the drones pushed back the Cabal's assault on Tellanon. With significantly greater numbers, these same drones may be the best chance to move against the Cabal's homeworld."

Aroganji's gaze moved on. "Slate?"

"I cannot yet say how tha Guard should move forward as I haven't heard their full case but Yip does have a point, as he had before."

"As ta how we move, I'm in agreement with Wrindanneth and Yip. We move as one. Battles need infantry just as much as they need advisors and generals. If we can help off tha field o' battle, then so be it."

Aroganji gave a curt nod. "So be it."

Summarizing, Aroganji said, "We talk with the Guard, let them know we are willing to lend our expertise as part of their mission, and decide how best we can aid in this cause together."

Washing his hands together eagerly, Slate added, "And we choose our artifacts!"

Now Aroganji smiled, adding, "And we choose our rewards from prior service."

ADVISORS

Moiling gray clouds run
fleet upon a rustling wind—
lambent full moon revealed.

"Abstract, please initiate contact with Eidelion." Aroganji sat in the cottage's small front room alongside Wrindanneth, Slate, and Yip. Late afternoon sunlight filtered through the windows, filling the room with warmth and cheer, flitting lightly upon their skin.

"One moment please." The Abstract's solicitous voice faded to silence with the attempt.

"Contact initiated. Eidelion will be available for communication in just a few moments."

"Thank you, Abstract."

The air veritably thrummed with the receipt of Aroganji's brief praise. "My duty and pleasure."

Slate grinned mischievously, the expression nearly lost in the tangled thicket of his beard. "What d'ya reckon his response'll be when he hears our acceptance o' his offer ta help?"

Wrindanneth smiled, his voice changing in an attempt to mirror Eidelion's. "He'll probably say something akin to, 'Your Light will add to our own' as his own radiance nearly blinds us."

Slate nodded in agreement. "I'm guessin' it'll be somethin' like, 'Tha Light has graced us with yer own.'"

Neither Yip nor Aroganji offered an opinion for they did not wish to voice any disrespect, especially for such an esteemed exemplar and friend. Their faces remained unreadable masks despite their disapproval.

"How about, 'May the Light's grace be ours'?"

Eidelion's smiling face appeared before them hovering in the center of the room. If he was offended in any way, no signs showed on his luminous face. If anything, he appeared more jovial than usual.

Slate stroked his beard consideringly, Eidelion's appearance taken in stride, reacting to his comment as a natural part of the conversation. "That might do in a pinch."

Wrindanneth laughed. "I should say so!"

His face now sporting a half-smile, Aroganji merely shook his head.

"Did ya hear tha beginnin' o' tha conversation or just tha end?"

"I just heard enough to formulate a reply. Nothing more."

"Then ya missed tha best part!" Slate laughed, his voice tinged with good cheer.

"Which was?"

"Fer better or worse, tha Guard and those that go with ya will have us by yer side as ya move against tha Cabal's bastion! We wish ta offer what little expertise we claim ta have as ya plan and make ready ta move against our foes! We wish ta be a part o' those plans and help bring 'em ta fruition!"

Eidelion smiled broadly and bowed his head deeply in appreciation. "The Light's gift is ours."

Slate smacked his forehead and sighed. "None o' us were right!"

Wrindanneth chortled. "But we were close!"

"Indeed."

Eidelion laughed, the sound brightening even the light of the sun streaming through their windows.

"When and where do you want us next?" Now that they had come to a decision, Aroganji wished to push onward, be of use, and put words to action.

Eidelion gave a short nod of appreciation and approval with Aroganji's driven expression of initiative. "Discussing how to move against the Cabal has become as much a part of my daily ritual as waking with the sun. Select members of the Home Guard meet each morning to plan and work out the details of the day's activities."

His tone firm, Eidelion added, "I suggest you join us for these meetings."

"I will relay the requisite meeting information that you will require to your Abstract."

Slate's brow furrowed. "Is it BYOB?"

"Pardon?"

Slate smiled, his voice full of mirth. "Bring yer own breakfast?"

Eidelion laughed. "Food can be summoned if you like. But"—here he gave a brief nod of acknowledgement—"knowing your eating habits, you might be better served by commencing breakfast a few hours before meeting time."

Wrindanneth snickered. "We wouldn't want to drain Illdrassil's reserves trying to summon enough food to fill your gullet, Slate! There's a war to run after all!"

Slate turned his gaze skyward, eyes lost in brief reflection. "Per'aps that's why me Mum was so eager ta have me leave tha delvin' and go huntin' Orcs."

Wrindanneth smirked. "There were other reasons as well I'm sure."

"Bah!"

Returning to the topic at hand, Aroganji asked, "Is there anything we need to do to prepare for the meeting?"

Eidelion laughed. "With your past successes, your reputation will precede you. Prepare to receive many questions."

More seriously, he added, "You have already reviewed Adar's summary report. The information and simulations therein provide sufficient background on our tactical evaluations to proceed with some degree of confidence."

Once more breaking a smile, Eidelion finished, "If not, I know you are all relatively quick studies."

Slate snorted. "I'm so quick, I don't need ta study!"

Wrindanneth shook his head unable to resist a retort. "In comparison to what? A comatose Ogre?"

Aroganji ignored both Slate and Wrindanneth, understanding that Eidelion's time was valuable and more effectively spent elsewhere.

"Until the morning, may your day be full and your actions fortuitous."

"Until the morn."

With those words, Eidelion faded into light.

Slate clapped both hands together firmly and stood. Heeding Eidelion's words, he said, "If Eidelion's right and I'm gonna be ready fer tomorrow's meetin', I'd better get started now!"

Wrindanneth stood as well, his tall form casting a long shadow across the room. "If you're cooking, I might as well eat something too."

Aroganji laughed, turning to Yip. "Looks like we're left alone by the Food Crew again!"

From down the hall, Slate responded to Aroganji, "Tha Hollow Leg Committee is convenin' fer those wishin' ta attend!"

Yip smiled subtly at Slate's words. "They will not miss us."

Aroganji nodded. "Of that I am certain."

"Shall we offer to teach them how to make a dish full of vitality and health?"

Aroganji chuckled. "You mean a *chi* cultivating and balancing meal from Chang Sen?"

Yip's reply was merely a mischievous smile.

Aroganji clarified, his voice full of cheer, "You mean something they won't eat?"

Yip laughed, replying in kind. "Of that we are certain!"

Shaking his head, the smile never leaving his face, Aroganji stood, motioning for Yip to do likewise. "It never hurts to try."

Moving fluidly, Yip stood with his friend as they walked together toward the kitchen.

Placing his hand on Yip's shoulder as they moved down the hallway, Aroganji said, "This may be our greatest adventure yet!"

Yip's grin returned as he replied, "And perhaps our most challenging!"

Looking up as they entered the kitchen moments later, Slate barked, "What're ya two laughin' about?"

Aroganji entered the kitchen first, the words ready on his lips. "Our next great quest."

"Really?"

Aroganji shook his head, replying, "Unfortunately, some challenges may be too great even for the likes of us."

Slate's chest expanded to its full girth. "Impossible!"

Yip's voice was a soft counterpoint. "Aroganji is correct. I fear this challenge is beyond us."

Wrindanneth squinted his eyes appraisingly sensing something was amiss. "What're you two getting at?"

Aroganji smiled brightly. "Trying to get you to eat a traditional herbal meal from Chang Sen!"

Slate coughed uncomfortably, taken aback. "That just might be impossible!"

A look of challenge appeared on Aroganji's face. "Does the difficulty posed by eating a meal that augments your constitution frighten you that much, Slate?"

"Speak fer yer own constitution! What aids or ails a Dwarf might not be tha same as a Man!"

Yip smiled, replying simply. "The energies that enliven your blood are the same as those that enliven a Man's. This food will serve you well."

Slate looked to Wrindanneth for help in a last desperate attempt to find something to grab on to before being pulled away, thrust into deadly rushing currents. "Bah! 'Tis tha food that serves me, and my tastes, not tha other way around!"

Rather enjoying the spectacle, and the situation it placed Slate in, Wrindanneth acquiesced. "Perchance their suggestion is a good one. Perhaps we should dine on some of the fine delicacies from Chang Sen this day!"

Defeat far from his mind, Slate growled, "Never!"

Cranking the pressure up, Wrindanneth rejoined simply and turned away from Slate toward Aroganji and Yip. "No matter. He has admitted defeat. Dwarves, though stout, are not made of as stern a stuff as they believe. What shall we prepare?"

Before Aroganji could answer, his mouth open to reply, Slate caved, giving in to Wrindanneth's ruse. "All right. But if yer veggie puffs and seaweed can't satisfy my gullet, then a real meal is what I'll have after!"

Yip bowed, saying, "If you are not satisfied, then I will prepare any dish you request."

"Now that's what I'm talkin' about!"

Yip smiled. "As am I."

Slate washed his hands together eagerly now in anticipation. "So what're we havin'?"

Yip bowed. "Perhaps an array of sautéed medicinal mushrooms, assorted vegetarian dumplings, some herbal teas, stuffed seaweed rolls, and a variety of hot soups would be a nice selection for your discriminating pallet?"

Slate glowered. "If it's discriminatin' yer wantin' then I'd discriminate against any o' those choices…save per'aps fer tha mushrooms." Lost in remembrance, he added wistfully, "I always did enjoy tha rich earthiness o' a well-seasoned 'shroom."

Aroganji laughed. "Yip's suggestions are rather tame! Would you prefer I add a few more choices to the assortment?"

Now fearful, Slate furrowed his brow and raised a hand placatingly. "Yip's courses should suffice! There's no need fer more!"

Wrindanneth smiled wickedly. "Are you sure? I hear variety is the spice of life."

Slate shook his head in measured, resolute disagreement. "Not fer Dwarves. Gold and spirits are tha spice o' life and I'll hear naught more o' it!"

Wrindanneth bowed with a flourish. "As you wish." He was overjoyed for the opportunity to watch Slate suffer through the foreign dishes as they were. That his bid for more torture failed in no way lessened his joy.

Turning to Wrindanneth, Aroganji asked, "Do you have any special requests for your meal, Wrindanneth?"

Slate raised his thick brows questioningly at the opportunity, interjecting, "Eh, Wrin? Care ta spice it up bit?"

Ignoring Slate, Wrindanneth shook his head and replied with a smile. "Only that Slate's portions be larger than mine!"

Slate huffed. "Ya don't have ta worry, Wrin. There'll be no leftovers on my plate. As fer ya, I hope ya have seconds!"

Nodding his head to Slate, Wrindanneth replied, "Until dinner then, Slate." Turning to both Yip and Aroganji, he repeated the gesture with a nod, saying, "Yip. Aroganji." Retaining an innocent expression all the while, Wrin waved goodbye and left the kitchen with aplomb.

Slate glared after him and muttered. "Tha scoundrel." Even lower, he added, "At least he has ta eat it too…"

Yip offered solicitously, "Would you like us to teach you how to make these dishes?"

Aroganji smiled, amending, "Delicacies."

Now that Wrindanneth was gone and Slate did not have to be on the defensive or otherwise put on any type of bluff, he replied thoughtfully with a shrug, "Can't hurt. If by some unexpected twist o' Brendle's beard it turns out that I enjoy 'em, then I'll have some idea how ta recreate 'em."

Aroganji nodded. "Then I will only summon the raw ingredients that we can prepare them together."

"What can I do ta help?"

With those simple words, Slate's gustatory adventures began.

The kitchen was filled with the succulent aromas of cooked mushrooms, sauces, teas, and stews along with steamed and stir-fried vegetables. Piles of steaming dumplings rested alongside variegated seaweed rolls, each with different treasures inside. Small trays with assorted dipping sauces—hot, sweet, sour, rich, savory, smoky, spicy, bitter, and others—rested beside deep bowls of soups and stews filled with aromatic spices and soothing broths. Herbal teas made from freshly crushed medicinals and tonics waited to refresh the pallet and restore the system.

Surprisingly, after his initial reticence, amidst the pervasive aromas and enticing sights, Slate ogled the diverse feast excitedly, licking his lips to restrain the free flow of saliva. "I hate ta admit it, but this looks ta be a feast worthy o' a thane!"

"Or a hungry Dwarf?" Aroganji half-smiled knowing the answer.

"Several!" Slate did not hesitate in his earnest reply.

Yip bowed. "Your anticipation does you justice."

Ready to bring Wrindanneth in to eat, Slate called, "Wrindanneth! Time ta meet yer destiny!"

Wrindanneth responded in kind from the front of the cottage, his voice filling the intervening space with a wave of sound. "I hope it's a good one!"

Slate planted himself at the kitchen's small table, positioning himself to best advantage for the meal. As he had assisted in the repast's preparation, his excitement had grown all out of proportion to his initial dread. Now, mere minutes from his earlier refusals, he waited as one who had not eaten in a great while, one who had been granted the opportunity to partake in the most delightful delicacies of his own choosing. Slate greedily piled food on his plate before Wrindanneth entered the room and before either Yip or Aroganji took their places at the table.

"I'm glad to see your curse suits you so well!" Wrindanneth laughed as he entered the kitchen, noting Slate's eagerness to condemn himself to the horrific throes of a meal anathema to his taste and constitution.

Ignoring Wrindanneth, Slate looked to Aroganji and Yip, asking, "Shall we commence?"

Yip smiled as he took his place. "Feel free."

And so he did.

To say that Slate ate with abandon would be an understatement.

He ate as one who had spent long years honing his skills in private, training with full determination and commitment in seclusion far removed from the public eye but finally given one and only one chance to display the skills he had carefully cultivated for so long. He ate with zeal, a fervor born of newfound sensibilities, and a single-minded focus.

He ate with the poise, economy, and efficiency of true mastery.

Food veritably flew into his mouth in a frenzy of masticatory adroitness.

Only when he finally pushed his last plate away, after having labored in silence for so long, did Slate realize that all eyes were upon him, carefully studying his every move, his friends' plates untouched.

Patting his paunch zestily with both open palms, he asked innocently, "Aren't ya gonna eat?'

Wrindanneth scoffed, "I just wanted to make sure I wasn't eaten!"

Aroganji laughed. "We wanted to make certain there was enough food for you!"

Smiling appreciatively, Yip replied directly without hint of sarcasm, "When one has the good fortune to see a master at work at his chosen craft, one should make every effort to appreciate the depths and beauty of his skill."

Wrindanneth snorted disapprovingly. "You do know this food is meant to be eaten slowly, savored, and appreciated both for maximal health and effect?"

Warmed by the cups of soothing tea, the steaming vegetables and dumplings, and bowls of hot soup he had consumed, Slate's face glowed a vibrant, ruddy red as he replied, "Didn't I?"

Wrindanneth snickered. "Only if you learned your table manners from a Dragon!"

Slate shrugged. "Azaelle seemed ta know how ta enjoy himself. Could be worse I suppose."

Wrindanneth shook his head. "I was thinking more along the lines of the Cabal's Spectral Dragon, Sarugauth the Dead!"

Yip declined his head before Slate offered his reply. "We are glad that you showed so much joy partaking of our modest fare."

"Modest nothin'! That rabbit food's tha best assortment o' victuals this side o' Brendle's forge!"

Lowering his voice, he added, "'Course we'll have ta keep this quiet. No self respectin' Dwarf would be caught by his beard eatin' such fixin's in public but more o' it I shall have!"

Aroganji smiled. "We are glad you enjoyed it, Slate." Turning innocently to Wrindanneth, whose own plate had remained untouched during the spectacle, he added, "Now we would like your impressions."

Eying his plate reluctantly, Wrindanneth began his own hesitating journey of self-transformation.

ART AND ARTIFICE

Fireflies passing in
the velvet spring night—
constellations without guide.

Dawn's light glimmered on the glass above Yip's head, effulgent hues refracted downward bathing his seated form in the full spectrum of white light. Rising smoothly from his bedroll, he moved easily through the fields of energy washing through and enlivening him, other forms much more luminous and vibrant than those emanating from the newly risen sun.

While his friends ate breakfast preparing for their impending trip to Illdrassil, he maintained his awareness and practice as he had done throughout the evening just as he would throughout the day. He did, however, contract his consciousness, increasing his focus on the immediate vicinity around the cottage, no longer pushing the limits of his capabilities.

All around, life stirred with the morning, a layer of newfound activity within the myriad processes of the air and soil that did not sleep only changed pace with the passing of the sun's light and warmth. Just as the vivacity of life suffused the environs, so, too, did his awareness.

The time to move had come once more.

This time, he would do it alone.

Before he did anything, however, he would help set in motion the next phase of their collective movements against the Cabal.

Only then would he act.

Only then would he have the assurance needed to strike out once more.

"Yip! Time ta stop sittin' and start walkin'!" Slate's summons was unnecessary though he did not know it for his friend already waited for them having moved silently to the sitting room in anticipation of the summons.

"I am waiting on you." Yip's words filled Slate's mind as if they were his own, an afterthought emerging from the depths of other inchoate musings.

Now used to such intrusions, for Yip would not yell or get upset but he would talk directly between minds when the situation warranted, Slate was not startled by the reply.

"Ya're outside?"

"I am waiting by the door."

Slate smiled, turning the situation around with a jest. "Come on! We can't have Yip waitin' on us! Let's go!" He motioned for Aroganji and Wrindanneth to follow him out of the kitchen, no longer needing to rouse Yip from his meditations.

Slate coughed pointedly when he saw Yip waiting down the hall-way. "Thought ya'd never get off yer mat and join us!"

Yip shrugged, replying with bland humor, "I knew you would eventually get off your chairs and join me."

Aroganji shook his head. "Are we ready to port?"

Slate grinned, never one to shy away from an opportunity to avoid exertion. "Beats walkin'!"

"Gather round."

With a brief surge of power and incantation, the view shifted instantly from their quiet street to the majesty of Illdrassil seen from outside her outer protective walls, the fiery light of dawn igniting her branches from the subtle luminescence of evening to the glory of morn.

Ahead, a cadre of Home Guard waited in front of one of the arching entrances melded through the shimmering bulwarks encircling the city's inner sanctum, the luminance from the rising sun overhead casting vibrant hues throughout the crystalline stone, a constantly changing tapestry mingling with the inner light shifting within. Behind, the entrance to one of Tellanon's many extradimensional gardens opened onto a view of an otherworldly jungle, a riotous profusion of organic shapes resembling irregular fungal inspired trees, flowers, vines, bromeliads, and undergrowth in more colors and tones than even the most fevered painter would have ventured possible. Between the alien garden and the outer wall, the paved lane glowed with the full illumination of the morn, sun splashes caught and held within each individual crystalline stone—lit with an inner fire, the boulevard was aflame.

Combined with the effect of the play of light on Illdrassil's boughs, the very air thrummed with electric allure.

Crossing the paved lane separating the unusual park from the periphery of Illdrassil's grounds, Wrindanneth walked forward naturally as though they had not just materialized from thin air. The Guard, despite the rarity of such an occurrence given the strictures on magical travel within the city, remained unmoved. In fact, the Guard appeared more of stone than the crystalline walls behind them for though the light played upon their shimmering armor, it was as nothing compared to the glory of Illdrassil and the flowing walls that shielded her.

As the party neared, scanned by the Construct as they approached, the two leading Guards, both stout Dwarves with wicked two-handed battle axes held at the ready, merely lifted their axes, gesturing for them to pass through. "You are expected. Follow the ghost light toward your assigned meeting place."

Wrindanneth bowed from the waist, not indicating the surprise he felt for they had never been granted passage so easily despite being expected on prior occasions. "You are most gracious."

Ahead, on the far side the of prismatic tunnel, a single bluish wisp light beckoned, flickering in the morning air. Between, a series of formidable Guard—Men, Elves, NUMEN, and Gnomes—remained poised and alert, their attention focused elsewhere, the group now passing through their midst but a swiftly passing dream.

Reaching the far side of the passage, the floating orb of light shifted onward, a flame without apparent source, guiding them toward fair Illdrassil and the mysteries held within.

Their thoughts turned inward, only Yip's attention remained on the timeless, paradisiacal beauty unfolding around them. There was too much delight here to ignore. The play of light on glassy stone, from bole to bower, told a story of celebratory expression, one that the mind's eye could not resist.

Daerdros waited for them ahead at the base of Illdrassil's immense, luminous trunk, her musical voice an ovation to the glorious morn. "Well met, Fists! The Light of your visages are as the newly risen sun!"

Yip bowed. "And yours is of its genesis."

Returning his bow with the grace and precision of a finely crafted song, she smiled with the compliment and ushered them forward, walking fluidly through Illdrassil's trunk without pause for fear of running into the solid wall. Likewise stepping fearlessly ahead through the fluid surface, joining her on the other side, the companions followed as Daerdros paused and said, "Given the import of these deliberations, members of the Guard and council will be present at this meeting."

Slate gave a short nod, understanding the implications. "And ya want us ta be on our best behavior."

A knowing smile was her only reply.

As Daerdros continued, she led them inward and upward toward the pinnacle of Illdrassil's crown. All the while, the sunlight refracting through Illdrassil's trunk lit the tree's massive interior in glorious, multicolored rays of light, shifting with the sun and clouds, the tenor and quality of illumination. This radiance and the attendant energies of Illdrassil herself filled the capacious central chamber of her bole with the interplay of a dynamic symphony that never ceased its music or awe.

"The meeting will proceed with some degree of formality. The nature of this dialogue will become readily apparent as you observe."

"Speak in turn, answering forthrightly and succinctly, for there is much to be discussed and more yet to be decided."

Wrindanneth smiled at Slate innocently. "In other words, do exactly the opposite of your normal inclination."

Not taking his eyes from Daerdros, Slate replied simply, "Speak fer yerself."

Waiting patiently, for she was used to their jockeying, Daerdros resumed after Wrindanneth and Slate settled down. Standing on a translucent lift floating toward Illdrassil's pinnacle, its sides open to the central chamber, they cut through rays of resplendence as she spoke, each with a different color and timbre. "There will be introductions though you are familiar with some of the participants."

"You will be honored to hear that most assembled requested your presence well before you decided to participate in these discussions."

Slate tightened his lips and inflated his chest to full girth proudly. Wisely, he refrained from making comment for Wrindanneth remained vigilant for just such an opportunity.

"What will be expected of us?" Wrindanneth was ready to take an active role in the discussion, to wait and be called upon as an advisor, or to merely observe. He would, however, like to know what was desired of them.

Daerdros smiled, choosing not to answer his question directly. "You are adept at speaking at liberty when given the opportunity. I am certain you will be given the chance."

Grand passages spiraled outward from the central chamber, these, too, bathed in radiant lambency—the graceful lines of Illdrassil's boughs and branches extending away through space.

Seeing all the people—Home Guard, Paratechnologists, diplomats, officials—moving through these corridors, Aroganji commented to no one in particular, "The denizens of Tellanon are fortunate to abide in the luminous shadow of such a place. Those who work here, granted the privilege to visit every day, are more so."

Slate nodded with a wide smile. "I could think o' much less agreeable jobs than havin' ta work in such a beauteous temple o' ideals."

Wrindanneth glanced at Slate innocuously and offered, "Like having to toil alongside you in such a place?"

Remaining unperturbed, Slate replied wonderingly, "Are ya readin' my mind, Wrindanneth?"

Continuing as though Wrindanneth and Slate had not spoken, Daerdros explained, "The others have already assembled. We will be the last to join."

Slate nodded. "All eyes'll be on us."

Finishing his thought, albeit immodestly, Wrindanneth added, "As always."

Slate smiled. "As it should be."

Aroganji shook his head. "The only thing that should be is that you both act with dignity and respect. Remember where you are and what is asked of you."

Slate laughed. "I am. Why d'ya think I'm havin' so much fun?"

Wrindanneth raised a finger. "I can answer that."

Aroganji shook his head. "Perhaps you would be better served if you did not."

Wrindanneth dropped his finger with an angelic smile and remained silent.

The crystalline lift finally finished its ascent at the apex of Illdrassil's central stem. Far below, myriad throngs of people moved through the coruscating waves of lights in miniature.

All around, the beams of the sun and the glow of Illdrassil's inner fires appeared brighter, more intense with the completion of their ascension. The very air thrummed with vitality—each individual walked through a luminous sea of sustaining light.

Stepping off the hovering lift, the passage before them sloped gently upward leading directly toward Illdrassil's crown and the fulgent luminosity beyond.

Slate shielded his eyes with one thick hand, squinting as he looked forward. "This place certainly wasn't designed fer Dwarves! It's so bright I'd have about as much luck findin' my way through here as I would findin' an Orc's sense o' compassion!"

Wrindanneth patted him on the back soothingly. "With all the glimmering gold and gems decorating your thanedom, I would expect that you would be the best prepared of us to deal with the overwhelming brightness of Illdrassil's upper reaches."

Slate shook his head. "We may have heaps o' gold and piles o' gems but few glow with a light as strong as this, reflected or imbued. Tha magical fires that light our halls're meant fer eyes used ta tha darkness o' tha undermount, not the full blaze o' tha sun."

Wrindanneth smiled and offered, "But your personalities dazzle nonetheless."

Ignoring his friend's sarcasm, Slate replied, "That they do."

Ushering them onward with a gesture, Daerdros ended further comment with her own. "This way."

Having granted them suitable time to appreciate the unencumbered majesty of Illdrassil's lofty heights, Daerdros's tacit call to carry on was understood and obeyed.

The lucent hallway curved upward around the outer wall of Illdrassil's trunk, still impressive in scale even at her peak. Given the fluid nature of her walls, no doors were visible, only the shifting colors of the walls' interior hinted at the spaces beyond. What those rooms may be or what purpose they might serve were riddles for another time.

For his part, Yip sensed the flows of energy defining and enlivening the space just as he sensed the living beings within and the overarching presence of Illdrassil all around. He also felt an assemblage of resplendent beings ahead, the gathered luminaries of Tellanon's inner circles. Each moment in such a sacrosanct place was a treasure, a gift he would willingly share with any who asked. His task was to ensure that such wonder persevered and was attainable by all.

For his part, Slate's eyes never stopped moving, roving over every surface and detail greedily. There was much inspiration to be had within Illdrassil. One day, perhaps if Brendle favored him, he would be fortunate enough to attempt to replicate some of her beauty in his own thanedom.

Aroganji was overwhelmed. The degree of possibilities, the amount of change and transition here—futures unfolding in a limitless cascade from such a focused nexus—only heightened his appreciation for Illdrassil's wonders. Here destinies were defined and made.

Wrindanneth reveled in so much power, so much energy, manifest in one place. If ever the divine energies had been crystallized and given definite form, it was here within Illdrassil's stalwart bole. If he could somehow learn the nature of this magic along with its actualization, his future would be all the brighter.

Only time would tell.

Daerdros turned, looking over her shoulder and smiled brightly, her grace a welcome accompaniment to that infusing the rarefied air, the soft tones of light playing across her face as she spoke. "We will soon be there."

Ahead, the hallway gradually ended, its outer course defined by the exterior wall finally joining the sweep of the interior. No door was apparent but for those granted leave to pass, the wall only held the semblance of solidity.

Though Yip sensed those gathered ahead, no sounds issued forth through the walls. To his mind's eye, the waves of energy moving through the walls masked the presence of those assembled, an unending waterfall of fluctuating force. He could, however, discern their individual presences and the strength manifest in each. This was to be a meeting of Tellanon's mighty of which these four, his friends and himself included, were in many respects the least.

"I will enter first and announce your arrival. Follow me through and the proceedings will commence."

Always testing, Wrindanneth asked, "And if we don't?"

Daerdros replied matter-of-factly. "Then someone much less tolerant than I will come to fetch you."

Slate's eyebrows raised. "That sounds excitin'!"

Aroganji shook his head. "And altogether not the sort we are seeking."

Yip bowed and motioned forward, putting an end to further discussion. "After you."

Her step as untroubled as the fey air, Daerdros walked forward and disappeared.

Following immediately behind her, Wrindanneth's boots were almost on her heels. Aroganji and Slate walked across the barrier side-by-side, neither overeager, both curious. Yip walked through the field of shimmering light separating them last and was therefore the final one to have his breath taken away.

In every direction, the verdant rolling hills of Tellanon fell away from their height, the city's colors heightened and accentuated by the soft hues of light filtering through Illdrassil's crystalline, nearly translucent walls. From the markets to the gardens, from the byways to the docks, the entirety of the city's organic arrangement was on full display in the morning luminescence, a wondrous patchwork tessellation of inordinate multi-layered complexity and synergistic expression.

Through her walls, Illdrassil revealed herself to them as well from where they gathered within the apex of her trunk. Vast limbs curved up above and below them, capturing the emanations of the sun and the ambient magical energies in full, blinding refulgence—stars born and realized in a blink of the mind's eye.

Cradled within her expansive bole, the room the Four now found themselves within was no less magnificent. Polished surfaces flowed together in perfect harmony with no signs of joints or flaw. The seamless wall, floor, and ceiling, blended together as naturally as the shifting waves of a tropical ocean tide, each capturing and playing with the radiance riding upon its surface in poetic opalescence.

At the room's center, surrounded by a host of Tellanon's elite, a floating representation of the Cabal's desolate planet awaited their attention, as ominous as the room was bright.

All eyes were on them, from the Home Guard stationed discreetly but protectively around the room's periphery to the members of the Protectorate spaced evenly about the Construct's representation of the Cabal's secret bastion.

Aside from Daerdros who now stood with them, other heroes from their past encounters with the Cabal waited for them including Éremon, Eidelion, Spreesprocket, Ruena, EMMA, Yrien, and Alderan. Like the Four, these stalwarts were there to voice their opinions and interpretations of the path ahead should their views be required. Beyond these friends and allies, none of the assembled worthies were known to them directly though the visages of the members of the Protectorate were familiar.

The gathered council members spanned the full extent of Tellanon's people and her interests. Before them, arrayed in their traditional locations, each position marked by a gently shifting aureate glyph on the luminous floor, waited Éremon's twelve peers.

Oroende, his visage lined with years of thoughtful consideration, held his place strongly, his skin radiant in the dazzling light. Inset with gold, gems, and the essence of stardust covering his skin marked his status as Ueralen, leader of the Thelios, the guild of Paratechnologists focused on material transformation and alteration.

Beside him to the right stood Rowena Bowspirit the city's foremost Aeromancer and fleet commander, able to read and shift the currents of wind and air with as much skill and precision as the finest of bards craft and guide an epic ballad. Her expertise in riding the currents on an airship and commanding her peers was only matched by her ability to facilitate in their design.

To Rowena's right stood Dizzywig Paddlepulley, Gnomish Paratechnologist extraordinaire, leader of the Sliced Bread Society, an erudite brain trust dedicated to furthering the degree and sophistication of magical and material comprehension across the breadth and entirety of mundane and mystical realms. Despite his lifelong dedication to Paratechnological research, he dressed without embellishment or obvious physical Paratechnological modification for, unlike many of his peers, he felt that the most remarkable transformations occurred from within. Despite these sentiments, there was, however, one minor exception to this rule. Beneath his robes, partially hidden by the long folds of his cloak as it fell over his shoulders, he wore a bright yellow t-shirt with a rotating three-dimensional image of a loaf of bread with a knife hovering above its surface. As the blade cut through the bread, the SBS's logo appeared beneath the slices in flamboyant calligraphy: "It doesn't get any better!"

To Dizzywig's right stood Jae'elthos, Iyela, Lorekeeper of the Anuvatari, the Children of the Light. His gentle countenance and flowing, silken hair glowed as in moonlight and appeared spun from the silvery radiance of stars. A deep and abiding peace settled about him, untouched by excitement or expectation. Although the room's air was still, his diaphanous robes stirred roused by an unseen breeze, hinting at the rustle of leaves in a soothing wind.

Beside Jae'elthos and to his right, his thick-bodied frame accentuated all the more by Jae'elthos's tall, lissome elegance, stood Vaendoer Thunderhammer, Dur'kazak and thane of the Thunderhammer clan. The Dwarves of the Thunderhammer clan had worked in direct collaboration with the Gnomes of Tellanon for many long centuries on activities that required the highest levels of craftsmanship, skill, and engineering expertise within a given Paratechnological endeavor.

To Vaendoer's right, standing immediately to Éremon's left, and completing the lower circuit of council members stood Whirlygig Sparksocket, his rampant hair and unkempt clothing underscoring the vibrant bustling energy and excitement of his presence even while keeping perfectly still. A thick ocular on a gleaming chain dangled from his neck while a translucent disk displaying an unending stream of numbers and images hovered in the air before him. Whirlygig was the lead Designer and System Administrator of COG, the Construct Organization Group, with direct authority over the Construct and its attendant artificial intelligence subroutines and processes. As such, he and his group governed, managed, and indirectly supervised much of Tellanon's infrastructure, organization, development, and functioning.

To Oroende's left stood Magdalia Miera, preeminent Theurgist, leader of the Light's Grace congregation, her radiant spirit almost as aurorean as Éremon's own. Her ebony hair was streaked with bright white bands that resembled nothing more than persistent flashes of lightning bolts in a dark night sky. The force and strength of her character were readily apparent without need for second sight.

His thick velvet robes billowing fluidly with each minute movement, Borus, Head Magistrate, lead Justicar, and Adjudicator for the people's will and the citizens' ethos, stood solemnly to Magdalia's left. His bald pate was partially covered by a loose, unadorned skullcap and framed by wispy gray hairs, clouds hovering about a shining snow-capped peak. His heavy, dark eyes gazed piercingly forward, full of intelligence tempered by the wisdom of many years, resting above jowls sagging with age but unbowed by time.

A sliver of a man, his alert eyes darting to and fro, fidgeted next to Borus on the left. His actions spoke of someone who would rather be somewhere else, whose business beckoned him urgently despite the import of his present summons. His gaze, however, took in all it surveyed with the zeal of one long imprisoned and starved for interaction only now free to enjoy the pleasures of company. Head of interspecies and interstellar diplomacy, chief facilitator of interstellar commerce, Noumel had the gift of tongues and a knack for setting people and situations at ease even if he himself never appeared to be. Changing weakness to strength, he had turned his apparent physical frailty to his advantage many times bartering deals for the city and her peoples.

To Noumel's left, full of figure and motherly, her rosy cheeks aglow with warm concern, Salia Proventure held her place with all the care and confidence of one welcoming oft requested guests to her home.

Citizen advocate and voice of the community, she put the concerns of her fellow citizens before her own. Mother to all and foe to none, her calling and cause were ensuring that the interests of the people were always at the fore of the city's dealings. Master healer and herbalist, she was known far beyond Tellanon's walls for her ability to cure the ails of those in need.

His long gray hair as disheveled as his simple, ill-kempt robes, Chutefunnel Knobwhistle, head of higher learning, intercollegial linkage and noetic exchange, intellectual prosperity, and citizen enlightenment, stood beguiled to Salia's left. His mind lost in higher order ruminations, his gaze only occasionally returned to the room and his fellow High Council members, although his mind encompassed them all in myriad equations governed by elegant symmetries.

Finally, to Chutefunnel's left and Éremon's immediate right stood Alain Ar'laen, called Brightblade, leader of the Home Guard, Tellanon's Master-at-Arms and principal defender, general, and Champion. Alain's skin shone with a light all its own, even brighter than the unfailing greatsword strapped upon his back. His form appeared fluid and chimeric, transitioning from one possibility to the next even when stable. A rarity even on Tellanon, Alain was an example of Paratechnology taken to its farthest limits. A synthesis of magical technologies and consciousness, Alain had given the body of his birth up in its entirety, merging his intelligence with both the expansive structures of his new form which were derived from his original cognitive structures and those of the Construct, expanding the limits of his physical self and conception, becoming not only a synthetic intelligence formed through the union of man and machine, but a synthetic being whose existence inhabited the boundaries between the real and the artificial, the imagined and the actualized. His body shifted at will and need, intimately linked with the Construct and its full capacities that he may enact and embody the needs of the city and her citizens for their defense and protection. He was the first and foremost of the NUMEN, the prototype for those who came long after, a position taken by choice, his mind not completely artificial unlike many of those who followed.

He was an incarnation of both the past and the future.

Many others, from strategists of the Home Guard, Paratechnologists, strong allies from other races, to representatives of the Keepers—officials, aids, and attendants of secondary but significant importance to those gathered—would assist with the efforts of these few after this strategic meeting. These ancillaries were not in attendance for their roles would unfold after the preliminary strategic direction had been formalized.

"Gathered luminaries, friends, and allies, I present to you the Four of the Flaming Fists, heroes of the realm, advisors to our cause, and agents of our past and future victories!"

"Speak freely and directly, for the Fists will honor you in like manner."

Indicating Aroganji, Wrindanneth, Slate, and Yip with an elegant sweep of her arm, Daerdros intoned, "Please step forward and make yourselves known."

Daerdros's words rang forth with musical resonance, requiring no song or verse to add to their lyrical quality, enveloping those gathered in a powerful wash of emotions, the synthesis of anthem and aria, ballad and verse.

Yip bowed his head humbly. "Yip Chi Chuan of the K'un Lun."

Aroganji followed suit, his vibrant robes flowing as harmoniously as his bow. "Aroganji, Fang Shih of Chang Sen."

Slate beat his gauntleted fist on his shining breastplate. "Slate, Bor'Banna o' tha Flintforge clan. Called Daer'Duin among my kin."

Declining his head slightly, Wrindanneth introduced himself simply as well. "Wrindanneth, Priest of Maeth Onai."

Éremon's powerful voice rang out in salutation, the acoustics of his words altered only slightly by the sound muting qualities of Illdrassil's iridescent walls. "We are privileged to have your company, perseverance, and insight with us, powerful tools augmenting our own, and welcome any assistance and guidance you may be able to provide in the days ahead as we continue to move together in common purpose."

All gathered members of Tellanon's ruling council offered their salutations in the manner of their own kind and inclination. Whether by bow, nod, or other form of recognition, the Four were granted warm, if formalized, welcome and greeting.

For Yip, seeing such an offering by Tellanon's mighty was not the humbling experience that it might have been for some nor did it fill him with pride for his sense of self was not relational. Seeing Tellanon's powerful elite acknowledge their deeds did, however, fill him with joy for it reinforced the Protectorate's commitment to the eradication of an evil far too dangerous to ignore. More importantly, in his eyes, the gesture represented the Protectorate's desire for a future where the possible was actualizable, where people were open to choice without fear, and opportunity of any stripe was dictated by the workings of the mind and imagination rather than the sword.

He did not need to look to his friends to know that similar feelings moved within them.

Here Éremon paused. "The heroic exploits of the Four along with the Home Guard and our respective allies against the Cabal are known to us. The honor they deserve is beyond our means to provide just as the value of the future they have secured is beyond our means to repay. We are not here, however, to reflect upon the past or discuss these concerns for there are more deeds of significance to be done, these with ramifications reaching far beyond Ea'ae's bounds."

"We are gathered here to decide on our future, on the destiny we choose for ourselves and the vision we will create for our progeny."

"We have each had sufficient opportunity to review the complete assessment of the Cabal's pernicious refuge and reflect upon its significance and how we should respond to its discovery."

"Your insight, forethought, and imagination are now required."

"What solution offers the greatest hope?"

"What path presents the brightest morrow?"

"Let us not be judged on this day to have not aspired to the highest of possibilities by those who one day take our place for their position is now ours to assure."

His voice diminished, growing firmer as he continued, "The path of our enemy is clear. In this decision, the clarification of our own path, at least if nothing else, we must now follow the course of our foes and decide."

"The time to choose has come. Our duty is and will always remain to decide guided by wisdom, justice, and benevolence even when such choice would be denied to us."

"What say you?"

"What will you conclude?"

"Where does the course of your thought lead?"

With that call to considered, inspired action, Éremon grew silent and, with him, the entire room.

Into this hush, Yip stepped forward sedately and bowed, one small man before many. "Today you will decide how to counter the Cabal's evil. I cannot know if, in this test of might, we will win or lose."

"Today you will choose a path to combat the evil of the Cabal's ideals. I cannot know if, in this test of vision and principle, we will win or lose."

"I do, however, know that victory is possible for we have succeeded in the past where others deemed impossible."

"So long as the source of the Cabal's might yet abides, so, too, will their evil."

"In this, though we may gain victory on the field of strife, as we do now after so many long years, we may yet have to fight another war when all is settled and appears calm, when those aware of the nature of the battle waged have long since passed and been forgotten."

"If it is human nature to dream, then I imagine a universe where Darkness gives birth to Light."

"While we must move against evil's manifestation, so, too, must we move against evil itself."

"If there is a way, we must move against Ur'Daus, the source of the Cabal's inspiration, lest we repeat the failings of the past and the losses of the future."

The Protectorate stirred at these words, holding their concern in silence.

Finally, when the room settled, Oroende raised his glimmering eyebrows inquisitively. "And how do you propose to accomplish this venture?"

Adding a question of her own, Magdalia Miera asked, "Are you suggesting that we attempt to address this issue concurrently?"

Yip bowed once more. "I merely offer what is and what may be. We are here to define our intent and discuss how we move today and tomorrow."

Unsatisfied, Rowena proffered, "Is this a mission you propose to undertake?"

Yip bowed respectfully once more. "This is a mission we should all consider together openly. If we succeed against the Cabal in the days ahead, then we may be presented with the ideal opportunity to take the next step in the future."

Wishing that everyone knew his own mind, Yip added simply, "This is a mission I will undertake regardless of the actions of this august assembly. This is the mission I have been on since I first set out against the Cabal."

Borus shook his head incredulously, his florid cheeks puffed. "You propose to do as one man what legions, entire worlds, populations, and their allies failed to do in the past?"

Yip shook his head slightly. "I merely propose to share my views, intent, and purpose that we may work together with common cause and purpose."

"Otherwise, I would not be standing before you today as I am."

Alain Ar'laen nodded, the gesture liquid and full of light. "Yip offers wise counsel. We must ever think not only of our next step but the one beyond, of our enemy and our enemy's keeper, of the source and impetus for our foe's power."

"Though we may not come to resolution on this day, nor should we for premature decisions are as dangerous as ill-conceived ones, Yip's concerns are very real. How to respond after our forces have moved against the Cabal should always be in our minds."

Alain Ar'laen bowed to Yip, the gesture as effortless as a breeze and just as ethereal. "Before we discuss these matters, however, we must come to consensus on the strategy to be employed against the Cabal, the enemy before us."

"Before I offer my own recommendation, I would hear yours."

Alain Ar'laen's otherworldly gaze shifted around the room touching each of the members of the High Council along with the gathered members of the Home Guard and Fists.

In response, Vaendoer Thunderhammer's gruff voice rang forth challengingly. "As he so willingly offers his opinion, I would hear Master Chuan's view on how the combined might of Tellanon and her allies should move against the Cabal in their fastness."

Untroubled by Vaendoer's words or tone, Yip stepped forward once more. "Though we face Ur'Daus's might directly, in this effort, as little life should be lost as possible for we have already paid a heavy toll with much more risk yet to bear."

"If Tellanon's defense and the subsequent surveillance of the Cabal's bastion are any indication, then a host of autonomous sentry drones in sufficient numbers should have the capabilities to overrun the Cabal's planet with little risk to our people, our allies, or our interests."

"In reserve, should these drones fail or need additional assistance, allied fleets could teleport in around the Cabal's planet forming a secondary perimeter to counter or capture our foes as required."

"If the host of microscopic drones teleported in first, blanketing the world as they arrived, our ships could safely move into position afterward whether the drones were detected or not."

"Any drones that yet survive from the initial surveillance mission could react in tandem with those staged around the planet's periphery."

"I would not risk moving against the Cabal until we have both amassed a swarm of drones determined to be large enough to overwhelm the planet's defenses, including a mantle of Darkness far beyond the likes of which was seen on Ea'ae, and then capture the planet on its own along with a separate fleet powerful enough to be deemed likewise. With these conditions met, the Cabal should have no means to counter our advance or hope to escape."

Concern for the people of Tellanon in her voice, by way of confirmation, Salia Proventure asked, "You would not engage directly with the enemy pitting our forces against theirs?"

His concern was her own. "Only if necessary. The less loss we take, the brighter our future."

Challenging him once more, Borus intoned, "You speak with surety. How can you be certain this is the most viable path?"

Yip bowed respectfully. "I cannot. I am limited by the extent of my own mind."

"I speak directly as I wish the world to be."

His eyes quickly coming to focus, mental calculations, evaluations, and simulations complete, Chutefunnel Knobwhistle spoke into the ensuing silence simply, curtailing further debate. "I concur with the essence of Yip's proposition."

For those interested in the visualization of his solution, Chute-funnel added, "Pertinent analysis shared along subchannel Delta Naught 01."

Nodding approvingly, Whirlygig Sparksocket said, "This certainly simplifies our discussion."

Much more realized than Yip's basic suggestion, Chutefunnel's optimized strategy presented a complete plan based on a continually refined analysis of myriad simulated eventualities in a series of organically unfolding scenarios built upon the core of Yip's idea—countless calculations and considerations performed and summarized in moments.

Satisfied, for this solution was very much his own, Alain asked, "Have we reached concurrence?"

Scanning the room, a chorus of ayes met his luminous gaze.

Leaning in to whisper at his shoulder, Wrindanneth said to Yip wryly, "That certainly was simpler than I had anticipated."

Watching the proceedings unfold, Yip merely smiled.

DREAMS

Eddies of vapor
swirling past in fleeting waves—
melting snow flies heavenward.

The deliberations continued for some time. Though a viable strategic
framework for their counterattack against the Cabal had been laid out,
the details of implementing that plan, the steps necessary to make it
actionable, had not been fully realized. Determining the ideal course to
most advantageously utilize key resources, guide and frame their
vision, and lever the proper agents became the major push of the
discussions proceeding from those of the initial, formative discussion.

From Eidelion and Spreesprocket to Wrindanneth and Slate, each of
them were asked entire litanies of probing questions on the guidance
and formation of both their past and the proposed initiatives, far more
than Yip had been subjected to in his initial interaction. By speaking
first, Yip had been saved much of the follow-up queries, but not all.

Even so, Wrindanneth, Slate, Aroganji, and Yip, in particular,
received many additional questions for their direct experience of the
Cabal's homeworld, limited as it was, was valuable corroboration of
the drones' findings. Though they only spent minutes on the world's
surface, the number and complexity of the questions posed suggested

they had visited extensively with particular emphasis on deciphering and understanding the whole of the planet from matters strategic to functional, covering the full breadth of its inner and outer workings.

As long as these considerations took, everyone understood that there would be many more to come.

Despite Yip's preliminary suggestion, the subject of Ur'Daus was one of many topics left largely for another day.

By the time they were ready to leave the lustrous chamber, Slate knew firsthand how a fried egg felt. He was certain that if he leaned too far either to the right or left, his brain would slide out his ears.

He was done.

This ordeal was far too much for a free Dwarf of sound mind and body to be voluntarily subjected to without imprisonment.

Better to waste away in a dungeon. Then at least his torture would be physical. Here he could not even see the source of the pain that was being visited upon him.

When at last the business of the day appeared to be nearing completion, the motions of the Protectorate recalling him to the chamber his mind had long since abandoned, unable to hold himself any longer, he shook his head and grumbled under his breath, "There'd better be a good meal after all this!"

Ever in position to catch him at an ill-timed moment, Eidelion placed an understanding hand on his armored shoulder. "There will be food served if you want it, but if it's peace you are after you will need to look elsewhere."

And so he did.

Before they could be cornered by any of the gathered elites, Slate turned to Aroganji and Wrindanneth and said, "If ya're stayin', it'll be without me. I need some air and nourishment in equal measures."

Aroganji smiled reassuringly, sympathetic to Slate's difficulty. Looking to where the members of the Protectorate remained locked in debate after the formal proceedings had reached an end, he knew that some time might pass before anyone wished to seek them out for the councilors' business was now internal. "I think our purpose has been served here for the day."

Looking to each of his friends, Aroganji asked, "If everyone is ready to take their leave?"

"Aye!" Slate answered unnecessarily, choosing the opportunity to push forward his need once more.

Smiling antagonizingly, Wrindanneth said, "I don't know... I think we should stay on a bit longer and make ourselves available for further questions."

"Wrin!" Slate's glare was intense, though his voice was muted so as not to draw attention.

Feigning reluctance, Wrindanneth sighed. "Very well." Squinting his eyes tauntingly, he added under his breath, "But you owe me."

Slate snorted. "Aye! A smack on tha head!"

Wrindanneth indicated the door with his head.

Smiling, Yip stayed in place. "Considering my dietary needs, I will stay and field any questions for us."

Placing one grateful hand on Yip's shoulder, Slate offered his sincere gratitude. "Thanks, Yip. Ya're a saint."

Sending his friends off with a wave, Yip did not reply.

While Aroganji, Wrindanneth, and Slate said their goodbyes, Yip held his position on the room's periphery garnering the attention of any who would have it merely by his presence. This calm stoicism gave Slate the quick exit he craved.

Sensing the Four's eminent departure from where he stood amidst the assembled councilors, Éremon raised a long arm, his voice reaching them clearly without resorting to a yell. "Fare thee well, Fists! The clarity of your vision informs our own!"

Watching his friends depart, understanding what Yip was about, Eidelion came to stand beside him, ready to lend support should any Protectorate call for the perspective of the Guard as well. Joining Eidelion at Yip's side were the other Guard, Daerdros included.

Walking down the glimmering passage toward the translucent lift that would carry them back to Illdrassil's roots, Slate stopped midstride and smacked his forehead, the sound of his open palm's impact echoing down the hallway's walls. "I forgot ta ask Ruena about visitin' Illdrassil's coffers ta select our items!"

Wrindanneth did not halt alongside Slate, his long gait carrying him forward toward the platform. Looking back over his shoulder, he said smoothly. "Not to worry. Seeing that your small brain was melting as it was overloaded by too much stimulation, I did."

His brow furrowed, resolving the contradiction of Wrindanneth's thoughtfulness couched in condescension, Slate gave a brief nod and resumed his walk down the hall unperturbed. "Thank ya, Wrin. That was almost thoughtful o' ya."

Wrindanneth gave a mock bow. "My pleasure."

"When're we goin'?"

Wrindanneth smiled. "As soon as you have completed the last course of your morning feast on the morrow."

Reaching the lift's edge, Slate clapped his hands together excitedly. "Excellent!"

Aroganji stepped out into space, his feet resting firmly on the lift's barely discernible surface, the first to stand on the nearly invisible lift. Addressing both his friends, he asked, "What will you select?"

Wrindanneth shrugged casually. "I will see what calls out to me."

Slate replied similarly, "Though tha thought o' artifacts are excitin', I cannot say there's somethin' in particular I'm pinin' after. I'll have ta see what catches my eye. Perhaps some storied armor or"—he grinned wickedly—"an axe that won't talk back."

Duraeleon's muffled protests could not be heard, but the aggravated jostling within its holster bespoke of his axe's sentiments on the matter.

"Maybe I'll need a few trips ta decide."

"And ya?"

Aroganji remained noncommittal as well. "I cannot say. Perhaps a tome of hidden lore may be of interest, though with access to Tellanon's store of knowledge such an item may be redundant. Perhaps Ruena's guidance will inform my selection."

He shrugged, adding, "Most likely, I will stumble upon an item of worth that I would never have conceived of needing or having."

Slate laughed. "Sounds like we're all in tha same position! No clearer than when we started!"

Wrindanneth shook his head. "And you expected differently?"

"There're few things I can count on with certainty." Slate held up his fingers as he counted off certitudes. "I can count on bein' hungry when others are full. I can count on bein' thirsty when others are slaked."

Here he smiled adding his third and fourth fingers "I can count on us muddyin' waters when they're clear. I can also count on us makin' somethin' that should be simple inta an odyssey fit fer a king!"

Wrindanneth smiled and said simply, "Then tomorrow will be an adventure. Perhaps like no other."

Slate nodded. "All my gear's packed and ready fer tha undertakin'!"

Reaching over his shoulder, he patted Duraeleon reassuringly, adding, "As ready and reliable as my axe!"

Though the Protectorate were not yet ready to speak of Ur'Daus, the Guard held no such compunctions. Available should they be needed, the Guard used the time granted by the Protectorate's ongoing discussions to ply their own questions of Yip.

Spreesprocket, multiple oculars, lenses, and orbs of unknown intent circulating about his brow like spy satellites, spoke first. "Did you have any indication that Ur'Daus's bonds were weakened while on the Cabal's world? "

"In particular, did you sense that the locale would pose a heightened risk if we succeed in our mission as currently proposed?"

Yip spoke slowly after a moment's reflection. "The *yuan-chi* was thin, drawn and wan in that place. With the Cabal's demise and the destruction of the *chi* voids, the *yuan-chi* should return and restore what damage has been done."

"However, until this occurs, those same *chi* voids allow for Ur'Daus's influence to extend far beyond the bounds of the nether realm that confines It."

"I sensed many of these voids. Ur'Daus's influence is great and will remain so after the Cabal's destruction unless countered."

"Without removing these voids, this world will remain a destination for those of evil intent and a source for continued manifestations of Darkness."

Spreesprocket nodded. "It is as I feared."

Daerdros asked simply, "Do you think destroying these voids will be enough to counter Ur'Daus?"

"The destruction of these voids will reinforce the bonds of Ur'Daus's prison, denying It strength and sustenance."

"So long as other voids remain, however, Ur'Daus will continue to have links to our universe, stealing life and potential from it."

"Should we manage to find and seal all of the voids created by the Cabal, somehow managing to destroy the agents of destruction in the process, the risk would remain that others could recreate what the Cabal has done so rashly. All the while, the threat posed by Ur'Daus would remain."

Eidelion's bright eyes darkened as he looked at Yip gravely. "What do you think must be done to rid us of this evil forever?"

"Darkness finds its resolution in Light."

Eidelion bowed his head. "As do we all."

Yip bowed in turn.

Ruena gestured toward the chamber's exit. "Would you care to join us for a meal?"

Aside from those accompanying Yip, members of the Protectorate remained at the room's center, engrossed in dialogue. "I would be honored."

Seeing Yip preparing to depart, Éremon called to him from where he yet stood with his fellow councilors, "Your words and wisdom were well received, Yip. Many thanks to you and your companions."

Looking to Éremon and his fellows, Yip replied loud enough for them all to hear clearly, "Thanks to you all for your open minds and kind hearts. Your clear vision will ensure bright futures for all fortunate enough to live on Ea'ae."

Bowing, he turned and left behind the smiles and acknowledgements of the Protectorate for the company of friends.

The shadows were long by the time Yip reached his quiet, cobbled lane, the bustle and energy of the day given over to the sedate repose of early evening. The tangled lines of limbs, columns of straight trunks, and irregular shapes of cottages intermingled in a maze of shadows beneath his feet as he steadily found his way homeward.

As evening settled across Tellanon, many of her people returned home with him, sharing the remainder of the day with friends and family, bridging periods of absence with conversation, relaxation, and merriment.

For him, the quietude of the streets mirrored the stillness of his mind. The many questions of the Guard had passed, their meal spent in continued wide-ranging discussions of strategy against both Ur'Daus and the Cabal.

In this discourse, as now, he had remained largely silent, only replying as needed when asked. His input was rather one of calm witness, an anchor about which consideration flowed, a presence ensuring focus.

Little more needed to be said for his intent had been expressed and the import of his words felt. From here forward, decisions would be made and actions taken based on his words and those of others.

His desire remained for the result of these deliberations to be as positive a world and as bright a life as possible for those living within it.

Though the arch of discussion may continue onward without his input, the course of action had not yet passed him by.

A MOMENT'S REFLECTION

Intertwined branches
framed by swaying leaves—
beauty defined in space.

"Yip?"

He opened his eyes and rose smoothly from his bedroll. The early morning sunlight transmitted evenly through the arching dome of his glassed room, green and gold luminescence filtered through the overhanging branches of an old oak, a gentle reminder touching his skin, lightly calling him to the day and events to come.

Without looking, he sensed Slate standing in the kitchen, facing him as he spoke, his friend separated by several paces and almost as many walls. With Slate, Aroganji and Wrindanneth sat around the table having just completed their morning repast, prepared for the events of the day.

Soft as the daylight bathing him, Yip replied as he left his room, walking toward where his friends waited, listening, "Yes, Slate?"

"Will ya be joinin' us in tha vaults 'neath Illdrassil?"

By this time, he had bridged the distance between them and greeted his friends with a smile. Understated, shaking his head, Yip responded softly, "I have another journey to make today."

Eager for confirmation, Slate asked, "And ya still don't mind if we take yer choice in tha items as one o' our own?"

Yip smiled warmly and bowed his head in assent. "You are as welcome to it now as you were when I first offered."

Slate clapped both hands together and washed them excitedly. Though nothing had yet been decided, he hoped that he would be the one to receive the choice of items once granted to Yip. "Excellent! Ya're as generous as ya are selfless, Yip!"

Aroganji did not let Yip's aside go without a question of his own. "Where will you go, Yip?"

Again answering simply, he replied, "On a journey of the mind."

Though Yip remained calm and poised as he spoke, Aroganji sensed an unusual gathering of purpose about his friend—the confluence of much energy, resolve, and intent, the release of which would express much dynamism and change. These fluctuations in potentiality left him feeling ill at ease and unsettled.

Despite Yip's innocuous words, there was much at risk here, both to himself and others, just as there was much to be gained.

His brow furrowed in an equal mix of concern and thought, Aroganji pressed, "Care to elaborate?"

With simple, innocuous words, Yip answered, "Whether or not I return, you will have your answer soon enough."

Slate snorted gruffly. "What in tha name o' Brendle's blade are ya hintin' at, Yip? Can ya not give a straight answer or are ya in preparations ta go riddle with a sphinx?"

Not wishing to dissemble, Yip answered directly, "I will return to the homeworld of the Cabal."

"Whatever for, Yip? Can ya not sit back and let others do what needs doin'? Can ya not accept tha role we decided upon?"

"By waiting, an opportunity not accepted may forever be lost."

Slate smacked his forehead full on with the palm of his head, his voice a surly growl. "Ya truly are wishin' ta riddle with tha sphinxes! Or perhaps ya want ta visit some long-lost relatives?"

Aroganji gazed into his friend's eyes deeply, probingly. "Then you put your life at risk for good cause?"

Yip's affirmation was his only reply. "Yes."

Wrindanneth scoffed derisively, his eyes sweeping over Slate and Aroganji in turn, offering the rare positive affirmation. "When has he not?"

Slate shrugged. "There's a first time fer everythin'." Pausing significantly, he added, "And last."

"And these actions will not risk our cause?"

"No."

Wrindanneth frowned with disapproval at the lines of objection from his companions. "Yip has every right to act on his own as he sees fit. It is his life to live, after all. In the days ahead, as our preparations grow more intense, such an opportunity may fall by the wayside. Let him be."

Slate gave a reluctant nod of his head and offered one mailed hand for his friend to take in his own. As Yip shook his proffered hand, he said, "So be it. I wish ya tha best o' luck, Yip."

Turning to Wrindanneth and Aroganji, the conversation a thing of the past, he asked, "Who'd like some pastries fer tha road?"

Aroganji shook his head hoping Yip's journey would not be bittersweet.

Yip left the cottage without hesitation, letting the door close behind him.

Though this might be his last time through the door, he did not look back.

All around, the subtle shifts of morning lit the streetscape in the warm hues of wakening, softening edges in diffuse shades, accentuating forms with bright possibility, lending the mind the opportunity to play across the landscape. Trees appeared more lustrous and vibrant, the movement of leaves lent an inner glow. Buildings shone as with a soft, unexpected inner radiance. The cobbled lane appeared to reflect on a bright future, leading the way tantalizingly forward, any path leading to relucent horizons.

Feeling the joy and reverence of the instant, the radiance of the morning, and the life and living energies that flowed within it, his own immediate future was not so lustrous.

Undeterred, he continued onward light in step, grateful for the moment.

A short walk along the lane under the shade of ancient trees, the sedate motion of the energies within and around them reflecting the gentle movements of their branches, brought him to the entrance to the neighborhood park. The stout, ironshod oaken gate opened onto a pastoral landscape of swaying grasses, old shelter lending trees, and gently sloping hills girded by clear streams.

Walking through the gate, looking off into the distance, he espied a place suitable to his need.

Aroganji could not leave well enough alone. Too much appeared to rest upon his friend's decision.

Watching Yip leave through the front door, a veritable storm of possibilities churned about his friend, the manifest changes of the Wuhsing swirling in his mind's eye. Yip was often at the nexus of such transitions, he seemed to gather change in an unending cloud. But these seemed particularly portentous, a dense haze of flux hinting that much more was potentially at play than he understood.

Always curious, he took it upon himself to investigate.

While Wrindanneth and Slate finished in the house, Aroganji slipped out after his friend, waiting some time for Yip to go ahead. He knew exactly where Yip was going. There was no need for him to hurry. Neither would he be able to avoid detection but he would take the opportunity to talk with his friend once more.

Calling out casually from the threshold, he said, "I have a brief errand. I'll be back shortly so that we can leave on time."

Slate replied from the kitchen, the deep tones of his voice filling hallway with bustling animation and enthusiasm. "Don't be long! We're expected!"

Smiling, Aroganji let the door close behind him.

The neighborhood park was but a short distance ahead. There he would find Yip. There he would get his questions answered. There he would ensure that closure was realized prior to the undertaking of risk.

Slate listened to the door shut behind Aroganji, its wooden frame echoing hollowly along the hallway.

He sensed something was amiss. Whatever was left unspoken, he trusted Aroganji to figure it out.

Of course, one man's problem was another another's opportunity.

Grinning cheerily, he sat back down to the table to begin another course of breakfast.

Eyes flicking briefly to Wrindanneth who now stood by the kitchen counter choosing to manually return dishes to the cabinets to pass the time, he asked, "Care fer another round while we wait?"

DREAM'S REALIZATION

Pink cherry blossoms
drift in the gentle spring breeze—
butterflies without branch.

Walking through the waist-high grass brushing against his legs, Yip approached the hill he saw from the gate, its lone oak sheltering the entirety of the hillocks' top. Eyes set on his destination, his mind encompassed the place.

He was, for the moment, completely alone.

This would change in short order.

He had read Aroganji's intent and knew his friend would be joining him. Aroganji's mind ever sought after resolution and clarity. He would never begrudge his dear friend his questions nor the opportunity for understanding.

There was much yet to be done before he began. He was, however, in no hurry. For his friends, he would gladly wait.

Immediately ahead, the knoll glistened in the morning light, golden sunbeams alight atop its grassy rounded crown, full of promise for the day to come. Framed directly within the rays of luminescence, the broad limbed oak spread its branches outward in verdant profusion.

This spot would do nicely.

Walking upward, the tall grass brushing against his legs, dewdrops leaving flecks of gray on the clean fabric covering his legs, he felt the moist, spongy earth give beneath his feet with each stride.

Would this be the last time he felt the cool morning air against his skin?

Holding out his right hand, he let the tall blades run against the palm of his hand as he strolled upward, in no particular hurry to reach the top, to take his place beneath the tree, to sit one last time within its shade.

Soon, the body would fall away as easily as the morn.

Aroganji crossed the stone-girded threshold, passing through the oaken gate, and entered the bounteous field of Yip's choosing. Eyes scanning the horizon, touching lightly upon the grassy, sparsely wooded hills and the festive streams tumbling at their roots, his search for Yip did not take long.

Between himself and his friend, variegated grasses swayed to an invisible wind, blades bedecked in innumerable lustrous diamonds, resplendent dewdrops not yet surrendered to the morn.

Without having to raise an arm to announce his presence, he knew that his arrival had been observed though Yip's eyes remained closed.

Expecting just such a welcome, he strode forward undeterred.

Taking a place beside Yip's welcoming silence, his shadow joining that of the convoluted oak and intertwining with Yip's, Aroganji stood beside his friend in like quietude for some time. Finally, when the rise and fall of his breath mirrored Yip's, he asked, "What is this truly about, Yip?"

Aroganji did not seek to express or allay his concerns, choosing instead to get to the truth of his friend's perspective without projecting his own.

Yip replied with questions of his own. "What truly is possible, Aroganji? What is the possible when no one mind can contain its totality? What are the limits of perception and of perception's influence? What is change and what can be changed?"

Aroganji remained silent, for these were questions too large for words, too extensive for simple answers.

"What if the aim of every mind was to find out?"

Aroganji smiled, replying, "We would live in a wondrous world."

Yip's reply was just as simple. "We do."

Aroganji returned to the comfortable silence he shared with his friend, not concerned about Slate or Wrindanneth, the impending errands ahead or other demands on his attention for these moments were the most significant of the day.

All else would unfold in time.

Finally, Aroganji asked, "You would give your life to exploration and understanding?"

Yip's gaze brushed his friend's for a moment. "That I have already given as best as I have been able in my own imperfect way."

"Then what?"

"Are the limitations of a man defined by him or something else?"

Aroganji laughed. "You would know better than I, Yip! You have given your life over to extending your limits as much as anyone I have known."

"I would give more."

"You would give your life?"

Now Yip's eyes locked on Aroganji's, the depthless gaze soft and full of warmth. "I already have."

Once more, Aroganji returned to silence, his mind adrift in the spaces between Yip's words—the realms of inner meaning, of implication and innuendo.

Finally returning from the quiet of his mind, Aroganji asked, "How, then, will you act?"

Yip's response was measured, thoughtful, and sure. "Darkness is the perversion of the *yuan-chi*, the universal energy arising from the seamless void of untold potential. Just as Light finds its destruction in Darkness, so, too, does Darkness find its destruction in Light."

Explaining gently to one already familiar with the concepts of energetic expression, he continued, "The expression of the Dragon's Gate is the direct manifestation of the creation of this universal energy from the limitless void of potential."

"Fueled by the mind, generative, celestial energies burst forth consuming their antithesis in radiant Light."

"What would happen if the mind did not direct this moment of creation but instead became it, wholly and totally?"

Aroganji shook his head. "I cannot say."

"What would happen if, in the moment of the generation of *yuan-chi*, the expression of this creation were not dictated by the resources of the mind and body but were instead determined directly by the mind's object, both its source and ultimate objective?"

Aroganji shook his head and did not answer.

"What would happen if a nearly limitless source of Darkness were exposed to such a unifying moment?"

Aroganji opened his mouth to reply but thought better of it.

He had no answer and sensed more was to come.

"What would happen if, in such a moment, the creation of *yuan-chi* were encouraged to continue unabated, flowing forth from the wellspring of the seamless void, unified with actor by body and mind, fueled by its depthless object and limitless source?"

Aroganji thought carefully for some time before finally relinquishing any pretense of apprehension. "I do not know."

Yip nodded in approval, his face bright with a radiant, peaceful smile. "Neither do I."

Ancient, gnarled branches swayed overhead rhythmically in tune with the sedate breeze. Moving in time, the tall grasses waved back and forth, their color only muted by the passage of the tree's shadows above.

Aroganji yet stood beside Yip as he had for some time.

As much as he enjoyed the glorious morning, Aroganji did not know what else to say or do, for he sensed that the time had come to say goodbye.

Unable and as yet unwilling to decide how to proceed, he stood beside his friend in silence.

Finally, he managed weakly, his voice full of unexpected and unbidden emotion, "So this is goodbye?"

As yet, he only vaguely understood Yip's plans with any certainty, but he did discern enough to infer what was to come.

Yip's return to the world of the Cabal was not merely to investigate the lay of the land but also to test another way forward.

Their plans of moving against the Cabal may now take place without Yip for he had found a parallel path, one that, if successful, he believed would be of greater benefit.

Aroganji did not begrudge his friend his freedom or the opportunity it presented. He only lamented his own potential loss. For this he was sad, for the last thing he should feel in the face of such selfless action should be something so small and selfish.

Just as he would have to let his expectations of the future go, so, too, would he have to drop such petty sentiments.

The work of making a better world always began with the self.

And the most positive actions were often selfless.

Reading all of this in Aroganji's eyes, Yip gave his friend some time before replying. "Was I ever here?"

"Will I ever be gone?"

Aroganji laughed.

Yip's reply was so typical, so representative of his friend that he could not resist. A puzzle for an answer, a riddle for a reply.

How else would Yip respond?

Smiling, he bowed deeply to Yip, maintaining his friend's warm gaze with one of his own.

The silent rapport of true, shared companionship would be his farewell.

Bowing in kind, Yip declined his head, bending his body from the waist as he sat, his appreciation palpable.

As Yip rose, returning to his erect posture, Aroganji turned and walked away. In his absence, the grass continued to undulate unimpeded.

Some dreams unrealized, some dreams not yet begun, Yip closed his eyes and let the body fall away.

DARKNESS UNVEILED

Stardust scattered
to the celestial winds.

So many points of light,
which shows the way home?

Yip's incorporeal awareness extended over the park imperceptibly, a haze of awareness spread across the landscape of the mind's eye. Within his perception, the luminous environs of the rolling wooded hills and burbling streams held equal sway with the wash of living energies that suffused the ground and air.

Within this purview, evanescent and all-pervading, an elusive complement to the vibrant *chi*, much like the *yuan-chi* itself, was an awareness like his own, only far more vast and subtle, its presence almost unmarkable due to its sheer scope and purity.

Illdrassil.

This presence was the one he sought, the profound splendor that reinforced and augmented the city's essence, the hidden wellspring of the city's grandeur.

Now he would ask it to do the same to his own.

Opening himself up, letting all barriers and bounds fall, he formed a cohesive vision in his mind of his plans and aspirations along with the means and methods through which he hoped to realize these ambitions.

Within this tapestry of hope, he clearly presented his conception of the way forward and Illdrassil's role in it—one of empowering and enabling, helping bring the daunting within reach, an endower of the possible.

With all this encompassed within his mind, he waited.

In time, Illdrassil stirred.

So vast was this movement, he only realized the transition after some time for many things were yet outside the scope of his awareness.

This movement was Illdrassil's response.

Once begun, the effect was almost instantaneous.

A seething wave of force overtook him, filling him beyond any capacity he ever imagined being able to contain, overtaking the bounds of what he would have defined as his limits, crushing his horizons under a wall of living energies. Unable to restrain the tide, he merely held on as best he could until it subsided.

In time, a period counted in lifetimes but perhaps more accurately judged in seconds, the influx stopped and he knew Illdrassil was done.

The vast presence left him brimming with power surging through his consciousness, leaving him to cope with his limits and frailties, illusions shattered and rebuilt.

Newly redefined by the transference, he adjusted to this new reality, one expanded and pushed beyond the demarcations he had recently known.

Before he could act further, he would need time to recover.

Relaxing as best he could, dispassionately riding the surging waves of force within, the raging torrent seeking to push him apart all the while, he waited, slowly gathering himself for action.

He abided in serenity for some time.

The morning passed around him untroubled.

His pains and difficulties were not its own.

Only when his mind was as still as the morn did he stir.

His essence now calm, he reflected the grasses that swayed, the trees that rocked, and the streams that flowed. Of one mind, in accord within and without, he dwelled in peace for a time, in no hurry to depart.

The future was in no rush to meet him. Nor did his future expect his arrival.

When he had watched long enough, he left the park and its people to their tranquility just as he had reasserted his own.

Visualizing a far different place, he bridged the gap between here and there and was gone.

In his absence, the depression left by the grasses accommodating his presence beneath the ancient tree gradually disappeared, leaving his only traces lost to the wind.

EMPTINESS'S END

Twin skies meet atop
shimmering waters—
Heaven and Earth conjoined.

No easily discernible signs remained of the struggle that had taken place over these desolate plains only a short time before. Tractless and unmarked, the victory they had achieved was lost to the past like so much else.

Gazing deeper, he could yet see subtle traceries of the conflict, but those signs that remained would fade soon enough.

Disembodied, his awareness covered a vast swathe of emptiness, a region filled nonetheless with the memory of what once was and what had so recently transpired.

Wary, he detected no presences or disturbances that would otherwise indicate the area was being monitored or defended in any way after the trap that had ensnared them failed to secure their end. The region was as abandoned by its masters as it was by whatever vibrancy it had once held.

Nonetheless, he remained vigilant lest his initial evaluation prove false.

The movements of the residual energies that persisted were strong, rushing currents feeding the numerous voids running unimpeded through the vacuity of space. Despite this, so unlike his initial experience on Al'Marr, the pull of these voids on his ethereal presence was negligible.

Energy currents passed through his celestial body unhampered, the extent of his awareness maintained by his will, the fullness of energy within untouched.

Though these fluxes did not touch his being, the movement of energy provided him with any number of unerring compasses to follow toward a suitable destination scattered across the dead world.

Choosing the quickest current, the one most likely to lead to the nearest *chi* void, he swooped across the landscape, floating above the devastation, unaffected and at ease. Just as the setting altered little as he progressed, so, too, did his mind.

Poised and ready, alert and at peace, he read the course of his destiny and moved forward undeterred.

There was hope to be had in endings just as there were beginnings to be had in the end.

Speeding across the land, the obsidian basalt passing below in a homogenous blur, he felt numerous irregularities in the distance. These blights were almost as abhorrent as the *chi* voids themselves—seething masses of corruption, abodes of Darkness, and the creatures drawn to it.

These were the outposts of the Cabal, some colossal and seeming without bound, others truncated and clearly delineated—all dens of iniquity. Each was a cancer on an already-diseased world.

A cure for these blights would arrive in short order.

Most of these outposts, from the miniscule to the mighty, were clustered around these singularities and the energies they drained inexorably, moths drawn to their particular noxious flame. These he avoided, risks that need not be tested.

The vortex he sought appeared alone in a desert of isolation, drawing in energy from an immense stretch of unbroken vacuous wilderness. Seething currents of celestial *chi* swirled and frothed about its event horizon before vanishing into oblivion—life's last breath before annihilation.

He would reach this terminus within moments.

Above, the boundless reaches of space stretched away without limit, untouched and untroubled by the events unfolding on one isolated, inconsequential rocky orb.

He felt similarly.

Stopping instantly, his destination within reach, he stared directly into the yawning edge of the abyss. A bright corona of luminescent energies churned in a violent luminous froth around the void's periphery, masking and defining the utter emptiness of the *chi* void within its brilliant heart.

Attempting to gaze beyond this chaotic field, he could see nothing for no energy escaped or expressed itself.

His future, while just as inscrutable, would end instead in brightness.

Though it may express itself in Darkness, his end would be quenched in the fullness of his purpose.

He had sealed the *chi* void on Al'Marr. Here, amidst the desolation, he would obliterate it, destroying the *chi* void and the living ocean of Darkness beyond.

Surging forward without hesitation, his study and preparation complete, he crossed the gap between his mind and the event horizon, igniting his essence as he did so in a blazing coruscation of Light.

Awareness complete, he plunged forward through the portal into the depthless sea of raging Darkness beyond.

THE FULLNESS OF LIGHT

Variegated clouds
bathed in golden light—
the moon ascendant.

Limitless living Darkness enveloped him, a universe of hunger, greedily suffocating his presence, crushing implacably inward. The breadth and potency of Ur'Daus's presence was beyond comprehension and expectation—unspeakable.

A fragile anchor between worlds, his presence bridged the space between the macroverse he knew and the one that imprisoned the terrible Creeping Shadow.

Amidst the utter, implacable Darkness, this tenuous anchor, the portion of him that remained in the world of Light, preserved him, sustained his memory of self, saving him from the utter cessation of oblivion.

Through this conduit he persevered, awash in the totality of ravenous Darkness. With unity of mind and purpose, drawing upon the entirety of the energy reserves granted by Illdrassil, he acted immediately before he, too, was suffocated, engulfed and swallowed forever, igniting the fires of the Dragon's Gate.

A single spark surged and flared, potential burning, expressing itself in Light.

Within the lightless depths, in a realm never touched by Light, the universe exploded in brilliance, empyrean flames fueled hotter and more intense than the highest Heavens.

Within the very substance of living Darkness, Light raged, celestial fury created within Ur'Daus's very essence, the consumer of Light destroyed from within by that which It devoured, unable to quench that which It consumed.

Holy fires fueled by insatiable Darkness, the Light of creation erupted unchecked, burning ever brighter and more intensely. Drawing on every source available, Yip drew in yet more energies from the realms of his birth, his will expanding with his purpose, bridging and drawing through more *chi* voids as the Light razed ever onward and more intensely.

As the universe exploded in impossible holy fires, lumination running rampant and without bound, he gave of himself, for Darkness is but the absence of Light and in Darkness Light finds its beginning.

In Light's presence Darkness and Its attendant Shadows disappear.

When he had given all and could give no more, he gave himself.

ENDINGS

Dust motes tenderly
catch the sun's rays.

Easing sunlight's
journey to the ground.

All across the shattered obsidian planet, among other far-flung blighted worlds, over long-drained edens, on shattered husks scattered throughout the stars, and among the empty reaches between, blinding indescribable Light burst forth, the shimmering afterglow of another dimension, and then disappeared, transient empyreal flashes burning away the rapacious portals into the darkest abyss, consuming the hungry gateways to annihilation.

When the incandescence faded, the once turbulent space around these *chi* voids quieted and was finally still. Within this stillness, energy that had once been pulled and drawn from afar, ravaged within the maw of oblivion, settled.

No longer devoured, torn, or pulled the energy of life rekindled.

Beyond these sealed portals, glimpsed for but the briefest moment, Light burned ever brighter.

With it, a new universe was born.

EPILOGUE

Celebrations

Wind rustling dry fall leaves—
a moment of peace,
hanging by a thread.

WALKING through the city in the clouds, Aroganji looked out at the horizon of clear blue sky. All around, Tellanon was abuzz in excitement with celebrations. Throngs moved through the streets in jubilation for Ea'ae's continued safety and prosperity.

He did not share in the feelings of merriment.

He could not.

His friend was gone.

Focusing outward once more, the great terraces, myriad open spaces, and expansive hanging gardens that covered much of the floating island were left unattended to move and sway in the breeze —a great green mantle granted soft repose while others rejoiced in the streets. Down below and in the skies above, along the island's fringes, airships moved and docked between moors of rope netting gently swayed with the wind, small spiders resting in their delicate webs.

He tried to imagine the city as it would be in Yip's mind's eye—the otherworldly metropolis shimmering like a torch ablaze beneath the noonday sun—men and magic, life and Craft, desire and intention, burning bright over the hillsides, pouring and flowing over the trellises and districts reaching for the sun.

This vision, too, eluded him.

Soon he would be in touch with Master Wei. In time this vision might be restored, if not in Yip then in others.

SPIRITS WERE high as the cool autumn air carried the occasional billowing white cloud overhead or around the floating city. Fall was a time of festivity and anticipation for the coming of winter and the opportunity to rest and recover that the cooler seasons afford.

As a major trade center, the city of Tellanon never truly slowed with the seasons, but as the air cooled and winter storms arose, airship travel within Ea'ae itself diminished, while fewer travelers braved the airways as they took care of more pressing business at home. Even so, citizens appreciated the more moderate pace of fall and winter, whether real or perceived, that the cooler seasons provided.

Of course what was true for most was not true for everyone, and, cold and forlorn, hot and stormy, summer or winter, the life of an adventurer varied little by the season. One quest leads to another, one success leads to further opportunity, and one hunt begins as the last ends.

In the fall, as the seasons paused between the past and future, Aroganji looked out upon his new home wondering where chance would next take him, where circumstance had taken his dear friend. Walking through bustling streets, in front of busy shops selling goods from the world over and far beyond, magical and mundane, past handicrafts and the works of artisans, by hawkers and streetside vendors, he took in the day with less pleasure and aplomb than were his wont, carrying a bundle of goods in his arms, trying to look forward to spending at least a short time home amidst his friends, those that remained, and his studies before setting out on the next endeavor.

Perhaps his friends' good cheer would rekindle his own.

He could always hope.

Rounding the corner to the tree-lined street that led to the house he shared with his companions, he noticed an unusual gathering of power in front of their small cottage. To his eyes, the wards that now surrounded his house looked like intricate smoky symbols floating and shifting slightly in the ether, gray and ominous, filled with hidden meanings and unknown threats.

Standing in the yard looking rather disheveled in his lustrous black great cloak, his frazzled red hair standing on end as power flowed around him, Wrindanneth gazed proudly at their cottage in apparent satisfaction, only looking up as Aroganji approached.

"You can never be too sure, I like to think," said the tall, lanky figure.

"Sure of what?" asked Aroganji.

"Your security, the safety of you and your things," replied Wrin.

"I trust *this* is safe?" asked Aroganji, wondering if his friend's paranoia, Wrin's concern for retaliation and safety after Yip's disappearance, might draw the kind of unwelcome attention they would rather avoid, enemies and local officials included.

They had helped secure the world's future and now Wrindanneth had turned his grand vision on their tiny little cottage, from the cosmic to the domestic…obviously the next logical step.

"Oh yeah, I've got the wards set only to respond to malicious or ill intent. They are perfectly safe."

"This enchantment is within allowable bounds provided by the Abstract?"

"Well…"

"Well what?"

"I haven't gotten confirmation on that yet."

Aroganji shook his head. "Haven't gotten or haven't asked?"

"Yes…"

As he expected. With a reproving half-smile, Aroganji asked, "And what will the neighbors think?"

"They'll never even know the wards are there. Besides, a man's security is better left in his own hands. I know there are several warded homes in our neighborhood."

"But their whole homes aren't warded nor are they warded like this..."

As he walked to the front door, Aroganji unwrapped a wreath of dried vegetables, grains, and flowers from his bundle and placed it securely on the front door. He then placed a large pumpkin and a variegated acorn squash on the small porch by the door to help celebrate the harvest season. With magic, crops grew anytime and anywhere, but the persistence of tradition carried on through the ages.

"Don't worry. I've got the wards set to recognize us. After all we've done for this city, the world at large, and the universe beyond, who would come here after us with hostile intent? If nothing else, this will at least give us some forewarning should someone from our past choose to pay us an unwanted visit."

"As long as it's safe, then we should be fine," replied Aroganji. He would look into the wards in more detail later to be sure. "Let's go inside to try some of these roasted Gnomish turnips I bought along with some Dragon's tears herbal tea. They should be perfect with dinner."

Wrindanneth sighed to himself as he followed Aroganji inside. "Did you happen to buy any cured ham or a nice cut of lamb?"

As Wrindanneth ducked under the eave, Aroganji could not help but smile to himself. Between Wrin's concern for their safety and his unrelenting focus on all things arcane, it was a wonder Wrin did not blow himself and everyone around him up in some wild experiment gone awry. Luckily for Wrin, his friends, and their associates, much of the guesswork involved in learning the subtleties of higher arcana was taken out of his hands due to his erstwhile association with Maeth Onai.

Having a god of magic as your guide made things a bit easier.

Stepping through the doorway, he sniffed and stepped back as a faint plume of smoke wafted through the entry while he peered inside. The stench was so profound that all he could think was that Wrindanneth must be working on some new mystical formula for monster repulsion.

At the same instant, a loud gong rang through the house, so loudly that Aroganji could hear his teapots rattling in the kitchen past the living room and study from the back of the house.

"How d'ya like my new doorbell?" asked Slate as he sauntered around the corner leading to the kitchen from the other side of the room wearing a grease-stained apron.

"Not nearly so much as your new perfume!" moaned Wrin with a sour face as he crested the doorway. "In the name of all that's holy, man, what in the world are you brewing in the kitchen? I'll never be able to go in there to work again. You've probably stained the walls."

"So ya smell it?" Slate brightened as he kneaded his hands together excitedly.

"How could we not?" yelled Wrindanneth. "You silly, bearded Cave Troll! Now I'm going to have to adjust my wards just to get rid of the stench!"

"Stench? What stench? That heavenly aroma is none other than tha finest Dwarven spirits, brewed and distilled from tha most exquisite ingredients this side o' Barad-Dur!"

Wrin and Aroganji groaned as they looked at one another.

Wrindanneth shook his head and muttered under his breath, "Smells like Orc sweat..."

"And how long is it going to take us to scour the smell out of the walls?" sighed Aroganji. "Perhaps I can make some expurgatory emulsions..."

"I may have just the spell..." muttered Wrindanneth as he started to go out behind the house to his research lab to look for the most appropriate ingredients.

"Perhaps we should just open the windows?" offered Aroganji civilly as he moved around the room quickly unfastening each latch and opening the shutters to let in more light and air.

Just then, as Slate muttered a disapproving oath under his breath while turning back toward the kitchen, the house rang out and shuddered with the peel of another even louder gong, followed immediately by a violent *whoop*—the sound of a great volume of air rushing in to fill a newly emptied space.

Aroganji turned to the door with a sinking mixture of surprise and despair, having heard a faint, distinctly child-like "Happy..." before the cacophony began.

"What was that?" asked Aroganji in alarm.

"Was someone at the door?" asked Wrin, bounding quickly back down the stairs while Slate disappeared to the kitchen.

Sighing inwardly, Aroganji slowly turned back to his friend, as a chill, unwanted realization slowly coursed through him. "So just what exactly does your ward do, Wrin?"

"Well…"

"You do know it is the custom in these lands for children to ask for treats on the first day of fall to celebrate the traditional time of harvest? You remember that's partly why I left to go to the market today?"

"Oh! That's today?" replied Wrindanneth innocently with a weak smile, opening the door and looking rather anxiously around the porch, noting the scorch marks where the pumpkin and squash had been.

"Yes," replied Aroganji, his sigh turning into a scowl.

Just then, Slate emerged smiling proudly from the kitchen, two foaming mugs held in his hands.

"Ale fer our guests!" Slate rumbled, looking around in confusion at his friends' expressions and the empty entryway, misconstruing the outrageous cacophony for his new doorbell.

"You see, should one of our enemies try to sneak up on us…" Wrin began.

"Enemies?" offered Aroganji.

"Well, if someone should try to sneak up on us…"

"No one's here?" asked Slate, the disappointment obvious on his face. He had hoped to share his new brew with someone who might actually appreciate the rich flavor and aroma.

"Not anymore," sighed Aroganji.

"Where'd they go?" asked Slate. "I've got just what they need ta lighten their spirits and celebrate tha start o' tha feastin' season!"

Everyone turned toward Wrindanneth, who had just finished his survey of the front porch.

"It works!" he exclaimed, still obviously avoiding the truth of Aroganji's sentiment. "We're safe!"

"Just what does that ward do?" asked Aroganji for the last time, more firmly than his prior admonishment.

Wrindanneth cleared his throat somewhat nervously. "You see, the ward opens up a portal, an extra-dimensional pathway, to one of any number of habitable worlds as cataloged within the Construct's planetary databases," responded Wrindanneth with only a minimum of chagrin.

"Can it take ya ta one o' tha nether realms?" Slate's thick eyebrows furrowed menacingly.

"Well—"

"Can you open another?" asked Aroganji, sternly cutting him off.

"Certainly," began Wrindanneth, slightly offended, as if his skills had somehow been brought into question. "I can recreate a portal along the same energy resonances before they fade..."

"Oh!" he said, looking around at his friends' scowling faces. "Are we going to hunt those miscreants down?"

Aroganji sighed, noting that happiness was the last thing being roused at the moment.

Quickly surveying his companions' faces, he sighed. "Looks like our next adventure is settled, then. Let's go!"

Following Aroganji and Wrindanneth charging out the door, Slate reluctantly set his ale down with a sigh.

Perhaps someone would be fortunate enough to enjoy a drink in his absence.

ALSO BY JOSEPH J. BAILEY

Zombies Forever

The *Unlikely Heroes* series:

Master of the Flying Broom - Sword Saint in Training

Demon Hunter - The Misadventures of a Fallen Holy Knight

Gnomegeddon – The Adventures of an Untried Gnome

Joe is also working on something else but really cannot say more on the matter at present.

HELP SPREAD THE WORD!

I hope you have enjoyed reading this book as much as I enjoyed writing it.

Whether these words transported you to another place, one you enjoyed wholeheartedly, or pushed you away without lasting impression, I would welcome your review wherever you may choose.

If you truly did appreciate this book, feel free to spread the word to your friends, family, and random acquaintances. I would also love for you to visit me at either my website or like me on my Facebook Author's Page.

If you would like to learn about future book releases, please consider signing up for my book announcement newsletter. I promise to use this information judiciously.

Many thanks and happy reading!

Joseph J. Bailey

RÓUCÍ

Assorted poems composed by Yip during his wanderings.

Dawn shrouded hollows
cool beneath the morning clouds.
Clear rays of sunlight
restore the brilliance of fall.

Roseate hues fill
the crisp autumn air.
Leaves crackle underfoot.

Dancing butterflies
kiss the new-risen flowers—
breath of spring alight.

Rain-swept trail glistening
with dewdrops from overnight storms—
traveled by more worms than men.

Verdant, variegated
moss blankets the forest floor.
I bed down for the evening.

Green ferns cloak the steep
mountainside in feathers.
A deer jumps and takes wing.

Cascading blue waves
break on forested ridges
overlooked by Thunder Hill.

Pearlescent white snow
layered upon bare branches.
Trees become coral.

Heady smell of earth,
dirt-encrusted fingernails—
a garden planted.

Large rounded gray rocks
protrude from the clear river—
casting lines, men fish.

Concentric circles,
clear fleeting intertwined rings—
Raindrops on water.

A small bundle of
pulled grasses held in hand
by an eager child—
the earth is ripe for planting.

Splashing through muddy
puddles with each step,
rain falls upward from the ground.

Diffuse silver light
alights on the window sill.
A whippoorwill calls its mate.

Cerulean waves
tumble, roil in succession—
mountains in the morn.

Jagged fractured rocks,
hidden recesses filled with plants—
life's fragile bloom emerges.

Yellow-green leaves strewn
across the sodden trail—
fragmented sunlight aground.

Emerald jewel
suspended from a branch—
a tree frog chirps in the night.

Raindrops murmuring
through the canopy—
below, the ground waits.

From one heavenly
body to another—
the moon shines its light.

Silver-hued moonlight
spills through an open window,
limned by spider webs.

Beneath the shadow
of a sunlit rainbow, a
waterfall flies in splendor.

Waxing silver moon

reflected on a still pond—
frolicking with clouds.

Green columns of light
pierce the canopy.
Boles support the heavens.

Wind whips and whistles
howling through the trees.
Raindrops drum against the roof.

Young hands play in mud
full of bright imagining—
untouched by the dirt.

A man bustles down
the open lane hurriedly,
walked by his two dogs.

Cool sand slips between my toes
as I wade the surf.
A sandpiper pecks for clams.

Shadows sway and dance
on a house's wooden sides
to the season's tune.

Scarlet-orange flames
waver and gambol.
Knees pop or is it the wood?

Backlit by the moon
fine mists descend from above—
I am surrounded by clouds.

Solid gray sweetgum,
round black hollow at the root,

home to dark envisionings.

Layers of mottled green
bridge the ground and sky
above a gurgling stream.

Beneath an old wooden bridge
meanders a still, wide creek
attended by flying birds.

Beacon in the night
clear luminous moonlight—
forest limned in silver.

Water striders flit
amid concentric circles—
suspended 'tween worlds.

Kaleidoscope rims
the overarching blue sky—
autumn leaves in bloom.

Cottonwood seeds flit,
miniscule fibrous white wisps
embraced by spring winds.

Snow falls in the moonlight,
drifting, swirling in air—
motes of starshine alight.

Multihued sunset,
gold sunbeams soar heavenward
arching over purple mounts.

A woodpecker drums
on the boles of trees.
Who echoes your call?

Warm diamonds dance
atop the rippling pond
untouched by the wind.

Lichen-covered rocks
line the embankment
in mottled flakes of gray and green.

Meandering streams
twist and turn serpently—
water wends aground.

Golden sunlight showers
the forest in lustrous light.
Heat burns away fog.

Gray branches laid bare
to the overarching cold.
Wind whistles without home.

Delta spreads outward
fluid capillary paths—
fans without a hand.

Gray ice flows gather
along banks laid bare by fall.
Thoughts still, thawed by time.

Straight roads run between
isolated hamlets
passing curved rivers.

Azure butterfly
flits at ease on the currents—
wingtips touch the sky.

Cool, even misle

shrouds the forest in a haze—
suffused by the green of boughs.

Clear raindrops litter
the pond's black surface—
ripples among the lilies.

Katydids and cicadas
celebrate the night
in a raspy chorus of sound.

Golden sunbeams blaze
bright with the new risen morn—
I can't see uphill.

Ochre sky flushed pink,
gray clouds on the horizon.
Sunset on the bay.

Electric sizzle
passing in cascading waves.
Cicadas at night.

A gray squirrel runs,
erratic across the trail—
I stand and watch, still.

Moss carpets the forest floor,
a lush green cushion
for the fog above.

Ringing static hum
rests lightly in the ears—
the soft sound of silence.

An untouched field draped
in shimmering dew,

broken by the beds of deer.

A black dog lunges
forward in excitement
to the squirrel's peril.

Silvery-blue leaves
sliced by the shadows of trees—
moonlight on the forest floor.

A chipmunk scurries
in and out of its hole
in preparation for fall.

Opening the window,
the smell of moist earth
evokes mem'ries of past rains.

Mountains in the mist
speckled by autumn leaves,
brushed by newborn sun.

Fallen fieldstone walls
ring open plots of land—
keeping out only farmers.

Heavy snowflakes fall
blanketing the forest floor—
blossoms without stem.

An interlaced grid
of variegated landscapes—
Man's activity expressed.

A line of thin clouds
in a graduated sky
parallel the horizon.

Coruscating waves,
light rolls over mossy rocks—
sun touched stream roils on.

A lone gray cabin
perched atop a green knoll
overlooks the sky.

An old apple tree
rests staidly in a hollow,
laid bare save for fruit.

Sunlight diffracted
in golden geometries,
spider webs take form.

Ice flows over rocks,
white crystalline rivulets,
waterfall caught in time.

Pale blue sky, purple clouds
dusted by pink sunrays,
Too bright, I close my eyes.

Lustrous green nimbus,
spring's expression unbound—
emeralds unfurled.

Churning ice-fed stream
cuts around a bend—
coherent turbulence.

Lambent golden dawn,
fierce light unexpected—
full moon broaches trees.

Yelping excitedly,

a dog runs through the copse.
Silent, the rabbit waits.

A squirrel darts
across the wooded lane—
the longest path to safety.

Hills on the horizon
turned blue by the setting sun,
mountains end, sky begins.

Yellow leaves lay flat
on the beaten trail.
Raindrops glisten like jewels.

Fierce winds funnel beneath
an arching stacked stone bridge—
mountain tops, open sky.

Blue mountains emerge
from swirling white mists—
islands amidst the clouds.

Open sky framed by
the fullness of green trees,
a river runs at my feet.

Raindrops glisten on
verdant water-laden trees
illumined by rays of sun.

A warm fire whispers
and pops as dried logs crackle,
burning away night's chill.

Light susurration—
snow falling through the bare wood.

Silence falls in a mute hush.

Water droplets build
gathering on the eave—
rainfall interrupted.

Bare limbs yield and sway,
angling toward the sun—
in search of spring, asleep.

Canvas whips wildly,
parasols take flight.
Dandelions in the breeze.

A woman and man
walk by bundled for winter—
fall's embrace eludes them.

Tree boles and branches,
opening bifurcations—
many halves make a whole.

Silence, broken by
a squirrel skittering on leaves—
roused, a dog gives chase.

Wood cracks and hisses
splitting and releasing fumes—
smoldering, fire warms chill hands.

An ocean of waves
white, tractless, and unbroken,
clouds stretch to the horizon.

Hoo hoo! Hoo hoo!' calls
beseechingly through the wood.
The owl's call echoes my own.

Rough hoary hemlocks
laid bare by the elements
bask in the drear fog.

Unfathomable—
the gulf between stars,
the distance between men.

Trees coated in ice
encased in lucent crystals
adorned for winter.

Swirling leaf descends,
glimpsed afar through mottled boughs—
golden mote in flight.

Heavy dusky clouds
laden with new rain
run aground upon ridges.

Purple and gold flowers
line the forest clearing
accompanied by ferns.

Pelted and soaked by
an unrelenting torrent,
I no longer need to bathe.

I wake, eyes bright, clear
ready and eager.
Who can say when our time ends?

Skipping across clouds
buoyed by cool air,
I am bathed in light.

Defined and described

by a beginning and end,
our lives have meaning.

Ancient chestnut stands—
remnant of ages past,
signpost for the future.

Tired and hungry
worn by the unending road,
I must keep walking.

Scents and hues of flowers
fill the air with vibrancy.
I am washed in spring.

I watch a man eat,
savoring each bite.
His hunger sates mine.

Snow drifts in white waves
overtopping my chest.
I am not eager to swim.

Lively blooming field,
air thick with flowers' bouquet.
Butterfly clouds drift above.

Hoary yellow birch
lord of the rhododendrons,
towering through time.

Framed by crowding trees,
wispy plumes float heavenward,
a river's breath in the morn.

A wood duck paddles
across a fog-laced pond—

black swaths cut through green algae.

Candles flicker with
each steady exhalation—
life's flame so easily snuffed.

Golden lights in the distance,
so clear in the night,
show how far I have yet to go.

Fog-haloed streetlights
limned by the shadows of trees,
expelled breath takes flight.

Mountain stream sheltered
by clustered rhododendron
lost in a green haze.

The art of choosing,
selection among options.
What will you decide?

Tumbled gray rocks flow
leisurely downstream,
passage marked by water's flight.

Layers of moss blanket
the mottled forest floor,
contours hidden beneath green.

A line of footprints
trail away over the sand—
a lonely gull calls.

Covered in pollen
a honeybee lays prone, still.
Flowers blossom unaware.

Two children lean forward,
arms dangling over rail,
following the water's flow.
The stream drifts onward, untouched.

Flying through a storm,
turbulence all around,
rain defines the horizon.

Full moon on the horizon
ochre sunset ahead,
ascent and descent in tune.

Water striders flit
drifting upon the clear rill,
suspended between worlds.

Heavy full moon lays
low in the midnight-blue sky,
forgetful of its zenith.

Rough concentric rings
rotate about a center—
a rock defined by content.

Striations in sand,
successive demarcations
map the ebb and flow of tides.

Butterflies twist and twine
swirling above the field—
sunlight in free flight.

Mountain ranges aflame
ringed by blue-gray haze—
the breath of countless trees.

Bare ashen branches
stripped by eager fall winds—
only a squirrel's nest remains.

Silvery-blue leaves
sliced by the shadows of trees,
moonlight on the forest floor.

Sea and sky commingle
silver joining blue—
corporal spanning sublime.

Moss springs underfoot,
giving and yielding.
Salamander skitters,
gliding over toes.

A cicada killer
swoops from the branches above.
Grasped tightly underneath,
the cicada returns to ground.

Black ghosts shrouded in
billowing gray fog—
the hushed silhouettes of trees.

Interdependent
entangled information—
the universe, alive.

Thoughts arise and fade
stirring of their own accord.
A man is not his thought
just as thoughts are not the man.

GLOSSARY OF TERMS
PEOPLE, PLACES, AND THINGS

Abyss – a general name often used for extradimensional regions home to Daemonic creatures of Darkness and despair. Also called nether realms.

Adamantium – an exceedingly strong magical metal.

Acolyte – an Initiate of the K'un Lun that has shown some attainment but has not yet been accepted as a priest.

Adar – a Paratechnologist from Tellanon.

Adrael the Black – an ancient Black Dragon slain by Ithilieon while wielding Duraeleon.

Aerdos and Aerlyn – Elven twins and heroes from ages long past.

Aerie – a name commonly used for the peaks and summits claimed by Dragons as their homes.

Aeromancy – the study of the air and its currents, the manipulation of its energies, and the fashioning of airships.

Aerya – literally, 'Light' or 'air.' An Elven term for the living energy of the universe. The concept of Aerya encompasses all forms of magical energetic expression in a single totality from the universal source to the personal creation—both *chi* and *yuan-chi*. See also *yuan-chi* and *chi*.

Aerya'ana – literally, 'those who bring the Light.' An elite Elven contingent named in honor of Yip Chi Chuan, trained in the ways of

Light discovered and shared by Yip, commissioned to spread knowledge and sanctity across the cosmos.

Aerya'anan – literally, 'Light Bringer' or 'one who brings the Light.' An Elven name for Yip Chi Chuan.

Aerya Etherum – literally, 'highest air' or 'highest breath.' Alternatively, 'first breath' or 'source of breath.' An Elven term for the source of the Aerya, the formless, boundless Void, source of limitless potential. See also Wuji.

Aeryaology – the study of living creatures that utilize magical energies as the basis of their constitutions.

Aeryasynthetic – a general term used to refer to those entities that utilize magical energies as the basis for their metabolism.

Aeryn – 'tree' in Elven. Also, a large, silver-boled tree named after the legendary Aeryn D'al for its similar, if diminished, appearance.

Aeryn D'al – literally, 'tree lord' in Elven. Also a derivation of 'magic lord' or 'Light lord.' A legendary, highly accomplished race of sentient trees. Original teachers of the Elves on Ea'ae.

Aeryn Sh'al – literally, 'tree heart' in Elven. Also a derivation of 'magic heart.' Enchanted wood sung from the heart of trees by Elven Iyela and fashioned into implements ranging from bows, swords, and armor to household goods like furniture, utensils, and living structures. Stronger than adamantine and able to carry powerful enchantments, the material of choice for Elven-wrought magical artifacts. Sometimes called Witchwood or Weirding Wood by Men.

Afternoon's Shade Inn – an inn in Shady Vale.

Age – any extensive period of time. Typically thought of as representing one thousand years though events of particular significance may also define its limits.

Airship – magically powered ships in as many shapes as the mind can imagine found plying the air currents and trade routes throughout Ea'ae and beyond. See also aeromancy.

Alaeron – a junior Paratechnologist on Tellanon.

Alain Ar'laen – member of Tellanon's guiding Protectorate, leader of the Home Guard, Tellanon's Master-at-Arms and principal defender, general and Champion. Once a man and a famed warrior, now a synthetic being joined with the Construct whose form and presence are owed as much to his imagination and will as his original physical form. First and foremost of the NUMEN. Also called Brightblade.

Aldael – the Indural's name for the Green Run.

Alderan – a guide, ambassador, and lorekeeper of the Elves of Yenaria.

Aleron – Elven noble and lorekeeper. Father to Llyewia. Husband of Nydia.

Allomorph – a being capable of taking on various shapes and guises, potentially augmenting its own intrinsic abilities, while retaining its primary core awareness, sense of self, and intelligence. The Jira S'al Alann are one such example.

Al'Marr – the homeworld of the H'era.

Aluran – literally, 'Green Glade.' The jungle village of the H'era Al'Marr.

Amakar – an ancient volcano located in the Drake Spires.

Anjali mudra – a gesture of salutation with both palms together at the chest.

Anubaraëthi – literally, 'Spawn of the Shadow,' or 'Shadow made manifest.' A general Elven name for greater sentient Daemons. Sometimes called Dread Lords.

Anubavaeri – literally, 'Spawn of the Flame,' or 'Spawn of the Fire.' An Elven name for powerful Daemons of flame.

Anuvaerya – literally, 'Children of the Light.' An Elven name for those Elves who have willingly left the bounds of the body to explore the realms of the mind and spirit. The existence of Anuvaerya is a closely guarded secret, known only to a few Elf-Friends outside the Elven people.

Anuvatali – literally, 'Children of the Dawn,' or 'Children of the New Morn.' An Elven name for the half-Elven children of Men and Elves born on Ea'ae.

Anuvatari – literally, 'Children of the Sun.' An Elven name for those Elves who first came to Ea'ae.

Anuvatari'aliana– literally, 'of one voice with the Children of the Sun' or 'friend-kin of the Children of the Sun.' An Elven name for those people of any race taken in by the Elves and taught something of their ways or those who are trusted and respected as Elf-kin.

Archaeus – the holy sword of Eidelion, forged from the rarified light of the sun, glows white when wielded by one of pure heart. Also known as the White Sword and the Bright Blade. Originally called Erudhaerya by the Elves.

Archfiend – a general name for a Daemon, particularly in reference to powerful Daemons that have usurped dominion over lesser representatives of their own kind.

Archlich – a particularly powerful Lich, often a powerful deceased practitioner of magic. See Lich.

Archmage – a highly accomplished or powerful magician.

ARMED – Allomorphic Recombinatorial Multidimensional Extravehicular Drones. A flexible, multi-faceted, shapechanging drone system invented by Spreesprocket. Also called sentry drones.

Aroganji – a Fang Shih from the lands of Chang Sen. A practitioner of magical proscriptions and formulae and friend to Yip, Wrindanneth, and Slate. Member of the Four.

Ar'thas – literally, 'Black Mountain Orcs.' A tribe of evil Orcs and their allies, hidden deep in the heart of the Drake Spires.

Aruene – desolate continent to the west of Dharia.

Aspect – a fragment of the Construct. Used to perform specialized duties for the larger Construct in Tellanon. Like a hologram, an Aspect is a smaller, self-aware representation of the whole functionality of the Construct contained entirely within the larger system but granted broad freedom, flexibility, and independence. Often given to and used extensively by citizens of Tellanon. Also called a Fragment.

Aurana – the deep-seated mental link shared between the H'era and the H'era D'ur.

Auros the Golden – along with Uzsanthal the Grim and Glaudron the Many Hued, one of the most powerful benevolent Dragons in all of Ea'ae. Father of Azaelle.

Ayle'ine Sea – the western boundary of Dharia. A vast expanse of open water dotted with wild, isolated islands.

Azaelle the Golden – a young golden Dragon of Auros's brood.

Azagothe – a Daemon lord of the nether abyss.

Baërn – literally, 'Berserker's Bane.' A magical ring given to Slate by Hoyt.

Baera – 'Brendle the All-Father' in the tongue of the Dwarves.

Baera'Dur – literally, 'Brendle's bulwark' in the tongue of the Dwarves. Called Dreadnaughts by Men.

Baeradun – a legendary Dwarven hero known to burst into flames.

Ba Duan Jin – the Eight Pieces of Brocade. A widely practiced and highly respected series of *qigong* movements with many associated benefits to health.

Bang tui – leg ties used to secure pants or stockings.

Barnaby Bilantré – a famous craftsman, aeronaut, and world-class aeromancer. Also known as Barney Black Eyes.

Beast Riders of Al'Marr – name for the feline beast riders of the Forlorn Forest who count their mounts as their brothers. Called the H'era in their own tongue.

Beyond – a general term for other dimensions in the multiverse, often in reference to the nether realms. See Abyss.

Blade Master – a highly proficient teacher of hand-to-hand combat in the Home Guard.

Blade Singer – see Caer'collas.

Blaeken Wode – literally, 'dark, bleak, or black wood' in the tongue of Men. An ancient forest on the continent of Kilaeron. Within its reaches, the Keep of Garen Muer houses the seal of Weis'liuhath.

Body of Light – another term for the *jalü*, celestial body, or rainbow body.

Bor'Banna – literally, 'bearded demon.' A name for the Dwarven masters of the axe, imbued by the remnants of power from Brendle's fire.

Borus – Head Magistrate, lead Justicar, and Adjudicator for the city of Tellanon. Member of the Protectorate and famed invoker.

Bot – short for robot, particularly with regard to Paratechnological clockwork devices made by Tinkerers that may or may not manifest synthetic intelligence capable of independent thought.

Braemen – captain of the airship *Shrike*, member of the nomadic R'yn Daer.

Brendle – The All-Father. Dwarven god of the forge and, in the eyes of the Dwarves, the creator of the known universe. More often than not, the brunt of Slate's curses. Called Baera in the tongue of the Dwarves.

Brendle's Flame – see Brendle's Spark.

Brendle's Spark – the remaining embers from Brendle's original flame and forge when Brendle first wrought the universe under hammer, anvil, and flame. The remaining embers even now bring forth life and magic into the universe. Also, the fires at the heart of the Daerdaana'Duin, the Bor'Banna's highest known skill, where the exponent merges directly with Brendle's flames. Also called Brendle's Flame. An analogue to Aerya and *yuan-chi* in Dwarven cosmology.

Brendle's Tears – the finest of Dwarven ales. Reputed to be so wondrous and flavorful that Brendle himself cries tears of joy and amazement with each sip.

Brightblade – see Alain Ar'laen.

Byear – literally, 'heart of flame.' Magical robe once worn by Mandros Gray Beard, famed archmage, now worn by Aroganji. Able to deflect a blade as well as allow full spellcasting, among other wardings.

C^3 – the Cogitation Clarifying Cap. A Gnomish Paratechnological device capable of reading and analyzing both simple and higher-order thought processes. Much more complex, convoluted, and cumbersome than using mind reading spells, the C^3 benefits from a certain Gnomish style and sense of eccentricity. Because of its complexity, convolution, and cumbersomeness, the C^3 is sometimes referred to as the C^6 or, more often, the C^0.

The Cabal –A sinister alliance of dark mages, fallen priests, extradimensional beings, and other creatures of might bent not only on domination but power. Known by many other names including the Order of the Lidded Eye, the Fallen, the Light Fallen, the Order of the Burning Eye, and the Order of the Hooded Gaze. Called Liúxīng Làngrén by the Priests of K'un Lun. Often symbolized by a blazing sigil of a closed eye.

Caelebeor – literally, 'Shadow's Grace' in the tongue of the Elves. A magical ring given to Slate by Hoyt.

Caer'collas – a Q'sharian blade master. Often called Blade Singers by those who watch their masterful interplay of magic and blade work.

Celestial body – see rainbow body, body of light, or *jalü*.

Cersaegian – Liege and eldest of the Fiersayne. Keeper of the Ghrem Weard. An ancient Black Dragon abiding in northern Maeron.

Champion of Light – a general honorific for those who have earned great esteem fighting the forces of Darkness. Also, a title for one of great accomplishment within the Dalaren Ka.

Master Chang – an exalted teacher of the K'un Lun.

Chang Sen – an ancient land of empire and intrigue home to unique ways and traditions found nowhere else in Ea'ae. Homeland to Aroganji and the Fang Shih along with Yip Chi Chuan and the K'un Lun.

Chen-jen – a true human being. Seen as the ideal figure in philosophical and religious Taoism. Chen-jen refers to someone who has apprehended the truth within herself and thereby attained the Tao.

Chi – *Qi*; breath, air, or vapor of particular significance in Taoism and Eastern medicine. From a Taoist perspective, the *chi* is the vital energy or life force that enlivens and pervades all things. *Chi gung—chi kung* or *qigong*—are exercises to build and strengthen *chi* flow. Along with *shen* and *ching*, one of the Three Treasures essential to human life. A less subtle and refined form of the *yuan-chi*, the universal potential. The fire that does not burn.

Chih-jen – a perfected human being. Another term describing an ideal person. A Chih-jen has realized unity with the Tao and is free of all concepts and limitations.

Ching – *Jing*; the germ or source of life. Along with the breath or vital energy (*chi*) and the mind or consciousness (*shen*), one of the life forces essential for the preservation and prolongation of life in the Taoist view.

Chuan – *Quan*; Fist.

Chutefunnel Knobwhistle – member of Tellanon's governing Protectorate, head of higher learning, intercollegial understanding, cross-communication, and numenal exchange, facilitator of intellectual prosperity, and citizen enlightenment.

Ciërna – literally, 'vision of the world to be' in the tongue of the Elves. An expression encompassing and embodying both how one would hope the world will unfold and arise, either individually or as a collective, and what may be required for the realization and actualization of this reality.

Circle – a powerful ritual magic employed by the leaders of Tellanon as a last resort. Used to invoke the Loel'dara.

Class M Fire – a general fire category used by Paratechnologists to describe fires of magical origin. There are multiple subtypes depending upon source, intensity, and required quenching response.

Cletus – Hoyt's pet Fairy Dragon.

Clockwork – a general name for a particular branch or type of Paratechnology focusing on magically animated contraptions of any shape, size, and function often resembling machines and robots but not limited to any specific shape. A particular specialty of Gnomish Paratechnological Tinkerers.

Coerdaerya – literally 'partner in Light' in the tongue of the Elves. A term used to describe two individuals bound together inextricably by *ciërna*, common vision, and common love.

COG – the Construct Organization Group on the island of Tellanon. The Paratechnologists in COG have direct responsibility over the Construct and its attendant artificial intelligence subroutines including the various Aspects and other specialized intelligence engines in addition to the management of the Construct's subordinate functions.

Common – see Common Tongue.

Common Tongue – a universal language used across Ea'ae to facilitate nonmagical communication. Also called Common.

The Construct – a powerful, centralized, multi-faceted sentient intelligence created by the Paratechnologists used to oversee, understand, envision, and facilitate activities in Tellanon. Administered and overseen by COG.

The Council – a secretive, informal band of wizards, priests, druids, and other wielders of arcane power from many different races focused on ensuring Ea'ae's continued safety and prosperity. Sometimes called the Council of Light.

Although an entirely different body, the ruling Protectorate of Tellanon is also referred to as the council or High Council.

The Council of Light – see the council.

Cozy Cabbage Inn – an inn in Tellanon known for its Gnomish delicacies.

Craft – higher magical skills. An umbrella term inclusive of various branches of magic including unique talents and abilities native to particular races, guilds, and tribes.

Cycles – the Elven equivalent for the lunar year. Based as much on the turning and changing of seasons and the ebb and flow of life as

Ea'ae's revolution around the sun. Called Soerlyn in the tongue of Elves.

D'al – 'Lord' in Elven.

Daeja – a trade city in central Var'Kera.

Daemon – a general name for extradimensional creatures with hostile intent or for those otherworldly creatures that feed and prey upon the energies of the living. Also called Infernals.

Daerdros – lieutenant of the Home Guard and Master at Arms. A Caer'collas, a Q'sharian blade master.

Daerdaana'Duin – literally, 'to become the heart of fire' or 'to become the heart of the forge.' One of the highest skills of the Bor'Banna, wherein the practitioner wreaths himself in the flames of Brendle's forge, becoming a direct manifestation of Brendle's power and one with its heat, energy, and vitality. In times of old, these warriors cloaked themselves in flames, striking down foes directly with Brendle's might. See Brendle's Spark.

Daer'Duin – literally, 'heart of fire' or 'heart of the forge.' Given Dwarven name for Slate Flintforge.

Dagron Iron Beard – a famous Dwarven Dur'kazak of old.

Dalare – 'Light' or 'One Light' in the tongue of Tol Aeron.

Dalaren Ka – the 'Knights of the One Light.' A chivalrous order whose members follow the ways of the Dalaren Mere, the Light's Path. Guardians of the Star of Elendial.

Dalaren Mere – the 'Light's Path.' The way of chivalry, faith, and the sword through the expression of the Light of Life.

Darkness – a general term for those beings opposed to the Light and Life it engenders and who would subvert, pervert, or otherwise mar Its presence and manifestation. Also a general term for the corruption of the energy of life, the Light, itself.

Dauren'Kas – 'the Bringers of Light.' A name taken by those Shaur'Daus who bring forth the Light of creation to negate the energy voids and Darkness brought forth by Ur'Daus and Its minions.

Dawrac di Gaydial – an alien Paratechnologist resembling an Ogre composed largely of stone and crystal.

Delving – a general name for any Dwarven city or outpost. See also undermount.

Deur Spricken Sprack – Gnomish for 'the Omnispark.' See also Phlogiston and Omnispark.

Dharia – the largest continent on the world of Ea'ae.

Dharma – cosmic law or truth.

Dhwer'werde – literally, 'Fate's Door' or 'Fated Forest.' A cursed forest surrounding the lands of Taerris'thule.

Dhyana mudra – a meditation *mudra*. To form the *mudra*, two hands are placed on the lap, right hand on left with fingers fully stretched and the palms facing upwards.

Diaspora – a general name for the large-scale exodus of various races of humanity from Ea'ae with the development of *faerviage*. Although not native to Ea'ae, Elves participated in these departures alongside Men, Dwarves, Gnomes, and other sentient races of Ea'ae. Many of those people who left have since reestablished contact with Ea'ae thereby encouraging interstellar trade.

DISCO – Daemonic Irradiating Stroboscopic Catastrophe Orb. A multifaceted Paratechnological orb capable of emitting multiple streams of high intensity magically amplified light suitable for the destruction of extradimensional creatures of Darkness...and dancing

Dizzywig Paddlepulley – member of Tellanon's Protectorate, Gnomish Paratechnologist extraordinaire, and leader of the Sliced Bread Society.

Doerdaana'Duin – literally, 'the dance of the heart of fire' or 'to dance in the heart of the forge.' One form of Dwarven axe work known for its fluid strikes and counters, commonly used by particularly adept Bor'Banna.

D'orauk managua al'zurka – literally, 'may your blood flow strong and pure.' A Dracodaeran expression of well-wishing for health and vitality, strength, and power. Often expressed at times of parting.

Dracodaera – a race of humanoid Dragon-kin. Hunters of Daemons and other creatures of Darkness. Originators of the Shaur'Daus.

Dracodin – an extraplanar being of some power resembling a humanoid Dragon.

Dragonflight – a group of Dragons living and moving together.

Dragons – along with the Aeryn D'al, one of the oldest races of Ea'ae. Steeped in magic and power, Dragons are feared by all who cross their path. As complex as they are storied, Dragons are as diverse as their characters and can wield power only rivaled by the gods themselves.

The Dragon's Gate – the way of energy creation, concentration, and direction taught to Yip by Azaelle the Golden.

Drake – Dragon.

The Drake Spires – also the Spine of the World. A series of lofty peaks running down the center of the Dharian continent. Named after the many Dragon lairs and aeries scattered throughout its heights. Ancestral home of the Yeren people.

Dread Lord – a general name for higher order, more powerful Daemons granted intelligence and power far beyond their peers. Called Anubaraëthi, Children of the Shadow, by Elves.

Dreadnaught – a Dwarven warrior specializing in heavy combat. Utilizing enchanted, rune-etched full plate armor along with two-handed axes, hammers, and maces, Dreadnaughts earn their place at the fore of the battlefield by fighting against the most implacable foes. Famous as much for their rallying battle cries and songs along with their fear inducing chants and dirges as their blades. Called Baera'Dur in the tongue of Dwarves.

Dread Steed – the otherworldly flying steeds of the Fyrskal.

Dream Stealer – Wrindanneth's own name for Maeth Onai. A reference to Maeth coming to Wrindanneth in dreams to partake of the choicest lore uncovered or discovered during his travels and research.

Drogu – an Orcish commander.

Drothman – a famous Dwarven hero.

Druids – protectors of the wilds, guardians of nature, and lovers of freedom. First students of the Indural.

Dunédâne – literally, 'deep delver.' Name for the Dwarves among their own kind and the Karadüm.

Dûnedar – a Dwarf from Slate's hold.

Duraeleon – 'The Light Bringer,' bane of Adrael the Black, ancient axe of Ithilieon. Wielded by Slate Flintforge.

Durden – literally, 'valiant heart.' A Dwarven rune that serves to protect against fear and indecision when properly enchanted.

Durin – a famous Dwarven hero from times of yore.

Dur'kazak – literally, 'fire shaper.' A Dwarven master smith skilled in the art and craft of metallurgy, elemental magics, and rune crafting known as Karaduen.

Durnok – literally, 'possibility reader.' One skilled in the reading and interpretation of possibility and chance, probable futures, cause and effect, and the outcomes of events. Often used as trackers, mercenaries, bounty hunters, and assassins.

Duuna'Dan – literally, 'rocks of the father.' The Dwarven name for the Green Run. The old, rounded hills, worn mountains, and boulders of the Duuna'Dan are thought to be the original handiwork of Brendle as he formed Ea'ae from the Void with the careful molding of his hands. Although no longer under their control, many Dwarven mining communities and outposts still dot the wilds in this region.

Duurn'Laden – a large northern Dwarven delving known for the depths and richness of its mines, the skill of its Dur'kazak and the quality of their craftsmanship.

Dwarves – along with Elves, Gnomes, and Men, one of the four most prominent races on Ea'ae. Dwarves are short, hearty, and solidly built and known for their ability to work metal. They excel at reading the earth and mining. Their keen knowledge of metals and runes allows for the creation of powerful works of Craft. Also called Dunédâne.

Ea'ae – 'The world.' Home to magical creatures and races of many shapes, cultures, and forms.

Echoing Fist – see Pai-lien Touch.

Ectoplasmic Reconnaissance Goggles – Gnomish Paratechnological visual enhancement device allowing the viewing and analysis of supernatural energies. Commonly referred to as ERG's.

EGAD – see the Every Gnome's Anti-Intelligence Device.

Eidelion – knight-captain and officer of the Tellanon Home Guard, leader of the Light's Guard, paladin of the Light, initiate of the Dalaren Ka, bane of the wicked, and wielder of Archaeus the White Sword. Known as Night's Bane, True Heart, and Dawn's Light.

Eiryna – a particularly fleet and agile Elven airship.

El'alen – literally, 'old home.' The Elven name for the Green Run. Named after the ancestral homes of their allies of old, the Dwarves.

Eldre'gheu – literally, 'old god.' One of the fourteen seals protecting Ea'ae from extradimensional incursion. Also the temple to the god once serving as the focal point of Taerris'thule.

Elf-friends – see Elf-kin or Anuvatari'aliana.

Elf-kin – Those people of any race taken in by the Elves and taught something of their ways. Sometimes called Elf-friends or Anuvatari'aliana in the tongue of the Elves.

Elixir field – energy fields in the body. See *tan t'ien*.

Elves – a fey race at home among the trees and dells of Ea'ae. Elves are a race of great Craft and knowledge that made peace with the land long before the coming of Men and Dwarves and many other sentient races. It is said that magic is the lifeblood of the Elves. Often called Lords of the Wood or Tree Singers by Men, although not all Elves are indeed Iyela. Those Elves on Ea'ae are the Anuvatari.

Embodied Cloven Crystallization of Refined Essence – A sentient crystalline entity with significant psychic ability. Also a well-respected Paratechnologist.

EMMA – a NUMEN serving Tellanon. Short for Energetic Mapping, Monitoring, and Analysis. EMMA's specialization is developing predictive models to visualize the magical energy currents flowing across Ea'ae.

Empen Wastes – coastal wetland wilderness of west-central Dharia composed of bogs, fens, swamps, lowland forests, and associated rivers, deltas, islands, and lakes. A vast, largely uninhabited region home to fey creatures and unusual beasts.

The Enemy – Ur'Daus, the Darkness between dimensions. Also known as the Creeping Shadow, Destroyer of Light, the Umbral Lord, the Devourer of Worlds, among many other names and curses.

ENNIS – see Epistemic Noetic Numenetic Integrating Summator.

Epistemic Noetic Numenetic Integrating Summator – a multifunctional Gnomish device with capabilities ranging from measurement and systematic evaluation of phenomena, data analysis, computation, and communication to independent reasoning, learning aid, and thought transference. Also called ENNIS for short.

Éremon – Exarch of Tellanon, august Consul of the ruling Protectorate, Fifth of Thirteen.

ERG – see Ectoplasmic Reconnaissance Goggles.

Erudhluin – literally, 'Heaven's Home.' One of many sacred groves tended and held sacred by Elven Iyela.

Erudhaerya – literally, 'Heaven's Light' in the tongue of the Elves. One of many names for the White Sword Archaeus.

Essence – the essential energies. The energies of life and magic and the source of their origination, especially when viewed wholistically.

Eyrdeas – the White Blade of Morn. The storied sword of Maeven D'lanaran. Called Taliaerya, Morning's Light or Dawn's Light, among the Elves.

Every Gnome's Anti-Intelligence Clandestine Apparatus version 3.1, Corvette Class – see the Every Gnome's Anti-Intelligence Device. Also EGAD.

Every Gnome's Anti-Intelligence Device – a Paratechnological defensive system suitable for espionage, surveillance, and camouflage added to items ranging in size from personal armor to airships. The Every Gnome's Anti-Intelligence Device replicates the surrounding environmental variables and superimposes them over the object protected by the defensive system rendering it indistinguishable from its surroundings. Sometimes referred to as EGAD or, more specifically and to add to the general air of confusion around Gnomish devices, as the Every Gnome's Anti-Intelligence Clandestine Apparatus version 3.1, Corvette Class.

Faerviage – magical voyage. A name for the magical ships capable of interdimensional and interstellar travel. Ships vary in form and function based on magical technology, need, and culture.

Fa jin – also sometimes called '*fa jing*'; a sudden wave of energy that surges through the exponent's body and into an opponent. A spontaneous energy release; to issue and discharge power.

Fallen – the Cabal or Liúxīng Làngrén.

Fang Shih – literally, 'a master of prescriptions'; a magician in Chang Sen. Traditionally, the precursor of Taoist sages and priests skilled in the use of various supramundane arts including astrology, astronomy, spirit healing, prophecy, geomancy, arts of love, the use of talismans and drugs, exercises for prolonging life, and enlisting the aid of gods.

Fang Shu – magical arts, especially as practiced by the Fang Shih.

Far travel – see traveling.

Fay Long – the Celestial Courtyard, highest peak in the K'un Lun.

Fiersayne – the brood and broodmates of Cersaegian.

The Fists – see the Flaming Fists.

Fizzlemiz – a Gnomish Paratechnologist. One of the foremost experts on alien technologies among the Paratechnologists.

The Flaming Fists – an honorific name granted to the adventuring band composed of Aroganji, Wrindanneth, Slate, and Yip. Sometimes called the Four, the Fists, the Four of the Flaming Fists, among other honorifics.

Forlorn Forest – the Emerald Jungle. A vast wilderness adjacent to Jenyuan Shulin and the Drake Spires. A region largely unknown and unexplored by most races. Home to the H'era.

Four Lands – a general reference to the four principle continents of Ea'ae. Although there are many smaller islands and land masses scattered across Ea'ae, Dharia, Maeron, Aruene, and Kilaeron are the largest and most prominent.

The Four – see the Flaming Fists.

Fraeü – literally, 'shadow's heart.' Magical robe once worn by Mandros Gray Beard, famed Archmage, now worn by Wrindanneth. Able to deflect a blade as well as allow full spellcasting, among other wardings.

Fragment – another name for an Aspect. A personalized portion of the Construct assigned to and intended to assist citizens of Tellanon in various capacities.

Freyda – Brendle's wife. Known for her patience and virtue.

Fria al'Othra – literally, 'eyes of true vision.' An Elven term for the universal perspective of the Iyela.

Fu – literally, 'return.' Returning to the root or source, the Tao. In Taoist meditative practice this return is synonymous with realization. The perception of the firmament from which the dynamic energy processes of *chi* flow, emerge, and return. An experience of the primal Emptiness or spacious void expressing the fundamental unity and equality of all things. See also Wuji and Taiji.

Fueron Mountains – a range of southern mountains near the city of Taerris'thule.

Fu-lu – Magical talismans, especially strips of paper, metal, or bamboo inscribed with symbols for protection employed by the Fang Shih.

Fyrskal – Guardians of the seal of Mihtig'leht and founders of Morowen. A chivalrous order of ages past that held to the ways and teachings of the Light.

Gaesia – sea-covered homeworld of the Jira S'al Alann.

Garen Muer – an ancient keep located in the heart of the Blaeken Wode.

Ghrem Weard – a common name for the nearly impenetrable northern cliff boundary of Maeron.

Gideon Goldsprocket – Flight Master of Tellanon. A Paratechnologist skilled in the ways of *faerviage*.

Gil-alan – a member of the Home Guard.

Gilaethe – literally, 'the light born.' Son of Nienael and a Wyaera of Tueran.

Gnomes – a race of short stature but of broad mind known for their creativity, imagination, and Paratechnological aptitude. Originators of Paratechnology, famed Tinkerers, often unable to leave well enough alone. Distant relatives of Dwarves.

Gnomeproof – a Dwarven colloquialism for foolproof.

Goran – a forest giant skilled in the ways of the Indural.

Gorthäk – a shaman of the Ar'thas.

Göerden – an armsman of some repute aboard the *Shrike*.

Grast – an evil Orcish tribal leader.

The Green Run – Man's name for the wilds of old, rounded mountains and ancient deciduous forests spanning the region from the western feet of the Drake Spires to eastern Var'Kera. Untamed and largely unsettled, this region is home to ruins, outposts, and creatures of every description. Called Duuna'Dan by the Dwarves, Aldael by the Indural, and El'alen by the Elves.

Gristnast – an Orcish sentry in the desolate wastes of Maeron.

Gromdek – a tribe of Orcs known for their skilled magic-wielding shaman.

Gruendan Weirndan – Champion of the Gleaming Blade, knight and commander of the Fyrskal.

Gründen – Thane of the Flintforge Clan. Kinsman of Slate.

Guai Lo – a Lung-wang, or Dragon king, from Chang Sen's past. Many artifacts of power have been made from his remains as well as his horde.

Guàn – monastery.

Guernden – a magical Dwarven hand cannon similar in appearance to an ornate rifle. Sometimes referred to as Dragon's Gullets for the fire contained in their bellies.

Günda – literally, 'Dwarf excrement.' An Orcish curse.

Guor' Uenaqe – literally, 'forge of our spirits.' Name for the harsh, volcanic homeworld of the Dracodaera.

Gyarxon – a race of psychic warriors who use their mental powers to travel interdimensionally seeking conquest.

Halls of Choosing – special locations spread throughout Tellanon that allow the visitor to select the pocket dimension of their choice to visit.

The Heart of Yere – a blazing red stone talisman that protects and guides its bearer. An artifact of the Yerens' and a piece of their heart and home.

Hellforge – a Daemonic smithy capable of producing fell items of great power.

Hellforged – a reference to Daemonic items made in a Hellforge. Most commonly weapons, armor, or arcane artifacts.

Henosis – a theurgical practice whose ultimate aim is unification with and expression of the Divine Light.

H'era – short for H'era Al'Marr.

H'era Al'Marr – the name of the beast riders of Al'Marr in their own tongue. H'era means 'children of the twin skies,' a reference both to the green canopy of their jungle home beneath the blue skies of Ea'ae and in remembrance of their homeworld of Al'Marr. Al'Marr means 'green sea.' Taken together, their name shows how the H'era find their compass and direction somewhere between the earth below and sky above their home—current and remembered.

H'era D'ur – 'Brother of the H'era.' Name of the sentient cat mounts with whom the H'era share a deep mental affinity, the so-called Aurana. Treated with much honor and respect, these mounts are an integral part of the H'era family groups and are considered an equal member in H'era society.

High Conservator – leader of the Dalaren Ka.

High Council – Tellanon's governing body of thirteen Paratechnologists and citizen representatives. Sometimes referred to as the council. See also Protectorate.

Holder of Secrets – a keeper of esoteric knowledge within the Home Guard. Also Keeper of Secrets.

The Home Guard – elite squadron of Tellanon's defenders and champions led by Eidelion.

The Home Reach – the fortress of the Home Guard located in Tellanon's center, part of Illdrassil.

Homeworld – planet of origin or primary habitation for a race, species, or group.

Hoyt – shop owner, gossip, and guide in Tellanon. Purveyor of fine goods, staples, information, and oddities. Wizard of some repute. Most often seen in his store, Hoyt's – Oddities, Found Goods, and Sundries.

Hröthe – literally, 'divine healing.' A Dwarven Karaduen offering a one-time boon of healing from a grievous or debilitating wound.

Hsiang Lung – a lush mountain range in eastern Chang Sen bordering the Q'ia Shan Sea. Home to Xian Shi, the school of the Fang Shih.

Hui-yin – an energy center located at the perineum called the Gate of Mortality and the Door of Life and Death. The seat of *ching*, the generative reproductive energy.

Human – see humanity. A general name for all sentient races on Ea'ae.

Humanity – a general name for all humanoid races on Ea'ae. Men, Dwarves, Gnomes, Indural, and other sentient races of Ea'ae are included under this broad description. As a naturalized race, Elves, too, are considered part of humanity although they are genetically distinct from the other humanoid races.

Humbol – a traveling merchant and airman. Friend and former adventuring partner of Hoyt. Captain and owner of the airship the *Rare Aer*.

Hürn – literally, 'evil's bane.' A Dwarven rune used for protection from evil.

Iera – literally, 'brother of the heart' in the tongue of the H'era. Uuraja's H'era D'ur.

Ilidian – Watcher of the Drake Spires.

I'ldaerya J'al Ishentaré – literally, 'the art of unbroken change.' An art unique to the Jira S'al Alann that encompasses an unending range of physical and magical transformations in response both to an opponent and the energies expressed by past and present teachers and adversaries.

Illdrassil – literally, 'Spire of the Heavens' or 'Tree of Heaven' in the Old Tongue of Men. The home of the High Council, Tellanon's ruling body and the Home Guard. A vast repository of magical energies that empowers the city in the sky.

Illendial – the North Star in the tongue of the Elves. Sometimes used as an invocation to guide and protect the spirit from assailment.

Imperial – centralized unit of currency used in many lands across Ea'ae.

Incirrinaen – highly intelligent cephalopodic organisms widely known for their heightened cognitive and mental abilities.

Indural – one trained in the magic, lore, and woodcraft of the forest giants.

Infernal – a Daemon.

Initiate – an ascetic just accepted into the K'un Lun.

Irielia – an Elven city in south central Dharia.

Ithil'alen – literally 'elden home' or 'eldritch home.' Elven territory in northeastern Dharia.

Ithilieon – a legendary Elven hero. Wielder of Duraeleon and slayer of Adrael.

Iyela – an Elven lorekeeper, wonder worker, tree singer, and shaper. Known for their ability to commune with the spirit of trees and request the boon of their heartwood, the Aeryn Sh'al. Called Tree Singers by Men.

Jae'elthos – member of Tellanon's Protectorate, Iyela, Lorekeeper of the Anuvatari, the Children of the Light.

Ja'lal – literally, 'dearest one' in the tongue of the H'era.

Jalü – a rainbow body. A spiritual attainment allowing for the direct transition and ascendancy of the body to Light and Mind. Also called celestial body, rainbow body, or body of light.

Jarvis Jenkins – a tailor of some repute in Tellanon known for his functional clothing, craftsmanship, and ability to meet his customers' expectations for unique garment properties.

Jenkins – a trader and merchant from Shady Vale.

Jenta – literally, 'to call' in the tongue of the H'era. To call oneself is *jentara*. To call a group or a people is *jentaro*.

Jenyuan Shulin – literally, 'forbidden garden forest.' The Forbidden Forest, ancestral home of the Aeryn D'al. See also Noes Al'amroth.

Jian Lu – one of Aroganji's teachers at the arcane institution Xian Shi in Chang Sen.

Jin – literally, 'power.' Also an opponent's experience of the energy manifest by another.

Jing – *ching*; literally, 'essence.' Along with *qi* and *shen*, it is considered one of the Three Treasures. *Jing* provides the material basis and fuel for the body and transmits genetic heritage.

Jing luo – the invisible system of channels or pathways through which *qi* circulates throughout the body. Also sometimes referred to as vessels and collaterals, conduits or meridians.

Jira S'al Alann – literally, 'People of the Imagining.' A race of changelings able to shift their guise and abilities depending upon their magical development and attunement. See also allomorph.

Jueran'al – literally, 'brothers-in-living-ideation' or, more simply, 'brothers in ideals' in the tongue of the Jira S'al Alann. The term refers to a particularly organic way of looking at those who share a common ground of thought and ideation created by shared goals and ideals reinforced through each other's commitment and communication to the continual development and expression of these underlying intentions.

Ka – 'Knight' or 'Paladin' in the tongue of Tol Aeron.

K'an and Li and the esoterica that follow – literally, 'water and fire.' In some schools of internal alchemy the interchange of *k'an* and *li* represent a combination of *yin* and *yang* whose interchange corresponds to the functioning of the Tao, both the macrocosm and microcosm, within an individual. After completing the large heavenly cycle represented by the microcosmic orbit and the fusion of the five elements, thereby opening all the energy channels within the body, the Taoist adept is ready to begin the process of energy sublimation of *k'an* and *li*.

Through various stages, the *ching*, the generative energy, is converted into *chi*, the life force energy. The power of the reproductive hormones is thereby transferred into the whole body and brain. The process is similar process to the yogic awakening of the Kundalini, except in the Taoist process the resulting energy is directed throughout the body continuously along the meridians instead of being directed solely upward to the head.

During the initial stages (lesser enlightenment of the *k'an* and *li*) this interchange focuses on the cultivation of the root, the *hui-yin* or perineum, and the heart *chakras* while the *ching* energies are transformed at the navel.

The next stage, Ta K'an Li (greater enlightenment of the *k'an* and *li*), involves increasing the amount of energy drawn up through the body while bringing the energy up to the solar plexus. The increased energy in this stage results from the adept drawing energy directly from Heaven (Yang, above) and Earth (Yin, below) while adding the elemental powers to those of the adept's body.

The following stage, T'ai K'an Li (greatest enlightenment of the *k'an* and *li*), involves further mixing of the *yin* and *yang* powers at a higher energy center in the heart.

From here the adept has several potential stages to follow. The adept goes through a process of sealing the five sensory organs to prevent energy loss. The *chi* is then converted into mental energy (*shen*), or the energy of the soul, to preserve and purify the body and spirit while controlling the emotions.

There are still other formulae available for the adept to practice. Among these are the congress of Heaven and Earth immortality. At this stage, the adept mixes *yin* and *yang* energies at the crown of the head to preserve and cultivate the body to allow the spirit to achieve immortality. As the energies circulate, the body, soul, and spirit mingle and unite with the universe. The spirit thereby returns to nothingness or the source.

Finally, one last formula in the adept's development is the reunion of man and Heaven resulting in a true immortal man. At this stage, the internal alchemist has overcome reincarnation, developed an immortal spirit and an immortal body to house the spirit and soul, and is reunited with creation.

Karaduen – a Dwarven word meaning 'Light's ward' or 'Light's seal.' Special Dwarven runes and symbols often employed by

Dur'Kazak and Kor'Dannan in the crafting of artifacts and the creation of spells and enchantments.

Karadüm – a type of particularly powerful stone giant in tune with the ebb and flow of the land's development and unfolding; usually guardians of a particular sacred place. Distant kin of the Indural.

Kazarhan the Stout – Dwarven lieutenant of the Home Guard, Kor'Dannan, and Dur'kazak. Wielder of the great hammer Raurdros. Master of Karaduen.

Kazzak – literally, 'marks of honor' in the tongue of the Dwarves. Symbols, tokens, and items of repute woven into a Bor'Banna's beard as badges of honor and accomplishment. Also common among other Dwarves.

Keep of Terraboer – the Citadel of Light. Home to the Dalaren Ka, the Knights of the One Light, and the Star of Elendial.

Keeper of Secrets – a select group of the Home Guard charged with guarding and maintaining Tellanon's secrets, hidden lore, and artifacts of repute. Also Holder of Secrets.

Khuerkanna – a famous Dwarven general known for his triumphant last stand against the Orcs and their allies in the Battle of the Broken Blade.

Kiervos – a large city-state in the plains of Var'Kera.

Kilaeron – wild continent to the east of Dharia.

Kiloboulder – a Gnomish unit of force, energy output, and weight.

Kor'Dannan – Dwarven Priests of Brendle given the keeping and wisdom of his fires, Brendle's Spark. Fierce warriors equally adept at healing and providing succor.

Koerdian Cave Bear – a species of gigantic cave bear particularly respected by Dwarves for their strength, perseverance, and indomitable spirit.

Kordas – Orcish blood beer.

Ku – pants.

K'un Lun – a mountain range often portrayed as a Taoist paradise, home to immortals. Home to the Priests of K'un Lun.

The K'un Lun – mystical priests from high in the mountains of Chang Sen. Also the Priests of K'un Lun.

Lael'darnael – literally, 'mission-view-survival-path' in the tongue of the Jira S'al Alann. A shared view and purpose developed organically together from the dictates and exigencies of the requirements for survival and success for an entire group providing the basis and direction for future action.

Landeiss – a large island nation to the south of Dharia.

Liao Qua – a large city in Chang Sen.

Li – literally, 'principle'. The expression of potential in form; the manifestation of inherent order distinct to each and every thing; the order of flow; the Tao in motion. Also pattern.

Lianel – literally, 'bowyer's heart.' A bow crafted by a master bowyer of the Elves melded and formed from his spirit and the spirit of a willing tree.

Lich – undead beings sustained by twisted magical energies.

Life – all living beings taken as a whole.

The Light – the ambient energy of the universe; the energy of Life enlivening all of existence. Considered holy, sacred, and heavenly. See also Aerya, *chi*, *ching*, *dalare*, Deur Spricken Sprack, Omnispark, Phlogiston, *shen*, Brendle's Spark, and *yuan-chi*.

Light Fallen – the Cabal or Liúxīng Làngrén.

Light's Grace – theurgical religious group on Tellanon led by Magdalia Miera whose activities focus on henosis, unification with and expression of the Divine Light on Ea'ae and beyond.

The Light's Guard – an elite force within the Home Guard led by Eidelion.

Light's Swath – the brilliant center of the galaxy encompassing Ea'ae.

Lightwell – the spontaneous, self-sustaining creation of life-giving energies formed through deft manipulation of the Dragon's Gate and the spontaneous creation of Light from limitless potential.

Master Liu – a revered teacher of the K'un Lun.

Liúxīng Làngrén – literally, 'falling star vagrants.' More figuratively, 'those fallen or straying from Heaven's path'. The Cabal, and those fallen priests associated with it, that have strayed from the path of Life, as referenced by the Priests of K'un Lun.

Llyewia L'oerllana – literally 'spring's first breath' or 'first breath of spring.' A lieutenant of the Home Guard. Elven Iyela, lorekeeper, and ambassador.

Loel'dara – literally, 'the Light's shadow beckons.' Tellanon's weapon of last resort and final line of defense.

Loesia – a cold, rugged region of lakes and mountains in the heart of the Northlands. Home to Wrindanneth and seat of Maeth Onai.

Loess – literally, 'Heaven's shielding.' A protective Dwarven rune meant for use against supernatural forces.

Master Loquan – a respected teacher of the K'un Lun.

Lords of the Wood – see Elves.

Lotus – see Pai-lien.

Lueciane Sea – the sea to Dharia's south. Lying directly between Dharia and Maeron, it surrounds the island nation of Landeiss.

Luereal – literally, 'troll's bane' or 'evil's bane' in the tongue of the Elves. The black wand of Q'ia'Li. Once in the possession of Hoyt, given to Aroganji. An exceedingly rare Anuvaeryan wrought artifact of witchwood.

Luerdan – literally, 'troll dung' in the tongue of the Dwarves.

Lung – a Dragon in Chang Sen.

Lung-hu – literally, 'Dragon and tiger,' symbolic of *yang* and *yin* respectively, and the fusion of *k'an* and *li* in the Taoist alchemical tradition which leads to the realization of the Tao. The Dragon rises from the fire and is therefore associated with *li* while the tiger arises from the water and is therefore associated with *k'an*.

Lung-hu-i tao – literally, 'way of the Dragon and tiger.' A colloquial description by exponents of other alchemical traditions for the mystical traditions practiced by the priests of the K'un Lun.

Lung-wang – Dragon kings; mythological Taoist figures. Dragons (*lung*) also correspond to the *yang* principle in Taoist iconography.

Macrocosmic orbit – the energy path encompassing both the internal and external energy paths. Completion of the macrocosmic orbit is signified by opening the energy gates completely to the passage of *chi* which ultimately leads to unification with the energies of creation.

Macrocosmos – see macroverse.

Macroverse – the totality of multi-dimensional existence, inclusive of all planes, alternate universes, and extradimensional regions. See multiverse. Also megacosm or macrocosmos.

Maeglan – a Dwarven Dur'kazak of the Flintforge clan. Uncle to Slate.

Maer'Din – a loremaster of the H'era. Keepers of the tribe's dreams, aspirations, and history. Their knowledge is brought to life through the dance of the Seura.

Maeron – a largely tropical continent on the southern side of Ea'ae.

Maeth Onai – a god of magic. Wrindanneth's exemplar and ultimate guide. Depending on his mood, sometimes referenced privately as the Dream Stealer by Wrindanneth.

Maeven D'lanaran – a champion of the Dalaren Ka and exemplar of the Light.

MAFS – see Magical Air Foam System.

Magdalia Miera – member of Tellanon's ruling High Council, eminent Theurgist, and leader of the Light's Grace congregation.

Mage armor – enchanted armor for magic users that allows the freedom and flexibility to cast spells while also offering some protection against physical or magical assault. Often made from robes or clothing typical of a given magical tradition.

Magic – the translation of the possible into the actual, the imagined into the real. The three primary components of magical practice are often understood as belief, faith that an individual can take an active part in universal creation; intent (or will), the shaping of this belief can guide in creation; and imagination, the vision or desired outcome made possible by belief and shaped by intent.

The wellspring of magic is universal energy. Depending upon the tradition, this source is known as *yuan-chi*, Brendle's Spark, Phlogiston and the Omnispark, Aerya, and Light among others. This universal energy is often understood as the source and fuel of life, the *chi*. Sometimes broken into greater and lesser magics referencing the differentiation between the universal source energy—*yuan-chi*, Phlogiston, Aerya, Light, and celestial or divine magics—and the intrinsic ambient energies of life—the *chi*.

See also *yuan-chi*, *chi*, Brendle's Spark, Phlogiston and Omnispark, Aerya, and Light.

Magical Air Foam System – a magical Gnomish Paratechnological fire extinguishing foam. Particularly effective against Class M magical fires. Also known as MAFS.

Magnus Flintforge – a distant relation of Slate. Innkeeper of the Afternoon's Shade Inn located in isolated Shady Vale.

Major and Minor Shielding – a complex combination of spells serving to protect the recipient from arcane damage and hostile spells, the Major Shield, while also guarding against physical damage, impacts, blows, cuts, and the like, the Minor Shield.

Mandros Gray Beard – a once renowned archmage known for his great enchantments and wondrous Craft.

Mantaed – a massive mantid native to Landeiss. One of the preferred mounts of the Wyaera.

Mazithras – a leading Paratechnologist.

Megacosm – see multiverse or macroverse.

Men – the youngest and most prolific race of Ea'ae. Native flexibility and intuitiveness allows Men to excel in many fields, progressing quickly through their chosen arts.

Mere – 'Path' or 'Way' in the tongue of Tol Aeron.

Meridians – see *jing luo*.

METS – see Multidimensional Examination Tracker Survey.

Microcosmic orbit – the primary channel for the circulation of *chi* within the body. From the perineum, the pathway follows the spine up the back, over the crown of the head, past the brow, across the tongue, down the throat, past the solar plexus and navel, back to the perineum. This energy meridian passes through several major energy points or *chakras* along its route.

The microcosmic orbit is divided into two primary channels. The governor channel runs from the perineum along the back up the spine to the crown and down to the roof of the mouth. The tongue touching the roof of the mouth serves as a bridge between the two channels. The functional channel continues downward from the mouth through the throat, the heart, the navel, until ending in the perineum.

When energy flows freely along the microcosmic orbit joining the two primary energy routes, the practitioner has completed the small heavenly cycle. When the circuits along the arms and legs are open and flowing in conjunction with the small heavenly cycle, the practitioner has then completed the large heavenly cycle.

See also *jing luo* and macrocosmic orbit.

Mihtig'leht – literally, 'mighty light.' One of the fourteen seals protecting Ea'ae from extradimensional incursion. Housed in a bastion in the far reaches of Aruene in the keep of Morowen.

Mithril – a particularly light, yet strong, magical metal.

Molly Flintforge – Magnus's wife and co-owner of the Afternoon's Shade Inn.

Morowen – the bastion protecting the seal of Mihtig'leht. Keep of the Fyrskal.

Mudra – literally, 'seal or sign.' A spiritual gesture and an energetic seal of authenticity. A physical posture or symbolic gesture meant to connect outer actions with spiritual concepts. In Mahayana and Vajrayana Buddhist cosmography, *mudra* help actualize certain inner states, anticipating their bodily expression, creating a connection between the practitioner and the Buddha or experience visualized in meditation.

Mui Fa Jong – literally, 'plum flower poles.' Vertical poles used in martial practice to train balance, focus, coordination, relaxation, and agility.

Multidimensional Examination Tracker Survey – an active evaluation and classification system for the type and origin of energies used by Gnomish Paratechnologists. Also known as METS.

Multiverse – the entirety of multidimensional space inclusive of alternate universes, planes, and dimensions. Also macroverse and megacosm.

Neana – a rainbow-hued magical tree species whose glimmering, diamond-flecked trunks soar to the heavens.

Negentropy cannon – a Paratechnological cannon that locally reverses the process of energy dispersal associated with a given object's entropy at the cost of localized energy injection into the targeted system. In essence, the targeted object explodes into a highly energized cloud of superheated plasma. Sometimes referred to as the Energy Accumulator or the Particulate Plasmifier.

New Unified Mental-Energetic Noesis – NUMEN. A synthetic Paratechnological being of great mental and physical capacity able to take on many shapes, forms, and functions. An extension of the Paratechnology developed in the TAMERS units without need of an operator as the NUMEN is guided by its own intelligence. Also, a play on words among Paratechnologists for their magical-technological creations that may one day supersede them.

Nether realms – extradimensional planes home to Infernals and other fiendish creatures. See Abyss.

Nienael – a lord of Tueran. Father of Gilaethe.

Noeldri – literally, 'flowing water.' A Dwarven rune granting grace and agility both physically and mentally.

Noes Al'amroth – 'the land where tears do not dry.' Elven name for the home of the Aeryn D'al. Called Jenyuan Shulin by the people of Chang Sen. Bordered by Ithil'alen, the ancient homeland of the Elves on Ea'ae.

Noosphere – the realm of the mind, the collective consciousness, or the sphere of thought. A general name for the metamagical plane allowing for the shared existence and interaction both within and between various synthetic intelligences. A Paratechnological creation of the highest order. Also references the sphere of thought, mind, or knowledge itself.

Noumel – member of the Protectorate of Tellanon. The city's chief diplomat, head of interspecies and interstellar diplomacy and trade.

Novice – an aspirant not yet accepted into the priesthood. Upon acceptance into the K'un Lun, the novice becomes an initiate.

Nüaerblun – literally, 'Dragon dung' in the tongue of the Dwarves. Often used as a Dwarven insult.

Nüaer'Daer – literally, 'life's heart.' A Dwarven term for Dragons.

Nüaer'Duin – literally, 'Dragon fire' or 'life's fire' in the tongue of the Dwarves. Among the Dwarves, Dragon fire is respected for its magical properties and power so like the heat of Brendle's forge.

NUMEN – see New Unified Mental-Energetic Noesis.

Nydia – Elven noble and Iyela. Mother to Llyewia. Wife of Aleron.

Oedenara – literally, 'Daemon's heart.' A crystalline gem found at the heart of some Daemons with powerful magical properties and of much practical use.

Omnispark – Gnomish conception of the ignited or expressed source of life unending, ever-changing and evolving, fueled by Phlogiston. Deur Spricken Sprack in Gnomish. Also called *yuan-chi*, magic, Aerya, Brendle's Spark, and Light, among other terms, by other races.

Orcs – a large, prolific evil race spread through the wilds and caverns of Ea'ae. Orcs are strong, aggressive, and full of guile, a race of warriors and shaman. Working in league with Trolls and Ogres, Orcs often lead their slower-witted brethren on the field of battle.

Oroende – Paratechnologist, member of the Protectorate, and Ueralen, leader of the Thelios.

Orogast – one of the lieutenants of the Home Guard under Eidelion. A Jira S'al Alann, able to change shape and form at will. Also known as Orogast the Elder.

Quju – a type of *shenyi* worn primarily by women

Pai-hui – crown energy center corresponding to the Sahasrara *chakra* in some yogic practices. The Yellow Palace. The spirit door.

Pai-lien – White lotus. The lotus is a significant symbol in the Buddhist and Hindu cosmologies. The lotus can represent a symbol of beauty; the various centers of consciousness (*chakras*) located throughout the body; the lotus floating in water can be seen as a symbol for non-attachment—as the lotus floats in the water and remains dry, the spiritual seeker lives in the world and remains unaffected by it; in Buddhism the lotus is also a symbol of the true nature of beings.

Pai-lien Touch – White Lotus Touch. A method of intervention developed within the Priests of K'un Lun that gives the recipient a chance to reform and remake themselves by granting visions of the summation of their experience, akin to a near death experience. Also called the Echoing Fist because the energies of the Touch echo through the chambers of the recipient's mind. Also called Shakyamuni's Palm because a master can use the Touch to cut through falsehood.

Paladin – a holy warrior dedicated to and empowered by the Light, vanquishers of evil, banishers of the unholy, adjudicators and arbiters, healers and almsmen. Many variants exist, some dedicated to particular deities and powerful entities, each with different talents, specialties, and ethos. The Dalaren Ka are one such group.

Paratechnology – literally, 'beyond technology.' The study of making the imagined real and actualizing the impossible. The art and science of applied magic and magical technologies. Paratechnological apprehension is shared across many races, however, the Gnomes' natural curiosity and creativity have brought Paratechnological expertise to its current refined state and have helped to spread its knowledge throughout the cosmos.

Pattern – the unique movements and shapes of *chi*, of limitless potential, indicative of the particular life force of an individual—the fingerprints of the soul. See also *li*.

Peran – Vicar of the High Lord Éremon.

Perfectly Polished Particulate Propeller – Beta Naught Mark Seven – a Gnomish frictionless toothpick invented by Spreesprocket.

Phlogiston – called Deur Spricken Sprack in the tongue of Gnomes. In Gnomish reckoning, the invisible spark of life pervading the universe akin to an invisible metastate of gaseous energetic conductance. Once ignited, Phlogiston fuels all life as the Omnispark. When manipulated by will, the Phlogiston gives rise to magic. Also called *yuan-chi*, magic, Aerya, Brendle's Spark, and Light, among other terms, by other races and traditions.

Plane – one of many distinct layers of existence in the larger macro or multiverse. Often synonymous with universe or dimension.

Plains of Kadoor – open grassy plains on the western section of Dharia. Part of Var'Kera.

Pocket dimension – a miniature space or reality created expressly for a specific purpose. In the case of the myriad pocket dimensions of Tellanon, these represent miniature universes intimately connected to Tellanon itself, extending its breadth and depth. More often, pocket dimensions are used to extend space within a given region, for example, to make the space within a bag or room larger.

Port – a shortened term for teleport.

Powers – beings of great might, often extradimensional in origin.

Priest – one who has been accepted fully into the Order of the K'un Lun. See Priest of K'un Lun.

Priest of Maeth Onai – an order of magicians from the cold Northlands that practices a unique blend of mundane and divine magics whereby divine energies are channeled to perform traditional and inimitable spells.

Priest of K'un Lun – an order of mystics dedicated to the practice of various esoteric and martial traditions found nowhere else on Ea'ae. The way of the priest is geared toward continual transformation and development within and without through the evolving practice of internal alchemy, meditation, and physical cultivation.

Projection – a general term for a multi-dimensional representation of an object. A magical hologram or depiction. Also a reference to life-like, immersive news feeds displaying current happenings and items of worth.

Protectorate – Tellanon's governing body composed of thirteen elected Paratechnologists and other citizen representatives governing matters of security, trade, diplomacy, research, and city form and function. Also called the High Council or council.

Current members include Éremon, Oroende, Rowena Bowspirit, Dizzywig Paddlepulley, Jae'elthos, Vaendoer Thunderhammer, Whirlygig Sparksocket, Magdalia Miera, Borus, Noumel, Salia Proventure, Chutefunnel Knobwhistle, and Alain Ar'laen.

Psion – a being gifted mentally and psychically.

Psionics – psychic mental powers and abilities as expressed by a psion.

Qì – *chi*.

Q'ia'Li – a highly regarded Elven magician of great power that transitioned to Anuvaerya in order to defeat an exceedingly powerful Anubaraëthi in single combat. Creator of Luereal.

Q'ia Shan Sea – eastern border of Chang Sen. A vast and sometimes turbulent body of tropical water dotted by islands and many atolls.

Qigong – literally, '*chi* work' or 'life energy work.' Generally, exercises to build and strengthen *chi* flow.

Qìxīnquán – literally, 'life essence-mind boxing' or 'life energy-mind boxing.' Another term often ascribed to the martial style of the K'un Lun.

Q'shar – A kingdom in far southern Dharia known for its fierce nomadic warriors.

Quai-lo – A widespread race of semi-intelligent insectoid predators. Large and ferocious, they resemble nothing more than vicious humanoid mantises.

Radok – war chief of the Ar'thas, the Black Mountain Orcs.

Rainbow body – a body of pure Light, a celestial or energy body. Called a *jalü* in esoteric tradition. See also *jalü*.

Rare Aer – Humbol's airship.

Rakshasa – a race of powerful feline Daemonic sorcerers in league with the Cabal.

Raour'Saqan – a Dracodaeran Shaur'Daus. Lieutenant of the Home Guard.

Raurdros – literally, 'evil's bane.' The great rune-etched hammer of Kazarhan, forged by Dwarven smiths of old, empowered by ancient runes of power, Karaduen, and other workings of enchantment.

Return stone – a magical crystal of concentrated energy used to transport the bearer to a predefined location—generally the starting point of a journey. Often used with airships to allow passage home without a portal.

Rhyllia – literally, 'the Mother Tree.' An ancient tree in the grove of Erudhluin held sacred by the Elves. One of the few surviving Aeryn D'al beyond the borders of Jenyuan Shulin.

Róucí – literally, 'pliant or soft poetry.' A simple three-lined poem consisting of five to seven syllables per line. Meant to capture the essence of a moment or the central character of an event, a few words to capture the entirety of an impression. Oftentimes, but not always, the final line heightens the moment of clarity provided by the poem through a sudden, unexpected transition, change, or image.

Rowena Bowspirit – Tellanon's foremost Aeromancer and fleet commander, member of the Protectorate, master pilot and craftswoman.

Ruena O'reine – archmage nonpareil, a principal magical instructor of the Home Guard, and a Holder of Secrets.

Ruen'elde – a name for the cadre of Archliches ruling Garen Muer.

R'yn Daer – a people at home in the skies as much as on the land. Native fliers, swashbucklers and rogues, they wander the skies of Ea'ae in search of fame and fortune.

Saedeus – Lich king, ruler of Garen Muer. Formerly an archmage of great repute and guardian of the seal of Weis'liuhath.

Salia Proventure – member of Tellanon's ruling Protectorate, citizen advocate, and voice of the community and its concerns.

Sarugauth the Red – a primeval Red Dragon allied with the Cabal. Bane of the Yerens.

SAVERS – see Self Actuated Variable Emergency Response System.

SBS – see Sliced Bread Society.

Sceaduwulf – literally, 'shadow wolf.' A spectral wolf.

Scierdyas – literally, 'Spectral Dragons.' Energetic beings very similar in appearance to Dragons summoned from the unholy nether realms of the darkest abysms.

Scimerian Gate – literally, 'Shimmering Gate.' A magical portal allowing entry into Tellanon proper from the loading docks. Also known as the Weirding Gate.

Seals – fourteen magical wards of untold power scattered equidistant across the planet forming a magical barrier protecting Ea'ae from extradimensional incursion and extraplanetary attack.

Seiza – a sitting position commonly used in Buddhist meditation along with the lotus and half-lotus positions. The practitioner sits on her knees with feet tucked under the buttocks.

Self-Actuated Variable Emergency Response System – a Paratechnological clockwork emergency response bot of Gnomish invention capable of independently responding to, assessing, and reacting to multiple life-threatening situations. Called SAVERS for short.

Senea – a massive, thickly trunked forest giant. Its magically reinforced wood is among the strongest on Ea'ae.

Sentry drones – a general name for Paratechnological defensive drones. See also ARMED.

Seura – the 'dance of dreams unborn.' A form of moving knowledge and history transmitted by the Maer'Din of the H'era.

Shade – a nebulous creature of Darkness.

Shadow – a general term for creatures of Darkness and their ilk. Those opposed to the energy of Life in all its manifestations and who seek to subvert, pervert, consume, or otherwise destroy the Light in all its manifold expressions.

Shadowkin – a general term for creatures of Darkness. See Shadow.

Shady Vale – a small hamlet in the western wilds of Dharia deep in the heart of the Green Run.

Shakyamuni – literally, 'sage of the Shakyas.' The historical Buddha Siddhartha Gautama, born into the Shakya, or Lion, clan before realizing the Four Noble Truths and discovering the Eightfold Path as a means to end suffering.

Shapers – see Yerens.

Shaur'Daus – literally, a 'Stalker of Darkness' in the tongue of the Dracodaerans. Draconic warriors wreathed in the fires of Heaven that do battle against the creatures of Darkness across the cosmos and beyond.

Shen – a deity or spirit; also the personal spirit or mind of an individual. One of the three essential life energies of man along with *chi* (*qi*) and *ching* (*jing*). In the Taoist meditative tradition, *shen* refers to both *shih-shen* and *yuan-shen*. Shih-shen refers to ordinary consciousness—thoughts, feelings, perceptions, and the senses. In contrast, *yuan-shen* refers to the spiritual consciousness that exists before birth and is part of the energy that pervades the entire universe (the *yuan-chi*). Meditation, or inner-alchemy, allows the Taoist practitioner to reestablish contact with her spiritual consciousness while eliminating the influence of the ordinary day-to-day consciousness.

Sheng-jen – a sage or saint. Taoist terms for an ideal man who has achieved perfection.

Shen-jen – a spiritual man. Another term used to describe an ideal man, a person who has realized the Tao.

Shen Po – master of the void palm, one of the fallen founding fathers of the K'un Lun, member of the Cabal, and one time teacher of Master Wei.

Shenyi – a long garment of Chang Sen much like a full-body robe with flowing sleeves tied by a sash at the waist. *Zhiju* are worn by men. *Quju* are worn women.

Master Shi – T'ien-shih of the K'un Lun.

Shih – master or expert.

Shrike – airship of Braemen, later of the Fists.

Shuǐ lù xiàn – literally, 'the way of the water course or water's path.' An inner teaching of Xīnyìquán embodying *wu wei*, *wu bu wei*, and non-resistance, the effortless passage and redirection of force and intent.

Singers – see Yerens.

Skael – a people of nomadic traders who travel the skies in airships plying their wares.

Slate Flintforge – a Dwarf of the land, Bor'Banna, and adventurer of some renown. Friend of Yip, Aroganji, and Wrindanneth. Member of the Four. In the tongue of Dwarves, known as Daer'Duin.

Sliced Bread Society – a Paratechnological think tank dedicated to furthering the depth and breadth of magical and material knowledge and understanding whose study spans the breadth and depth of the mundane and mystical. Driven by the motto, "It doesn't get any better!" Also called the SBS.

Soerlyn – Elven years. See Cycles.

Span – a unit of distance roughly equivalent to a league.

Spreesprocket Goldpulley – a lieutenant of the Home Guard, Gnomish Paratechnologist, and warrior nonpareil.

Squarepeg Springwidget – highly skilled Gnomish Paratechnologist of Tellanon.

Star of Elendial – a magical artifact of great power housed in the Keep of Terraboer. One of the fourteen seals protecting Ea'ae from extradimensional incursion.

Star of Illdrassil – small crystalline fragments of Illdrassil that grant magical boons to members of the Home Guard.

Stasis box – a magical storage box, often enclosing a pocket dimension for added storage space that ensures the freshness of stored food.

Super sack – a magical Gnomish bottomless bag. Super sacks are often cluttered, disorganized, and very difficult to retrieve items from within, especially within a short, highly critical period of time.

Synthetic intelligence – a Paratechnological term for the sentience resulting from the merger of two different intelligences. Typically, one intelligence is natural and the other is artificial, one is organic and the other is disembodied or a metamagical complex arising from technical sophistication, or one intelligence is formed explicitly to merge with and augment another. Far different from the Abstract and Construct's relationship with citizens, for example, wherein one intelligence serves another directly and indirectly, synthetic intelligences are the result of a complete union between two disparate awarenesses, the resulting union having complete access to the knowledge and capabilities of both. Most typically, one intelligence is created explicitly to merge with and augment another, extending the field of sentient consciousness into directions and dimensions only limited by the imagination.

Also a reference to any created intelligence.

Sythaeran Quadrant – a region of space containing the planet known as Al'Marr.

Taerris'thule – literally, 'old home.' Formerly a religious city and home to the seal of Eldre'gheu. Sometimes referred to as the City of the Fallen Gods.

Taiji – alternatively, Tai chi or T'ai chi. Literally, 'supreme ultimate' or 'great absolute.' Undifferentiated or unlimited potential. The source of existence. The primordial state of emptiness from which potential and existence arose and returns. The great, undifferentiated beginning. The wellspring and return of possibility.

Taliaerya – literally, 'Morning's Light' or 'Dawn's Light' in the tongue of the Elves. Known as Eyrdeas, the White Blade of Morn among the Dalaren Ka. The storied blade of Maeven D'lanaran.

TAMERS – see Transmorphic Actionable Multidimensional Exo-Robotic System.

Tan t'ien – an elixir field. The primary energy centers of the human body located at the navel, chest, and forehead. Often a specific reference to the elixir field near the navel. The seat of the *shen*. Alternatively, *dantian*.

More generally, *tan t'ien* can also refer to various energy centers throughout the body through which energy is successively refined. Depending on the alchemical system, the number and purpose may vary. Typically, one *tan t'ien* is located at the navel, another is found at the heart, and one is situated between the eyebrows. Most commonly, the lower *tan t'ien* at or below the navel transforms sexual essence, or *jing*, into *chi*. The middle *tan t'ien* in the center of the chest transmutes *qi* energy into *shen*, or spirit. Finally, the higher *tan t'ien* at the forehead, or on the top of the head, transforms *shen* into Wuji, the infinite space of void.

Tao – literally, 'Way.' Also refers to the way of Nature or Heaven. The mysterious, elusive source and guiding principle behind the phenomena of the universe. The unnamable spring from which *chi* and all existence flow. Also Dao and Wuji.

The Tao that can be told is not the eternal Tao;
The name that can be named is not the eternal name.
The nameless is the beginning of Heaven and Earth.
The named is the mother of ten thousand things.
Ever desireless, one can see the mystery.
Ever desiring, one can see the manifestations.

These two spring from the same source but differ in name;
This appears as darkness.
Darkness within darkness.
The gate to all mystery.[5]

Tao-Shih – a Taoist priest in religious as opposed to philosophical Taoism. Supervisors of various religious rituals and ceremonies, leaders of congregations, and scholars.

Tellanon – literally, 'Heaven's Landing' in the Old Tongue of Men. A spectacular floating island city in the sky, a center of commerce and diplomacy, and a starting point for both interstellar and interdimensional travel. Home of Illdrassil, the Home Guard, and Paratechnologists on Ea'ae.

Temple of Eldre'gheu – see Eldre'gheu.

Terala – a massive, sentient man-eating spider.

Thaelos – an Elven-trained archer aboard the *Shrike*. Braemen's second.

Thaiel Lui'nost – Elven lorekeeper and sage.

Thane – traditional leader of a Dwarven clan.

Thelios – a guild of Paratechnologists focused on material transformation and alteration led by Oroende.

Therion – an ancient hero known for many exploits including cleansing the seal of Eldre'gheu.

The Thirteen – euphemism for the council.

The Three Pillars – a code of ethics or core tenets of the K'un Lun which guide and support their actions and activities. These moral pillars fall into three general categories reflective of the three primary regions of human endeavor: morality of deed, morality of mind, and morality of spirit.

Furthermore, within each ethical pillar, actions are elucidated by additional secondary tenets. Morality of deed includes expressing humility, loyalty, respect, righteousness, and trust in all actions. Morality of mind entails evincing courage, endurance, patience, perseverance, and will in thought. Morality of spirit includes internalizing, manifesting, and actualizing contemplation, insight, compassion, wisdom, and serenity through freedom of thought and expression.

Three Treasures – the three essential substances of the human body. The three treasures are *jing* (*ching*), the material essence; *qi* (*chi*), the vital energy; and *shen*, the spirit or soul.

The Thunderhammer Clan – a clan of Dwarves residing upon Tellanon known for their technical expertise and cooperative working partnership with Gnomish Paratechnologists.

T'iao chi – harmonizing the breaths. A Taoist breathing technique that serves as preparation for further Taoist development exercises.

T'ien – celestial; Heaven.

T'ien Ming – the celestial mandate or mandate of Heaven. The right to rule granted by Heaven to just emperors.

T'ien-shih – celestial master. Also a title borne by the leaders of some schools of Taoism.

Tinkerers – Paratechnologists focusing on clockwork devices melding magic and technology in forms often resembling complex mechanical devices. Most often associated with Gnomish Paratechnologists due to their strong imaginative mechanical tendencies.

Tol Aeron – a lush, temperate mountainous island far to the south and west of Tellanon off the western coast of Dharia. Birthplace of Eidelion, home of the Keep of Terraboer, the Citadel of Light and the Dalaren Ka, the Knights of the One Light.

Transmorphic Actionable Multidimensional Exo-Robotic System – A multi-functional, transforming exoarmor system created by Spreesprocket. Also known as TAMERS.

Traveler – a magic user capable of teleportation.

Traveling – teleportation or any other form of instantaneous travel whether inter- or intradimensionally.

Tso-wang –meditation characterized by objectless attention or pure awareness coupled with inner and outer stillness—the universe expressing its own enlightened true nature. One of many contemplative approaches employed by the K'un Lun.

Tueran – a largely Anuvatali city that is also home to humans, Dwarves, Gnomes, and Elves located on the southern island nation of Landeiss.

Tuio Shou – literally, 'pushing hands.' A name for the two-person training routines utilized in some internal martial arts.

Tyraethe – homeworld of the Tyraethians.

Tyraethian – reptilian humanoids originating from the planet

Tyraethe known for their extreme physical prowess, highly developed code of honor, cultivated ethical systems, and complex moral conduct.

Ueralen – title for the leader of the Thelios, a band of Paratechnologists focused on transmutation and alteration of matter.

The Umbral Lord – see the Enemy or Ur'Daus.

Undermount – a general name for any Dwarven city or a Dwarven occupied region. Typically located in the bedrock beneath mountains. Dwarven fastnesses and attendant halls and byways that grow within the roots of the hills. Also called delvings, though delvings are typically smaller in scale.

Ungar – literally, 'earthen might.' A Dwarven rune granting physical strength and endurance.

Uraera Al'on – literally, 'strengthener of intent' or 'gatherer of will.' A form of magic practiced by the Anuvatali that weaves webs of enchantment around allies, augmenting and expanding upon strengths and abilities.

Ur'Daena – literally, 'the axe's lament.' The uniquely Dwarven art of the axe. Many styles and forms are known, each generally ascribed to a specific family, clan, or thanedom. Variations in styles from the use of great two-handed war axes taller than a man suited to the openness of the battlefield to forms of double-bladed combat better suited to the close quarters of a mineshaft are all practiced with distinctly Dwarven fervor.

When practiced by a master, a Bor'Banna, these styles rely as much on channeling the remnants of Brendle's original creation magic through the axe as physical prowess for their efficacy. When wielded by a true master, the axe of the Bor'Banna is said to glow with the light and heat of Brendle's original forge.

Ur'Daus – literally, 'The Darkness.' Also known as the Enemy, the Creeping Shadow, the Devourer of Worlds, the Umbral Lord, the Great Devourer, and many others. A fathomless Light consuming Darkness trapped between dimensions in ages long past.

Urduen – large Dwarven-fortified city-state of north central Dharia.

Uuraja – leader of the beast riders of Al'Marr, feline lords of the Forlorn Forest. Father of Uuraru.

Uuraru – young son of Uuraja, hereditary lord of the Al'Marr. Named Evensong for his skill in weaving music and magic.

Vaellorea – a grand Elven tree of wondrous form and silvery hue. Kin to Aeryn D'al.

Vaendoer Thunderhammer – member of Tellanon's ruling Protectorate, Dur'kazak, and thane of the Thunderhammer clan.

Vanduen – literally, 'divine regeneration.' A Dwarven Karaduen that enhances healing capacities, speeding recovery and repair from exhaustion and injury.

Vapor of Golden Quintessent Life – a sentient gaseous Paratechnologist with significant psychic ability.

Var'Kera – a land of open grasslands and rich, rolling forests, home to many great kingdoms, and the typical mooring below Tellanon.

Verakesh – a mage in Braemen's employ, pilot of the airship the *Shrike*.

Vöer – Troll in the tongue of the Dwarves.

Vöerdan – literally, 'Troll saliva or spittle.' A Dwarven insult.

Void – the wellspring of creation. The limitless potential underlying all existence. Source of the Tao and *yuan-chi*. Also Wuji.

Void palm – an unassailable attack directly upon the life force of an opponent.

Vorath – an amorphous, mist-like intelligent predator that reads the thoughts of its prey and feeds on their essence.

Vradek – Orcish gruel made from ground bones simmered in blood.

Vyaera – literally, 'wanderers along the path.' An Elven term for those sharing the same path, quest, purpose, or journey.

War of Shadows – one name for the first war with the Cabal and their dark allies waged on Ea'ae in the distant past.

Warren – a general name for the complexly convoluted and often interconnected structures typical of Gnomish homes. Also a name for large, extended Gnomish families.

The Watcher – elusive denizen of the Drake Spires; Ilidian.

Master Wei – an accomplished teacher of the K'un Lun. Yip's primary instructor and guide through the ways of the priesthood. Teacher of the Five Excellencies, master of the Moonlit Mind, keeper of the Echoing fist, and Sheng-jen.

Weirding Gate – see Scimerian Gate.

Weirding Wood – see Aeryn Sh'al.

Weis'liuhath – literally, 'wise light' or 'light of wisdom.' One of the fourteen seals protecting Ea'ae from extradimensional incursion. Housed in a fastness secluded in the lost forests of Kilaeron in the keep of Garen Muer.

Whirlygig Sparksocket – member of the Tellanon Protectorate, Paratechnologist, and lead Designer and System Administrator of COG, the Construct Organization Group.

Wieru S'al Alann – literally 'Way of the Imagining,' 'Way of the Imagined,' or 'Way of Imagining.' The path of self-transformation and actualization taken by the Jira S'al Alann. This way encompasses the techniques, knowledge, and skills necessary to live, survive, adapt, and change in a mutable world.

Witchwood – see Aeryn Sh'al.

Worgs – massive wolves used by Orcs as mounts in lieu of horses.

Wrindanneth – friend of Yip, Aroganji, and Slate. Priest of Maeth Onai. Member of the Fists.

Wu – literally, 'nonbeing; emptiness.' The fundamental character-istic of the Tao. Also refers to a Taoist imbued with the Tao so that he has become free of all passions and desires (empty). Also the absence of qualities perceivable by the senses.

Wu bu Wei – literally, 'not left undone.' The creative completion and natural accompaniment to wu wei. Knowing when and how to act and not to act in intuitive harmony with the Tao. The active, creative complement to the passive stillness of *wu wei*. Taken as a whole, by not acting, nothing is left undone.

Wuji – alternatively, Wu Chi. Literally, 'boundless,' 'ultimateless,' 'limitless,' or infinite. The Ultimateless, Void, or Infinite before the Great Ultimate, Taiji, before differentiation. Synonymous with Tao.

Denoted in Zhan Zhuang standing meditation *qigong* practice as the initial and fundamental stance for practice.

Wu Wei – literally, 'without action' or 'non-action.' A description of 'effortless doing,' 'action without action,' perfect equilibrium, or harmony with the Tao. The complement to *wu bu wei*, or 'not left undone'. Together, *wu wei* and *wu bu wei* form the creative, harmonious passivity and intuition needed to know when and how to act or not to act.

Wu Xin – literally, 'energy gates,' points in the body where internal and external *chi* come into contact. The five primary energy gates include the face, the center of the palms of the hands at the Laogong points, and the Yongquan points on the bottoms of the feet. Energy can also enter through the navel at the *tan t'ien* and through the skin at the pores through special *qigong* practices (i.e. via Fu Xi or skin breathing).

Wu-hsing – alternatively, the Wu Xing, literally 'the five movers,' 'the five elements,' 'the five virtues' (Wu-te). Also represent the five phases of transformation or the five energies that determine the course of natural phenomena. These 'elements' correspond to abstract forces and act as symbols or metaphors for basic characteristics, properties, and interactions of matter. The five symbolic elements are water, earth, fire, metal, and wood.

Master Wuping – a venerated teacher of the K'un Lun.

Wyaera – literally, 'wanderers along the sky,' or, more loosely, 'sky striders,' or 'cloud walkers.' The Riders of Tueran.

Wyrm – an ancient or powerful Dragon.

Xi Wue – a Fang Shih and respected teacher at Xian Shi.

Xian Shi – a school in Chang Sen dedicated to the arcane study of *fang shu* and *fu-lu* and the development of young Fang Shih. Located between the Hsiang Lung Mountains
and the Q'ia Shan Sea.

Xīnyì – literally, 'mind-to-mind,' 'mind to intent,' or 'mind to thought.' A higher order of teaching rarely employed by the Priests of K'un Lun in which a priest directly shares his knowledge and experience with another.

Xīnyìquán – literally, 'heart to mind fist,' 'mind to thought or intent boxing,' or, more loosely, 'mind-to-mind boxing.' The term used to describe a primary component of the martial tradition employed by the Priests of the K'un Lun. Not so much an internal or external martial style, practitioners read and feel the *chi*, the intention and spirit of their opponent, anticipating, redirecting, and manipulating their opponent's energies and intent before and during expression.

Yaozi – a term for 'kite' in Chang Sen.

Ydrael Faer'Leirn – a fabled archmage and author of a magical tome of high magics given to Wrindanneth and Aroganji by Azaelle.

Yenaria – literally, 'House of Dreams.' Elven city linked to Tellanon.

Yerens – a noble race of yeti-like creatures. Singers of the world-song. Called the Shapers of the True Song, Shapers, and Singers.

Yi – any open cross-collar garment worn by both men and women in Chang Sen.

Yin-T'ang – the gateway to Heaven; a primary energy center of the body. The point between the eyes along the brow corresponding to the Ajna *chakra*.

Yip Chi Chuan – an Acolyte of the K'un Lun. Friend of Wrindan-neth, Aroganji, and Slate. One of the Flaming Fists. Called Aerya'anan, 'Light bringer,' by the Anuvatari.

Ylldel – literally, 'Mountain Father.' The Indural's name for the mountain home of the Karadüm in the Green Run.

Yrien Al'nori – member of the Home Guard, Anuvatali Uraera Al'on.

Yuan-chi – the primordial energy, the inherent unrealized potential, of the universe; the celestial or divine *chi*. In some Taoist cosmologies, the personal spirit *shen* is thought to arise from the union of *ching*, the essence, with the universal primordial energy of *yuan-chi*. The *shen*, the result of this union, enters the newborn infant with its first breath. The *shen* resides in the body in the *tan t'ien* (navel), where it determines thoughts and feelings until leaving the body at death.

Yuan Ser – a journeyman amongst the Fang Shih. Not yet a fully accomplished master or archmage in the rites and traditions of the *fang shu*.

Yuan-shen – universal, original, or primordial awareness, spirit, or mind.

Yu-jen – literally, 'feather man.' An alternative designation for Tao-shih.

Zabuton – a flat padded mat used for sitting. Sometimes positioned under a *zafu* in meditation.

Zafu – a round cushion used for seated meditation.

Zhan Zhuang – standing like a tree or post; a form of standing meditation used in various systems of *chi gung* (internal energy work).

Zhiju – a type of *shenyi* worn primarily by men in Chang Sen.

Zhiyuan – a term for kite in Chang Sen.

REFERENCES FOR MORE IN-DEPTH INFORMATION AND FURTHER STUDY

1. Blofield, John. *Taoism - The Road to Immortality*. Shambhala: Boston. 1978.
2. Chia, Mantak. *Awaken Healing Energy through the Tao*. Aurora: Santa Fe. 1983.
3. Chuen, Master Lam Kam. *The Way of Energy*. Simon & Schuster, Inc.: New York. 1991.
4. Cleary, Thomas (trans.). *Opening the Dragon Gate*. Tuttle: Boston. 1996.
5. Gia-Fu Feng & Jane English (translators). *Lao Tsu/Tao Te Ching*. New York: Vintage Books. 1972.
6. Liang, Master Shou-Yu and Wu, Wen-Ching. *Qigong Empowerment - A Guide to Buddhist Taoist Medical Wushu Energy Cultivation*. Dragon Publishing: East Providence. 1997.
7. Schuhmacher, Stephan and Woerner Gert (eds.). *The Encyclopedia of Eastern Philosophy and Religion*. Shambhala: Boston. 1989.
8. Suzuki, Shunryu. *Zen Mind, Beginner's Mind*. Shambhala: Boston. 1973.
9. Watson, Burton (trans.). *The Complete Works of Chuang Tzu*. Columbia University Press: New York. 1968.

ABOUT THE AUTHOR

Through such simple questions as, "What if we lived in a world where our beliefs were real, tangible, and actualizable?" Joe explores the possible through thought, fantasy, wit, and character.

Including influences such as Shunryu Suzuki, Tolkien, Krishnamurti, Iain M. Banks, Laozi, Stephen R. Donaldson, Philip Kapleau, Raymond E. Feist, Edward O. Wilson, Dan Simmons, and David Bohm, Joe creates existential fantasy filled with rich worlds, concepts, stories, and ideas.

Joe holds an advanced degree in environmental management from Duke University, where he also studied religion with a focus on meditative, experiential, and transformative traditions. Additionally, Joe graduated with (dubious) honors from the Tellanon Institute of Noetic Knowledge, Education, and Research (TINKER), but has yet to put this knowledge to good use.

When not at play with his family, he enjoys reading, writing, and relaxation. When he can, Joe also practices various martial traditions in which he has attained the victim level of proficiency.

Joe's website

ACKNOWLEDGMENTS

I would like to thank my wife for her patience, love, and support; my beta readers for their willingness to enter worlds unlike any other; my friends for listening to my all-too-frequent updates and ideas; Ashley Davis, my editor, for helping realize my vision; and all the readers who took a chance in reading my work.

Thank you!

COPYRIGHT